The Fugitives

Book Three
Of
The Eleusis Cycle

D. Brumbley

Content Warning

This book contains content that some readers might find triggering, such as:

Combat violence
Mass casualty events
Sexual content (explicit)
Dom/Sub dynamic
Arranged marriages
Infidelity
Genetic experimentation
Apocalyptic scenarios
Pandemic / disease
Institutional gaslighting / emotional
manipulation
Forced pregnancy
PTSD / trauma responses

Read with Care

To all of you
who are weighed down by challenges
you haven't overcome.
Yet.

CONTENTS

PROLOGUE

Time was a funny thing. Wanting more inevitably led to feeling like time was moving too quickly. Wanting time to move quickly led just as invariably to feeling like every hour was a lifetime.

For Maria Kaplan, time was not kind, not since the Eleusis Initiative was disbanded and shut down with no hope of bringing it back. She had returned to her work as a committee member for other Consortium projects and re-opened her psychiatry practice so she was seeing patients again. That was some small consolation for what she lost, at least, since she did enjoy having patients. Projects. Experiments. She wanted more knowledge, and even after what happened to Stephen, she couldn't change. She *wouldn't* change. Especially because those rats ran off with the Twist and effectively halted her chances of getting to Eleusis.

What she hadn't expected, having been relegated to an essentially civilian life, was to be called into a meeting with the previous directors, Vance and Gehrig. She didn't know what they had done with themselves after the project was disbanded, though she knew they had remained in high leadership.

Eventually she was going to work her way back through the ranks, it would just take time. Time and patience. One she hated wasting and the other she had very little of since the collapse of her prestige and authority. The rest of the world needed to forget how terribly the Initiative had failed. Once that happened, once they started to forget, Maria's life would get better.

"Good to see you again, Doctor." Vance said as he shook her hand, though the hard set of his face sent a different message entirely. "I'm glad to see that you've been keeping busy the past . . . what has it been, fourteen months or so?"

He was standing when she entered the room, but there were two figures seated on the other side of the small conference room. A man and a woman whose faces Maria had seen hundreds of times, but never, ever in person.

"Please allow me," Vance continued, "to introduce you to Dominic Alpert and his wonderful wife, Sara."

The Alperts stood at the introduction and moved toward Maria. Their posture and bearing told a psychiatrist of her training everything she would ever need to know about them. Confidence and a lifetime of political work flowed in every gesture and expression, everything about them poised and polished to a high shine. Of course, the Alperts had only been members of the Consortium Board of Directors for most of their lives, following both sets of their parents. Both their mothers had served as Chair at one time, as had both of them, though Dominic had only recently taken that position. Their identity was in their blood as much as in their bearing. "It's a pleasure to meet you, Dr. Kaplan."

"The pleasure is all mine, Mr. Chairman." Maria said warmly as she shook the man's hand, and then his wife's in turn. "Please excuse my surprise, I certainly wasn't expecting a meeting like this to start out my morning."

"Ah, the element of surprise. Some weapons of war never lose their efficiency." Dominic gave her a warm smile and indicated a seat at the table before he and his wife took charge of the proceedings. It was strange to see Vance outranked by anyone, but he and Gehrig seemed content to sit back and merely support the Directors for the time being.

"We're familiar, as I'm sure you know, with your record of service in the most recent Eleusis Initiative. Like all the survivors of the project, we've scrutinized your performance closely and come to some conclusions which will require you to make some drastic changes in your current work. You're here this morning so that we can discuss those changes and ensure you understand what is expected of you going forward."

Drastic changes? Again? Maria didn't like the sound of that, especially following the statement that she'd been scrutinized, though her work could stand up to scrutiny. Her personal life might not stand up so well. "I see." She said cautiously, though she realized she couldn't exactly say no to whatever the Board was about to command of her. Ultimately, she wanted to get to Eleusis, just like everyone else. She was capable of kissing anyone's ass and acting like she enjoyed it to get there.

Maria looked at Mrs. Alpert, but the woman just smiled at her in a knowing way. It unsettled Maria even more, so she turned her attention back to Mr. Alpert. "I'm sure I can serve the Consortium in whatever way you decide is best."

"We are perfectly confident in that." Dominic's lips curved in the same kind of knowing smile, as he watched her for another few moments in relative silence. He seemed to enjoy watching her squirm. Recognizing such pleasures in herself had made it all too easy to recognize them in others.

"There are three items of business that require your attention. Your other research and experiments will need to be placed on hold in favor of these, though of course what you do in your spare time is entirely your business." The knowing smile hadn't left his face as he reached out and tapped a command panel on the table between them.

Out of the table rose a small vial she recognized, since it had been locked in her highly-fortified, retina-secured lab just the night before. The reddish liquid inside looked like nothing more than diluted blood, but it was slowly becoming much more than that, with Maria's constant refinement.

"I believe your notes refer to this one as a Binding agent, though they do not describe any results you've found with it from human trials. You've been admirably careful about your record-keeping." He actually smiled at that, and there was no sign of anything but approval from Vance or Gehrig as they glanced at the vial. "On a scale of one to one hundred percent reliability, what kind of results have you obtained with it so far?"

They saw a little more reaction out of her when something that she considered one of her prized projects was somehow in front of her instead of back at her lab. Clearly she was not happy it had been taken and she had no notification or warning about it. Her first reaction was to ask in anger about how they had taken her research, but she managed to control her emotions, her expression and her thoughts before anything came out of her mouth.

"Since the Eleusis Initiative has been disbanded, I haven't had much opportunity for human trials." She replied carefully as her eyes flicked from the vial to the Alperts again, though she could tell that they already knew more about it than she wanted them to. "I've spent a lot of the fourteen months since the . . . tragedy. . . developing this further. I've removed most of the hallucinogens from the original formula. Initially the purpose was to further the obedience response, by confusing . . ." She realized he hadn't actually asked her about her research, just how well it worked, so she cleared her throat and started again. "In my latest trial, it showed an 87.73% reliability."

They were clearly impressed by that number, and seemed perfectly at ease to listen to whatever else she wanted to tell them about it. "And in order to bring that response to within acceptable reach of full compliance, which I would place at 99.9% for this case, what kind of resources do you think you would require?"

Were they really thinking about backing her research? Giving her access to what she really needed and the answers she really wanted? Animals were one thing. She needed human trials. Human participants. Their brains were different, and she needed to adjust the formula accordingly. "I need research assistants, but only one or two, to analyze trial data. A bigger lab. And most importantly, I need test subjects."

Dominic expected that, and he nodded with the same satisfied smile on his face. "Would two hundred test subjects be sufficient to make a start, or do you expect a mortality rate during initial trials that would require a larger quantity before you can ensure that the mortality rate declines?"

Two hundred people? They were going to give her two hundred people? And resources? Maria was too stunned to speak immediately, but excitement flooded her thoughts afterward at the very idea. She wanted to reach for her communicator and call . . . "Two hundred should be enough to begin, yes. I may need to request replacements if there are complications."

"Of course." The way he let the sentence trail off, it was unclear what the answer would be right away. "It's possible from time to time, as your obedience metrics improve, that we may send you subjects for the trials. You should adjust your initial rubrics, however, to show that all the two hundred subjects you will have to begin with are decidedly against any form of obedience. It will be interesting to see the effects of your binding agent on such minds."

He nodded to Director Vance as he settled back in his chair. "Hugo will be seeing to your accommodations for this particular project and you will be reporting to the board through him. Victoria will coordinate your work on the second initiative," he grinned as he used the word, "for which we require your services. You may consider this one your means of payment for the resources you require for your work on the binding agent, since we both know that project involves just as much play as work."

"Second initiative, Sir?" Maria's tone was careful, since she didn't know what else the Directors expected from her, but she was already pleased to know that she would get adequate time and resources to work on the binding agent. Even though it wasn't only *her* baby. She and Stephen had worked on it together.

"According to our closest estimates, there were 1,324 members of the Eleusis Initiative alive on the station on the day it was destroyed, not including senior staff such as yourselves and others who escaped by way of the Twist. In spite of the many technical glitches we experienced as a result of the rebels' tampering in the weeks that followed, we estimate that nearly 1,250 of the same managed to escape the station in various spacefaring vessels. Of these, we know of at least 140 who crashed across the world and were discovered, a ship of 37 which attempted to defect back to the Consortium rather than returning to Earth, and four populations of recovered survivors totaling 389 people, many of whom are now dead."

He didn't say what they had died of, but it wasn't hard to guess, since they had been "recovered" by the Consortium.

"This leaves roughly 680 people who returned to Earth and have not yet been recovered, in over a year of searching for them. This is not a number that can be tolerated."

The man across the table from her didn't look particularly angry, but his smirk was gone and everything about his posture was still as a stone. He was not the kind of person whose bad side anyone wanted to be on. "You will work with the subjects we send you to glean information about the whereabouts of the surviving rebels, and you will apply your mind and practice to determining where the rest of them would go. All information about current results and work in tracking the rebels will be made available to you. You are to think as they would, so that you can inform the board as to what they would do in any given situation. We want them found and exterminated, along with their stolen equipment, before the next phase of the Eleusis Initiative moves forward."

Hearing that was also pleasing to Maria, since she had a particular bone to pick with several surviving rebels. She'd know if they were dead. They weren't.

Her own expression hardened and she gave the room a nod. "I'm sure it's no surprise to you that I have a personal investment in making sure the rebels are found. Rest assured that I'll do whatever it takes to get the information."

"We're sure you will." Somehow he managed to make the vote

of confidence sound like a threat. "We will be expecting thorough reports of your progress on both fronts. Please understand, the Board is of the mind that progress needs to be made in both these areas quickly, so that when we begin to move into the final phase of operations, everything can be undertaken without concerns of underlying problems. Any final questions?"

Maria nodded as he explained things needed to move quickly, and she shook her head when he asked if she had any further questions. The meeting had been a surprise, certainly, but now she was pleased with the surprise. "No final questions, Sir. Thank you very much for the opportunity. I'll send reports as progress continues."

"You will be earning the opportunity, Dr. Kaplan." He cut off her gratitude quickly. "You have three days to close your practice and your current work, after which you will report to Hugo. He will take you to your new laboratory and see that you have everything you need." He stood up from the table as his knowing smile returned, and nodded at Vance as he got to his feet. "He's also got another surprise for you. That other initiative I said we wanted you to work on earlier. I believe that project is prepared just down the hall?"

"Yes, Sir." That was a first. Maria had never heard Vance call anyone 'sir,' but Dominic was the political leader of the known universe, after all. "I'll take her there to review the case now."

They were all about filling her plate completely, weren't they? Maria got up from her chair as soon as the directors did, and she walked behind Vance as she exited the room behind him and Gehrig.

"You two certainly love the element of surprise, don't you?" Maria looked back at the opaque glass room where the Alperts remained. "Just didn't want to warn me?" Both Vance and Gehrig were her superiors, but she had been very familiar with them while working with them on the Initiative.

"You don't deserve warning, Maria." It was clear that as quiet and obedient as Vance had been with the Alperts, he had lost none of his awareness of his position over Maria. "I advised the Alperts against assigning you to this kind of work, giving you these kinds of resources. You were the primary reason for the failure on Nine, even though it's never been publicized as such and never will be. You take these experiments of yours too far and end up creating monsters you can't control."

"*I* am the primary reason for failure?" She looked over at Vance with shock and disgust. "You cannot blame solely me for that disaster. You . . ." She shook her head and let out a laugh. "You know what, it's not worth fighting with you over what is done. I will be working on this to the best of my ability. That's all that matters now."

"Your abilities are best kept in limited contexts. And we will be ensuring your context remains extremely limited." Vance clearly wasn't thrilled about the entire meeting, but like everyone else in the world, he did as the Alperts commanded.

"Here is your last project." He turned a corner and badged them through a door into a medical triage unit, then walked past the attendant nurses at the reception desk without so much as a second glance.

Near the back of the triage center, Vance stopped at a glass wall that divided the hallway from the examination room, where Maria could see someone lying in a bed under a sanitized white blanket.

"It was deemed appropriate, given your new responsibilities, that you also be cleared to care for him personally. You can read his full report yourself at your leisure, but the highlights are simple enough. He was kept in an induced coma for the first eight months of his convalescence, but failed to emerge from it after the medication was removed. During the fits in which he has emerged since, he has been entirely incoherent, though his brain waves in recent weeks are returning to those recorded from him prior to his . . . incident. All conventional methods have been attempted to bring him back to consciousness, and he is therefore being released to your medical care so that you may attempt whatever unconventional treatments you deem necessary."

Medical care? Wasn't she being released from her patients? Maria moved closer to the room and ignored Vance after he said the man would be under her care, since she had to see the man.

What she wasn't expecting was to see *him*.

Maria ran the rest of the way into the room and immediately went to the side of the bed and picked up his hand gingerly. "Stephen? You're alive?" When she heard Vance and Gehrig step up to the doorway, she looked back. "He has been alive all this time and no one told me? He's my husband!"

"Technically not true." Vance said from the doorway. "You were married under the protocols of the Initiative, which were declared void by the Initiative bill that passed just prior to the explosion. Therefore you had no rights to information regarding his welfare or condition." Vance stepped back toward the hallway. "I'll send you a message with details of your assignment in a few days. Pack what you can fit on a cart. And your 'husband,' of course."

Maria glared at Vance and thought about things she wanted to do to the man, but she instead turned her attention back to Stephen. She moved to sit on the edge of the bed and moved his hand into both of hers, instead of just one. She looked him over carefully, but it was hard, considering the last time she saw him he was unrecognizable. It seemed, however, that he had received the best care and restructuring the Consortium could provide, since other than the scars, his face looked more or less like himself. Even scars could be seen to, eventually.

"Hey, you. I thought you were dead. You shouldn't keep secrets like that, asshole."

Vance and Gehrig left her alone, but in the time she spent by his side, there was no sign of activity from him. There were steady numbers from the monitors above his bed and the occasional twitch of his muscles as the sleeves over his arms and legs flexed his muscles for him to keep his body toned and active even in disuse.

"Dr. Kaplan?" A man's shaky voice came from the doorway, clutching something unseen in one of his hands and looking as though he was about to pass out from stress. He was dressed in a doctor's coat, but it looked like he had either stolen it as a secondary school prank or he hadn't been wearing it for very long.

Maria looked over at the shaky voice. She didn't know what was causing the man to be so nervous, but she didn't really like the idea that he was nervous in the first place. She also thought it was funny that Vance and Gehrig and everyone else had no problem referring to her by the name she had taken, Dr. Kaplan, but Vance had gone out of his way to say that her marriage was void. It wasn't void to her. "Yes? Can I help you?"

"I . . ." He swallowed as if that would help his nervousness, then took a single step inside the room. "I'm Kunal. They told me I was supposed to be one of your . . . assistants." He made the word sound like the most terrifying thing in the world, but then he lifted his hands to reveal a tube-like shape.

"I was told to do this." He lifted the vial in his hand, which had been inserted into a small syringe, and injected the dark red contents efficiently into his own forearm before removing the needle and turning back to face her.

Clearly he hadn't been given much more by way of instructions as to what to do or what had been in the syringe, since he looked terrified that he had somehow killed himself, visibly shaking as he stood in front of her.

"You should really ask for more information before you do something like that." Maria said with a shake of the head, but she let go of Stephen's hand slowly and put it back down on the bed gently. "Even if someone won't give you more information, at least you asked." She crossed her arms and got up from the bed to get closer to him, her eyes scanning him up and down as she waited for the chemical agent to take effect. "How do you feel?"

"Fine." He said quickly, but his mouth kept moving afterward, and he couldn't take his eyes off Maria no matter how hard he tried. "Really sweaty, a little sick, slight shortness of breath, increased heart rate . . . possibly attributable to a history of panic attacks beginning in early childhood and increasing in severity until late adolescence . . ." Once he started, he couldn't stop answering her question, identifying everything about himself in which he could find any fault in order to try and diagnose his current state. He was a doctor, after all.

Maria got closer to him and put a hand on his shoulder. "I can tell you what's wrong with you, as long as you stop trying to diagnose yourself." She waited until he stopped talking, then reached out to grab an unused towel off the table behind him. Maria politely dabbed at the sweat on the man's forehead.

"You injected yourself with a research project of mine called the Binding Agent. I really should come up with a better name, I'll have to work on that. I do have a counter-agent, but it's not nearly as effective as what you just used on yourself. That particular vial, as all the ones I have currently produced, are mixed with a distilled cocktail that greatly enhances suggestibility in very specific ways. It means that you listen to me. You want to listen to me." She gave him a small, but somewhat pitying smile. "Because your body will find reward in my touch and attention if you do what I say." Maria showed him by touching his forehead with just her fingertips after she dabbed the sweat away. "Do you understand now?"

Every twitching muscle in Kunal's body immediately relaxed after the single touch from Maria, but while the relief in his body made its way through his entire frame and into his eyes for a moment, another heartbeat's comprehension sent his eyes flaring into a deeper panic. All the same, panic or no panic, he did understand. He understood exactly the kind of power the woman had over him with a single application of the drug he'd been given. "Yes, Doctor." He almost whimpered, since he couldn't refuse to answer her question. "I understand."

"That's good." She said gently as she touched his forehead one more time. "I have no desire or reason to harm you, so you don't need to worry. I need your assistance with this drug and to further its development. If you're dead, you're no good to me. So don't die." She took a few steps back after that. "You have no reason to fear me. I'm not the one who told you to inject yourself, am I? No. We can be friends, Doctor."

"I . . . I would . . ." He stuttered a little without moving from where she had left him, though he had taken half a step forward instinctively to follow the source of his only reason for living. "I've read some of the reports from the Eleusis Initiative, Dr. Kaplan. I was given security access to override normal redactions and read experimental logs for the behavioral conditioning that was employed there. I saw some of your experiments, though I haven't read them all yet. I'm . . ." He tried to keep from continuing, but it was pointless. "I would like to be your friend. I can't imagine anything worse than being your enemy."

That actually made her laugh. "I have enough enemies, Kunal. Most of them are down on Earth." Maria looked over at Stephen again and back at her new assistant. "We'll focus on the Earth ones first. The others will come later. Ultimately, we just want to get to Eleusis, don't we?"

"I want what you want, Doctor." Kunal said eagerly, the chemicals in his blood reaching their full effect beyond any kind of resistance he could offer. "Anything you want me to do, I'll do it. Just tell me."

"Good." She replied gently before she stared at Stephen a little bit longer. "Right now I want you to stay with Stephen and let me know if anything changes. I need to go back to my unit and pack up to move. But I want to know if there are changes."

The man rushed to the foot of the bed and whipped out his communicator, ready to monitor everything about the man just because she had told him to, as if it was the thing he had wanted most to do since childhood. His eyes were still panicked and his forehead was covered in fresh sweat, but his eagerness went deeper than he could rationally explain. "Yes, Doctor."

Maria watched them both carefully for a moment and then turned to walk out. She didn't have a choice. This was her opportunity, her way to prove herself and to get herself and Stephen back in the right direction. It was her only opportunity to make sure she could have a life on Eleusis. Now she had to make sure her drug was successful and the rebels ended up dead.

1

SPRING

"Come on, keep up!" Orion yelled back over his shoulder as he jogged up the path. The mornings were finally bearable under a few layers of clothing, and the last lingering cold of the long winter felt good after making a full circuit of the mountain valley they presently called home. "Or do you want me to just pick you up on my next lap around?"

"Your legs are twice as long as mine!" Anna yelled after Orion, and though it wasn't untrue, it also wasn't entirely the reason she wasn't able to keep up with him. Running for exercise was not one of her favorite activities, even though she was back to decent shape after the birth of her twins. Not to mention that Orion was genetically altered to be far superior to her, and it showed.

She paused as he kept going, but she told herself that she was only planning on pausing for a quick breath. "You are insane! Stop running so fast!"

He eventually relented near the top of the rise, and went backward a few steps, panting heavily, so that he could let her catch up with him. Once she did, he put an arm around her shoulders and walked with her the rest of the way to the overlook. "There's no way I'm ever getting used to this." He stood casually behind her, looking over the world below.

Their home was on the eastern edge of the Rocky Mountains, in a hollow a hundred kilometers from the nearest occupied ranch, let alone any kind of civilization. The emptiness of the world never ceased to strike him, the ruins of a city and various highways visible in the distance. The ruins were one of hundreds of ancient pockmarks on the surface of the world. Remnants of a time before humanity had destroyed itself in a violent fit of disease and fear and panic. "There's too much of it to get used to. At least that's what I keep telling myself."

"It's not nearly as pretty when my ribs are on fire and I'm

sweating like a pig." She teased as she leaned into him heavily so he was supporting her weight, since her legs felt all wobbly. "I'm a girl from the midwest. Things are flat there. We don't run up mountains for fun." Anna looked out over the view anyway, and he was right about it being a lot to get used to. It was both beautiful and frightening at the same time, since most of it looked so desolate. "I do hope that one day it will be full of life again. Even if I won't live long enough to see something like that."

"Well, if we keep on popping out twins, we could end up repopulating the whole place by ourselves. Enough to fill a high-rise somewhere, anyway." He nodded toward the horizon where a partly-destroyed skyscraper was visible through the clear morning air. "That one looks pretty good. Bit of a fixer-upper, maybe, but nobody's perfect."

Anna let out a whine and shook her head. "No, don't talk about babies. My uterus doesn't want to hear anything about babies, I just got my ass back under control." She turned around in his embrace and leaned against him with her front instead of her back. "Especially don't wish twins on me again. Other than these milk-enhanced tits, there's little benefit to popping out multiples at once."

"Well, you got two over with at once. It's not like being pregnant was your favorite thing in the world." He leaned down to kiss her, even though they were both still breathing heavily as they waited for the morning air to cool them off. "And your tits didn't need any enhancing, but that's not a complaint."

Anna smirked and pulled Orion down into another kiss. "I'm glad you have no interest in seeing them altered." She was still sweaty and panting for breath as she looked backward at the view and then back at Orion. "You know, there are *much* better ways to work up a sweat. Just sayin'."

"Whole different kind of cardio. I'm a big fan of that kind too, but unless I'm fucking you up against a wall, it's not much of a leg workout. Gotta get some distance stamina in there too." He grinned down at her and slipped his hands under her workout clothes, glad as always to have her back more or less to her pre-pregnancy self. "I also need to just reaffirm once in a while that I can still run faster than you, for those inevitable times when I piss you off."

"I'm not *that* violent." She defended quickly, but she grinned when he slid his hands under her clothes. "I would think your giant legs would ensure you can outrun me easily." Anna panted as she kissed him again between breaths. "Okay, so, mister giant are you going to carry me all the way home?"

"All the way? I don't think so." He relinquished his hold on her, but immediately picked her up by the waist and tossed her over his shoulder, holding onto her with an arm behind her knees as he began to continue down the path off the mountainside. "Part of the way, maybe."

"My legs thank you, monstrous man." She groaned in pleasure even though it wasn't a comfortable position. At least she wasn't running anymore. "I also have an excellent view of your ass. I love this ass."

"I've tried to take good care of it. Honestly, that part is easier down here than it was upstairs." It was true enough. One of Orion's favorite things about living on Earth was how much easier it was to stay in shape, since he didn't have to worry about changing gravity all the time making life easier on him. He was still nowhere near most of the other rebels who had been born and lived most of their lives on Earth. But he was certainly stronger than he previously had been, as was evidenced by the length of time he was able to carry Anna down the mountainside. "What have you got going on the rest of the day? I know we talked about it last night, but then the grain alcohol kicked in and I honestly don't remember much after passing out."

She laughed but she didn't say anything until he actually put her down. Once he got part of the way down the mountain he needed a break. "I'm going to stay with the kids this morning since I've been away the last few mornings. I'm even going to make you a real breakfast and everything like a proper wife." She smiled as she looked over his sweaty body. God he was hot. "Then I'm going out to help with our house so we can move by the end of this week."

"You really think we can get in there that fast?" He helped as much as he was able on the construction of their new house, but he was consistently outdone by the rest of those working on it. He had many talents, but it turned out that construction wasn't one of them.

He had, however, had a major hand in planning out the house's design, since he did have a mind for efficient use of space. With a community of eight hundred people, space was a prevalent concern, especially since ninety-four of those people had yet to turn a single year old. "I thought we were still waiting on windows for the upper floors?"

"They got in early. Like, two o'clock this morning early. There's another delivery coming sometime today with more." She was still grinning, since she was so excited to finally have their own place. More or less. They were going to live in a small house next to Logan and Mercury since they all wanted the kids to be raised together. "I just want to get out of the underground. It's disgusting and deafeningly quiet. I hate it."

"For a girl who grew up in the middle of a corn field, you've got some pretty low standards for deafeningly quiet." He had to agree, though, since the underground bothered everyone. When they had first arrived, Gordon (no, Jason, Orion had to remind himself) told them the place was called the Labyrinth, and it had more than earned its name. The extensive underground complex built into the heart of the mountain was a good and secure home, but it continued to give Orion the creeps. "I'm with you, though. It'll be good to be back up in our own space again. Have a door we can shut and a separate place to keep the kids."

"It'll be kinda weird to live next to Logan and Mercury, but I think it's a good idea. The kids should grow up together. Right now they just cry together, but it will be good." Right? It was the most civil and mature way to go about things. God, she felt old. "I'm also talking to that dickhead Jason again. I want to go home and see my family. It's been more than a year. The Consortium has no fucking idea where we are."

"Every time you do, it's like he's got a whole stable of reasons that he keeps picking out at random. But I think Logan's coming around to your way of thinking." He and Logan had never been and would never be friends, but they interacted more often than Anna and Mercury did, which was to say they actually spoke to each other by choice from time to time. Orion was one of the drivers and conveyance officers for the rebels, which was a fancy way of saying that he drove trucks and occasionally flew the one and only helicopter they had at their disposal. The job involved taking orders from Logan and occasionally driving the man around, but they managed to establish a more or less professional relationship. "He was talking the other day about starting up more recruiting efforts once the rest of the block housing is built aboveground. We'll have a lot of space down in the Labyrinth for more people to relocate."

"I just want to see my family." All practical reasons aside, once she realized where they were, the need to go home got worse every month that passed. "I want you to meet my family. My dad, if he's still alive. Not to mention, we need more doctors. Mercury, Barry, and Michael can't handle our population. Not when living out here is this hazardous. Between injuries and babies, Mercury and Logan hardly see each other. I'm not a fan of the woman, but it's shit to be overworked like that."

"You're right enough about that." They had tried to train up a number of nurses to assist the doctors in taking care of the population, but it was still a ridiculous amount of work to go around. "White will cave. He has to, with spring coming on. He might have thought this war would be over by now, but at some point, he's got to just own up to the fact that he hasn't pulled off his end of the bargain. We need more people, we need more resources, and we're gonna need a whole lot more of everything to fight this war." Orion was almost always practical first and feelings second, but he squeezed her hand as they walked. "I also want to meet these siblings of yours. They sound like a lot of fun."

Anna squeezed his hand back and she looked down at his hand as it engulfed hers. "I'm glad we got some time together this morning." They were pretty fortunate, they got more control over their time than most. Kids were hard enough, but she and Orion were figuring it out together and he was a great dad. "I'm not a fan of you potentially running into a lot of my exes, but that's unavoidable."

"So you've told me." He had always found her accounts of her life down on Earth incredibly entertaining rather than something to judge her by. "I'm not too worried about it. Whoever it is we run into, I've had more of you than any of them, and I'm going to have plenty more. Is there a word for the opposite of jealous? That feeling where you feel sorry for some poor bastard who's never gonna get the chance to fuck the most amazing woman alive ever again?"

"God, you are the best. You sure know how to make a woman feel good when she just ran up a mountain like a loser and had to be carried back down." Anna pulled Orion into another kiss before she would go any further. When the kiss broke, she pulled back slightly and looked into his eyes. "What if we never make it? What if we never go to Eleusis? Are you going to be happy here?"

He couldn't give her an answer right away, but as he held onto her hand, she could tell the only reason he was hesitating was because he wanted to make sure he said the right thing rather than speaking without thinking. "If we never make it to Eleusis, it'll be because we lost, and sooner or later, the Consortium will find us here. So long as we're on this planet, we're on borrowed time. I don't want to just borrow time with you. I want to make it ours. And that means getting somewhere we can have it all to ourselves."

Anna wasn't entirely convinced they really had a chance to win. Jason couldn't crack the Twist, and he wasn't the only one who had tried. They were all stuck in a limbo, and most of them were wondering how things would end up. Death or Eleusis. "I want that too. I'm just worried that we'll never get there. We don't realistically have the people or the resources to fight the Consortium. So we're sitting ducks."

"I prefer to think of myself as a sitting leopard. Or maybe a tiger. Something that ought not to be poked with a stick, one way or another." He kissed her and turned back toward the entrance to the Labyrinth with a sigh, as they passed a few other people out for similar early-morning purposes on their way in. It was just too tempting to find any excuse to get out from the subterranean confines. Any excuse at all. "We'll get there. It's just a matter of finding the right way, that's all."

Anna still wasn't entirely convinced but she gave a placating nod anyway. "I'm glad you have more confidence about it than I do." She held tightly to his hand as the subterranean darkness took them again. "Come on, let's go rescue our kids from Gwen."

It was close quarters belowground, but that morning with so many people coming and going to get out for a little while, it was even worse. They squeezed into a small elevator with five other people, and he pulled her in against him in the corner just to touch her scandalously the entire way down the dozens of stories they plunged below the surface. By the time they got down to the level where they lived, they were the only people left on the lift, but that didn't mean he stopped touching her. "This is our stop." He glanced at the lift door as if nothing was weird. "Come on, what are you waiting for?"

"I'm waiting for . . ." Anna was trying to think up an excuse to linger on the elevator so he would keep up the touching. "Um . . ."

"Naptime. The word you're looking for is naptime." He kissed her again but moved away, since they needed to relieve Gwen. The woman was busy and had done them a favor by watching their kids while they went on a run. For the rest, though, their kids had minds very much their own, and their naptime routines were the clock by which the rest of their lives were set.

Anna whimpered when he pulled his hand away and forced herself off the elevator, since they were on a 3-day dry spell. "No fair. You big tease."

"This elevator can't handle what I plan to do to you, baby." He backed away with her hand still in his, as they headed down the stone corridor toward their rooms. "As it is, there *will* be neighbors complaining. Not that I care, so long as it's not the kids. Anybody else can bitch and moan as much as they want."

She didn't say anything else as they walked the rest of the way, but before they went inside, she stopped him. "Just tell me your plans." Anna whispered urgently. "Just to tide me over until naptime."

He stopped with her and leaned down in the low corridor (in which he had to walk partly stooped, at least until they got into their unit) to kiss her neck and whisper against her ear, even though the sound still echoed in the impenetrable silence of the lower corridors.

"This is the first morning I've had off to be home with you, and one of the last days we're going to spend down here belowground. I'm going to set the camera for the kids, then take you into the bathroom and bar the door to soundproof it. The whole damn compound is gonna hear you screaming my name through the pipes and think the place is haunted by the horniest ghost that ever spooked the underground."

Anna smirked but she shook her head. She definitely wanted to be screaming in the bathroom, but she didn't want to think about a ghost when she did it. "Alright, alright. Dirty talk doesn't usually come with horny ghosts. Always with the jokes. Let's get inside then."

"Hey, there's nothing wrong with horny ghosts. Who am I to say they can't do as they like?" He opened the door and let her inside first, obviously not finding any problem with his plan.

"Everybody still alive in here?" He asked in a gentle voice as soon as he had the door closed. It wasn't hard to be heard throughout the unit. The place echoed like it had been designed for the acoustics, not to survive a nuclear holocaust.

"Still alive!" Gwen called out from the bathroom where she had both babies in the bathtub at once. "They decided to wear their breakfast food, since they still haven't really figured out the whole keep-it-in-your-mouth thing." Gwen was soaked with bath water from the splashing babies, but she didn't look like she cared. Most of her time was spent watching babies, after all.

There were nearly a hundred babies in the complex and Gwen hopped from one family to another whenever she was needed. She was young, single, and she didn't need nearly as much sleep as everyone else. She was also building up a reputation for her house calls, but the people involved didn't usually mention it too much. Not everyone who had children together was happy about the match, after all. The Initiative hadn't asked for people's opinions when they got put together for procreative purposes. Gwen had earned a reputation for enjoying some of the discontented men in the companionships.

Gwen barely looked back with her bright blue eyes when Orion approached the bathroom doorway, her sun-kissed blonde hair clinging to her skin from the splashed water. She didn't want to look away from the tub too long because she didn't want one of the babies to slip under the water. "Leo hates plums, by the way. He spit it all into my face."

"Well that was rude." Orion stayed by the doorway to watch the scene, mostly because the bathroom was only so big and certainly hadn't been designed with the need to bathe infants in mind. "Not cool, little guy. Appreciate the plums. They don't make those back where half your genetics come from. Show some respect."

Leo splashed excitedly at the sight of his father, which only further soaked Gwen sitting on the floor, but she laughed anyway. "Alright. I've had enough of this." She grabbed a towel, picked up Leo, and wrapped him up all while keeping an eye on Lynnette as well. "Come get your son. He should be good and clean by now."

"Yeah, we'll see how long that lasts." Orion said as he took the squirming little boy. He was a blur of constant motion, but Orion managed to wrap him up tightly in the towel to contain him, if only temporarily. Gwen and Anna could hear Orion threatening the little boy all the way down the hall. "Boy, I swear, if you pee on me again, we are not gonna be friends. You understand that? Not friends. Friends don't pee on friends. It's just one of those things."

Both Anna and Gwen laughed as Orion walked away with Leo, and Anna stepped into the bathroom to help Gwen get Lynnette out of the tub next. The girl was more sedated than her brother, though they were equally smiley. Leo already had four teeth and Lynnette barely had two on the bottom.

"Thanks for watching them this morning, Gwen." Anna took the towel-wrapped baby and tried to dry her off. "I nearly killed myself on that run, but you know. Whatever makes Orion happy."

"You seem to have that effect on him. Means he spends his time running laps and not running around." Gwen said with a smile as she got up off the floor and grabbed a spare towel to pat herself dry after being splashed so many times. "Do you need me to hang around? I told Logan and Mercury I'd pop over to their unit as soon as you and Orion got home."

"No, I think we've got it from here. Thanks again, Gwen." Anna said with a sedated smile, though she was always unsettled by comments Gwen made. Of course she was going to keep her husband happy. She certainly didn't want a snipe like Gwen to come along and take him. Especially since Gwen was young, fun, spontaneous, and all sorts of bendy Anna wasn't. "I better check on Orion and Leo before Orion gets peed on. Gwen is leaving, Orion!" Anna yelled out, so he would know what was going on.

"I know, the acoustics told me!" He answered from the other end of the hall, where they could hear Leo laughing in spite of a few frustrated grunts from Orion. "Thanks for watching the rugrats! We'll make sure they're more annoying for you next time."

"I can handle it!" Gwen said with a grin and gave Lynnette a little wave before she headed toward the door. "You know where to find me." She was looking at Anna but she knew Orion could hear her too. Orion had never once shown her any interest, but she wouldn't mind tackling a giant if he did. However, she wasn't one to go around with the *happily* married. With that, she stepped out and headed through the halls to get to Mercury and Logan's unit next.

Orion shook his head as Anna walked into the children's room so they could get the children dressed. Finding baby clothes had been as much of a challenge as everything else living out on the edge of the world, especially since the community needed so many of them, but Leo and Lynnette were among the oldest of the children. They ended up getting most things first and then handing them down to others as they grew out of things. "That woman is trouble, but you have to hand it to her, she found the one gig that nobody in this whole place is gonna turn down. Nobody says no to free babysitting."

"I don't think it's really free. It's just that neither of us are offering what she wants to get paid." Anna shook her head and got Lynnette diapered and dressed. Anna was pretty handy with fabrics, so whenever she could get her hands on some, she was capable of making clothes for anyone who needed them. It was a skill that she had needed growing up as the oldest of so many children. "If you ever consider paying her, come find me first. I'll change your mind."

"Never once crossed my mind." He smiled over their kids at her. "Don't forget, I more than had my fill of the bimbo game way before I even met you. It doesn't interest me." He picked Leo up once he was dressed, and went to stand by Anna with his free arm across her chest to hold her back against him while she held Lynnette. "No amount of free babysitting is worth that. And I say that as someone who is very earnestly a fan of free babysitting. Seeing as it gives me more time with you."

Anna turned her head just enough so she could lead him into another kiss, even with both babies in their arms. "I used to be her. Chasing after everything I could. I don't want to even think about it, I want you."

"You've got me, wife." He never shied away from touching her every way he wanted to whenever they actually had some time together, and even with the kids in their arms, that moment was no exception. They'd had some incredible fights over the course of their year on the ground, but life away from the Consortium had given them an opportunity to get to know each other on their own terms. They had been able to develop their relationship in the ways they wanted, not the way they were forced to. Orion wouldn't have it any other way.

"Hey, hey! Your mother is allowed to bite my ear. You are not, dude. Not okay." He squirmed to get Leo away from the side of his face, but it only made the little boy laugh.

Anna laughed loudly and gave Orion another kiss before she backed away. "Come on, let's go get them some toys and I'll work on breakfast." Anna was happy with Orion, and she loved seeing him as a wonderful father to their children, but sometimes she wondered if he would ever take anything seriously. Anna wasn't known for being the most serious person herself, but Orion was always playing things off, and it drove her nuts sometimes. Just like every other couple, they had their ups and downs. They had each other. That was really all that mattered.

A few levels away, Logan and Mercury's unit was a very different place. It was still fairly early in the morning, but as soon as Gwen was given the go-ahead to enter the unit, she could smell breakfast already come and gone, and she could hear white-noise still roaring in a back room with the children. The front room of the unit served both as an office for Logan and an impromptu examination room for Mercury, and there were none of the children's toys and general chaos that Anna and Orion's unit had at all times. For them, their children either went to someone else's house for daycare or remained back in their bedroom.

"Mercury is finishing up her shower." Logan said from the desk nearby, where it looked like he was reviewing a series of reports, standing out in sharp, shining contrast to the relative darkness of the rest of the unit. The couple took living underground to heart in the way they kept their unit, ostensibly in the name of conserving energy and maintaining a sedated atmosphere for their children. "There's leftover biscuits and some eggs if you haven't already had breakfast. Help yourself."

"Thanks." Gwen said with her ever-present smile as she went to get a plate and filled it with the food mentioned. She kept herself busy all the time, so a full meal was a rarity she cherished. "I was too busy battling Anna and Orion's twins to eat. The closest I got was pureed food that was either spat or thrown at me." She shrugged, since she wasn't that bothered by it, but she took her plate and moved to stand by Logan's desk. "Mind if I ask what you're working on? You look very focused."

"I do try to be." He said without looking away from the screen. "It's the most recent manifest for the supplies arriving today. I'm checking it against outstanding requests and figuring out how to disappoint the smallest number of people." He moved a few more items to a new method of organization and sighed. "Then I can have other people do the disappointing and wait for the screaming and whining to start. Sort of like your job, in some ways."

Gwen laughed at his deadpan joke and nodded as she took a bite. "I guess you have to know who isn't as affected by disappointment. Some babies will just find another toy and move on, other babies cry for hours." She looked over the reports briefly as she stood next to him, but then her gaze drifted so that she was looking just at Logan. He was such a gorgeous, strong man, but so . . . stoic and unreachable. He never looked happy. Was he happy? He and Mercury had a strange dynamic between them that Gwen couldn't figure out, but neither of them looked very happy most of the time. So few smiles. "I heard Mercury had a long night. Mrs. Graham finally went into labor, huh?"

"After much prodding and a slight assist with medication, yes. She had a little girl about four hours ago." He still didn't take his eyes off the screen or his work, in spite of how close she'd gotten with her plate of food. "I'm sure she would appreciate any help you can give her with the newborn, but I would also advise you to wait until Trevor goes to work unloading the inventory later this afternoon. That way Mrs. Graham won't get any ideas about your motives going there to help."

"Oh, Trevor and I have never danced the dance. Don't worry about that." She teased as she took another bite and kept looking Logan over. If he was going to ignore her, she was going to look. "They were married before they got here. And they weren't matched. It makes quite a difference, you know. It's the matched ones who act out more often. Trapped in their choices by babies, as it were."

"Yes, I'm familiar with your credo." He said with a glance just barely to the side that nonetheless targeted her without even looking directly at her. "There are more than a few divorces in progress, not that I can even bring myself to call them unfortunate, since they've really been just a matter of time. But you have hurried a few of them on. I also understand that no fewer than four of them have also extended marriage proposals to you. I don't imagine you're actually going to take any of them up on that offer, are you?"

Gwen smirked. "Four. Yeah, that sounds about right." She shook her head, even though his glance had been short and he wasn't looking at her again. "No, I've no interest in marriage right now. That would ruin all this fun I'm having." Gwen didn't advertise the reason why she wasn't afraid to hop about so much, since it was technically illegal, but she wasn't worried about joining the mothers' club. Not soon, anyway. "And it is so much fun. You don't look like you have enough fun, Mr. Bickford. You should try to have more."

"My fun isn't your concern, Ms. Pierce." He had established very early on in their working relationship that he was going to keep himself at a distance and expected her to do the same, but that clearly never stopped her from trying. "And if your fun gets to the point where it threatens the peace of the community, it will become my concern. So far you've done an admirable job of avoiding that, and even with the divorces currently in progress, I will thank you to continue your discretion."

He could hear himself when he spoke, hear the man he had become over time living in the mountains and taking care of the people who had somehow become *his* people. He wasn't sure exactly how or when it had happened, but ever since they had arrived on Earth, nearly everyone in the community had looked to him for the final word in all things, and it weighed on him heavily as the months went on. "What time is your next engagement?"

"Not until this afternoon." She took her half-eaten plate and went to get rid of the rest, since his pseudo-threat was a little unsettling. Gwen had absolutely no interest in getting kicked out, especially since she would probably end up dead. She was from the area formerly known as California, so she'd traveled a great distance in her short life. "One-thirty." She added, since he'd asked for a time.

He nodded approvingly when she actually answered as he had required, but he still wasn't looking at her. "Mercury will appreciate the chance to catch up on some sleep after last night. I'll be leaving shortly for the day, so you'll have the unit to yourself."

He finished the list he was working on and sent it off, then checked a camera on one side of the room to make sure the twins were still sleeping soundly next to each other in their crib. They weren't fully sleeping through the night yet, and Logan had been up most of the night with them until they finally gave up the fight.

He got up from his chair and switched off his interface before stalking across the room, still in a loose t-shirt and pajama pants from the night he'd passed with the children. "What do you need from the requisition?" There were advantages to being the babysitter for the leader of the entire community, and Logan made sure to keep them in Gwen's good graces as much as possible, just for the relief she offered from the children from time to time.

"Chocolate? Is there chocolate this time? And maybe some more fabric? I am hoping to find some blue fabric." She kept her distance, but she still watched him carefully. "Are you sure that you don't need some sleep as well?"

"I'm on my way to get some now. You know where the monitor is." He stopped at the doorway into the hallway that led back to the sleeping chambers, framed by darkness as always, as he considered her request. "The blue fabric I might be able to manage. Leave me some notes as to what you're hoping for and I'll get you whatever I can accommodate. I'm not so sure about the chocolate, but I'll let you know."

"Thanks. Logan." Gwen said gently before she grabbed the monitor as he disappeared.

Mercury stepped out of the bathroom quietly once she saw their bedroom was dark after her shower, and she went about getting her clothes quietly, since she didn't want to wake Logan. She heard Gwen's voice when the woman arrived, so she knew that the boys were being monitored. Mercury wanted to check on a few patients before getting some sleep, though it felt like she could never get enough rest. Or time. For anyone or anything.

"Come to bed, Mercury." Logan's voice came from the bed, when he saw by the dim light that she was heading for her clothes.

Mercury startled a little when she heard Logan's voice, but then she turned and walked toward the bed. "I thought you were asleep." She whispered. She always felt like she needed to whisper when their babies were asleep.

"No, I just came back in. I was reviewing tonight's reported inventory." He put out a hand to take hers as she got closer, then pulled her in beneath the covers gently before he covered her up with the sheet. It was a far cry from the luxurious room they had shared on Nine, with the entire world shining and spinning just outside their window, smooth sheets and perfect quarters free of a single speck of dust. The underground was well-designed, but the perfect darkness and smallish rooms gave the darkness a sense of overall claustrophobia that only went away under the closer constraints of the sheets over their bodies.

He took some time getting comfortable there with her against him, but eventually came to rest with his head on their pillow and her head on his chest. "Did the shower help?"

"Somewhat. The water turned cold quickly, so it wasn't as relaxing as I had hoped for." She admitted honestly but Logan was warm, and her body instantly relaxed against his. He was clothed and she wasn't, but she didn't care. Especially when his fingers scraped up and down her back underneath the blankets in a constant caress. "That feels nice."

At that admission, he kept it up, and pulled the blanket up around her tightly to make sure he kept her warm. "They brought back a few more hot water converters on this trip. I've made sure that not all of them are being installed in the surface houses. So maybe there will be some improvements down here with our supply." The station had allowed for many things to be unlimited, even if other things had been in short supply. It was still an adjustment for both of them, since in his life of privilege he had never particularly wanted for anything that couldn't be delivered within a few weeks of ordering it. "You've had a long night. You need to get some sleep."

"I haven't seen you all week." She mumbled against his skin, since he was definitely helping her relax, and she was starting to get warm. "Living like this is so hard." Mercury admitted in a vulnerable whisper, since she was a little worried he would turn into her hardened leader and tell her that everyone was dealing with the same problems. She wasn't looking for privilege, she was just so tired. "I'm trying to help as many people as I can, but it's . . . a lot."

Mercury didn't want to admit that it was too much, but it was. Admitting that it was too much wouldn't change the situation, though, so she thought it was pointless to even mention it. "We're also running low on treatment medication. We need a lab to produce more." The only way she could prevent everyone from getting sick all over again was to treat. And they were running low on the supply they had stolen before leaving the station.

"The chemist team is working on ways to synthesize what they need, and the import tonight should bring in enough to see us through another few months until they can get up and running." He said just as quietly. A few people had skipped their treatments, just as Logan himself had a few times, in favor of others who were more likely to need early interventions, but it was just hard. All of it was hard. "They're confident they'll be able to start producing from some raw materials soon. And there's two more nurses already trained in the convoy coming in." Two more nurses would only help a little, allow those already working to take just a little more time off to rest and recover before getting back to work, but it was something. It was never enough, but it was always something to help them stay more or less on their feet.

"Don't worry about any of that right now. Just worry about getting some rest. Gwen's got the boys and she's not going anywhere until this afternoon. Which means neither are we."

"I heard her talking a little bit." Mercury opened her eyes again, but all she was greeted with was darkness. It wasn't very comforting, but being close to Logan was the comfort she truly needed. "She doesn't think you're fun."

That got a low chuckle from Logan as he moved in to kiss her neck. "Hopefully you disagree."

"Mmmm. We've both been much less fun recently. But she doesn't know you like I do." Mercury enjoyed his kisses on her neck, and she moved into his touch eagerly. Most of her pregnancy had been spent recovering from what happened to her at the hands of the Kaplans, but she had managed to slowly work her way out of it with Logan's attention and help. She was still quieter than before, and definitely more fearful, but she still managed to function as normally as she could under the circumstances. She trusted Logan and a few others. That was all that she needed. "Most people are afraid of you. You're very serious."

He ran his hands over her a little more once she moved in against him, and even though she couldn't see him in the near-pitch-darkness, she knew him well enough after almost a year and a half of sharing his life to know what his expression looked like. "It gets things done. And if it means people don't like me, I can live with that. So long as things get done." He said it resignedly, since even after so long, he didn't like to admit how much he enjoyed the power his position had given him. He tried as hard as he could to remind himself that underneath it all, he was nothing more than a farmer on a power trip. But it had been a long and sustained trip. "The only person here whose opinion I really care about is you."

"The only person, huh? Well, that gives me a lot of power, doesn't it?" She teased gently, but she responded to his touches by moving closer to his lips and kissing him gently. Mercury still tasted like minty toothpaste, but she hoped he didn't mind. "I love you. I don't get the chance to say that much anymore. We never see each other."

"No, we really don't." He returned the kisses, his hands still wandering over her to take in the feel of her greedily. Time had changed a lot of things about them both and changed a great deal about their relationship, but it hadn't changed how much he loved her. It had just changed some of the methods of how. "I love you too. And if I manage to pull off the surprise I have in the works, you and I will both get some time away from here pretty soon."

"Surprise?" She replied curiously, but she didn't want him to stop touching her. Mercury loved to be desired by Logan, especially because he was so attentive to her needs. When they had a chance to be together, anyway. "I like surprises. But I like having you here more." She punctuated the statement with another kiss, and her hand slid under his thin shirt so she could touch his skin. "I want to see you more. I miss you."

He let her touch him however she liked, even though he knew they were both tired after the day and night of running ragged. Still, being away from the kids and having time to themselves was its own kind of very small vacation, and he wanted to enjoy as much of it with his wife as possible while they could.

"I miss you too. Constantly." He moved to oblige when she pulled his shirt over his head, but his huge hands didn't leave her body for any longer than they had to. "Did Christoff get the flowers to you yesterday?" Logan hadn't officially adopted the boy, but he was one of the few orphans that could actually run around for himself, since he'd been a part of the Labyrinth residents before the rest of the fugitives had arrived. He'd gotten the boy his own small unit right across the hall from the one he shared with Mercury, and the boy had been an eager errand-runner and general-purpose spy for Logan ever since. He and Renata had spent quite a lot of time together, and Logan was fairly sure the boy was as much in love with his secretary as he was afraid of Logan himself, but both made for powerful motivators of obedience.

Flowers . . . Mercury had to think about it for a moment. She remembered seeing Christoff momentarily but she was so busy that she hadn't paid the boy much mind. "Yes, they were beautiful. I forgot to bring them back with me, though. I may have left them with Mrs. Graham." Mercury kissed Logan with as much heat as she could muster. "She'll appreciate them after what she's gone through." Yvette Graham had had a troublesome pregnancy with too many instances of early labor, but she'd managed to hold out long enough that the baby was born without complications. Mercury had her worries, but the baby was under Barry's care now. "Thank you for thinking of me. I wish I had sent you something in return. I think about you all the time."

"You were busy bringing a new life into the world. I think

you've got a valid excuse." He grinned, and kissed her harder, pulling her down against him so that he could wrap his arms around her back. "I think about you constantly. I know I'm not cut out for the baby-bringing business, but I'd love nothing more than to be around you every day."

Mercury relaxed a lot more when he talked like that and when he wrapped his arms around her securely. She didn't know why, but she got a little teary when she heard him say it. "I worry a lot. I don't want to drift apart."

"We're up in the mountains. The only things drifting anywhere around here are the clouds, and we're a ways below them right now." He moved her onto her back on the bed so his kisses could wander over the rest of her neck and shoulders, though his touches were still slow, enjoying her rather than devouring her. They both lived in a perpetual state of being exhausted, and for a long while, he had been very careful not to push her or ask any more of her than she offered.

His tone turned a little more serious as he leaned down against her, his hands wandering over her within the warmth of the blankets. "I've pushed away everyone else in this settlement because I want them to see me as nothing more or less than their governor. But I never want that from you. I don't want any distance from you at all."

She placed her hands gently on his face and pulled him in for another kiss before she hooked one of her legs around his waist, just to keep him close. Mercury wanted him close as often as she could, since she *needed* him just as much as she wanted him. "I don't want distance from you either. But you don't need to keep yourself so far away from everyone else. I don't like them thinking you're cold and heartless. You're not. We're not old people. We shouldn't have to live with the world on our shoulders all of the time. I want to enjoy my life too. It's been hard to do that."

He nuzzled her neck as he pressed himself against her, his body quickly remembering exactly how much he loved to be near her. No amount of time could change his attraction to her. "I think the only times in my life I enjoy anymore are with the kids and with you." He held himself up with one of his fists in the sheets beside her and manhandled her with the other, the space between the sheets turning heated. "But much, much more with you."

"Mmmmmm. I just want to make you happy, Logan." Mercury's hands wandered down his sides and she kissed him just as passionately. "You had a long night too. But I don't want to sleep." She tugged at his pants, but she rarely removed any of his clothes without his permission. "I want you. I have missed you so much. I don't want to miss you anymore."

He moved to let her push aside his pajama pants, then laid himself against her with another heated kiss. Things had changed between them since their first stolen nights together, especially since the destruction of Nine, but every time with Mercury was just like the first for Logan. No matter how long he spent with her, no matter how devoted they were to each other and how much time passed, he still found her as much an incredible mystery as the day they had met. He understood her, and she understood him, and he wanted to be everything she needed him to be. "I never want you to miss me." He moved against her slowly as her body responded to him, clasping her against him as if the rest of the world would try to take her away.

"Then . . . you can never leave this unit again." Mercury stuttered before she moaned and wrapped her legs around him to keep him close. He felt so good. A wall of muscle and heat, he made her feel stable, protected, and still sexy. Somewhere in the back of her mind she knew Gwen was out there and it was a small unit, but she was jealous and possessive enough that she almost hoped Gwen would hear them. Logan was hers. "That's the only way I won't miss you."

She heard him chuckle and felt the sound rumble against her chest before he leaned down to kiss her again. "Alright, then. I'll stay here, you'll stay here, and we'll do away with the entire concept of clothes forever." He certainly wanted her that much, from the way he was touching her. "I'll give the order that we're not to be disturbed for a year, and supplies are to be delivered to us by the door."

"Perfect." She agreed as her body turned as needy, since every touch was erotic. He knew just where to touch her, and she responded every time.

He kissed her deeply instead of sharing all the thoughts that came into his mind, his touch working against her with the ease of long familiarity. Most of what they had were memories. Memories of a time when things had been new and easier, in some ways. Memories of the fire that had existed between them when they first realized how drawn they were to each other, and always had been.

The draw he felt toward her hadn't changed, the need he felt for her that was only satisfied by her presence. But time and circumstances had pushed them apart, no matter what their own desires on the matter were. They both had responsibilities they couldn't and wouldn't unload onto other people. But as he heard her moans increase in pitch, he wondered all over again if he could just put everything else aside, tell someone else to take the reins for once, tell someone else to pick up more shifts so that he and Mercury could have more time together.

Mercury's mind was entirely on the present, everything else pushed aside for once under the weight of her husband. "Logan." She worshipped his name with her moans, and every touch she returned to him was desperate. What she did think about was how much she missed him and missed this, the fiery intimacy they had together, and how grateful she was that he was willing to be intimate even when she knew he was exhausted. "Logan . . ."

The sound of his name wrapped inside her moans was a drug he would never have enough of, and he kissed her lips as he sent her careening over the edge. He wanted to take in every part of her pleasure that he could, take her to himself in every way, and he didn't relax his assault until she was shuddering beneath him with the aftershocks of the moment. "Think about that next time." He whispered against her ear as her own moans echoed back to her in the enclosed stone space.

Even his whispers were sexy, especially when it was that kind of command, and it made her groan in pleasure even more. When the world kept her busy, it was hard for her to remember little things like that, but Logan was beyond anything she could have imagined or anticipated. She loved him, she was addicted to him, and while she hated the way they were forced together, she couldn't regret it completely. Without the Initiative, she never would have been with Logan. Never would have fallen in love with him. "I will." She promised eventually, but she didn't stop touching him. "Will you think about it too when you think about me?"

"Every time." He promised in return, content for a while just to lay against her and feel the heat he had inspired in her body warming the bed and every part of him. The darkness of the room was near-complete, but the red of her hair still came through as it splayed out along the pillow behind her head. Why couldn't he stay in that moment? All he wanted was to look down at his wife and see her satisfied against the bed, with no constraints, no one asking her for anything, no one pushing her beyond her limits, just relaxation and contentment, if only for an instant.

As he looked down at her and she finally realized he was watching her, she squirmed a little bit under his scrutiny. Unlike Anna and the stubborn fifteen pounds that had lingered for a while after her babies were born, Mercury had sprung back to normal quickly. Probably because she kept so busy in the first place. "You know what I like thinking about even more?" She reached out for his hand and then tugged him closer. "Feeling you inside of me."

It had been too long since they'd been able to talk to each other or be with each other the way they once had, and her eagerness for him brought up all kinds of memories for Logan. Times when he had tormented her into begging for him just to make it that much better when she had him, times when he had woken her up in the middle of the night to be with her even when they were both still half-asleep.

His touch on her and the way he moved were slower, more sleepy and relaxed for the moment as he kissed her, moving against her easily. "There's nowhere I'd rather be in the world." He whispered quietly, rocking himself against the most sensitive and satisfied parts of her. "I want you." He said in no uncertain terms through the kisses that burned a trail along her breasts. "Every minute of every day." He had taken to keeping his beard slightly more rugged and ragged in their life in the mountains, and the coarseness of it was a signature to her skin. "Every second of every night." He breathed as he finally slid inside her with a groan of absolute satisfaction.

Everything felt right when Logan was finally inside of her, and now she was moaning for an entirely different reason. "Every second I'm alive. I want you too." Her voice was ragged already from his previous torture, but he could hear how her desire dripped from every word. Her hips responded to every movement he made, and it was bliss. Hearing his groans and moans was everything she wanted to hear.

Even tired, there was something desperate about Logan that needed her too much to pay attention to his own body's fatigue, and their lovemaking was as fierce as it had ever been as a result. He was greedy for her, wrapping her up in his arms and driving her own moans higher and higher as if they were the only thing keeping him breathing. Everything he had, he gave her, holding nothing back and for once delaying nothing. He needed her too much to play any of the games that they both enjoyed so much with each other. She was the only peace his world knew anymore, the only thing that truly made sense, and it was a delicious feeling to lose himself in the world of her. Being completely satisfied, falling apart to a depleted nothingness, was a heaven he doubted he deserved, but relished anyway as he panted against her skin. Each breath was a caress of its own as his beard swept over her chest.

Mercury fell apart all over again in delicious ecstasy, heightened by Logan's pleasure, and she clung to him as her orgasm rippled through her body with every tiny movement he made. She was happily in a more exhausted and relaxed state, and yet she still clung to Logan just to make sure that he would stay right there with her. She knew that he wasn't going to leave, but too many times had they rushed off into responsibility when they should have just stayed and cherished each other a little bit longer. Mercury wasn't sure how it was possible, but the connection that she and Logan had was so much more than physical. She felt like she was a part of him as long as he wanted her to be, and she needed that as much as wanted it.

"That . . . was amazing." She replied haltingly, but she wanted him to know that being with him was the best thing in her life.

A growl was all he could manage in response for a long time, until he finally rolled them to one side with her legs still wrapped around him. It wasn't the first time he'd kept her on top of him as they settled in to sleep, but it had been a long time. His touch along her sides and back was sleepy and sated, but it kept her body tingling even as their shared exhaustion worked its way through both of them.

"I want more." He said through the irresistible haze of satisfied sleep taking them over. "I want you for days, not just once in weeks."

"Mmmhmmm." She said with her own sleepy response and a nod, and she kissed him soundly even as her eyes got heavier. Mercury should have known she could only push her exhausted body so far, and she definitely pushed herself way past her limit. "I want more too. I'll come find you." She promised, even though she knew it might be hard to keep that promise. "Every day."

As he drifted off to sleep, he remembered a time when that

had been true. When they had gone to find each other in the clinic on Nine, when she would come and find him at the office the Initiative had provided him for hours at a time. Days when he had always gotten a full night's sleep and when agenda items could always be delegated, when there were always enough doctors to see to her caseload if he had indisposed her.

There in the Labyrinth, no one was forcing them to stay, there were no locks on the doors unless they put them there, but there were so many more draws on their time. The water might not work, the lift might break down, the rations might be down to bare daily portions and power consumption might be limited by generation capabilities. Everything was limited except their freedom, but their freedom was put in its own constraints by every other limitation. Everything came down to time, and it always fell short. "I love you." He mumbled against her cheek as he pulled the blanket up over her back and his caresses slowed.

"I love you." She replied as he encased them in the blankets, but she couldn't open her eyes again. Someone would come knocking eventually, but right now, they had each other. It was enough.

* * * * *

Jason laid back on the floor looking up into the eyes of the infant staring down at him, both of them appearing gravely serious. "Oh come on, don't you think I've already tried that? What am I, a beginner? Of course I did a map of the power inverters before I synced it to the grid. Well, yeah, I could have missed something, that's possible. I'm pretty good at this stuff, though." The baby seemed to think he'd said something funny, since she smiled and tried to claw at his eyes. Jason just screwed them shut. "Alright, alright, if you think it's a good idea, I'll look at it again. I'm telling you, though, I've been over it twice. You're gonna have to do better than that."

The baby giggled again and tried to get her hand to his mouth instead, and Jessie looked over at Jason on the floor with their baby girl as she washed a small pile of dishes. "Seems like you have quite the helper there. Only I'm pretty sure she's more concerned with her next feeding than she is with power inverters."

"Hey, just because she's not saying it in so many words doesn't mean she isn't interested." He turned his head to avoid the baby's assault, but she quickly crawled right over his neck, leaving him to make strangling noises as he finally picked her up and rolled her down into his arms as he sat up. "You already know all the answers. You're just not that articulate. Must be frustrating." He picked the girl up and carried her over toward the sink so they could both be closer to Jessie. "Has she been alright today?"

Jessie nodded and looked over at their little girl in Jason's arms. She was older than most of the other babies around, but she still looked small and scrawny for her age. Jessie blamed it entirely on Jason, but she wasn't sad about it. "She's back to normal for now. I just hope she doesn't get sick again before we get out into a house."

"That should be within a couple weeks. They've made a lot of progress in the last week on the first few rows." He worried every time he saw the deeply incisive looks from Rebekah, the mumbles and attempts at phonemes that were much too advanced for a tiny human of only eight months. Every time he heard her say Mama and mean it, clipboard notes flashed through his mind that he had discovered in the days following the fall of Nine. His own test notes from the researchers who were the only people who could in any sense be called his parents.

His infancy had been a great deal more rigorous and less loving than Rebekah's, and he didn't want her to have the same experiences of understanding the world just a little too soon. "Especially with the shipment coming in tonight, things should speed along. We'll get some windows for this little girl to look out of and for me to draw the curtains on when she goes to sleep and I finally get some time alone with her beautiful mother."

Jessie laughed softly as she turned her attention back to the dishes. Time alone was nearly unheard of since they'd returned to Earth, and even when they were alone, she could see that his mind was preoccupied with the puzzle that remained unsolved.

The Twist.

He talked about it with their infant, he talked about it with her, he talked about it with his team, she didn't know when he *wasn't* thinking about it. Even when he wasn't working on the Twist, he was working with Tatyana and her connection to the rest of the rebels, scattered as they were. Jessie remained silent about it, mostly because she knew what he worked on was important. Eventually it would come down to life or death for all of them. Jessie stayed home with Rebekah and worked from their unit. She mostly made and mended clothing, and she made evening meals and delivered them to the compound's guards and doctors, who had no time to stop for themselves. "It'll be nice to be in a house. Even a small house. Just to get away from this maze."

Jason didn't mind living underground as much as he knew most people did, but he knew that was his oddity, not everyone else's. "I got a notification from Logan that the inventory for later is actually better than they had originally thought it would be. Anything you want me to steal out of his files for you?" He made a game out of messing with their fearless leader, since Logan had maintained his own authority over the fugitive settlement; rather than ceding it to those allies in the cause who had already been in residence in the Labyrinth when they arrived.

"Sugar?" She asked as she rinsed off a glass and set it aside to be dried. "I didn't get to make you a cake for your birthday, even though you said you didn't want one." Sugar, along with everything else, was in limited supply and they rarely had enough to use it on desserts. "You didn't even come home on your birthday, so I figure I can make you a cake eventually."

He felt guilty all over again for that, since he really hadn't intended to work straight through it or spend so long away from home, but things got from him more often than not in recent days. He always felt like he was so close to cracking the Twist, but it was just a little out of his reach. Tatyana had been a help for some parts of it in the initial stages, but when he had gotten to the point of actually getting the thing to engage, there was no one he could turn to for help with the equations. He'd been obsessive, but he didn't know how not to be.

"I can make that happen." He said quietly, then kissed her shoulder as he stepped away with their little girl to keep Rebekah from clawing at her mother to be held. "I'm going to keep away from the workshop for a couple days, if that's alright. I'm stuck again and there's really not much point in me going back until I've gotten some distance from it."

Jessie washed the final dish in the small tub that passed for a sink, then turned her attention to drying the dishes. "Are you sure? The last time you said that, I woke up to an empty bed in the middle of the night. Though the distance did help you, that half day. You figured out . . ." Jessie couldn't remember all the technical terms. "The thing that keeps the one part cool enough to keep moving without showering the room with sparks."

"The heat sink that I thought was a cross-field stabilizer." He filled in the blanks for her, remembering his incredible screw-up that he was lucky most people didn't understand well enough to recognize as a potentially catastrophic mistake. "I'm serious this time. I need to . . . stay away from it for a while. Otherwise I'm going to engage in too much pathological destruction and that would not be good for the future of humanity." He'd had to stop himself several times already from venting his frustrations on the machine directly when it didn't do what he thought it ought to.

"I'm sure Rebekah will be happy to have you home. She likes all the toys you've made for her." Jessie gave him a sedated smile when she looked back at him on the floor with their daughter. They were able to get toys in shipments from time to time, but most of the things that Rebekah had were made from pieces of things that Jason found and created, little dogs made from discarded circuits held together with stripped wire, a boat made from screen glass and polished console housing, and dozens more. "I think she's starting to figure out that the shapes go into the holes, but clearly she's way too young to figure out which go with which."

Jason had his doubts about that, given some of the other traits the girl had shown, but he kept his silence on that particular point. "Is she the only one who'll be happy that I'm home?" He was distracted much of the time, but he wasn't blind to the impact his distraction had on his wife and on their relationship. There was a lot that had come between them in the months since their return to Earth, and only a few short months before that for them to really gain a foundation with each other in the first place.

"No, of course not. I'm happy you'll be home." She replied quickly, but she barely glanced up at him before she continued what she was doing. "I don't know if there will be much for you to do." Their unit was small, and it didn't take a lot for Jessie to keep it clean. She was used to taking care of everything, since Jason wasn't really around to do anything. "I'm sure Tatyana will need you for something or other." There was the slightest sharpness to her tone, but she didn't think Jason was cheating on her. Although she knew Tatyana would love it if he did decide to be unfaithful. He spent plenty of time with the skinny Russian ballerina, after all.

"She already had her chance to pitch a fit at me taking time off from the Twist work. I let her speak her peace and then came home." He had a deeply complicated relationship with Tatyana that had gotten worse and more complicated over recent months. "Mostly I worry that she's going to try and figure the damn thing out while I'm home. It's out of her league and she knows it." He put Rebekah down on the carpeted floor to play with some of the plastic mechanical toys that he'd brought home and stood back up, momentarily keeping his distance from Jessie, since she seemed to prefer it that way. "She reminded me that everybody's required to help unload and disperse the inventory once it comes in tonight, but after that, we can come home and be shut-ins for a while."

Jessie nodded and continued about her tasks, it was just easier to keep to her schedule than to look at him when he was attempting to dissect her thoughts from across the room. "She's never had any reason not to come find you if she absolutely needs to while she attempts the Twist on her own." Jessie wasn't trying to hurt Jason with her distance, it was just the best way she figured out how to cope with his workload, as well as reminding herself that he was working on saving humanity. "It's important work. The future of humanity literally depends on it."

He checked on Rebekah again briefly, but then crossed the space to stand near her, and reached out to put a hand on the side of the drying rack of dishes to stall her a moment. "I'm trying to be here, Jess. It's where I want to be."

"I know." She looked at his hand before she looked up from her task. "I never said I thought you didn't want to be here." Jessie actually looked into his eyes, but it didn't last. She couldn't just look at him without guilt. Wanting more than she knew he could give, hoping for things that wouldn't happen, there was a smorgasbord of guilt to choose from. "You just aren't most of the time. Rebekah and I have adapted. You deserve a break, though. So I'm glad you're taking one."

All he could do was nod, since she hadn't really given him any leeway in her statement or any indication that she actually wanted him there. "You shouldn't have to adapt to an absentee husband." He'd had a number of revelations over the course of being on Earth, not the least of which was realizing that his typical obsessive behavior was not endearing to anyone, no matter how noble his intentions. "From now on, I'll limit myself to a workday with the Twist. No matter how much time I spend on it, I'm not getting any closer, whether it's eight hours a day or eighteen. So it's pointless to make it eighteen. Not if the price is a wife at home I can't talk to."

"I'm not trying to be hurtful." She replied gently, though she was just being honest. Honesty didn't exactly come with a pillow-soft-casing to lessen the blow. "I just don't know what to talk about. Maybe we don't have enough in common." They hadn't actually been matched, after all, so maybe they weren't compatible after all. It was something she thought about often after so long of basically single-parenting their infant daughter. He clearly had a lot more in common with his group of Twist co-workers. With Tatyana. "We've been back on Earth for over a year. I feel like I knew you better on Station Nine than I do now."

Jason kept an eye on Rebekah as she rolled and crawled across the floor, but there wasn't much the girl could get into by way of trouble. "We had work to do on Nine." He said almost wistfully. "We had somebody to fight and something to push against. Out here on our own, all any of us have had to push against or fight is each other." He knew he was just as guilty of that as anyone else, but that didn't mean he hated it any less.

"I had this great vision that this war would be over by the time Rebekah was born. We would get the Twist, get to Eleusis, break the Consortium's hold on the place, and start a new future for humanity. I knew it wouldn't be that simple, but I never imagined it would be . . . this kind of silence." He sighed, since everything was resting on him, and he was failing. "Even now, I keep thinking I'll finally get the damn thing up and running and be able to hand over operations and strategy to Logan and Reed and Tatyana and Haley. Step back from it and just help where I'm needed. Spend more than an hour at home here and there."

"You infiltrated the Initiative for the Twist and to do what you're doing, not for me or for Rebekah. And I understand that. I do." She reminded both him and herself. "And I guess I signed up for a new life, and I have one. I'm trying to be as patient as you need me to be." She sighed and glanced over at Rebekah as well. "We were just so close before." She had once felt like his reason for living, she felt special, and she didn't feel that way anymore. "The only way I've learned to cope was to move my focus elsewhere. Rebekah."

Jason could understand that, and he actually smiled slightly at the sight of their daughter across the room. "I did tell you so. I told you that you'd be an amazing mom." He knew that Rebekah was the main thing that kept them together, but he hoped it wasn't the only thing they had left. "I've never had . . . this. I know that's not an excuse, and I'm not trying to make it one. I've just been so focused on the rebellion for so long that I never learned how to do this. That doesn't do you any favors." He looked back at her, but she wasn't meeting his eyes, so he just looked back at Rebekah.

He paused and turned to look back at the clock on the stove nearby. It was only four o'clock, but there wouldn't be too much daylight left to them so high up in the mountains and early in the spring. "Does she have a coat or a blanket we can wrap her up in? There's something I'd like to show you. It won't take too long."

It said a lot about how much Jason hadn't been there that he didn't know that she had a coat and he didn't know where she kept it, since she kept it in the same place. Jessie had made almost all of Rebekah's clothes, after all. She nodded and went to a tiny closet to grab Rebekah's coat and a blanket just to be sure. "I mended the coat you had that got burned. I found some scraps that matched the color closely, so it's not that noticeable." Jessie pulled his coat out of the closet and held it out for him. It had been hanging in there for over a month, but she assumed it was because he thought it was a lost cause when he came home with it. "I got the smokey smell out of it too."

"Wow. Thank you." He looked over the coat with a sedated smile, since clearly it wasn't a particularly happy moment, but he was still grateful. The real reason he hadn't used the coat in a month was because it had been that long since he had actually left the Labyrinth. He pulled the coat back over his shoulders gratefully, then helped her as much as he could with Rebekah and carried the girl himself to the lift. Rebekah seemed incredibly excited by the impromptu trip, and Jason buttoned her inside his coat just to keep her secure and able to look out from his chest to see the world. "I wanted to show this to you when we move in a few weeks, but tonight seems as good a time as any." He gave her a tentative smile as the lift reached the surface, since they were only a few floors below ground.

There were a few defensive twists and turns to the natural cave in which the Labyrinth entrance was situated, but once they were out in the open air of the afternoon, the world immediately felt much less constricted. The entrance of the Labyrinth was wide enough to admit trucks and various supply vehicles, and the road ran down a dirt path that was usually disguised so that it couldn't be seen from the air until it reached the cul-de-sac they finished paving a few months earlier.

On either side of the long, arcing stretch of road moving away from the Labyrinth itself, there were multiple ranks of housing. Some of it was in the form of row-houses all in a block and some of it in smaller, individual houses for those who already had families. Construction work was everywhere, and was the main activity of the vast majority of the fugitives, whipping up housing for themselves as quickly as possible. Many of the townhouses were complete and many of the construction workers lived in them as they worked on the rest of the homes, and those closest to the Labyrinth were the last ones to complete. Jason and much of the leadership elected to move last so as to take care of the people before themselves.

He angled them toward one of the houses a few rows up from the entrance to the Labyrinth, situated higher on the mountain slope with a view of the entire hollow valley below. The house had a roof on it and walls, but it was still mostly cinder blocks and much of it was covered in tarps to protect it from the elements. No one was working on it at the moment, but the entire place smelled of sawdust and fresh glue, spare nails and screws were scattered around the workspace.

"This one is going to be ours." He eventually said, even though it seemed relatively obvious, given the fact that he was leading them to it. Even so, it was strange, since the house was slightly larger than most of those farther down the hill, just as the other dozen or so houses nearby were, to house the leadership of the settlement. "There's four bedrooms, and I made some alterations to the floor plan a couple weeks ago that I hope you like. The rooms aren't divided yet, but the rooms aren't what I wanted to show you."

"Four bedrooms?" She wasn't expecting to have that many bedrooms, and they only just had Rebekah. "You're planning on a bigger family."

"I'm . . . leaving the option open." He gave her a subdued smile. "I'm not planning anything on my own when it comes to a family. But when we talked about it before, you always said you wanted kids. Plural. I wanted to make sure we had room for that if that's something you still want."

"It's still something I want. I do want a big family." Jessie didn't know if he would ever be around often enough to actually logistically make it happen. It required enough time to have sex at the right times, after all. "I just don't know how it's going to work now." She admitted as they stood in the house. She looked at Rebekah zipped up in his coat and she looked up into his eyes again. "What did you want to show me?"

He stepped through the framework where they would eventually live, and led her toward the back wall of the house, facing away from the branch of the street that ran in front of the space for the broad porch. Off the back of the house, there was a strange frame that made it look as though the entire back yard, ramping up the mountainside at a dramatic angle from the back door, would be eventually covered somehow. There were timbers driven into the ground on either side of the yard and a few of them a dozen meters away up the hill to make a frame, but while everything was exposed to the cold mountain air, the entire skeleton was recognizable by the trellises that stood in half a dozen ranks on the incline.

"The next few shipments," he said by way of explanation, "are going to have a lot of glass in them, since we picked up a reliable supplier and route coming down out of Washington. Most of it will go to finishing off the rest of the house windows and replacing some of the components underground, but I put in an order for enough to make this into a greenhouse. There's enough spare parts down below that I'm going to rig up a regulator to keep it at the right temperature year-round, but I'm completely clueless when it comes to what kind of grapes are best for this kind of thing. So I haven't started looking for seedlings or vines that could be transplanted." He had done all of the design work without consulting her, but he hoped it would be a pleasant surprise for her when they finally moved into the house. Something to make it a home for them.

"Wow." She said with genuine surprise, since the last thing she would have imagined as part of their house would have been a greenhouse for grapes. Her life on a vineyard seemed so far away, almost as though it hadn't even been her life in the first place. It felt separate from the life she had now. "I, um, that's great. Thank you. It would take a long time to grow and make anything, though. Do you . . . think that we'll be here that long? Or are you suggesting that we take the wine to Eleusis and let it age there?"

"The climate where we're going on Eleusis should be pretty

perfect for it, actually." He said with a tentative smile, still unsure if she actually liked it or not. "Mediterranean climate, off a large body of water, hilly landscape, plenty of rainfall, high sun exposure. Though I'm not sure how the difference in sunlight quality will impact the grape production. I'm sure they'll adapt." Just as they all had, in their own ways.

"We can start them here and take them with us once we get our vineyard set up there. There are a few sites I've found around the area they've already tried to settle that look like they'd be good, depending on which one you like best." He looked around the yard and at the houses to either side of them. "Though our neighbors will be a lot farther away there, if I have anything to say about it. Give us some room to spread out and make the world our own."

At least he didn't say that they wouldn't get there, since she was afraid that she was going to live hiding in the mountains for the rest of her life. Jessie wasn't exactly sure how they *would* get there and avoid getting killed in the process, but that wasn't part of her duties. She wasn't a part of the figuring out process. "I hope we can. Someday."

"I can see it." He said quietly, bouncing Rebekah a little as she tried to claw out of his jacket and get her hands on the beam near him to the shiny screws. "I haven't told the rest of the team yet, but the targeting systems for the Twist, the visualizing, target frame referencing systems, I've gotten them working. I just can't make it make the connection, open the bridge. But I can see it."

It was more than he'd had for the past year, and more than he had even expected, in his less hopeful moments. "It targets by the Consortium's own systems already in place there to help frame it. But they can't take them down because they have to use them for the one they still have working. They don't even know I'm using them. But I can see it. Eleusis. And if we can see it, we can get to it. I just don't completely understand it yet."

"I'm sure you will. You've never once found a problem you can't solve." She looked over at him for a moment and then back out at the framework for the greenhouse. "If we never get there, I'm okay with that. I never thought I'd have what I have now, and I do. Everything else is a bonus."

He hoped she meant that, but he wasn't sure, given the distance between them. "I want it all for you." He hoped she knew he meant it as he looked over at her. "I may be away a lot of the time, but that hasn't changed."

Jessie looked at him for a moment longer and sighed before she moved closer to him so she could make sure that Rebekah was still tightly bound in her coat. "Do you?" She met his eyes again. "I don't think I am the most important thing in your world. I don't know if I ever was. It's okay, really. I just . . . I don't know." She ran her fingers over Rebekah's cheek and she kissed the baby's forehead.

"It's not okay." He put a hand out and took her by the front of her coat to hold onto her, hoping she wouldn't pull away. "You are the most important thing in my life. Past, present, or future. I just need to do a better job of showing it."

She looked down at his hand holding onto her before she looked up into his eyes again. Her heart hurt again, wanting him and wanting more, even though she knew she couldn't have it. "I wanted more. More time with you. But it hurts more if I want more. And I already suffered enough before, living with a family that despised me and a mother that hated me. I don't want that again."

"I never wanted that for you in the first place." He said without letting go. "I still want more, for both of us. I don't want suffering, I don't want . . . I don't want either of us to be alone. And you have been, because I couldn't do what I thought I could do. That's why I'm saying, I don't want to keep doing crazy days with the Twist anymore. I need to be home. I want to be home. You're the whole reason I'm doing any of this anymore."

"I don't want to be alone." Jessie spoke softer and softer, since she had a hard time talking about it. She still didn't believe him about being his reason for doing anything, since she knew that he had been devoted to the cause long before she came into the picture. "I want you around. Rebekah needs you around too. We're just so far apart. I don't really know what to do from here, Gor . . . Jason." She felt guilty all over again, since she still had moments when she wanted to call him by the name she knew him first. The man she fell in love with was Gordon. The man who had left her alone with their baby so often was Jason. She wasn't so much a fan of his.

"I'm sorry." She said quickly, since she didn't want him to get mad. Jessie had mended some broken chairs and tossed broken dishes because of his anger in recent days toward the Twist. He'd never hurt her or Rebekah, but his anger could still reach levels that were uncomfortable for her when frustration was high, even if it was never aimed at them.

He shook his head when she apologized. "I don't know what to do either. I just know where I want to be, and it's not bashing my head against the Twist every single day and night." He had to bounce Rebekah a little to keep the little girl from getting frustrated, but for the time being, she was playing with the buttons on the front of Jessie's coat as he held her close. "And I can be Gordon to you if you prefer that name. That one I at least chose. Jason is what got assigned to me because I was tenth in the lineup."

"I liked the way things were, but I don't want you to change your name for me." She stood still there in front of him. "I just want to be in love again. With you, if that's possible. Though I don't know if it is. How do I know that we won't just drift back into this in two months?"

"We don't." He answered honestly, even if it wasn't the answer she wanted to hear. "But no one does. All anyone can do is decide." He reached up to brush his fingers along the side of her face, but it was a tentative touch, since he was just as scared of her pushing him away as she was of him on general principles. "On the other side of the summer, it will have been two years for us. In that time, my mind hasn't been changed."

Jessie didn't pull away from his touch, but she didn't answer it either. "Two years and we rarely sleep in the same bed at the same time." She replied with obvious concern and worry. "I'm okay with being whatever kind of wife you want me to be, but don't pull me back into loving you unless you can be involved. If you want a different kind of relationship, then I need to know. I'm not looking for divorce, but I don't want to expect something I'm not going to get."

"I don't want something different." He assured her, wishing silently that there was some way of proving to her that he meant what he said, since he knew all his actions had been to the contrary. "The life I want is us being left alone to do whatever we please. I'm going to hate the Consortium for as long as it takes to destroy them, and I'm always going to work to bring them down, to make things better for the rest of the world. That's who I am. But that doesn't mean I have to be away from you and Rebekah to do it. There's no part of what I do that I don't want you to be a part of."

"I want to believe you." She whispered with a defeated shrug, but she focused her attention on Rebekah and ran a hand over the little girl's cheek. "Maybe we should start over. Maybe we should take things slow." They certainly hadn't taken their relationship slow before. "You said there will be four bedrooms, maybe we should stay apart for now until we can figure this out." Jessie was far more convinced their relationship wasn't going to get any better than she was that they were going to recover from over a year of neglect. Her mother always told her she wouldn't keep anyone happy, after all.

All he could do was nod, and he drew his hand away. "If that's what you want, we can do that." He glanced around at the frame as if to look at their future bedrooms, but he could see the front of the house through parts of the frame, and there were people coming down the street from some of the finished houses, heading down toward the road. "I, um, I can take the couch down at home for now. It'll make it easier for me to hear Rebekah at night that way." He told himself that that was the reason he'd be on the couch, but he knew he was just avoiding the full weight of what he himself had also been told all his life. That he would never be able to make a true and honest connection with anyone.

"That couch is terrible." She shook her head and stepped back as he drew his hand away, though she didn't want him to. Part of her wanted him to keep fighting for her, to tell her to stop being stupid, even though the rest of the evidence was stacked against her. "Sleep in the bed. It's not like we've never slept in a bed together. It'll be fine."

He let that drop for the time being, since nothing he said changed what was going on between them. At least she didn't completely hate him. He had dealt with that before, and knew how to handle it, but feeling that from Jessie would have been a turn of the world that he wasn't sure he could make it through. "Come on, let's see where everyone's going. Maybe the shipment's on its way in."

Jessie followed after him and halfway down, she reached out for one of his hands, even though the other was keeping Rebekah secure. If they really wanted to fix something, they had to start somewhere. She missed him. Desperately. But she hated feeling as though the depth of the emotions were one-sided, and that was how it felt all of the time. Just like with her sister's husband, Jessie felt like she cared for someone who wouldn't feel the same kind of love back.

He paused half a step when she took his hand, but he looked over at her with a smile and held her hand tightly as they walked. As they turned a corner of the house to get onto the street, he lifted it to kiss the back of her knuckles, stirring memories for them both of their first days together. Jason never thought he would miss Nine, and he didn't for its own sake. What he missed was the chance to be with Jessie, the relative simplicity of living with a well-constructed plan before that plan actually managed to mostly succeed.

As they finally got to the main road, they saw the convoy in the distance entering the valley. There were no fewer than a dozen semi trucks, all driving in perfect intervals with each other, unmarked, with all their axles on the ground, clearly heavy-laden. A general cheer went up, and Jason couldn't bring himself to blame them. It had been months since they'd been able to get a shipment of supplies, especially one of the magnitude in front of them.

"Pretty sure there's gonna be sugar in there somewhere." He said with a tentatively-teasing smile over at Jessie as he squeezed her hand.

She gave him a small smile in return, since the sugar wouldn't mean much if she made a cake and he wasn't there to enjoy it. "What kind of cake do you want?" Jessie still wanted to please him, she still wanted to make him happy, she still wanted him to want her and really show it. It was silly to believe, before she met him, that she would find someone who *wanted* her. He had given her a taste of that reality and disappeared.

"I had a kind once when I was traveling that was actually raspberry." He mused as he thought about it. "I've never seen it anywhere else before or since. I know we've got some raspberries left in storage. Do you think that would work?"

"Sure, I can make you a raspberry cake if you want." It was a bit of a strange request, but if he wanted it, she would make sure he had it. "I know a good glaze to go with it. Hopefully you'll enjoy it." She gave his hand another squeeze as they got closer, and Rebekah was wide-eyed with all the commotion. "There are a lot of trucks this time. Wow."

The final vehicle in the convoy pulled up along the side of the street at the very end of the cul-de-sac, a long truck that seemed like a mix of an army assault vehicle and a tour bus. There were two dozen men and women inside, all of them armed and all of them dangerous but happy to be off the bus. They didn't wear uniforms, but their clothing was nondescript and their eyes still had the look of soldiers. Some of them, Jessie had seen before, but most of them were new, coming in from other sites that were held and supplied by the rebels all over western North America. From the way all the trucks parked in perfect rows on either side of the broad street, it was clear they had all been operating under automation. They all shut themselves down at the same time, and their back doors came down to allow them to be unloaded.

"I wonder what that means." Jason said beside her, still holding her hand but looking doubtful as he watched people approach to sort through the available resources. "Either we've taken on somebody else's supply route, which means somebody else doesn't need it anymore, or they were just really fortunate this time. I'm not betting on the second."

He wasn't tasked with helping load or unload, so he didn't feel the need to rush to the trucks to lend a hand. They watched the proceedings for a while as the soldiers got off and immediately met with Logan and the other central leaders, though Jason could see that Tatyana was conspicuously absent. "Either way, we'll see if we can figure out . . ." he stopped mid-sentence at something he'd seen in the middle of the soldiers greeting people below, but his eyes were darting around, since he had lost track of what he thought he saw.

"Figure out . . ." She wasn't watching Jason as he spoke but she turned her attention to him when he stopped talking. Jessie was trying to figure out what halted his attention, but when she looked down, she spotted Tatyana first. God, did he really still . . . have a thing for her? Or was a fire rekindled? He spent a lot of time with Tatyana, but she thought that maybe, just maybe, he was seriously past her. Apparently not. "Is she smiling? I really don't like it when she smiles." She mumbled before she looked back at Jason again. "Do you need to go?"

He shook his head, but he still wasn't looking away. "It's not . . ." she hadn't seen him speechless very often before, and when he was, good things never came from it. "I didn't know it would be him."

Eventually he nodded down to the street where she saw Tatyana, and she saw the tiny woman picked up briefly by a man roughly Jason's height who was wearing sunglasses and a hat that obscured his face. Clearly the man and Tatyana were friends, but he moved on quickly from her and looked around the crowd. When the man's eyes came to rest on Jason, the expression on his face was just as fixed as Jason's, and he began moving through the crowd to climb the hillside toward them.

"Do you remember how I told you I had a lot of brothers?" It had been a long time since they had talked about anything personal, but she was one of very few people he had ever talked to at any length about his own family, such as it was.

"Yes, you said that." She fixed her gaze on the man approaching them, but she knew that she didn't know him. Especially since most of his face was still covered. "Am I about to meet one?"

He nodded without taking his eyes off the man approaching, but he swallowed again anyway before he continued. "The oldest. Except he's not . . . Brothers isn't the right word for it. It's just the easiest one to use."

The man got up to them, and she could see when he got there that he was so nearly the same height as Jason that there was no distinguishing them. He took off his hat and unwrapped the pragmatic scarf before he took off his sunglasses and looked over at Jason with a smile. Once his face was visible, Jessie could see what Jason meant, but that didn't make it any less unsettling.

Where Jason's face was narrow and his cheeks almost sunken with his chronic malnutrition, the man facing them was full and healthy and obviously older. His face was harder, more weathered, with the hint of cracks around the corners of his eyes that suggested a man well into the prime of his life. At the moment, he was clean-shaven, just as Jason was, but there was a slight dusting of a day's growth that she had never noticed on Jason's own cheeks. Both sets of eyes were precisely the same mid-grade shade of brown, the curve of their eyebrows was the same; their nose, their mouths, their chins, even, from Jessie's vantage point beside them, the precise curves and formations of their ears and the shade of their hair.

It was as though Jason was looking into a mirror that would show him what he would have looked like had he been permitted to grow up healthy and free of his childhood tortures.

"Aren't you going to introduce me?" Even the man's voice was the same, though his accent was slightly different than Jason's, a touch more British and less American without being fully devoted to either.

She knew Jason well enough to know what he looked like when someone was trying to push his buttons, and he just glared before he turned back toward her. "Jess, this is Alexander. He usually goes by Xander, unless that's changed in the last three years?"

Xander's smile was at once both harsher and more open than Jason's, less sinister but rougher by nature. He only wasted it a moment on Jason before he looked over at Jess, with the unsettling impression that she was looking right into the eyes of her husband. "No, it's still Xander. Pleased to meet you, Jessie. You're a rare creature, to put up with this one."

Even though she and Jason weren't in the best place in their relationship, Jessie would always be the first to defend him even when someone wasn't actively attacking him. Jessie held out her hand so that she could at least shake the hand of her husband's . . . clone? "I'm not that rare. We'll see how pleasing it is to meet you, though."

In spite of their recent discussion, Jason smiled at that defense, while Xander seemed surprised. The same kind of dark intelligence was behind Xander's eyes, the same kind of suspicion about everything in the world around him, but not the fear and borderline paranoia that her husband bore.

"Very interesting. And this must be the spawn." Xander glanced down at Rebekah, then gave Jessie a broad smile, more open and free than any Jason had ever given anyone, before looking back at Jason. "I'll be around a while this time, J. We'll have to catch up a little later, once all the cargo is unloaded. Where's Kenneth?"

"He never checked in." Jason answered, though Jessie had never heard the name Kenneth before from him. "I thought he was with you."

"I thought he was here with you." Xander looked mildly worried, but finally shrugged. "He'll check in if he wants to. I just assumed he'd be here, since you were. I haven't heard from any of the others."

"I doubt we will, at this point." The smiles on both men's faces were gone in an instant, but Xander didn't seem surprised. Jason shrugged as well. "They've made their choices."

"So have we. Fuck 'em." Xander took a step back toward the trucks. "Anyway, I'll be around. We'll talk later."

"Can't wait." Jason said with no enthusiasm whatsoever, but it only amused Xander as he turned around and headed for the trucks.

"So you're not friends, I take it?" Jessie asked as she watched Xander walk away. She found it odd that even though they looked so similar, she didn't find herself attracted to Xander. Did that mean that she loved Jason more than she realized? Even after the last year? "I don't know what that smile was about after he looked at Rebekah."

"He's surprised I had a kid." He glared after his 'brother.' "As far as I know, I'm the only one of all of us who has. Xander decided not to a long time ago, and the others all had their own reasons." He finally looked away when Xander was some distance away before he looked down at Rebekah just to watch her. "But no, I wouldn't call us friends. I'm probably closer to Xander than any of the others except Kenneth, but Ken almost never comes around. He and I lived together for a while right before I went to Europe." He sighed and reached out to play with Rebekah's hand and tuck it back inside her sleeve. "Xander is the oldest, and tends to think that means he's in charge of the rest of us. No matter how many opportunities I've taken to disabuse him of that notion. Most recently by going up to Nine."

"I think that's just a tendency of older children. Clones or not." She ran her hand over Rebekah's hair and pulled her coat tighter around herself. "Don't listen to those comments. It doesn't make me special because I love you. You have had love in more places than me."

"It does, actually." He looked over at her sharply, since she had said it so casually. He started walking with her back toward the Labyrinth to get Rebekah back inside and out of the cold. "What I had before you were an opportunist who loved me in her own twisted way, and a diagnosable psychopath who only loved me so long as I was willing to go looking for a martyr's death. Neither is exactly the kind of thing people write poetry about." He took her hand again as they walked, hoping it was okay. "You've never been just something I've had before."

Jessie held his hand once he took hers, but she didn't make any effort to get any closer to him. "People don't write poetry about me either." Jessie said as they kept moving toward the Labyrinth while Rebekah started chewing on her father's jacket. "He looks like you, but he's not you. You've always been there to protect Rebekah and me. You've given us a home. It's more than some people get." She looked down at their joined hands before she looked up at him again. "Even if we weren't together, I would still defend you. And I will always be in love with you."

He smiled warmly, and when they got into the lift inside the Labyrinth, he pulled her with him against one of the walls to hold her as the lift descended. "I have a lot of talents, but poetry isn't one of them. I never had any desire for that to be otherwise before I met you. But I wish I had that kind of talent, for you. Only way I could ever do you justice." He looked her in the eye and kissed her once, tentatively and gently, but he couldn't not kiss her after that meeting with Xander. "I love you. And this little one too." He poked the back of Rebekah's head between them. "There's never going to be a time when we're not together, if I have anything to say about it."

It felt like it had been so long since they had really kissed, even though he had given her a few cursory goodbye kisses here and there. It hurt, wanting him and not knowing if he would just keep losing interest, but he made her happy when he was actually around. "I love you too. I can't keep doing this, though. Wondering what day I'll see you, or wondering if you're so bored with me that you and Tatyana . . ." Jessie just cut herself off and shook her head. "If we were a priority, then I thought you'd show it more. That's why I think two years into this and you're already bored. I can't help but wonder the worst."

He opened his mouth to deny anything happening between him and Tatyana, for the hundredth time, but he knew that would just turn into another fight, so he let it drop. He already told her that there was nothing between them, but he needed to do better in order for her to believe him. "I'll show you that you are a priority." He promised quietly as the lift stopped. "In the meantime, I think this one needs new pants and a nap."

Jessie nodded and reached to take Rebekah out of his coat so she could take care of their daughter. "I'll take care of it. You should get some rest." She pulled Rebekah back into her embrace as they got to their floor. "I'm sorry for making your day more difficult. I didn't intend to do that."

"You didn't." He didn't fight her on taking Rebekah, since just an hour earlier, he had gotten home from working for twelve hours straight on the Twist with no success, and he really was tired. "I'm glad that we got a chance to really talk." He closed the door of their unit behind him, then went to take her hand again after she put Rebekah down on the floor to get what she needed. "I've missed you. And I'm sorry." He squeezed her hand and moved in for one more kiss before he pulled away to head for the bedroom. "I am going to get some sleep, though. I'll be up to help with her tonight."

Jessie nodded as he headed for the bedroom. "Sleep well." She didn't let herself cry until she heard the door close and he was separated from her and Rebekah. After being attacked on Nine, it had taken Jessie a long time to trust being around Jason and then after they got to Earth, everything went to hell anyway.

After grabbing a clean diaper and changing Rebekah, she showered the little girl with both her tears and her kisses before she started to nurse her. "I hope he comes around, little one. I miss him so much."

2

"Yes, I said Vancouver." Xander said impatiently, glaring over at Logan. He met the man only half a day before, but after taking orders from him the entire night long while they were unloading cargo, he wasn't Xander's favorite person. "Something significant about that to you, Bickford?"

"Not in this context." Logan admitted before leaning back in his chair. He wasn't going to bring up his own limited experience in Vancouver given the rest of the audience present. Anna and Mercury, both of them nearby, already knew plenty about it. As for the rest, there were some things it was just better that people didn't know. "Just wanted to make sure I heard you right."

"Good. Now, if there's no more fucking interruptions . . ." Xander glanced around the room until he felt satisfied, then continued, eyes flicking to the various leaders gathered in the room. Jason and Tatyana he already knew, and Reed, who had run the Labyrinth facility for years before the rest of the fugitives from Station Nine showed up. Haley was an unknown quantity, but she looked like she could prove to be an interesting prospect if pressed in exactly the right ways. He could think of a few ways he would consider very right where she was concerned. Her and Tatyana both.

"We had three hundred people outside of Vancouver running supply chains, picking up what they could, keeping it in warehouses for later distribution, managing our supply routes all over the continent. The whole place got drawn out on a wild goose chase and the majority of their personnel got shredded once they were out in the open around Shasta. A few of the ones I brought back with me were the ones left behind. We emptied the place out once we heard them sound the mayday and hauled it here. Stopped up in Deseret for a while to make sure nobody was trailing us and went over the inventory again to make sure there were no surprises."

Anna shook her head, but she wasn't as surprised as she knew she should have been. The Consortium was looking for rebel havens and destroying them. One by one. The only survivors she'd ever heard of were just lucky bastards who weren't close enough to get slaughtered.

"As much as that sucks for Vancouver and for all of us on the whole, at least we have more people here now. When they find us, we're going to need all the manpower we can get." She knew it was only a matter of time. The Consortium had far more resources and people, and in the mountains if they were found . . . even at about a thousand people, they would not stand a chance. Especially because at least a hundred people were under the age of one and another solid hundred were children of various ages that were from the families living in the Labyrinth before the Consortium decided to make a goal out of hunting and murdering rebels. "We need more."

"More is just going to make us more of a target." Reed snapped back, cranky as ever and clearly less afraid to show it that day than previously. The older man had been grumpy ever since the fugitives arrived more than a year before, and very nearly busted a blood vessel when they announced they were going to build housing and a road on the surface right outside the entrance to the Labyrinth. *Might as well paint a 'come fuck us here' sign on the top of the mountain while you're at it,* he said at the time. His attitude had not grown more open since.

"The more people come here, the more the Consortium is going to look and the more likely it is that *somebody* here is working for them. Which means it'll only be a matter of time before we get bombed to hell and back. What we need to be doing is getting that damn machine working!"

"That's been in progress. As you already know." Jason responded quietly, since he didn't have more of a defense that he could mount on the topic. "With my brother here, I'm hoping the work will go a little more smoothly. He's the only other person in this time zone that I'm aware of who has an IQ above two hundred."

"No offense taken." Logan almost growled back, but they were all accustomed to being insulted by Jason from time to time. The man did typically back up his boasts, though. The Twist was the only thing Logan could remember seeing him fail at when he put his mind to it. "Whether we get the Twist working or not, the end result is going to be the same. If we don't get it working, we're going to need more people who are willing to fight and who can manage resources while the rest of us work against the Consortium. If we *do* get it up and running, we're going to need more people to pour through it so that we can take Eleusis and keep it. Either way, we need expansion. And not just a few hundred more people. We need movement. On a global scale."

"You are correct in that." Tatyana agreed with Logan, although clearly she had a 'but' hanging in the air. "It takes time to get people gathered. Especially to do it without being noticed and especially without getting killed. Every time we try to move rebels, the Consortium gets the information and they're dead within months. Our best bet to grow our cause is to recruit first, build up a significant force and weapon supply and *then* try to continue to move rebel forces globally."

"And just because our best weapons are here right now doesn't mean we invite the whole damn world to come spend the night." Reed said adamantly, dearly hoping that someone would suggest a relocation that didn't involve his precious maze.

"It does for now." Logan said quickly, glaring at Reed to make sure the man backed down, which he did, predictably enough. "When I looked last week, our closest cells were out near Shasta, a small community in Deseret of maybe a hundred people, and three down in the Painted Desert district. If they've found the Vancouver haven, they're going to eventually work their way through the rest of the western districts. If we begin slowly moving our people from those outer cells back here, having them make supply runs along the way to bring resources with them in small groups, we should be able to move inconspicuously. It'll take time, but it'll be safer, and it will give those of us here time to start scouting out new locations for a stronghold."

He gave Reed a pointed look before turning back to the rest of those present. "The Labyrinth is about as good as it gets when it comes to security, but we need to either find some way to make progress with the major governments or start putting things in motion to get them ousted. We don't have the access to start with space. We have to get a foothold here on Earth first."

"We definitely need more weapons." Kameron Fitch often kept quiet and to herself, but she was in charge of security since Carl was still MIA on Eleusis. Orion helped her as often as he could, but he was needed more in transportation than dealing with weapons. "I don't care if I get pieces of shit, that I can manage to figure out. I just need more. We can't protect ourselves if we don't have any fucking firepower."

"The best source of weaponry is taking directly from the Consortium." Jason stepped in, since that was an area where he could actually contribute. "But getting a large quantity of it all at once will involve tipping our hand to them to reveal a fairly huge security flaw they still haven't patched since the fall of Nine."

"How big a flaw?" Xander was immediately interested, but also clearly skeptical.

"Big enough that I can take over the piloting of any ship in their fleet at any time." He said quietly, with a small shrug afterward. "So yes, I could do what you're all thinking right now, I'm just not interested in killing millions of innocent people along with the few hundred cocksuckers we all wish were pushing up daisies right now. I haven't been able to identify a good enough opportunity to push that button yet. It's a trick I'm only going to be able to play once. And there's no guarantee it'll even work, since as soon as their ships go off the reservation, they'll know there's a weakness they need to fix."

"If you can do that . . ." Reed was incredulous, but he was trying to rein himself in. "You could put every warship they have out into an unrecoverable orbit all at once, while they're unmanned. You could take every single . . ."

"I've run all the contingencies." Jason shot back. "Long story short, they don't end in our favor. But for weapons supply, I might be able to work something out."

"We're not trying to murder any more innocent people." Mercury inserted with obvious concern on her face. Normally she was quiet support for Logan, but she couldn't believe what some people were hinting at. "They're not criminals up there. It's not us versus them or them versus us. We're all equally victims of the Consortium."

"Some of us more than others." Reed turned his glare on Mercury. "Not all of us had our every need provided for us the whole time we were growing up."

"Breathe another vicious word against my wife and we'll start counting how many breaths you have left, Reed." Logan's voice didn't even have to change pitch for it to be obvious he meant every word of his threat.

The only person taken aback in the gathering was Xander, just because he had barely met the overbearing Midwesterner. As he looked around and saw a lack of shock on everyone's faces, he actually laughed. "Alright, alright, little tension. No need to be ripping each other's throats out. Let's save that for the throats that deserve it. Red is right. We're not in the business of killing more innocent people than we can avoid. Some are inevitable. That's just what happens in a war. None of us are stupid enough not to understand that."

He looked over at Jason with an approving nod. "See what kinds of contingencies you can come up with only focusing on diverting supplies, weapons, and ships that you can permanently disable remote control on. See what it looks like."

"Still not a solution to the central problem we still need to solve." Logan countered. He wasn't blind to someone trying to appear as though they were the one in charge, and his position wasn't one he was going to relinquish. "We need a long-term strategic foothold. Everything we have is a stop-gap measure right now. We need long-range focus."

Anna looked at Logan and stared at him for a moment before she looked at Jason. "If we can send an envoy to where Logan and I are from, we can get the whole town here if we need to. And all of their resources. I mean, my father alone had like ten guns and enough ammunition . . ."

"Ten guns? Great! We're saved!" Reed had clearly been pushed past his limit, but he was also quickly ignored as Logan steamrolled him yet again.

"Bringing the town brings a lot of risks with it, but it also sets a precedent." Logan waited to make sure everyone was listening before he continued. "If we take the town, then it's going to leave a hole three hundred miles wide in the middle of the district. People are going to figure out what that means and where everyone went, and they'll start realizing that rebellion is an option. None of the rest of you come from anyone who cares." He knew it was something harsh to realize, but it was true. "Your families miss you, or missed you, when they were alive, but the communities you were a part of are either dead or a loyal part of the Consortium. They're not going to ignite this revolution. Our people would, if given the chance."

Anna felt a little hope, even though it emphasized everyone else's harsh realities. She couldn't help it, though, she wanted to go home. She knew that everyone at home would want to be a part of the rebellion.

"You can't take a big group." Tatyana started to say. "If you get killed on the road, we can't take a large loss."

"Well, I'm glad we wouldn't be missed too much." Logan laughed at Tatyana's eternal pragmatism. "We wouldn't need anyone more than the four of us, maybe a few others to keep an eye on security, whoever you think is best," he nodded at Kameron, since she was one of the few people he was comfortable deferring to around the settlement, "and maybe a couple people to help with the kids. It may take a little while to work our way through the community, so we should plan for anywhere between a week and a month stay."

Fitch looked around at the group and then looked back at Logan. "We should probably take a few more than just a handful. If we can bring a load of supplies back with us, then we should. We just got that old bus working again a few days ago, and it's been in a junkyard for at least ten years. It'll blend in with any of the normal traffic, if there is much traffic in the first place."

"That proves how little you've driven midwest roads." Logan gave her a friendly smile. "There won't be much by way of traffic. And a bus won't raise any eyebrows. A tank would raise eyebrows, if there were any to raise in the first place, but a bus will be fine. As long as we're fairly sure it'll make it the whole way."

"It'll make it." Jason promised. "I did the final checks and the fixes on the guidance myself."

"Oh, the way you fixed the Twist?" Reed never missed an opportunity to pour some salt when there was a wound around.

Xander's arm had been resting peacefully in his lap the entire conversation, but it shot out and shoved Reed backward until his chair sent him tumbling across the concrete floor with a scream, but Xander didn't so much as even look at Jason again afterward.

"We'll make the arrangements for who goes, then." Logan said with a look back over at Anna. "You think the rest of your siblings will still go camping by the lake over Easter weekend?"

Anna nodded, though she couldn't believe he was actually asking her, because that meant they were really going home. She couldn't wait to tell Orion. "It's tradition. They won't break tradition. Even the last year my mom was sick, we still went."

"That's where we'll get to them, then. If the Consortium's had them under surveillance for a full year and change after what happened on Nine, I'll be shocked. All the same, we'll talk to them by the lake and then work our way through the rest of the families one at a time." He looked around at the rest of those present, including Reed, who slowly got back to his chair in prudent silence.

Anna tried not to jump for joy since she had wanted to go home for so long, but she held it back to a nod as she looked around quickly. "Good, good. Sounds great. So are we done talking about everything for now?"

"For now." Logan said before anyone else could. "There's still a lot left to figure out while we're gone. We need a larger movement. And keep me updated on your hijacking work."

"Will do." Jason agreed as he got up, along with just about everybody else.

Anna just about bolted out of the room, but she decided to go up to Logan and give him a hug, even though she knew it was out of the blue. "We get to go home!" She whisper-yelled, but she couldn't hold herself back.

"We get to go home." He smiled as he hugged her, though it was rare for the two of them to have an extended conversation anymore about anything besides Lynnette. "Is it bad that I'm almost as excited to get my old clothes back as I am to see Liam and Larissa?"

"Your hat!" She gladly took his hug because it made her feel that much closer to home. "I swear, I wanted that hat more than anything. I wanted to steal it from your head a hundred times. I want my old clothes. My favorite perfume. Pictures. I can't wait to see them either, but you are so right. Getting my things back will be amazing!"

Logan grinned as they stepped back and headed out of the room. He squeezed Mercury's hand once he had it again and shrugged. "It was a good hat. I really like that hat."

Mercury's smile was subdued as she walked with Logan out of the meeting, and Anna darted out in front of them so she could run to Orion and tell him her exciting news. "She never has a problem showing how she feels, does she?"

That made Logan laugh, since it was Anna she was talking about. "No, when it comes to that, she's never really had much of a filter. We've both wanted to go back and see our families ever since we touched down, it's just . . . it feels like it's been long enough to be safe now. Finally. I know the Consortium is still looking for us, but if we haven't been back home in a year, they can't still have eyes on our families, can they?"

"It's unlikely." She held tighter to Logan's hand. Mercury wanted him to go back and see his family as well, but she was always worried about leaving their safe home. Even if they really did need more supplies and another doctor. "They wouldn't waste valuable resources to watch a bunch of farming families that think their loved ones are dead. Not this long, I don't think. They don't even know we've survived. So that would be quite a gamble to waste resources and time."

He appreciated her agreement because she had a much more logical mind than he did, so he knew he wasn't just being overly optimistic. "I'm excited for you to meet everyone. You'll like Larissa, and though I can't promise you'll like two of my brother's wives, you will probably like Rachel, at least."

Mercury shook her head a little at the very thought of someone having so many wives. "Do you think he's really happy that way? With three women vying for his time? I would hate being in a marriage like that."

"So would I. But for somebody like Liam . . . you'll understand when you meet him, I think. I don't know what it's turned into since we've been gone, but he needs that kind of stability around him. The whole point was to make sure they could keep him in line and help him manage the farm on his own. He's a talented guy, just . . . used to run a little wild." Logan was smirking fondly as he thought of his brother and all of Liam's shenanigans.

"Well, I'm not sharing you." Mercury said resolutely as she turned to kiss him on their way back to their unit in the labyrinth, even though she didn't want to go back. She didn't want to get back to work. She wanted to just . . . exist with Logan and their boys. "But I'm happy to meet your family."

"I'm not sharing you either." He told her when they got to a part of the path where nobody else was nearby to overhear. They spent too long in a relationship where they'd had to share time and themselves with someone else, and Logan never wanted to go back to feeling that way. He still struggled sometimes with the person he had become, but at least he only had to be one person. "And who knows, knowing my brother and at least a couple of his wives, Dec and James might have some more cousins to play with by now."

Even when she didn't want to go back to work, being a doctor was a part of Mercury that was always ready to assert itself.

"Especially considering your fertility and he's your twin brother, I can't imagine he has *no* children. He probably has several. Your sister too, if she is married . . ." Mercury paused, since she realized in the middle of her statement that things worked differently on Earth, that babies usually came before marriage, so it was probably rude to assume that someone *had* to be married. "I just mean it's likely that she is also similarly fertile."

He smiled at her stumble, since it was easy to forget sometimes just how different their backgrounds were. "I'd be really surprised if she and Cory aren't married by now. They seemed to be getting along really well when I left and in the few messages I got up on Nine. There's just a lot to find out. A lot we'll have missed." He didn't say it sadly, since they had missed out on what was going on with their families on purpose, so that nothing could ever get traced to them to endanger them or their loved ones. "It'll be strange to be home again. It feels like a different world."

Mercury actually looked upward as if she would see through everything all the way up to her home station, but then she looked back at Logan again. "It is. For me." She missed her parents terribly, and she wished that her own family could see her children and be with her, but if anything the Consortium was definitely watching her parents. Her father was a part of the Consortium, after all. "I'm glad we're going back for your sake. It'll be good to see you in your element. Hopefully you'll be able to relax a little more."

"Maybe." Relaxing was not his strong point, so he had his doubts. "With this offensive that Jason mentioned, possibly bringing down ships and supplies directly from the Consortium, things are going to get a lot more complicated for him to pull off something on that kind of scale. It'll be a huge distraction for the Consortium, and I think it would be a good opportunity to get a message through to your parents. Maybe Orion's family too." They were able to see, through Jason's surveillance and ongoing access, that her father was still in his position over Station Six, where she'd been raised. Orion's family were all still in their previous pursuits, though they all clearly believed that Mercury and Orion were dead. "I know they'll be excited to find out that you're alive."

"I miss them so much." She felt a stab of pain in her chest as she thought about her parents, but she did her best to ignore it. "They wanted me to be happy." When she thought about what her parents wanted, it was a conflict in her mind between what she knew and the haunting words of Stephen Kaplan telling her to investigate her life and her parents. She had resolutely refused to do so. "I wish they could meet you and Declan and James."

"They will. They're grandparents. They should know about that. Have a chance to know their grandkids." He didn't want to get off the lift and get back to work, but he knew they both had a great deal to do if they were going to leave within a few days. "As much as I hate the Consortium, I've always been glad they left your father in his position even after what happened on Nine. Just like I've been glad they left my family alone."

They watched news sources and found as many indirect means as possible to keep tabs on their family without doing anything that surveillance would pick up. Liam's signature had appeared on bills of sale for the farm produce, along with Larissa's, and there was a plentiful amount of public documentation showing her father issuing statements of various kinds to the citizens of the station he supervised. "I thought for a while they were just leaving them alone as bait, but now I just wonder if they have bigger problems to deal with."

"Or they don't know if we're watching, so they can't know if going after our families would do any good to get what they want." Mercury had been soured on the Consortium entirely after Kaplan turned her into his plaything. She knew not all the people were bad but it felt like all the leadership was like Kaplan.

"I should check on my patients." She mumbled so softly she almost couldn't hear herself. "I don't want to. I want to be with you." It was only after she arrived on Earth that she started to dread her job, but it was so hard with so many patients and limited resources.

"This will be a vacation for us in a lot of ways." He stepped out of the lift, but stopped against the wall of the stone corridor to hold her, since he didn't want to get back to work any more than she did. "No patients pulling at you, help with the kids coming along, a chance to see something other than grey walls and smell something besides sawdust and sweat." So many limitations were the guiding characteristics of their lives, inescapable and omnipresent. "A little work to do in talking to people, but I'll take care of most of that. You need to get some decent rest."

"I don't know if decent rest is possible, but I'll try, as long as you're with me." Mercury gladly stayed in his embrace a little longer before she kissed him warmly. "But you have to keep a shirt on. Otherwise you may look a little too much like a rugged farmer from the cover of a smutty romance novel."

"Been reading a lot of those, have you?" He grinned as he moved his hands over her sides. "Now I'll have to lose the shirt at some point, make sure I complete that mental image for you."

Mercury blushed a little bit, as she usually did whenever he encouraged her in one sexual way or another. "Make sure to take a picture then. Because I want to be able to revisit that." The blush in her cheeks turned deep crimson, but she kept smiling. "They have an extensive library here. I've tried to pick out some things that will be enjoyable to read between patients."

He kissed her again after that mention, but he thought mid-kiss about just how far the distance was between the people they had been and the people they had become. When he first met Mercury, her sexual experience was incredibly limited and mostly clinical in nature. Any kind of erotica would have been considered almost irrelevant when compared to medical journals and other forms of research. "I'll make sure there are pictures for future reference. So long as you share some of the interesting ideas you pluck out of your literature."

"You really want to know?" She teased as she brushed her lips against his, and even though her kiss was warm instead of heated and passionate, she didn't want to get him all worked up when they had to part ways. "There's little I have found that we haven't tried. But it's still incredibly sexy to read something dirty. Or to hear it." She whispered the last bit against his lips before she kissed him once more. He had turned her into a more sexual being, mostly just by way of her attraction and addiction to him. She *always* wanted him.

"Well then if it's something we haven't found yet, all the more reason to hear about it." He wrapped his arms around her back and held her for a while, content to take a few seconds of a vacation from the world. "Though I'm glad to hear we've been thorough about trying new things. If you don't run across something we haven't done yet very often, I'd say we're doing something right."

"Mmm. Well, we've been pretty boring for a while. I miss a lot of the things we had to leave behind." Mercury wrapped her hands around his neck and played with his hair at the base of his skull before she kissed him again. "I'm not glass. I know you worry about me. But you don't need to worry so much."

"I know you're not." Logan said with a chuckle against her lips. "You know, there's more than just people out in the district." He pulled her in to whisper against her hair. "There are shops in the little town we're gonna be passing through. If you know where to look. Which I do."

"Oh really?" She replied with a smirk that she wouldn't have ever developed without Logan and his extremely creative mind. "We should go to these shops. Definitely."

"I'll make sure we have some time to." He promised, reaching up with a thumb to trace the line of her smirk, which he loved. "Now come on, the sooner we get this day over with, the sooner we can get the boys to sleep and the sooner we can get back to having a night to ourselves." He slapped her ass playfully when he was finished, hard enough to send the sound ringing down the corridor but not enough to really hurt.

She liked it, of course, and it made her smile broadly as she stepped away from him. "Now you're just teasing me, Mr. Bickford." She kept backing away, since she had to get to her clinic. "I'll see you tonight. I'll wear whatever you want me to wear."

He looked her up and down, clearly thinking about it intently. "Start with the green top and the red skirt. We'll see where it goes from there."

Mercury nodded, though she would never leave without him expressly telling her to go. "It's been a while since I've dressed up for you. I'm excited." She grinned and ran her finger across his cheek. "I better go. If I can get away, I'll find you."

"I'll be in my office upstairs. And I'll make sure I'm alone for as much of the day as possible." He nodded off down the hall with a final smile. "Go on. I'll see you soon, even if not soon enough."

* * * * *

Tatyana stayed back with Xander as the group dispersed, but she didn't say much until they were alone. Everyone was either happy or upset about the decision, and she didn't want to discuss it further with anyone else. Except Xander.

"Will you want to go with them?" She asked curiously. He just arrived but she didn't know what he anticipated his role to be. "Depending on Jason's decision to go or to stay, and Logan definitely going, we'll need strong leadership to remain here. Reed is bipolar at best."

"Reed was a good man in his time. It's not his fault he's gotten his ass kicked by the Consortium longer than the rest of us." Xander put away his tablet in a backpack that was never more than arm's reach from him, then tossed the pack back in the chair he just vacated. "And no, there's no fucking way I'm going out there with them. They talk a good game about what they think they can get out of their families and their town, but I'll believe it when I see it."

Tatyana agreed with Xander on that, since she basically thought that Logan and Anna were letting their emotions get the best of them. "I hope they make it back. It won't help us if they die. But they're walking straight into danger. They will be lucky if it isn't a trap."

"We have something to gain either way." Xander doubted that would be a popular perspective to have, but he had been working with Tatyana long enough to know that she wasn't most people, even if most of what he knew about the woman had been by way of long-distance communications.

"If they come back with a few hundred more enthusiastic fighters, great. If they get killed out there because they walked into a trap, less great, but we know for certain that the Consortium is still capable of watching every family for signs of our survival. If they survive and get back here safely, we can start letting people go home to their own families and keep the cycle moving." He didn't seem to have many things in common with his brother, from what Tatyana could see, but in that way, they were the same. They were always four steps ahead of everyone else at minimum.

"He kept wondering if you were really going to show up." Tatyana said without much explanation, because she didn't need to. "But it's a good thing you did. Or else we would never get the Twist stabilized. He can't figure it out. We need fresh eyes with another version of the same genius brain." She smirked as she looked at him and sat on the edge of the table recently been vacated by the rest of the leadership. "Thank you for showing up. He was turning into a giant pain in my ass."

"Jason's never been anything *but* a pain in the ass." Xander moved to one side of the room, which doubled as a mechanical central point for the Labyrinth and therefore had watch-panels for the various systems that kept the sanctuary running. "I'll take a look at it as soon as the inventory distribution is finished and the Vancouver people are settled, but I'm not making any promises. Jason may be a pain in the ass, but he's also smarter than I am, even if it's not by a big enough margin for me to admit that to him. As far as I've seen, his math checks out. Hopefully it's like you said, a fresh set of eyes is all that's needed."

"He's been working on it day and night. Sleeping in the lab. Honestly, I'm a little surprised he still has a wife. He doesn't really go home very often." Tatyana shrugged, since she didn't care if he stayed married or not, but she had long given up on trying to seduce Jason. He was too lost in the Twist and his wife, even if he would end up losing her anyway. "And he keeps telling me no. So we are both annoyingly frustrated in the lab."

"I'm sorry, you're a gorgeous foreign badass with a bossy personality and you're looking for me to feel sorry for you because the one guy you've still got a thing for won't fuck you? Please tell me you're joking." Xander's look could only have been more condescending if it had been on Jason's face. Xander's features didn't have as much practice with condescension as his younger copy. He'd had too much work to do all his life to waste time talking to fools.

"Yes, I do want you to feel sorry for me." She replied with a laugh and she shook her head. "No, I just wanted you to know a little more about your brother and his apparent dedication to solving the Twist. No sleep. No sex. No wife. No daughter. No affair. Just work."

"You say that like I should be surprised." He found something wrong with one of the settings on the lights and did a few seconds' worth of work with the interface, after which the lights dimmed a little and she could see the efficiency rating in the corner of the screen jump twenty points. "For the vast majority of his life, Jason's had no wife, no daughter, no affairs, just fucked-up relationships and work. Mostly work. It's the whole reason you two got along so well in the first place. You're both career workaholics who happened to enjoy each other's genitalia."

"I didn't see anything wrong with it before." She shrugged again and jumped down from the table. "Should I show you to your unit? Do you need anything?"

"No, I know my way around here pretty well. I stayed here a few months back in the sixties." He finally gave her a smile, since he thought it was fairly adorable she thought he might need any help. "Where are your quarters? Or do you stay and sleep in the lab so you can be closer to Jason while you're wearing him down?"

"I'm not wearing him down. And haven't even gotten close. He thinks I'm too crazy anyway." She motioned out of the makeshift conference room so that they could go down deeper into the labyrinth. "My unit is close to the lab. Fifteen floors down."

"I'm down on Fourteen. At least we got the nice floors before the flooding and the really weird shit deep down starts." He had done his own exploration of the place in times past, and he didn't look particularly happy to be stuck back underground. "Oh well. Nobody promised when we decided to turn rebel that there would be anything glamorous about it. Maybe if we can get the Twist working we can take some of this construction work and start building luxury penthouses on Eleusis. I could use something with a hot tub right about now."

Tatyana never allowed herself to think about life on Eleusis, since she never thought that she would make it that far. Somewhere between Earth and Eleusis, she expected she would die. That was what she was prepared for. Nothing more, nothing less. "The hot water is unreliable here anyway. It would make no sense to even install something like that. The beds are comfortable at least."

"There's two kinds of beds. The kind that's good for sleeping and the kind that's good for sleeping *with* somebody. Usually not the same bed, in my experience. I don't want anything soft if I'm gonna have somebody riding me on it. Throws off the whole thing." Xander switched easily between English and Russian, though his Russian wasn't as good as Jason's and he clearly hadn't spent much time in Russia to perfect it. Still, he knew quite a bit, and didn't have any of the hesitation that usually came with someone picking up the language for the first time.

She raised an eyebrow as she looked him up and down again. "Are you expecting to have a visitor join you in your bed?"

"Plan for the apocalypse, but also plan for the best night of your life. Reality is always gonna be somewhere in between. I just like to be prepared." Xander replied easily, though his expression was unreadable.

"I see. Well, I did not test your bed. I do not know how soft it is or is not. You'll have to figure that out." She continued walking through the hall until they got to the lift. "Jason is taking time away from the Twist. I will be going back in the morning. I can show you what we have accomplished."

"*Accomplished* seems like kind of a strong word for something you haven't gotten working yet, but whatever you say. I look forward to it." He got into the lift and pressed the appropriate floors, but he was giving her a once-over when he turned back around. "You don't have somebody you're planning on taking time away for, I'm assuming?

Tatyana laughed, but she liked his attention. Clearly she was already attracted to his appearance, and the healthier version of the face she knew was even more attractive than Jason's. "I'm too crazy for most men to tolerate."

"Most. Wonderful word. Immediately makes people wonder if they're in the minority group. Solid manipulation tactics." He grinned back, since he appreciated a devious mind, but his grin didn't linger too long. "There's a difference between being crazy and being dedicated to the point where dedication becomes pathological. I'm guessing you cross that line once in a while, but that's the only way anyone like us still knows they have a line at all."

"I live on that line, mostly because I cross it more often than not. I'm here dedicating my life to a cause I think will kill me. And I accept that." Tatyana looked at him with a defiant expression, since she knew who she was and her purpose. "Jason likes to say I'm gladly marching toward my death. I just happen to not care if death is the price I pay to make things happen."

"I've always found that apathy is its own kind of joy, so he's not wrong." He was still looking her over as the lift stopped on his floor, and he didn't move to get off right away. "You've been a good leader for the European divisions, Grey. I respect that. It takes people who don't give a shit about anything but their focus to really change the world."

"Thank you. At least someone does." She said with a nod before she returned the looks that he gave her. "I'm not done yet."

He raised an eyebrow at that statement. "With what? Saving the world or constructing your fantasy for the night?"

Tatyana just smirked. "Both. You're more attractive than he is, he can't keep any meat on his bones. And I like the look in your eyes."

"You like what you think you see. And you like it because I'm not him." He challenged easily, then looked her over one more time, apparently to get the image of her fixed in his own mind. "The look in my eyes might surprise you, once you get to know what's behind it. Lucky for you, I'm not going anywhere for a while."

"Lucky for me?" She stood in the way of the lift door, forcing it to remain open. "Why don't you tell me something behind your eyes, then? I do like you."

"I told you, I need to see to my people and the inventory first." He turned in the hallway to make sure she wasn't following him. "They've had a shit time of it and they just lost eighty percent of the people they ever cared about in the world. So did I." There was pain there, of a kind that Jason never would have shown. He would have looked at the losses of their people and called them casualties of war, statistical probabilities come to pass and resources that needed to be allocated elsewhere. Xander *felt* it. He felt the loss of his people, even as he talked to her about the hypothetical pragmatics of the possible death of the party sent to the midwest. "When my people are settled and we're holding steady to wait for the Bickfords and Al-Jabbars to get back, then, if the sky doesn't start falling, you and I can see about getting a drink and we'll see how long you want to look at these eyes of mine."

"I see." She stepped back into the lift so the door could close. She didn't blame him for wanting to do things his way. It still didn't feel great to be rejected by the same damn face. "Let me know if you need anything."

Xander nodded, since he didn't expect her to be happy about getting brushed off, but priorities were priorities. Of everyone else involved in their rebellion, he expected Tatyana to understand that. "I imagine when we get to that point, I'll be letting you know about all kinds of things." He gave her a faint smile as he moved back toward his unit, everything about his walk and bearing proclaiming him as everything Jason never was and never would be. Confident from head to toe, strong, experienced, and dedicated down to the last drop of blood in his body.

Tatyana didn't say anything else or smile back at him, she just let the doors close so she could go to her unit and get a little bit of sleep. The most important thing was getting the Twist to work. If he could do that, then nothing else mattered.

3

"So wait, we're actually going? Like I should start packing assless chaps and start measuring my head for a cowboy hat?" Orion reached up and ran his hands around the crown of his head, trying to imagine what he'd look like wearing one. "I'm not sure where I put my chaps, but I'll figure it out when we get there. I can't believe Tatyana and Reed actually agreed. Was Reed drunk?"

"He was his usual kind of mean, so I'm gonna guess no. He's usually nicer when he's wasted." Anna shrugged but she was happy about Orion's excitement. "Let's hold off on the assless chaps. They're kind of useless for someone who has never even ridden a horse, but I'm sure we can find a horse for you." She beamed and pulled him into a kiss. "I'm so happy!!"

He picked her up easily in the middle of the kiss and held her in mid-air with her legs wrapped around his waist. It was a fairly common thing for them, since it was just easier for him to kiss her that way. "I'm excited to meet your family. I still can't wrap my head around somebody related to you by blood being a complete asshole all the time, so Ben is gonna be a fun specimen to study." He chuckled and kissed her again. "And I'm just looking forward to seeing what kind of place could produce somebody as awesome as you. I need to see the source of this for myself."

"Ben will take some getting used to." Anna laughed and mauled Orion again with her lips, but then her smile faded slightly. "They are going to be mad we lied this whole time. And the last time they saw me, we had just celebrated my marriage. To Logan. So that's kind of awkward."

"Little bit." He knew that was a pretty deep complication of them going back to her home, but it obviously wasn't going to stop them. "They'll get used to it. It's been a long time since you've seen them or they've seen you. They have to expect that some things have changed. Your little brother Danny might be married by now. Things change pretty quick down here."

"He might." Clearly she hadn't thought about Danny being married and suddenly she was more uncomfortable with the time she lost with her family. Nearly two years had passed since she and Logan left on a shuttle. "In my mind they haven't changed, but time never stops to wait for us."

"Well, it's not like you've been standing still either. Things are a little different all over." Orion shrugged, which bounced her a little against him, then kissed her one more time before he put her down. "I'll be glad to meet everybody. And I know they'll be excited to see you again. No matter what has or hasn't changed. They're still family."

"You're right about that." She got lost in his dark eyes and smiled at him before she grabbed his hand to hold it. "I haven't really changed, though. I mean, we nearly died, we had children, that sort of thing. But I don't *look* different, I don't think. Logan has changed a lot more than I have."

"Your hair is longer." He said as he tugged it down her back. "Plus there's the augmented boobs that you really shouldn't forget about. Otherwise, yeah, you look about like I remember you from when you first got onto the station. Rough and ready to kick some ass."

"That's right." Anna said with a proud grin. "And my hair is only longer because you said you like it better that way. I like it long too, but ultimately I want to look better for my man." She poked at his side playfully. "The boobs too, but that's only temporary while breastfeeding. Unless you knock me up one right after another."

"Well, nature is the only one stopping us right now, so if that happens, it's not like we didn't know it was a possibility." It was incredibly strange for Orion to have switched over so completely to the Earth mentality of having as many children as possible, but even with everything staring them in the face, he couldn't bring himself to not want more children if they were capable of having them. The world as it was needed them, and if they were ever going to build the human race on Eleusis, Eleusis was going to need people just as much as Earth. "Hopefully we'll just do it one at a time from now on, though. It turns out I like kids, but twins are a fucking lot of work."

"They really are." Anna agreed quickly and she hauled him down into another kiss. "I can ask around, you know. If you want me to go looking for a contraceptive. I know they exist, even if they're illegal. Technically everything we have is stolen anyway."

Orion didn't have a straight answer for that right away, since his own feelings on the subject were complicated. "My only problem with having more kids right away is worrying what's gonna happen to us in the next few months. But I've been wondering about that since we got to Earth, and it's starting to feel pointless to even worry about anything until we start really making a pain of ourselves with the Consortium. After that we're all gonna be targets all over again, but who knows when that's gonna be."

"For all we know, it could be another year and a half before they get the Twist figured out, and even longer before we can even do anything with it. It doesn't make sense to wait on having a life until we're some kind of safe." They never would be, that was something Orion had come to terms with even back on Station Nine. It was just harder to maintain his peace with that sentiment when there were kids to worry about as well.

Anna nodded at that rationale, but it wasn't the first thing that came to mind. Anna had been raised on Earth. People died for stupid reasons. A car accident that didn't get help fast enough. Food poisoning. Snakebite. Rabid dog. Even the occasional report of rough wanderers that went through and stole, ravaged, and raped. Her entire life was wondering if she would survive one week to the next and never once allowing herself to live in fear of death. Death was always going to be closer than she wanted it to be. "I've never felt completely safe in my life. My parents never did, no one here on Earth really does. My mom died and left small children behind, and I don't think she would say she regretted any moment. I kind of believe you can have a full life, but I don't know about a safe one."

"I kind of think safe and full are mutually exclusive anyway." He shrugged and spun her around a few times as they walked. "If you haven't gotten shot at a few times in your life, you're doing something wrong."

"Except you probably haven't been shot at by your brother who thought you were a deer sneaking around behind him." Anna laughed, since she had too many stories and there were still a lot of stories that she hadn't told him. Not because she didn't want to, just because they didn't always come up. "I was making out with one of Ben's friends, too. He swears that wasn't the reason why he shot the tree full of buckshot."

"Yeah, it probably was. I took one of Khadi's boyfriends on a hop between stations once and made sure the guy was puking for most of the rest of the day. I told both of them that it was because of technical problems. It was *not* because of technical problems."

Anna looked at Orion and dropped her jaw. "Shame. Shame on you!! That was mean." She smirked afterward, though, and shook her head. "I did give a girl food poisoning once. The girl who was interested in Ben before Susan. She totally knew it, too. My reputation only went further downhill from there."

"I think you mean downtown." He glanced down at his own crotch with a grin back at her. "God, I can't even imagine what we're gonna be like when Lynnette starts dating. It's gonna be a mess."

"Who says she's going to get to date at all?" Anna shook her head. "Nope. I'm not letting her. I know what boys think about. And what they do. Nope."

"Yeah, no. That's just . . . no." He had never really considered what it would be like to be a parent before, and certainly hadn't fully realized what it would involve. Including but not limited to homicidal feelings toward future potential boyfriends of his daughter.

They got to the truck he was supposed to drive down to the new exterior community and he paused by the driver's door with one hand up on the handle to hang off. "So when are we leaving? I need to know how long I have to prepare myself against getting beaten up by brothers-in-law."

"It won't take too long to get packed up and ready to go. And there is no reason to put it off. Maybe a day or two?" She couldn't stop grinning. "I was thinking maybe you could ask and see if Fitch and Melissa want to come too. We could use the backup manpower and Melissa is always complaining about being stuck around the same places and never seeing anything. This is definitely going to be a change of scenery."

"I'll ask, I'm sure they'll want to come along." He let out a deep breath and shook his head, since he couldn't believe they were finally . . . *doing* something. Anything. They had been sitting around in the mountains looking over their shoulders for so long he started to forget what life was like any other way. "It'll be good. For all of us. Give you a chance to say a decent goodbye to your home. Not even the kind that necessarily has to last forever, since who knows what the world is gonna look like on the other side of all this. Just, you know, a chance to see everything again."

Anna's smile dimmed at the thought of saying goodbye to everything all over again, but she knew she would have to. "They'll come back with us. They have to. Staying there doesn't make any sense when Eleusis is possible for all of us."

"I hope you're right." He pulled her in for one last kiss, but he had to get to work. "I'll let you know what Kam and Melissa say, and I'll be back in a little while to start getting our stuff together. It's gonna be weird. The twins have never been more than maybe a few kilometers from where they were born."

"Keep your radio close so I can talk dirty to you without someone overhearing." Anna teased as he got into the vehicle. "I love you, Mr. Al-Jabbar."

"You call that dirty talk? I'm not impressed." He picked up his earpiece from where he'd left it in the console of the truck, and tucked it into his ear while still grinning down at her. "I love you too, Anna. See you in a little while."

* * * * *

"I don't think I even need to ask," Kameron hedged as she sat down at the table where Melissa had a warm meal for the two of them while their daughter took a late nap. "But there's a group that is going out to the midwest. Orion said he thinks it would be good for us to go, but there's a risk involved with the Consortium . . ." Kameron took pauses while she spoke to see if Melissa would freak out, but since the baby was asleep, she figured her wife would probably keep it down. "You know, if they are watching then we might be walking into a death-trap. That kind of thing."

"Sounds like the kind of thing somebody needs to be around to shoot if it happens." Melissa tossed the comment over her shoulder as she walked back to the stove to get the rest of the food. "I was with Priscilla when they asked her to go along for babysitting. I figured they'd ask you to go along too, since it's Orion's wife pushing things." Melissa had never been outwardly jealous of Kameron's friendship with Orion, but there were a lot of times where it felt like Kam had ordered her priorities by what Orion needed just because they'd been friends for so long.

Kameron turned around and looked at Melissa with an expression that said she didn't want to start that fight again. "Come on, Mel. I'm asking if you want to go, I'm not saying that we're going because Orion is."

"It seems like asking for trouble." She brought the rest of the food over and stepped back to take her hair down and put it back up, since it had gotten messed up while she was working on dinner and getting the baby to sleep. Her arms and mostly-exposed torso were covered in brightly colored tattoos that made even something as simple as putting her hair back into a work of art, and she seemed a little more relaxed once her white-blonde hair was back under control.

"I mean, seeing their families again, I get it. I don't really feel the need to see mine, but if they want to see theirs, that's one thing. Trying to recruit the whole district all at once is . . . that's just asking for something to go wrong. All it takes is one person who doesn't want to join in against a rebellion to make one phone call and the whole place will get bombed off the planet."

"With that kind of mentality, it could happen to anyone at any time. How do we know with all of the strangers that just arrived here we don't already have a snake?" Kam got up from her chair and went over to get close to Melissa, and she reached out to grab her gently by the arm. "I thought it would be good to get away from here. We could even find a way to get rings." She looked down at Melissa's bare hand and thought about all the times she wanted to make it obvious that Mel was taken. By her. "Maybe even get some new clothes. Get you some more supplies for all those tattoos that people keep asking for."

Melissa glared back just slightly less playfully. "Bribery? Already? That was fast." She pouted a little, but took the hand Kameron had placed on her arm and looked it over, equally empty of rings. "If we go, can we just . . . can it be just us that goes? Anna and Logan might need to take their kids to meet their families, but Kassie doesn't have any family out there to meet. She should stay here, just in case. Unless we're going all the way to St. Louis, and even then . . ." They knew Kazuo had surviving siblings somewhere in the midwest who had gone into hiding, but after the events on Nine, one of the few retaliations they heard of had been the killing of Kasumi's grandparents. No one could confirm it, though.

"We're not going to St. Louis, even if they wanted to go that far." Kameron wouldn't dare take that risk, especially if they had Kassie with them. "I don't . . . we've never left her."

Melissa rubbed Kam's arms as if to soften that idea. "I know.

But we both know this is a war. When you go off to fight, you're not gonna take her with you so she can ride these hips while you're shooting people." Her hands moved down to the aforementioned hips to hold her closer.

Kam groaned loudly, since she didn't want to leave her daughter behind, but she also didn't want to admit that her wife was right. "I fucking hate it when you give me logical explanations for shit." Kam definitely didn't move away from Melissa's touch. It always felt better to lean in. "We don't have to go if you don't want to go. You know I'll still work on getting you supplies and a ring regardless. You're mine. I want people to know."

"You're the one I want people to know is off the market." On Earth, and especially with the people they had encountered since coming down with the rest of the refugees, a badass like Kam was in much more demand than Melissa was, and that was fine by Melissa. "And if you're going into something dangerous, then of course I'm going with you. I may not be as good in a fight as you are, but I can still watch your ass. Both for fun and for safety."

That got a small smile out of Kameron, and she looked Melissa over head to toe. "You're the living work of art with a damn fine ass. Don't even deny it." Fitch smiled a little bit more, but she still didn't like the idea of leaving Kassie behind. "We haven't really had a chance to enjoy some time alone. And I really want time alone. Who would we leave her with?"

"I could ask Jessie if she'd be willing to let Rebekah take on a roommate for a little while, but if not, I'm sure I could get Erebi to watch her. They've been sort of taking in everybody else's." Melissa's voice turned sympathetic as she talked about Erebi, since the two of them had been through a kind of hell that Melissa didn't even want to contemplate. They had gotten pregnant back on Nine, then she'd had terrible problems near the end of her pregnancy, only to prepare for a child and take their beautiful baby boy home and have him die just a few weeks later.

It had been a terribly hard time for them, but rather than allowing their grief to weigh them down and drown them, they had started taking on other children for a few days or a week at a time in order to give other parents a bit of a break and a chance to catch up on rest. They claimed it helped them to cope with what happened, but Melissa wasn't sure she could have done it herself. "She's got a hell of a lot of playmates, that much is for sure."

"We'll ask them first. I know Erebi loves Kassie." Kameron

stepped in closer to her beautiful wife and reached out to run her hand along Melissa's cheek. "I know that shit is hard since I'm heading up security. It should be Carl . . ." She said with a shake of the head, since she missed Carl a lot. Especially because his wife was Kassie's aunt. "I know it pulls me away a lot. But I'm always trying to get right back here." Kameron loved her daughter, but she loved Melissa to her soul. They'd never had an official ceremony, but as far as Kameron was concerned, Melissa was her wife.

"I knew what I signed up for with you, Beautiful." Melissa said with a warm, slow kiss. "You deserve your position, and you've done a hell of a job keeping this entire community safe. We're a bunch of misfits out in the ass-end of nowhere, but you manage to keep us all from being found and you kick the ass of anybody who gets out of line. You're amazing at your job, and Kassie is easier than any of my little brothers and sisters ever were to take care of. If I've got any complaints, it's just that our house isn't done yet."

"It's almost done." She reassured Melissa, but she was a little dazed by the kiss. "You are such a good kisser. Fuck. It just scrambles my brain."

"Good. I like your brain the way I like my eggs." She kissed Kam again heatedly, since she missed her all day while she was gone in meetings and planning sessions. "I'll talk to Erebi later tonight when you inevitably head out to go do more official things with guns, and I'll let you know what she says.I also picked out a bunch of interior items for our house and got some of the carpenters to start working on them for us. I wore that one tank top and the leggings I got a few months ago that forced you to forgive me for the crib thing." Melissa smiled mischievously, since she had gotten more than a few favors out of people by way of her provocative clothing.

Kameron gave her a playful glare. "You wore that and a bunch of sweaty men got to see it and I didn't? How the hell is that fair?"

"Because you get to see everything that's underneath it, and none of them do." She swivelled her hips just a little against Kameron's after that, and kissed her again.

"Damn right I do." Kameron murmured as she kissed Melissa greedily and moaned a little against her lips. "Not unless we want another baby, and if we do, I get to be there for that too."

"Wait, why am I automatically the one who's gonna carry a

baby if we want another one?" Melissa looked taken aback, and pulled away from the kiss. "These tits are big enough already, thank you very much. I bust them out for nursing a baby and I'm gonna need a back brace."

Kameron rolled her eyes and looked down at her own body. "It's true, I don't have that problem. I just have better but not crazy tits right now." She pulled Melissa back in, because she wanted to kiss her some more. "Fine, fine. I can carry the babies if it would make you happy."

"We'll figure it out once Kassie gets out of diapers. Maybe by then I'll start feeling like my clock is ticking and I'll want to volunteer for the next round of baby-making. Right now, the only thing I want to make is time with you."

"The food smells great, but you smell better." Kameron said as she held tightly to Melissa to keep her close. "You smell like vanilla." She moved her kisses to Melissa's neck, and right to one of her favorite spots. "And something else . . . " Kameron couldn't decipher the other smell, but she didn't care.

"Lilacs." She tilted her head back to enjoy Kam's attention to her neck. Being home or hanging out with friends all day, while taking care of the baby, made for some very long days. "Priscilla and I found a bunch of them up on the hillside this morning, and we gathered a few bushels of them so I could start breaking them down for ink and scent. Throw a little in with some of the coconut oil we got in last shipment and they work just like perfume. I already traded three vials for favors."

"You better keep some." Kameron said as her hands snaked up underneath Melissa's shirt and she grazed her fingers along the front of Melissa's bra. "Damn bra. Always in the fucking way."

"This is what I get for making you dinner. You come home all needy with sabotage plans to make my food cold before we get to it. I see how you are." She leaned down to kiss Kam again, though, clearly encouraging her, barrier or no barrier. "Come on and get it, then, gorgeous. That baby isn't gonna sleep forever."

"I'm sure the food will taste great. Later." Kameron got Melissa's shirt off before they made it back to the bedroom, and Kameron's shirt came off as they walked through the door. She was happy to have a sleeping baby. And a smoking hot wife.

4

The bus for transport had been restored and the engine entirely rebuilt, along with its navigation. All Orion had to do was be present in the driver's seat to monitor their progress and make sure the bus didn't completely derail itself. He was glad for the curtain between the driver's compartment and the rest of the bus, since it allowed him to gawk at the beautiful countryside in peace. He was especially grateful for it when Anna came through and unceremoniously plopped herself into his lap.

"You're interrupting my book." His tone carried mock indignation, as he pulled her in closer with an aggravated sigh. "Geez. The nerve of some people." He leaned back to grin at her as his hands moved over her thighs. "About half an hour out. Things looking familiar yet?"

"Not really." She leaned in, enjoying his caress on her thighs. "Though it'll look familiar eventually. I hope." Anna felt pretty free at the moment, since Logan was keeping an eye on Lynnette asleep in her carseat, and Gwen was handling Leo. "I'm glad Gwen came along so I can harass my husband who says he's reading a book."

He nodded back toward the windshield, where there were a few lines of text projected near the bottom of the glass, then gave her a vindicated look. "I used to read quite a lot, thank you very much. My old hops from Three to Prime were at least ten hours of drift time. A guy can only take so many naps before *Les Miserables* sounds like really interesting reading. In the original French, I might add."

"Wow." She said with raised eyebrows, clearly impressed. "I didn't know you knew French." Anna turned to face him completely, straddling his lap as well as her short legs could manage. "So say something sexy."

Orion grinned at that challenge, but his accent was perfect, and his baritone voice slid through the words as if he had been born to them. *"L'amour est l'emblème de l'éternité, il confond toute la notion de temps, efface toute la mémoire d'un commencement, toute la crainte d'une extrémité."* He pulled her down into a kiss afterward, as if to seal her request in place. "Love is the emblem of eternity. It confounds time, erasing both the memory of the beginning and all the fear of an ending."

"Aww." Anna swooned with genuine warmth, and she kissed him back with heat. "You are more and more impressive the more I learn about you." Anna looked up into his dark eyes with a grin and she nipped at his bottom lip teasingly after. "I don't know a foreign language. I'm sorry."

"Well, you never needed to. Makes sense. If I wanted to talk to my grandparents growing up, I had to learn Arabic on one side and French on the other. I started picking up a little Spanish with Carl, but I never got very far with it. Just enough to know when somebody's talking shit about me. As far as I remember from school, though, pretty much every direction but the tribal territories south of you is English until you hit an ocean or a pole."

"Something like that." Anna looked into his eyes again for a moment, then rested her head against his shoulder after she scooted further up on his lap. "You are so much smarter than I am." She wasn't used to feeling insecure about herself or even particularly vulnerable. "Seriously. So much smarter."

"That's not true. I've just had a lot more free time." He sounded just as off about his statement as she had about hers, he just had different reasons for it. "I've been flying long stretches since I was sixteen and I got to run my first solo flight. Once I showed I wasn't going to crash anything, they started giving me boring ferry jobs until I could work my way up to some of the more complicated outer-orbit freighter jobs."

"But even the more complicated jobs required maybe, *maybe* one hour in ten of what I'd actually call hard work. The rest is dead space letting inertia do the work while I watched the controls. So I've quite literally spent ninety percent of my professional life doing absolutely nothing and getting paid for it. Then there's the last year or so, and I've never worked harder in my life, though I know this is pretty much exactly the level of work you're used to. I've just had free time. That's the only difference."

"I don't know if that's true, since it takes intelligence more than time, but you can believe what you want and I'll believe what I want." Anna took a deep breath of Orion's scent and just remained there, holding onto him. "I wasted most of my 'free time' having sex. I worked hard on the farm, sure, but I wasted time too. I'm not sure what my life would have looked like if I hadn't spent so much time chasing boys."

"I wasted my fair share the same way. I didn't always make all those long shuttle rides alone, you know." He chuckled against her cheek. "Though zero-gravity sex is a lot more of a novelty than something to make a habit out of, honestly. Some fun possibilities, but generally just more of a mess than it's worth."

"More mess?" Anna cringed at the thought, and then chuckled. "Talk about waste, those muscles are better put to work than just . . . floating."

"I'll stick with gravity-based sex, thank you very much." He pulled her in to grind against him from the way she straddled him. "You nervous? You usually only come and get me like this when you're worried about something."

"Are you saying that I don't look for sex any other time?" She replied defensively, since she didn't think she was *that* needy. "Can't I just want to be with my husband?"

"You absolutely can." He rolled with her defensiveness, since he was used to it whenever he called her out on something. "But it's okay to be nervous too. And it's okay to need somebody when you're nervous. Believe me, if we ever go back to see my family, I'm gonna be shaking in my jumpsuit beforehand."

Anna was quiet for a long time before she finally leaned back enough to look into his eyes again. "I'm scared of going back home and facing things I left behind. My things aren't even at my father's house. My life is piled into a room in the Bickford house that I shared with Logan for a month before we left." She looked pained as she thought about the life she had left behind, even though it felt like it was something made up in her head. "Things have been endlessly complicated between the four of us. I'm happy with our marriage. I love you so much. But none of that was here at home. It's going to be filled with things that Logan and I have shared our whole life."

He could understand that, and he pulled her into a kiss to silently let her know that he'd heard her. "I've been trying to think the past few days about what I can do to help make that better for you, but I honestly don't know. I want to be with you through all of this, I want to get to know your family, but you've already told me how happy everybody was when you married Logan. All I can do is be here for whatever you need me to be." He didn't have that kind of history with Mercury, and strangely, he and Mercury had actually had a chance to talk about that fact earlier in the trip out of the mountains. They had only gotten married just before they met Logan and Anna and the four of them had been cross-matched, turning all of their lives upside down forever.

Anna kissed him several times and afterward she pressed her forehead to Orion's. "I hope you don't take offense when we get there. They don't know you. And some people won't be happy that Logan and I aren't together anymore. Not that I think we could even be together should someone try to enforce some crazy law or something. He's . . . changed a lot. I'd spend a lot of time smacking him around for scowling so much." Anna sighed heavily and kissed Orion again. "I don't know what you can do to help. I just want to get there, see my family, and drag them all back to the mountains with us and move on."

"I just hope they're all open to being dragged. We could use all the help we can get. Frankly, if there's anybody who can kick the shit out of the Consortium, it's gonna be a whole countryside worth of farmers. Your people take precisely zero shit from anybody." He hugged her tightly, and kissed her again as his hands rubbed her back. "It's gonna be good. You'll see."

"It's not only the whole thing with Logan." She was glad for his hug, though, and she hugged him back just as tightly. "It's the midwest. They're, um, not going to be very used to seeing . . . well, a freakishly tall dark-skinned guy."

"Oh, so it's a racist thing. I keep forgetting that's still a thing down here sometimes." Both on the station and in their mountain retreat, there were people from all over the world represented and getting along just fine, even if it was just by necessity. "Well, I'll hold off on the *Salaam alaykum* for the time being." He grinned, and the dimness of the cabin coupled with the fact that the sun was setting outside made the brightness of his smile a contrast against the rest of him.

"I like hearing you speak in whatever language you like. I don't care. I just wanted you to know." Anna kissed him harder and nibbled on his bottom lip. "I wouldn't have gotten some really cool tattoos from Melissa in Arabic if I didn't like the way it sounds when you read it out loud."

"It is still my favorite poetry." He leaned in to kiss her neck. "Your body and the tattoos on it, not Arabic."

Anna smiled again when he kissed her neck, and she tilted her head back so he could further explore her skin with his lips. "I need to stay as close to you as I can. I don't want to get sucked back into the life I left behind, I want to stay with you in the life I have now."

"Speaking on behalf of the life you have now, you're not going anywhere." His kisses got racier and rougher with that declaration, and he wrenched the collar of her shirt to have more room to kiss her before he leaned back to look up in her warm eyes. "We should probably send in somebody they don't know to let them know we're coming. The whole gang of us walk in there all at once and they're gonna get twitchy before they know what's happening. You did say they freak out pretty quickly over strangers, and like you said, I look pretty strange."

"You want to go in first?" She was confused by that, but she didn't know if it was because his kisses were distracting her or she just didn't understand why he was volunteering himself. It could be a trap. "But what if the Consortium is watching?"

"No, I mean send somebody in who doesn't look threatening but who also doesn't look like somebody who they think is dead." He clarified quickly. "If the Consortium is watching, then we're fucked. There's no real way around that at this point. But even if they're not, I don't want you to go in there first and get shot because your family thinks you're some kind of Consortium plant or doppleganger or some shit. I'm sure they hate them just as much as we do right now."

"Do you think anyone else is going to want to risk their life for us?" She said with an edge of doubt, since she didn't think anyone else would be willing to go in first. "If I know Logan at all anymore, he'll want to go in ahead of everyone else."

"Right. Because Logan has been so even-tempered and easy to predict the last year." He looked at her like she was stoned.

"I didn't say he was. I'm just saying he won't want anyone to go in ahead of him. Mostly because his brother isn't going to believe anything other than seeing Logan face-to-face." Anna shrugged and went in for another distracting kiss. "We can ask what everyone else wants to do, but I'm certain he'll want to go in first."

"He will." Logan's voice came from the door to the driver's compartment, but as he stepped in, he didn't so much as look over at Anna and Orion in the driver's seat. He just stepped to the forward side of the compartment to look out at the prairie sweeping by on the side of the endlessly-straight roads. "How much farther to the lake? I was hoping we would get there before sunset."

It wasn't awkward at all that she was straddling Orion's lap, her shirt askew, and Logan was just standing there. Not awkward at all. Anna wasn't going to let that force her off of Orion's lap, though. Logan was the one who had walked in unannounced. Anna pointed toward the GPS and then the timer next to it. "There's the countdown, big guy."

He glanced over at the GPS and his scowl deepened, but his eyes turned to the landscape again rather than to Anna and Orion. "If you park us far enough away up the hill, then most campers will see us coming at least, realize we're not trying to sneak up on them. I'll go down on my own and make sure everyone gets past the brunt of it, then signal for the rest of you to come the rest of the way down the hill. With any luck, Larissa and Cory will be around." He adjusted the sides of his coat absent-mindedly, running his hands over some of the portions that had become threadbare over the last year and a half.

"Yes, Sir, boss-man." Anna said with a playful smile, but when he didn't smile, she just got annoyed. "Okay, seriously, I'm not going to let you off this bus if you don't act even a little bit happy that we're going to see our families again. Seriously. I will kick your fucking ass. Liam is going to think you've been brainwashed if you don't retain even a little bit of personality."

"I'll be happy when they decide not to pull the trigger. I know Liam and Ben, at the bare minimum, will have some kind of weapon on hand as soon as a strange bus from the other end of the continent shows up." He did spare a glare for her at her comment, but then turned to go back into the main section of the bus. "Just tell me when we get there. Jason's back home on the satellite feed watching for anything anomalous, but he hasn't seen anything worth worrying about while he's been busy erasing us from the footage."

"We'll be there soon." She said after that, since he wasn't going to relax even a little bit. "Is that all you wanted to talk about?"

He turned and looked back at her, his eye contact solid and unwavering, as if he was purposefully ignoring everything else about the image in front of him in order to focus on just her eyes. "Did you have something else? Lynnette is sleeping in one of the seats in the back."

She shook her head, but once he met her eyes, she felt a stab of guilt that she knew shouldn't exist anymore. Anna and Logan weren't married anymore. No one back home knew that, but she and Logan did, and that was what mattered. However, she still felt guilty. A tiny part of her still felt like she was cheating on her best friend, especially knowing that they were about to be back in the life where they had promised so much. They promised they would never give up and they would stick together no matter what. So much for those vows. "Let me know when she wakes up and I'll come back to feed her."

He gave her a cursory nod and headed back through the door. He took a moment to himself after he closed it just to get himself back together. Knowing that Anna was with Orion was one thing, and he'd had plenty of time to put himself in the frame of mind where he could watch her stay with other men and remove himself from the situation. It was another thing entirely to see her right in front of him all over another man.

He went back to Mercury in the seats they shared and he looked down at Declan, who was watching the world fly by with bright-eyed interest as they drove. "Did he actually finish his milk for once?"

"He did." Mercury said with a smile, but when she looked up, she could see something clouding Logan's expression. "Is something wrong? What happened?"

"Nothing's happened. We're just getting close." He sat beside her and leaned back after looking around to make sure the other three children were accounted for and taken care of. Gwen still had Leo, Lynnette was still asleep, and James was asleep in Priscilla's arms, on his way to being put down for a nap. "When we get there, I'm going to go down first, just to make sure they know we're not some kind of ambush."

"What?" Mercury didn't like hearing that, but she knew she should have expected it. She tugged at her shirt to make sure it was in place after feeding Declan, but she didn't care about that as much as Logan putting himself in danger. "Alone?"

"I'm not going to risk anybody else being a victim of my family's itchy trigger fingers when this entire thing was my proposal in the first place." He knew Anna had been the one to suggest it in the first place in casual conversations, but he was going to conveniently ignore that fact so long as it allowed him to take responsibility. "If I go alone they're not likely to do anything stupid before they see who I am. If there's more than one they're likely to feel threatened, especially with a whole bus behind us."

Mercury let out a small sigh. "Alright. If you think that's best." She clearly didn't like the idea at all. "I would gladly go with you, if you'll let me."

He hesitated before he answered that, since he didn't like the answer any more than she was going to, but it was still the only answer he could give. "If I go with you before I explain what's happened, at least in broad strokes, then they won't think it's me."

"Oh. I see." She turned her attention back to Declan in her arms who was still watching the scenery. Declan, more than James, looked like her with his red hair and fairer skin, which was fitting for his name. Though he would have been James, had he been born first. "We'll wait for you on the bus."

It was the longest twenty minutes of Logan's life as he saw more and more that the countryside looked familiar. Orion finally turned off the road and took the long dirt trail that led into the countryside and away from the highway, other tracks nearby showing that the area had seen a few visitors recently.

Logan felt like he was watching a movie he had seen a dozen times before, even down to the way the bus rocked and skipped where the road was uneven. He knew the broken fence lines before the campground and the lake beyond came in sight, and he could almost feel it in his bones when he knew Orion would turn off just past the crest of the hill, only moments before he actually did.

Below, in the basin with the lake at the bottom, there were no fewer than four dozen campers and RVs, spread out all around the lake as space and the campground permitted. A large solar sheet had been spread on the hillside to provide power to the entire campsite, but there were also a dozen fires burning along the shore. For the most part, people were sitting around in the quickly-growing shadows of the evening, but there was a game of football in the distance that stopped just as soon as Logan's bus came into sight. All around the campsite, people turned toward them and got up from their chairs, though no one made any attempt to get closer.

"Alright. Here we go." Logan heaved a deep sigh, kissed Mercury, then Declan, before he got up. "I'll wave you down in a few minutes."

Mercury felt insanely nervous as Logan got up to leave, but she didn't say a word to stop him. Everything would be alright. His family wouldn't hurt him. Would they? He trusted them, and she trusted him.

Larissa was one of the first to see the bus, and while Cory was talking about something else with Ben, all it took was a nervous tone for her to get the attention of both her husband and her brother-in-law. "Cory? Ben? There's someone out there."

That phrase alone got both men up and moving, looking up the hill where Larissa pointed to the bus that stopped a few hundred meters away. Cory wasn't sure what to make of the sight, and the look on his face was more confused than anything else. "That's a cross-continental bus. They don't even come through here but every other week, and they sure as hell don't come to the lake."

"Go get Liam." Ben said to no one in particular, before he ran toward the large camper where his family's luggage and supplies were stored. Cory didn't waste time complying, with one look at Larissa and a squeeze of her hand before he ran off to find her brother. Strangers meant trouble, and trouble was something that needed taken care of, and quickly.

Larissa stayed by the fire with her family, two of her sisters-in-law, their babies, and the rest of Cory's siblings. She was tremendously nervous, but a few of their neighbors, men with guns, were nearby and watching closely.

When Cory found Liam he was helping Bree with supplies for s'mores, and they were both laughing and holding hands until they saw the look on Cory's face. Bree immediately knew something had to be wrong, since Cory was shit at hiding his feelings. "What happened? Is someone hurt?"

"Bus just pulled up. Cross-continental. Nobody we recognize." Cory didn't wait for permission before brushing past the two of them to get to the chest up high in the incredibly-fancy camper, where he knew Liam kept their rifles.

"Whoa, whoa, calm down, little brother. Sometimes a bus is just a bus." Liam was clearly in too good a mood to be ruffled by even Cory's panic, but he did take the rifle his brother-in-law gave him and headed for the door along with him. "Just keep the safety on and keep your finger off the trigger."

"I can handle a rifle, Liam." Cory was wound a little tighter than Liam was in many respects, but then, he had his reasons to be.

By the time they got outside, a small picket line formed at the outer edge of the campers. Some of the armed men in the camp decided to stay where they would have some small amount of cover, most of them out in full view with their guns so that anyone approaching would see. Liam and Cory barely made it to the line when the doors of the bus opened in the distance and a single person stepped out. When the doors were closed again behind him, the man started walking down toward them, hands out to his sides, but he was too far away to recognize.

"Could be armed under that coat." Ben said nearby, holding his rifle pointed at the ground but still very much at the ready.

"Only if he's a suicide bomber." Liam shot back with a laugh. "He's got about thirty twitchy rednecks down on this side of the hill ready to make sure he never gets through a metal detector again. So unless he's bulletproof and he's got laser fucking vision, I'd say he's got the look of a guy just wants to talk."

Bree was just about the only woman nearby, but she wasn't about to leave when something exciting was about to happen and Liam knew better than to tell her to go back with the others. "That coat looks kind of familiar." Facial features were harder to see from a distance than a coat, but she felt like the approaching man was familiar. "He's coming down alone? From that big bus?"

"Looks that way." Ben was starting to relax just a little with the man's oncoming non-threatening posture, and tensions all along the line started to ease even more when the man reached in slowly to open up his coat and show that he wasn't carrying any weapons beneath. "He looks a lot like . . ." Ben continued, but then drew up short of actually speaking his mind, as he glanced over at Liam.

Faces all along the line turned toward Liam the closer the man got, and as the man approached, it was easy to see that his own face was turned toward Liam as well. When he was a little over fifty meters away, the figure stopped and slowly lowered his hands.

"If you're gonna shoot me, Liam, now's your chance. But you were always shit with a .22, so I hope your aim has improved."

"What . . . the . . . *fuck?*" Liam looked across the space at the figure who taunted him, unable to allow himself to believe what he was looking at. He handed off the rifle he'd been holding to Bree beside him, and brushed out past the rest of those along the impromptu line to approach the man. "Last I checked . . ." he called out across the space, "ghosts don't have death wishes."

"Can't say that's something I know much about." Logan called back, as rifles all along the line were lowered and released. "You know, seeing as I'm not a ghost."

"The fuck you're not." Liam was close enough to recognize everything about his brother, even though Logan was leaner, his face harder, than he had been a year and a half earlier. "We saw the station explode. Saw every ship go down."

"Didn't I teach you not to believe everything you see on the fucking news?" Logan took a few steps closer to his brother, his heart twitching with a dozen different emotions. "We're alive. Most of us got off before the station went boom."

Liam stopped and took a deep breath just to steady himself as he looked up at a face he didn't think he would ever see again outside of a mirror. He shook his head over and over again as the fact of what he was seeing set in. "I should've known you were too stubborn to die."

Logan smiled at that, and it was the first open smile he could remember feeling on his own face outside of his private chambers with Mercury in a very long time. "Yeah, you really should have." A few steps erased the distance between the two men, and they took each other in a back-breaking hug as more of the line began to advance on them both.

Bree had remained back as Liam and Logan spoke to each other, but as soon as they were hugging, she bounded forward with tears streaming down her cheeks. Bree dropped the s'more ingredients so she could hug Logan as soon as he was released by Liam. "Larissa is going to lose her mind. She didn't believe the news reports, she's always said that one day you would just show up . . ."

Logan returned the hug, though he was confused as to why Bree was by herself with Liam, until he saw Larissa nearby and all other thoughts went out of his head. His little sister had turned into someone he barely recognized in the time that he'd been gone, having inherited their family's height. When he left, she was a tall young woman, but still young. He had not been prepared to come home and find out that his sister was well and truly a woman. "Holy shit! Rissa?" He didn't even register the fact that Liam was laughing at him from nearby as he went for their little sister.

"Logan!" She bolted toward her brother and jumped up onto him for a hug, even though she had grown quite a bit taller and filled out. She was definitely a woman now. "I knew you were alive. They kept saying there was no way, but I knew it!"

"Oh my god, what the hell happened to you? You used to be microscopic!" He swung her around in the hug and put her back down on her feet, but still didn't let go of her. "God, it's good to see you two. I thought . . ." he was breathing heavily from the emotional rush of seeing his entire family again, and he hugged Larissa again to make sure she was really there. "I thought a lot of things. I can't tell you how good it is to see you."

"Well, not *too* much has changed. Except this." Larissa held up her hand to show her beautiful sapphire wedding ring. "And Liam has like ten kids now." She teased as she looked over at Liam, since she couldn't help herself.

"Ten?" Logan looked over at Liam almost in accusation, but oddly, his brother didn't seem fazed.

"Three. She exaggerates a lot more now that she's got Cory to back her up." Liam glared at Larissa, but nothing could wipe the smile off his face. "Rachel got pregnant a couple months after you left, but that was about the time when we stopped getting your letters. Bree was a couple months after that, and Margo just had a baby a few months ago."

"Wow." Logan grinned and smacked his brother on the arm. "Guess that's what a little focus will get you, huh?"

"You have no idea, brother." Liam laughed and gave Bree a scandalous look as people started coming up from the camp to see what all the fuss was about. He looked the other direction at the bus in the distance, and gave Logan a confused look. "Are the rest of your friends shy? Is Anna with you?"

Logan's smile fell a little at that, but he nodded. "She's with me, but it's not what you're thinking." He turned away and waved to the bus to come on down, at which it started rolling down the hill at a sedated pace while he turned back to the crowd. "It's complicated. But the short version of the story is that Anna and I aren't together anymore. A lot has happened. For everybody."

"You're not together anymore?" Larissa couldn't imagine what possibly could have pulled Anna and Logan apart. "But . . . that doesn't make any sense, Logan." She thought back to her brother's wedding, and how happy he was on that day. His smile had been more true and full than she had ever seen, even at his first wedding.

She was about to say something else when Cory caught up with them and stepped up behind her. Larissa immediately turned toward her husband as he watched the bus with wide eyes. He could see Logan standing there, but Larissa knew who he was waiting to see. "He said they're not together. Anna and Logan."

"What, like she's not here?" Cory's brain was clearly incapable of fully processing the information the way she had intended it. "Did she actually die?! Where is she?"

"No, she's not . . ." Larissa didn't have to explain anything, since as soon as the bus was close enough, the door opened and Anna came running out of it. She headed straight for Cory, since he was the one she could see.

"Cory!" Anna was yelling before she even got close, and she was crying as well, but she couldn't help herself. Pregnancy had made her crying reflex a thing that she couldn't get rid of even after her babies were born.

Cory immediately jumped right at Anna to catch her halfway, and was sobbing himself in the process. As he was swinging her, though, they were bombarded with the rest of her siblings, every one of them piling on to get a piece of her, including Ben, who was the next closest one nearby. Danny no longer forced her to stoop to hug him, but Emily and Ginny were still short enough that they had to jump up onto her, all of them latching onto her until they were an indistinguishable mass of a family.

Anna was crying and laughing and kissing and hugging, at a loss for words as she looked at her family. She had missed them all so much, and she wondered why the past version of her ever thought that leaving them behind was the right or best thing to do. Though the past version of her hadn't known that the Eleusis Initiative was just a ploy for human experimentation either. "You've all changed so much . . ." She was still crying and smiling as she looked around, but eventually her eyes settled on Ben. "Dad? Is he . . ."

"He's here." Ben looked sad as he said it, but his face was just an echo of all the others around her. "He's in bad shape, but he wanted to come to the lake. He's always loved these trips, you know that." He nodded back toward the camper Anna recognized from her own childhood years, no part of which had changed. "I was there visiting with him a little while ago, but I think he's sleeping now. Liam helped us out and hired a full-time nurse to take care of him. British guy. Pretty dry, but he does a good job taking care of Dad."

Anna stared at the camper for a moment and nodded, since she knew if her father was alive, he wouldn't be in good shape. She felt guilty for hoping he was alive because she selfishly wanted to see him when she knew he was probably in a lot of pain. "Do you think I can see him when he wakes up? Or . . . would it be too much?"

"I'll talk to him and Oliver first. Make sure he's prepared for it." Ben had taken on the role of family protector while she was gone, even though he had placed himself in that role more than once even before she left. "Not really sure how anybody can prepare to hear that their daughter is actually alive, but I'll do my best."

Cory looked over at Logan as he spoke to Liam, Larissa hanging on as if he was going to disappear if she let go. The sight made him smile, but he turned a confused look back at Anna. "Logan said you two aren't together anymore. What the hell happened up there? Where have you two been for a year?"

"I'm sorry." Anna started to say, but there was nothing she could do to change what had happened. "The Consortium used their Matching program on all of the Initiates." She shook her head. "Turns out the thing works. We didn't intend on breaking up, but that's what happened. We're with other people now. I have twin babies, Logan is the father of one, and Orion is the father of the other." It was strange to even say Orion's name to her family. He had never been a part of her life in the Midwest. "I can't really say where we've been. Not until we're sure that no one is watching or listening."

Ben nodded seriously, immediately understanding the risks, but he still smiled, which was more testament than anything else as to just how much time had passed and how much had changed.

"Orion?" Danny asked with a laugh, looking around for support even though he didn't seem to get any. "I know you went to outer space, but did you have to marry an alien while you were at it?"

"I think I'd make a pretty good alien, thank you very much." Orion said with a broad grin, descending from the bus slowly to let them get a good look at him. "I come in peace. I'd say take me to your leader, but I'm not really that big on leaders these days."

Anna looked back as Orion came out of the bus, and Anna

rushed to his side, even though she was sure her family would find it weird. Especially with Logan nearby with his own family. "The babies are asleep, but we'll get them out shortly."

Mercury watched as more people got off of the bus, but she wasn't going to get off until Logan came back and gave her permission to do so. He needed time with his family, and she could force herself to be patient even when she didn't want to be.

After Orion came out and introduced himself to Anna's family, Logan knew his brother and sister would notice the change in him, no matter how he tried to hide it. He moved along the side of the bus to get a look at Mercury and wave her out. He knew she would wait, and he was smiling as he found her, openly happy in a public setting for the first time since they had come to Earth.

"This is Mercury." He said as she made her way to the front of the bus to get off with James in her arms. "We had twin boys about six months ago. Declan and James." He said with a significant look at Liam and Larissa. "The seventh, unless you had a boy before him and beat me to it."

"We're starting at the beginning of the alphabet and working our way down." Bree explained as she remained by Liam's side. She didn't know if Rachel and Margo would show up or wait back at the campsite, since it was hard to get three babies anyplace all at once. "Anders, Beckett, and Chrissy. We'll get to J eventually." She looked over at Mercury and she honestly couldn't believe what she was seeing. Logan's new wife put her and any other woman around to shame. "Nice to see another redhead around."

"It's very nice to meet you as well." Mercury said politely before she looked back toward the bus briefly. "Declan also has red hair. James looks much more like Logan. Lynnette does also, she and James look more like siblings than James and Declan do."

"Which means the next round is bound to take after their mother." He pulled Mercury in close against him with a kiss first to her cheek and then to James'. "Thank goodness." He turned and nodded to his brother and sister. "This is Larissa and if you needed me to introduce this guy as Liam, then we have some pretty massive problems."

"No, I see the similarities." Mercury said with a smile before she turned her attention back to the baby in her arms. "It's very nice to meet you all."

Gwen came out of the bus with both Lynnette and Declan in her arms and she came up behind Logan and Mercury. "Hey tall people. Your babies are awake, clean, and ready to make their debut."

"In this crowd, you're going to have to be more specific." Orion grinned back at her and took Lynnette from her once she got close enough, and turned to look down at Anna. "You never told me you were a shortie among your own people. Criminy."

"Hey. That's mean." Anna said as she bounced Leo once he was brought out as well. He was more wild and wiggly than his sister had ever been. "It's in my genes so you're just going to have to accept mediocre sized children."

"I think I'll survive mediocre-sized children." Orion held Lynnette like a football in the crook of one arm as the rest of her family tried to decide how to handle the giant in front of them.

"If they get taller than you, they're gonna have to start calling them something other than human." Ben said with a dark smile on his face.

"Oh right, you're the mean one." Orion grinned and pointed down at him with a laugh. "I'm gonna like you. I'm deciding this now, just getting it out of the way."

Anna rolled her eyes both at her brother and Orion, but she would rather them throw barbs playfully than glare at each other. "So, um, will you all let us stay? We'd really like to spend time with you for a while. Explain everything we can."

Ben looked confused, but he nodded haltingly. "Yeah, yeah, of course. This is . . . I mean, this is the spring camp. Of course you can stay." He looked past her at the bus. "Unless you've got another small army coming or something, then there might not be room."

"No, we don't." Logan said from nearby, since the babies and the inspection of them had brought conversation more or less to a lull. "We were kind of hoping the small army was right here already. But we'll get to that."

5

Ben went ahead of Anna into the camper, and nodded toward the rear bedroom, which was the only place anyone could get privacy on board. Anna could hear the coughing Ben described once she was just outside the bedroom, and Ben's face took on the same shadow that had been there ever since their father started getting sick years before.

"I'll be right back." He reassured her, then stepped through, careful to keep the door mostly blocked as he did.

It wasn't Ben who came out a moment later, though, and it clearly wasn't anyone who belonged in the midwest. He was tall, built lean, with thin features and glasses, which she hadn't seen on anyone since Station Nine.

"Oh. Hello." The man's voice was a pleasantly deep timbre, and his accent was unmistakable as soon as he opened his mouth. There were several Brits back in the mountains that she knew well enough to recognize the accent when she heard it. "You . . . must be the sister Ben's informed me of on this bit of a note." He held up the small scrap of paper Ben had written in haste just to let him know what was going on. "Oliver Masterson, at your service."

"Not at my service, but thank you. Oliver." Anna said as she looked the man up and down again. "You must get five marriage proposals a day out here, don't you? That accent . . . goes a long way with a farmgirl."

"So I've found." He gave her a tentative smile, but it wasn't the kind of eager grin most men she knew would have given her for that kind of comment. "I've had some interest in the eight months I've been tending your father, yes, but I keep rather busy both with Joseph and with the house in general. Ben, Cory, and Danny started working on a second house on the property last summer, so they've been rather busy. So I mostly take care of the first house and help Susan watch Emily and Ginny. Doesn't leave a great deal of time for accent-swooning."

"Probably not." Anna stepped up a little closer, since he was between her and her father. "I don't know you, I don't know if I can trust you, but I do want to see my dad. Regardless."

"No, of course. Of course." He stepped out of her way as well as he could, but he did have to slide past her in the tight confines of the camper. "He's had quite a lot of ups and downs since I was hired, but he's an exceptionally stubborn man, your father. I would almost say to the point of being British, but don't tell him I said that. I know he'll be overjoyed to see you. I've heard all manner of stories about you. Most of which I've been assured are true by reputable sources. They've all missed you terribly."

Anna nodded, since she had missed them too. Her family. Her friends. Even just her neighbors. "He won't be *too* overjoyed, though, right? I don't want to kill my own father."

"No no. Steady as a cliff, that man is. You could parade a stripper convention through his front door and his blood pressure would never spike beyond tolerance. He'd just critique them and tell them how farm work is better than pole work." Oliver smiled, clearly fond of Joseph and his unflappable nature. "His main concerns at this point aren't his blood pressure or his respiration. The tumors have started to exert pressure on his lower spine. Once the process starts the way it has, it's a bit like squeezing a tube of toothpaste. They begin at the base and eventually work their way up. You'll not do him any harm."

"God, that was a visual I could have done without. My dad being squeezed like a human tube of toothpaste." Anna winced and looked back at Oliver. "Thanks for taking care of him. I know Ben and Susan needed the help. I should have been here, but I haven't been." She sighed and then looked around the camper. "A few things changed in a good way, but ultimately, I wonder if I would have been better off staying here on Earth. Even though I never would have met Orion down here. What we went through was a hell that I am sure no one would choose again."

"No, I'm sure they wouldn't." He agreed, his polite smile disappearing quickly. "My, um, my wife was accepted to the Initiative at the same time you and Mr. Bickford were. She and I had only just gotten together before the acceptances were sent out, but she elected not to go. When we started to hear about the loss of communications, some rumors of the attack that you all suffered up there, we were glad she didn't go. Especially when Nine . . . well, when we all thought the entire complement of the station was on its way back to Earth as a meteor shower." He saw that that particular image sat with her about as well as the tube of toothpaste, and looked the slightest bit sheepish. "Sorry. A morbid sense of humor is something of a prerequisite for a hospice nurse."

"Apparently." A small laugh escaped Anna anyway, since it was kind of funny. And terrible. But also funny. "It's alright. Laughter is about the only thing that can help anyone survive anything." She let out a sigh and looked into his eyes momentarily. "Is she here with you? Your wife?"

His smile didn't return with that question. "No. She died shortly after Nine exploded, back in London."

Anna's smile disappeared also, and she felt genuine concern for a man she'd just barely met. "I'm so sorry." He didn't clarify how his wife had died, sickness or otherwise, but Anna knew that a lot of trouble had broken out after the rebellion on Nine. They heard about riots and uprisings that ended up in mass murder by the Consortium to keep control. She was afraid to ask how his wife had died, especially if she was at least partially responsible by fleeing for her own life.

Oliver didn't say anything else right away, but when he did open his mouth to speak, Ben came out. Oliver immediately went silent and the words remained unsaid to let Anna and her family have their time together.

"He's awake and ready for you. Just be gentle with him." Ben asked as he moved out of the way, holding the door open for her to slide in to see their father.

Anna gave Oliver a small parting smile of gratitude, even though she felt guilty for his wife. She looked up at Ben afterward, gave his arm a squeeze, and slid past him so she could see her father. She knew she wouldn't be prepared to see him in such a state, but she was still selfishly glad he was alive.

"Daddy?" She said softly as she nearly tiptoed into her father's room.

"Anna." She heard his weak voice from the bed, but it was hard to tell exactly what kind of shape he was in. He was covered mostly in blankets, but his hands were exposed, and they had the look of some of the eighty-year-olds she saw up on Station Nine. His face was thinner than she had seen him last, but his eyes were still bright and clear, aside from the pain that she could see behind them. His smile was more labor than it had once been, and she could see the lines that set in during the time she'd been away. "Ben told me . . . I didn't believe . . . you're here . . ."

"I'm here." Anna replied softly as she went to the side of the bed and took one of her father's frail hands in both of hers. Hers were warm and full of life, and his were far from it. She leaned in to kiss his cheek and his forehead, her eyes full of tears. "I never should have left. I'm so sorry."

"You did what you thought was right. I was proud of you for doing it." He said weakly, his eyes still mostly closed as tears ran out the sides into what was left of his beard. He smiled up at her when she pulled away, working his lips a few times before he managed to produce sound. "When we stopped hearing from you, we tried to figure out a way to get up there to rescue you, but we got blocked every step of the way. We got so far as making some friends out in St. Louis, but right before we were supposed to take off, they disappeared. When we saw what happened to Nine, Ben and I thought you must have had something to do with blowing it up."

Anna nodded and gently wiped at her father's tears, since she didn't want him crying over her, even though she was crying along with him. She sat down at the edge of the bed and kept ahold of his hand, since she didn't want to let go. Anna did glance back once, and as soon as she was sure the door was closed, she looked at her father again. "Yes, Logan and I along with a lot of other people helped take Nine down. They're still looking for us, though. We didn't come back right away because we knew they would be watching you and everyone else. They have been watching for a long time. They showed us images and videos from home to keep us in line."

"We took out some of the watchers we could find." He said slowly, clearly being careful not to start himself in a coughing fit. "That's part of the reason Ben wanted to get working on building a new house up on the far side of the horse enclosure. Wanted to build some place we knew for a fact nobody had come through and tried to bug just to keep tabs on us. People kept stopping by trying to act like they were looking for work and we would find out they were armed or had some kind of uplink with them to plant shit in the house . . ." He shook his head. "We haven't had any of those for months, though."

Anna glanced back at the door again. "And Oliver? Ben is sure he's trustworthy?"

Her father let out a soft exhalation and a smile that would in other circumstances have passed as a laugh. "I think he must've vetted about two hundred nurses before he settled on Oliver. But he's a good man. The Consortium killed his family. His wife and unborn daughter. If that doesn't make a person hate the whole damn government, I don't know what will."

Anna winced, since it only confirmed and further solidified the guilt she felt. "We heard about the riots. We heard about what the Consortium did, but it was after we had already arrived here. It was too late. God, I feel terrible."

"It's not your fault." He squeezed her hand as well as he could, which wasn't saying much. "Nobody really knew what the Consortium was until that happened. Until that guy White sent out his broadcast and turned the world upside down. No one understood how far things had gone. That they're already on Eleusis and they were just fucking with the rest of us . . ."

He couldn't hold off the coughing fit forever, and it was worse than it had been before, bad enough and violent enough that Oliver opened the door just a crack to see if he was needed. It eventually did subside, and Joseph nodded to Oliver to let him know he was alright, and the door closed again.

"Things have changed so much down here, Anna. I don't know where you've been hiding out, maybe you already know that. But things are so different. Supplies don't move like they used to. People pass through all the time asking for a quiet place to live, take a few acres somewhere, anywhere they can get away from the cities. Anywhere out from under somebody else's thumb. It's chaos."

"The Consortium is trying to keep their power and the rest of us just want them to go away." She said gently as she went back to holding his hand when his fit had passed. For the moment. "We have something they want. And need. And we are trying to get to Eleusis. We just need more people and supplies." She was trying to be as reassuring as possible, but she wondered if it helped at all.

"Things have changed for everyone." Anna continued softly. "Logan and I aren't married anymore, but we do have a daughter between us. I married a man named Orion Al-Jabbar. The Initiative matched us together initially . . . it's a long story. But I love him a lot, and he's good to me. He's smart and strong, funny. Almost too funny sometimes. We have a son. My twins have two different fathers and that's crazy, but it's all because of what we went through."

Joseph opened his eyes a little wider to look her up and down, but he had never been the type to need to be told something twice. He just took in the information and studied her face as she spoke about it. "Muslim funny guy, huh? I guess they had them from all over the world up there." He let out a breath to control his cough and he squeezed her hand again. "I've never known you to be conflicted about things for long, Anna. Whatever it is about everything you just said, you'll figure it out, in time. I'm sorry to hear about you and Logan. I can't even imagine what that must have been like."

Anna looked into her father's eyes for a moment before she looked away, since she knew how much he loved Logan and the Bickfords and he was there for their happy wedding. The day that the whole town had been waiting for, considering the friendship Anna and Logan had for so long. "We tried really hard. Things got really bad. Logan and I didn't even really talk about it. He's with the woman that was Orion's wife before me." She still had a hard time calling Mercury by name, but she tried not to over-analyze why.

"Logan and his wife have two boys together too." Her voice was softer, since it felt harder to speak, as though the truth and reality was heavy on her tongue. "It was so hard. Loving one person, falling in love with another. Fighting the Consortium, only to have them trap us, drug us, intervene in every possible way. Orion and I decided to sever ties with Logan and Mercury romantically. We love each other. Even if it came from having no choice."

Joseph shook his head and closed his eyes against the pain of knowing that someone forced his daughter through something like that. "I'm so sorry, Anna. You always had the biggest heart of all of us, but that doesn't make it easier to have it torn to shreds like that."

Anna shook her head. "I'm just glad we made it out alive. We have beautiful children, and they're all well and happy. I'll have to bring them to you so you can see them. Lynnette looks so much like Logan. And Leo is just trouble. Although he is handsome." A small smile ticked up the corner of her mouth and she squeezed her father's hand a little bit more. "I love you so much. I am so glad I can see you. Talk to you. I missed you so much."

"I missed you too." He sounded sad as he said it, though, but he tried his best to squeeze her hand back. "I don't have long, Anna. I know I've thought that for years, but now there's actually a medical professional around who's willing to give it to me straight. Doc Weber always beat around the bush on things, but Oliver is refreshingly honest when it comes to my life expectancy. I don't know how long I'll be around to help you do what you need to do, but whatever we can give you, you know we will. Everyone here, not just your brothers and sisters."

"I hope that people will want to get involved. It's the only way we're going to be able to stop young people from dying before they've really lived. It's the only way for any of us to get to Eleusis." She was crying all over again when he said he didn't have much time, even though it was obvious that he didn't. "How, um . . . how long did he say?"

He shook his head. "Not long. His best estimate was a few weeks if I agreed to stay home from the lake this year. Obviously you can see how that conversation turned out." He gave her an attempt at a smile. "I just wanted to see someplace peaceful again before I go. The past year, this lake has felt like the last place on Earth the world hasn't been able to touch."

Anna nodded quietly as more tears slid down her face, since she was so grateful to get home in time to see her father before he was gone forever. "You picked a good place. Mom loved it out here too."

Joseph was quiet for a long while after the mention of her mother. He had always been quiet about her after she'd died, but Anna could almost feel the man in front of her looking through something he would never come back from, looking at life from the other side of death even though he was still alive. "She'd have been proud of you too. Of what you did in standing up against the Consortium. I want to tell you to stay safe, to stay out of harm's way. But I'm not gonna do that. Because I know she wouldn't do that. She would tell you to kick their ass from here to the moon. Which is exactly what I know you're capable of doing."

"I will. I promise I will." Anna said as she leaned in and kissed her father's cheek again. "I'm the favorite because I'm the most like her, right?" She asked teasingly before she kissed his cheek once more.

He smiled at her teasing, but more tears fell. "You always have been. I've always been grateful it wasn't me you took after. I lived my life as a pushover compared to her. All I wanted was to run the farm, turn a profit, and catch a decent-sized fish once in a while." He started to cough again but managed to suppress it, fighting it down before he could look back in her eyes. "The world doesn't change because of people like me. It changes because of people like you, and your mother."

"You loved each other so much because you were different, but you are what she needed and she was what you needed." Anna wiped at his tears again and smiled down at her father. "I don't want to wear you out any more before I bring the babies in to see you. They've got to meet you before you decide to whisk away and go see Mom."

"I'd like that." He agreed through the exhaustion she could hear in his voice. "I love you, sweetheart. Give 'em hell, and don't ever change."

Anna gave him another smile and a kiss so he could get some more rest. "I love you too. Always." It sounded so final, but she honestly didn't know if he was going to die before she was able to bring in her children, and she didn't want him to die without hearing her tell him how much she loved him. She didn't start crying again until she walked out of the small room, and she leaned back against the door. Ben had gone, probably to handle another crisis, but Oliver was still there. Even though he was a stranger, she couldn't stop herself from sliding to the floor and crying like a little girl.

Oliver slid to the floor along with her, but he was a few feet away across the narrow space, just to let her know that he was close by. "I'm glad that he got to see you. I think that's about all he's wanted in the world for a while now."

"I knew . . ." She tried to say, but it was hard to talk between the sobs she was desperately trying to keep quiet so her father wouldn't hear her. "I knew he might be gone. When we came." Anna wiped at her eyes, but it didn't do much good since she was still crying. "He could have . . . he *should* have had a full life. Too many people die too early." She glanced up at Oliver, briefly thinking about his wife and unborn child before she looked at her hands again. "How . . . how do you do this? This job?"

He shook his head, looking at his hands instead of watching her cry. "I've been doing it since I was ten, and I watched my own parents die slowly. It took my dad three years since he was too sick to work until he finally gave up. It only took my mum another year after that. She had spent most of the time after my dad got sick making sure I was taking lessons, and she made sure I got sent off to a nursing school on the coast right after she died. I went there for two years to finish my program and I've been doing it ever since. I've attended fifteen people."

"You're a saint." She replied softly through the tears. "I . . . we've always been so close. It was hardest leaving him behind, in all of this. Ben is strong and clear-headed, and I've always been too emotional. In good ways and bad. He always said Ben was born to temper me, and he always teases me about being a little too crazy. Now he's going to leave us too."

"Everyone does. Now or fifty years from now." Oliver said darkly, then shrugged afterward. "That doesn't make it better, or easier, or okay. But for me, it helps to remember, just so I don't forget that life is about living before that day comes. Not living in dread of that day, whenever it'll be. Only people living in space get handed a number and told that's when they're going to expire, and that's only when they've fucked up beyond all tolerance. Nobody knows how long they have. I've always figured there are worse things I can do with my time than to help people pass the last parts of it as peacefully and painlessly as possible."

Anna knew there were parts of the world where people ritually practiced assisted suicide whenever they received a terminal diagnosis and had set their affairs in order, but it had never been something that caught on in the North American districts, for the most part. It wasn't something she'd ever seen from people around her, at least. But from the way he spoke, it sounded like he had assisted with a few himself.

"As lives go, your father's had a good one. He knows it and he's grateful. I hope I can say the same when I get to where he is."

"I wanted to get to Eleusis. I wanted to take him there." Anna buried her face in her hands and stayed that way. "I saw it. With my own eyes." Anna knew she shouldn't say such things to a stranger, but she was in a bad place. "It's beautiful and real, and that's where we all should be."

"I've seen some of the pictures that were dumped along with the broadcast. It looks amazing." He agreed, looking wistful after hearing she had seen it for herself. "I'm not sure it's a world I'm really cut out for. If humanity as a whole manages to get there and set up shop, I'll be unemployed for the next 40 years or so."

"People will still need someone like you around." She finally looked up and while she looked like a complete mess, she temporarily stopped crying. "People still die, even when there are the world's greatest doctors and equipment." She just stared at him for a moment and her expression turned sorrowful. "I'm sorry about your wife and baby. I know you probably hate me. Maybe all of us. We started a rebellion when all I really wanted to do was live."

"I don't hate all of you." He said as he shook his head. "You just lit the fuse that's going to burn the world down. It's not completely the fuse's fault when there's so much ample fuel around to set the place on fire."

"I didn't even know we were a fuse. We just wanted to get away. They were planning on killing us, and I . . ." She was pregnant at the time, but so was his wife. She had no argument. "It doesn't matter. I'm so sorry."

"I told you, I don't blame you." He shook his head and wrapped his arms around his knees. "The Consortium is just like every other dictatorship in history. The only difference is that most people didn't realize that's what they've been this entire time until your people called them out for everyone to see. There've been dictatorships before, there will be others after it, but it's inevitable that it will fall eventually. Whether it's by us or by someone else, I don't know. Hopefully by us."

"Hopefully." She finished wiping off her spectacularly splotchy face and looked at him again. "Would it be wildly inappropriate to hug you? I . . . can't really talk about all of this with anyone else. My husband likes to make jokes a little too often, Logan is . . . unreachable. My family has no idea what happened to us. It is nice to just talk to someone who isn't involved with anything."

"No, I'm pretty flexible when it comes to professional boundaries." He said with a slight smile, though his manner was still exceptionally subdued. He didn't move from the floor, but he did reach out with long arms to pull her into a hug. It was only awkward because they didn't really know each other, but he was clearly a man who was practiced at giving hugs. He was accustomed to being there for people when they needed someone to talk to, to work out their problems with.

It was awkward until Anna told herself he was someone her family trusted with her father's life, and that was more than enough to convince her to trust him. Anna hugged him back tightly, probably too tight, since it hurt her arms a little but it felt good. She took a deep breath and let it out slowly to attempt to calm herself further. "Are you going to move on? When he's . . ."

"I don't know. I make it a rule not to go looking for other contracts while I'm still working on one. I'm pretty morbid, but I do have my limits."

"You can come with us, you know." She said as she slowly extracted herself from the hug. "We don't have dying elderly people, but we have a lot of babies. If you'd want to change your work a bit."

"I'm not sure how well I'd do with humans at the other end of the spectrum. But I suppose a lot of the skills are the same. Comfort them when they're whining, change diapers, give baths, keep them from dying as much as humanly possible . . ." He nodded. "If you're here to recruit and take volunteers, and if there's the possibility that I can help pull the plug on the Consortium, then yes, count me in."

Anna smiled a little as he agreed to go back to the mountains with them, and she went in for one more hug. "Thanks. For listening to me. For wanting to help. But mostly for helping my dad."

"Yeah, of course." He squeezed her back in the hug, and got up from the floor first so he could help her back to her feet. "Just let me know what I can do. I did actually mean the whole 'at your service thing' when I introduced myself."

Anna shook her head again. "You're not my servant or anyone else's. But we can use all the help we can get." She looked back toward her father's room and tears threatened again, but she needed to go check on her family, not fall apart again. "I should go check on my babies. Can you let me know when he's rested enough for visitors again?"

"I surely will." He nodded back as he headed back into the room, where her father was already sleeping again. "It was lovely to meet you, Anna. I'll send Ginny when he's awake, she tends to be the one running messages back and forth between us back at home."

Anna nodded and headed out without saying anything more. When she stepped out, Ben was standing there talking to Logan, and Anna felt really embarrassed that she looked like she had been sobbing, because she definitely had. "He's asleep again." She said to clarify to Ben, but her cracked voice made it sound like she was going to start crying again. Just when she thought she was okay.

Logan nodded sympathetically, for once, his hands in the pockets of his coat. "We'll bring the kids by later so he can see them. Rachel's got Lynnette right now over by the fire, and I'm pretty sure Orion still has Leo."

She couldn't talk for a moment, but then she looked back again. Anna thought about her father and one of her most recent memories of him was walking her down the aisle to marry Logan. "I just . . ." God. Was she that pathetic? "I'm sorry. I'm just falling apart."

"It's home." Logan could understand, of all people, since he was getting his fair share as well. "It's a lot to handle. We knew it would be. But as far as I can tell, pretty much everyone in the camp is already talking about exactly how they're gonna pack to come west with us. Which means we were right to come."

Anna took a few deep breaths, but she just looked back and forth between Ben and Logan before she said what she wanted to say to Logan. "I know you didn't convince them to let us come for me, but thanks. I wouldn't have gotten a chance to say goodbye."

"It was partly for you." He said with an even expression, unreadable even through their years of friendship, the face of the stranger he had become. "Partly for the children, partly for the people and the resources. Partly because it was the easiest way to push the rest of them to let us start somewhere. Reed would never have let us leave the Labyrinth if he had his say about it, let alone bring anyone back. We don't just need the people here, we need the whole fucking world on our side. This is just the best part of the world to start with."

"You're right. It is." Anna stepped past her brother to hug Logan, even though she knew she was an emotional wreck who should go let her emotions sort themselves out, but she needed people. Anna always needed people. She couldn't handle things well on her own. "He looks so bad. He . . . it's . . ."

"I know. Ben was just telling me." He told her as he hugged her, patting her back as he sighed. "He's been fighting it a long time. You Princes are tough to kill, even for a planet that's got killing people as its main defining feature."

Anna turned into mush in Logan's embrace, since she had missed it and missed him, her best friend. The way they ended things hadn't been an ending. It had been a book with the last half ripped straight from the spine.

"This is really fucking hard." She mumbled into his chest, and the scent of him hit her hard, since she hadn't realized how much she would miss it. Logan was at least taking it seriously, whereas she was a little concerned that Orion would just try to make her laugh to help her out of it.

"Yeah it is." He agreed wholeheartedly. "They look at me like I'm from another planet. And not Eleusis." He said quietly enough that only she could hear it. "Even Liam doesn't know me anymore. No matter how much I know I've changed, I never expected that."

"We've all changed." She hugged Logan tighter. "You've changed, but you're still Logan. You're still loving and devoted, strong and smart. You just unlocked a different part of yourself that you didn't know existed." Anna stepped back slightly and looked up at Logan again. Apparently Ben disappeared as soon as she went to Logan for a hug. "I miss being your friend." She admitted softly, since she was afraid to admit it to him, as though he might tell her that he didn't want to be friends again. "We are amazing friends."

"We are." He agreed, though there were more years of pain behind the brief admission than just the one they had spent in the mountains. "We'll be alright. Whatever else the world gives us at this point, I'm not sure it can top anything that's already happened."

"I don't think anything could be worse than what we've endured." She didn't want to challenge the universe to try, but they were dealt a pretty rough hand. Anna reached for Logan's hand and then squeezed it gently. "What did your siblings think of Lynnette? She looks so much like you."

"Rachel's got her right now. They're saying she looks a lot like Chrissy, but I haven't seen the little girl yet to make my own judgment." He squeezed her hand once and let go again with a brief look up at the camper. He took another look around at the campsite on the whole, all of which was either abuzz talking about their arrival or waiting their turn to come up and greet them personally. "Rissa was telling me they think she might be pregnant, but they're gonna wait until they get back home to make Doc Weber actually run a test. Don't want to step on anybody's vacation."

"What? Really?" That brought a smile back to Anna's face, and she looked around as if she was going to spot her brother or Larissa, but she would have to find them again later. "So we did a good job, putting those two together?"

"I think we did." Logan's smile was cautious, since they hadn't been around to really see a full picture of what the last year and a half had been like for everyone, but he looked hopeful, which was more than normal. "She seems happy. And they were married a while ago even without knowing for sure if they could get pregnant, so that says a lot, I think."

"I knew he would just fall in love with her. Your sister is the sweetest. She's just shy sometimes. They just needed a push." Anna looked from his eyes to his smile and back to his eyes again. "I like seeing your smile again."

The smile lingered as he looked out over the rest of the camp, thinking to himself about the fact that something they did looked like it was actually working, for once. "Don't tell anybody it still works. I have a reputation to maintain."

"Right. Right." Anna still smiled at him anyway and nodded toward the fire. "Don't tell anyone about my breakdown either. Especially not my husband. Considering he'll probably just try to make jokes to make up for it."

"I'll keep it to myself." He took a step away, since his family's camper was in the other direction, and he planned to go spend some time with his brother for the evening before they started making their rounds of the rest of the campsite. "I'll see you in a little while. Give my best to your father when you take the kids in to see him."

"You don't want to see him?" Anna said after taking a few steps away, since she assumed Logan would come too. "I'm sure he would like to see you too."

"I'm not sure he would." Logan's smile turned a little sad. "We both know how complicated things were to get us here, but I made some promises to him that I wasn't able to keep. If he doesn't have much time left, he doesn't need it to be taken up with disappointments."

Anna just shook her head. "You're Lynnette's father. And he has no idea all of the things that happened, but I explained a little bit. He doesn't blame you. *I* don't blame you. I was the one who made the decision, Orion and I did, in the end. You take too much guilt on yourself, Logan."

"Not the first time I've heard that." He said without giving any indication that hearing it again would change his mind. "I'll see you later, Anna."

Instead of going toward the bonfire where she knew her kids were, Anna went to the bus to unload more of their things. She saw Orion there alone, since apparently everyone else decided they needed to take a break for the evening. She walked up to the bus slowly with her arms crossed, since there was a bit of a chill in the evening air. "Hey, you. Still working hard?"

He hadn't expected to see her back at the bus so soon, and he smiled as soon as he stepped down with another armful of gear, mostly for the kids. "Well, everybody else headed out to go make friends, our children have been lovingly kidnapped, and Mercury's off comparing notes with Doc Weber and her daughter, getting up to speed on things that sound very complicated. So I figured I'd get things squared away for us. How's your dad?"

Any smile that had appeared on her lips at his explanation and upon seeing him was gone at the mention of her father. "He's . . . barely hanging on, to be honest."

Orion had been afraid of that, given everything she had told him about the man and how sick he'd been before she left, and he nodded sadly. "I'm sorry, baby. But I'm glad you got to see him, at least for a little while." He wiped off his hands and stepped over to pull her into a hug, just to make sure she was alright.

Anna accepted the hug and held tighter to him, since apparently she was all about getting hugs from anyone she could get them from. She buried her face into his chest so that she wouldn't start crying again. "He's going to die. I can't . . . he's always been my biggest supporter. I hoped he was alive so I could see him, but it's not enough. I wanted more for him. I wanted him with us on Eleusis."

"Maybe he will be." Orion said with a slight shrug. He knew that he and Anna differed when it came to their religious beliefs, and even Orion didn't hold his beliefs particularly strongly, but he did always leave himself open to them. "Your brothers seem like they've been taking notes from him. As soon as they got the idea that we're here to recruit, Danny and Cory started making the rounds of their friends and their friends' parents all over the camp. I haven't seen either of them since. They're just off and working. Kinda like somebody else I know."

That brought a little bit of a smile back, but he couldn't see it, since she was still hugging herself to him. "It's so hard. Being here.

Especially being here and being with someone who isn't Logan. Everyone keeps looking at me like I have brain damage when I say we're not together anymore."

"Well, they're not wrong. You do have to be a little bit crazy to be with me. Comes with the job description." He ran one hand through her hair just to keep her close, sighing in a way that let her know he was being serious, even through his jokes. "I have to say, this is the largest collection of strange looks I think I've ever gotten in my life. I'm used to the giant jokes and people double-taking whenever I actually get close to them, that part's never bothered me. But they're all looking at me like I brought some kind of voodoo with me and sprinkled you with it to pull you away from Logan."

"Logan and I have been friends since we were little. Everyone thought we would end up together. We kept missing each other somehow, and remained friends for the longest time. They're used to seeing us together, at least as friends, and now we're hardly even that. I told him earlier that I miss being his friend. He's changed a lot, but he's still Logan." She sighed again and looked up at Orion. "I don't know how you don't just win them over. You're probably the nicest person I know. Except when you first met me, but I get why you were mean to me."

"Yeah, I was definitely an ass." He shook his head and leaned back a little to look down at her. "I'm not . . . part of this world. In any sense, honestly. I get along with everybody back in the mountains because we've all got shared history, we all know what we've all been through. It feels the same out here, it's just a language I don't speak. And that's okay, I really don't know that much about this part of the world aside from what I know through you. They all look at me the way you did when you first met me out in St. Louis before we lifted off. This space freak who's hopping around the place looking like he's never planted a seed or milked a cow in his life. What good could I really be to humanity? It's a fair question."

"Maybe we need to be one of the first ones to start breaking down those barriers." Anna pulled Orion down by his arms so that she could kiss him. "People in space want to go to Eleusis. People down here want to go to Eleusis. We're never going to learn how to get along unless we try to understand each other."

"I try." He said with a quiet smile, since they had talked more than once about some of their disconnects in understanding each other. "I like to think I do a decent enough job most of the time. All I'm saying is that I get it when the rest of your people look at me like I'm green instead of brown. Maybe once the shock wears off, I'll have a chance to get to know some of them better."

Anna kissed him again and pressed her forehead to his as she kept him hunched over to her level for just a second. "Wanna go with me somewhere?"

He looked confused, since he had been driving and there was absolutely nothing close by, in any stretch of the word. "Sure, where did you have in mind?"

"I camped here every year for as long as I can remember." She grabbed his hand and started walking before she picked up the pace to run. "I know a lot of fun places around here. And our children have been lovingly kidnapped, as you said. I might as well show you around."

"Alright then. I'm always up for a tour." As they got away from the bus, she could tell that he had some small anxiety about being away from things; but that was one of many things she had gotten accustomed to understanding about her husband. He wasn't naturally at home with wide open spaces. Being up in the mountains had helped, he had admitted more than once, but there were still times when she caught him looking down the valley at all the space and he would back unconsciously against a door or a corner just to reassure himself that there were physical boundaries to the world.

He felt the same way as he ran off beside her into the gathering darkness, but he was still there beside her, up for whatever she wanted to show him. It was a huge world, and it wasn't going to get any smaller just because the size of it intimidated him.

Anna headed toward the woods between the campsite and the road back toward the town. She didn't dare go past the woods, since she didn't want any chance of being seen on a main road. She knew every tree and every bush.

They stopped abruptly right before the treeline got thicker, and she turned around to look up at Orion again. She was breathing heavier from running, but she looked happier. Her hair was free and wild, her cheeks red. "This place was always trouble for me. I had my first kiss here. My first kiss with a girl here. The first time I let a guy touch my tits. I didn't lose my virginity here, though." She walked slowly through the thick trees until they seemed to enter some kind of secret hideout. There was a small pond glittering in the darkness, completely encircled by the thick trees. On one side of the pond, there were half a dozen abandoned, open trailers, some more worn by weather and age than others.

She was actually surprised that they were all empty. "Usually kids sneak out here with blankets and . . . enjoy the stars."

"Just the stars?" He smiled at the nature of the place, and the stories he could almost read off the weathered boards and long-rusted trailer hinges. "Somehow I doubt the stars are all anybody enjoys out here." He started walking with her along the edge of the pond, passing the trailers and a single incredibly-old pickup truck. Weeds had long since grown straight through the truck's engine and cab, but the back was made out of steel, and was still more or less solid, the weeds hacked away from time to time by ambitious teenagers. "And I'll bet the adults sneak away back here just as often as the kids do. I know I would, if I were camping out here."

"It doesn't look like anyone has snuck out here yet, but that's probably because everyone can't believe the dead aren't actually dead." Anna squeezed Orion's hand tighter and looked out across the water. "We came here to fish too. My friends and I. It may have turned into skinny dipping by the end, but we caught dinner *first.*"

"Catch it, then go give the survivors a free show. I like it." He smiled at the pond, wrapping around a corner where he could see a few other private spaces that people cleared away over the years. It was a different place than the one he had grown up in, that kind of intimacy not only condoned, but encouraged, in the interests of people finding families for themselves as early as possible.

"We'll have to make it a goal to be the first people to go skinny-dipping on Eleusis. I guarantee the Consortium thugs who are already there have sticks shoved too far up their collective asses to have even considered it." He plucked at the sleeve of her jacket as they walked, already encouraging her to strip down casually without pausing their walk.

"Their loss. Skinny dipping is fun." Anna was glad to get rid of her jacket if that meant that she would have Orion's hands on her instead. "I suppose you didn't have much opportunity, did you? I mean, outside of a pool."

"Even pools, I've never had much experience in. I can swim, since we had to learn in basic, but there's not much use for it."

They were both dressed casually, with plain shirts and unremarkable pants. He tossed her jacket over his shoulder as they strolled around the lake and reached out casually to unhook the bra she wore with a deft flick of his fingers through her shirt. "Always looked like a lot of fun in the movies, though."

She raised an eyebrow and laughed softly as her bra went loose underneath her shirt. "You're a little *too* good at that, Giant. Should I be worried that you've been out here often?" She teased, since obviously he'd never even seen the place.

"I have a limited skill set in life. Getting your clothes off made the short list." They rounded a corner in the trees and came up on a trailer that looked like it was relatively recent, with the paint job on the wood still mostly intact and the slats still mostly present. He tossed her jacket along one edge and stepped closer to her to run his hands up her arms from wrists to shoulders. His touch promised to keep her warm in spite of the chill of the night. "I wish I'd had a place like this to go to as a kid. As it was, I stayed in the barracks. So it was mostly about convincing girls I was worth taking back to their place."

"I know that you and Mercury had enriching childhoods, but I don't know I would trade all of this for more education. I love Earth. Even if it is killing me. Or was." Mercury was able to give everyone in the mountains treatment medication in a diluted formula that held off the dying part, but left them vulnerable to illnesses. It was the best Mercury could do with the limited supply and her resources, but a little went a long way. Until there was no more, and it would run out soon. "I love the wide open spaces and all the unknowns. And I love being out here with you."

"Part of me is always going to be looking over my shoulder for a security camera." He turned her around and backed her up against the trailer, leaning down to kiss her as he lifted her up and put her backside onto the trailer. "I think I probably would have made the trade, if I could've had all this. Learn to fly a plane that actually uses aerodynamics to get off the ground. Bed every farmer's daughter I could get my hands on." He smiled and tugged her shirt up over her head, taking her bra with it.

Anna's nipples responded to the cool breeze that tickled her skin, and she let out a slight gasp at the feeling. The breeze hadn't played any factor on the station. Out in her homeland, the smells, the sights, everything made her think of a version of her that had existed before the present. Before the Initiative. "Every farmer's daughter? Who says I would have shared?"

"Well, I would've stopped bed-hopping willfully once I got to you." He smiled and ran the backs of his fingers down over her chest slowly, letting the breeze do its work and enjoying the attentive results. "I could've been the strange foreigner your parents try to warn you about. Too exotic and outside the lines for them to be willing to have over for dinner on a Sunday night."

"If you're not invited to Sunday dinner, I'm not going to Sunday dinner." She moaned softly as he ran his long fingers over her skin. Even in the darkness it was a stark contrast, his skin against hers, but it didn't seem as obvious before as it did now. Anna didn't care what Orion looked like, but she was reminded at home how different he was than in space where there was such a variety of ethnicities. "Aren't you going to take off your shirt too, my exotic lover?"

"If you want the shirt off, or anything else, you can come and get it." He teased, his hands moving to the clasp of her pants. It had been a long time since they'd had the chance to be quite as spontaneous as they were being at the moment, but it was a pleasant change of pace as far as Orion was concerned.

"Well, then. Fine." She batted his hand away once he had opened the clasp of her pants, and she wiggled out of her pants only to lunge at him and roughly attack his shirt so she could get it off. Once it was off, she grinned up at him triumphantly. The breeze ran against her bare skin again and she shivered, which didn't help her aching nipples. They desperately wanted his attention. "I love this. Running off with you. I miss sneaking away."

"You and me both. I never thought I would actually miss the maintenance tunnels." He put his hands on her waist to hold onto her, as he leaned down to kiss her bare neck. "Or the early days in the Labyrinth, going down to the cisterns and fucking you through the echoes. Those were some good times."

"I've missed you talking like that." She arched her back as he kissed along her skin, and she hurriedly worked to unbuckle his belt so she could get his pants off. "I fucking love your dirty mouth."

The mouth she loved moved over her breasts as soon as his pants were unclasped, and he pushed off both his shoes as she shoved his pants to the ground. "Even on Eleusis, when we get there," he teased along her shoulder as he stepped out of his pants to climb up onto the trailer with her, "when we win this war and build our house out on that hilltop, with a private fucking deck the kids aren't allowed to play on, I'm never gonna have enough of you. Under these stars or any others, I'm always gonna want more."

Anna moaned a little bit louder when he said that, since she excited to think about her life with Orion on Eleusis. "I can't wait for that." She said between moans as he teased her. "I love you so much, you know that?" She turned around and confused now that she was surrounded by memories and pieces of home and of a different life, but her feelings about Orion certainly hadn't changed. "I'm sorry today hasn't been a great day, it's hard to be here. Even though I missed my family so much."

"Today is turning into an incredibly good day. I don't know what you're talking about." He was careful of where he laid her down on the trailer, getting a cursory look at the thing to make sure it wasn't going to hurt her, but once he was convinced, his kisses turned rougher, his hands more insistent as they warmed her skin. "I love you too. Out here in the middle of nowhere, up in space, the mountains, on Eleusis, everywhere there is. I want this life with you all over the fucking universe."

Anna loved hearing that too, that he wanted her and their family more than anything. She did too. She wanted him and their family wherever they could have it. They had their problems, but who didn't? No marriage was perfect. She loved him. He loved her. They would figure things out. Anna didn't let him get away with torturing her without getting some in herself, and so she reached out to stroke him as soon as she had him naked. Anna felt as rebellious as she had always been, and yet it was better. Orion was her husband. "I hope we don't get caught." She teased.

The contrast of his grin was bright against the darkness, and his moan was an extension of the breeze as it snaked through the high trees around them. "You're a terrible fucking liar."

Anna giggled. "Okay, I totally hope someone catches us so that they will know how much I love having sex with my husband."

"*There* she is." He kissed her hard and rocked his hips against her hand as she teased him, before he worked his way down the trailer and his kisses were on course to drive her insane and give the pond a show it wouldn't soon forget. He wanted to get her screaming, and wanted to see what it would take to make the outdoors sing the way the maintenance corridors had back on Nine.

She was trying not to show Orion how excited she was about the idea of having his mouth on her most sensitive places, but every kiss he planted on her body gave her chills in anticipation. "You are such a tease."

"You can only call me a tease if I don't deliver." He said just before he began doing exactly that, pulling her underwear aside, to give him full access to torture and please her as he wished. Being so out in the open was something new for him, somewhere they couldn't be monitored on a camera or by any kind of microphone, but anybody who knew where they were could walk up on them out of the thick trees. Anything was possible on Earth. Anything was possible with Anna.

"Oh god . . ." She moaned when he really got going, since Orion definitely knew how to make her squirm and have her shaking and trembling. "Fuck . . . babe . . . that is *so good* . . ."

It had been too long since he had the chance to torture her without worrying about waking the kids, without worrying what they were supposed to be doing, what needed to be done . . . the moment was a vacation for them both, a chance to leave their life behind just for an hour and be themselves again. It was a chance they got too seldom, and never lasted long enough. He was going to make things last as long as he possibly could for Anna.

He knew exactly how to take her apart, exactly what would satisfy her and how to keep her there. He knew everything he had been able to discover about her in the time they'd been married, in a year and a half of fighting and feasting on each other night and day as much as they could. Every moan that escaped her was another building block between them, a link tying them together. It was something they could give each other, something they could keep between them, something they could hold onto no matter what else they were dealing with. He spread her knees apart as he pushed her to the edge of her tolerance and beyond, and he wanted to hear just how loud the trees could be when it was his wife's voice ringing off them.

Anna couldn't help but push herself up into his mouth and when he decided not to tease her anymore and push her to the end, and she was definitely not quiet about her pleasure as she shattered to pieces. "Fuck! Orion . . ." She worshipped him by moaning his name as he kept her orgasm rippling through her.

He rode the edge of it as long as her body could take it, only drawing back from her when her body turned to panicked spasms and desperate groans beneath his lips. He rolled backward to lie flat against the trailer for a moment, clearly satisfied with his work, his fingers still sending aftershocks through her to keep her blood boiling in the cool of the night breeze over them both.

Anna was heaving breaths as he continued to tease her, but she wasn't so easily defeated. It took her a few minutes, but she eventually moved away from his touch to climb on top of him, though it was a little bit comical. Her body felt like melted honey. Anna's hair had mostly fallen out of the tie in all of her writhing pleasure, so it was a mess around her face as she moved to situate herself on top of Orion. "That . . . you . . ."

His fingers raked her back and sides as she snuggled herself against him, every move of hers on top of him turned him on, and he was rock-solid beneath her pliant body. "I love it when you go wild. Have I ever told you that?" He asked through a smile, his every touch inviting further wildness.

"You do, do you?" She said between gasps, since she was all too happy to go wild for him as often as he liked. Especially since it wasn't the first time he'd told her so, and she liked hearing him tell her how much he liked it. "I'm glad you do." Anna didn't hesitate to slide closer and tease his cock with her warmth, and as soon as she had some control of her body, she moved to take him in. Slowly. Just to torture him.

He groaned loudly, clearly relieved not to have to censor himself for once, and his hands roamed over her chest and neck to hold her close, while he growled under the heat of her. "Every damn time." He breathed as she took him, his eyes rolling back as she worked her magic on him. "Every damn time I think I can't want you more, you prove me wrong."

There were times where Anna was bursting with joy after things Orion said to her, and that moment was one of those times. Anna loved being desired, most certainly by her husband, and to hear that even after more than a year together that he wanted her *more* only encouraged her to blow his mind. They weren't a perfect fit, she was short, he was ridiculously tall, but they figured each other out. They fit because they wanted to fit. They wanted to please each other, and Anna was sure as hell going to make sure he never forgot this moment by the lake. The trailer creaked beneath them, but Anna did not slow or take it easy once she really got moving. "*You* are the one . . . who drives me wild."

It was far from the most comfortable place they'd ever been together, but Orion relished the moment anyway, even knowing the bruises and scratches he would have after being ridden on an old trailer by a gorgeous woman. There was something simply primal about it in a way that nothing else captured, and he knew as she ground her hips into his, it was something he could absolutely get used to.

For just a while, nothing else in the world mattered, but at the same time, it was the world that was present in their lovemaking. They had been living in fear underground for so long that being up and out in the open, even isolated as the pond was, felt like a liberation. And Anna was the ultimate expression of freedom he could imagine. "Fuck, baby, just . . . fuck, just like that." He held her tight as her hips rocked his world, gasping into her hair as the world and the stars above it spun in his vision at the pace Anna set.

Anna was gasping herself as she rode him hard, but she basked in hearing his groans and his dirty mouth. Every curse she could pull out of him only encouraged her to fuck his brains out. "I love you . . . so fucking much . . ."

He normally wanted to take control, to take her however he wanted once she had pushed him beyond the point of return, but that night he was content to lie back and let her ride him straight through the orgasm that had him crying out her name into the dark. It felt like something in him had been completely taken apart and left bare for the world under her sorcery, and he wouldn't have it any other way. Her hips continued rocking against him until he was nothing but a pile of shuddering breaths, his lips quivering as he panted cool air to try and catch his breath. He couldn't even begin to talk, so he resorted to pulling her down into a kiss just to groan against her lips. "I . . . Mmmm." He rocked beneath her slowly, unwilling to let the moment completely fade between them even though he felt as though he had been deliciously destroyed.

Anna smiled contentedly and wrapped her arms around his neck as she rested flush on top of him. Both she and Orion were sweaty and panting, but Anna felt so incredibly wired and happy that she wanted to savor every second. "The best." She said without hesitation, since being with Orion was incredible. It was one thing to have great sex. It was out of this world to have great sex with someone she loved as much as she loved him.

He was anything but shy about letting her know exactly how satisfied he was, and the long, lingering kisses he left on her neck and shoulders were a lazy declaration that she had completely tamed everything about him, at least for the time being. "I still don't know if I would trade childhoods." He mused when he could talk again, kissing below her ear at a spot on her neck he knew she liked. "But if I could trade with somebody down here to have those years here with you, I'd make that deal. No question."

Anna smiled brighter and showered him with her own lazy kisses. "I wish we had more years before." She agreed as she hugged herself tighter to him. "I probably would have fallen in love with you too fast and pretended that I didn't for months, just because I was stupid and rebellious like that." She ran her fingers across his lips before she kissed him again. "But regardless, I wish that our love story would have started differently. Chasing the sexy, tall man instead of how it happened. We would have had so much fun."

"We still do." He insisted as his hands ran over her backside, rocking her against him even though they were both still sensitive from the moments before. "I just need to make sure all your midwest exes out here are aware that you have been well and truly claimed by this giant right here. And I don't care how many ponds I have to fuck you by to make sure they get that message loud and clear, I will do it."

Anna laughed and then kissed him heatedly. "I don't think any of my exes are going to come looking for me. I'm all yours, big guy. As long as you still want me, I'm yours."

6

The fire was a very different place with so many new faces around it. Liam leaned back in his folding chair to stretch, even with Brianne still in his lap, and cracked his neck a few times before he picked up his beer.

"Not a chance." He said absently. "If we involve your parents, we might as well wave a flag in the Consortium's face and let them know we've got some prisoners for them. I know they're not in it intentionally, but they're some of the richest people on the planet. Kind of people the Consortium is always gonna be watching."

"They could really help, though." Bree replied quietly, even though he had a valid point. She plucked the beer from his hand and took a swig, even though he was likely to tell her to get up and get her own. It wasn't her night to take care of the babies, so she took advantage of her freedom with Liam. Especially because they were on a vacation of sorts. "Isn't that what Logan said was needed? People and resources?"

"People and resources that don't have strings attached to them." Liam corrected, glaring at her for the booze theft before he took the beer back himself, one arm firmly anchored around her waist. "I'd love for them to be able to come along, believe me. I think your parents are probably some of the most decent people I've met, outside of a couple things they've done that are shady as fuck. But do you really think they'd turn on their own world like that? Go voluntarily live as rebels against the people who made them rich in the first place?"

"I don't know what they would do." Bree admitted, but she hoped that the grandparents of her child and her own parents would side with her over money and the Consortium. However, they had openly sent Brianne, their most beautiful daughter, out to Liam as some sort of prize, since they did believe that rich should marry rich. Fortunately, she didn't have any intention of actually seducing Liam for any of his money. She just liked him.

A lot. "I would leave it all behind. Especially if it meant being able to eventually get to Eleusis with the people that matter most." She gave him a hard kiss. "I'd live in a cave with nothing, naked, even, if you were there." She said with a grin against his lips.

"Well now you're crossing over from deprivation to my BDSM fantasies." He was happy to return the kiss, though, as he pulled her in tighter on his lap. "I mean, I'd even like to be able to say some of your brothers or sisters would come, but I'm not even sure about that. I just don't want to give them the chance to try and sell us out."

"I know." She said softly, since she didn't want to run away and tell her family nothing, but they really didn't have much of a choice. "You're right. We can't take those kinds of risks. My family is an unknown variable, and there are too many lives at stake. I'll go without even saying goodbye. Where you go, I go."

"They'll know where we've gone. And they'll make their own choice." He shrugged and kissed her again, then looked out to the fire. "I think I know what Margo will have to say about all this, but I don't imagine Rachel is going to have a problem with picking up and running. She's been planning on it since Nine came down, I think."

"She's the smart one." Bree replied with a shrug, since she had no doubt in her mind that Rachel was smarter than all of the rest of them, and then some. Rachel was insanely smart. And beautiful. It was a little unfair, but Bree didn't hold it against her. "Margo grew up here like you. She won't want to go, but it's not like she's going to stay without you and Chrissy."

He had some of his own thoughts about what Margo would or wouldn't do, but he kept those to himself. "Lucky for me, you and Anders both pack light. I'll just throw Anders in my backpack and throw you over my shoulder and be on our way."

"Very funny. Also very caveman of you." Bree said with a grin as she stole his beer so she could drink the rest of it. "I'm going to get a couple more of these. The cooler is over by the way-too-pretty babysitter. Where did Logan find that one?"

"He claims the babysitter came with the hideout." Liam shrugged, but didn't bother hiding the fact that he was looking the woman over himself. As pretty as she was, though, he was more interested in the fact that Brianne was checking her out first. "Why, you looking to collect one for yourself?"

"What if I am?" She looked back at Liam even though she'd

gotten up from his lap. "There's no one that young and gorgeous around here that I can touch. Everyone around here has lived around these parts too long. Either they're my friend or they're no one I want to tangle with. *That one*, though, I mean, look at her."

"I see her." He agreed with a grin. It was always a fine line for him to walk with his wives when it came to talking about who or what he was attracted to, since none of them looked anything like each other. "Let's get our business in order out here and get ready to move first, but you go ahead and take a closer look if you're interested. Far be it from me to deny you anything or anyone." He kept his voice low so that only Bree could hear him, but he doubted anyone else around them would have been surprised by the conversation. Especially if they knew Bree at all.

"Really?" She turned her attention back to Liam, since she was surprised to hear him encouraging her. They had been involved in some similar activities before they were married, but nothing since. Not that it stopped Bree from admiring a beautiful woman, but she hadn't had a chance to really admire someone in a long time. It was the first time they were seeing new people in a long time. "You would be okay with that?"

"Okay with what? Making you happy? Yes, I'm very okay with that." He leaned back in his chair to relax once she got up, and cracked his knuckles behind his head. "Just be low-key about it. She might be attached to somebody back in the mountains. I'd say to feel her out first, but I think you'd get too much of the right idea."

Bree laughed softly. "If only Rachel would have been okay with it in the first place. But nooooo . . . neither of them want to share in the fun. They're missing out." She smirked at him and wandered over to the cooler where she grabbed a couple of beers next to the blonde vixen. "Hi. I'm Bree."

"Gwen." She took another drink from her beer. She had the night off since Logan's and Anna's families wanted to take care of the babies. Anna ran off with Orion somewhere, but there were enough people around to take care of the babies. Gwen was glad for the break, even though she loved all four babies. They were the ones she watched most often, after all. Her attraction to Logan was enough encouragement for her to want to watch his kids often. "Nice to meet you."

"Ditto." Bree looked Gwen over as discreetly as she could manage. "Night off, huh?"

Gwen nodded and looked away but her eyes settled on the Logan lookalike. "It's so weird that Logan . . . Mr. Bickford is a twin." She shook her head and mumbled into her beer bottle. "Criminal, really."

"Liam is more fun, though." Bree said with a grin that was proud, since she really did love her husband. He was a good husband and he was the strong foundation that the three of them needed when trying to figure out a marriage with multiple wives. "Three wives and he's still not half as serious as Logan."

"Three wives? Fuck. They're lucky." Gwen admitted as she looked over at the woman standing next to her. Redhead.

"Thanks. I think I'm pretty lucky. He could have picked Rachel, brains and beauty, but he decided all three of us were a better package."

Gwen's eyes widened as she realized who she was talking to, one of Liam's wives, and she looked the woman over a little closer. "Do Bickford men have a thing for redheads?"

Bree just laughed. "Nah. Rachel, Margo, and I, we all look incredibly different actually. Liam just likes beautiful women. He doesn't really have a particular flavor." She beamed and handed over one of the unopened beer bottles. "Can you go give this to him? I told him I would get him another drink, but I forgot that I have to go check on the babies."

Liam watched Brianne work her magic on the new girl, and he had to grin. She was a sly one, his redheaded minx of a wife. But he wouldn't have her any other way. "Babysitting and drink service? You're the total package." He gave Gwen one of his winning smiles when she got up closer to him with the replacement beer, and took it from her with a grateful nod.

"Your wife basically commanded me to do it." Gwen said with a laugh and she sat down in an empty chair nearby with her drink. "I didn't know Logan had a twin." She repeated to the twin himself, but she couldn't help but steal a few looks. "You smile much more than he does. That's nice."

"That's because I got to be the fun one growing up. He had the serious thing handled. Didn't need my help on it." He looked her up and down in return for her own looks, but kept most of his attention on his beer. "I'm guessing in whatever situation you had growing up, you were the fun one too."

"Still am." Gwen said as she nursed the beer a little bit more. "God, it's been a long time since I've had beer, though. We can never get it in . . . well, where we're living. Alcohol is watched too closely on the market. I miss it."

"Oh, well we're gonna have to make sure we bring the whole cellar, then." Liam laughed just thinking about the stock he had back at his house. "You guys are gonna love us. At least while the booze lasts. I've got a wine cellar that runs for about a mile and a half, and liquor storage that runs almost as far. Always wanted to make sure we were prepared for a party at my house." He glanced up to see Logan talking to Mercury and Doc Weber, since Mercury had quickly fallen in with her own peers there outside of civilization. "I'm glad you like the beer. We've got better stuff back at the house that we'll break out for the going-on-rebellion party."

"Better stuff? I think I might kiss you." She replied teasingly before she followed his gaze to his brother, and her smile faded slightly. "You better not get me in trouble with the boss, though. I like watching his kids." And Logan. She liked watching him too.

"Is that what he is? The boss?" That made Liam laugh, but he knew it wasn't a very big stretch to think of his brother as being someone in charge of things. "I don't think I can bring myself to call him that, so hopefully it's not an official title or something."

"It's kind of official. He's pretty important back home." Gwen finished the last of her beer quickly, since she really wanted to enjoy her alcohol to its fullest, and that meant more booze. "I'd really like to see him loosen up." Gwen looked back at Liam and there was definitely mischief in her look before she got up. "I'm . . . kind of a thorn in his side, unless I'm watching his kids. He doesn't like the trouble I cause back home. But I can't help it if people like to find me for a good time."

"No, I imagine you could help it if you wanted to. It's just more fun not to." He knew a fair amount about making his brother's life into a living hell, and he didn't mind having someone else around who appeared to enjoy nettling Logan as much as he once did. "I haven't had a chance to really get the full story from him. Of everything that happened up there. But I know my brother, and whatever it was, it did a number on him. He was never this serious before."

"I guess you wouldn't really have had time to hear the story yet. Considering we just showed up here." Gwen motioned toward someone by the cooler and they knew a fellow drinker when they saw one. They tossed her a beer across the fire. Gwen caught it easily and grinned at the unknown person across the way.

"Guess they matched your brother up with his bombshell wife there instead of Anna and the Consortium pulled a bunch of shit to drive the first relationships apart and push the new ones together. They were spying on you and everyone out here and everything. That's why it took so long for us to come out here, we figured the Consortium was watching."

"There hasn't been much to watch. But if they had their eyes on us, then they saw us hold funerals for the two of them." He nearly teared up thinking about that occasion, but he shook his head. "With all the shit they dropped the day Nine blew up, I'm surprised the Consortium is even still flying. I guess because at the end of the day, they're still the ones with all the best toys." He took a long swallow of his beer and closed his eyes, before he rubbed at his face in the heat of the fire. "I'm glad you all came back to recruit us, but I'm still scratching my head as to what kind of actual difference it's gonna make."

"It'll make a difference." Gwen said resolutely, since she agreed with Logan. "The more people, the better. And morale has been sinking since they arrived, but it'll help to have new people around. Anyway, would you rather stay here and know you're going to die by CV or take the chance of getting to Eleusis with the rest of us?" Gwen clearly was on the train to Eleusis. "Trust me, we've got a much better chance of getting there than the majority of the Consortium does anymore. They've got better toys, but we've got the one they want."

"You've got a Twist, then." Liam said with the same kind of incisive look that she had seen so often from Logan when he was picking apart a problem. Liam might have been the fun twin his entire life, but he hadn't been a stupid one.

"Am I that readable or that drunk?" She looked around and looked down at the bottle in her hands. Gwen wasn't sure what number she was on, but she was amazed that she hadn't opened the one that had been tossed to her yet. "Can you open this for me?"

Liam gave her a skeptical look, since he doubted she actually needed help, but it wasn't in his nature to stand between a person and their alcohol. He took the bottle from her and snapped the top off deftly. "It's the only thing that would make anybody think they could win against the Consortium at this point, and clearly you all still think you can. Which means you've got a way to get there, you just need the actual people to fight once you do."

"Pretty much. I'm shit with a gun, though, that's why I get to take care of all the babies." She smiled and gladly took the beer back from him. "Do you need help?" There was a short pause. "With your babies?"

"I've got three wives, two of whom enjoy babies. We've got a pretty good rotation going, thank you." He was still smiling in spite of declining her offer, though. "You have any of your own, or do you prefer to jump around and take care of everybody else's so you can give them back later?"

"Waaaay too young for my own babies." She said with a smile, since she knew that there was almost no such thing as being too young for babies on Earth. But Gwen had been dreaming of Eleusis since she was little, and she wasn't going to let babies get in the way of that. "I'm twenty. Ran away from home just after I turned fourteen, ran into rebels by dumb luck when I was fifteen, been living in the camp ever since. I'm from California. My parents . . . well, that's a story for another time. Basically I have the right medications to make sure I don't have a baby before I want to. And yes, I know it's illegal. And no, I don't care."

Liam didn't seem as shocked by that news as some people had been. "I've never seen the point in people getting angry about that. Yeah, it's illegal, and yeah, I get why, but I'd rather people who didn't want kids not have them at all. The rest of us in the rest of the population are doing what we can to multiply and replenish, no need for everybody else to be going overboard with it too."

He was clearly adding that information to the rest of what he knew about the blonde as he looked her over, but he truly didn't seem to mind it much. "I got a shot myself once. Just after some shit happened to Logan. I didn't want to spring having a kid coming into the world on him at the time, and I needed to be free to handle shit for a while without being tied down by a pregnant girlfriend who would need things from me all day long. So I made a few calls and got a shot. It was supposed to last for a year, but it didn't hold up that long, apparently, since I got Bree knocked up within a couple months of getting married and Rachel wasn't far behind."

"Sometimes they give out diluted doses so they can sell more." She shook her head but he didn't seem upset about being a father. "You're happy with your babies and situation, though, I hope."

"Oh yeah, of course I am. I actually like having kids, weird as that is to say." He laughed, since he felt like the last person in the world who would actually enjoy having children. "I don't get to see them that much, though, which my wives are fond of telling me is the reason why I actually like having kids. They're cute kids, though, all three of them. Chrissy is still a whiner and somebody still has to wake up with her every night, but she's still pretty cute."

"They usually are. Whiners, I mean. I'm not surprised you have cute kids. Logan's kids are super cute and he's attractive like you." Gwen took another swig of beer. "Did your wife really just disappear? What's it like? Having three at once?"

"Kids or wives?" He said with a mischievous grin. "Either way, the answer's the same. I don't think of it as having three at once, since I almost never really do. The kids, sometimes. They're in the same place most of the time, with whoever's taking care of them on any given day. The wives I almost never see more than one of at a time. And that's by design."

"So, what, everyone gets a couple days? Or a week each? Either way, doesn't that get exhausting?"

"Two days each and then one to myself, then everybody all over again." He laughed again, since he knew how it sounded to everyone but those involved. Even to him sometimes it sounded absolutely absurd. "We tried it before with everybody getting a full week to themselves and I would just go around and around, but that ended up being too long away from them at a time. And a week is a long time to go without a decent night's sleep, for whoever's watching the kids. So chopping up the week seems to have pretty well done the trick lately."

Gwen shook her head but not because she was judging them, really, she'd just never seen polygamy work. "Hey, whatever makes you happy. They get a hot husband, and I imagine all your wives are hot too."

"They are, now that you mention it. And every one of them is too smart for me. So I'm pretty fortunate that way." He put his beer aside in the grass next to his chair and sighed, since he didn't take enough opportunities to really remember just how awesome his life was. For the most part.

"Well, congrats to you." She tipped her beer at him and then took a big gulp. "Is three wives your maximum number, then?"

"I don't know. I've been asking the universe to put a few more days on the end of every week for a while now, but I understand I'm not alone in that. So if the universe ever decides to actually grant that kind of wish, I could consider it. As of right now, there's only so much of the sun to go around." He shrugged as he looked over at her, since he could tell she was interested in the position, if it was going to be open.

"I've talked about the possibility of a fourth with them before, but we haven't really been married that long as it is. Plus, I don't know anybody out here I would seriously consider. Everybody's come to pretty much the same consensus that I'm insane and Logan was just as insane for coming up with the idea in the first place."

Gwen about choked on a gulp of beer when he said it was Logan's idea. "What? No way, I don't believe that for a minute. Even when the man doesn't get action for weeks, he doesn't look in any other direction other than Mercury. No way he came up with a polygamous marriage."

"My hand to whatever gods you believe in." He put his hands up in the air and then put them behind his head to relax. "Bastard cornered me at his own party and told me he had gone behind my back to arrange a marriage with all three of them in a single night. Didn't want to leave the planet and leave me to fend for myself. Tied me down three ways just to make sure I wouldn't go anywhere or fuck things up too badly."

"Huh. Wow." She finished off another bottle. Gwen knew she was drinking too fast, but she didn't care. Getting drunk felt nice. She was lightheaded already. It felt freeing. "Never would have guessed that. He should really consider it. He and his wife are way too busy for each other."

"Yeah, speaking as a poly myself, if he's already too busy for one wife, he's twice too busy for two." He hadn't gotten a chance to talk to Mercury yet, but he had gotten a very distinct impression from their first conversation, and he had to shake his head as he sought her out in the crowd. "And there is no excuse for any man to be too busy for his wife."

"I told you, he's in charge. And she's one of too few doctors. They go days without seeing each other sometimes." Gwen looked down at the empty bottle in her hand and she turned and tossed it effortlessly into the bucket where everyone else was tossing their empties. "Too bad he doesn't even notice me. Oh well."

Liam just laughed. "Wow. I've been dealing with my brother's fan club for most of our life, but you take the cake. I thought that would sort of simmer down after he got married, but apparently not. Good luck barking up that particular tree. Logan is a serial monogamist. Always has been, aside from a few drunken nights he would beat the shit out of me for telling you about."

Gwen pouted at that, since she really didn't want to hear that she wouldn't be able to see what Logan Bickford was hiding in his pants. "Simmer down? Have you looked at yourself in a mirror? Marriage does not make either of you less attractive. At all."

"I don't know. Some days it gets pretty ugly." He grinned over at her as he thought back to a few times when things had gotten either particularly crazy with his wives or particularly messy with the kids. Things were never simple, that much was certain. "Besides, isn't there a war to fight or something? I would think that would distract you from scratching an itch most of the time."

"A war doesn't mean much if there's nothing important waiting for you on the other side of it." She replied with a shrug before she got up, even though she was a little wobbly. "Anyway. Nice to meet you, Liam Bickford. I'm gonna . . . go somewhere else. Staring at your face is not . . . it's nice, but I . . . nevermind. See ya around."

He laughed as she got up and headed off, since she was clearly losing coordination in a hurry. "I'll take you up on that offer sometime, you know." He said as he took a sip of his beer. "Of help with the kids. Everybody needs a break from the kids sometimes."

That was a sting that she wasn't expecting, so she just nodded. "Sure. Yeah. Whenever. You know where to find me."

He watched her go, partly to make sure she didn't stumble herself into the fire and partly because it was just that nice to watch her leave. Gwen hadn't been gone long when Bree came back with her own replacement beer to slide herself back into his lap.

"Mmm . . . good timing." He adjusted himself in the seat so her ass would be deliciously flush against him, and she could feel that he had pointedly missed her presence. Either that or somebody had piqued his interest in the meantime. "How're the kids?"

"The kids? Oh, I'm sure they're fine." She said with a playful grin, since she had actually just gone off to give Liam a chance to chat up the pretty blonde. "So, I guess you like her, huh? My ass seems to think you find her interesting."

"I like her well enough. Your ass is an excellent thinker." He didn't mind holding onto her tighter, since it was far from the boldest they had ever been in a public place before. "Turns out, it's actually Logan she's got the hots for. But I'm pretty sure she'd be up for whatever she can get, even if it's with the carbon copy."

"Logan doesn't pay attention to anyone. Maybe his new wife, I don't know. He didn't even notice Anna until they actually got married." Bree shook her head and turned around on his lap so she could kiss him. "It's getting late. Do you want to go back to the trailer?"

"No, I don't want to go back to the trailer." The kids would be back at the trailer, and it was Margo's night to watch them, and he really didn't want to deal with Margo that night. "You remember how last year I said I was gonna take you out and show you the pond, but then you were too pregnant to do anything but exist when we actually got out here?"

"I do remember." She leaned in and kissed all along his neck while her hand discreetly snuck between their bodies to stroke his attentive cock between them. "Are you going to show me the pond this year?"

"I'm going to show you the pond right now." He said with a moan, moving one hand up to the side of her face as he kissed her. "Go get us a blanket, it's a mess out there and I intend to make it a hell of a lot worse."

Bree didn't move right away after he told her to go get a blanket, since she really, really liked to tease him. She stroked him a few more times and kissed him heatedly before she backed off of his lap slowly. "I suppose I can grab a blanket."

"Quickly." He said with a playful glare as he got up after her. He abandoned the chair where it was and headed out into the dark, just waiting for her to catch up. The blonde had put a few too many thoughts in his head, and every one of them was about to be his redhead's problem to deal with.

And if his redhead really wanted the blonde that much . . .

All that did was increase the problem in his pants, and he didn't need that as he ran off toward the pond. He would think about that later. He would give that lots and lots of deeply dedicated thought later.

7

Orion shook his head as Mercury handed Leo back to him, and he settled the little boy on one of his knees as he made the final adjustments to get the bus in motion. "I didn't expect it either. But apparently they knew what they were talking about." They had a few more people on the bus than they had on the way out from the mountains, since Anna's younger, unmarried siblings decided to ride with them. They wanted to spend a little more time with their sister, and a few of Logan's friends had come along as well, to catch up with him and explain the way things had been for the past year since the explosion of Nine. "From the way they're talking, there's gonna be more than enough people coming back with us to make Reed's head explode. I expected maybe four or five dozen tops, but they're talking about four or five hundred."

"Four or five hundred?" Mercury looked a little queasy at the thought, since she didn't have the energy to deal with that much population growth, although they would be coming with additional medical staff that she was grateful for. "That's definitely a lot. I guess they really know their friends and neighbors." She watched Orion with Leo and smiled a little bit, since he really was great with children. "Are you sure you don't want me to take him back to his carseat? I know there is no official police force down here, but it's still unsafe for him to ride with you. Even if you are just going to plug in coordinates and watch the road."

"Oh he's fine." He gave Mercury a playful glare and nodded to a seat next to the driver's area that was unoccupied. "Have a seat and put a blanket down or something, we'll let the boys play while they catch up back there." He did have to hang onto Leo for the first few minutes of the drive to get them back to the road. After that, it was as she'd said, and he entered the coordinates and let go of the wheel.

Mercury pursed her lips a little before she moved and took the unoccupied seat with Declan in her lap. She ran her hands through her son's hair and she looked over at Orion again. "It is really unsafe. I won't remind you again, but you should know that as a medical professional, I really advise against this."

"And as a pilot, I accept and acknowledge your advice, while completely ignoring it." He laughed once the vehicle was fully back on autopilot, and turned the released chair to swivel toward Mercury so the boys could mess with each other. "Doc Weber and her daughter seem nice. They'll be a lot more helpful than most you've already got out there."

Mercury nodded and watched Declan and Leo carefully from where she sat. Declan was a few months younger than Leo, but they were both big boys. "They're very knowledgeable, both of them. They've also been researching CV from the information they've had access to here on Earth. It's fascinating. I wish I had the time and the resources to delve into that again, but I don't know that I ever will. Especially because we're all fugitives and the Consortium might be able to track my research." She reached down to cushion Declan as he wiggled and wobbled with the movements of the bus. "I enjoy being able to help people, but everything that I wanted as a doctor . . . just isn't feasible anymore."

"You'll be able to get back into research." Orion watched the kids as well, but focused on corralling them with his boots rather than manually intervening. "I heard the new guy, Xander, talking to Jason before we left. He was yelling because Jason's been so obsessed with the Twist that he hasn't given a shit about anything or anyone else. With Xander pulling the strings, though, I imagine we'll all get some better toys and tools here sometime soon. And the Consortium isn't gonna track you without Jason knowing about it, no matter how obsessive he gets."

"I don't know. I got so close to cracking something. I think if I got into it again, they would see it somehow." She stared down at Declan and shuddered a little as she thought about Stephen Kaplan and his haunting warning to her before he drugged and raped her. "They have so many ways to watch." She reached out and brushed Declan's hair across his forehead before she looked over at Orion again. "I wish we had a chance like this. To go home, see our families, bring them into this and save them."

"We'll have our chance." He sounded like he believed it when he said it, and the smile on his face was full of easy confidence. "It's been easier for us to keep up to date on them, at least. We'll know where to find them when the time comes, and we'll know that they're alright. Even if I'm not happy my sister actually decided to start dating. The guy she's with is a joke."

Mercury smiled at Orion and she hoped for his sake he actually got the chance to tell his sister what he thought before she made any big changes to her life. "I hope you're right. You seem a lot more confident than most. I'll take that." She looked between the boys and back up at Orion. "I miss talking to you. You've always been so easy to talk to."

"Well, pretty soon we're gonna be neighbors. That'll probably make it just a little easier than it is right now, considering you and I are running all over the neighborhood at this point." He glanced over the controls, taking in every specific measurement of the vehicle with a single look as well as the road. "We need to just come up with some kind of massive kid-proof bin to put between the two houses, dump the kids into it and let 'em fend for themselves. Somebody cries, somebody will go out and take care of it, otherwise just let 'em crawl around in there and make trouble."

"A massive bin. That's your solution to childcare." Mercury replied incredulously with a laugh as she shook her head. "Only *you* would say, 'Just put them in a big bucket. They'll be alright.'"

"Hey, they would! I mean, yeah, they'd get in each other's way and crawl all over each other, but that's life, right? You gotta figure out how to navigate other people sometime. Might as well be when you're learning how to crawl." He grinned down at Declan, who was pawing at Leo's face as if trying to figure him out, though Leo was completely ignoring him. "See? They'd be fine. They've got this."

Mercury looked down at the boys together and she just watched them for a while. She wondered, briefly, what her children would have looked like if she and Orion had stayed together. Things were so different, and she certainly didn't regret her life at all, but it didn't stop her from wondering how things might've been if she had the life she chose instead of the life that the Consortium chose for her. "You're a good father, so you must be doing something right. Even if that means putting your children in giant bins."

"Hey, stay away from the gears. You're not old enough to know how to work those yet." He redirected Declan with the tip of his foot until the boy got distracted with a part of a chair.

"Motherhood suits you too." He said with a cautious look up at her, though he was smiling the whole time. "I always enjoyed watching you with babies, even if they belonged to other people. Getting to see you with your own has been a lot of fun."

Mercury watched Declan for a moment quietly and nodded. "I love spending time with both of my boys. I just wish I had *more* time. More time to be a doctor. More time to be a mother." She glanced back toward the rest of the bus for a moment, even though the partition prevented her from seeing the rest of the riders. "More time to be a wife. There was a reason why I avoided dating or getting involved with anyone. I don't think I'm good at being all three things at once."

"That's not on you." He gave her a sympathetic smile, since he and Anna had had some of the same conversations. "If we were, I mean, not that I'm wishing we were still working for the Consortium now that we know what a bunch of fuckbags they are, but if we were, you know, still just on rotation, still piloting ferries between stations, still bringing babies into the world, still just doing our thing . . . then we'd have time for everything we need to do. Everything we want to be. Your caseload would be monitored and reduced due to diminished capacity, you'd have had a decent amount of maternity leave, the whole package."

Mercury nodded and sighed again. "My mother would have been there when the boys were born." She missed her parents a lot, but she knew there was nothing that could be done about it. "I know that the Consortium just wanted to use us and kill us." She replied softly, since she didn't want anyone else to hear her. "But I liked my life. Before the Initiative. I had a fulfilling life. I didn't get sick because I was overworked. My life was managed. I desperately want that. Order. I need some kind of order."

"Too bad we're in the chaos business right now." He nodded down at the kids who were trying to pull themselves up on the various support bars and levers that made up the front portion of the bus. "Kids, rebellion, a Twist that doesn't work, there's a lot of chaos to go around right now. Not that I think the people leading us are doing a bad job, they're doing the best they can, Logan, Jason, even Reed. We're just stuck between about half a dozen hard places. There's no clear way through that."

"Logan seems confident that we'll find a way. I'm sure he's right." She continued watching Declan instead of looking at Orion again, since she didn't want to doubt Logan by showing even the slightest bit of worry in her expression. She wanted to believe they would succeed. Win. Beat the Consortium at their own game. But she truly didn't know how it was possible. "I'm glad we're going back to the town now, though." She decided to change subjects just a little, since she didn't want to think about the possibility of never making it to Eleusis. "I didn't like all of those people watching my every move at the camp. I felt like an alien."

"We *are* aliens." He said with another laugh. "We're not from this planet. I'm pretty sure that's the definition of alien. They look at us that way back at home too, they're just more accustomed to seeing us around, I think. Doesn't stop them from staring."

"That's not comforting. Telling me that I am an alien." Mercury muttered as she finally looked over at Orion again. "Logan doesn't look at me like an alien. You never did."

"Yeah, well, I have an excuse. We're the same kind of alien." He grinned even though she didn't seem too happy about it, and he shook his head. "Logan, on the other hand, is his own kind of alien. So that's his excuse."

Mercury was quiet again, but clearly she was thinking about how she should respond. "I wasn't expecting his family to dislike me. I know they weren't expecting him to come back with a different wife, but it wasn't as though this was my plan either. I know I'm strange, but I never thought I'd end up being jealous of Anna. His family loves her."

"If it makes you feel any better, her family aren't my biggest fans either." He was clearly more bothered by that fact than he really wanted to show, since he wasn't looking at her as he said so. "I mean, she's been going around the last day or so expecting all of them to be mad at her for not being with Logan, but it seems like it's me they're mad at, for existing."

"We're already victims of the Consortium. Living on a planet we've never known. Our families are still at risk and still think we are dead." Mercury didn't know what Logan's family expected from her, exactly. "We've given up our whole lives. Everything we have ever known. We don't need their hatred and disdain just for loving Logan and Anna."

"Well, whether we need it or not, I guess." He tried not to linger on the way the others viewed them. "They barely met us, and the two of them not being together is kind of a lot to process. It'll take them a while to get used to it. But I'm sure they'll come around." The road turned smoother the farther they got from the lake, and they moved on some of the nearly-indestructible highways that crisscrossed the world.

The sun was still rising ahead of them, since everyone wanted to get an early start back toward the pieces of nowhere Logan and Anna's people called civilization. "Look at it this way, just a few more days out here for everybody to get their lives in order and then everyone will be back in our house, and it'll be their turn to be the weird ones."

"We're still the weird ones." She mumbled as Declan started to get fussy. Mercury, even while working, had managed to keep her supply up, so even when she wasn't home at least her sons were drinking her breast milk. It helped ease her guilt at being away a little bit. "I should probably feed him. I swear, these babies never stop eating."

"They really don't." He hadn't realized that she was still feeding her boys herself, but they were a little younger than Leo and Lynnette, after all. Still, Orion was impressed. He looked her over once in spite of himself, but he wasn't sure if she noticed him doing so or not. "I've got a blanket up here somewhere, I think."

"Don't worry about it." Mercury said as she grabbed Declan and turned slightly, but soon enough Declan was attached to her, so there really wasn't anything for her to 'hide'. It wasn't like Orion hadn't seen her breasts before anyway. "He gets hot under a blanket and it makes him cranky. He'll be fine like this."

Orion tried to tell himself that it was no big deal to see Mercury bared in any context, but he had to exert a very concerted effort to keep his eyes forward or on Leo. He *had* seen her before, that was part of the problem. He had been one of the first and only to see her completely bare, one of the first to actually make her want someone to see her that way. There were a lot of firsts behind her nakedness, however partial or casual. "At least he actually stays put. These two can be a problem the whole time until we added in a bottle."

"James is worse."

"Then it's a good thing his mother is the hardest working woman on the planet." Orion managed to make and keep eye contact at that, giving her a confident smile. He had to scoop up Leo afterward, though, and placed Leo on his knee to look out at the racing countryside.

"Not the hardest working, I am sure, but I try my best." Mercury ran her hands through Declan's red hair and she smiled as she looked down at him. She loved her sweet babies. "I'm a little sad I have missed watching you deal with the messy parts of parenting. I'm sure blowouts are more entertaining with your commentary behind them."

"Wow. Those are the parts you're sad you've missed? I take it back. You *are* the strange one." He balanced Leo with one massive hand wrapped around the boy's midsection and held him aloft in a way that never failed to make Anna nervous, so he could only imagine how much it would freak out Mercury.

"This kid . . . has peed in my face so many times I've stopped even getting offended. But his blowouts I can deal with." He brought Leo back down to where the boy was teetering on his knee with the world rushing by outside, trying to escape with no actual hope of doing so. "Lynnette's are something else. I've gotta call Anna in for those."

"Really? You call for backup? You?" Mercury said with a laugh, but she just looked Leo over carefully. "He really does look just like you. Such a handsome little guy."

"Better get used to hearing that, mini-me." He grinned down at Leo, who seemed entirely oblivious to the conversation in favor of the outside world. Orion's expression grew a little more serious the longer he looked at his son, though.

"You never have answered me on the genetics questions I asked." He didn't say it as an accusation, just something to put out into the open. "I don't know if my parents had to do anything medical with me when I was little, but the more I see him turning into my old baby pictures, the more I know that one of these days, whatever modifications were made to me will come around and bite this kid in the ass. He's already trying to walk when he should barely be crawling. And if he's anything like his dad, it's only going to get worse."

"You talk about genetic modification as though it's a curse." Mercury said carefully. "I don't really have the equipment to give him a thorough test. His genetics come from both you and Anna, after all." She looked down at Declan who had fallen asleep while nursing. "Babies mature at different paces even when they don't have parents who were genetically modified. Some babies skip crawling altogether." She cradled Declan differently so she could reach out and touch Orion's arm lightly. "As soon as I can give you more information, I will. But Leo isn't showing any signs of deformity or mutations that are going to hurt him. He's longer than most babies his age, but that's inevitable with you for a father. That's not a bad thing."

He smiled at the fact that she was trying to comfort him, but he wasn't entirely at ease. "I broke both legs three times when I was a kid, and both arms at least twice. My right I broke four times, but that was because I favored that one. My mom told me when I got older it was because they said I had a calcium deficiency, but my doctor said that wasn't quite right. It's because I grew faster than the rest of me could develop to support it. And that was me in space running at about sixty percent Earth gravity for most of my childhood. I can only imagine what he's gonna be like down here on the ground."

He shook his head, since there was no use stressing about unknowns. Life being a pilot had taught him that. But the lesson was also useless. All they had were unknowns, and consequently all they had was the stress that came with them. "Could be nothing, though, I'll agree with you on that. Just feels like it's never going to be nothing with us. Not when the Consortium's had their hooks in us before either of us were even born."

"I never really looked into my own genetics. Not closely." She said cautiously as she pulled Declan away from her breast and tugged her shirt back into place. "Right before we left . . . Stephen Kaplan told me that I should." Mercury's voice shook a little as she mentioned Stephen Kaplan, but Orion didn't know what happened to her. He would never know, if she had her way. She didn't want him to think she was weak, or worse, think less of her for allowing herself to fall victim to the Kaplans. The withdrawal she had suffered through from the drug had been enough punishment, not to mention the mental toll ever since. "I've always thought there was more my parents never told me, but they also encouraged my medical pursuits, so I imagine they always knew I would find out someday. I just haven't wanted to look into it."

"Well, considering the source of the tip, I can understand you being reluctant." Orion was around, but just barely, for Logan completely losing his mind and destroying Stephen. It seemed too personal a beating under the circumstances, but it wasn't something he was going to bring up. "I had a chance to talk to Carl a couple times before Nine went down, about what Aiko discovered about him." It was still incredibly hard for him to talk about his friend, and a large part of the reason why Orion hadn't been personally capable of committing to leadership or talking to Jason without being hateful.

At first, he held out hope that Carl and Aiko could have survived for a little while on Eleusis, long enough for them to get the Twist to Earth and get it to work in time to mount a rescue. But more than a year later and Orion's hopes had long since dried up. "Her theory was that they created Carl and others like him to see just how much humanity could take. How much humanity could be, when it was pushed to its absolute limits. She thought I was a minor expression of the same question. Which makes sense, since in spite of all expectations, I've grown another twenty-five millimeters since Nine." He hadn't mentioned it to anyone, including Anna. He had quietly taken some of his pants to be remade and made no other fuss. If they stayed in the mountains much longer, his old uniforms would need to be remade as well.

"I'm not stopping. I guess I'll deal with the consequences of that when they start causing me problems. If I keep going at current rates, I'll start running into heart problems by the time I'm thirty, like classical Gigantism." He shook his head, since he was rambling and he knew it. "My point is, I've never thought you were a part of those kinds of experiments. You're not . . . the way you were designed, you're not reaching toward something. You are something." He smiled, since he did mean it as a sincere and heartfelt compliment, even if it was a cause of anxiety for all of them who had to deal with being altered. "I hope that's what you find when you look into it. And I'm sure James and Declan are better for it."

Mercury hadn't known about his continued growth, and it did make her look at Leo again. "You're not going to die when you're thirty." She put all her confidence into her tone, confident that she could help him avoid the future he was describing. "I promise I will find a way to help you. Even here, with limited resources. Leo and Lynnette need their father. The world would be less without you in it."

"Well, it would be shorter. We can agree on that. I do fuck up the average for everybody." He smiled about the prospect of his own mortality, but that was nothing strange for him. "There are a lot of other things in need of that brain of yours. I've got time, don't fret about me."

"The other things aren't as important as you. Other than Logan and the children, you are more important to me than anything else. I know we're not in a romantic relationship anymore, but I still care for and about you. I always will."

Orion smiled, since he appreciated where the sentiment came from. If anything, being on Earth and in such strange situations had brought them closer as friends over the preceding year, even if they hadn't seen that much of each other. "Well, right back at you. And if you figure out a way I can somehow pay back the application of that beautiful brain to my particular problem, please don't hesitate to let me know. Though I'm really not sure what would measure up to something quite like that."

"I don't require payment to help one of my best friends." She smiled at him and leaned in closer to him to kiss his cheek. "I should go trade babies with Logan, I'm sure James will be hungry soon."

"Can you grab a bottle for this one on your way back? It's been a while, and I think he's just too distracted right now to know he's hungry. Once he figures it out, it'll just be a meltdown." Orion smiled warmly at her as she got up, since Mercury with a baby was just one of the most perfect images he could conjure up in the universe. It was every bit as right and correct as a star having planets or a planet having moons.

Mercury nodded and went as quietly as she could so the sleeping wouldn't be disturbed, and to make sure Declan stayed asleep. When she got back to the baby seats, she gently buckled Declan in and sat down next to Logan in his seat for a moment. She could see James wiggling in his sleep, so she knew that she had timed things right.

"Hey." She whispered as she shook Logan's arm gently. Mercury didn't blame him for falling asleep, and if James needed him, crying would have woken Logan up. "Declan is asleep, James is waking slowly. I'll take him and feed him. I just wanted to let you know I was switching them."

"Alright." He said sleepily as he pulled her in close. "Are you doing alright?" Logan asked without even opening his eyes. "I didn't really get a chance to see you much this morning."

She nodded and kissed him gently since he pulled her in closer. "I've been up front with Orion. Trading stories about how much your family and Anna's hate the both of us."

"They don't hate you." Logan said without sounding like he was surprised she thought so. "They just met you. If you'll recall, even I took a couple days to come around where you were concerned."

"You were forced to sleep with me while you were married to the love of your life." Mercury nearly winced at saying it out loud, but Logan hadn't chosen her from the beginning. He hadn't chosen her in the end either, even though she wished he had. "I know you weren't my biggest fan."

"That's not what I meant." He defended quickly, since he didn't mean to bring up the fact they hadn't been together by choice in the first place. "I just meant that once I started talking to you, really started to know you, I fell in love with you quickly. They just haven't had that chance yet."

Mercury nodded slowly and looked toward the boys because she needed the distraction. "You should get some more sleep. I'll take James up and feed him."

He pulled her in for another slow kiss instead of letting her go and squeezed her hand afterward. "Just give them time. I love you. So will they."

"I love you too." Mercury said first and foremost, and she kept her forehead pressed to his after his kiss. "I just worry. You're here in this place where you fell in love. You didn't have that with me. We didn't choose each other, not from the beginning, and by the end . . ." By the end, Mercury had made it clear who she wanted, but Anna made the declaration they all stuck with. "I love you so much. But I don't know if I can compete with a lifetime of memories." Mercury didn't know why she was bringing this up on the bus, but everyone was sleeping around them, and she wanted to say it before she lost courage.

"You don't have to compete with anything. Or anyone." He was still partly asleep as he said so, but his grip on her was firm enough. "You're mine. That's the beginning and the end of it for me."

"Okay." Mercury conceded softly and kissed him gently. "Go back to sleep. I'm going to take James up to the front."

"Declan and I will be here." He promised sleepily, before he closed his eyes completely and relaxed into the seat.

Around him, people from his past abounded, people whose names and stories she had heard from him in bits and pieces over the time they'd been together. She walked through ghosts to get back to the front, and she grabbed a bottle from a cooler near a sleeping Anna, his clearest and closest ghost.

Orion watched the world move by through glassy eyes, but he

glanced back at her with a smile as she came through. "Welcome back. Leo was starting to get fussy up here without you."

"I'm sure he didn't miss me that much." She said with a glance back at Logan's family and friends and before she closed the partition between the driver's suite and the rest of the bus. Mercury held out the bottle, though she looked down at it afterward. "Will he drink it cold? I can feed him too, you know. If it wouldn't make Anna angry. I'm used to feeding both boys at once, and Dec didn't drain me dry, he hardly drank anything before he went to sleep."

"He doesn't usually like them cold." He did his best to reposition Leo on his lap as he took the bottle, since he would at least try first. "If he decides to be picky, I'll hand him over, but go ahead and take care of Jimmy first. Then maybe we can trade."

"Jimmy?" She questioned as she shook her head and put James on her breast. "Don't let Logan hear you call him Jimmy. He's not a fan of that nickname." She laughed anyway, though, and she was glad to see James didn't fuss too much.

"Oh come on. Jimmy is a great nickname. Jimmy, Jim, Jimbo, come on, they're country-folk, they should be coming up with these on their own, not needing my help to make it happen."

"Jim maybe." Mercury chuckled as she watched him try to feed Leo, but it wasn't going extremely well. "We'll leave it at James for now."

He sighed heavily. "Fine. Be that way. But seriously, Jim and Dec? Those are nicknames meant to be had." He looked down at the squirming infant on his lap, who was more interested in inspecting the bottle than drinking from it. "Not much we can really do with yours, dude, sorry. Lee, maybe? O? Maybe we'll just go with O."

Mercury laughed softly. "Isn't Leo kind of a nickname already?" She reached out her free arm and nodded toward Leo. "Hand your large son over. I'll feed him. You need to focus on the road."

The switch ended up necessitating that Mercury was left bare during the actual handoff, but Orion did his best to keep his eyes on the children between them, even if he didn't fully succeed. "There you go, picky." He took James and put him on his knee the same way Leo had been a moment before, as if he was one of Orion's own children.

Mercury had fed Leo before when she and Logan had cared

for him and his twin sister on a few occasions, though it was rare. She smiled down at the grumpy baby, and while he had been bottle-fed for a while, he still knew how to take to the breast. He seemed happier when he had a steady supply of warm milk. "Much better, huh, Leo?"

Orion smiled over at the sight of her, and worked on getting a burp out of James. "One of these days, they're gonna be the ones saving the world." He said with a look down at the baby, staring back up at him like the strange creature he admittedly was. "I kinda look forward to that."

"Me too." Mercury ran her fingers across Leo's face as though he was her own baby. He looked so much like Orion. Mercury didn't have anything against Anna, but Mercury liked Lynnette for the same reason. Lynnette looked like her brothers and her father. "Such a sweet boy." She murmured as Leo's eyes fluttered open and closed as he suckled. "Once this expedition is over, we'll go home and enjoy our new houses. I look forward to a new normal that way."

"Normal. I wonder what that would be like?" He grinned over at her and settled back with James who was quickly awed by the things flying by them.

"I hope we get a chance to find out." Mercury settled back as well, since Leo and James were content and it was a moment to relax. Just for a little while.

8

Anna was awake even before the bus stopped moving, since she knew the bumps in the road well enough to know they were close to the Bickford estate. She opened her eyes and looked at the estate in the early morning sunrise. Her eyes burned with the tears she didn't know she needed to cry, but they slipped down her cheeks anyway.

So many memories flooded her at once that it became difficult to breathe, let alone stop herself from crying. She looked over where she thought Logan was sleeping in a seat not far, but when she looked at him, he was awake. And watching her.

Anna quickly wiped at the tears and tried to give him a smile. "Still looks the same." She whispered across to him.

He nodded slowly and looked back at it himself, a small smile on the corners of his mouth. "Honestly I'm surprised Liam didn't burn the place down while we were gone." He said it as if they had stepped away on a day trip and left his brother without a babysitter rather than the entire life-changing adventure they'd survived. "He didn't paint last year. Some of it's wearing through in patches. Not that I suppose it matters at this point."

The mid-morning sun was obscured behind a cloudy spring sky, but the mansion still stood like an icon of civilization in the middle of nowhere. The hangar off to one side was closed, housing dormant farm equipment that would soon need to see use for spring planting. One of the hangar doors opened as they approached, since they could easily leave the bus inside along with the rest of their farm equipment. The hangar door still bounced in exactly the same way when it opened, and Logan couldn't put a precise name to the way that simple thing tugged at him.

Anna remembered playing as a young girl in the hangar, even though they weren't supposed to. She remembered getting cut on her leg climbing over one of the large combines, and she couldn't help but reach down and itch her leg where she'd gotten stitches, though the scar was gone.

"I'm glad he didn't." She finally said, though her throat felt dry. This was supposed to be her house. Her life. She'd imagined having sex in that hangar, with Logan. It never happened, but the thought was in her mind just the same. "I love your house."

"It always seemed too empty to me." He said without looking away from the machines in the hangar, each one of which he had worked on personally and knew intimately. "I considered once just telling everyone in the district they could move in, just everybody take a wing or suite or something and have at it. Just to feel like the place was actually alive. My lawyers advised against it and I was too young to tell them to just go fuck themselves." He shook his head and scoffed at himself once. "I should've just done it."

"Liam could put a dent in it with his kids." She replied with a small smile before she stared at him for a moment. "I'm sorry." She whispered even softer as her eyes filled with tears again. "I didn't realize . . . I didn't think . . . it would be this hard." Or hurt this much. "This was supposed to be ours."

"Technically it still is." Logan said with a brief, humorless laugh. "Liam told me that he and Larissa refused to file a death certificate for either of us after Nine. So we're still listed on the property as joint owners." He shook his head at how silly such things sounded to him after everything that happened. The people who were supposed to be governing the world had turned things like law and order into tools of manipulation and nothing more. It didn't matter whose name was on a document or what a statute said, all that mattered was why.

"I don't think living in it together for a couple weeks makes it mine." She looked away from him and continued wiping at the tears that wouldn't stop no matter how stupid she felt. "We would have been happy here. We would have had a good life." Anna knew the very day they were living at the moment would have been a very different day, had she and Logan never gone to space. They would have had a limited clock, and perhaps never known about Eleusis, but being involved with Eleusis had already taken an immeasurable toll on their lives. They would have been happy.

She could tell from the lack of response that she spoke out loud some of the things he thought to himself, but he eventually just nodded and looked back over at her as the bus parked itself in the back of the hangar. "A really good life." He eventually echoed, as he stood up in the aisle of the bus, still looking out the windows.

"There are times when I wish I could close my eyes and pretend none of it happened." He said in a low voice, since people farther back behind the children's seats were getting out of their seats and getting their things together. Farther into the hangar he could see other vehicles coming back behind them, Liam maneuvering their family camper in place. He wondered if it would ever be used again. "Pretend there was no Eleusis, no Consortium, no CV, nothing beyond this farm. Life used to make sense here."

Anna wiped at her face yet again and nodded, since she had wished the same thing more than once. Their lives were complicated simply because they tried to do a good thing. They thought they were going to be a part of something that would give their families a better future. That would give *their* children a better future. Longer, fuller lives.

"Even with the CV, dying young wouldn't have been as bad as what we've already been through." She admitted a little too freely. "My father doesn't have regrets about his life. I do." If anything, she regretted the way things ended, because she and Logan were barely even friends. Anna knew she could have made things better for him. Easier, even.

Logan turned to pick up Declan gingerly since he was still asleep, but Priscilla was there to take him instead, shooing him off the bus to go see his old house without being encumbered by an infant. He thanked her and gave Declan a brief pat before he turned away to go behind Anna toward the front of the bus while Priscilla and the others gathered up the children's supplies for the visit.

"Regrets are something I feel like I'm getting used to these days." He said quietly, since he wanted to continue the conversation, but they had their present surrounding them as well as their past.

"How do we get rid of the regret?" She asked just as quietly, since she didn't want Orion to know how upset she was. She knew he would be supportive, but she didn't want to talk about it with Orion. He could be understanding, but he couldn't understand. At Priscilla's prompting, Gwen took Lynnette, but Anna didn't like giving up her baby. She wanted a distraction from all of the memories.

"If you figure it out, let me know." Logan answered without

looking back at her.

When they got up to the front of the bus Anna could hear Leo crying, but Orion had Leo up against one shoulder and had the situation pretty well in hand. He smiled at her sympathetically, since he could see that it had been an emotional homecoming.

"Kid didn't really understand the concept of me needing both hands to park this thing. I put him down for a couple seconds while I was getting situated and he decided that was an insult he could not abide." He stepped outside the bus with the rest of them, still bouncing Leo, and nodded toward the open hangar door. "I'm gonna go walk him, see if I can get him to calm back down."

"Do you need me to take him?" Anna asked quickly as she hurried after Orion, but it was obvious that she was just trying to avoid going inside of the Bickford house and seeing things that she didn't think she would ever be ready to see again. "Gwen took Lynnette . . ."

"No, it's okay, I've got him." He held Leo down a little farther so Leo could see that Anna was there as well, but Orion was still smiling in spite of the boy's crying. "I know this is rough." He said with his voice lowered, not that there was any chance of anyone hearing him over the sound of Leo crying. "I've got this screamer, don't worry about it. Just show Gwen and the others where we're gonna set up shop for the next couple days and have fun getting back into jeans that actually fit you right. We both know you've been waiting for that ever since you came upstairs."

Anna searched his eyes even though Leo was still crying, because she wanted him to tell her to stay with him or take Leo or *something*. She was terrified to go into the house and fall apart all over again, but Orion just gave her a reassuring smile. She pulled him by his arm for a kiss, hard and rough. She needed to keep herself grounded in the present. "The house is massive. I'll make sure there's someone directing or there are signs up or something. It's easy to get lost. If you want me to take Leo, I can . . ." When Orion shook his head, she just nodded. "Alright. I'll . . . try not to spend all day digging through old clothes and boxes."

That just made him laugh. "If you do, it won't be a wasted day. I imagine we're mostly just going to be sitting around waiting by the phones for people who have questions and coordinate people bringing supplies. I got two calls from people already this morning asking whether there's space for them to bring up tractor trailers.

Your people move fast."

"People will bring anything and everything they can as long as we think we won't get spotted for it." Anna was sure that Reed and Jason would be biting their tongues once they saw the people and resources that were coming home with them. "Thank you. For keeping me grounded. I'm having trouble, and I'm sorry."

"Nothing to be sorry for. If it makes you feel any better, I promise to absolutely, one hundred percent lose my shit if I ever get the chance to take you to Three." He tugged her in against him with a hand around her waist, and he rubbed at her back for a moment as he kissed her, though none of it seemed to make Leo much happier.

"Go ahead. Take him on a walk. He'll be happier." It was hard to listen to Leo screaming on top of everything else and she was grateful again for Orion's flexibility. Anna watched him walk out of the hangar with Leo longingly. When she turned around, Mercury was walking alongside Logan with James in her arms, and suddenly it was too much to see Mercury holding Logan's hand as they walked toward the house.

Anna hurried after them, but only to rush by Logan without looking at him. "I'm going to go in and start going through my things. If you could tell Gwen to direct baby traffic, that would be good. Orion is going to try to soothe Leo and get him back to sleep."

"Sure. I'm going to set them up in the back living room downstairs for the time being, just so you know." Logan nodded toward the center of the house. "I figure there's that one garden suite of rooms nearby where all of us can get set up for the next few days, so it'll make for a decent nursery. The one with the elk horns hanging over the arch and the case of chess sets, you remember?"

Anna remembered. Logan's father got angry when they pulled out the chess sets, but he sat down and taught them all how to play chess. Liam didn't care, and Anna ended up using her chess knowledge later for sexual purposes, which was certainly not his father's intent. "I remember. I played chess drunk on my fifteenth birthday in there. I hope my dad still doesn't know about that."

"I'm sure he'd just laugh if he did." Logan certainly had laughed at the time, and he smiled in nostalgia. "I'm gonna get everybody settled and make some phone calls, but I'll be up to help clear out the room in a bit. Unless Liam or his wives have done any kind of inventory on the house while we were gone, I'm probably gonna need your help to make sure we've gotten everything that could be useful."

Anna nodded and glanced up at him again before she power-walked ahead of them. "I'll just be working away. See you up there."

Mercury could tell that Anna had been crying from the way her face was red and splotchy, but she didn't say anything until she was out of earshot. "Is she going to be alright?"

Logan nodded, unsurprised by the question. Mercury was always worried about everyone, it was part of what made her such a good doctor. "As much as any of us will be." He gave his wife a reassuring smile and squeezed her hand as they walked. "There's just a lot going on here for us. I think part of it is knowing we're going to have to leave again. Seeing it one more time is just that much more proof that this life isn't real anymore."

"It must be hard. I understand." Mercury replied sympathetically, since she knew it would be hard to leave her home again too. It was harder still, though, to know that she might never see it again. She wasn't close to her home, and it would take a lot more to get her back there. Earth was it, or Eleusis, if they were lucky.

"There's a lot of history for you here. Are *you* alright?" She held his hand tighter as she thought about what he said to her earlier that morning, about her belonging to him. She didn't want to compete with his past.

"I will be." He promised as they stepped back inside the front door of a place he had long since said goodbye to. The main entry was still every bit as grandiose and eye-shattering as it had always been to him, even when he had played as a child on the three-story bannisters and sat on top of the carved lions' heads to do his homework just because he could. "I never really expected to come back here. I made my peace with it when I left, thinking I was headed for Eleusis and I was doing the right thing. It's been a lot between there and here."

Mercury looked around as soon as they stepped into the house, and it was clear she was surprised by how intricate and fancy and *large* everything was. "I don't think anyone will have any problem finding a place to sleep here."

That understatement helped ground him, and he was grateful for it as he smiled back. "No, I don't think so. Usually the problem is making sure you don't get lost."

He led her off in one direction down a back hall behind the massive staircases. "Even when the place was built, it only used about a tenth of the total capacity of bedrooms. And since then I don't think it's ever gotten above a third of the way full, even at max capacity four generations ago. Then most of that generation died off all at once in a sickness. My grandparents moved away early, and they ended up being the inheritors. Came back after everyone else was gone, raised my dad and his brother until his brother died. Then us. If I believed in curses I would say the place is cursed to never be at max capacity, but I don't. I just think it hasn't had the chance to really stretch its legs yet."

"Maybe we can come back here, if Eleusis doesn't work out." She shrugged and continued to look around. "Eleusis was once my dream, but I don't care about it as much anymore. I just want to have a good, long life and practice medicine until I can't anymore. I want all of that with you."

He didn't answer right away, but she'd known him long and deeply enough to know the silence was because he didn't agree with her. "I left here in the first place because life on Earth is never long enough." He still looked around in the hallway at all the things that were the same, and his eyes lingered on the few things that were different, obviously touches of Liam's wives and their decorating preferences. "And I still don't think it is. But I'd rather live short years here than be dead in a fight we can't win."

That was the sticking point for him in the mountains. Unlike most of the rebels around the world and most of the established rebel leadership, Logan didn't just want to fight and make progress for their cause. He wanted to win, and he would accept nothing less.

"Life on Earth isn't going to be a death sentence if I can find a cure." She reminded softly, even though she didn't like pushing something with him if he didn't agree. Mercury let go of his hand slowly, since she knew he had a lot to attend to.

"*When* you do." He corrected, since he wanted her to know he had every confidence in her. Even the corridors around them seemed to echo his confidence, since they belonged to him every bit as much as any medical office belonged to her. The way he walked, the way he carried himself, everything about him had changed to the look of a man completely at ease in his surroundings. It was a little disorienting, but that was only because she had never actually seen Logan in a place where he was completely comfortable before.

A few twisting hallways later, he brought them to a comfortably-appointed living room that was almost as large and grandiose as the entryway they'd come through, with doors visible beyond in elaborate scrollwork frames leading to half a dozen bedrooms. The elk horns he had referenced a few minutes earlier were displayed in huge and grotesque twelve-point glory above the hallway leading to the bedrooms, as a centerpiece of the room.

"Liam will get in here in just a few and help get everything cleaned out and the plastic off things. I'm pretty sure the water to these rooms was turned off a long time ago, but he'll get all that running too."

Mercury nodded and bounced James a little as he started to wake up in her arms. She kissed their son gently and looked around some more. "We'll be alright until he gets here. We'll just wander for a bit."

"Don't wander too far. It's a big place." He gave her a small smile and a brief kiss, then gave James a kiss as well in the hopes of keeping the boy at ease. "But it's also yours as much as it is anyone else's. So if Brianne or Rachel or Margo, or . . . well, let's face it, just Margo, if she tries to give you any lip about it, this is yours, and they should know it. I'll be back down soon. I doubt I have that much to get besides some clothes that are already boxed up anyway."

She nodded and bounced James a little bit more. "Take your time. You want to be sure to take everything that means something to you." Mercury gave him a small smile and started to wander just a little. "Come on, James, let's see if we can find any embarrassing family photos . . ."

Logan was laughing as he walked away, but his laughter died as he walked through the corridors, completely alone in a place that felt abandoned to him for most of his life. It had taken him a lot of getting used to even as a child. His house never really seemed to end, there were rooms upon rooms and entire wings of the compound covered in plastic that hadn't been touched for decades. Sure, there were machines that periodically ran through the entire estate to dust and vacuum and generally ensure that the place didn't go completely to crap, monitoring the foundation and the windows for structural problems, but that wasn't life. That wasn't use, or worth.

His room was well removed from the parts of the house that Liam and Larissa inhabited, and it was a long, familiar walk to get there. The floorboards still creaked in exactly the same way, the windows let in exactly the same quantity of light as they always had, and at the end of the hallway was Anna, just as she had always been in his youthful dreams.

He damned the Consortium more in that moment than ever before, even in his most violent fits of anger aboard Nine. They hadn't just taken away everything he had finally gained for himself before he left. They had twisted everything he had ever wanted.

"Hey." He said to announce himself, though he was sure she'd heard him coming.

"I'm in here." Anna replied without even seeing him, but she didn't get up from where she sat on what had been her side of the bed. She was wearing his letterman's jacket and she had a yearbook open in front of her. Clearly she hadn't gotten that far in going through her clothes.

He walked in slowly once he got to the room and saw the book open in her lap, but he stepped up beside her to look over her shoulder anyway. "Always thought it was insane at the time that they still bound a book for the sake of eighty-two graduating seniors who had never once been in the same place at the same time. I get it now."

"We did a lot of things together, even if we didn't always do it at the same time." She said without looking up. Anna tried to suppress the shiver that ran down her spine at the sound of his voice. Wearing his jacket was bad enough, but she loved his jacket. Anna flipped through the pages slowly and laughed at a few of the comments that had been left for her. Most were lewd, but she definitely held the title of 'class slut'.

He laughed along with a few of them and shook his head at others. "That one's not true. There were thirty-four guys in the class, and I know of three at least who you did not, in fact, sleep with during high school."

"Your brother. I did not sleep with your brother. Or Christopher, of course." She said with a laugh and shook her head. Anna flipped through some prom pictures, one of the few times where the majority of them got together. It was a short dance followed by couples running off to do unspeakable things with each other more privately. Anna went stag and ended up going home with one of the lesser-known young men in the class, though she thought it was fun and exciting at the time.

"You two looked so great." Anna paused on a big picture of Logan and Melanie. "I was so jealous of her, but you were good together."

"We tried to be." Talking about Melanie had been hard for him even before they left Earth, and it was never something he was going to do by choice, but she did look happy in the pictures from prom. He tried to remember her like that, the way she had asked to be remembered in her note. "I've got the rest of our school stuff around here somewhere. I'm pretty sure I had that stuff in a box before we even graduated. Aside from the jacket, of course." He and Liam had both worn their jackets for months even after graduation, since they wanted to let go of the schoolwork, but didn't want to let go of the friendships and the feeling of freedom and fewer responsibilities.

"It looked comfy and inviting." She said to defend herself, but she got up from the bed and shrugged it off to hand it back to him. "I'm sorry if it smells kind of girly. I found my favorite perfume and put it on before I found the jacket. Now it's kind of been trapping it in." She replied with a nervous laugh, since they both could smell the perfume as soon as she took off the jacket. "I didn't even get to the closet where our clothes are."

He held it in the air between them after she handed it back to him. He wanted to give it back and tell her she could keep it, but he kept his mouth shut and left it on the side of the bed. The house robots would dust it or put a plastic sheet over it or something. He couldn't bring himself to care. No robot would be able to remove the feel of Anna from the room, especially with her perfume infusing everything.

"I tasked one of the lift carts on the way here, but it has to come from storage at the other end of the estate. You know how slow those things move. I figured we'd both have at least a couple loads of things we need to take down." He looked over the room with a sigh, trying to decide where to start. All thought of what was useful or practical was difficult to keep in mind when faced with an entire room's worth of childhood whimsy.

Anna nodded and stepped inside the closet so she wouldn't have to look at Logan any longer. She looked at their things, hanging as they had left them, but dusted by robots, as though no time had passed. She ran her hands along his clothes, along the clothes he wore to their wedding, and she pulled a sleeve closer to her so she could smell it. His aftershave lingered just a little bit. Anna was fighting tears again, but she turned to her side before Logan could see her. She ran her hands over her own clothes, her wedding dress, and instead of crying she yanked it off the hanger and tossed it out of the closet.

It hit him on the way out, and he stood there for a moment as if it had injured him. He stared down at it with memories pouring through him. Eventually he had to close his eyes and push through the memories to step into the closet and take in the sight of his things.

"Well," his voice sounded somber and dry, but it almost always did in recent days, "I've always heard it said that you should pick a wedding dress by how it looks on the floor, since that's where it belongs anyway."

"I hate this. I hate it that all of these memories feel tainted because of the Consortium." She was crying again and now she was sitting on the floor with clothing she had pulled down off the hangers in anger. "They ruined this. All of it. Just because they wanted to fuck around with people. With us." She had her hand on lingerie that was given to her as wedding gifts and she threw it all out of the closet. She wanted to burn it. "I hate this."

He stood by his clothing with his head bowed, hanging on by jackets and t-shirts that felt familiar the way a life in a book felt familiar, not a life he himself had lived. "They can ruin it, but they can't change it." He eventually said through his own sighs. He wouldn't cry over the past, but he would let it hurt. Not like he had any other option.

"I thought in the beginning they would try to make us hate each other. Try to miscommunicate things, play us off against each other, drive us apart somehow. But they never did. It took me a long time to figure out why. It hurts more this way. And that's what they wanted. To make sure they got their own way by the most painful method possible."

"They still drove us apart." Anna finally pushed herself back up, since she didn't want to sit there and cry in his closet. "You were my best friend. And I might as well have been dead to you, after everything happened. Even after Lynnette was born . . . it should have been happy. And it felt sad."

"Just because they're going to be torn." He shook his head, since he wouldn't allow the essence of their daughter's existence to become a grief for them. "No matter what we do or how well the four of us get along, all four of our kids are going to feel conflicted their entire childhoods. Let alone all the boys and girls with divorced and hateful parents back home that we've been dealing with. That's what the Consortium created, a mess of chaos where there should be living families."

"We were supposed to be a family." She said so softly she could barely hear herself, but the silence in the closet was deafening. "I lost you up there. I lost the one person I've loved longer than anyone or anything else." Anna shook her head and found an empty box, ironically, a box she'd brought with her into the Bickford house with her things. She started with the clothes that were already folded, grabbed them, and threw them into the box.

"You're never gonna lose me." He didn't start packing when she did, as he looked at the clothes in front of him and the boxes filled with childhood memorabilia that no longer mattered. "Even the Consortium can't do that."

"They already did." She shook her head and tossed more clothes into the box before she abandoned the task to get out of the closet and back into the bedroom. Instead of looking around, she went to one of the shelves attached to the wall where there were wine bottles lined up. Leftover wine from their wedding. They wanted to keep a few bottles for their first anniversary. Fifth. Tenth. They would never get there, so there was no sense in leaving the wine. Anna dug around in the shallow drawer of his bedside table. There was a pocket knife with the tool she needed to get the bottle open.

It was so quiet in the room he heard the knife click open, and he started to step out of the room just as she managed to dig into the bottle and pop the cork. She always had been stronger than she looked. One of many things he had always loved about her.

He looked past her at the line of bottles and felt himself getting angrier. Everything in the house was a representation of things they would never have. It had been a long time since he'd had a drink. It was too limited a commodity in the mountains for him to keep it for himself. But he was damn sure going to drink the wine they'd been given for their wedding. "I don't think I have any glasses up here. But save me some of that."

Anna was about to tell him to grab his own bottle, but instead she took an angry gulp and held out the bottle to him. Once he took it, she backed to a wall and then slid down to the floor. "Who needs a glass anyway. I'm going to drink the whole fucking thing."

He went to join her against the wall as he took his own drink. "I already had your first anniversary present." He said afterward, taking a second drink before handing it back to her. "I got it set up before we left Earth, while you were over at your parents' getting packed. Liam and Larissa were going to handle all the details for me, get it arranged so that they could ship it up to me before we took off. I was going to take it across the universe and give it to you on our way to Eleusis." He shook his head as he thought about it. "It was a collection of pictures of us, a dust collector to sit on a coffee table or a mantel someday and hold onto our whole timeline, from being kids in Mr. Unruh's class all the way to our wedding pictures."

Anna didn't know if she should laugh or cry again, so she took another drink before she handed the bottle back to him, though she was taking it more than handing it back. God, she needed to be drunk. "Is . . . is it still here?"

"I don't know if they actually had it made after we left." He looked around the room as if for the first time, then saw a box just above his head on a shelf and took it down. He sighed when he saw the return address, since it was the place he knew he would have ordered the prints from, but the box had never been opened. After a moment of hesitation and another swig from the bottle, he took off his wedding ring and used it to cut through the shipping tape. "Yeah. It's here." He put the ring back on slowly and pulled the small book out of the box, tossing the box itself aside on the floor as he handed it over.

Anna took it from him slowly and flipped it open to a picture of the two of them, not even five years old, swimming in a small inflatable pool with Liam and a few of their other friends. Anna was topless, and it made her laugh. Five-year-olds didn't really care, and it wasn't as though a five-year-old Anna was trying to impress the boys. She was trying to be like them. "My mom bought me a new bathing suit for that party. Just to try and convince me to keep my top on. I wanted to be like the boys."

"She should've stuck with a one-piece if she wanted you to keep your top on. Even then, I think you'd have found a way around." He chuckled along with her, especially at a few of the other pictures included. One was of the whole group of them, including Ben and Larissa and Cory, on top of a combine Logan's father was driving. It had only gone a few hundred meters and hadn't actually done anything, but it had been a magnificent ride. "Pretty sure I pissed my pants that day for the first time in a few years."

Anna laughed again as she looked at the picture and ran her finger over it slowly in the plastic. "You look a lot like your father. I didn't really realize that. It's been so long since I saw a picture." She reached out for the wine and took another gulp. There were a few pictures of them fishing, one where Anna was proudly holding the largest catch and was halfway covered in mud. She had really loved doing all of the tough and dirty things until she turned into a young woman. Priorities changed after she got boobs. "My mom made the best fish fry in the world. I miss her food."

"She did, you're right. God, I had forgotten about that. Mom always kept somebody on hand as a cook." Their family cook had been one of the few people the three siblings had been able to trust in the years after their parents had died, and Logan was suddenly sad that he didn't even have a picture of the woman or others who had helped them over the years. The picture of Anna was too good to resist smiling at, though, and the next one was no better. It was hard, at first glance, to tell if it was Liam or Logan in the picture hiking by the lake they had just left hours before, but Logan knew the look in his own eyes. Liam had always been more lighthearted. Logan was taking the hike seriously, standing above everyone else on a rock with Anna nearby as his partner in crime. "Trying to get as far away from camp as possible before one of us got a call. I still say we could've gotten farther if Ben hadn't been dragging behind the whole damn time."

"Ben didn't like the outdoors until I found a different hobby. He hated that I was better at a lot of things." She shrugged, but she was sure Ben was over it by now. She hoped he was, anyway. The wine was getting lower and lower, but she refused to stop drinking. "We did so many things together. After my first kiss when I was nine, my mom told me not to fall in love, because she had high hopes that I would marry you. She said you were such a gentleman and a well-mannered boy and she loved you. Even when we were little. I told her it would be like marrying Ben, and that you were terrible at throwing a baseball."

"I still suck at throwing things. Unless I'm just trying to break them. Then I'm incredibly talented." He took another long swig, but left the last of it for her. "And my parents never got around to telling me anything about who to marry. But my lawyer wanted me to marry you almost as soon as my parents died. Not right then, but get engaged or something. That was when I fired him. I thought he was just trying to lock down any kind of strings to make the place look more secure, and besides, I think you were teasing Martin Edwards around that time. I didn't think you'd ever go with me."

"Why would a lawyer tell you to marry me? My family is poor. Well, not poor. But certainly not rich." Anna finished off the wine and turned her attention back to the photos. "I loved you even when I told my mom I didn't. I always wanted to come over here to see you. Not Liam. He's way too annoying. Though he did try to kiss me once at a party, did I tell you that? Totally grabbed my boob and told me he didn't see what the big deal was."

He was beginning to feel the effects of the wine, and looking over the pictures made it a little too easy to feel the same as he had back when the pictures had been taken, when he first started noticing Anna himself. "That son of a bitch." He clearly hadn't known that before, and looked incredibly affronted by it. He also looked down at her chest without making any apology for it or hiding the fact that he was looking. "Your tits have always been a big deal. He should have fucking known better."

"As soon as they started coming in, I knew they were going to be a big deal." She added with another laugh as she looked down. Somewhere in her mind she wondered if she should chastise him for looking at her, but it wasn't as though he didn't know her breasts intimately already. "I have great tits. He doesn't know jack shit. Also, in dodging his kiss, he kissed me on the ear. It was gross."

Logan rolled his eyes, but he was laughing anyway. "He was worthless with women until he was about seventeen. Seriously hopeless case. They loved to go out and have fun with him, that was fine enough, but they couldn't stand to stick around him for longer than that. And if he kissed you on the ear and thought these tits of yours weren't worth sticking around for and making a big deal out of, then he was an idiot. Complete idiot."

"You never were, though. Never an idiot." She stared into his eyes for a moment and she found that she desperately wanted to kiss him, but she didn't allow herself to move in closer. "More wine?"

"Yes." He agreed almost desperately. "More wine is necessary."

"There goes our one year . . ." She got up and jumped up clumsily to grab another bottle. "Here's to the five years that will never exist." She grabbed his pocket knife again and uncorked the bottle. Anna took a gulp and was glad that she could enjoy the flavor now that she was drunk enough not to care about anything else.

When she handed it off to him, she picked up the pictures. She flipped through years and years of memories until it got to their wedding. Anna stared at the two of them kissing at the ceremony, getting cake in her face, and when he easily yanked the garter off her thigh with his teeth. "If we had married earlier, do you think we would have lasted?"

"Yes." He said without any hesitation whatsoever, almost pre-empting the end of her question. Clearly it wasn't the first time he had wondered about it himself. "I think if we had gotten married sooner, both our lives would've been . . . incredibly different. We'd have three kids by now at least, Mel would've married Jake Harvey, or her parents would've convinced her to marry an older man for his money and the security. Something that wouldn't have gotten her killed, either way."

He shook his head. "Neither of us would have applied to Eleusis, neither of us would've ever had any reason to leave the planet. And right now we'd be packing up our family to go to the mountains to join up with the rest of the rebels or doing something else to try and support them however we could. Because in this life or any other, there's no way we would've just laid down and put up with their bullshit."

"I'm sure as hell not going to sit back and do nothing." Anna looked at the pictures closely, at the happy people in them, and she wondered what she would say to them if she could go back and tell them something. "I'm sorry I was so stubborn and I never told you how I felt about you. I fucked around and experimented because I was stupid. I wanted you but I wanted you to want me first. It was so stupid." She knew she was saying stupid a lot, but it was how she felt about everything. "You're home to me, Logan."

Logan knew what she was telling him, they had confessed everything to each other long since, but it was a different kind of regret on the other side of everything they had been through.

"Before all this, I could regret being stubborn and let it go." He looked back up at her with eyes that were only slightly glassy with the buzz of the wine, not nearly drunk enough to be completely off his judgment. Not nearly as drunk as he wished he was. "Because I could look back at the years we hadn't been together and feel angry at myself and then turn over and fuck you in the middle of the night and no longer give a shit about anything that had happened before then. Because you were right there. Because you would always be there for me to make up lost time with. And I wanted to make up for all the time we lost. I wanted to make up for being an arrogant asshole who was convinced the meaning of life was showing the world you could do things on your own. That you didn't have to rely on your best friend who you were also in love with just to look like you had your shit together. I wanted to make up for all that. Forever."

Anna stared at him, again on the edge of tears, but she reached out to take his hand. Anna entwined her fingers with his and held tightly to his large hand. "I miss you. I still love you. We never figured out closure. How are we going to figure that out?"

"I don't know." He didn't resist holding her hand, and tugged her back down to the floor, since she never sat back down after getting the second bottle of wine. "I've started believing that nothing ever closes. That would be too easy. That would mean things have some kind of magical beginning and middle and end and that's not life. Not even if people die, depending on the person." He shrugged and sighed again, leaning his head back against the shelf. "We love each other. That's as much a part of who I am as anything else. More, sometimes. It's never going to be untrue. You can't close something that's true."

Anna was sitting too close to him, since she could feel his body pressed against the side of hers, but she didn't move away. "You still love me?"

He didn't seem to respond to the fact that she sounded so incredulous, but he didn't move away either. "You shouldn't be this surprised. You know me better than that."

"I thought I did. But I never thought I'd wonder about so many things about you." Anna stared at their joined hands and wondered, for the first time in a long time, if she had made the wrong decision picking Orion. She loved Orion. Adored him, even, but they also had their problems. Everyone had their problems, but not everyone had been locked into a unit and forced to make a decision about a spouse under duress. Anna looked over at Logan before she rested her head on his shoulder and continued to hold his hand. "We never got to make our own decision."

He very nearly let out a whimper at how good it felt to have Anna close again, and he leaned his face against her hair. "No, we didn't." He agreed, feeling a little relieved to finally say out loud what he had been thinking for a long time. "We were thrown in with people who hated what happened every bit as much as we did, who it was impossible to hate and impossible not to love, under the circumstances. But there was nothing free about what happened. I love Mercury, and I love our children. But they're the product of a trap. Our whole lives right now are the product of one big fucking trap we walked right into because we thought we were doing the right thing."

"I still don't know what the right thing is. For anything." Anna shivered as he pressed his face into her hair, and lifted up her head and turned toward him. He was so close. Anna looked into his familiar eyes, even though the man behind them had changed more than she had changed. Anna looked down at his lips before she looked into his eyes again.

Was it the right decision to be with Orion when she still felt deeply for the man she had married first?

"Logan." She said softly before she leaned in and kissed him.

Chaos twisted his insides into knots within knots at the first brush of her lips against his, conflicting responsibilities and obligations tearing at him from all sides until his heart was spinning under the single touch. But the longer she kissed him, the longer he failed to resist and he kissed her back.

He felt the entire world fall silent by degrees. Even his own thoughts had the volume turned down on them, the unheard sound of the world outside the two of them fading away to a dim awareness and then to absolute nothingness under the force of the touch.

It was a silence he hadn't experienced for a long, long time, and he deepened the kiss between them, wanting the silence to wrap around them both and drive out every other force in the universe. When he was kissing her, nothing else existed. When Anna was nearby, it was impossible for anything else in the world to matter, to convince him that it required his attention. All they had was the present, and there was nothing inside him but the instinct to hold onto it, to claim it as his own for as long as he could.

His hands moved down over her to her waist to pull her in on top of him as he kissed her hard, as if he could make the Earth stand still with the force between the two of them.

A moan escaped Anna's lips against his as he pulled her into his lap. She ran her fingers through his hair and gripped the back of his neck with an urgency of need that she could not ignore. Her whole body felt magnetized to his, and her kisses were the same way. "I miss you so much." She replied quickly between kisses, since kissing him felt right when she wondered if it was supposed to feel wrong.

He needed . . . he didn't know what he needed, but he knew Anna had it. The book nearby was an extension of his thoughts, emptied of everything he was, everything that he had become, just for a moment, so in his mind he could be the person he could have been, just for a little while.

The man who brought Anna back to that room and who threw her wedding dress on the floor, exactly where it was now. The man who had watched with a grin as she brought in all her things in boxes, just as they were now. The man who had locked his arms around her and half-carried her across the room, the man who drove her down on the bed with his weight on top of her as if he'd just taken her prisoner for all time.

He thought it, he remembered it, he felt it, he was that man again, dropping her onto the bed beside his letterman jacket and kissing the life out of her as he felt her squirm beneath him. He needed it back. He needed it all back.

She needed him just as much as he needed her, and she was not going to stop until she had him. *This* man was *her* Logan. The Logan who she had flirted with endlessly for years, and who gave her crooked, warm smiles, who looked at her with an intensity that took her breath away.

Anna's thoughts had started to get fuzzy with the wine, but they were clear and sharp as she looked up at Logan between their frenzied, intense kisses. This was the life they were supposed to have. This was the way things were supposed to be, the two of them against the world, as they had so often been their entire lives.

She clawed at his back against his shirt until she forcibly pulled it up and over his head and tossed it over by the discarded wedding dress. He was bare chested and hovering over her as her chest heaved with deep breaths. His body was solid, his chest was rigid and perfect, and she paused in her kisses to run her fingers over each line of his chest. Her lungs constricted with how much she had missed him. "You're still so gorgeous."

He had hesitated in his kisses for the briefest of moments as she touched him, the sensation of her hands on his bare skin enough to sharpen his world into its own kind of razor focus, but it only encouraged him. He pulled her up forcibly on the bed to rip her shirt off over her head, some of the fabric actually tearing in the process because it got in his way. Her bra didn't stand a chance either, and he nearly tore it from her shoulders just for existing before he had her on her back again with his lips burning a trail down her chest. "Liam was a fucking idiot." He growled against her tender skin as his hands explored her in turn, moving frantically as if they couldn't touch enough of her at once.

Another moan escaped Anna's lips and her back arched at the sensation of his lips exploring her skin. She forgot, temporarily, what it felt like to have his facial hair teasing her and driving her wild. It felt incredible. He felt incredible. "God, I love you and that fucking beard." She said as he teased around one nipple. "And Liam is *still* a fucking idiot."

He was a starving man at a feast the way he explored her, and while his tongue teased her in all the ways he knew would drive her wild, his hands were not idle in ripping her rough pants from her waist. He knew they annoyed her to begin with, and they were another part of the life that he wasn't thinking about. One more thing he wasn't interested in being a part of with Anna warm and gorgeous beneath him. They needed to get back to the life they had wanted, the world they had wanted to create for each other. Somewhere warm and alive, not cold and harsh like the places they had been forced to inhabit for what felt like lifetimes.

Anna was left in just her thin underwear, but she wasn't going to let him strip her bare without taking him with her. She attacked his belt and pants, kicking them off the bed before she teasingly felt along his boxers. Anna grazed his groin and groaned when she felt how hard he already was. "God, Logan . . ."

It had never taken him long to need her, and especially with her hand on him, that moment was no exception. He needed the silence of a world that made sense, and Anna was the only part of his entire life that ever had. It was their bedroom, and the time they spent away from it had been someone else's life, someone else's choices. How could they have ever done anything but build a life for each other? How could he have ever been anywhere but there with her? He rolled to the side to let her handle him as she pleased, but his kisses returned to take her lips as he handled her the same way, muscled fingers teasing her through the scanty fabric of her underwear.

Anna whimpered at the feeling of Logan's fingers attacking her, so she desperately tugged his boxers down and away so she could stroke the length of him. It was all so very different than being with Orion, but she couldn't even think about Orion. Logan consumed her every thought in the moment. "Oh, babe . . ."

Somewhere in the back of Logan's mind, a catalog was rolling off to list all the things he was not at that moment. The way Anna handled him, the way she took without asking, without needing to ask, the way she took because she wanted and not because he told her she was permitted to want, drove him crazy. He knew there was more behind the list, more substance behind all the things that he wasn't, but he couldn't feel anything but Anna. He remembered everything about how she felt, how she moved, how her moans echoed in his mind and stirred up the living ghosts of every other time he had so much as imagined her against him. There were entire worlds of her in his mind for him to get lost in, and every racing beat of their hearts pushed those worlds closer to the surface of reality.

"Anna . . ." He breathed into her hair, his warm breath and the heat of his skin was the only defense she had against the slight chill of the new spring around them in the abandoned wing.

Hearing his voice that way, heavy with passion and desire, made Anna crazier. She was desperate to get out of her own underwear, and once she did, she wrapped both of her legs around him to slide her heat as close to him as she could get just to tease him. "I need you, Logan. I want you. I want you so much." She gasped between touches and kisses, since she really was undone with the heat between them.

As soon as she had him inside her, Logan wished he could make the world stop. He wished he could see his entire life flash in front of his eyes in that moment and then blink it away and be done with it, without regrets. His arms moved over her back to clasp her against him, since gravity wasn't enough. His kisses and his movements against her were slow, relishing the moment and only stoking the urgency of the fire between them, but he had no desire for things to be over in a flash. He wanted to drive her insane and feel the world turn bright again inside her for as long as he could make it last.

Anna thought a lot about their wedding and the bliss that followed, even though the time had been short in comparison to everything else. She was perfectly happy in the time she was married to Logan before they went up into space. She was happy in a way that held nothing back, and that lack of complexity she had only found with Logan. Even being with Orion came with its own web of troubles. Being with Logan again felt good, it felt right, and she clung to him and the moment between them.

Anna slowed herself, mostly because she wanted to make love to the man she had loved for so long. Anna kissed along his neck, his jaw, his cheeks, and his lips, slow and steady and heated. "I love you." She said against his lips, because she did. She still loved him, and she didn't know if she would ever be capable of not loving Logan Bickford.

"I love you." It was the only thing he could say in return. The only thing that was worth saying. The only thing that mattered in any language. Saying it, hearing it, feeling it, showing it, was life. Anything else was death. His hands moved over her body to take in everything about the feel of her, losing himself in her. He never wanted to find himself again if he could stay there, never wanted to come back from being lost. She was too right, too perfect, and as his hips dug into hers and her moans escalated, it was music to the soul he sometimes doubted he even had. If he had one, it belonged to her. It belonged to *them*.

Anna didn't know how much more she could take after the tension continued to build bit by bit, and her grip on him tightened as the pleasure coiled and teased her. She shuddered and trembled as she tried to fight it off, but as soon as he increased his pace just a little bit, Anna was gone. She was hit with a powerful wave of pleasure as he drove into her, crying out his name over and over. It felt amazing. Perfect.

It was all he could do to keep from coming apart himself at that feeling, but he wanted to savor her too much to let go quickly. His kisses moved over her throat as she cried out beneath him, as if he could inhale the force of her pleasure and keep it for himself. She was his, if only for a moment, as completely as another person could be someone else's. His hands moved over her legs to savor the feel of her wrapped tightly around his waist as she invited even more of him. He wanted all of her. "Come and get some more." He said breathlessly against her neck, his pace showing her no mercy as he rocked against her.

Anna whimpered as he commanded her body and her mind, and she wanted more. She wanted so much more. "I want it all. Every . . . I want . . ." Her body trembled, though she could feel he was going to push her over again. She wanted it. So badly. "Fuck, so fast . . . it's coming so fast . . ."

Once he had her where he wanted her, it was pure instinct to keep her there, wrapped in a world where they were the only things that mattered until even time was irrelevant. During a single, short respite, he moved to his back on the disarrayed sheets, only to continue his assault on her in different ways. He wanted to see her shake, wanted to see her driving herself down against him the way she had when the world made sense.

Anna adapted all too easily however he wanted to move her, take her, and fuck her. She was glad to be on top, though, as it gave her more control. Anna gripped tightly to his shoulders and tossed her hair, though it still draped around her face as she rode him as hard as she could. "Fuck." She hissed as he hit deeper inside of her, and she didn't have time to think about anything else before she was climaxing again.

Even when they first began to be honest with each other about their feelings, Logan already knew Anna would be the best thing that ever happened to him, the best he'd ever had, simply the best in every aspect of his life. He had never once been wrong, and he'd never once been able to wrap his head around just how good she was at everything she did. He knew as soon as he was on his back it had been a mistake in his strategy, but he couldn't bring himself to regret it. She was going to send him over his own edge in a matter of moments, but it didn't matter, because he would be there with her, the way it was supposed to be, the way it should have been in the first place.

The world was . . .

The world turned to something peaceful and powerful as he lost himself in her, crying out as his hands clutched at her in involuntary spasms to lock her against him.

Everything in the world was right. Every single thing that had ever been and would ever be was right, in that single moment.

Anna didn't settle until she was sure she had pulled every bit of tension out of his body and turned it into pleasure. Her body was covered in sweat, her hair sticking to her face, but she gladly rested her head against his shoulder and kissed along his jawline.

Even his sweat tasted good on her tongue, salty and perfect. She kept her hands moving over his perfect chest and torso, wanting to memorize every touch.

"That was amazing." She said softly as she ran her fingers across his lips. "I want to do that all day long."

It was a long time before Logan could talk again, but eventually he reached up an exhausted hand to caress her sides, massaging her back as she clung to him. "All day and all night too. And all the next day. And the next. And the next."

"And the next and next." She added with a warm smile before she gave him a heated kiss. It felt so right in that room, together, as they should have been. Anna was doing her best not to think about anything other than Logan and the amazing feeling of being together. "I don't know if we can hold a candle to our wedding night. I don't think I slept more than an hour that whole night. You were insatiable."

"I had proper motivation." He said in his own defense, his hands moving roughly over her ass to draw another groan from both of them. "When we left here, I was actually looking forward to being stuck in a spaceship with you for a few years on the way to Eleusis. Nothing to do but lie around and fuck my gorgeous wife for months and months on end? Yeah, fucking sign me up."

Anna laughed, though it was a little more subdued than her previous laughs, just at the mention of Eleusis. She ran her fingertips over his forehead and searched his eyes as soon as his gaze met hers. "I'm not that drunk." She assured him, since she knew the decision she'd made, though she didn't want to think about what it meant for the future or what repercussions would come from their actions. Anna wasn't ready to feel conflicted again. "I want more of this. More of you. It feels too right not to want more."

"It does." He agreed completely, since it didn't just feel right, it felt like a dream that he had stepped back into after too long being awake. "I want more too. Not just this, but more of you. All of you."

She nodded and wiggled her hips a little just to remind him what all of her meant. "I want all of you too." Anna stole a few more kisses from his lips. "We're an unstoppable team. Between us, we made a rebellion happen. We saved lives. We're the unstoppable partners, and amazing lovers. I want more."

"I've never known how not to want you." He reached up to

brush her hair off to one side of her head so he could see her clearly. "Right now, I just want more of this. Not more of what's going to happen when we leave this room, just more of this."

"I'm not going anywhere." She had no desire to be anywhere else. Not right now. The door was closed, at least, and she doubted anyone would come looking for them. Not in their place. Anna grabbed his hand after he brushed away her hair, and she kissed along his palm. "Nothing exists outside of this room right now. You're mine, I'm yours, and that's all that exists here."

* * * * *

By the time either of them finally came to any kind of exhausted rest, Logan could hardly move and couldn't have cared less. His phone had fallen out of his pocket nearby where Anna had thrown his pants, and he could see a few messages that had come through, not from Mercury, but from back in the mountains. It had been well over a couple of hours, and he knew better than to think they would be left alone forever.

"We have to go." He said more reluctantly than he thought he had said anything in his entire life.

Anna groaned and curled into Logan even more, since she didn't want to go. She didn't want to move from the bed or his side, she just wanted to stay there cocooned in his warmth and strength. "I don't want to." She mumbled into his skin, and her hands didn't move from touching him. "I want to stay here."

"So do I." He said almost breathlessly, since he was just as incapable of convincing himself to move as she was. "But we can't." He had to force himself to say it, even if it was true. "Our life now is out there. This is the life we didn't get to live. The one we have is out on the other side of the house."

Anna took a deep breath as she allowed herself to think about reality again, the reality that was outside the door that kept them in their own little world. The reality that her name was not Anna Bickford. It was Anna Al-Jabbar. The reality that he wasn't her husband, he belonged to Mercury.

Anna clung even more to Logan as she thought about how she felt, and what she could do. "We have choices on Earth." She eventually replied softly into his skin. "I know we don't want to hurt them, but if we still want this . . ." Anna ran her hand over his skin, savoring every second she could touch him. "We can have it." Anna moved so she could kiss his lips again, and she did so with a slow heat, but passion nonetheless.

"They deserve to know the truth." She finally replied cautiously, since it wasn't all that she wanted to say. "But maybe we should wait to tell them until we're sure if we want more of this or if . . . you . . . we just need to get this out of our system." Anna didn't want to sneak around, but she also didn't want to upend everything until she knew exactly what she was going to have to tell Orion. She also didn't think that she just wanted this to happen once, and if anything, she definitely hadn't gotten Logan out of her system. It didn't feel like saying goodbye.

"This isn't something that's going to change for me." He answered as he shook his head, but it didn't sound like he was fully contradicting her. "But what's outside isn't going to change either. We can change what we do from here, not what we've already done." That included the hour of the past they had just re-lived with each other, but it also included the spouses and children that were waiting for them out in the rest of the house. "You're right, though. This needs . . . time."

Anna nodded and sighed as she kissed him once more. "What I do know is that I want to make a decision that's free of being in a trap." She ran her hand down the side of his face slowly. "I love you. I love him. But I want to make a decision on my own. I think we both deserve that."

"We do." He was conflicted about a lot of things in his life, but he wasn't conflicted about that. They did deserve a choice, and they did deserve a chance. "We deserve a lot of things, and I'm going to fight for every fucking one of them." He rested his forehead against hers, as his hands moved lazily over her back, trying in vain to hold the weight of the rest of the world at bay.

Anna couldn't stop kissing him as soon as he brought his face closer, since she was not going to pass the chance of kissing or touching him when she had the option. "No matter what happens, I'm on your side, Logan Bickford." She replied against his lips. "You have a lot of people on your side, but me more than most. We are an powerful force together."

He treasured every kiss they shared, every moment of borrowed time they got to spend together, but he treasured that knowledge more than anything. Logan looked back into her eyes so he could see the dedication there, the ferocity for which he had always loved her.

"Never think you've lost me." It was something between pleading and commanding, the tone gentle but firm. "No matter what happens, no matter where we go or what we do from here, you will never lose me as someone who is on your side. Wherever I am, I will be fighting for you, and for our future. Until the Consortium rips this heart from my chest, it's yours. Always."

She stared at the intensity in his gaze, and Anna nodded as she took a deep breath. It was easier to have to leave the room knowing that even if they didn't choose to be together, they would still be important to each other. "I won't doubt you again. I promise." She said sincerely, since she wanted him to know she trusted and believed in him no matter what. "I was angry before. And hurt. It kept me away, it caused a wedge. I don't want that, even if we don't . . . stay this way." Anna didn't want to think about not being with Logan again, even though Orion had an equal share of her heart and her love. "I will always fight for you too. And our daughter. And our future."

He kissed her for what felt like the last time all over again, but then stood up with her still in his arms, and set her down slowly, the world feeling colder with the first smack of space between their bodies. Everything seemed heavier when he wasn't holding her, everything seemed just . . . wrong. But it also felt familiar. The weight of it, the complication of it, was something to which he had long since permitted himself to grow accustomed, but it was all much heavier, much more complicated, after having stepped away from it, even for a little while. "I'm . . . going to shower off. And see if some of my old jeans still fit."

Anna nodded and watched him walk off, but she couldn't let him shower alone, not when it was *their* shower, and so she joined him and stayed with him until the water started to turn cold. Once they were out and dried off, Anna tried not to be weighed down by all the things she knew she should. Instead, she happily tried on her clothes and found they fit. "Who says I have a new-mom ass? It still fits into these jeans!" She twirled around in her bra and her well-loved jeans, ripped in all places. "It's those stupid mountain runs. I hate running in the mountains."

"So do I. Must be why I don't do it." He said with a weak smile, but it did feel good to be back in his own clothes after so long in Initiative uniforms or secondhand clothes. If anything, he had actually put on muscle over the course of their time away from home, and his worn-in jeans and simple t-shirts just looked that much better on him. The jacket he pulled on over his shirt was tight across the chest where it never had been before, so he left it hanging loose, since it was still comfortable. "Good thing I've got the one Larissa and Cory made me downstairs. This one looks like it's close to being done."

"But you still look so sexy in it." She said with a smile as she went digging for a shirt. Most of her clothes other than her t-shirts were definitely more scandalous than uniforms. "Did I really dress this . . . slutty? I mean, these are really asking for it." She replied with a laugh as she pulled a red sweater over her head, the V in the front cut especially low.

He laughed at the pieces of her wardrobe that scandalized her in a world after having children. "You were never asking for it so much as offering freely. And nobody minded." He looked at her in the sweater and reached out when she got close enough to run his hand all the way down from her neck to where the V ended just past the line of her partly-exposed bra. It was strange to see her in the clothes they had worn on Earth, comfortable and themselves for the first time in a long time.

"I had some friends who decided they would keep tabs on the seasons by how short your shorts were. Right about now is when you'd be breaking out your warmup shorts and you wouldn't stop wearing them until about November."

Anna laughed, though her cheeks flushed as he reached out and ran his hand down her cleavage. She liked it. A lot. "I *was* offering it freely. Often." She met his eyes and gave him a smirk. "Not anymore. Only the select get a taste. But I can wear the shorts if you want me to."

"The jeans do your ass just as much justice." He assured her, since the jeans and the sweater made more sense given the lingering chill outside. "But take the shorts. You know, for running in the mountains." He knew that was something Orion did with her, so it was very much a mixed reference for them both. But him telling her what to do felt like a shadow of his relationship with Mercury, and that mixed in uncomfortable ways in his mind.

"Fine." She smirked as she added shorts to the couple bags of clothes she had collected for herself. "Only because you asked nicely." Anna teased him afterward. He had explained to her the nature of his relationship with Mercury, even if Orion didn't know about it. If he wanted to tell her what he wanted her to do, she didn't mind, but Anna was still herself. Complying would still come with her own sarcastic and teasing edge. "We'll have to come back. I didn't get that much packing done."

"Neither of us did." He picked up the backpack he had stuffed full of some of his clothes, and pulled it over his shoulder with a sigh. "I'll bring the yearbook. Let everybody downstairs get in a good laugh at us." He picked the book up off the shelf and shook his head. "We'll get the rest of our stuff tomorrow."

Anna stepped up next to him as he went to the door, and she reached out for his hand and slid her hand into his for one more moment. She pulled him into a kiss as soon as she held his hand, and she nibbled on his bottom lip afterward. "I know I'll be thinking about you. I miss you already."

"I've been missing you since we got to Nine." He said quietly, since the closer they got to the rest of their lives, the more of a betrayal every word sounded like, even if it felt more like a return. He didn't know what to think anymore, especially with Anna still hanging onto him the way she was. He ran one hand up over her body slowly one final time, as if to take in the memory of her body by touch. "And I'm gonna keep on missing you."

"I'll be here tomorrow." She promised, even though she wasn't sure if he would show up or avoid the place entirely knowing she would be there. Anna stole one more kiss. "I love you, Logan." She breathed softly before she watched him open the door slowly. Reality was on the other side. Guilt. The pain of being torn between two loves all over again. But this time they had the opportunity to make a final choice, and they both needed it. Even if it would be painful.

9

Orion couldn't believe his eyes as they sat near a window of the living room where they had been placed for temporary housing. They had been there a little over two hours, and already there was a parking lot of people showing up in front of the hangar, mostly folks who had empty semi trucks or other massive conveyances to transport people and goods, all of them lining up to await the results of the entire district's galvanized efforts.

"Unfuckingbelievable." Orion shook his head for the hundredth time as he watched people gather, talk, sometimes take off again at impossibly dangerous speeds to rip away along the endless roads. "These people are insane. There's a clinical diagnosis you could make here." He glanced back at Mercury. "I mean, I know it's not your area, but still, insane."

"What part of it is insane, exactly?" Mercury asked with a laugh at Orion's perpetual shock. They were doing pretty well, managing the four kids between them, especially without any help. Soon, though, they would have to attempt to get the four babies down for a nap, and that was likely to present a challenge. "The amount of people or how quickly they work?"

"Both. They always talked about this place like it was completely abandoned for hours and hours in every direction. But there were at least three hundred people at that campsite, and there's easily fifty trailers out there already. I didn't know there were that many people out here with this much . . ."

"You can call it junk. It won't hurt our feelings." Liam laughed as he watched the work outside, which Rachel had already taken charge of. The woman was better than he deserved most of the time and it was a pleasure to watch her lead. "A lot of those trailers have probably been sitting around for at least a decade without seeing much use. But we'll give them all a once-over before we leave, to make sure they at least survive the trip."

It was strange to see someone who looked so much like Logan

without it actually being Logan. He sounded like Logan. He was definitely *not* Logan, though. Nothing about his manners or speech were even close to Logan. "You're very efficient. I think it's great." Mercury complimented with a smile.

"Yeah, well, we've got a long history out here of moving fast when somebody pisses us off." He chuckled, and there was almost nothing of Logan in the sound whatsoever. It was too lighthearted, too casual, for anything she had ever heard from her husband. "Excuse me, I've gotta go make some more calls. I'll be right down the wing if you need anything." He gave them both a nod and headed off with his hands in his pockets and a spring in his step.

"That guy is entirely too happy." Orion pointed after him as he left and went to round up Lynnette as she attempted to roll to her death off the pillow.

"He looks like Logan, but they are not even close to similar. Except in their determination." Mercury looked toward the doorway and then turned toward the children again. "I'm surprised he talked to us, really." Mercury wanted to sit there with Orion, but she knew she really should befriend Logan's twin. "We have lived such different lives than they have."

"I think he was surprised we knew how to take care of the kids." Orion said with a laugh, since the way Liam looked at them was less hateful and more pure comedy than most of the rest of the midlanders and their reactions. "Like we shouldn't know how to deal with tiny humans because we're not actually human or something. If they shit, can we not wipe it up?"

"I know I have cleaned a lot of baby poop." She giggled, since she couldn't help herself. "A *lot* of baby poop. These babies are pooping machines." Mercury looked out the window again and hoisted Declan up a moment afterward. "Do you think you would have liked a life like this? On a farm?"

"Nope." Orion answered without any hesitation. "I mean, maybe, if I had been born here and this was my entire life. Fish can't exactly hate swimming, it's just what they do. But I don't . . . yeah, no, I don't think I would've enjoyed it. I would've been one of the guys I've heard Anna complain about who act like they're too good for this place and meet some girl from the cities online and move away as fast as possible. That's part of the reason I became a pilot in the first place, so I would know there's always more places I'm gonna go than where I am."

"But what if this turned into our life all of the sudden? Would you be unhappy here with Anna? This is the life she knows. The life she loves, I think." Mercury didn't know much about what Anna loved, but she took a stab at it. "She's kind of . . . all over the place. What's the term? A 'jack of all trades'?"

"I think you're looking for 'Attention Deficit,' actually." He chuckled, since he had given Anna grief for the tendency more than once. "No, if we were stuck here for some reason now, I think I could deal with it. I mean, I know exactly shit about what I'm doing, but I can drive anything that moves, no reason to think I can't figure out a combine or a tractor." He shrugged and jumped to save Leo from himself again, since the boy was trying to move faster than was prudent. "What about you? They do need doctors out here."

"It would be a lot harder here. I suppose I could relieve some of the stress from Doctor Weber but it would be hard to travel all over the place. Especially with small children. And I hope for more children, since I want a large family." She looked down at Declan and over at James before she looked at Orion. "I don't want to sacrifice being a good mother."

"Well, with a house like this, you could convert a whole fucking wing to be a clinic and still have room for about twenty nine kids. And their kids. And possibly *their* kids. And if these people can get here within forty-five minutes with a twenty-year-old bus, they can damn sure get up here if they've got a sore throat they need you to look at."

"You're right. I would probably be able to manage that. Especially in this house. It's beautiful and massive." She looked around the room for a moment before she went to scoop up James too as he started to whimper on the floor. "I can't really imagine what it would be like, living here with Logan."

"And his clone." Orion flicked a glance at the doorway, counting off on his fingers. "And his wives. All three of them. And the kids. All three of them. And whatever more he's got on the way at some point."

"That is certainly a more social atmosphere than I'm used to. Or comfortable with, really." Mercury looked at her boys again. "I'm not good at making friends or meeting people. I never will be. But I hope I'm a good wife and mother at least. I'm trying to be someone more than a doctor. Even though I miss being *just* a doctor sometimes."

"You *are* a good mother." He knew from watching the way she interacted with her boys, and he had known it since long before she'd even gotten pregnant. "And you'll keep on being a good mother no matter how many more kids you have."

"I hope so." She sat on the floor with both of her boys and she looked toward the door again. "How do you think we can help them? This is a hard time. I don't know what to do, but I'm terrible at doing nothing. I want to do something."

"I don't know. I didn't think about the fact that we would mostly be watching the kids." He looked out the window at the growing groups of people coordinating efforts on the front lawn, and jabbed a finger at the window. "Hey, there they are. Damn, I thought it was Liam and his one short brunette wife at first. But no, that's definitely Anna. Looks like they carted out some boxes and they're mixing with some old friends."

Mercury watched as Anna and Logan interacted with their old friends, Logan was shaking hands and patting backs and Anna was hugging people left and right. They were standing next to each other like they belonged together, and they looked happy and relaxed. They looked like they were in their element, greeting friends and reminiscing. Both Anna and Logan were smiling, which was another thing Mercury had a bit of a hard time with. It was hard to get Logan to smile, but here he was, smiling easily with Anna. "They look like they fit right in."

"Well, it's their world. It makes sense that they would." He caught the note of pain in her voice, though, and it was echoed in his own. He liked to see Anna happy, but it was a distinct kind of happiness that didn't include him or Mercury. Not only that, it was a happiness that wasn't going to last, because they were going to go back to the mountains. Weren't they? Staying would be a death sentence.

"They definitely don't make jeans that tight up in the mountains, that's for sure." He was more and more fascinated as he watched, since Logan and Anna were good friends not just with people near their own age, but people Orion would have considered superiors back home. Older men and women with enough age on them to have teenage children of their own, talking to Logan and Anna both like peers and long-lost friends rather than the young people that they were. It made Orion's head swim a little to watch such a complete lack of hierarchy at play. "They look like they might as well have never left."

Mercury definitely didn't like to hear that, but she knew he was right. They looked like they belonged together, and they were perfectly content in the situation around them. Partners. They looked like they were partners in what they were doing, greeting people, even when they started to help, they talked to each other first and then went to help people together. Mercury didn't like the way Anna smiled at Logan as they went to help, or the teasing way that Anna bumped into Logan's side. When did they become such good friends again, anyway?

"She looks beautiful, even in jeans and a sweater." Mercury had never owned clothing like that, it wasn't practical, so she never had a reason. Apparently Anna had a reason.

Orion gave her a sarcastic look at that, since obviously he agreed and he thought Anna looked beautiful, but the note of jealousy in Mercury's voice was something he never thought was justified. "She does. But you really ought to look in a mirror once in a while. You could walk around in a burka and a parka at all times and still be gorgeous. Though if you did, you might die of heat stroke. Those things are hot."

Mercury looked back and gave him a halfhearted smile, but her attention was drawn to Logan again. At least until he and Anna moved out of view and she turned away from the window. "I appreciate your humor in an attempt to distract me." She sighed and bounced Declan a little. "It has always been easier to talk to you than anyone else I know. Including Logan. It's hard to get through to him sometimes. At least it is for me. It looks as though Anna makes him smile a lot easier than I do."

"It's home making him smile. This is his kingdom." It was Orion's turn to sound just a little unconvinced, since he very much hoped it wasn't Anna making him smile so easily. The more he watched them work in tandem, the more he remembered all the times Anna talked about hating the loss of her best friend, and maybe that was what they were returning to. He had no idea. He had to be happy about that, right?

"Besides, there's a difference between making somebody smile and making them happy. Give me a room and an audience full of people who don't mind dirty jokes about a blind plumber and I'll make lots of people laugh for a little while. Doesn't mean I make them happy."

"I don't know, people like to tell me laughter is the best medicine." Mercury seemed unconvinced it was the best medicine, since clearly she knew there were much better ways to manage pain and problems, but she didn't look up again.

"I dug up your medical file on my mobile device." She said quickly, so she could change the subject and sound interesting again. Medicine was the one thing that made her interesting and unique. "When we get back to the mountains, I'd like to take current blood samples, if that's okay. And some x-rays. I want to see how your bones are doing now, in comparison to the last full-body medical history the Consortium has on file. I found a little bit of research on slowing down bone growth. It's a temporary solution for your problem, at least, until I can figure out a permanent one."

"So that I don't start having disagreements with ceiling tiles?" He already did in some rooms, but he smiled and kept that fact to himself. He was accustomed to having to hunch over, both in space and on Earth. "Sure, you can have whatever you want, I can always make more." He turned away from the window to pick up Leo and Lynnette, taking them over to where he had laid out blankets to see if they would go to sleep for a while. "I'm really not the highest priority we need to worry about, though. If I grow a few more centimeters, nobody's gonna die unless they're living on my forehead when I try to walk around. If they are, they've got bigger problems. I'm probably not the best use of your time."

"Stop saying that." She said a little too sharply, though she only glanced at him before she got up to get blankets for her children. "I decide what the best use of my time is. Stop trying to convince me that you're not important." Mercury grabbed a few blankets from her bag and looked at Orion again. "You are important to me. And I don't want you to die or get sick because of something the Consortium did to you."

The sharpness from her wasn't something he was accustomed to, but she could tell that he backed down immediately. "I'm sorry. I'm grateful for your help. I don't mean to seem otherwise." He finished wrapping up his children and sat down beside them as they wiggled and attempted to chew on their swaddles. "You're important to me too, and I know how thinly you've been stretched. I just don't enjoy the thought that I'm adding to that in any way. I'd like to alleviate it as much as I can."

Mercury's expression softened as she brought her boys close to Lynnette and Leo and she wrapped them up too. James didn't even fight before he was drifting off, since he enjoyed being wrapped snugly. "I'm sorry. I'm just tired of being told that I do too much. I know that I do, but being a doctor makes me happy. It makes me feel useful." She glanced over at the window even though she couldn't see out the window from the floor.

"I don't have a lot of things that I'm good at here." Mercury felt ashamed to admit it, but in space, she was good at everything. Good at her job. Good at her art, good at cooking. But everything was measurable. Everything was accessible. When she cooked before, she could monitor temperatures and portions and ingredients. In the mountains everything was unreliable, and she rarely had everything she needed. Photography and painting weren't hobbies people took up in the mountains. The resources weren't worth risking anything to get, and a finished painting served no purpose in a world focused on survival. The only thing she was useful for was her medical practice, and even that was incredibly different from anything she had endured in space. "I feel overlooked. And foreign. If I say I want to help you, I do. Please don't stop me from doing so."

"Okay." He agreed quietly, giving her another apologetic smile. He looked down at James and smiled at him drifting off, then looked at both of his own, who were going to be trouble, since neither of them were succumbing to the warmth of the blanket very quickly. He grabbed his phone from nearby and sent a quick message to Priscilla to see if she was close enough to help, but he wasn't sure where she and Gwen had wandered off to in the city-sized house. "Though I have to say, in my own defense," he picked up Lynnette, who had chosen that moment to be fussy, while he waited to hear back from Priscilla, "the only reason I overlook you is because you're about half a meter shorter than I am. It's really not intentional. I overlook everybody."

Mercury shook her head and turned her focus to Declan. She picked him up again to rock him gently. "I'm taller than your wife is. She doesn't get overlooked by anyone."

"She tends to be a little louder than you are." He said with a smile. "Tends to draw attention."

"She does, that's true. Even through the air vents you can hear her." Mercury said flatly before she continued to rock Declan. "Did you need to go somewhere? I can watch over the four of them if you need to go." Mercury saw him send a message, so she assumed he had somewhere he needed to be.

"No, I was asking Priscilla where she was so she could help

rock one of these two to sleep." Leo had gotten out of his swaddling while he worked on putting Lynnette to sleep, but Orion couldn't bring himself to care. If attempting to crawl around haltingly kept the little boy happy and quiet for a little while, then that was fine. Lynnette wasn't going to take that long to go to sleep. "Knowing those Priscilla and Gwen, it's entirely possible they found a farmer to take a ride on in the back of one of those trailers. But that's me making assumptions about people again."

He went to a rocking chair off to the side of the room and sat down, rocking gingerly, since he never had been able to get accustomed to them. In orbit things needed to be stationary, preferably bolted to the floor so that shifting gravity wouldn't send a couch flying through an airlock or something. Rocking chairs were a novelty he had never really experienced for himself prior to coming to Earth. "Do not make me sing to you, little girl." He said in a deeply threatening voice, glaring down at the baby in his arms as if she was in serious trouble. "I'll do it. Do not force my hand. You will regret it."

"That little girl must have you wrapped around her finger if you're willing to sing to her." Mercury said with the smallest of smiles. Being the only girl among three brothers, Logan was equally wrapped around Lynnette's finger. She was definitely the princess among the little ruffian boys. "I think you should sing to her."

"That's just evidence that you've never heard me sing." He said with a playful smile up at her, then turned his eyes back to Lynnette.

"I know." She said with a note of sadness in her voice. Mercury didn't care if he was a terrible singer, but not knowing what it sounded like further reminded her they barely had a chance to get to know each other before everything changed so drastically. "So will you sing for me, then?"

That got a genuine smile from him, and he released a deep breath as he settled into the rocking chair a little more, still looking down at Lynnette. "See, Lyn, she's what we call a glutton for punishment. She just doesn't know it yet." He glanced up at Mercury again with the same smile, but resigned himself to the request. Orion lifted Lynnette to kiss her forehead once before he snuggled her back in place against his arm to hold her before he started singing.

The tune was a slow, undulating kind of tune, hypnotic the way a small space station was hypnotic, slight swells and dips as the rotation evenly and subtly changed the relative force exerted on those within. The song was in Arabic, at the lower extremity of Orion's vocal range, but his voice wasn't as terrible as he made it out to be. She hadn't had a chance to do much studying of Arabic in the brief time they had been together, but she recognized enough of the words to understand the gist of the lyrics after they repeated for a few verses. *"Sleep, sleep, sweet little girl, Sleep in the dark 'til the cloud moves away. Sleep, sleep, sweet little girl, until we have moonlight to brighten our world."*

Mercury was quiet and she smiled as she listened to him. She was glad to see that after a few repetitions, it soothed Lynnette, even though she wasn't completely asleep yet. Mercury looked down at Declan who was also asleep, and she bent enough to kiss his forehead. She whispered her response to Orion when he stopped. "You made it out to be much worse than it was. My ears are still fully functioning." She looked at Lynnette again and back up at Orion. "Nowhere else around here or back in the mountains is she ever going to hear something as unique and beautiful as that. Your heritage is a gift to her."

His smile dimmed a little, but he kept his voice down as he answered, speaking in smooth tones to let Lynnette continue to drift off. "I guess time will tell what their heritage from us will be. Gift or curse. But I hope you're right. I really do."

"It isn't a curse." Mercury replied resolutely, but she really wasn't able to say anything else before she heard Priscilla coming toward them. She could hear the young woman giggling, but the noise died at the doorway. "Looks like the babysitter decided to show up after all the hard work is over."

"No way." He shook his head, still smiling a little, and nodded soundlessly at Leo on the floor as Priscilla tiptoed into the room. "That one needs a nap, if you could. I think we've got the others." He looked back at the doorway to see who had come along to share her giggling, but whoever they were, they stayed behind rather than coming in and getting closer to the aliens and half-aliens.

Priscilla nodded before she picked Leo up and re-wrapped him in a blanket so he would be nice and snug. "Sure. I've got it, Gwen is supposed to come give me backup soon. Everyone else is outside helping, I think I saw Anna and Logan out there."

"We saw them too. We figured they'd be busy. Thanks again for the help." He smiled at her on her way out to the hallway with Leo, and by the time he looked down at Lynnette again, she was asleep. He moved slowly to get up from the chair to the makeshift bed that had been set up on the far side of the room. Getting her down beside James was easy enough, and Orion just stood there for a moment over them, shaking his head.

"Still hasn't sunk in." He whispered low as he went back to the other side of the room with Mercury. "I've gotten it through my head that I'm a rebel and a traitor, but not that I'm a dad."

"I imagine it will take a long time to get used to it." She put Declan down on the other side of Lynnette so she was surrounded by her brothers. "But there is definitely no denying that you're a father. Your little man is going to out-cute my rolly little boys."

"I doubt that." He grinned down at her kids and reached out to tug on a few stray strands of her red hair. It was up, but only in a ponytail, since it was easier and more efficient not to waste time on braiding or fancy hairstyles, but there were still a few stray bits that he could tweak. "You've made some seriously cute kids. Mine's just gonna be a brown giant in a sea of pale child adorableness."

Mercury laughed softly. "You always know what to say. You are such a charmer. Everyone will be in trouble if Leo is as smooth as you are." She smiled warmly and reached out to give his hand a friendly squeeze before she nodded toward the door. She could hear someone running toward them, and she could only assume it was Gwen. "Now that the other babysitter is here, do you want to go get something to eat?"

"That sounds good, actually, I haven't had anything since that granola bar on the bus. I wouldn't be surprised if we go wandering in this place and there's a full service cafe operating somewhere." He saw Gwen on the way in and smiled with a finger over his lips to remind her to be quiet, since the babies were asleep. "Tag, you're it." He high-fived her on the way out of the room with Mercury, and didn't even look back.

10

Anna wondered if the sky was playing tricks on her when she woke up and the sun was shining. They thought that getting ready to go would only take days. It was now a week and a half later, and on this day, everyone else was ready to go to the mountains. Except on this day, this bright, sunny day where the birds sounded happy and the world seemed cheerful, her life was a little emptier.

She laid there in the bed next to Orion, who still didn't know what had happened the week before, and she hadn't really talked to Logan in a few days. She couldn't talk to anyone the day before, not when yesterday morning, she woke up to the information her father had died.

Anna ran her eyes along the ceiling and slowly turned onto her side and into Orion, even though he was still asleep. She hadn't cried. She was too stunned to cry, but now she could feel it. Today was her father's funeral, and instead of the rain she would have expected, the sun still rose. It still shone. And it brought her to tears. Quiet, body-shaking tears.

Orion had been doing his best since the day before to be there for Anna, but he found out very quickly she wasn't an easy person to support. He cared for the children for most of the time they'd been in the midwest, and it meant he had only sporadic sleep. The night before, though, Gwen and Priscilla had taken all four babies for the night, so it took a while for Orion to wake up from such a deep sleep. At her shaking, though, he slowly came to consciousness, and put his arms around her slowly, eventually remembering what had happened the day before. "Morning already?"

"The sun is shining." She mumbled into his side and between her tears, as if the universe was being cruel to her. "One of the most important people in my life is dead. God, I'm an orphan." Anna cried even harder knowing she was an orphan and her biggest cheerleader in her father was gone. The last thing he told her was to hold tightly to the things she loved most. "I'm happy he's with my mom. Or, at least, I'm going to tell myself he is. But he's gone."

"I believe that too. That he's with her." He held her, rubbing her back as she cried. "But you're not an orphan. Orphans are made by parents who abandon their kids. I don't think there's anything your parents wouldn't have done to try and stay with you just one more day, either of them, if there had been a way to manage it. They're still your parents, wherever they are."

"Our kids will never know him. Or her." She still trembled with her sobs as she clung to Orion. "Your parents are the only grandparents they have left."

"Who they also may or may not ever meet." Orion was very conscious of how unlikely it was for them to ever get in touch with his parents or Mercury's ever again, but they were at least still alive. "That being said, Leo and Lynnette would be big hits back home. My mom loves babies."

Anna held tightly to him until her eyes hurt too much to continue crying, and then she sniffled while she was in his embrace. He was so good to her. So strong and supportive. She was feeling worse and worse about sleeping with Logan, but also missing Logan at the same time. "I hope they get to meet your parents someday." Anna replied softly, still clearly heartbroken.

"I hope so too." He smoothed back some of her hair that stuck to the side of her face with her tears, his fingers moving behind her ear and down her neck in slow, soothing movements. "In the meantime, they'll hear all about their grandfather and grandmother from you, and they'll learn from what you learned from them. That's a form of immortality in itself."

Anna was grateful for his support, and she accepted it readily even knowing that he might not give it to her if he knew what happened. What did she want? Did she want to tell him right now? What would she tell him anyway? She didn't know what she wanted, and she was so unbelievably torn all over again. All she knew was her heart was broken.

"I should get a shower. The Bickfords are being gracious and helping us, but I need to help." Logan and Liam had insisted on bringing in all the food and things that would be needed for the funeral visitors. The funeral wouldn't be much, but they would drive her father out to be laid next to her mother. Everyone had been housed in the Bickford mansion since returning from the campsite, but they'd made a few runs back to the Prince property. Anna thought she said her goodbyes to home. Now they would go back one more time.

"Alright, I'll be right behind you." He kissed her one more time as she got up, and she could see him going around the room gathering their clothes as she got into the shower. He moved around efficiently and purposefully, as always, to help her get everything ready to go. The more he could do for her to help, the better.

Anna was in a daze as she showered, and she barely even noticed the water changing from hot to warm as Orion stepped in and showered with her. He didn't like it nearly as hot as she did. She did turn to face him once he was in the shower with her, and she moved toward him so she could pull him into a kiss. "What if we fail? What if we leave behind our children too young or too soon for Eleusis?"

He helped her pull her soaked hair back behind her shoulders into a long, dark line down her back, and returned the kiss. "I guess at this point, the saying 'failure is not an option' would sound pretty standard-issue military of me. But that's kind of how I've felt about it ever since you and I saw the Twist with our own eyes. If we fail and never make it to Eleusis, or if we die trying, it's going to mean a worse life for our children. For everyone's children, but especially for ours, if the Consortium gets their hands on them. But ever since we participated in evacuating Nine, we've been all in with this. There's not a lot of middle ground left for people like us."

Anna nodded woodenly, though she was worried they would fail, even though it wasn't going to stop her from trying to get to Eleusis no matter what. "I didn't sign up for a war, even though I'm not backing down. I just . . . all of this is a lot. And I'm kind of fucking up at dealing with it. I'm not nearly as strong as I think I am."

"You don't look broken to me." He reassured her with a caress to her cheek. "I know you didn't sign up for a war. I did when I enlisted. Not that I actually knew the Consortium was at war with anybody, I just thought I was doing the patriotic thing. The family thing, with my brother and my dad and my grandparents and everything all being servicemen. But I know none of you thought that was what you were signing up for when you applied for the Initiative." He sighed and smoothed her hair back again under the hot water. "I love you. Peace or war, we'll handle it."

"I love you too, Orion." She looked up into his eyes, even though there was pain and conflict in hers. "You're too good for me. I don't deserve you." Anna meant it, he just didn't know how much.

That was a very new kind of sentiment to get from his wife, and she could tell that he was shocked by it, but he actually laughed once, even though he clearly wasn't in the mood to be amused by anything with her father's death hanging over everything. "And you tell me *I* make bad jokes. That one's terrible. I'm good *at* plenty of things, but I don't think anybody should ever accuse me of being just good. You know me better than that."

"You are." She pulled him into another kiss, heated and needy, since his affection was still something she craved, even if she was conflicted about who to fully give her heart to. After the kiss, she stepped into him again, and as soon as he wrapped his arms around her, she felt a little more secure.

He held her tight under the water, grateful the Bickford estate had the world's largest water heater. "We'll be alright, baby. I know it feels like we're in over our heads, since we absolutely are, but we're going to do what we set out to do here. Give the Consortium a kick in the ass and give humanity the home it deserves. Where people won't have to bury their parents before their own children are even walking."

"God, I hope so." Anna held onto him a little bit longer before she took a deep breath, trying to be strong again. "Alright, I'm going to get out and get dressed. Can you check on the children?"

"Sure, let me finish up here and I'll be out in a minute. I think Gwen should still have the camera. I didn't hear any blood-curdling screams last night, so I'm guessing Leo didn't have another one of his nightmares."

Anna shook her head, since she didn't understand how a baby could have nightmares, but Mercury had assured Orion that it was normal by this age, except that she had called them "night terrors". They certainly were terrible. "Hopefully he slept through alright. I feel like my breasts are going to explode, though." Normally Anna was able to pump in the night, but after everything with her father, she hadn't had the energy to wake up. "I'll go pump them some breakfast too. I'll keep my communicator with me if you need anything."

"Sounds good." He gave her one final kiss on her way out of

the shower, then for good measure, leaned down and kissed both her breasts in quick succession. "No exploding. That's an order."

She gave him the smallest of smiles before she got out of the shower and got to business. She passed by Gwen on the way out after giving her the pumped milk and thanked her for her help. Gwen didn't say much other than that Liam's sister would be replacing her to take care of the children while she took some time to herself as well. Anna barely registered any of what was said but she nodded and went on her way.

It was difficult meeting with her siblings again, crying for another couple of hours after all the planning was complete, and finally stepping out to get some fresh air before she was completely dehydrated from crying.

The Bickford house was a complicated maze of rooms, but Anna had years of experience to learn at least half of it, and once she stepped out into the backyard, she knew where she was and where she was going. Anna wandered from the back porch, fenced in and beautiful, toward Logan's mother's garden and out of that to a small grove of fruit trees. She had picked apples in the grove nearly every year and it was where she once broke her arm competing with Liam to get highest in the trees. She won, but the cost had been falling afterward and breaking her arm in two places. Still, she held it over Liam's head for a year - he got beat by a girl. He claimed she only won because she was smaller than he was. It was probably true.

Anna wandered to the very tree where she had broken her arm and she was surprised to see Logan on a bench nearby. She thought she was escaping to get some time alone, but she was surprisingly glad to see him. "I didn't think I would run into anyone out here."

Logan was already dressed for the funeral, in a perfectly black suit in a fashionable style. She'd only seen him wear it a few other times, for other funerals in the years before they'd left, but it was tighter on him than it had been before. The pants were a perfect pitch black, the shirt was black with white buttons and the jacket was the same light-denying dark as the pants. Two silver strands hung down from his collar in a stylized bolo, bound with a hunk of silver and black that she knew had been in the Bickford family about as long as the house, if not longer.

"I thought the same. Great minds, I guess." He said without smiling, even though she could hear the mild joke anyway. "I'd ask how you're doing, but if you're out here, that speaks pretty well for itself."

She nodded and sat down next to him in her own black attire, except she was wearing a necklace with blue sapphire stones that had once been her mother's. Her dress was just as eye-catching as the rest of her wardrobe, and it hugged curves she hadn't had before having children, but there was nothing to be done about her wardrobe now. It was all that she had. Short and cleavage-exposing. "Ben is a hell of a lot stronger than I've ever given him credit for." She stared at her black flats on her feet. "He worked out everything. All I could do was cry."

Logan shook his head. "Ben gave up on the world being a pleasant place when your mother died." He sighed deeply as he looked around at the trees, taking in the peace of the spot in the middle of a great big vast nothingness. The house always felt dead to him, abandoned, but in spots like the small orchard and his mother's garden, he always felt like the solitude was appropriate. He was the intruder, borrowing silence from a place where it grew as naturally as the apples on the branches. "He never got over that. He's been looking at everything in the world like it has an expiration date ever since. Makes him an asshole and a fatalist, but on a long enough timeline, it sets accurate expectations."

"His heart was so broken when she died. He was her little man." Anna shook her head as she stared at her feet. "There's this gaping hole in my chest, and I can't imagine what it felt like for him as a child. I loved my mom, and I miss her every day, but I was so much closer to my dad."

"You're not built from the same stuff as Ben." Logan said quietly, his tone making it clear he meant that as a compliment. "Ben is one thing or he's another, but whatever he is, that's what he is and changing is not an overnight event. People like him, your dad, Rissa, they're sure. Solid." He included Mercury on the list silently, but he wasn't going to bring her up in the present context. "I'm probably built more that way than is good for anybody. You move easier. Bend, adapt, flex around to whatever you need to be in the moment. People like you are the reason the human race has survived as long as it has, honestly." Logan put an arm around her and rubbed at her shoulder, to let her know he was there. "I'm sorry."

Her eyes burned again with tears even though she could have sworn she didn't have any more to cry. Anna slid into his side and buried her face into Logan's black shirt. She took in the scent of him, his cologne and soap, and wrapped her arms around him as he held onto her. "Your family is doing so much. Thank you. This would be a fucking nightmare without you."

"I'm just glad to be back in a place where I'm actually able to do something." He said quietly. "Even if it's for a little while." They both knew they were going to have to go back to the mountains, and soon, but the sigh that followed had a little more than just the pressing nature of their situation.

"I got a call from Jason earlier this morning around four. He said there's been a few manually-selected sweeps of our area by satellite and communications monitoring systems. He was able to make sure they saw only what he wanted them to see, but if someone's doing manual sweeps, then all the more reason for us to vacate the area. I told some of the other squad leaders from the district. Everyone's going to be ready to move by nightfall."

"I'm sorry this caused a delay." Anna spoke softly, though she pulled away as soon as it was obvious he was all business again. "Ben said he kept everything out of the local news about my dad so no one would have any reason to think I would show up for his funeral."

"That sounds like Ben." Logan nodded as she pulled away, and got up afterward to let her have her space there in the trees. "When we were growing up, all the research about Eleusis was rediscovered; there were a few reports that came out publicly. They published the telemetry, habitability, they were called the Paradise papers. I remember reading about some group saying Eleusis was actually heaven, the place people went when they had led a good life." Obviously he didn't believe it, and the group that preached it had gone silent as more was learned about the place by scientific means. It had still been the belief of some for some time. "Times like this, I wish it were true."

"I do too." She agreed wholeheartedly, since she had desperately wanted to take her father with them to Eleusis. "Then I could imagine my parents there with your parents, shooting the shit, laughing and having a good time. They were good friends."

"I'm sure they still are." That idea got a small smile from him, even if it was much-sedated under the circumstances. "Whether that's on Eleusis or somewhere else entirely, who knows. Death seems a little too common and petty to me for it to come between things like friends or lovers. Just my opinion."

Anna nodded and turned her attention to watch him instead of her feet as he got up and moved away. "Remember when I broke my arm falling out of that tree?" She nodded to the one closest to him, and she looked up near the top, as if she would see the ghost of her childhood self up there. "It was nice to gloat over Liam until I fell and busted my arm in two places. My dad asked me afterward if I thought it was worth it. I said yes, even though having my arm in a cast sucked."

He nodded, since he did remember. He'd been worried about her at the time, seeing as there had been a lot of blood and screaming. "Bragging rights last longer than a cast, as I recall you saying."

"They sure do." She stared up into the tree for a little bit longer before her eyes trailed down the tree slowly and landed on Logan again. "Liam told me that I wasn't strong enough to hang out with you two anymore. Girls weren't supposed to hang out with boys. But you were my best friend. So there was a lot at stake in that climb."

"You've always been strong enough. No matter what you've attempted, or what people have thrown at you." There was a cloud of self-reflection in his eyes as he looked first down at the ground between them, then up, scanning the skies through the budding leaves to look for any visible stations in the unblemished blue of heaven. There were two visible at the moment, shooting their way across the sky like tiny snowflakes between stars. "Whatever's happened, whatever happens from here, one thing anyone who knows you knows better than to do is underestimate you."

Anna got up from the bench and walked the short distance to Logan, since she didn't want to be away from him when she had a moment to be with him. "I'm only strong enough when I have a reason to be."

"That's going to be always." He squeezed her hand and smiled to reassure her, the morning breeze catching a few wisps of his hair, shaggy as it had gotten, to whip them around his ears. "You've got plenty of reasons you're never going to be without."

"You are one of my reasons." She tilted her head up so she could meet his eyes again. Orion was significantly taller than Logan, but they were both taller than she was. Anna reached up with her free hand to run her fingers along his loose strands of hair. More than anything and anyone, Anna felt like she needed Logan to keep her grounded. He was a part of this life, the life where her family was, the life where her heart ached because her father was gone. He knew her father, whereas Orion had barely met him, along with everyone else that mattered to her. Orion was doing his best and Anna loved him more for it, but he still didn't understand her loss. He didn't understand her and her family the way Logan did. "I've missed you the last few days."

"I've missed you too." He admitted quietly, still looking around at the trees before he looked back at her. "I think the longer we stay here, the more everything else feels like someone else's life to me. Like there's some other Logan Bickford who decided to throw up a middle finger to the Consortium and run away to the mountains to help lead a rebellion. Like it's somebody else's war. The guy who grew up here can't fight a war. Hell, I can barely keep my own crops in good rotation every season, let alone . . ." he shook his head again, since he had to cut himself off from such thoughts. "I know it would be impossible to stay. And it's not in me to run away and choose something else the way some of our people have. It just . . . standing here, in these trees, it doesn't feel like my life. Even if it is."

"I know. This. This feels like my life." She said softly as she hesitantly stepped into him, but she wanted so desperately for him to hold her. Especially now. "Even with my dad gone, being here has made me happier than the Consortium could ever make me. This is the life we were raised with. I still want Eleusis, I still want a life there, but I want to build a life like this one. The life that I love. And miss."

He put his arms around her to hold her in against his chest with a sigh that took a long time to leave him. What she'd said was the heart of the trouble they were in, even if neither of them had realized it until they'd come home. The life they wanted was the life they had come back to, however briefly. Victory would mean they could have that life again. "I can't think of anything I would love more than that. Growing old on Eleusis, watching the kids grow up and make lives for themselves, watching the world put itself back together. Raising a crop and fighting with the damn farm equipment, but doing it under a different sun and a different sky."

Anna felt like crying all over again once he was holding her against his broad chest. "What would we plant, do you think? Eleusis apples?" She said with a smile as she looked up at the Apple trees.

He didn't quite laugh, but he did return her smile. "Apples are a lot of work, and involve a lot of broken limbs. But we'd have to have them nonetheless. Have to make sure Lynnette has the chance to win some bragging rights of her own one of these days."

"She will. I don't know what I'm going to do if my daughter turns out to be extremely girly and afraid of mud." Anna was glad to see his smile, so she reached up and ran her hand along his cheek. "I love this beard. And you."

They were well away from the house, and he wasn't wary of holding her tight out in the open as they were, so he turned his face to kiss the inside of her palm. "There's no way she's going to be scared of anything. Not with you as her mother. Just because you're not in school anymore doesn't mean you stopped being the best kind of cheerleader. You still have the skirt in there to prove it."

"That skirt is way too short. She's not allowed to wear it." Anna laughed back at him. It was nice to feel something other than sadness. The open air, the breeze, the memories, and feeling Logan solidly holding onto her made things more bearable. Even if the weight of her father's death was still heavy on her shoulders. "I only joined because I wanted to make sure you were watching."

"Oh, I was watching." He looked her over with another smile and a brief kiss, since they wouldn't be out in the orchard for long enough to do anything about the memory of her in her cheerleading outfit. "We'll get there. She'll grow up on Eleusis with skirts you and I both disapprove of, going after guys we both hate, and generally causing trouble even across the galaxy."

"God. Across the galaxy? That's too far. She can't have a driver's license or a flying license. Nope. I won't let her." Anna pulled him down into another kiss, since the first one felt so good. It sent warmth all the way down into her toes.

Logan personally doubted that Lynnette would stay out of the driver's seat for very long, given who her step-father was, but he didn't say anything of the kind as the kiss deepened. It was too beautiful a moment for him to want to shatter it by talking about anything outside of it. "She's our daughter. Trouble is in her DNA. Just a good thing she's got professionals like us around to teach her exactly how to manage it once she gets into it."

"You? A professional of trouble?" She teased him as she held tightly to him, since she was not willing to let go. Anna and Logan definitely got into a lot of trouble together, but usually it was Liam who started it, Anna who refused to be shown up, and Logan who went along to make sure no one died as a consequence. "I distinctly remember at least a hundred times where you started a sentence with, 'Anna, this is probably not a good idea . . .'"

"In my defense, I was usually right." He stood by his cautious nature, even if he absolutely had been along for the majority of the adventures that had gotten her in trouble as a child. "Not all the time, but usually." His hands moved over her back and her backside as his grip on her loosened, but only because they did have somewhere they needed to be, and soon. "I'm sure there will be a hundred more. Especially if we decide to continue . . . this . . . when we get back to the mountains." They'd talked about it once, just as they had both gotten lost in the frenzy of remembering the life they both wanted, and they had seen each other a few times while they were there in the house, 'going through their things' to move out, but neither of them had said anything definitive on the subject.

"I know I want to." She remained in his loosened grip. "I know we both have changed. It was impossible to survive what we went through and not change. But we're good together. We're good for each other. I want to discover all the new things about you and be with you some more. Don't we owe it to them and to each other to know for sure what we want?"

He nodded, but the look on his face was still conflicted. "I doubt either of them will see it quite that way."

"I know." Anna released a heavy sigh before she looked up into Logan's eyes. "I love you both. But I had to violate my marriage vows to even get to know Orion. I never would have fallen in love with him if I hadn't been forced to put aside the love I already felt for you. It sounds terrible, and it *is* terrible we had to live through it. It doesn't mean I don't love him. I do. But I still love you. I can't ignore that, and I need the opportunity to choose for myself. If you don't, if you want to be with Mercury, just tell me. We didn't even get to talk before it all happened. The Consortium would never let us talk about anything. But now you can. You can tell me how you feel and what you want to do. I'm still going to be your friend, your partner, and your supporter no matter what you say."

Ever since they had gotten back to the estate and reconnected, Logan felt like he was back on Nine with the decision between Anna and Mercury hanging in front of him all over again. Before, something had taken him almost physically away from Anna, placed him with Mercury against anyone's will, at least at first. They both acknowledged that.

But he had made his choice, hadn't he? Anna had chosen Orion, and he had chosen to be with Mercury. Now Anna was asking him to reconsider their old life, the life they had both thought they wanted, and it was . . . a shadow of himself that he wanted back.

"I want that chance too, Anna." He said quietly, less energetically than she had, but no less certainly. "I know . . . a little too much about myself after everything that's happened. As much as I know, though, I know that we've always been good for each other, and good together. Not that Mercury and I aren't. Or that I think you and Orion aren't. It's just . . . different." That was the biggest problem, in his mind. He was happy with Mercury, he was just cranky and distant all the time because they led a stressful life. There was nothing about Mercury that made that worse. All she did, she did to make it better, and he was grateful for her every day because of it. "When we get back to the mountains, we need to tell them. And hope that they don't hate us forever for it."

"They probably will hate us for a while." Anna said softly, since she could feel the guilt prickling every sense she had, and it did not feel good. "I don't want to hurt him." Anna didn't necessarily want to hurt Mercury either, however, she didn't particularly care for Mercury in the first place. Their opinions and personalities differed quite starkly.

"He will be angry. Furious. Maybe he *will* hate me." Anna didn't want Orion to hate her, but she didn't know what to do about her still-split feelings for Logan and Orion unless she had a chance to make a decision on her own without the threat of death. "I don't want him to hate me. But I don't want to lose this between you and I either. Not if we want to see if we want to be together. We made vows to each other before we made vows with them."

Logan could only nod, since he agreed with everything she said, however much it hurt. "Let's get home first. I don't want to talk to them about it out here where they're both uncomfortable enough as it is. Our families haven't been as welcoming to the two of them as I was hoping they would be, and unfortunately, this isn't going to make that any better."

"I know." Anna agreed, since she could tell most of her family didn't care for Orion no matter how often she told them about how great he was. "I wish I hadn't been afraid to talk about how I felt until now. Right now, though, I just need to survive this funeral."

11

Figuring out how to get everyone down to the Prince estate in the smallest number of vehicles had been a logistics feat Liam didn't want to try to wrap his head around. He left it to Logan and Rachel and hopped into the van with Bree and most of the children in the vicinity, allowing Logan and Anna and their spouses to drive together in relative silence.

Gwen tagged along to help manage all seven tiny children, all of whom were strapped into a plethora of car-seats with various forms of entertainment to keep them busy. He wasn't sure how it happened, but after half an hour on the road, all the babies were, by Gwen's report, either asleep or content with their on-the-road entertainment.

"And you're sure you're not a witch?" He asked the rearview mirror, one arm around Brianne beside him and the other resting lightly near the wheel, though the van was piloting itself just fine without his direct assistance. "Because I'm pretty sure putting seven kids to sleep single-handedly is grounds for being burned at the stake. Or thrown into a lake, whichever you're more in the mood for."

"I never said I *wasn't* a witch." Gwen smirked as she caught his eye in the mirror. "Do you really want to burn someone at the stake if they are capable of wooing your children into contentment? I mean, it *could* be a spell. Or it could be that I'm a baby whisperer. Does it really matter? I can make them cry if that would make you happy."

"No!" He quickly lowered his voice and waved her off. "No, no, for fuck's sake, leave them alone or just . . . keep doing whatever you're doing. I'm just saying, there's something supernatural about that. But bring it on, I've got no problem with that kind of witchcraft."

"It's not the first time I've been called a witch." She laughed softly and looked over all of the babies again. "But that's a story better left a secret."

"Most stories are." He chuckled and sighed, settling in for the drive down to the Princes' ranch, his hand idly playing along the side of Bree's neck and caressing over skin made bare as soon as possible in the warming spring. They were both in black, but Bree, like Anna, had very little by way of modest clothing, and a little black dress coupled with a shawl was the best she could do for a funeral. "I know I've got my share."

"It's interesting to watch you with all three of your wives." Gwen said rather bluntly, but she knew Bree wouldn't care. In fact, Bree gave Liam some sort of smirk that Gwen could tell was suggestive, but she didn't pause. "With Bree here, you touch her like you want to devour her all of the time. With Rachel, you touch her in more supportive ways. You hold her hand, stand next to her and put your hand to the small of her back. She seems less on the PDA, but likes being touched. Margo, well, she likes to do the touching. She leans into you, she kisses you proactively, but usually she blushes if you do something to her in public. Even a butt smack the other day turned her crimson. It's just interesting. You know your women. You know their limits, likes, dislikes. How do I know *you're* not the witch? Wizard? Whatever the fuck it is."

That made him roll his eyes again, but he looked at her in the rearview mirror even as his touch continued over Bree. "If I was a wizard, it wouldn't have taken me so long to figure out how to deal with all three of them. Though I admit, this one didn't need much magic. Still doesn't." He said with a caress that went straight down the center of Bree's chest and back up again along the hollow of her throat, teasing at her relentlessly as she leaned against him in the front of the van. "The other two were a lot more of a challenge to figure out. More error than trial."

"You've managed to work it out." Gwen shrugged just as Declan started whimpering so she reached over and popped a paci into his mouth. He quieted almost instantly. "In a couple of years. That's impressive."

"He's a good listener." Bree explained afterward, looking back at Gwen briefly. "If we take the time to tell him we like something or we want something, he goes out of his way to make it happen. And he doesn't talk about us to the others, at least not disparagingly. He did plot with me for Rachel's birthday present, but she loved it, so it works out."

"And Margo helped me with yours. Not this past one, the one before." His touch never ceased, but also never got directly scandalous, just tracing the edges of the skin that was already available to his touch as if memorizing present boundaries. "Besides, plotting is one of your strengths. If I ever need to do something sneaky, believe me when I tell you, I'm going to you first."

Bree grinned proudly before she chewed on her bottom lip. She knew that they were on their way to a funeral. It was supposed to be a sad day. Funerals just made her happy to be alive, though, which definitely made her want Liam in ways she shouldn't want him at the moment. She leaned across the center console and kissed him before she whispered into his ear. "If we want to invite her over, we should see if she is interested. Turn up the heat a little, Babe."

"You're bad." He whispered back into her ear, but it was far from a criticism. He kissed her again and ran his hand up her back to her hair, which was in two braids at the moment. He pushed the console up from between them, and tugged on one of her braids with a gentle pull to her shoulder, turning her in the seat so she could lie back with her head in his lap and her legs tucked up into the seat she had vacated. Once he had her where he wanted her, he looked in the rearview again at Gwen. Bree was partly out of sight for her, but he doubted it would matter soon. His hands got a great deal more bold in the way they wandered over Bree, but his eyes remained on Gwen. "So you said you were raised on the west coast. Tell me about yourself. What was that like? I've never known anybody from that part of the world. Too many blasted zones."

Bree shivered at his touches and she smirked as she gave him a few teasing ones of her own. She was in his lap. How was she supposed to keep her hands off of him?

"I, uh," Gwen watched Liam's fingers trail along Bree's cleavage and it was obvious how much Bree liked it, since she responded like a cat, nearly purring at his touch. "It was amazing, being close to the beach. A beach that was never crowded." Gwen watched his fingers slip under the edge of Bree's shirt. "It's way more free-spirited than the mountains."

"They get pretty weird up there, or so I've heard." His hand continued moving idly over Bree's chest as he spoke, as if there was nothing else going on but the conversation between them.

The way Bree was moving said otherwise. "But I think I could've done with a beach. If it was never crowded, I'm going to assume wearing any kind of bathing suit was optional for you most of the time, yeah?"

Gwen was not expecting him to ask that, but she was distracted enough there was a pause. "Optional. Yeah." She glanced down at herself but then she looked back at the two of them. What was Bree doing? Surely she wasn't doing anything . . . "I'm confident enough with my body I don't mind either way. Suit or not. But when I still lived out west, I was younger than I am now."

"Ah. Well, missed opportunities, then." He moved a little against Bree's touch, adjusting to get more comfortable and rock into her hand to encourage her further as his hand massaged over her ample chest. "From some of the things we saw in the leaked video during the fall of Nine, the settlement on Eleusis is already on the coast. We'll just have to make sure the establishment of the first nude beach on a new planet is high on our list of priorities. Make up for some of your lost time in California."

Gwen was too stunned to speak, especially because she wasn't sure if she was purposefully getting a show from the two of them or if they just didn't care who saw them feeling each other up. "Your brother would shit a brick if he thought a nude beach was happening under his watch. He hates me enough as it is because I'm a . . . what should I call myself? A bed-jumper? Homewrecker? That's the one."

"My brother's capacity for shitting bricks should have single handedly made him the masonry capital of the universe long before you ever came around. But the world keeps on spinning anyway. So will Eleusis." His hand moved beneath Bree's shirt to cup her breast and tease along her nipple in exactly the way he knew she liked, and it drew exactly the kind of moan from her he expected. He didn't even look away from Gwen in the mirror as he did it, looking as relaxed as ever. "And he doesn't actually hate you for fucking half the men in town, if that's your usual MO. The whole time we were growing up he was crazy in love with Anna, and you'd have to go a few states away to find a dick she hasn't sucked. Don't let him fool you. If he lets you stay around, he doesn't mind you."

"He sure scowls at me a lot for not minding my presence." Gwen's cheeks flushed as Liam continued to tease his wife, since she couldn't help but wonder and imagine what it would feel like if his hand was on her instead. She was trying not to look bothered and she tried to ignore it, but it was hard to do either. "Do you two always put on a show for a car-full of infants?"

"They're still rear-facing. You're the only one watching." His grin apologized for nothing, his hand teasing its way down over Bree's chest toward the hem of her little black dress. Though his touch was, as of yet, only teasing, without showing off his wild wife completely. "Besides, I thought you said things were more free-spirited where you come from?"

Her cheeks flushed even further, but not because she was embarrassed. She was getting turned on. "They are." She watched his hand a little closer, but when it was his turn to groan from whatever his wife was doing to tease him, Gwen definitely felt her body react to that. His groan was incredibly sexy. "This isn't the coast, though." Her voice was a whispered rasp, but clearly she was paying attention.

"Nope. Just a van." He leaned his head back against the seat with a glance at the controls just to make sure things were still smooth. The road was moving by quickly and the van's engine was humming contentedly as they moved, cars far ahead and behind in the caravan, all of them out of sight. "And if there's one thing I learned, it's never to waste travel time. God, I used to love the days when we had to go into town to go to school."

His hand got bolder at the fond recollection, smoothing the black fabric of Bree's dress down between her legs where there was no barrier to her husband's explorations. "There was this unmanned bus that would go around two days a week throughout the year to pick us all up out in my neck of the district, and there was this one set of twins that Logan could never stand. Holy fuck, talk about an education, those two never quit." He smiled down at Bree with another groan at her own insistence. "Kinda like somebody else I know."

Gwen shifted uncomfortably in her seat and she crossed her legs tighter as though it would make any difference to the part of her that was slick with excitement. She definitely wanted to lean forward some more to see if she could catch a glimpse of the part of Liam she wanted, but she stayed put. His hand certainly seemed to know what to do with Bree, since she was writhing and making all kinds of little noises. "So, um, do you do that? Like, between your wives? More than one person at once?"

He chuckled at that question, and the sound set him at a much greater remove from his brother, however similar they looked. "No, never went that way. We asked Rachel once if she wanted to join in, but she said she'd rather not. And we would never ask Margo." He said without any further explanation, though his reasons were fairly obvious from the time Gwen had spent in the Bickford house watching him and his wives.

"There was this one marketplace meeting I had to go to last fall, after the harvest. Bree just had Anders, so the four of us decided the two of us would go in for the week and Rachel and Margo could watch Anders for a little while. Rachel was about to pop, but we figured we'd be back in time." He groaned again, and Bree's dress inched up a little more to allow him to tease her more directly. "This one . . ." he teased Bree until he got a slightly louder moan from her, "took a liking to the daughter of one of the other farmers at the market. Sassy little thing, wicked attitude. We had her for a midnight snack a few times that week. And breakfast, once."

Gwen didn't expect to hear Liam had invited anyone else into his bed that wasn't one of his wives, and so her eyes widened at hearing him say they had invited someone else. Because Bree wanted to. She really should have expected that Bree was just as fluid as anyone she knew from the coast, but she just hadn't expected to find someone like that in the midwest. Was this show because Bree had 'taken a liking' to her too?

"Sounds like a good time." Gwen chewed on her bottom lip as she watched and her breathing quickened slightly. "Was she a redhead too?"

"No, she was Latina, actually." He managed to take a little more control of Bree than he allowed her to have of him at the moment, and grinned down at her as she continued to writhe against his hand on the front seat. Gwen could see from the way he touched her that he was in no hurry, but whatever he was doing, it was working for Bree in a hurry anyway. "She likes all kinds. Apparently both coasts are a little more free-spirited that way." He looked back at Gwen in the mirror again as Bree's moans increased in pace and pitch, though she was keeping her voice down for the children's sake. "But I'm that way too, so maybe I was just born in the wrong place. I should've come up on the coast."

"Maybe you should have." Gwen was leaning forward, since

she couldn't stop herself from getting just a little bit closer. She wanted to reach down and do to herself what Liam was doing to his wife, since she was tense from watching. "Do you . . ." She was a little nervous to ask what she wanted to ask because Liam was Logan's brother, but she couldn't stop herself. "Do you consider me a snack?"

Liam grinned and didn't answer the question right away, though he did continue watching her as Bree's moans escalated. Once she was on the downward spiral, he was quick about finishing her off, setting her entire body spasming on the seat beside him. Bree's breaths were fast and barely-controlled as her back arched in the freedom of the release. He waited for her to begin to recover as he caressed her hair with his free hand before he looked back at Gwen. "I don't think 'snack' would apply to you. The girl at the market was someone we knew we wouldn't see any more of after that week. As I understand it, we're gonna be in some pretty close quarters up in the mountains. That would make you more of a seven-course meal than a snack, I'm thinking."

Gwen couldn't prevent the whimper that escaped her throat at that opinion. She looked Bree up and down, her dress hiked to her hip, relaxed and satisfied, and Gwen knew she definitely wanted to jump in with the two of them. "That sounds . . . like fun." She finally replied as she met his eyes. "Too bad it doesn't start now. It was cruel to make me watch."

"First thing you should know about me. I'm a mean-spirited bastard." He tossed Bree's dress back down over her thighs and proceeded running his hands over her chest as she came down from the relaxed high. "Are you saying you're gonna have an uncomfortable ride the next forty-five minutes? Am I understanding you correctly?"

"You may be mean, but you're sexy regardless." She replied as she found her courage, but she smiled. "Well, both of you. But yes. Very uncomfortable."

Bree, who had been quiet for a number of reasons, smiled up at Liam. He was still hard and suffering from the same tension as their new blonde friend. "Aw, babe, she called me sexy. Don't be mean to her."

He gave Bree a look Gwen could see was both deeply loving and deeply amused. It seemed in their particular relationship, the two feelings were far from mutually exclusive. "I'm always mean."

He let her get herself adjusted until she could raise herself up into a kiss, then turned to look over his shoulder at Gwen instead of looking at her in the mirror. The way she had her legs crossed tightly and kept shifting herself on the seat made him grin before he looked at Bree. He reached down and unlocked a lever on the side of her seat, which allowed her seat to swivel around to face the rest of the van, then clipped the same one on his own, though he didn't turn around yet. "Well, if you think I'm being mean, go be nice, then."

Bree raised her eyebrow, even though she was still smiling. "Why can't *you* apologize? I'm enjoying my afterglow."

He grinned again, since Bree continued to surprise him no matter the circumstances where they found themselves. He spun her chair for her, taking a last glance at the controls to make sure things were set before he turned to face Gwen, slouching comfortably in the seat as the van swayed hypnotically along the road. His suit pants were undone and the part of him she had imagined by way of his twin for so long was casually hanging out, waiting for someone's attention.

Clearly Liam didn't have a strong preference who he received that attention from.

"She's a bad one to piss off, so if she says I should apologize, I guess I'd better get to that." He sat casually in the seat as he watched Gwen and her reactions, the look on his face finally reminding her just a little of his brother. They both watched people intensely, picked apart everything they did. It made Logan a good leader. It made Liam a good lover. "How exactly do you prefer people make things up to you, if you have your preference?"

"Ummm. . ." Not once had Gwen imagined she would actually be in the situation in front of her, and she was actually so stunned she didn't know how to respond at first. "I . . ."

Bree got comfortable in her chair as she watched, clearly enjoying the chance she had for a show. "She said she was uncomfortable, Dear. Perhaps you should see how uncomfortable she is. I'm curious to see myself."

Liam's smile grew into more of a grin, distancing him a little more from her fantasies of Logan and pulling her more into the reality that was in front of her. He watched Gwen squirm just a little more in her seat, then raked his eyes over her from top to bottom, taking in the clothes she had partially borrowed from Bree's wardrobe. The black shirt was long on her, but Gwen was bustier than Bree was, even if she was shorter, leaving the shirt tight around her chest. The black skirt at least, she had brought with her just in case, even if it was shorter and more playful than was typically considered decent for a funeral. Liam finally reached out and took Gwen's hand slowly from where she had them resolutely clasped in her lap, then tugged her toward his swivelled chair. She leapt into his lap eagerly.

He spun her as she crossed the narrow space between rows, and pulled her ass down into his lap with his hands on either side of her waist, so she was mostly facing Bree. She said she wanted to see for herself, after all. "You'll have to let me know when you're feeling a little more comfortable. But in my experience, things get worse before they get better." His hands slid over her thighs, running over the skirt covering the outside of them before slipping over the thin fabric to caress just along the inside of her knees. He spread them slowly and gently as he got a feel for the way her body moved.

Was this really happening? Gwen couldn't believe even the physical evidence of her senses telling her she was really in Liam's lap, but the stiff member between them was definitely real. Gwen didn't stop him from exploring whatever he wanted to explore, and she shivered in pleasure as he ran his hand along the inside of her thigh. "I didn't wear, um, I mean, I don't . . ."

Bree smiled as she watched, her eyes scouring the beautiful young blonde. "I think she's trying to tell you that she doesn't wear underwear. But she's so *jittery!*" Bree got up from her chair so she could get closer. She never was good at being patient or staying away. When she boldly reached out to touch Gwen's cleavage, she nearly giggled at the intake of breath she heard as a response. "And so sensitive."

"I can't imagine why she'd be nervous." He chuckled beneath her back, his touch on her thighs growing bolder to give her a taste of the strength she had so often imagined feeling from Logan. He was so much larger than she was in every way, a farmer and a fighter, and his control over what he wanted to do to her was absolute. "What, is this not the way you imagined your day when you woke up this morning?" One of his hands moved up to tug her hair backward, until she was resting her head against his shoulder. It exposed most of her to Brianne and left the rest of her completely at Liam's mercy, while she felt the stubble of his cheek scratch a quick burn against the skin of her neck.

"No, I certainly did not expect this." Gwen replied breathlessly as Bree slid her hand in to touch her breast underneath and Liam continued to tease her with light touches to sensitive skin. It was definitely getting worse, but it was a good kind of bad. They were both excitedly teasing her, and she was trying to keep her eager squirming to a minimum.

Bree moved in closer and continued teasing Gwen's nipple before she leaned over Gwen so she could whisper between Gwen and Liam. "Is she really wet?"

Once the question had been asked, Liam wasn't shy about finding out the answer, his hand moving against Gwen's core beneath her skirt. His fingers slid inside her almost possessively, taking hold of her in a way that pressed her ass back against the hardness she could feel between them waiting for her. After so long on the sexual offensive when it came to making herself available to the men in the mountains, his take-charge way of handling her was a drastic change. "Ooooh, apparently she enjoyed watching you and your afterglow, baby. I think she wants a piece of it herself."

"Of course she does." Bree giggled and kissed along the opposite side of Gwen's neck as her hands got bolder in their teasing. Bree reached behind Gwen's ass and stroked Liam a few times too. "Do you want it too, Babe? You need some love."

Liam rocked his hips beneath Gwen a few times in response to Bree's hand. He leaned his head back against the headrest to enjoy both her and the way Gwen was squirming on top of him. "I don't know. As much as she talks about getting around back in the mountains, she's a tight one. I might do some damage." His hand continued to stroke her masterfully as he teased, his strong fingers stroking against her insides as his palm teased her clit with every movement. The teasing left her legs shaking involuntarily as he stretched her out to lay back with one leg on either side of his knees.

Bree was relentless with both of them, and her hands kept moving between Gwen's sensitive breasts and Liam's hard cock. "Please, Babe? I wanna see her lose it with you. You are so sexy to watch." Bree grinned and moved closer to Liam so she could kiss him, and within her kiss, he could tell she found the whole scene incredibly arousing.

He groaned against Gwen's neck as he tortured her and he looked back up at Bree after she drew back from a kiss. Bree was straddling his leg and Gwen's as she helped him torment the woman, and he couldn't help the rush of heat the entire scene brought. They were all keeping quiet for the sake of the rest of the sleeping car, but he somehow doubted Gwen would be able to stay that way long under the assault from both of them.

"What do you think, Ms. Pierce?" He shifted himself so that instead of being in Bree's grip, Gwen was sitting along his slouched abs and he was exposed beneath her, his pants undone by his wife and shoved to the floor. The heat and hardness of him was there against her for the taking as his fingers continued their assault on her. "Come and get it." He said against her ear. "If you're so inclined."

Gwen was wound so tight she didn't have to be told again, and she was amazed when Bree moved away to watch. She didn't hesitate, though, and she raised herself up and quickly slid down on top of him so he couldn't tease her with an inch at a time. Gwen didn't expect his size, but she still groaned in pleasure as he filled her completely. "Fuck." She hissed, since she was so close to climaxing already. "You are massive, Liam Bickford."

That was something that never got old to hear, but it certainly wasn't the first time he'd been informed of that aspect of his physiology. She was every bit as ready for him as it was possible to be, though, and he leaned her forward on his lap so he could grip her by the waist and rock her against him. Liam's hands moved below her skirt to get a firm grip on her ass once it presented itself. He gave a louder growl of pleasure at the feel of her once she had all of him, and his touch on her only increased in violence and possessiveness the more she rocked against him. "Good god, woman, that is a fucking vice-grip." He let her do most of the moving, to make sure she took what she could from him and nothing would hurt her, but every sound she made only encouraged him further.

"That's . . . because I take care . . . of it." She was all too eager to bounce on top of him, since it felt so fucking good. She hadn't slept with anyone the entire time away from the mountains and she was sure as hell making up for celibate time. Every few moments she would look to see Bree watching them, and she knew Liam had to be watching his wife too, especially when Bree started to touch herself. That only excited Gwen more. She loved adventurous people.

He let her keep control just to get a taste of what she liked, how she liked her men in that particular position, but eventually his grip on her hips intensified and he scooted forward on the driver's seat. He almost shoved her forward until she fell with her hands on Bree's knees to keep her balance. The angle gave him all the leverage he wanted to slam himself into her as hard as the space would allow, riding her as her hair fell along Bree's breasts and her hands were forced to grip Bree's thighs to keep her balance. He loved how involved Bree always was whenever they took in a 'snack' as they had called them, but he was impressed with Gwen's restraint in keeping herself from falling apart. He loved a woman with something to prove.

Gwen would have lasted longer if Bree hadn't started a new attack as soon as Gwen was within reach again. Once Bree started kissing Gwen's neck and playing with her nipples again, Gwen was done for. She did her best to be as quiet as she could, but her moans were still too much to contain as a fierce climax ripped through her body.

Liam buried himself inside her as he unleashed his own in the course of her orgasm, and held her there pressed into him with one hand on the side of her neck. Her pleasure was delicious, and the way she shuddered over and over again made her unique of all the women he'd been with in a long time. They were all aware of her 'birth control' situation after their first conversation, but that was rarely even a consideration on Earth. "And that was only the first orgasm I've gotten out of you." He said as she tried to catch her breath. "Believe me, I get meaner."

"That was two." She tried to say as matter-of-factly as she could, but she was in orgasm-land where everything was either warm and fuzzy or it just wasn't a problem.

"Two, Babe." Bree repeated and she pulled back and didn't tease Gwen again, but she seemed equally happy to see both of them sated. "You really went to town on our pretty blonde here." A few of the babies were making noises as though they were awake, but they weren't making any actual complaints. Yet. The babies were facing away, so none of them could see who was awake or not. "Good thing she's on birth control or you could have made another kid just there. I know your faces."

"Good thing is right." He pulled Gwen back against him by her shirt so she was flush against him again, as he ran his hands over her legs and chest just to further enjoy her while they shared their own afterglow. "So how do you like the flavor of the midwest?" He was still inside her, still loving every small nuance of the way she moved against him as they began to recover.

"I'm glad . . . the midwest is coming to the mountains." She said with a contented groan, since no part of her yet felt solid. "I really hope that's not a one-time thing." Gwen looked up at Bree, and Bree shook her head and smiled.

"No way. Next time we get naked and we will have more space. I hope. I haven't heard much about where we're going to live in the mountains." Bree looked at the two of them and giggled before she got up and grabbed Liam's face so she could give him a wild kiss. "God, you are the best husband in the world. I love you for being so flexible. Both figuratively and literally."

"You're a hell of a lot more flexible than I am. Both literally and figuratively." He grinned up at her and ran one hand over her while his other hand was still busy exploring Gwen. "You're gonna enjoy her every bit as much as I just did. And getting both of you on your backs in a bed . . ." Liam growled at the image in his mind, and ground his hips into Gwen one last time before he allowed himself to leave her. "We're going to have some very, very good nights."

Gwen nearly collapsed to the floor, but fortunately Bree helped her back to her seat where she laid out the best that she could. "Fuck, I'm going to be sore." She didn't sound the least bit sad about it, but it had been one hell of a ride. "You should thank someone for that cock. I don't know if God is appropriate, but damn."

Bree laughed again. "You'll get used to him. At least, I hope you'll want to."

Liam didn't even bother to pull his pants back up as he leaned back in the chair, satisfied and unwilling to move other than to relax as he watched Gwen attempt to recover. "Is that what you think you are?" He shot at Brianne with a teasing look. "Used to me?"

Bree smirked at her husband as she looked him over, taking in every part of him that was exposed with an always-hungry look. "Well, I don't get sore nearly as often as I did when we were first together."

"And when you do, it's because you come at me with those fucking claws of yours and tell me you want it rough. You can't fault my dick for that, that's all on you." He pulled her into another kiss that then trailed down to the inner curve of her breasts.

Bree moaned softly as his kiss trailed down her sensitive skin. "You are the most versatile lover on this planet. I won the lottery with you." She replied with another moan. "Just don't tell Margo."

"They both know about the girl at the market." He shrugged, since he knew the situation was very different, but he wasn't going to talk about that in the afterglow he was feeling at the moment. "She wasn't happy about that one either, but that's between me and Margo. Satisfying all three of you is pretty close to the top of my list of priorities, and when it comes to you, that means . . . like you said, some versatility." He winked up at her and leaned back to look over at Gwen as his hands trailed casually over Bree's legs. "Some fucking *good* versatility too. If you're this good when we catch you off guard, I look forward to how you do when you actually come over expecting to get fucked."

"Mhm." Gwen just laid there for a moment before Bree tossed her a towel so she could clean up, since Liam left a mess. "I'm all about having more fun like that. You know, as long as it's just fun." Gwen wasn't actually looking to be a fourth wife, even though she had asked him if he was looking before. He said he wasn't looking. She wasn't either. "Fun is what I'm about."

"That's up to Mrs. Bickford here." He kissed down Bree's chest again and adjusted the way he sat on the chair to get a little more comfortable as he looked back and forth between the two of them. "That's how we decided this was going to work early on. She's a wild one, and I love her for it. But when it comes to me being wild, it's gonna be on her terms and only on her nights. If I'm with one of the other two, it'll be best for you to keep your distance. Those are the boundaries." He grinned at how worn out she was so quickly, but he knew they had taken her without any real preparation at all, and he had certainly shown no mercy for her first time with him.

Gwen just held up her hands as though she was surrendering. "I won't bother you. If you want me, you know how to find me. Otherwise, I'll stay out of your hair." Gwen didn't actually pride herself on destroying marriages, the ones that were already broken were usually the ones where men showed interest in her. Liam's life was messy enough without her, she wouldn't make it harder for him. "Childcare with benefits."

That got a loud laugh from Liam, but she could see he was looking at her hungrily, even as satisfied as they both still were. His eyes said it was only the beginning of what he wanted from her. The fact she could see his body beginning to react all over again to Brianne's light touches and the sight of Gwen's still-panting recovery was only a promise of things to come. "You think you're capable of babysitting the controls for a little while?"

"Uh, sure?" Gwen got up slowly and tugged her clothes back into place before she turned her attention to the controls instead of the sexy man and his reacting cock. "If you trust me. I can handle it."

"Good. Just make sure we don't die." He slid out of the chair and onto the floor between the front seats of the van and the second row, stretching out languidly as much as the width of the van would allow. "And you . . ." He pointed up at Brianne with a grin that needed no explanation. "If you think I'm gonna waste any time where the babies are mostly asleep, you're insane."

Brianne let out a soft squeal of excitement and joined him on the floor where she happily sat down on his midsection with her dress hiked again to her hips. "It is one thing to watch. It's entirely another to have you to myself. Especially with an audience." Bree leaned down and kissed him passionately. "I love you." The words she said were given to him with sincerity and tenderness, and she certainly never passed up an occasion to let him know how much she loved him. She was wild and crazy. She knew it. But she was also fiercely loyal to Liam and she would stand by him and their family to her dying day.

As Bree rode him, slowly and deliciously as she somehow knew he wanted, his eyes moved up to Gwen past Brianne's shoulder and the flaming red hair that came with it. His wife's lips were moving over his chest as she started to ride him harder, her chest pressed against him completely until his mouth was gaping with pleasure. In his eyes, though, Gwen could still see the promise she had looked for so many times in Logan's, that he was there with his wife, but he would have more of her in the future. It was one more kind of ownership, a different kind of commanding presence than Logan's, but with its own kind of authority born of a visible desire.

When he thrust up into Brianne to pull an audible gasp of pleasure from her, his eyes were on Gwen, each move, each gasp, another promise and threat all rolled up in a single delicious package.

12

Jessie couldn't believe the news when Jason told her, and she still couldn't believe it when she heard the new arrivals were incoming. She stood next to Jason as he watched, keeping more and more to the background of operations than he had in a long time. Jason worked less on the Twist than he had before, but Jessie was still somewhat distant, even though she didn't want to be. She just didn't trust him not to lose himself in it all over again. Yet.

Jessie watched as the caravan came in, holding Rebekah tightly, since she still wasn't sure there wouldn't be some bad apples in a group of hundreds. "That's certainly a lot of people that Logan brought back. What does your brother think?"

"He thinks we're all dead." Jason said flatly, but he sighed afterward, his eyes darting from one of the newcomer vehicles to another, taking in faces wherever he could. "I've run background checks and communications profiles on every one of them as thoroughly as I can, and I had a team of a dozen people helping just sift through everything. Aside from the one whistle-blower we found in the whole mess and they dealt with," swiftly and without mercy, as Logan had assured them Midwest justice always was, "I didn't find any evidence of any problems. And I've got a handle on every phone and piece of communication-capable equipment coming into this place. But yeah, he thinks we're all dead, regardless."

"Wonderful." She replied just as flatly as she continued to watch. Rebekah flailed her arms in excitement, though, since to her it was just a flurry of action that was fun to watch. "Well, it'll be nice to have Gwen and Priscilla back. Unless they're so taken with the newcomers that we need to find a new sitter."

"Logan told me something about that not being an issue anymore with all the newcomers. Not sure what he meant by that, but here we are." He sighed again, but when he looked over and saw Rebekah flailing, he smiled anyway and reached out to take one of her hands as she watched the seemingly never-ending caravan of vehicles.

The passenger cars came through first, but the tractor trailers and buses were starting to come through the far end of the valley, and Jason had to blink a few times just to take in the sheer quantity of materials and goods coming into the mountain community. Logan had been vague on details because he didn't have an accurate count of everything, but Jason could tell from the dozens and dozens of trucks it was going to take days just to get a handle on everything. Let alone get everybody settled. Cars were beginning to park in designated areas, which meant it was time to get to work.

"Alright, Personnel team, go say hi to somebody and let's start getting people and their luggage settled. Bravo team, start rounding up drivers and getting rough sketches of inventory, we'll make up a full plan later on once everything's in and accounted for. And if anybody sees Bickford, tell him to come find me once this circus gets cleared up."

Jessie watched Jason as he ordered people around, and she looked at their daughter again for just a moment. "You know, her future husband could be among those newcomers."

That clearly wasn't a thought that had crossed his mind before that moment, but he nodded and looked a little more warily out at the flood of cars. They didn't have quite the density of infants they'd had there in the mountains, but Jason groaned when he saw a carbon copy of Logan get out of a van with three children just to himself.

"I hadn't considered that." He said honestly, eyeing the tiny children as if they'd done something to be worthy of him being wary of them when it came to his daughter. "Do you think that's something we should set up for her early? Not something we'd enforce on her or anything like that, just some kind of arrangement we could steer her toward? I know of several places that do that and it seems to work fairly well for them."

"I don't know." Jessie said cautiously, but she obviously didn't think it sounded like a terrible idea. "I would have wanted it, only my parents never made it happen."

"I couldn't understand why it made sense when I heard about it at first. A few years later, I understood a little better." He was still fairly close-lipped about his past, even though she knew all the major details of what he'd been through. "It's something to keep in mind, though. These folks typically fuck around until they get knocked up and then stick with the one responsible for the knocking up. Not the best method of finding a spouse, if you ask me."

"These folks." She replied with a laugh. "You know that these are mostly my people, right? I didn't live *that* far away from where Anna and Logan are from." Jessie, however, had no interest in contacting home at all. They could think she was dead all they wanted, she truly did not care. "I slept around as much as I was afforded the opportunity to do so."

He turned toward her to kiss Rebekah on the forehead, then leaned in and kissed Jessie as if the touch would help erase the past neither of them had reason to remember anymore. "Most of the point of everything we're doing here is to make a better world for the next generation. I'd like to think we can make a better situation for Bek here than the one you or I had to deal with for ourselves."

"I hope it will still be good for us too." She replied softly after the short kiss broke. Jason's lookalike caught her eye as people moved to deal with the influx of new arrivals, and she watched him carefully as Tatyana moved next to him. "You didn't tell me how the testing went last night."

Jason's face fell at the change in conversation, but he shook his head. "Xander thinks he saw some progress with some of the initiation sequences he ran, but statistically, they look about the same as all the others. Startup is fine to a point, target sighting is fully functioning, the lock looks good, power levels are within thresholds, but no bridge. He was pissed last night that the midwesterners were coming in so soon because it meant he was going to have to step away from it a while. But he's optimistic." Which was something Jason hadn't been about the Twist for what felt like a long time.

"That's good." She gave him an encouraging smile before she looked out again. "I better go check and make sure there's food ready for them. All of those people are going to be hungry, and thankfully we have enough for now. Hopefully they brought a lot with them that will last."

"From the looks of it, they brought everything any of them have ever owned." He watched the trucks roll in, since there seemed to be no end of them. "I'll be around helping with inventory, but I'll be back home as soon as I can be." He said with a last kiss, both to her and to Bekah between them. "I know they're your people, but be careful with them, alright? They're gonna have a lot of assumptions about what it means to be here, and you're better equipped than anyone to help them understand. Just be wary of them."

"They probably would have told me to be wary of you, if it was the other way around. We'll be fine." She assured him and she grabbed his hand before he could get away too quickly. "I love you." Jessie was doing her best to repair their relationship from her end, and talking more about her feelings, good or bad, was one of her methods.

He was surprised, given her distance lately, but he smiled anyway and squeezed her hand. "I love you too, Jess." He lifted her hand and kissed the back of it before he pulled away to get in motion, but she could see that the smile lingered on his face even as he got some distance.

Tatyana was near Xander when Jason came down into the madness and she looked up to where he was standing with his wife previously. "She really does not like me, does she? She won't even come down and say hello?"

"She's with the team working on housing and provisioning. She's got her own work to do right now." Jason said with a slight glare. "But no, she doesn't like you. Never has, to my knowledge. Any problems down here so far?"

"Not that I've seen." Tatyana saw someone motion a truck in their direction, and Tatyana knew what that meant. Weapons. She actually grinned as the truck moved their way. "I guess Bickford came through. Who would have thought?"

"We did. Otherwise we wouldn't have sent him in the first place." Jason gave her another dismissive glare, then looked up at Fitch. He hadn't heard much from her or, frankly, from any of the others the entire time they'd been gone, but he assumed that had been because they were equal parts enjoying themselves and actually working, so he was content with a small lack of information. "Pleasant vacation, Commander?"

"I was with my wife, drinking booze and eating shit I really should have said no to." Kameron laughed as she looked at Jason. "It was a good vacation, but we're glad to be home. Melissa nearly ran out of the truck just to get into the Labyrinth so she could see Kassie." Fitch loved everything about her inked wife, and she hoped that they truly had another sixty years to be together.

"I'm here with the weapons." She held out a handwritten list of the inventory, since she was far more organized than people gave her credit for. "Nothing was loaded up into this truck without me knowing. The only weapons unaccounted for are personal items that some people insisted they keep with them, mostly handguns. Some shotguns and knives. I thought the handwritten list was the better option, considering I wasn't sure what kind of security we had out there and I would hate for the Consortium to know what we have."

"Probably the best call to make under the circumstances." Jason took a quick look over the list to take in the volume of armaments the people had brought with them, and he gave her a surprised look both at the list and some of the weaponry he could see beyond her in the truck. "Good fucking grief, did one of these people own an armory or something?" He set the list on the ground and took his data core out of his shirt, activating it quickly to scan and digitize the list with a few quick commands.

"Just about." She laughed as she glanced over at the truck. "Let's just say that these people are very . . . anti-government." Fitch looked around and waved at a few of her new friends. Kameron's filthy mouth and carefree attitude made it easy for her to get along with people. Most people, anyway. "And fucking paranoid at that, too. The good news is that most of them know how to use this shit. So they don't really need training. Hell, *we're* going to need some training with the big stuff. They have jerry-rigged some crazy shit in some of the other trucks."

"Crazy shit is what some of us do best." Ben said as he popped out behind Kameron, looking around at the entire town under construction and the path beyond where he could see people being led into what he assumed was the Labyrinth. He was wearing a handgun in a shoulder holster beneath one arm, taking no chances about walking into an unknown place unarmed. Paranoid was a nice word for it. "Ben Prince. You must be Jason. You've got 'pretentious asshole' written right across your forehead."

He hopped down out of the truck and looked around at some of the others present, apparently putting faces with names. "We brought along a few crates of sim-guns along with the actual artillery, figured it would be best not to waste ammunition teaching a bunch of would-be colonists how to shoot people."

Jason wasn't impressed, and just nodded as he continued his review. "How prescient of you, Mr. Prince." He leaned to one side without taking his eyes off the inventory. "The title is actually *all-*

knowing asshole, but pretentious works well enough."

Kameron rolled her eyes as she stood between them. "Please don't start a dick-measuring contest *right in front of me*. I'm sure you both have satisfactory dicks. I mean, you both have kids. So they work, at least." She glanced away from the two of them and took a deep breath as she glanced and saw Xander and Tatyana as they headed toward the truck. "Where did you want to store this stuff, Jason? I think it should be accessible, but I hesitate to leave it up here anywhere."

"There are some upper levels within the Labyrinth that we haven't touched, just because the lifts don't run up there. It's all ramps and stairs. X and I talked about turning it into an armory, but we didn't really have the inventory. Clearly no longer a problem." He was still in shock at the sheer quantity of artillery that came with the midwesterners, but he wasn't going to permit himself the fool's hope of thinking that it would actually do them any good if the Consortium found them and decided to attack. The only way arms like the ones on the truck would be any good would be on the offensive in a place where the Consortium didn't expect them. But it was certainly better than nothing.

"You have this one in mind for a killing-people type position, Fitch?" He nodded over at Ben, clearly not fond of the man on first sight, but then, he wasn't fond of anyone besides his own wife.

"He's a better shot than most I've seen, which is saying something, considering he's never had military training." She looked back at Ben and gave him a small smile, since she didn't really have a problem with either of them, but most people did. Fitch could handle the likes of Jason and Ben. "I did a preliminary scope of the talent by having a contest. They had all this great shit and I wanted to shoot some of it. A contest is something people usually like to get involved with. Ben here came in second place."

"Then why is he riding shotgun with you instead of whoever won first?" It was Xander's turn to fling a question at her from the truck as he looked over the equipment. He was much more the hands-on type.

"Cuz Orion never leaves his wife and kids if he can help it." Kameron said with a smirk. Orion wasn't really known for his sharp-shooting, especially since he had been in charge of transportation the entire time in the mountains, but that was only because he didn't like to get involved with a gun unless he had to.

"It's his super-genes. So it's cheating. Somehow."

"Right." Both Jason and Xander said at the same time and in exactly the same tone, though neither man seemed amused by the surround-sound. It was Jason who continued, regardless. "Well, whatever he's appointed to depends on you, Fitch. I trust your judgment." Jason gave Ben a dismissive glance and handed back the paper inventory, having gotten all he needed. "Any cooks where you come from?"

Ben gave a snorting laugh. "I assume you're not talking about food or meth. But yeah, there's a few I went to school with. I never got quite that deep into things. I already tipped Kameron off to them, though."

"Good. We'll need them working with some of the chemists that we've already got on staff. Bullets and grenades only go so far."

"We've got a few DEWs on hand too." Ben said with a smile. "Some of us took personal defense a little more seriously than others. Especially the Bickfords. They had all the toys."

"And kept most of the best ones for themselves, I expect." Jason was surprised about the nowheresville folk having directed energy weapons, but he wasn't going to complain.

"I'll get more information from Liam, if I can." Kameron glanced toward the Bickford bunch, which included her tall friend, since Anna, Logan, Orion, and Mercury tended to stick together when they had their kids. "Seems like a decent guy." Kameron was quiet for a moment and then she looked a little more serious as she turned her attention back to Jason. "What about the Twist? Figure out anything more?" Kameron had a personal investment in making sure the thing worked again. Her daughter's aunt was on Eleusis. One of her best friends was on Eleusis. She only hoped they were still alive somehow.

"Closer. Still no cigar. Believe me, we wouldn't be out here talking about gun inventory if we had that thing working already." He heaved a sigh and gave the inventory a final look. "Xander can show you the vault we were planning on making into an armory, you and your people can outfit it however you like. With this kind of firepower, though, make sure you post a couple guards on it at all times. I don't want somebody who just came from the middle of nowhere getting any ideas of going on a shooting spree because living underground doesn't agree with them."

Kameron nodded and looked over at Ben. "Come on, Prince.

You and I can work this out together, right? You know your people, I know ours, we'll set up a schedule and get all the weapons in one place. Sound like a plan?"

Fitch was unlike anyone else Ben had ever worked with before, and if he had to draw up an exact antithesis of his own wife, he couldn't have done a better job, but he found himself getting along with her decently well nonetheless. He nodded and headed back into the truck. "Whatever you say, boss. I'll get started with some of the small arms, just point me where we're going."

Tatyana watched as some people started to unload the weapons, and she hopped into the truck. She peeked around the corner to smile at Xander. "Do you have a request? I'm sure you can have whatever you like. You should be armed, you're the brains we need to stay intact."

"There are several hundred brains in this operation, and I would prefer all of them remain intact." He watched the rest of the newcomers, all of them looking around in wonder. Faces said a lot about a person, and anyone who was looking around for weaknesses or particular elements would stick out from those who were simply looking around at a new place just because it was new. "That being said, I'm a sucker for a Beretta 92 revival edition, or a good long-scope rifle. I try to have one of each."

"Let me see what I can find." Tatyana wandered through the truck and stayed inside for a while before she came out with a long-scope rifle. "Well, here's one." She tossed it to him and smiled, since he caught it easily. He seemed very at home with a weapon, and she was okay with that. "So do you think Bickford really brought home a rat somewhere in this group?"

"With these numbers, I'd be surprised if it wasn't a whole nest of them." He had been overruled in his concerns, but being overruled hardly made those concerns evaporate. "The odds of a breach here are just too damn high. No matter what they collected, no matter what Jason managed to wipe on their way here, every single piece of technology they brought with them is a liability that has the potential to point straight to our location. All it takes is one fucking kid with a microchip that somebody forgot about and the Consortium will have the coordinates it needs to vaporize the area."

He inspected the rifle the entire time he spoke, clearly comfortable with multitasking. Xander seemed to find it to his liking and he adjusted the scope to his preferences, targeting the top of the mountain beneath which the Labyrinth was hidden. "The only thing that'll render those kinds of odds irrelevant is if we finally crack that damn Twist. GPS doesn't mean shit if the tech involved is on another G."

"Well, we're getting close, aren't we? We opened it long enough the other night that I thought Jason would jump through the hole." Tatyana picked up a gun for herself and then looked it over. "We're close." She answered her own question before she looked at Xander again. "We'll get there."

"Close is never good enough." He and his brother did have that much in common, they were both men of absolutes. But then again, they were surrounded by people of similar inclinations. "We need . . ." Xander stopped, then turned back to Tatyana as she saw the wheels spinning in his mind. "What if the problem isn't on our end? What if the problem is something with Eleusis that's causing the bridge to falter every few fucking microseconds? If it's not something we're doing on our end, and we could get something through to help stabilize the connection, it could extend the operable time of the window. The Consortium's monstrosity has a whole fucking complex built around it, they could have any number of auxiliary functions that weren't accounted for in the data Jason grabbed."

"How do we fix a problem on their end? Especially if we don't even know what kind of problem it could be? How do we know we would even have the tools? Are you suggesting that someone just hops through on the hope that it could be stabilized?"

"No, not a person. With it only staying open for seconds at a time, there'd be no way of guaranteeing a safe transition. I don't want people getting shredded in the process. Which reminds me, I need to work on some safeguards for it. Or go over the ones Jason said he made up but never implemented. Anyway, no, I think we need to work up a few dozen anchors. As small as we can make them just to make sure at least one of them gets through intact. If they do, and I'm right, we can pair with that anchor for a location lock instead of having to scan every time and keep scanning so we don't end up in the middle of space or the crust of the planet." They'd had that problem more than once before they managed more or less to lock down the area where they wanted to arrive. But the opening site continued to hop around with a radius of roughly a mile, including vertical jumps far above the surface of the planet and drops that were just barely subterranean. "Eliminate as many variables as possible."

"Well, you're the genius. I'll just follow your lead." Tatyana replied as she kept her new toy close. "Come on, let's go try it now."

At that suggestion, Xander looked around at all the strangers who were picking up crates of ammunition and entire racks of firearms. Tatyana could see him visibly convince himself not to be as paranoid about them as he wanted to be before he turned away and slung the rifle over his shoulder, looking back over the same shoulder more than a few times. "They'd better be worth the risk we all took to recruit them."

"They are. Because we're weaker without them, even if there are a few bad eggs. Paranoia only takes you so far. Kicking ass takes you the rest of the way." Tatyana walked alongside Xander as they headed back toward the Labyrinth without any explanation to anyone, including Jason. If he showed up, they would clue him in. If he didn't, he would have to wait. "What do you hope for with Eleusis, anyway? Everyone has to have a reason."

"Wow. Most people start with your favorite color and work their way down slowly until they get to the roots of your soul. Way to dive right in headfirst without checking the depth first." Xander smiled as they walked, though he didn't look over at her to answer the question. "I want what everybody wants for Eleusis. A second chance for the human race, something free, something that hasn't been corrupted by thousands of years of human shit piling up all over the map."

From the way he stopped, it was clear he wasn't finished, and he stalked up the hillside toward the entrance to the Labyrinth, as if the ground offended him. "Mostly I just want it to be over." There was exhaustion behind his voice and his eyes, so similar to Jason's but haunted with very different ghosts. "The natural state of humanity isn't war, it's creation. But we've been fighting a war against the world and against our own lifespan for so long we've started to forget it can be any other way. I want the war to be over."

"Let's say we take over Eleusis and somehow fuck the Consortium. It's never over." She said plainly as she looked at him again. "Because as long as some of those people exist, they'll fight for power. The best we can do is keep the power as long as possible." Tatyana kept up with him no matter how he altered his pace, but she didn't try to get closer to him. Being rejected by him after his arrival had kept her away. "I never expected to make it this far. Maybe living on Eleusis won't be so bad if I don't actually die. I'm not expecting that I'll live, but it will be interesting if I do."

"Believe me, I understand the feeling of making it farther than you think you will." There was a deep amusement behind his words, and it was one more way in which he was like his brother. They'd both expressed how amazed they were to have lived as long as they had, though neither of them ever said explicitly just how long that was. "And even if there's always going to be assholes struggling for power, at least for us, for our own sakes, the war will be over. I've been fighting and living on the run for longer than I care to think about. Peace will be . . . something new. Something to look forward to."

"For a while." She agreed as they continued through the Labyrinth to the lifts so they could go down to the Twist. "But what is there to do, if there's nothing more to fight for?" Tatyana seemed genuinely concerned. If she wasn't going to die for the cause, she didn't know what purpose her life had. She had been working so hard toward vengeance and restitution that she didn't know what she would live for after that.

"There's always something to fight for, even in peace or when you're actually left alone." He shrugged, looking down at her across the narrow lift as it descended. "But there's also things to get out of bed for. I think that'd be good enough for me."

"What gets you out of bed, other than the need to fight?" She questioned as they got onto the lift and went down as quickly as the old thing would allow. "Are you hoping for a family? A wife? Or a husband? I totally could have read you wrong." She teased, since she knew he had interest in women, though he could be interested in men also, she wasn't sure.

"I doubt I'd make a very good husband. To a woman or to a man." He teased right back, since he was going to let her keep wondering. "Honestly, I don't know. This war is the only thing I've ever known or cared about. Anything else is an adventure. The only reason I know how to live like a human being is because I've gotten good at pretending to be one."

"You are one. Even if you were made instead of conceived. In the traditional sense." Tatyana looked down at the new gun at her side and she ran her fingers over the metal, fully familiarizing herself with the weapon. "Sometimes I wonder if it would have been better to be like you and your brother. I don't mean the part where he was tortured. I just mean the part of not having parents. It would make this whole thing much less painful."

"I've wondered if that's true." The lift reached its destination and he continued his brisk pace toward the Twist, his concentration on their goal clearly not distracting him from the conversation at hand. "If there is some kind of god watching over this mess, I can only imagine their reason for giving most of us families is so we would have an inborn reason to give a shit about anything besides ourselves. It took me a long time to start doing that. It's made things less painful, sure, but it does it by putting the whole world on the other side of the petri dish." He shook his head, since contemplating his existence wasn't something he enjoyed doing if he could avoid it. "I was sorry to see what happened to your father, when Jason sent out the broadcast to the world. He was a good man."

"A good man who was just trying to do the right thing." She replied without any emotion behind it, because she had heard the sentiment too many times. "How many of those people do we have here? How many people have been made worse because of the Consortium and the Initiative? Even if we make it to the other side of this war, I wonder who we're going to be left with because of what they've done."

"We'll be left with the same thing every war leaves. Corpses and a mess to clean up." He went to one wall where there were bins filled with discarded technology, none of it active or powered in any way. He started sifting through the collection of spare parts for pieces that would serve his needs, a long-discarded communicator here, a wristband there. All of them were capable of tracking, and all of them could be useful.

"Here, see if you can get these to hold a charge, I'll work up a code to make them useful." He had dozens of small devices he wanted, it seemed, and he quickly pulled down a workstation to jump back into the coding where he and Jason had lived for weeks.

Usually Tatyana was the one bossing people around, but she was good at making *people* do what she wanted, not technology. She went to every port she had available to connect the tech to a power source, and hoped most of it still worked. "Anything else you want me to jump around and do, *Sir*?" She replied sarcastically, but with a smirk anyway.

"Well, if you're inclined to jump, I'm sure I could come up

with a few ideas." He shot back with the same smirk. Normally it was the two of them and Jason all working in the lab together, and the fact they were in the lab by themselves was a rarity. Whenever Jason wasn't around, the world was an easier place to live in. With a few final keystrokes, she could see his written codes installing in all of the available devices, though some of them completed quicker than others because they were so archaic. He turned while he waited and faced the Twist, through which he could see her with the last of the devices. "If this works, we're all gonna be doing a lot of jumping for a very long time."

"If it works, then you're the genius you advertised yourself to be." She smiled at him through the Twist arch before she looked up at the Twist itself. It always fascinated her that a fairly simple structure could send her to another world. "I have a secret collection of hard alcohol with your name on it if you manage to get this thing to work."

"A rebel among rebels. I knew you were my type." He grinned through the opening at her and then reached across to begin the initialization sequence for the Twist's operation, which dimmed the lights in the room and all over the complex, since it was drawing not just on their own power grid but the generator for the entire Labyrinth. It was the only place the rebels controlled at the time of Nine's destruction that was capable of powering the Twist at all, given the huge demands at stake.

As the software fed to the tiny tracking machines, the Twist came to life with a rush of heat and crackling light that was a far cry from the brilliance and majesty Xander knew it held when it worked smoothly. Even so, he still admired the violence of it as it pushed and pulled him through the room in tremendous waves of pressure and force. "Twelve minutes to midnight, Eleusis time." He said out loud as he worked on the targeting to get it close to the safe zone they identified for their probing. The machine fought him at every turn, but nothing about it surprised him any longer. He expected the difficulty. He also expected to win.

Tatyana stepped closer to the Twist as though she dared it to do something spectacular, and even though the heat coming off of it was uncomfortable, she remained close. "Should I start throwing things through?"

"Not yet." He went to pick up a few of his own, spinning them between his fingers as he waited for things to stabilize, at least to the point they achieved the night before. "If you can see the tall grass or the trees, start throwing. If we end up in the lake again, it wouldn't help us much to stabilize there."

Tatyana waited and waited, and just when she thought they wouldn't get it stabilized, she saw trees. She didn't wait for his okay, she just started throwing things through so something would get through that could help them. They really needed to catch a break.

Xander held back just a little longer, watching for the flickering movement of the Twist as it tried to stabilize within the grasses, but it occasionally sliced through trees, sliced through blades of grass that began collecting on the floor of their laboratory along with piles of others that hadn't yet been incinerated. When it came to rest at the edge of the trees, he tossed a few of his own through, some of them turning to shredded pieces as the passage flickered and nearly died.

Once they were out of pieces reprogrammed to anchor, Xander moved back to the interface by the wall, but stopped when he saw that Tatyana wasn't moving. He pulled her back with him with a hand clenched to the back of her shirt, just to get her out of the immediate danger zone. She could see him tinkering with the targeting system and the effects his work had on the Twist itself, but very quickly, it appeared as though the connection completely flared out of existence. He actually growled in the humming futility of the power coursing through the room, but he didn't stop working.

It took a number of stops and starts, but she could see more than ever the echoes of the Eleusis landscape reoccurring in patterns, the same view of a tree, the same scars in the landscape the failed gate had torn as the portal began to lock itself in place. The minutes were tense as they passed, with Xander's eyes flicking back and forth between the Twist opening and the screen, until finally, the other world came fully into focus.

The stillness of it was almost anticlimactic, the ease of the air on the far side of the portal as the Twist's basic programming kept unintentional particles or insects from passing through, but had no trouble letting the fresh air of Eleusis waft through with its strange and powerful scents.

"What. The. Fuck. You . . ." Tatyana looked over at Xander but then stared at the Eleusis landscape. "Is . . . this real?"

He let out an exhausted sigh, since it had been easily one of the most stressful hours of his life while they worked. "You owe me a drink." He went up to the doorway and looked through it with her, finally satisfied enough with the control interface to trust that it was open and would stay that way, at least for the time being. "Go on. You of all people deserve the right to go first. Just get your ass right back in here."

Tatyana looked through and actually hesitated, since she wasn't sure she could go and convince herself to come back. She looked over at him and took a few steps closer. "It's completely different, just staring at it. I . . ."

"Go." He commanded one more time, his voice a little more stern even though the expression on his face was understanding. "I'll make sure it stays open for you from this side. Go take a breath of what we're fighting for."

She went ahead after he told her to go again, and when she stepped through, she stood there in the grass and took a deep breath. It was after midnight on Eleusis, but Tatyana didn't care. Tatyana tilted her head up to the sky and kept breathing deeply before she started whispering in Russian.

She spoke to her father, and took a moment to thank him for all he had done to bring humanity across the stars.

The Twist behind her was nothing more than an oval opening in the air, with part of it digging into the ground itself. On either side of it, she could see two pieces of hardware they dropped earlier as anchors, with other bits and pieces scattered all around in the tall grass. Whatever they were doing, it had worked, and she was there, breathing an atmosphere she could already feel was more oxygen-rich than Earth, with a difference in air pressure between the coastal plain and the mountains that made her ears pop.

The stars were all wrong, but they glowed in ways no one on Earth had ever seen before. One of Eleusis' moons hung in the sky, a tiny, distant spot of pockmarked light floating in the sea of stars. It was quiet, in ways the worries of Earth could never allow her home planet to be, dark in ways the known fears of Earth would never again allow it to become. It reached out and offered endless fields and forests where no human foot had ever stepped, begging to be known.

"I wish you could come through." She replied loudly when she turned back and looked toward Xander who was on the other side. "It's not nearly as fun by myself, it's so beautiful here."

"I'll make it on the next trip." He smiled, watching her take it all in. "Though believe me, the prospect of getting stranded there with you is tempting."

"Can't be that tempting." She replied as she bent down again to touch the grass, though she knew she had to go back through. Tatyana only had her gun, and she wasn't sure they wouldn't be discovered somehow. "I'm coming back through."

He stood out of the way so she could get back through the open doorway unhindered, but she could see the awe on his face at what they managed to do. She had just stepped across the galaxy as easily as stepping over a threshold, and though he understood the science of it, he was still left in amazement. He reached out and put a hand on her arm as she came back through, moving his grip up from her forearm as if verifying that she had physically returned. "Feels pretty warm there. We'll have to remember to pack accordingly."

"It is warm." She smiled brightly as she came back through, but almost immediately, she looked back longingly. "Jason is going to lose his mind. He's been trying to get Aiko and Carl back for so long."

That dampened Xander's mood again, and he shook his head. "He needs to realize he's likely to find a couple of shallow graves at best. Nothing at all at worst. Just because he hasn't been able to find any record of them in Consortium databases being captured, tortured, or held doesn't mean they survived. They weren't exactly prepared when they got shoved through."

"I don't know. If anyone can survive without being prepared, it is probably those two." Tayana wasn't usually optimistic, but she also wasn't entirely convinced that Aiko and Carl were dead. Xander took some time before he powered down the Twist, but when he did, she let out a sigh. "It is definitely time for alcohol."

"I could not agree more." He hadn't completely let go of her once she got back to Earth, and he looked her over once as she remained close to him. "Fair warning, I turn into a mean drunk. Though maybe mean isn't the right word for it. Rough, maybe, might be the right word."

Tatyana laughed and stepped out of his hold, since she wasn't exactly sure why he was hanging onto her in the first place. "I can handle it. I'm not as fragile as I look. Don't you know my reputation by now?"

"I make it a point never to put too much faith in reputations." He followed her out of the lab, locking up the room on their way out as always. They just got the damn thing working, and he wasn't going to let anyone interfere with it. "I prefer to judge things by my own experience."

"Well, I worked hard on developing my reputation, thank you very much. I may be small, but I am in no way fragile." Tatyana didn't look back at him, but she felt like she was on a kind of high. Xander got the Twist to work. She stepped onto Eleusis soil. Things were looking up. "Just so I know, as a mean drunk, does that mean you're going to try to take a swing at me or something?"

"If I did, I'm sure you'd handle me without too much trouble." She could see his smile and feel the same kind of high running through him as was running through her. They got back to the lift quickly, and he let her select their destination, since he didn't know where she'd hidden her stash of alcohol. Once the lift doors were closed, he turned toward her again. "No, what I mean is a little more like this."

He pulled her by one arm and shoved her back against the sheet-metal wall of the lift hard enough to rattle the moving platform, then stepped in against her with his hands going for her waist. Clearly the man didn't have a problem with aggression in any form, and his touch had a kind of savage curiosity to it.

Tatyana's surprise was clear on her face when she looked up at him. He mentioned he might be interested in her after he first arrived, but things cooled off since then. Mostly because he'd rejected her, and she hated that. "You already said no to me once. What makes you think I still want any piece of you?"

"First off, don't put words in my mouth. I didn't say no, I said there were things to make sure of first." His hands moved over her sides as he settled himself in against her, clearly in a fairly vulnerable position if she did feel inclined to get violent with him for his attention. "Those things are now seen to, and sorted." There weren't many instances where his slight british accent came through, but every so often, it became just pronounced enough for her to remember it. "And if you're not interested, then say so."

Tatyana looked up into his eyes with a hardened expression, though she couldn't say she wasn't interested because she still was. "I don't like to be rejected." It was the only version of no that she could give, even though it wasn't no at all.

"Nobody comes to mind who does. Good thing I'm not the rejecting type. I'm just the type that gets shit done." His hands moved farther down over her hips as he rested against her, forcing her head back if she wanted to look him in the eye. "I want some of that alcohol you promised, and I want you. Whether that's tonight or after you think I've been sufficiently punished for wanting to work, it's not gonna change."

She didn't say anything until the lift stopped on her floor, since her alcohol was locked away in her unit with her things. Tatyana finally moved her hands so she could graze them over the top of his hands. "Show me, then. Show me how much you want what you say you want."

He gave her a slightly warning look at that, but he was still smiling. "I don't like the implication that I'm a liar." That said, she barely had time to feel his hands tighten on her hips before she felt herself picked up between them and whirled through the air until her back came up against the still-open doorway of the lift. He stepped into her and kissed her hard, keeping the lift door open as it tried to close with her in the way, forcing her against him with every attempt. He hadn't been kidding about how rough he was, but he certainly wasn't treating her like a fragile alabaster princess either.

Tatyana ached for that kiss. She kissed him back just as rough and her fingers dug into his clothing as she gripped his torso to keep him close. Tatyana wasn't into something sick and twisted like she was replacing Jason with his brother, because that wasn't true. She just happened to be incredibly attracted to the way they looked, even though they still looked different. Her kiss was needy and heated, which said a lot about how she felt. She had gone so long without a sexual partner that she was eager to jump up onto him right there.

The lift rang out a warning bell to tell them to remove themselves from the doorway, but Xander ignored it. He didn't want to move from the moment with the way she was returning his kisses. As long as he had known of her, even if he had very seldom met her in person, he knew just how wild and ruthless Tatyana could be. Ever since he'd gotten to the mountains, he had wanted to find out more for himself. He finally pulled away from the doorway to walk down the hallway, still holding her against him with his hands on her ass to let her hang off him. He took one look to make sure the low-ceilinged passage was clear and he kept kissing her as he made his way along it, waiting for her to let him know exactly where they were going.

Tatyana only paused when they made it to her door, which had a security system she installed herself. She swiped her hand over it and punched in a few codes before the door opened. "This is home." She said simply before she closed the door behind him.

"Your home is a lot like you." He teased as his hands roamed over her. "Begging for someone to come along and make a mess of it."

"Do not make a mess of my home." She said sharply, but she wasn't actually threatening him. Yet. "You can make a mess of me, but not my home. In fact, you'd better."

13

Anna was quiet the entire day after they returned to the mountains. The day after, her family and Logan's family helped move Anna, Orion, Logan and Mercury out of their units in the Labyrinth and into the houses that were finished while they were gone. Anna sat at the small table in their new kitchen and stared down at the coffee in the mug in front of her. They had been back two days, and she still hadn't said anything to Orion. He kept asking her if she was okay, and she hadn't been able to give him a straight answer.

She didn't even hear Orion come out of their room and she nearly jumped out of her chair when he touched her shoulder.

He took his hand away when she flinched, but returned it to her shoulder when she settled to caress along the back of her neck and lean down to give her a brief kiss. "And here I thought the military was the only thing that could give somebody the thousand-meter stare. How long have you been up?" He went to get himself a cup of coffee as well.

Anna took a gulp of her coffee, but it was almost cold. She hadn't been able to sleep. "A long time. I couldn't sleep." She looked over at Orion and as she stared at him, she almost decided to say nothing. She almost decided to tell Logan that they should just keep it a secret, pretend it never happened. "I need to talk to you."

"Whooo boy." Orion said as he poured coffee for himself, hesitating with the pot still in his hand as he looked her over. "That's a conversation starter that never has a happy ending." His eyes flicked off to one side where he could see the camera monitors for their children as they slept, but neither of them stirred. He and his wife tended to wake before most of civilization. "Should I put some rum in this to prepare for this conversation?" He had discovered rum for the first time out in the midwest, and decided it was going to become his drink of choice, therefore making him a space pirate.

"I think you're going to want to skip the coffee altogether." Anna said softly and pushed her coffee away. "This is hard. I don't . . ." She sighed in frustration, since she didn't know how to say anything that would prove to him the depth of her feelings for him and try to get him to understand. "I'm confused."

He looked down at the cup of coffee he poured before she told him to skip it, and looked back up at her with a raised eyebrow. "About coffee?"

"No, about . . . life." Anna looked down at her hands, since she couldn't look at him. "Fuck, I . . . Going home was so fucking hard, and I . . . everything I chose for myself was staring at me and what the Consortium chose for us . . . I love you. God, I love you so much, but I . . . I slept with Logan."

He was frozen by that admission for long enough that the steam coming off his coffee began to fade, his expression surprised but otherwise blank. Eventually he agreed with her suggestion, since he took the coffee cup and put it aside near the pot, looking anywhere but at her. "Wow. That's . . . okay, wow. I um . . ." Anna could almost see him looking for a joke to make about it and coming up empty, and he eventually just shook his head. "So you . . . this whole time when you've been saying nothing's wrong and it was just hard to go home, that was all just bullshit, then."

"Nothing is *wrong* with how our relationship works, it just . . . we didn't choose this. Did we? I mean, we were fucking trapped." Anna was staring at him now, even though he wouldn't look at her. "I don't even know what to think, but I know that it is hurting you right now, and I'm sorry. Not that hearing my apology makes any difference. I just . . . I still love him too. I love you both. I never had a chance to really decide for myself, and I need that chance. My whole life was Logan before I went into space. That doesn't just vaporize when there's no fucking closure."

He looked at her sharply when she talked about closure, and there was something in his eyes she never thought she would see there. He was one of the most mild-mannered and easygoing people anyone in the mountains had ever met, but she found out in that moment what it looked like when he got angry. Furious. There were no jokes, no terrible puns that made people laugh anyway, no trace of a smile waiting to banish any sense of worry to farther down the road.

The anger had to come up through every one of those layers of his personality to show itself in his eyes, but somehow it managed.

"You weren't worried about fucking 'closure' when we first got here from the Station. You weren't worried about it when your *husband* turned into a fucking control freak and an asshole who picked a fight with the only superpower left in the world. Where was this a year ago?"

"A year ago I was still reeling from the fact that I wasn't dead. And I loved and still love you. I didn't want to think about the fact that I still had feelings for him. It was painful." She pulled her hands back into her lap, and she held them together painfully. "You have been so good to me, and you don't deserve this. But what if you would be happier and could be happier with someone else? Mercury was your perfect match. Don't you wonder what could have happened if the Consortium had just left you and Mercury the fuck alone?"

He looked at her with the same angry expression on his face for a little longer, then did the last thing anyone could have expected. He started laughing, shaking his head as he looked down at the ground to enjoy a joke only he thought was funny. "You know, yeah, I wondered that a couple times. Mostly on the station, once or twice down here. Down here it's mostly been when we run out of toilet paper or some stupid shit like that and I miss orbit. But I don't need to ask what it would've been like for me and Mercury. We would've been fine."

"But that's not what happened. It's not what we chose, either of us. We chose you. You and Logan." The anger in his eyes was back as he stared over at her across the table. "Forced or not, we all made a choice, and where we come from, that means something."

"We made a choice to be involved in the Initiative too. If someone told me before I left that going up meant losing Logan, I never would have gone up. That's what I have to deal with inside my head, and I just don't know how to. I don't know how to reconcile the life I would have chosen for myself and the life that we have." Anna wasn't making anything better the more she talked, but she didn't know what else to do other than to talk.

"I don't know what I would have done if the Consortium had trapped all *four* of us in a room together and told us to make a decision. It kills me, not knowing what I would have done. I mean, fuck, Orion . . . you laugh almost all of the time that I get angry or I cry. We fight way more than I ever thought we would. I don't love you less for it, but I wonder where we would end up ten years from now. Are we going to hate each other for stupid shit like that?"

"Do not turn this around on me, Anna." He said with a harsh glare she had seen him give others but she had never been on the receiving end of. "This isn't about what I laugh at or when, this is about you fucking your ex and sounding like you're about to walk out on me to buy a house on Memory Fucking Lane."

Anna remained silent for a while, since she didn't know what else to say. She wasn't changing her mind, not when she had a chance to find out if the life she'd left behind was the one she still wanted. The Consortium wasn't controlling her now. "I'm not trying to turn it around on you, Orion."

He stared back at her for a while as he ingested the information, but eventually shook his head and turned away to lean on the counter. She could almost read his mind as he looked around the room, thinking about the home they finally had to themselves after so long waiting for it, and now . . . "In ten years, we might both be dead, along with everybody we care about. If not, and us fighting is the biggest problem we've got to deal with, then I'd say that would be a pretty fucking great life. And we would deal with it, the same way we've dealt with everything else. But apparently you think there's a better option."

"I didn't say that." Anna said defensively. "I said I don't fucking know how I feel. I'm sorry that I don't know. I'm sorry that you're in the middle of this. I don't want you to hate me, and fuck, I . . . I just . . . he was my best friend my entire fucking life. The person I wanted to be with more than anyone else in the world. I'm sorry I can't just turn it off. It's more complicated than that."

"Complicated. Right. That's a word that always puts a positive spin on things." He still wasn't facing her and didn't turn around during her defense, sighing at the countertop as the world changed around him. "So what do you want me to say, exactly? 'Sure, honey, I totally understand, go on back to your ex-husband and let me know how that other life you *actually* wanted with somebody else works out for you'? No, not fucking likely." He finally turned around to look at her again, but he shook his head. "I'm assuming Logan's gonna have the same conversation with Mercury about this today too? You two coordinate on that during your last 'let's be spouses again' session?"

"I don't know what Logan is doing today, Orion." She sighed, since she didn't know what else to say. Anna felt like shit, but she knew she would. She had no idea if she was doing the best thing for them both or if she had just been overwhelmed by a past that she longed for and a future that she missed. Either way, the damage had already been done. "I haven't talked to him since before we got back."

"Yeah, sure. With all the moving yesterday, I'm sure you were too tired to come up with places to sneak off to. The Bickford place was easier." He spat the surname, but then sighed, since he couldn't sustain the venom in his voice for very long. "I guess it's a good thing most of our shit is still in crates. It'll make it easier to move out." Even when he was angry, he was trying to look on the bright side of things, it was hardwired in his nature.

"No, you don't have to . . ." She finally looked around and sighed. "I can go back to the unit. You can stay here."

"Lynnette is your and Logan's daughter." He said sharply, having clearly made up his mind. "It only makes sense that she stay here with you two, in a decent house. I'll . . . get a crib set up for Leo so we can move him back and forth." He was clearly making up plans as he went along, but he'd been forced to think on his feet for most of his life.

That was a stab that she wasn't expecting, since she never imagined that Orion didn't want to be a part of Lynnette's life. "You don't want to be her father anymore? She's had two fathers her whole life." Anna said with more than just shock, since Lynnette and Leo were a package deal.

"She's had two fathers because her father was married to someone else, and I was happy to be her father because I was married to you." He shot back without hesitation. "I love her like she's my own, but you're her mother and Logan is her father. If you're gonna be with him, I'm not gonna complicate that for her. This entire family is fucked up plenty as it is. At least one out of the four of them should be allowed to grow up without needing a theoretical physics degree to explain her family tree."

"They sleep together. They spend all day together. I'm not separating them." Anna said firmly, though she was only being sharp because she didn't want to cry. "If you don't want to take care of her, then you can come here to see Leo. I'm not separating them because of this. They're just babies."

"Then I'll take them both when I take them." From the angry look on his face, it was clear he had no intention of spending any more time in the house than necessary.

"Fine." She replied with resignation and she got up from the table and grabbed her coffee to dump it out. "I'm sorry." She repeated as she stood at the sink where she'd dumped out her drink. There was nothing else she could say, but that was not even close to being enough.

"Yeah, you said that already." He stood leaning on the counter for a long time without saying anything, stuck inside the fight and unwilling to leave it. If the argument was over, then so were they, but it wasn't as though she was giving him much of an option. She had made up her mind, and he wasn't going to be the guy who begged and groveled for her to reconsider her choice. Eventually he just let out a long sigh and pushed himself away from the counter, away from his wife. "I'll come back for my crates later. I'm going for a run."

Anna didn't want to watch him leave, but she turned around to look at him anyway. The tears that she fought were already silently falling down her cheeks.

The only stop Orion made on his way out the door was to look at the monitors for the children again to make sure they were still sleeping soundly. He had to stop to put on his shoes by the door, but he didn't look up at Anna again until he had them on and he was standing by the door leading out onto the front porch.

"The Consortium might have forced us together, but nobody's been forcing me to do shit for over a year now. I've been here with you because I wanted to be. I've been trying to fight this war because I want to fight it. If the time comes when you get conflicted about Logan, I hope you tell him sooner than later. For me, I wish I had known about this a year ago." He sighed one last time and put his hand on the door. "I'll see you, Anna."

Anna didn't say anything. She couldn't. She didn't regret the time she had with Orion, and truly, she didn't know what decision she would have made. Anna didn't even understand her own feelings, or how she could want both men. How she could want to be with Orion and Logan both, but that was impossible. Now Orion was gone, and her heart was breaking, because she did love him so much. She had no idea what would happen with Logan, and she could very well end up alone, but there was no changing the path she was on now.

Unexpectedly, she was again Anna Prince. She wasn't Orion's wife, and she wasn't Logan's, since they were going to tentatively test things out. She was in a limbo that she had created, and already she hated herself for it.

* * * * *

When Mercury got up, Logan was nowhere to be found in the comfortable master suite they'd only had a single night to enjoy. By the time she had herself awake and left the room, she found him standing in the hallway, looking through a peephole they'd had installed on the boys' room door so he could see them directly. It was still much too early for them to be up, and they had appeared asleep on the monitor, but Logan was standing there watching them anyway, fully dressed for the day with his hair already dry. Had he really been awake that long? Had he slept?

Mercury felt like she looked like a mess as she ran her hand through her hair, since she hadn't even had a chance to do anything but collapse in their bed after moving. She looked Logan over with a smile as she slowly walked toward him. "You're already dressed? I thought you were going to stay home today."

"I'm not sure what I'll be doing today." He said in a low voice, since they were just outside the children's room, after all. That kind of uncertainty wasn't like him at all, but she knew him well enough to see that he was troubled by something. He was usually working, not just standing around contemplating things.

"Okay." She said with a concerned expression, but she usually didn't like to push him when he was clearly mulling something over. "Can I make you something to eat?"

"No, thank you, I'm . . . not hungry." He shook his head without looking at her at first, but he finally pulled his eyes away from the boys' room. "I've called Gwen to have her come over and watch the children for the morning. I wasn't sure what kind of plans you had, but I thought it'd be best to have her here to assist." He took a deep breath that told her he wasn't finished, and his hands actually fidgeted a little before he put them in his pockets. That wasn't like Logan at all. "There's something I need to talk to you about."

"Sure. Okay." Mercury felt nervous, since she didn't know what would cause him to fidget and tell her that he needed to talk to her. Mercury tugged a hair tie off of her wrist and then pulled her hair up, since it was such a mess. "Where do you want to talk? Is someone hurt? Did the Consortium find us?"

"No, no one's hurt that I'm aware of, and the security scans covering our route back here all came back clean. As far as Jason and his staff can tell, we weren't seen." He reassured her in a low voice, then turned toward their living room around the corner. He still wasn't looking at her as he moved, and he didn't sit down in the chairs. He looked like he wanted to pace, but forced himself to remain in one place as he turned back to face her.

"I've been trying for a while to figure out a way of talking about this, and there's nothing I can think of that will make it any less terrible or any less painful. More than just about anything else in the world right now, I wish there was."

Mercury stared at him and the more he talked, the more uneasy she felt. "Please don't hedge around something that has you this uncomfortable, Logan. Tell me what you need to say. You're making me nervous."

He wished he could say something after that to alleviate her anxiety, but that was his entire problem, since there was nothing that would do any good. "I slept with Anna while we were back at the estate." He said quietly. "Being home again had both of us thinking about the way life had been before we went up to Nine, the choices we made, the things that happened between there and here. All of us were forced into making choices we had no intention of making before we joined the Initiative. Even if those choices were made by all of us, and we kept making that choice when we got down here, everything about what we went through has been shadowed by the Consortium."

Mercury couldn't breathe as soon as the words were out of Logan's mouth. She immediately had to sit down, since she never once thought Logan would actually . . . cheat on her. With Anna. Anna. Why did the woman have to wreck her life? Anna hated her as soon as they met, and Mercury tried to be as kind as she possibly could.

"The Consortium put us together, but I *chose* you. I chose . . ." She had to pause and take a deep breath, since she was having trouble thinking clearly. "We talked about a life together long before anyone made a choice. You said you wanted this. You said you wanted a family with me."

"I did." It wasn't clear if he was just admitting that he had said those things or if he had wanted those things at the time and no longer did. "I meant what I said. I thought . . ." Logan wasn't often at a loss for words, and there were very few times when she had seen him stumble over anything, but he was clearly at a loss for what to say in his own defense. He had none. "I love you. I've never lied about that. Even if the Consortium forced us together in the first place, the way I feel about you is real. The life that we have is a good life. But it's not the one that either of us planned to begin with. That life was taken away, from all of us."

"The life that either of us *planned*? That's what you're telling me is the reason for all of this?" Mercury stared at him as her chest continued to throb. "I planned to be a well-known and renowned doctor as a part of the Eleusis Initiative. I planned an entirely different life, and here I am, the mother of *your* children because we wanted it together. My entire life is somewhere else. I never *planned* to be on Earth, in the mountains, running myself ragged trying to be a doctor, a mother, and *your* wife. You cannot tell me that you love me if you would do this to me. That's not love. That's selfishness."

"It's being realistic." He said sharper than he intended, though his tone quickly softened again. "Your plans for the future before the Initiative were about your own place in the world. A place I'm going to be fighting to make sure you have no matter what happens. The life I had imagined never had anything to do with Eleusis. I've known Anna since we were children. The relationship I have with her isn't something that's ever going to go away, for either of us. You've known that since all this started between us. Not unless that ending is something we both have the chance to choose for ourselves."

"Then I deserved to know I was going to have to share. If you always intended to go back to Anna, then you should have told me before we built a life together." Mercury finally found herself capable of taking a deep breath and she stood up. "Do not talk to me as though I misunderstood, or tell me what I should or should not know. Clearly you have made your choice. Get out of my house."

Logan knew he shouldn't have been surprised by that order from her, but the force with which she delivered it was still a little startling. She had always been a strong woman, but he knew he had gotten too accustomed to submission from her, even if that submission was far from being her natural state.

He nodded slowly to let her know that he would, but he didn't move immediately. "I won't be far away." He promised, though he doubted she wanted to think about the possibility of needing him for anything at the moment. "All I'm going to ask right now is that you not think this is something I came to lightly. Or easily. I know that doesn't make anything better, but I want you to know it anyway." He started to move away toward the door, not taking any of his things with him, but then again, none of his things had been unpacked from the day before.

"That's worse." She said as he went to the door. "It means that even with everything between us and everything we've shared, you determined I'm not good enough for you." Mercury stared at him for a moment and moved in the opposite direction of the door. She wanted to get away from him. "I gave you everything."

There were a number of things Logan wanted to say in response to that but he kept his mouth shut, as had so often been the case in the disagreements he and Mercury had gone through over their year and more together. He knew she had given everything, but so had he. They had both fundamentally changed who they were in order to be with the other, given each other their children, their position among the rebels. The sacrifices had been mutual, but pointing that out wouldn't have done any good at the moment.

Instead of saying anything, he just looked back at her for a long moment and headed obediently out the door. Staying would only make things even more painful for them both.

* * * * *

Orion's run lasted most of the morning. He went up to the ridge where he and Anna ran for the past few weeks and decided it was better to walk the rest of the way. He stopped almost every other step, looking out at the planet that felt more foreign than it had the night before. Anna had been his connection to the place, his means of understanding it, much of the time. It was her home, and he could feel like he was sharing it so long as he was sharing it with her. His children had been born there. That by itself should have made it home. But it didn't. It wasn't. He belonged in space. He belonged in the empty places, two hundred kilometers above sea level. Instead, he was a fugitive, and felt like one for the first time since they had touched down in the mountains.

There were a dozen messages that came in over the course of the morning, mostly from some of his coworkers who heard through the grapevine about what happened. Logan had left Mercury's house and gone into the Labyrinth, but almost as soon as he'd left, all of his things had been left out on their front porch, just as all of Orion's things had been left out on his. With him missing in action and everyone concerned clearly upset about something, people hadn't had a difficult time putting two and two together to make two very different couples.

He didn't want to go back to the Labyrinth to get a unit set up. He didn't want to go back and live on his own for the first time in almost two years. He knew he would, he knew he had to, in order to get away from Anna and the house he imagined she would shortly be decorating in tandem with her ex-new-husband.

He got requests from various departments to go down and help move the trucks around that had come in the day before, but he couldn't bring himself to come down off the mountain, so he ignored them. If they really wanted to find him or they were really concerned about him, they would find some means of finding him. For the time being, Orion just wanted the silence of the ridge and the unlimited world beneath him.

Eventually, in looking through all of his messages, there was just one that he realized he had almost been waiting for, but which he still didn't see. He had managed to make a number of friends over the year they'd spent in the mountains, and Kameron was still there somewhere, but she clearly hadn't heard what happened yet. For all the time they had known each other, though, there was one person he considered an even closer friend.

It would be fairly stupid of me to ask if you were alright, so I won't. Since I'm not either. He typed out to Mercury honestly. *Is there someone around to help you with the boys?*

It was approaching fifteen minutes before he finally received a response. *Gwen is taking care of them. I took over Barry's shift in the clinic.*

Orion wasn't surprised by that in the slightest, since she was absolutely the type to throw herself into work in order to get past anything emotionally damaging. *I've been blowing off the world all morning up on the ridge. You're a better person than I am for continuing to do something that's actually useful.* He sent the message and then looked back out at the outer slope of the mountains leading away from their sanctuary, utterly untouched by humans except for the single access road far in the distance. *I'm going to talk to Reed and get a unit set up in the Labyrinth with a couple cribs for when I take the kids. Beyond that, the world looks pretty hazy right now.*

Should I have seen this coming? Mercury sent the first message and then followed it up with another. She didn't have any patients at the moment, but she wished she did. *I mean with anyone, not just Anna. I work all of the time. The boys take a lot of work. Did I push him into her? There has to be a reason why he thinks that being with someone else will be better than being with me.*

Orion shook his head, even though he knew she couldn't see him. *This is their history talking, and there's a lot of it. I'm not saying that makes it better, but it's not something either of us did, or that we could've seen coming. I thought we had all made our choices and were happy with them.*

So did I. She typed back, taking a seat on the edge of the desk at the front of the clinic. *I feel very alone now. Also very angry. I wish that I could take my children and go back and stay with my parents. They would know what to say.*

I'm sure they would. He sent back immediately. *I wish I could see my family again too. Let them meet Leo. Khadi would spoil that kid rotten. She's a sucker for babies.*

He didn't send anything more for a long while, but his next message was longer. *I thought we were past this. When you and I were first Matched, we were both all-in, and I had no regrets whatsoever. Never doubted. Then we got into the Initiative and life turned into chaos, but I thought we were past it. That's what I'm angry about. That I thought we were all moving forward with our lives in spite of everything that happened. I get that going home was hard for both of them, but I didn't think they would want to go back to what it felt like in the Initiative, when we were all struggling about the fact that all of us love both our match and our spouse.*

Mercury didn't know if he was admitting that he still loved her, and she loved him too, just . . . not the way she loved Logan. Mercury had jumped in and hadn't looked back. It wasn't in her to look back. Progress was rarely made when looking back at what could have been. *I don't regret my sons, but I never would have pursued a family with Logan if I thought there was no future. This is worse. He told me I knew about everything between him and Anna as though I should have expected something like this to happen. I don't accept that. You don't marry someone expecting something like this to happen.*

Neither do I. Anna and I have even been talking about the possibility of having more kids. She's always said she wanted a big family, and after seeing hers, I agree it looks like fun. And now this. He didn't even know what else to say about it, honestly. *I wouldn't have stayed with her once we came to Earth if I had thought she was still conflicted. Even a little bit.*

Mercury sighed and looked around the clinic before she just dropped her head into her hands. She couldn't answer Orion right away because it was just too hard to think about her new reality. Ten minutes passed and she finally answered again. *I'm glad you didn't hate me after what happened up there. I'm glad we're still friends. You're the only real friend I have.*

That's not true. Barry is pretty much the president of your fan club. And Jason's always seemed pretty fond of you. Such as he is. No one was fond of Jason, but it was better to be on the man's good side than the alternative. *I understand why you feel alone, but you aren't. We're still in this together. As always.*

She nodded even though he couldn't see her, and she stared at the screen on her communicator for awhile. *I've been working on some research between patients. You still owe me some blood samples so I can analyze your growth. You can stop by anytime.*

I'll come by the clinic in a little while. I'm coming down off the ridge right now. They want me to help rearrange the midwesterners' stuff.

You don't owe anyone anything. If you need to stay away, then you should do that. Really. Mercury looked up when one of her regular OB patients came in, and she stood up from the desk. *I have a patient to see. Let me know if you do want to stop by.*

It was another hour before he got down to the clinic, and when he did, the day they'd both had was obvious in everything about his appearance. He was dressed in shorts and a tight t-shirt that were perfect for running but not exactly for any other kind of work. The cold air of the mountains came in with him, and the remnants of the solitude he'd been locked in for the past few hours.

"Table for one." He said with a forced smile as he approached her at the front desk. "I'll have a type O negative and a rum and coke, please."

"You can have the rum once I'm done taking your blood." She replied with her own small, strained smile. Mercury let him into one of the small exam rooms and got her supplies ready. "I read some very promising research about the pituitary gland and the human growth hormone. It was mostly research after the fact, but it's still helpful. I need to rule out anything cancerous, though."

He nodded, since he'd heard plenty about that possibility from their time on Earth and in speaking to those who had grown up on Earth. Various kinds of cancer had been around for centuries, but there were still a few kinds that were more difficult than others to correct. "Whatever you need." He sat in the exam chair and took a rubber band before she even got back to him, tying it efficiently around his arm with his teeth. "Have you had any chances to take a look into your other research?"

"About Leo, or about me?" She asked as she brought over the needle and skillfully inserted it as quickly and painlessly as she could manage. Mercury looked at his eyes briefly before she grabbed a test tube, the first of a few.

"Either one. I just like to stay up to date on the most recent marvels in medical science."

She smiled a little bit and focused on getting the blood samples she needed. "I need to discuss things with Barry before I really know what to look for as far as Leo goes. He knows much more about little people than I do. I am used to taking care of them before they're born and immediately after." She clicked another test tube into place.

"I did look into my own medical file a little bit more. I already knew I was created with a very specific genetic code and specifications, but I . . ." Mercury just shook her head. "They went to a very well-renowned geneticist. He did a lot of early Earth research, and he was also heavily involved with the Eleusis Initiative, but then he was in a shuttle accident. His pilot was drunk and they crashed into the side of a station."

Mercury clicked the last tube into place, took the sample, and prepared some gauze and a wrap so she could wrap it around his arm. "There are some strange things I noticed in my coding. I'm already CV-immune." She said it nonchalantly, but she was still stunned with the information. "I didn't know that. They never told me that. Also, there are other markers I didn't recognize. One was closely associated with healing and general immunity to pathogens. It . . . Carl has something similar in his medical information, I did a search to see if anyone else has it whose information we have. His looks different though. More active."

"Well that means James and Declan probably are too, then. That's good news." It meant that wherever they were, wherever they had to make a life, her children wouldn't have shortened life spans just because they lived on Earth. "Also explains why you've never had so much as a cold the whole time I've known you. I know you told me early on that you almost never get sick, but it's good to have understanding behind it, I would think."

"It's more than that, though. It's . . . like I'm genetically programmed to survive." Mercury knew it sounded ridiculous, but after going through Carl's information extensively, she was a little worried about what her body could do. She also didn't know how the dormant things would be triggered. "Your friend can heal from a rainstorm of bullets in hours. That's not healthy. That's superhuman."

He glared over at her as he rubbed his arm over the gauze. "If you're thinking about going out in a rainstorm of bullets, I'd still recommend you take an umbrella. Preferably a bulletproof one. I know you bounced back really quickly after the twins were born, but not every limit needs to be tested."

"I'm not saying I'm going to test it. I'm just saying it's a part of my genetic code. His is active, which explains a lot of other problems but mine . . . someone put it there for a reason. My parents put it there for a reason. I don't know why."

Orion didn't know much about it that could be relevant, so he shook his head. "I don't know either. Hopefully one day you can talk to them and ask." He got up from the exam chair, but didn't seem in a hurry to leave. He'd spent the entire morning in solitude, after all, and Mercury was the one person who wasn't going to try and offer sympathy by way of social platitudes. "You could probably talk to Jason and have him break into the Consortium's databases for genetic sequencing. Guy could probably do it in his sleep. It'd give you a wider base of information to draw on when making your conclusions."

"I will do that. Thanks for the suggestion." Mercury made sure his arm was nice and wrapped before she stepped away to grab a water bottle and a small package of homemade cookies. She didn't know when he'd eaten last, and she could tell he was a little dehydrated. His blood flow was slow. "A token of appreciation for donating your blood to my scientific research."

"So if I stop by next week and give more blood, I can get more cookies?" He held up the bag with a hopeful expression. "Because I make blood all the time. I can't make my own cookies."

Mercury gave a small laugh, but she was grateful for his humor. Even though it didn't change the pain she felt. "You don't need to give me blood for cookies. Though you really should eat those and drink the water. I don't want you passing out in my clinic. It scares people when they see someone unconscious in a medical setting."

"Wouldn't want to scare people." He popped open the pack of cookies and ate one whole as he looked at the door to leave, shaking his head. "You were my first stop coming in from the ridge. Hopefully Reed's got some rooms left over after the influx of the midwesterners yesterday. I know some of them slept in their cars and campers last night, but I think that was just because there were so damn many of them to get assigned. I doubt any of them want to do that permanently."

"I don't know, it's been really busy. I don't think there is any space left. That was why they wanted us to move out." Mercury was a little sad he was getting ready to leave, but she put the samples away properly and washed her hands. "Stay with me. The boys usually sleep close to me anyway, and I'm not ready for them to have their own room. Regardless, we . . . I have extra space. And you waited just as long as I did to get out of being underground."

"I don't . . ." Orion said immediately, but it was clear the rest of the sentence wasn't going to say that he didn't want to do that, even if he was hesitating. "I thought about asking you, if it would be alright. I just worry about people getting the wrong idea. I don't want everybody in this place to think the four of us just . . . trade each other back and forth whenever we feel like it. But I'd be grateful for a couch. So long as it's a fairly long couch."

"What do I care what people think? It's not going to change what happened. It's not going to change the truth. You're my friend. I'm their doctor. If they have a problem with me or if they would like to discuss something with me about my personal life, they can come find me." Mercury had never been as blunt as she was at that moment, but she was more angry about the situation than she had ever been angry about anything in her entire life. She was taking back the control she had given over to Logan and then some. She didn't care what people thought about her personal life. "If you want to stay on my couch or on the floor, that's fine. I won't force you to, clearly. I just thought it would be easier for the both of us to have a friend around."

She could see he was a little surprised at the anger he saw in her, but he knew it wasn't directed at him. "You're right." He agreed with a nod. "It would be easier. Plus, I find I don't sleep well if I don't hear a baby crying every couple hours or so. World just doesn't feel right anymore without it."

"Don't worry about them." She said softly, the anger evaporating out of her voice. "I can take care of them. I like taking care of people."

"I know. It's part of what makes you a great doctor. That and the free cookies." He popped another one into his mouth with a weak smile. "I'm gonna go move some trucks. But once I'm done with that and nobody needs anything else moved for the night, I'll . . . go move my stuff. Is somebody watching the kids all day?"

"Gwen has them now. I'm going back home in a few hours, since Barry wouldn't give me the whole shift. He's against working to escape something like this, but I'll take what I can get."

"One more thing you and I both tend to have in common. I just take long walks first." He tried to smile again, then shook his head. "I'll go relieve Gwen if you'd rather stay here a while longer."

"You would do that for me?" Clearly her children didn't belong to Orion and he had no reason to take care of them, but she was touched he was offering. "They can be, well, you saw them. They can be troublesome."

"They don't scare me. I'm bigger than they are. For now." He tried again to give her a brief smile, then stepped back toward the door. "I'll send you a message when I get to the house. I'll take measurements of the couch . . . maybe talk to a couple of the carpenters to see if they can work up one that's about . . . fifteen feet long. Want to make sure I don't grow out of it too fast." He gave her a smile and paused for a moment with a look of gratitude on his face. Not a single mention of what had actually happened to them both that morning, no talking through their emotions, no need to do either. They both understood. They both knew what was happening. They both knew what they were feeling. They both knew how much it hurt.

"Maybe an adjustable couch, then?" Mercury smiled back at him. She really was so grateful Orion was still her friend after everything else that happened. She needed a friend, now more than ever, and he was one of the best ones to have. "Thanks. For watching my boys. Hopefully they don't give you too much trouble."

"One of my other middle names." He shrugged with a slightly wider smile. "Means something different in Arabic. Don't work too hard, and remember to eat lunch. I'll find out if you don't, and then I'll be forced to bring the boys over to force-feed you."

Mercury let out a short laugh. "You still know me pretty well, don't you?"

"I think so." He smiled from the doorway, then turned it into a playful glare. "Sustenance. Or else. I will find out. I'll see you at home."

14

Liam thought, from time to time, that the living situation they had at the estate had been complicated, with each of his wives having their own wing of the house with their own style and their own preferences, shuffling babies back and forth, trying to keep things as simple as possible.

Boy, had he been wrong about that.

Getting settled in the Labyrinth was an entirely different world, not just of complication but of situation. He had been assured by Logan that due to his children's age, he and his family would soon be the recipients of one of the homes under construction, but in the meantime, they had been given three separate units all at the end of the same corridor (after a great deal of protest from Reed, who didn't seem to understand the concept of plural marriage and its implications terribly well) none of which were large enough to suit anyone's preferences.

After some discussion among the four of them, they had all come to the decision that the units wouldn't be assigned to them individually, but would be assigned to certain purposes. One would be for the children and whoever's night it was to watch them, one would be for Liam and whoever's night it was to be with him, and the third room would be for whoever's night it was away from both. Liam himself didn't mind too much the idea of not having a room of his own, and had assured the three of them that his seventh night he would spend taking care of the kids. It was going to be a precarious arrangement for all of them, but he was hopeful that they could make it work, at least on a temporary basis. Living out of a suitcase was going to get old in a hurry.

The night after they moved in had technically been his night alone, since it had been decided arbitrarily that his rotation with his wives would be based on the order in which he started dating them. He had, per his own stated intentions, spent the night with the children in the room they had hastily set up as their nursery, and the night had been less than smooth. Still, by two in the morning, after a night spent moving all their necessary things down into their rooms, setting up beds, setting up cribs, and fighting with one child after another to get them to sleep, he had managed to finally lie down and get some much-needed sleep, even if it was on a twin mattress in a tiny side-room of the unit.

His first thought on waking up just three hours later was that he had no idea how long he had slept. He felt slightly rejuvenated, but that could have meant he had slept only a few hours or that he had slept two days, there was no immediate way of knowing. There was no sound of crying from any of the three bedrooms in the 'nursery' unit, and there hadn't been a knock at the front door. There was only the white noise echoing from all three rooms to help the children stay asleep.

A flick of his communicator on the nightstand showed him the time, at which he groaned, but he couldn't be too angry about it. After all, it wasn't as though he'd been trying to soothe all three children or do everything else on his own.

He put his communicator back where he'd found it and turned back to the other side of the twin bed, most of which he took up with his own bulk. The forever-warm body pressed up against him had been just as tired as he was when they went to sleep, but as he pulled the sheet up around them and put his arms back around her, he felt her move instinctively against him in ways that had been among the first reasons he'd been unable to ever get enough of her. Technically his night 'alone' could belong to anyone of his choosing, and he rarely chose to sleep alone.

"You awake?" He said in a low voice that had no chance of being heard anywhere outside their blankets.

Margo curled into him even more as he wrapped his arms around her, since she could never get enough of Liam. She absolutely hated sharing him, but she could not get enough of him. "I don't want to be awake." Margo replied in an equally low whisper, since she didn't want to make any noise. "But if you are awake, then it's not so bad."

"Sorry I take up so much room. They said they'd get some larger beds down here tomorrow. Apparently this used to be a barracks or something, so they're not exactly used to people sharing." He moved his face down into the blankets to kiss her sleepily, stretching a little before he relaxed again, his hands running over her back and her backside with equal ease to hold her tightly against him.

"You've always been this way. I'm used to it. At least I'm not pregnant. That would be troublesome on this mattress." Margo was the thinnest of his wives, though she now had a little more definition after having a baby. "It just gives me more reason to snuggle."

"That and the fact that it's a hell of a lot colder up here in these mountains than it was back home." It had taken them longer than usual to get the babies to sleep in part because they had to dig through boxes to find appropriately thick pajamas, since even underground it seemed like the chill of the outer world permeated down to them. He moved against her again, since she was always so warm, and he was greedy about stealing every bit of it from her. At the moment, she was trapped between him and the bunched-up blankets against the wall at her back. "Place is honestly better than I expected, though, even if it's got problems."

"Better than you expected? I'd hate to think what you expected." Margo wiggled against him and tilted her head back so that she could find a way to kiss him. "Logan gets a house with one wife and two kids and we get this? We're going to be tripping over each other. Or . . . hearing each other."

He chuckled at the last comment, though he knew she was serious about it, and he returned the kiss as his hands wandered comfortably over her. "These doors are designed to hold out bombs and bullets in the event of an attack. I'm pretty sure they can hold in screaming. And we'll get into a house before too long. They had dozens up there that're already done, they're just working on getting things straight, and we just got here." He made no attempt to act as though the way she moved against him didn't have an effect on him, and he continued kissing her as they spoke. "Besides, Logan is like, president of this place. Not a job I'm jealous of, but it does come with perks."

"I don't think Logan is going to be much help to us." Margo said flatly, since she was still upset on Liam's behalf that Logan let his brother and sister think he was dead for more than a year. "Logan doesn't always know what's best. He vastly underestimated you for your entire life."

"Yeah, well, he's been busy overestimating himself. Math's gotta shake out somewhere." Liam had never particularly resented his place as the 'younger' brother or been jealous of Logan's authority, but he had been surprised, since his wedding, to find how easily he fell into some of the roles Logan had always taken care of previously for the family. He had certainly leaned heavily on Larissa and his wives, but he had found himself more capable than he had expected to be, all in all.

"Anyway, whatever else he's been up to, I believe him when he says he'll get us moved soon. And if not, I'll just have to go topside, claim some real estate and start doing the framing myself. Might work out better that way anyway, since I could make sure your suite's got room for a couple of our favorite features." The two of them had gotten together the first time in a hot tub at his house, and it had been a joke between them ever since that anything shower, tub, or bathroom-floor-related was very much their thing. They had certainly made a mess of theirs back at the estate often enough.

That brought a smile to Margo's face, and she kissed him heatedly at the reminder. She loved reminiscing with him, thinking about all the times they'd spent together where she was with him without thinking about anyone else. She liked the fact that she was his first 'regular', and one of her fondest memories was when he told some guy to fuck off because she was his girlfriend. She liked hearing she was his girlfriend. And then his wife. Though she did not like sharing the title. "I never thought I would enjoy it so much. You were my first in a hot tub."

"Yeah, and I'm never gonna stop being surprised about that. I hadn't done it before either, but the way you came at me, I figured you were a pro." He chuckled low in his throat and laid a little more on his back so he could pull her on top of him while they talked. "Of course, speaking of people overhearing other people, I didn't think I was ever gonna hear the end of it from Larissa. But hopefully after living at the Princes' for a while, she's a little more sympathetic to how hard it is not to get overheard when somebody's blowing your fucking mind."

Margo laughed again and easily took her place on top of him. He was so masculine and gorgeous, two days a week was never enough time, but she did her best not to talk about that. She wanted him. That was just going to have to be enough. "I'm glad I was capable of blowing your mind. I know I haven't been as creative recently."

"We've all been stressed lately, with the kids. Things get a lot more complicated with them around. Good thing they're cute." He smiled and pulled her into a long, lingering kiss, his hand caressing along the side of her face tenderly to let her know how much he cherished having her there with him.

Margo kissed him back with just as much need and emotion as she possibly could. "I have missed you. I always miss you, Liam."

She could feel the slight reservation she got from him after that comment, since he knew as well as she did what she meant by it, but he didn't stop kissing or touching her. "I'm never far away, Margo." He said in as loving a tone as she had ever heard from him. "I love you. There's no need to miss me. Especially when you're right here on top of me." They couldn't see each other very well in the darkness, but she could feel the teasing smile on his face as he kissed her afterward.

By the time Margo and Liam emerged from the room they were sharing, the babies were awake and Rachel was taking care of them while Bree was making breakfast. In a frilly little apron that she insisted she bring with her. It only made Margo want to roll her eyes, though she didn't. She had no idea what he saw in Bree. She was wild and crazy and Margo didn't like the things that Bree encouraged in Liam. He was fine without Brianne's insanity. Rachel was at least level headed and private, even if she was a little too bossy.

"Good morning, sleepyheads!" Bree's voice, as usual, was much too cheerful for so early a morning. Liam was smiling. That made her cheerful. Rachel was glaring at her over a mug of coffee at Bree's shrill morning greeting. "So we're not in our house and our selections are limited, but I'm making pancakes!"

"I can handle limited. So long as pancakes are within limits." He picked up Chrissy and slid her into a chest carrier she seemed to enjoy, since she wasn't quite up to crawling yet. He gave brief greeting kisses both to Brianne and Rachel, though that was as much as he ever did with any of them in front of the others, by way of saying good morning. He stopped to take a particular whiff of the pancakes Brianne was cooking, cradling Chrissy's head the whole time, then gave a particularly satisfied sigh of anticipation. Afterward, he went over to the counter where Rachel was leaning with her coffee and grabbed a cup for himself. "You two sleep alright? It's quiet as a recording booth down here."

"I was thinking about too many things to sleep very well." Rachel grumbled between sips of coffee. "Also, this is the worst coffee I've ever had, so it's a good thing we brought a lot of our own. I'm not handing the good coffee over to a bunch of strangers I don't know. They can drink their junk and we can drink ours."

"I'll make sure to bring down a crate of the good stuff when I go up to take another pass through our personal inventory later on. For now . . ." He took a sip of his own cup and choked it down with a grimace. "Oh wow. You are not joking. If caffeine wasn't an end in itself . . . sheesh." He saw they didn't really have much else to put in it either, but he did drop some synthetic sugar into it to make it a little more palatable. Even so, his next few sips were accompanied by the same kind of grimace as before, which had Chrissy laughing at him. "Oh, that's funny, you little sadist? Wow. Real loving of you. Wow."

He took another sip and made an even worse face because it made Chrissy laugh, but then went to sit near Margo as they all waited for the pancakes to be finished. "I thought they said they wanted to have some kind of big meeting somewhere down here today, but then I got a note this morning saying that all meetings in here had been canceled pending a forthcoming announcement. Then a message that there was nothing to worry about. I'm taking that as mixed signals. Did you all get that?"

All three of his wives nodded, but it was Rachel who spoke up, after a glance over at the boys playing on blankets on the floor. "Logan was supposed to meet with me this morning, so I could see where I could help. I went to his house. Gwen told me that he and Anna were out somewhere, and his house wasn't actually his house anymore, but he would be at Anna's house. What happened?"

It was Liam's turn to look surprised instead of disgusted by the coffee. "Damned if I know. I'll find out what I can, though." He pulled out his communicator and tapped a quick message to Logan, still shaking his head. "If the alien kicked him out and Gwen said he'd be back at Anna's house . . ." Liam looked over at Brianne with a knowing look, since she was already looking at him after hearing the news. "Then maybe you weren't hearing things after all. Also, if that's true, your hearing continues to freak me the hell out."

Brianne gave him a smirk and turned back to her pancakes. "He's better off with Anna anyway, even if it made the other people angry. Logan and Anna belong together."

Rachel almost looked sad by the way Brianne responded. "They're still people. They have feelings. And children with Logan and Anna. They're a part of this family even if you don't like them. Also, what are we possibly going to accomplish if we're looking at everyone else as 'them'? That's how the Consortium got us into this mess in the first place."

Liam clearly agreed more with Rachel than he did with Bree on that particular subject. "If they are back together, it's gonna divide some people. I've heard a lot of the orbit people look up to Logan and Mercury particularly for making things work between them. If the gold standard fu . . ." he cleared his throat to try and stop himself from swearing in front of their children, ". . . unctionally fails, there's not much hope for everybody else. Even if I agree that Anna's good for him personally, it'll still make waves."

"Still. Logan's happiness should matter more than what everyone else thinks." Brianne didn't let up on her opinion, but no one expected her to. "I mean, if someone has something to say to me about how my relationship with you goes as one of three wives, it's not like I'm going to care."

"Can't think of a reason why you should." Liam said with an amused smile, giving each of the three of them a loving look in turn as he sipped at his coffee. "I want him to be happy too, but as twisted around as his whole situation's gotten, I don't even know what that's gonna look like. I'm sure he doesn't either right this second." He shook his head. "I'll make him my first stop of the day. Only da . . . . arn person in this world besides the six of you I'd put before good coffee."

Liam gave Rachel a wink at that shared priority, then looked back over at Margo, since she'd been quiet the entire conversation. "I'm probably gonna end up spending most of the day going through inventory, dealing with Logan's love life and checking up on everybody else from the district, since I'm supposed to be an . . . overseer or . . . manager . . . something, I forget what the title's supposed to be." He brushed it off at the time, since it had clearly been important to Logan but not important enough to Liam to care. If Logan wanted him to help out in making sure midwesterners had what they needed, that was a job he figured he could do easily enough.

"Do you need help?" Margo asked hopefully, since she wanted to spend as much time with Liam as she could, and back home, they had other responsibilities that kept her from spending most days with him. "I can help with whatever you need."

"That's the plan." He said with a smile, then turned the same smile on Brianne to accept a plate of pancakes, which he handed over to Margo beside him. He did his best to make sure he went last in just about everything they did as a family. "Since Rachel said she's gonna go report to Logan, I'm assuming you've got the kids for the day?" He said with a look up at Bree.

Bree gave him a friendly salute and smiled at him before she glanced over to the boys on the floor and went back to plating pancakes. He could hear the mischievous smile in her voice while she made up another plate. "Maybe I'll see if Gwen can come help me."

He almost glared at her for that, but he managed to stop himself short before he did so. An incoming plate of pancakes helped him keep his features from being quite as open as hers. "If she's watching Logan's twins, it would make for a handful. But it's good to make friends in new places. We're going to be living and fighting with these people for a good long while, after all." He thanked Bree for the pancakes and dug in, looking over at Margo.

"With as many new people as they're going to have running around, all of us could probably slip into whatever kind of role we want. I handed over what we had left of the crop and a lot of our emergency supplies so they can put them in with the general storehouses, but there's all kinds of crazy going on around here. If we want to help in construction, carpentry, even if we want to join a supply caravan and start running out to risk our necks bringing in goods, we probably could. Though I imagine all three of you would line up to snap my neck if I even acted interested."

"We have more to lose if you go do something like that." Rachel said with a tone that meant she would rather tie him up than let him go too far away. "Stick to something a little more safe, will you?"

"I'll try. No promises." He smiled over his pancakes, and focused on them for a while, laughing at Chrissy as she found the action of chewing utterly fascinating. He sat back in his chair as he ate, messing with Chrissy with tiny bits of syrup on the end of his fingers for the girl to taste. He looked over at Margo as he messed with their daughter, one arm around the back of her chair. "What do you think you want to look for, opportunity-wise?"

"I don't know, I suppose I'm as good as anyone at doing grunt work. Or I could help clean. Mend clothing. I'm sure there's a lot of mending that could be done. People from orbit probably never had to do that."

"No, I'm sure they had machines for that. Hell, I wouldn't be surprised if they got dressed by automation up there." He shook his head, since Logan tried to tell him that Orbitals really weren't that different from those raised on Earth, but Liam still wasn't buying it. Especially after watching Mercury and Kameron eyeing the farm equipment in their hangar like it was diseased. "I'm sure we can get you set up in that without a problem. Or anything else you want, honestly." His other two wives had always been fairly set in what they did with themselves, Rachel with her brilliance in just about everything she did, and Brianne with her dabbling in a dozen different businesses, most of them having something to do with public service or entertaining. He'd never met a woman more excited about the prospect of planning somebody else's wedding or party, when she was given the chance. Margo, on the other hand, had always been more . . . fluid.

"Maybe I can make clothes too, everyone always needs clothes." Margo said with a nod, since she wasn't sure before how she could contribute and now it felt like she had something. "Do we need to get going?"

"Yeah, no reason to put it off. Gotta go face my idiot brother sometime." He got up once she was finished with her pancakes, and plucked Chrissy up out of the carrier to hand her off to Rachel, since Bree was busy cleaning up. "I'll let you know when there's decent coffee back in stock. Let me know what you hear going around and where you end up." He briefly remembered Gwen's commentary about him and his wives as he put his hand to the small of Rachel's back, supporting her lightly as she hefted Chrissy into place. The thought just made him smile.

Bree paused in her cleaning to kiss Liam before he left for the day, and then Rachel followed suit. Both of them never had the jealousy or hurt in their eyes even kissing him one after another that Margo did even just as a bystander before he got to her. Margo gave them all a brief smile, went and gave her daughter a kiss, then walked out with Liam.

He took her hand as they walked and spun her around in the narrow corridor between their suite and the lift. "I would say I could just hang out with you for the whole day, but Rissa tried to teach me the whole sewing gig one time when I was younger and it turned bloody pretty fast."

"Your hands are too big for it." Margo said with a laugh before she twirled right back into him. "I wish you could too. It's nice to have some time without kids and with you. But I know you need to go talk to Logan. Are you still upset with him over the whole . . . pretending to be dead thing?"

"Yeah . . ." He didn't sound a hundred percent sure of being angry as they got to the lift, where they were joined by other midwesterners. They knew all of them by sight, but Liam just gave them all a friendly wave and settled toward the back of the lift car so he could pull Margo in against him. "Honestly, I'm still pissed at some of the stunts he pulled on me when we were kids, let alone faking his own demise for over a year. That baggage isn't getting dealt with anytime soon."

Margo nodded quietly and easily remained close to Liam, since there was nowhere on the earth she would rather be. "Do you actually think we'll make it to Eleusis?" Margo whispered her question, since she didn't want other people to hear her doubt.

Liam didn't look fully confident as he answered, but he did rest his hands on her hips to hold her close. He kissed her first instead of answering the question. "I might be pissed at him, but I believe him. He wouldn't have roped us into a fight he thinks we're gonna lose. If he thinks we'll get there, we'll get there. Just a matter of when."

Margo nodded in spite of her own doubts, and kissed Liam again before the lift stopped to let them out. She held onto his hand as he led the way. That was how their relationship was, Margo was always tentative and unsure, and Liam led the way. It may not have been how he was with his other wives, but she liked being led by her confident and strong husband. "I hope you're right."

They wandered for a while just to get a sense of the layout for the upper floors of the Labyrinth, which were much more extensive than the residential core of the place. They found a different way through some of the back hallways to get up to the level Liam decided he was going to call the parking garage, which wasn't even a third of the way full after the the influx of midwesterners, shockingly enough.

They found their trailer and climbed in among their supplies, to look for a few things to make home feel a little less like a cave. As usual, Liam didn't miss an opportunity during which they were left alone in a private place, setting both Margo's mind and her body just a little more at ease than either had been earlier that morning.

When they calmed a little against the back loading door of the trailer's interior, he kissed her one last time with a smile. "We're gonna be okay here. I promise. It's just gonna take some time to settle in."

Margo curled into him easily and held tightly to him as though hanging onto him meant life or death. "I didn't want to leave home. We were happy there. No one was chasing after us. I know why we're here, but it doesn't mean it isn't hard. I didn't even get to say goodbye to my parents."

"The parents who ask to borrow money before they ask how you're doing or how their granddaughter is doing?" He had never been fond of her parents, but since marrying Margo, they had gotten even more bold. They were both old, for Earth-born humans, though neither of them was in particularly bad health yet, on account of how young they'd been when they had Margo. All three sets of his in-laws were that way, except that Brianne's father was old enough to have started showing some signs of deterioration. He was rich enough to afford the best doctors on the East Coast, though. Margo's, not so much.

"I didn't say they were perfect parents." She replied a little defensively, though she didn't have much defense for her parents, nor did she really want to defend them. They'd sent her after Liam for his money in the first place, but she never cared about getting any money. Just getting Liam. It was a common thing, for families to chase after the Bickford name and fortune. "But they're the only ones I have. I've never known any other life than living close to home. I'm not very good with change."

"I'm not sure how I'm going to do with the change either. But we're gonna make it work, all of us, together." He kissed her again as he rubbed her back, glad to have a moment off to themselves for a while. "Home is where family is. Even if that's underground, for the time being."

Margo clung to Liam while she had the chance to have him completely to herself. "I love you so much. I'll do my best to adjust, I promise."

"I love you too. And I believe you." He said with a smile and he grinned under the kiss he gave her before they got up. He picked her up and set her physically back on her feet so they could get dressed. As he tugged on his shirt he caught a glimpse of a bin of Margo's things. "Hey, there's your machine over there, and whatever else got tucked in with it. Even if they've got some already, I'm sure they'll be glad to have extras, and I remember you liked that one." He finished getting his pants on and kissed the back of her neck while she looked in the bin.

She went through the bin and sighed as she looked through the unfinished clothes, fabrics, and tools she had to go with her sewing machine. It had been particularly difficult to leave a lot of things behind, but it was also difficult to set up a new life somewhere else without knowing if they would be uprooted days later. "I do like it. You gave it to me for my birthday."

He smiled at the memory and kissed her again as he tugged his shirt into place. "Come on, let's go make ourselves useful. I'll see you later tonight." The promise came with a smile that promised a great deal more to come just between the two of them, as always. He helped her get the machine out of the bin and packed it into a bag so it would be portable for her. They parted ways at the entrance to the parking garage where it separated into the various larger facility units near the surface.

"You need a hand with that?" The words were almost unintelligible to her at first, just because the accent behind them was so thickly African, but when she turned to follow the sound, the man's body language was understandable enough. He had a hand outstretched to take the machine for her and another toward her, his smile bright against his dark skin.

"Um, alright." Margo held out the heavy machine, and she gave him a warm smile. "Thank you. That's very kind of you." She held out her now-free hand so she could shake his hand. "My name is Margo."

"Jela." He said as her hand almost completely disappeared inside his own. The man wasn't particularly tall, but it was clear he was in construction and he was clearly built for the job. He had a barrel chest and a set of arms that looked like they might be able to lift a house on their own, so he clearly had no trouble with her sewing machine. "You look a bit lost. Are you with the group that just got in yesterday?" His accent didn't get any lighter as he spoke, but he fell in walking beside her easily, clearly assuming she knew where she was going.

Margo nodded as she kept her supplies close to her chest, but she was still glad to see someone friendly. It made things a little easier. "I was going to find someone to see if it would be okay for me to mend and make clothes."

"Oh, you're in luck. I know who you need to see." His grin was huge and genuine as he gently changed their direction, pointing out to the entrance of the Labyrinth and the road leading out into the valley. "Deirdre and her match are in charge of clothing requests and repairs. They've got a pair of Turkish sisters working for them, but they'll be happy to see somebody else willing to help. They keep yelling at me for ripping my shirts and jackets every time I come to see them, though, so if they don't look happy to see us, don't worry, it is because of me, not you."

Margo laughed softly. "Well, maybe you need to get some clothes that fit you. Has anyone ever measured and made clothes just for you?"

That got a look of amusement from her cheerful new friend, and he laughed as he shook his head. "Outside of Nairobi, we get mostly hand-me-downs from the city, we don't have much in the way of custom-made clothes."

"Wow, you traveled a long way." Margo replied with wide eyes, since she hadn't expected him to have traveled so far to be there, even though his accent said that he certainly wasn't from North America. "I have a lot of fabric." She said as she held out her bag of fabric and supplies. "I can make you something, if you want me to. That way you'll make less trips to get your clothes mended."

"You always make new clothes for people who give you directions?" He seemed amused, but as he moved, she could see that he hadn't been kidding about his clothes being often mended. He was wearing a set of stiff jeans that had been patched in half a dozen places, and not always very well, with a shirt that was torn in so many places it was barely salvageable, though it looked like it had once been a very respectable button-down dress-shirt. "If so, you must be both very popular and very busy."

"No, actually, I don't get the chance to make many clothes. Usually ours are bought." There were a lot of other things she had to help with around the Bickford estate, and so sewing turned into more of a hobby instead of a necessity. Liam could afford their clothes and Rachel and Brianne had more expensive tastes than she did. She made a few things for Chrissy, but not much else. "I wished I had more time back home. But now I do. So I would be happy to make some for you."

"If you make me better clothes, I won't have an excuse to come by to have mine mended and see you again. That would be a shame." He grinned over at her, then shrugged as they walked. "But I've always been told it's rude to say no whenever someone offers to give you something, so I won't. Maybe you can let me repay you when those in charge decide where you'll be living. I can make sure I get myself reassigned and say that I helped build you a house."

"Oh, I . . ." Margo was a little stunned he was telling her he wanted to see her again. "I think we already have a house in order. Maybe. I'm not sure." Margo's cheeks flushed a little bit in embarrassment. "My family is related to Logan Bickford. My husband is his twin brother. We have a big family, I'm one of his three wives and we each have children, so they're trying to get us a house quickly. I think."

"Oh!" He clearly hadn't realized that she was married and hadn't assumed that was the case, and she could see his eyes flick down to her hand to look at the wedding ring he hadn't even noticed. "I'm sorry, I didn't realize, I just thought you had come with everybody else."

Margo tried to laugh it off, but she wasn't laughing at him, just the misunderstanding. "It's alright. I'm flattered that you would be interested. We can still be friends, though, right?"

"Yeah, of course, of course." He said quickly, since he didn't want her to think that he was just helping her because he was interested in getting something in return. "Sorry, I was kind of set back there a bit. I was really hoping for the not-married thing. That, and the Councilman really, really doesn't like me, so now you're certain to make me nervous by proxy." He still wore the same teasing grin as before, but he kept slightly more distance between them as they walked than initially.

"You were really hoping for the not-married thing?" She replied with a laugh. "You just met me. You don't know if I'm crazy or not. And I'm a little scared of Logan myself, so you're not alone. I don't care what he thinks, though. So even if he doesn't like you, we can still be friends."

His opinion of her clearly only went up at that announcement, and he nodded his enthusiastic agreement. "Alright then. And he is very scary. And a little bit crazy. Good man, but crazy. Though I suppose that must run in the family. I can't imagine what it must take to juggle three wives."

Margo's smile dimmed and she looked away. She didn't think Liam was crazy, since she adored him, but she definitely didn't like being one of three wives. "I don't know what he really thinks about it. He says it keeps him on his toes." She looked down at her supplies again to avoid looking at the nice stranger. "I don't think the other two mind so much, but two out of seven days with your spouse is hard. I wish I had more time. All of the time."

"That would be hard." His smile disappeared immediately as soon as it was clear he had struck a nerve, and they walked in awkward silence for a little while. "Back in Kenya, my father was a thief." He said out of nowhere, since it didn't seem like the kind of thing a person generally said just to make conversation. "In Kenya, this is a mark against the criminal and their family. Once it was known he was guilty, my mother and brothers lost their jobs. I was able to negotiate with the Initiative before I accepted my commission to the project, and they arranged for my family to have jobs again, in exchange for me going to space."

"I had not thought about going, and I had not thought about being matched once we arrived. The woman they matched me with was from one of the Stations, and had been looking forward to being matched her entire life. I was not the man she had in mind. She split most of her time between me and another man she met within the Initiative. I could not fault her for it, but even though our relationship was selected by others, I still missed her. I can't imagine what sharing must feel like under other circumstances."

"It's not unheard of here." She shrugged, but obviously she was still not okay with it. "Liam was dating us all at the same time, and Logan arranged it before he left. I didn't want to lose someone I loved, and I didn't know if I could ever find someone else." Margo chewed on her bottom lip as she spoke honestly. "Sometimes I wonder how he can love all of us the same. We're so different. Sometimes I hope he's thinking about me instead of them. I get jealous very easily, but I've learned to be silent about it." Margo shrugged again. "I'm sorry it happened to you too. Missing someone is painful."

"Yes, it is." He said without saying much else, sharing a sympathetic smile with her as he turned aside past a small row of houses, after which a larger, low building came into sight. There were people coming and going, everyone carrying something, from a basket of clothes to a case of tools.

"This is the Lodge. Right now it's where everything happens around here besides what's already underground." He went in with her and guided her through the chaos inside, since there were dozens of different kinds of workshops, all set up without any clear boundaries between most of them. The station he led her to was unoccupied at the moment, but he set her sewing machine down on a small table across from another one that was older and less intricate than her own. "Deirdre usually comes in about mid-morning, but you'll like her. She's a very nice person. I'm sure she'll see to it that you've got plenty to do, and she'll take good care of you."

Margo nodded and finally looked up at him again. "Thank you, I would have wandered for a long time." She looked him over before she dumped out her fabrics and spread them out a little. "What about your shirt? If you pick a fabric, I can make one for you. I just have to take measurements."

"Um, I don't know. What's not going to get torn and snagged all the time while I'm doing construction?" He looked over the different fabrics, but he hadn't been joking when he said he wasn't used to getting things for himself. Standing around and getting her things together gave her more of a chance to really get a good look at him, and there was no deception in the man's face as he looked them over. He looked exceptionally clueless about what he was seeing aside from the textures he could feel.

Margo reached out and grabbed a few flannel patterns. "I can make you a shirt out of this." Then she grabbed some denim. "I can make pants out of this, with lots of pockets so you have places to store whatever you need."

He didn't have a problem with either fabric, so he shrugged and gave her something closer to his earlier smile. "I'll trust your judgment. You know better than I do." He held his arms up a little awkwardly, having never been measured for anything in his life, but he was in her hands.

She grabbed her measuring tape and a stool so she could get accurate measurements. Nothing about her movements or her touches was the least bit scandalous or inappropriate, even though she did have to get his inseam measurements for the pants. She was quick about it, though.

When she went to get his inseam, he did clear his throat and look away, and she'd been with Liam too long not to know a man avoiding something when she saw it. He also breathed a sigh of relief when she left the area and stood up. "I feel like a mannequin that should be going into a window somewhere." He had stayed as still as possible throughout the process so she could get whatever she needed, but for the most part, his eyes had been hidden from her view so she couldn't tell where they were lingering at any given moment.

"You would make an attractive mannequin." She wrote down all the numbers she needed to make his clothing just right. Margo double-checked her work to make sure, and then she finally stood up straight and backed away. "Okay, I think I have everything I need. They'll be ready in a couple of days."

"Thank you." He said genuinely, with a smile to match. "And I meant what I said about you telling me when they settle on which house is yours."

"Sure. I can do that." She smiled at him as well and set aside the fabrics for his clothes. "It was nice to meet you, Jela." Margo knew she sounded awkward saying his name, but she tried her best.

He smiled at the way she got it not quite right, but he didn't correct her, and he got her name just as wrong, since Rs weren't his strong point. "Nice to meet you too, Mah-go. I'll see you around."

She nodded and watched him go before she sat down at the workstation. No one had given her any instructions, but she knew if she sat down and started working, either someone would interrupt her or she would get his clothes finished faster. One way or another, she would be working, and she needed that focus more than anything.

She didn't need to think about the attractive man that had flirted with her. She didn't *want* to think about how unhappy she was about being involved with a resistance, that she wanted more time with Liam, that she felt like her life would never feel fulfilling enough. All she wanted to think about was the hum of the sewing machine and to watch its precise stitches.

15

It had been . . . the longest day of Logan's life. What was worse, he knew by everyone around him taking a break from their work to eat that it was only lunchtime. He had gotten quite a lot accomplished when it came to making sure everyone from the midwest was settled, but it still felt like time had slowed to a crawl. At the end of the day, if it ever arrived, he knew he would be able to go home, to a different home. But even that comfort didn't help him.

He finished putting together the priority list of those who would be moved into houses first of the midwesterners when he heard his door open and close. When he looked up, it took him a moment to remember he had indeed requested a meeting with Gwen.

"Ms. Pierce." He said formally, setting his tablet aside with a sigh and nodding toward the chair near his desk. "Thanks for coming. Please have a seat."

"Seriously, still calling me Ms. Pierce?" Gwen approached the chair and smiled at him before she sat down. "I've seen you with some serious bedhead. Enough to be called Gwen. Please?"

"I'll think about it." He said without sounding like he was going to think about it at all. She had seen him in various emotional states, and she had seen him really and truly angry, but she'd never seen him quite so . . . stoic as he was at that moment. "Are you aware of the most recent count of children under the age of one year, as of the arrival of the other midwesterners?"

"Yeah, there's a lot." Gwen said as she slumped a little in the chair. "Around a hundred. Which is insane. Talk about hormone-city once these kids turn into teenagers."

"My plans aren't about what's to come in thirteen years when we have to start worrying about mass puberty." He sighed and shook his head, since that wasn't something he wanted to contemplate. "I'm more concerned about the next year or so.

However long we'll be staying here."

He leaned back a little in his chair, not exactly to get comfortable, but just to trick himself into thinking he could put some distance between himself and that eventuality. "If all hundred and sixteen of the children were under your care, directly, twenty four hours a day, seven days a week, how many staff would you need beside yourself in order to adequately monitor them?"

"Holy shit, twenty-four hours a day? Okay, I like kids, but that's insane." Gwen was shocked he would ask so much of her, but she couldn't even imagine the staff. "I mean, you're asking about a twenty-four hour daycare, right? I guess . . . one adult to every two kids. That means at least ten staff-members on at all times, no matter what. People would have to be flexible to be on-call if the numbers got too high. They're mostly infants, so one person can't really handle more than two at once. If we're going to offer the service, then we would probably have to do it for the few older kids too, right? I take that back, at least fifteen people at all times, five to ten who would be backup on-call."

"So if I understand your math, you'd need roughly twenty five people per shift, three shifts per day, let's say four shifts just to be safe in numbers and call it somewhere around a hundred people you'd need to have for the sake of flexibility. Does that sound about right?" He didn't seem surprised at her shock or at her estimates, and as well as she'd gotten to know Logan, the mere lack of any kind of correction or condescension in his question was an exceptionally high compliment.

"Something like that." Gwen said with a nod, even though she still couldn't really believe what he was asking her. "Are you really considering that? I mean, it couldn't be just anyone. I would have to go through White and do extensive checks. I don't want any crazies around babies."

"Good. Get started." He didn't draw out his permission any longer than necessary. "He's also going to show you where we've allocated space for the whole operation. You'll oversee everything about it and report to me." He laid it all in place and gave her a moment to ingest it before he continued. "Any questions?"

"No, I . . . um . . . I won't let you down, Logan." She said gently as she sat there stunned. Gwen was usually full of jokes and sarcasm, but she was really quite touched that he trusted her with something so big. "Thanks for giving me the chance. Even on a bad day." Gwen tried to give him a reassuring smile before she remembered something and took out her communicator. She whipped through it quickly and tapped on a video to show it as a hologram.

"When I was watching the boys today, they thought it was funny when I played with that hat you brought back with you. It got left behind, so I was playing with it." The video was not showing her, but the boys, who watched her and laughed when she played peek-a-boo with Logan's hat.

Even when he was watching them at first, he didn't crack a smile, but the sight of them laughing at her finally did get the smallest hint of one from him. "It's a good hat. I missed that hat."

"One of them will be the most handsome boy wearing that hat. Well, both of them will, but they'll obviously have to fight over it." She teased as the video ended and she tapped a few times to send it to him directly. "They're happy boys. Most of the time. They have their bad days. Everyone does." Gwen felt bad for Logan, and while she would still definitely like to take his pants off, she knew he was going through a hard time. Gwen was the last person to try and judge anyone, and she wasn't going to judge Logan either. "You've had a rough day. Things will get better. They always do, somehow."

That mention removed the smile on his face, but when he spoke, it was far from the harshest he'd ever been with her. "The details of my personal life don't concern you beyond the welfare of my children while they're in your care. But thank you. I hope, in this instance, that you're right." He looked at his communicator to accept the video file she'd sent him, tucking it away for later re-watching. "I'd recommend you consider Anna's sister-in-law Susan for one of your shift supervisors. She's excellent with children and she takes precisely no shit from anyone. Anna's younger sisters could be put to work helping as well. They're young, but almost pathologically helpful, and they're very fond of Susan."

Gwen nodded and took notes in her communicator for his recommendations. "Sure, I'll get in contact with her." She tapped a few more times on her communicator and looked up at him again. "Is there anything else?"

"Just one more thing." He seemed to get even more . . . Logan-ish when he said it, every trace of happiness or joviality that she'd seen from him out in the midwest apparently was leeched out of him by whatever it was he needed to say. "Since you're now reporting to me directly, I can tell you this with the expectation you won't repeat it. To anyone." He never doubted her confidence before, but the final thing he needed to talk to her about was potentially uncomfortable at best.

"Xander and Tatyana managed to get the Twist working last night. They made a stable connection to Eleusis. Tatyana's already been through to make a test run of it and returned safely."

"No shit?" Gwen was even more surprised to hear about that than she was about an unexpected job in baby management. "That's awesome! I guess we really need to pick up the pace with recruiting, but you did a good job bringing all of your family and friends. I think so, anyway."

He nodded, but that clearly wasn't the end of what he had to tell her. "We do need to pick up the pace on recruiting, you're right, and if you have any ideas of how we can go about doing that, I'd be open to hearing them. Besides advertising to the entire world we offer free daycare to rebels." He said with the tiniest of smiles, though the expression evaporated quickly.

"It also means that once we've done some reconnaissance and solidified some of what we think we know about the Consortium's presence on Eleusis, we'll soon be going to war. Not just us, but every cell across the world is going to start pouring through this place on our way to the other side of the galaxy. I know better than to think you're interested in picking up a gun and marching off on the front lines, and I can respect that. But what war means is that some of the children you'll have in your care will be orphans by the time all is said and done. I will be relying on you and your staff to oversee care and placement for those who find themselves in that situation."

It was far from pleasant to think about, but Logan knew better than to think they would get through what was to come unscathed. "Is that something you'll be willing to do?"

Gwen was pretty amazed at Logan's talent for making a hard situation even harder, but she wasn't weak or particularly tender-hearted, even though she was a generally happy woman. "I spend a lot of time with a lot of these babies." She said first and foremost, and she was being serious, not funny, when she said it. "I see their firsts sometimes before their parents do. Their first steps. First laugh. I've taken care of sick babies, sad babies, babies that struggle to develop. I'm not a doctor by any means, but I've cared for a lot of babies. I don't only care about their physical well-being, I care about *them*. You can't take care of these little people and not fall in love with them, it's just impossible. Whatever happens, I'll make sure they're cared for."

There was an almost visible shift she could see in the man as she watched him nod his acknowledgment, as if the responsibility for the children had moved from his shoulders to hers, making him lighter. Or if not, it was at least shared, and that made things easier, if only just a little. "Thank you." He sighed again, glad that they were past that part of the conversation. "What else do you need from me to get you started?"

In a switch, Gwen smirked, since she really wished that he would ask her that question in a different context. "Oh, I don't know, I really like . . . oh, you meant for the babies." She teased, and her smile remained. "If you could have a team of people bring all the baby supplies and furniture to the area you've already claimed for us, that would be great. Oh, and paint. I want to make it a cheery place for babies to stay, especially considering they could be with us days at a time or more. That's all for now, I think."

He gave her a sarcastic look after her purposeful stumble, and shook his head. "I'll get a team working on it." He gave her a pointed once-over once he'd said so. "Also, if I find out that you're using your new position as a means of making connections with the fathers who come to drop off their children, we'll need to have a different kind of conversation."

Gwen rolled her eyes. "Look, I won't proposition anyone. But I'm a flirt. If a guy looks good, I'm going to give him a compliment. If he comes back looking for more and I'm interested, then I don't think you have any right to control who I do or do not sleep with. But when I'm on the job, I'll keep my comments to a minimum. Sound like a compromise?"

"I can accept that." He got up from his chair to see her out, but it wasn't a large office, so quarters between them were relatively close. "I'm hoping that with the option of childcare made available to everyone on a reliable basis, some of those couples who've been having trouble dealing with the stress of life out here and the stress of handling children at the same time will be able to take a much-needed break once in a while and begin to re-establish some . . . damaged relationships. That becomes difficult when the babysitter presents herself as a distraction." He smiled as he said it, though, since he knew he wasn't going to change her, and he wasn't even angry at what she'd done most of the time. He couldn't completely argue with the logic of her existence, even if he didn't agree with it. "So yes, keeping it to a minimum will help tremendously. Thank you."

"No problem." Gwen said with an answering smile, and she turned toward Logan again as he reached to open the door and her back was to the open door. "You know how to contact me if you need to. Or want to." Her grin turned playful up until she backed herself into someone standing outside the door. "Oh, I'm sorry . . ." She apologized before she even had a chance to turn around.

Liam laughed as she righted herself, one hand out to steady her in case she stumbled again. "I know the song says 'back that ass up' but that doesn't mean you shouldn't still watch where it's going." The difference between the brothers had never been more apparent than in that exact moment, Liam dressed in a yellow shirt and faded jeans, a constant grin on his face, Logan in dark slacks and a grey shirt, his expression a constant storm of dour anxiety. Liam was about to knock on the door, and while Gwen recovered herself, he looked back over at his brother. "This a bad time?"

"No, it's perfect. I was actually about to look for you." Logan shut the door of his office behind him as he stepped out into the hallway to leave, taking a moment with his back turned to lock it up behind him.

Gwen took her time to step away from Liam, since she hadn't seen him up close since the bus ride with Brianne. Her cheeks instantly flushed, but not out of embarrassment. He told her then that she was only a guest at Bree's request, so she hadn't once tried to reach out or say a word to any of them, but she couldn't help how her body reacted in the moment. Especially from his brief touch. "Nice to see you again, Liam."

"Ms. Pierce. Always a pleasure." He said in his usual light-hearted way, grinning at her while his brother's back was turned. The formality sounded very, very different coming from him than it had coming from Logan, especially with the scalding look he gave her afterward as she retreated.

She looked him over as well, since she couldn't help herself. He was gorgeous. He was definitely one of the best lovers she'd ever experienced, and she wanted it to happen again. Even if she wasn't completely sure it would. "Same goes for you. You know how to reach me if I'm needed."

"Bree's got the kids today and tomorrow, but she mentioned that she might call you up to see if you're free." He couldn't resist teasing her just a little bit further, but he broke off as Logan turned back around, and gave her a wave as they walked away the other direction, apparently intent on their own business.

Gwen resisted the urge to pout and gave them both a wave before she bolted off faster than Logan had ever seen her run. Especially away from someone with a penis. It was torture to be around Liam, and Gwen needed to go take care of the tension that she already felt before someone called her up for some kind of baby duty.

* * * * *

When Mercury came home later that night, it was to the sound of the boys laughing and the smell of spaghetti. The boxes of Logan's things that were set out on the porch by her earlier that day were now stacked on Anna's porch next door, but there was nothing on her porch. Clearly Orion hadn't wasted any time putting the reminder of things as far away as possible.

Inside the house, there was a communicator set on its side to play a program with puppets and bright colors, near which both her sons were hanging from bouncers that were suspended from a ceiling beam. The living room of the house, the central entryway, and the kitchen/dining room were all in a row by the front door, the massive archways between rooms making the entire front of the house into what felt like one huge room. The boys were suspended, at the moment, from the apex of one of those archways, and Orion had twisted the two of them together until their bouncers were constantly spinning and spiraling the boys out of control in hysterical fits of laughter, only for them to get wound up in each other all over again and start the process all over. They were both red-faced and out of breath as she closed the door behind them, but she could see Orion just smiling at them from the kitchen, where he finished up some of his work over a pot.

"That's definitely a sound that never gets old." Mercury said with a smile as she walked in and put down a computer and her bag on a small table near the door. "Whatever you're making smells wonderful."

"It's this incredibly fancy recipe I've learned down here on Earth called Spaghetti and Hot Dogs. Supposed to be some incredibly high-class, upper crust stuff. Also garlic bread." He remembered the garlic bread as soon as he said it and hurried over to the oven to pull out said bread. "Slightly browner garlic bread than I had intended, but I'm sure there's some fancy Italian term for it that would make it seem okay." He set the bread out to cool and went back to plating the spaghetti noodles and the sauce with hot dogs. "How was the clinic?"

Instead of sitting down, Mercury walked over to the boys and showered them both with kisses before she said much of anything. It was strange to have Orion in her house, the boys, and everything appearing domestic and good, but there was consolation in it. Usually Mercury was worried when she got home about one thing or another. Worried about if her unit would be a mess, worried that she'd left the boys too long, worried about dinner or laundry . . . not that she expected Orion to do her laundry or anything. Logan hadn't demanded those things from her, but she had taken it all on her shoulders. Just the fact that Orion was making her dinner made her smile.

"It was steady but not too busy. I didn't get much research done, but Jason sent me some files he found, so I'll do some reading once the boys go to sleep." She turned away from the boys and walked over to where Orion was cooking. "This is really nice of you. Thank you. Can I help?"

"Um, sure, I didn't really go looking around for drinks. Once I found the pasta and got going, it was this and then the boys and I just kind of didn't get to it. Kinda weird how a house with exactly the same design has everything in different places." It was an uncomfortable thing for him to experience, but he was trying to just push past it.

"Sorry, I know it's still a mess." She felt bad he had to go searching for anything, even though she was still grateful he had anyway. "What would you like to drink? A lot of the people that came back with us brought that carbonated drink in different flavors. We have some." Apparently Logan had been feeling nostalgic in a lot of ways, but his carbonated drinks were left behind. "Or filtered water. I think there is also some alcohol."

"No, I'm . . . sort of putting off the drinking binge for now, I think. Eventually it'll hit me, and I want to make sure I'm really stocked up for it." He had never been a particularly big drinker the entire time she'd known him, unlike Logan's tendency to become a borderline alcoholic from time to time. "Some of the lemon-lime stuff they had out there would be good with this, I think, if you have it."

"Alright." She agreed with a nod before she moved to pour their drinks and put them on the table. Mercury didn't know if he would want to sit next to her, but she put their drinks near each other. After she was done setting the table, she finally went and took off her shoes and her white coat. It left her in her pale blue scrubs, but she wore scrubs often, so she knew he wouldn't mind. "How was your day? You know, considering."

"Not terrible. You know, other than the obvious." He focused on serving out their food while she got settled, and he wasn't too far behind her with the plates. He went over to the twins as he spoke, resetting the episode of the program and spinning them one more time to keep them entertained so he and Mercury could have some hope of eating in peace. "Got a lot of the midwesterners' stuff put into order in the hangar, went through the armory with Kam," he let out a low whistle. "Allah have mercy on anybody who decides to piss off a redneck, that's all I can really say about that."

A small smile crept to her lips, and she was still smiling as she looked up at him when he leaned over to set the plate down in front of her. Even if it was a meal that was very different than any they had shared in orbit, she was happy to share a meal with him nonetheless. "I'm glad we're prepared. At least somewhat. They're going to restock all of my medical supplies tonight. I looked over the inventory, it's extensive. That eases my mind a little. And their doctors will be working the night shift tonight."

"That's pretty huge in itself. Maybe you'll all be able to get set on a decent rotation now. Especially if . . . well, if we can get some more recruiting under way." He knew he was getting ahead of himself, but he didn't want to get too far ahead of himself. He looked over Mercury's shoulder at the boys to make sure they were alright, and started mixing up his own food.

"There was one other big piece of news that came out of today. Kam told me they're not telling anyone yet so the councillors have time to formulate a real and actual plan, but she told me, and I don't honestly care if anybody would be pissed about me telling you." He glanced at the door and the windows, just out of precaution, not out of any real fear. If there was a threat, they'd all know about it very quickly. Their drills every other week on preparedness measures were ridiculously thorough. "Xander and Tatyana finally cracked it. They made a stable bridge to Eleusis."

Mercury certainly wasn't expecting to hear that, so she looked incredibly surprised as she looked over at Orion. "Wow, really? Wow . . ." She was stunned into silence for a moment. "What about Carl and Aiko? Did they find them?"

He shook his head. "No one's gone through except Tatyana, just to make sure it was stable. Crazy . . ." His lips formed around a word that he tried not to say around infants, and he broke off without finishing his statement. "They've been meeting most of the afternoon trying to put together plans of how to proceed, now that we actually can." He took a bite of the spaghetti, still thinking through it himself. "I expect they'll suddenly find that any bastard can drive a truck and I'm more useful with a gun in my hand. I can't say I'd argue. Kam already told me she's going to be leading the first team herself, however they decide to get things started. So I expect to go along."

"Oh." Mercury picked up the bread first, but was suddenly feeling less hungry. She was worried about anyone going, let alone Orion, her one remaining real friend. She knew it was a selfish feeling, but she found that she hadn't been selfish enough for the last year. Now she wanted to be, and losing a friend was not on her list. "I hope you'll be alright."

He paused in eating his spaghetti and pointed at her with his fork. "Don't. Don't do that. Not the 'It's likely you're gonna die' eyes. I know that look. I'll be fine." He assured her with a teasing smile. "It's kind of what we've both been training for all our lives. Just thought I'd be getting out of a transport carrier when it happened, not going through a portal in the Rockies."

"Things are very different now than what we thought would be happening when we went to Eleusis." She said softly as she turned her attention solely to her plate. "Everything I dreamed for my life turned into a nightmare."

"Hey." He reached across the corner of the table between them to take her hand and force her to look him in the eye. "We're gonna be alright. We made it this far."

Mercury nodded, but still refused to maintain eye contact because she suddenly felt the real need to cry. Her life was falling apart, she still couldn't keep up with her work, and now they were supposed to be ready to go to Eleusis? Eleusis, which was a hostile environment for them, Eleusis, with no home, nowhere to live?

How was she supposed to work with that? The tears burned in her eyes. "Everything has been so hard already. I'm not ready to be a combat doctor. I'm not ready to try and live on an unknown planet with my two children . . . alone. I can't do this."

"No one's going anywhere until we're ready." He said without letting go of her hand. "If I'm right, it's gonna be a while before Eleusis is any place for children. There's too much we don't know, about the planet and about the Consortium's resources there. If the last year has taught us anything, it's that we need to be prepared before we move. On anything. Nobody's running into a war tonight."

Mercury wiped at her eyes and glanced at him once more before she looked away again. "I'm sorry. I'm probably overreacting. I know we're not going into a war tonight." She sniffled and stared at her food. "I'm glad you're here. I don't know what I would do if I were alone in this house with the boys. I . . . if I'm not busy, I have a hard time being alone. It makes me feel vulnerable."

It was a huge change for Orion to see concerning Mercury, though he didn't know the reason behind it. The version of her that he had once known, a strong, independent, yet socially-awkward and isolated doctor was quite different. She didn't feel strong, and when she was alone, she had flashbacks to what happened to her before they fled the station. Reminders of how powerless she was, and it made her often feel inadequate. She was unable to protect herself, and certainly unable to protect her children.

"You're not." He reassured her, though she could tell he was a little confused at the change in her apparent level of personal confidence. They had all changed, though, and he was going through his own fair share of personal insecurity after the events of that morning. After the way Logan had treated Anna on the station and ever since, Orion was questioning everything about the way he himself had treated Anna, if she seemed to think Logan had actually been the one to do a better job of it, given that track record. "We've got the whole complex around us and every kind of security net the eggheads can come up with keeping this place safe. And for you specifically, vulnerable would not crack my list of the top fifty words I would use to describe you."

"I can't defend myself. I can't stop someone from coming in here and hurting the boys or taking them from me." Mercury shook her head and wiped at her eyes again. The boys were content and fascinated with the colorful puppet show and she was falling apart at the table.

She had never really expressed an interest in learning how to defend herself before, but after giving his surprise a moment's consideration, he supposed she had never really had a reason. The station where she'd grown up had been so closely monitored that even her carb intake was thoroughly watched, let alone private security. After the events of Nine and their exposure in the open on the mountains, he could understand that sense of security being gone forever.

"I can teach you, if you want." He offered quietly. "You've never been weak, and honestly, your kind of mind has made some of the most terrifying people I've ever had my ass beaten by. I know the first rule of medicine is to do no harm, but the first rule of self defense is do as little harm as necessary in order to resolve the situation. I don't personally see a conflict there."

Mercury sniffled in silence for a moment before she finally made eye contact. Her eyes were red and puffy, which was in stark contrast with her pale complexion, but she nodded. "Please. Please teach me. I need to know . . ." She hesitated, because she worried if Orion knew anything about what happened to her he would think less of her for allowing herself to enter the situation. A situation that had altered the rest of her life. "I need to be able to stop something from happening. I don't . . . I don't want to be a victim again."

He nodded confidently and squeezed her hand again. "Okay. Ass-kicking class officially starts in the morning. Don't be late." He smiled faintly to try and encourage one from her as well, but it clearly wasn't going to happen. Instead, he stood up and moved his chair around the corner to set it next to hers, and pulled her into a hug with the table at his back. "We'll be alright, Mercury. All of us. Even the tiny humans. I believe that."

She easily fell into his side and hugged him tightly, since she needed the comfort and the feeling of stability. Orion and Logan both had offered her different kinds of stability and protection, but Orion had never once ripped it out from underneath her. Even after things failed to go the way they originally planned. "I hope you're right. I desperately want you to be right."

"I like being right. It's usually something I'm pretty good at." He held onto her with no sign of letting go, but eventually moved one of his hands to lift the braid of her hair against her back. "Haven't lost your touch for braids, I see. Been a while since I saw one of these on you."

"My . . . Logan preferred my hair loose." She had no reason to be ashamed of doing something differently to please her spouse. Only Logan wasn't her spouse anymore. Mercury wasn't exactly sure about the legalities, but it wasn't as though anyone was enforcing any law other than the law the rebels established amongst themselves. Regardless, as far as she was concerned, Logan was not her husband. He would never touch her again. "His preferences no longer matter to me. So I'm doing it how I prefer."

"Well, it looks good." He tugged it one more time to try and put a smile on her face, then let her go enough to look her in the eye. "I'm not saying go all the way to dreadlocks or microbraids or anything, that might be a little extreme, but it looks good. I'm more used to this than the other thing." He smiled and squeezed her shoulder as James started whining a little behind her in the archway. "Here, I'll get him, you go ahead and finish eating. There's a bottle with his name on it on top of the fridge." He patted her shoulder one last time before he headed into the kitchen to retrieve it, leaving his own food for the time being.

Mercury watched him as she attempted to take a few bites of the dinner he made for her, and her heart softened as she watched him with her son, a baby that didn't even belong to him. Orion was sweet, tender, and he made her baby smile. "I hope there's nothing I ever do to lose your friendship, Orion."

He looked over at her in surprise, but he chuckled and just smiled afterward. "Why would that happen? I'm a tough guy to get rid of. Kam's been trying to piss me off for years, I just get her back worse and we move on with life. You're not getting rid of me." He leaned back in a chair with his legs crossed and James settled into the bend of his knee as he propped the bottle into the boy's mouth as James tried and failed at holding it himself.

"There's a lot that has happened. Things that I'm ashamed of. I worry what you of all people would think if you knew everything." Mercury kept her voice quiet, still upset by the idea of being alone, vulnerable, and going to war. It was a struggle to eat, even though it tasted good.

"We've all had to do things since the Initiative that we're not proud of." His smile faltered at the topic, but he couldn't lose it completely with the little contented child in his lap. "I know you better than to ever think less of you because of situations we've been forced into beyond our control." He looked up at her with another attempt at a reassuring smile and a shrug. "Turns out I'm a halfway decent thief. Didn't know that until I started going out on supply runs last fall. Not only that, I kind of enjoyed it. Getting something over on people who've got it better than they're equipped to appreciate. Not my favorite thing I've ever learned about myself, but it is what it is, I guess."

"You make a good thief. You've helped keep us alive after all of this time by doing the runs. That's never something I'm going to hold against you." She said with a small smile as she took another bite. "You made me dinner. No one usually makes dinner except me."

"Well, you're certainly better at it than I am, nobody's gonna dispute that. But if you're gone and I'm home, I can put something together. I still make a mean peanut butter and . . . whatever kind of jelly substitute we have hanging around." He nodded toward the table. "I may or may not have stolen the sauce for dinner from the storehouse. You could blackmail me with that if you wanted to."

"I have absolutely no interest in blackmailing you, Orion Al-Jabbar. You matter too much to me." She meant it completely as she took another bite, since she knew she needed to eat. "Thank you for everything. Really. This is so kind of you."

"Hey, you're the one giving me a place to live. The least I can do is pay rent." He replied with a broader grin, since none of them were paying anything for their homes. Besides the entire effort and labor of their lives, of course. "They woke up about an hour ago, so they should go down pretty early for the night. Are they still getting up for midnight feedings or are they sleeping through yet?"

"Declan wakes up most nights. James is a good sleeper for now. Sometimes they both get hungry, but don't worry about them. I still breastfeed at night, since Barry has been covering the night shift most nights." She gave him a small smile. "They both like to use me as a pacifier to sleep, but I don't really care. I like to have them close. Some people say I'm spoiling them, but I'll never have this chance with them again once it's gone."

"No such thing as spoiling a person this tiny." He bounced James a little on his leg. "All they care about at this point is if they're clean and fed and entertained. World is a pretty simple place. That's what's fun about taking care of kids most of the time.

When you're taking care of them, your world is as simple as theirs. Just for a little while. Then of course they start screaming and crapping their pants and it gets a little less fun. But that's alright."

"I'd rather have their problems sometimes." Mercury commented as she continued to mull about her own problems. "They are loved by their mother and father no matter what." Unlike what he did to Mercury, she did believe that Logan wouldn't abandon his sons. She took another bite off of her plate and got up after she finished chewing. "I'll have to save the rest of this for later. It's very good, I'm just not hungry."

"Well, between you and James, that makes one of you. He chugged this thing." He held up the bottle that was already empty and set it aside on a table nearby. He wasn't going to second-guess her on eating dinner, since he couldn't blame her for not feeling hungry after the conversation.

Mercury put away the leftovers and she looked at his abandoned plate. "I can take over if you don't mind watching them while I grab a shower once you're done eating. Some hot water would feel incredibly nice. If I can get any right now."

"I haven't used any, so it should be all yours. And we have our own individual ones per house now." It was the first time that had been the case for either of them in their entire lives, since they'd been utilizing community water their entire childhoods growing up on the stations and living in the Labyrinth. He stood up and handed off James gingerly before he went back to his own plate.

"I won't use it all, so you can have plenty." She promised as she turned her attention to her boys. "This is your house too."

* * * * *

It was well after sunset when Logan finally came home, and Anna could hear his heavy footsteps on the front porch before he opened the front door. He wasn't sure if the children would still be awake or not, but he hoped he could see them before they went down for the night. At first there was no sign of movement just inside the hallway, but his boxes were all piled just inside, stacked neatly and closed, since clearly no one had gotten to them just yet.

"Anyone home?" He said quietly, since he didn't want to wake anyone if the children were asleep.

"Hey, you." Anna said softly, though she approached from the babies' room at the back of the house. She was holding Lynnette

287

on her hip with a soft smile. The baby girl's hair was wet, so clearly she had been recently bathed. "I'm glad you're home. I missed you." She stepped up without permission or hesitation and kissed Logan immediately, since she was going to throw herself into things as much as she could. Anna had given up Orion to be with the man in front of her. She wasn't going to hold back.

He held her tightly in the kiss, glad for it after the day he'd had, mostly spent trying to keep busy and get something done. He took in a deep breath once the kiss ended before he even opened his eyes. He sighed before he looked at her, as if in that moment the world was able to change for him and allow him to be home. "Where's Leo?"

"In his crib. I gave him a few toys so I could bathe Lynnette in the tub without him drowning her with his splashing. He's alright. You know how he is, he cries like nothing else if he's unhappy. We'd know."

"I do know that." He rolled his eyes, and it was as though he could feel the weight of the day falling off his shoulders. "I've got . . . quite a lot of news from the day. I'd rather start with yours."

"I tried to get as much unpacked as I could." Anna looked around the house. Lynnette held her arms out toward her father, and Anna smiled as she passed her daughter over to Logan. "I unpacked some of your things, but mostly mine and the children's. I did hang up a lot of your clothes, though." She looked around at the sparsely furnished home and back up at Logan. "So I've been working my ass off to make our house pretty." She replied with a sarcastic smirk before she kissed him again. "I made dinner. Chicken pot pie. Not very much chicken, but I know it's one of your favorites. And let's face it, it's easy."

"Probably for the best." He gave her a teasing look as he walked with her back toward Leo's room, looking over the decorations she put up in the meantime. He grinned at the hook she put up for his hat just off the entryway, since he remembered the video Gwen sent him earlier about his other children wearing it. "I always loved your potatoes, though. And heaven knows we've got plenty of those hanging around."

"They're very versatile. Expect to see a lot of potatoes." She replied warmly, as she looked around the room as well. She'd put up different pieces of artwork for the children, as well as a few photos, since there was one point in time when they had the supplies to develop a few photos. "There are more pictures up in our room. Larissa gave me a bunch more. A big one of us at our wedding." Anna had a few pictures she'd carried around since before they even went to orbit, but thankfully her family and his had given them some more.

"Trust Larissa to be armed with scrapbooks." He was amused by that, and smiled as he looked around the house, everything still freshly painted, but still home nonetheless. "Did she or any of your family come over at all? I wasn't sure if they'd know where to find you, and the only one I saw today was Liam."

"Yeah, Larissa came over and Susan and my little sisters. They all helped a little bit. Larissa said that she's been feeling sick, so Susan definitely thinks she's pregnant. I think they both are. They cried like newborn babies when they helped me hang up the wedding photos. They kept telling me how happy they are for us."

He smiled at the thought, since he was glad to hear that Anna was getting support from both their families. "Part of what I did today was assign Gwen to head up a centralized place for community child care. So instead of her and all the other babysitters going around to everyone's houses like chaos, people will be able to bring their children in and have them looked after, day or night. I told her it'd be a good idea for her to utilize Susan and your sisters for help. Seeing as Susan's already got two of her own and Ben working security under Kam, I'm sure she'll need all the help she can get."

"What do you think about your sister, huh?" She went up to him and smirked. "Do you think my brother knocked her up? They are so good together, aren't they?"

"They seem to be." He got into the room with Leo and bounced Lynnette as Anna checked on her son, who seemed content in his crib with his toys for the time being. "Cory's been taking charge with the little ones a lot more, and Ben allows it, at least from the way they acted at home. Cory hasn't said anything to me yet about wanting to go into security or anything else, but I'm sure they'll find something to suit them soon enough. Before we left, he just seemed concerned about Danny and your sisters having a chance to finish their education."

"Cory was never very comfortable with a gun. He can use one, but he'd rather not." Anna hefted her big baby boy and gave him a few kisses to get him giggling. "I think we could use more teachers around here. He's really smart."

"I'll see what he says. The kids from the district are going to need somebody to coordinate their lessons even up here." The vast majority of the children in their population were under two years old, but they would need to take care of the entire spectrum of ages, after all. It wasn't something Logan had ever imagined being necessary to a rebel cause, but it was obvious everything in the world was more complicated than he once thought. Life itself was more complicated. "I also saw that nurse Ben hired wandering around making house calls in the Labyrinth for booster injections. Oliver, I think his name was. I'm glad he decided to come with us. He'd have been a liability otherwise, and the medical staff can use all the help they can get."

"He said he would be glad to help take care of the babies too. He's really kind." Anna replied with a gentle tone. "I barely know him, but he was willing to comfort me and let me cry on his shoulder after I visited my father. His wife and unborn child died when the Consortium decided to retaliate after uprisings started. He had every reason to hate me, and instead he comforted me."

"Seems like a good man." He carried Lynnette against his chest as they got back out into the family room, where there was a section walled off for the children to explore safely. "There . . . may be more of those uprisings soon. If the rest of the councilors and I have our way." He set Lynnette down and made sure she had a toy to keep her entertained. "They got it working. Xander and Tatyana. Last night."

"Really?" Anna was both surprised and excited, since she was anxious to get to Eleusis, even though she wasn't entirely convinced they ever would. "Did they see anything? The compound?"

Logan shook his head and went to the display console set up in their home, both for entertainment and for more pragmatic purposes like communication. In a few gestures, he pulled up a visual of Eleusis that had been classified above top secret until the fall of Nine, and which the world now referenced as casually and easily as a map of Earth itself.

He zoomed in on the area of the compound along the shore of an inland sea in the southern hemisphere, and turned the map to show a three-dimensional image of the surrounding geography. "The compound is down here where the slope off the hills gets close to the coast, just a few dozen meters or so above sea level. They've got our Twist set to come down here, about two clicks up the coast."

He pointed to a spot where the mountains were in much higher contrast with the sea, cliffs over a hundred meters high plummeting to the water in a sheer dropoff. There was a broad meadow between two mountains, looking down on the compound from afar but too far away to be seen by anyone inside or on patrol. "We're not telling anyone yet until we can finalize the plan for occupation going forward. Most of my afternoon was arguing with them about how to proceed."

"That doesn't sound fun." Anna put Leo down with Lynnette and tried to pull him toward a chair. "Sit down, I'll give you a massage, and you can tell me how the argument ended."

That wasn't an offer he could refuse, so he took off his coat at last and set it nearby. He pulled her down into a kiss first, but then settled back into the chair. "It ended with them finally realizing they were all being too hasty, and that we need to send a purely exploratory team through for intelligence first. The idea is to get sensors in place that won't be detected by the Consortium compound, so we can watch for patrol movements and find a suitable place to set up our base of operations planetside. But we need to know a hell of a lot more about the area than we can find out from just these geography scans."

Anna nodded and thought over what he said as she started to rub his shoulders. It was probably an impossible task, but she would try anyway. He needed to relax. "They've been waiting for a while to strike against the Consortium. But not only do we need intel, we need more people."

"I keep telling them we need to centralize our resources, at least for the Americas, but I seem to be the only one who thinks so." He was clearly annoyed, but he was doing his best to relax under the massage. "When I brought it up today, they all looked at me like I was stoned and reminded me they're already humoring me by bringing in the entire midwestern contingent. You know, not like all of them are going to help with things or anything."

Anna rolled her eyes, since she agreed with Logan's proposal, not that anyone would particularly care about her opinion. "It's because they're too afraid of bringing in a spy or being caught by the Consortium, but at some point the benefit outweighs the risk. As it stands, we risk more by doing nothing to bring in people. We have over a hundred babies here alone. We can't depend on the people we have here to bring down the Consortium on Eleusis. Half the people here have never actually fought or killed anyone.

We need more people. We risk the Consortium if we do, but they're going to find us eventually if we don't. It's only a matter of time."

"Not only that, but the majority of the actual fighters, the rebels who've been a part of this since before we even went up to Nine, aren't here. The ones Carmina didn't take years ago," he'd gotten that entire history from Jason not long after arriving on Earth, "are still in Russia, Jakarta, Perth, Johannesburg . . ." he shook his head, since they wouldn't do anyone any good scattered all over the world. "Assholes had enough balls to send out a message to the entire world dropping all the Consortium's secrets, but they can't buy a damn plane ticket."

"We can't exactly go to them, what with near a thousand people and a motherfucking Twist." Anna shook her head, but she moved her hands up to the back of his neck. "There's a solution we just aren't seeing. For now, we'll just have to investigate Eleusis and hope we don't get fucking killed. Or caught." Anna leaned in and nipped at the side of his neck before she kissed his skin. "You never did tell me what *my* job is going to be, Boss Man."

He smiled, though his emotions at the nickname were mixed, since that was a little too much like the relationship he had just walked away from. Even so, he pulled her around in front of him so that she could straddle his lap in the chair. "You want me to assign you to something? You've been pretty good about jumping all over the place wherever you think you're best suited so far."

"Well, I'd like a suggestion at least." She replied with a laugh before she kissed him, since straddling Logan's lap meant kissing and all sorts of touching. "You seem to know where to put everyone else."

"Knowing where to put you and where to put you to work are two very different things." He returned her kisses, his hands running freely over her otherwise. They were both back in clothes they'd worn growing up, and he couldn't have been happier about that aspect of their life at the moment. "I thought a while back about putting you in charge of Labyrinth operations. Reed knows the place better than anybody else alive, but his mechanical skills cap out at an etch-a-sketch. Then I figured if I did actually assign you to that, you'd kill me in my sleep for keeping you underground all the time, so I decided against it."

Anna laughed against his lips and kissed him harder. "I want to go to Eleusis. Please?" She added on the end, since she wouldn't go without his say-so. "I know it's dangerous. And Lynnette and Leo don't need their mother running off to an unknown world. But this is what we've been working toward, right?"

He glared at her, but clearly it was something he had thought about already, since he didn't look completely affronted by the idea. "You really want to be one of the first people going to explore the place and run into everything that could possibly go wrong? Don't get me wrong, you're probably the single most resourceful person I know, but the data we've been able to get on the planet itself is pathetic. Jason thinks it's because the Consortium has been more concerned with walling off their compound and setting up their own personal palaces, and I tend to agree with him. But seriously, we know almost nothing about the wildlife, the plant life, even the aquatics of the near sea. We're not even a hundred percent sure what to expect from the weather, though we're probably closer to eighty on that. It's gonna be one big chain of 'what the fuck is this' the whole time you're there."

"Doesn't that sound kind of exciting?" She asked tentatively, as though she thought he might look at her like she was crazy. "I mean, isn't that kinda what we signed up for in the first place? Sure, we didn't sign up for *no* information, but I think it would be kind of fun. Extreme camping or something. Eleusis is so beautiful. I want to explore it more. Find out more about it. Find a place for us to build a house and everything."

He sighed, since he clearly didn't see it with the same adventurous spirit that she did, but the last year and more taught him more about trepidation than excitement. "Alright, I'll recommend you for the initial recon team. We won't send anybody through until Gwen can get her child care center set up, so she'll be able to watch the kids while you're gone. Right now the plan is to send in a team of a dozen people for three days."

"Don't sigh like that." She scolded teasingly before she kissed him again. "We need to rebuild your sense of adventure." Anna trailed kisses to his ear where she nibbled on his earlobe like she knew he liked and she nipped at his neck again. "A few rounds of sex in a semi-public place should help."

"Where did you have in mind?" They hadn't been married long enough to start getting really adventurous with their sex life prior to going up to Nine, and once they had gotten there, things had been more about the survival of their relationship than pushing boundaries. "Just about every place around here is some kind of public. Though it is getting warmer. We could go up to some of the lookout trails near the satellite tower."

"Yes. Yes to that." She sat back a little bit on his lap so she could look into his eyes, though they paused every so often to make sure the two babies weren't going to injure themselves. Now that she had his gaze, though, she just smiled. "God, I missed looking into your eyes. You are fucking gorgeous, Logan Bickford."

He had missed so many things about Anna without even realizing he missed them, but he especially missed her foul mouth and her thoroughly direct nature. It was as refreshing now as it had been while they were growing up. "I missed you too, Anna." He raked a hand up over her chest to her neck as she looked at him. "All of you. Whatever you do, don't change a fucking thing, okay? I've got a feeling I'm gonna need my ass kicked by you for more than just my lack of adventure. Just don't hold back on me. Ever."

Anna grabbed his face between both of her hands and she kissed him passionately before she pressed her forehead to his. "I never have been one to hold back, and I never will. I'll kick your ass whenever you need it." She laughed against his lips and held his face for a little bit longer. "And fuck you like a wild woman whenever you want it. Don't forget that part too. I'll interrupt your meetings and everything. Just to keep you guessing."

"I know better than to guess with you." He took her by the front of her shirt to pull her into the kiss that followed, and groaned under it in anticipation of the night to come, even though they needed to get the kids to sleep before he could have his way with her. There always seemed to be something in their way, but Logan tried to accept it as the reality of their situation instead of getting angry about it. "I'll try and remember the guy I used to be. I'm not sure if he's still inside me or not. But if he is, I'll see what I can do about getting back in touch with him."

"We're both different than we used to be, but not completely. You're still Logan. My Logan." She moaned softly as he kept her shirt in a tight grip and kissed the breath out of her. Was it bedtime yet? "No matter how you've changed, it's okay. You don't need to worry about being different. I am still crazy in love with you."

"Well, you came pre-crazy, so you're already halfway there." He kissed her roughly, and took a deep breath as if he was having trouble breathing afterward. "I love you. I love this. All of it." He leaned in to kiss her neck as he hugged her against him, groaning under the embrace until it sounded like Lynnette started whimpering. "I'm going to go get some of that chicken pot pie. But I'll be back to help with these two as soon as I can inhale some of that."

"Good. Go eat as much as you want." Anna stole one more kiss before she slid off of his lap, though she desperately wanted to be back in his lap as soon as possible. "We're okay up here. The sooner I wear these two out and get them to bed, the sooner I can fuck you like the fate of the world depends on it."

"In that case, put those rugrats on a treadmill." He grinned over at them, and stopped to kiss them both on his way to the kitchen, his step and his heart lighter than he could remember feeling in a long time. It didn't take away what had happened, or what the two of them had done to get their time together, but they had done it to be together, and they were.

Even so, as soon as he was away from Anna, he started wondering about Mercury and the boys, where Orion had gone after leaving Anna. It was information he had no right to, but that didn't stop him from wondering, and feeling the pain of what he'd done every moment he was on his own. They were going to be that for each other in days to come, the means by which he and Anna forgot, even for a little while, the promises they had broken. But they had their reasons.

The world had to be one they *chose*, or else what was the point of living in it?

16

Kameron stared across the table at Melissa and watched her with Kassie. Melissa was so good with their daughter, she always made Kassie smile and laugh, and she was far more patient with her than Kameron was, overall. Even though Kassie had come from Kameron, Melissa was a much better mother.

She was thankful for Melissa for everything, considering Kass might not have a parent at all if Kameron and the rest of the group didn't make it back from Eleusis. Carl and Aiko hadn't made it back, and Kameron could only hope they were still alive. Somehow.

The risk was high that the Twist wouldn't last long enough for them to investigate very long, but a team had to go. There was no reason to stay behind, not when they needed more information.

Kameron glanced up at the clock on the wall, then looked at Melissa again. One hour. She had one more hour to watch her wife and her daughter for what might be the last time. No one knew the real risks, but she knew that every time she left, it might be her last. "Watching you two together is the best part of my day."

Melissa looked up only briefly, focusing most of her attention on Kass. "Then maybe you should stay. Have a few more days where you can watch us both."

"You're not going to give it up, are you?" Kameron continued to watch them even though Melissa wasn't looking at her. "I thought you'd be okay with this by now. I'm head of security unless I can get Carl back, and I need to get my friend back. He would do this for me."

"This isn't about what he would do for you. It's about going across the galaxy with no guarantees of coming back. Let alone coming back alive." Melissa sighed and bounced the little girl a few more times, then tried another spoonful of baby food to see if she would take it. "You're gonna say that everybody who's going is risking something and everybody has to risk something to get things done here, but tell me how she's . . ."

Melissa shook her head again and pulled back her white-blonde hair so it would be behind her shoulder and out of her way in trying to feed Kass. Her hair hadn't been cut since they escaped from Nine, and it was nearly down to her ass, but she still didn't want to cut it. "There's just too much we don't know yet. Why can't they send through a drone or something to do the scans? Why does it have to be a dozen of you, all with families that will break if things go bad?"

"We don't have good enough tech. And even if we did, it's much easier for the Consortium to pick up tech on their scans than personnel." Kameron got up and moved her chair so she was sitting right next to Melissa, and she took her hand. The one that had a ring on it, finally. "Look, no matter what happens, you know I'm going to be fighting like hell to get back here to you and Kass. Mostly to you, but don't tell her that." Kameron reached up and ran her finger across Melissa's cheek. "No one knows what's going to happen. And the Twist isn't that stable. But even if we get stuck, we'll make it back."

"Stuck. Sure. Half a galaxy away." She took a deep breath and didn't return the touch Kam had given her, but she didn't push her wife away either. "Protecting us all here in the mountains is one thing, but assaulting the Consortium is something else. It feels like we've been out here getting ready for so long, but we're never going to really be ready."

"This *is* protecting us. If we can fuck up the Consortium before they find us, then we can actually survive. They're still looking for us. And we may be a needle in a haystack, but we're not impossible to find if they're thorough enough going through the hay." She still ran her fingers over Melissa's cheek. "I'm sorry. I'm sorry that you're some kind of fucked up army wife, I don't know. But this is who I am. I can't sit back when this is what I do. This is my life. I'm not good at anything else, Mel. But I'm sorry that you have to deal with it too. I hate hurting you."

"You're not hurting me." She said quietly, still unable to make eye contact. But she put Kass in her high chair, where Kassie always seemed to be content with life. "I just . . . never signed up for a war in the first place. I know you did, and I love you for it. Especially because you chose to fight this one instead of the other one. It's just not something I ever thought I'd be a part of. So when shit like this happens, I wish I could help, but I'd be worse than useless on something like this. Unless some kind of dangerous local wildlife needs a tattoo."

"You're not useless. You're a better mother to Kass than I would ever be. That's why you're here with her and I'm the one going across the universe. Because losing me wouldn't be as bad as losing you." Kameron moved her touch to Melissa's neck. "Please look at me."

She turned, but she was glaring at Kameron when she did so. "That's not even half true. You're her mother and she loves you." She looked down at Kam's chest with the same glare. "It's *your* tits she just barely stopped sucking on, not mine. You're literally the reason she exists. The only reason she's got left." She squeezed Kameron's hand, not trying to be mean, but just being honest, as she had always been with her foul-mouthed, abrasive beauty of a wife. "You're not going to find your friends on Eleusis, Kam. It's been over a year. Aiko was pregnant when she left, and you told me Carl had some kind of specialized superformula he had to take all the time just to stay alive. I know you want there to be a chance, but whatever chance there was of them surviving, it's been gone since we blew up Nine. The only people who are gonna get anything out of Eleusis are us. Maybe."

"I'm trying to be as realistic as possible, Melissa. I know it's likely they're dead, but I can't count them out completely. And I can't stay here when they need someone like me for this. Just staying here hoping for the best isn't going to do anyone any favors." Even though Melissa was angry with her, Kameron leaned in to kiss her. "I love you. Please don't be mad about this. Please."

Melissa returned the kiss, and melted into it as she almost always did, angry or otherwise. "I can't go down there to watch you go. I'm sorry, I just can't. I'd be standing there at the edge of the room the whole time yelling for you even louder than she does. You know I get loud. I'd spook the Eleusis wildlife without even being there."

"Okay. You don't have to be there if you don't want to be there." She kissed Melissa again and again, each more passionately than the last. "Just thinking about you here is going to get me home. And if anyone hits on you, you tell me who they are and I will fucking mess them up when I get home."

"Hey, you don't get to be the only one screwing with people

who hit on me. I do that very well on my own, thank you very much." She glared back, her accent a little thicker than usual, since emotions were running high. "There were two midwesterners at lunch who wanted to take me out to dinner. One of them actually said yes when I asked if my wife and daughter could come along. Brave guy."

"You're mine." Kameron said sternly, since she definitely had jealousy issues. She wasn't ever going to want to share her wife unless she absolutely had to. Sperm was going to be necessary if they wanted another baby. Kameron cupped Melissa's breast and teased her nipple as Kam kissed her again. "I love you more than anything in the world. I hope you know that."

"I know it." Melissa reassured her, one hand answering her caress with one of her own, hanging on tightly to the collar of the uniform Kam wore. "I love you too. I'll get better at the whole army-wife thing. As long as you're aware that you'd better come back immediately fuckable. By which I mean completely uninjured or at least only scratches and bruises."

"Immediately fuckable. I promise." Kameron kissed Melissa a few more times. "Once we have a home on Eleusis, all this shit will get better. I'll step down from this position. Sit behind a security desk or some shit. Anything you want. Anything that will make you happy. Once we get to Eleusis."

"I want you to be happy." Melissa added with a brief glare, since she didn't want Kameron stepping out of what she loved doing, where she felt her purpose was. "If that involves you getting shot at . . . I'll . . . just . . . self-medicate like any other good stay-at-home mom. The midwesterners brought back some pretty good shit for after this little one goes to bed. You better believe I will be indulging if you end up stuck anywhere." She clutched at Kameron for a few more kisses, but eventually let go. "I hope you find your friend. They seemed like nice people."

"They are." She ran her thumb over Melissa's bottom lip after all the kisses, and she glanced at the clock once. "I still have time. Maybe I can give you a proper goodbye? Just to hold you over until I get back."

"Nothing's gonna hold me over. Even if you come back in an hour." She batted her long blonde eyelashes at her gorgeous wife, and held her hand as she stood up. "Besides, this one is about to go down for her nap. I'm pretty sure my moaning through a 'proper' goodbye from you would keep her up." She smiled one more time and pulled Kameron in to nuzzle her face against her chest. "Come back. In one piece. Remember, you promised."

"I promise." She reassured Melissa before she gave her one more long and lingering kiss. "I'll be home soon." Kameron squeezed Melissa's hand before she walked toward the door, but she stopped and looked back once at Kassie and Melissa before she gave her wife a reassuring smile and walked out the door. Kameron felt like she couldn't breathe as soon as she was out of her unit, but she was also strong enough to believe her own words. She was not going to make her wife a widow. Kameron didn't want to leave, but she believed what she said. It was necessary.

In the wide room that housed the Twist and all its paraphernalia, there were dozens of people milling around making final preparations. They managed to erect barricades around the Twist itself to guard against the initial blast of its activation, but everyone seemed more concerned about double and triple-checking packs and weapons to make sure they were sufficiently armed, both with guns and with science.

"Kam." Orion said from one side of the room, holding up a pack that was already packed. "You're welcome."

"Thanks, big guy." Kameron jogged over to him and took the bag that was offered. "You're a lifesaver. I certainly didn't want to go back home for anything. Melissa is already pissed enough."

"Yeah, that happens." He helped her get buckled into it, then started going over armaments with her so she could get up to speed. "Final count of us is an even dozen. Tatyana's on point, you've got the alpha squad, Xander's got beta. I'm with you, so is Koskei." He nodded toward the other side of the room, where he was clearly avoiding looking. "Anna's backing up Xander."

"Well, you're on the best team there is. I'm way better than Xander or Tatyana." She said with a weak smile, since she knew why he was avoiding the other side of the room. "Don't worry about her. Let's just keep focus and look for Carl. Stupid women are all over the place."

Orion returned the smile just as weakly as he checked his artillery to make sure everything was in order, then tightened the straps on his pack before facing Tatyana and Xander, who were busy with final adjustments to the Twist interface.

"I know a lot of you are hoping to get your friends back today." Xander said with a glare at the group in general. "I hope that happens too, since from what I've heard about those two, we could use them. But they're not the reason for this trip. We stick to our primary objectives, scout the area, place the improved anchors, and get back here within the window. The last thing we want to do right now is stay so long we tip off the Consortium to our presence." Which was why every one of their guns had silencers and every bit of the technology they were going to leave on Eleusis had masking devices. They were going to need the element of surprise like they needed oxygen.

"We understand what we're going there for. We don't need a lecture from you, Xan. You've got the best of the best here." Kam glanced over at Anna and back at Xander. "And I'm only talking about fighting skills. Actual intelligence aside."

That just got more of a glare from Xander, since Anna was on his squad, after all, but Koskei spoke up before Xander could fire back on her behalf.

"What assurance do we have that the Consortium doesn't patrol this far out, exactly?" He said without any fidgeting or last-minute doublechecking, and stood near the Twist with his hands tucked into his pockets.

"Prior to establishing a bridge lock on the planet's surface, the Twist enabled us to do some surveillance of the area." Jason explained, reaching in to correct something Xander had done with a glare before turning back to Koskei. "In the weeks of observation we were able to do, we never saw signals from Consortium tech any more than a click from their perimeter, and even then it was only a few incidents. Also, from what I've been able to intercept from Eleusis orders to the present staff in residence, their primary objectives right now are focused on construction within their perimeter and some kind of experimentation they're doing within that facility. So if they are interacting with the planet itself, it's only in the most cursory fashion."

"So basically, they're still thinking like Orbitals." Orion volunteered. "Leeching off the planet while denying the fact that they're actually part of it."

"Couldn't have put it better myself." Jason smiled back at Orion, immediately in a slightly better mood. "All the same, scans can be wrong and patterns can be broken. Which is why those guns you're carrying have bullets in them."

"We're as prepared as we'll ever be." Anna interjected as she held her gun tightly. "As long as one of those fucking storms doesn't show up." She remembered learning about the storms in her flight training, since it was a simulation often used to teach them how to fly through without getting fried. She hadn't survived most of the simulations and she didn't think they would do well even on the ground. "Those things looked nasty."

Jason glared at her for that. "You had to say something." He shook his head and looked back at his instruments, setting some final calibrations. "Four hours." He said quickly. "That's how long we can safely tax our power reserves here and maintain the connection. Which means you'll be back in three and a half."

"Three and a half hours." Kameron said with a nod. "You better believe we'll be back. I got promised a prize with the best tits ever if I come back unharmed. So, you know, gotta cash in on that."

"Whatever gets you moving." Jason said disinterestedly, punching in the last few orders before turning and nodding to the barriers. "Everybody get behind something and be ready to move when we say move." He moved himself to stand on the other side of the Twist's opening, out of the area that would be affected by the portal's opening, and pulled the control mechanisms with him.

The lights dimmed, the Twist came to life, and the majority of the people in the room watched as if they were about to see the most incredible magic trick in history, since the majority of people hadn't seen the machine at work before, even though everything in all their lives depended on it.

Fitch didn't know what to think when the arch lit up and crackled a hole across the galaxy. She had seen some weird shit in her life, but this topped the cake. She stared for a moment as the heat hit her in waves and the entire thing kept shooting out sparks. "Thing's got a temper like Zeus when he's fucking drunk off his ass. That is crazy!" She yelled over to Orion as they waited for it to stabilize.

"You should've seen the big one!" He yelled back, ducking lower because he was that much taller, his hands clasped behind his head as they waited. It felt more violent there belowground than it had on Nine, but he was pretty sure that whatever faults the Consortium had, they were better at many things. Better than a bunch of rebels cowering in a bunker.

When it finally did level out, he put his head up tentatively with the rest of those present, looking at a half-lit field of muted colors and a grey sky. Xander was the first one to actually start moving toward the portal. "We've got about half an hour until dawn. Once the sun's up, we need to keep cover. Give us thirty seconds for point watch and if you don't hear screaming, move your asses and follow." He jumped through the portal immediately after Tatyana, guns out and eyes peeled for any possible danger in the dimly-lit world.

Anna looked over at Orion as she waited for the okay, since she was on Xander's team and she would be following after him once he gave the go-ahead. The last time Anna saw Eleusis, she'd been with Orion, and she remembered distinctly they had talked about fucking on the mountain and claiming land for their own. She knew it wasn't right to think of it now, but she couldn't help it that she missed him. She loved them *both*, but it didn't matter now.

He didn't look back over at her, but she knew him well enough to know when he halfway glanced at the middle of the room between them, he was checking to see if she was still there in his peripheral vision. Clearly she was on his mind as well, even if he was still too angry about what had happened to actually look at her directly. "They don't look nervous." He said to Fitch beside him, as Tatyana and Xander wove back and forth in the grasses, looking for threats but not finding any. "After you, Commander."

"That's one hell of a title." Fitch shook her head and headed out ahead of Anna and Koskei but she definitely made an effort to shoot a nasty glare at Anna. "You're being nicer than I would be." She mumbled to Orion as they stepped through the portal, and she couldn't help but stop and stare as she looked around.

Orion thought he would feel something as he actually passed through the portal, and he was almost disappointed when he didn't. All that changed was the air pressure around him, and his ears popping, but the air itself was . . . different. He thought he had gotten accustomed to the purity of the air in the mountains on Earth, but there was something about Eleusis that was just . . . clear. He could smell the grass, familiar yet strange, and a dozen other scents that stung his nose and confused his senses with their alien perfumes. The grass itself was . . . tangy . . . in a way for which Earth simply had no equivalency.

"Planet's gonna make me hungry." He grumbled low in his throat as he looked around. Everything was so close to being familiar, but the trees grew just a little higher than they should have in the distance, their leaves just a little darker than he thought they ought to be, like they were just a few shades of green away from black.

"Well, don't go chomping around on the grass. I don't know what Aiko knows. It might kill you." Kam looked around with a watchful eye and her gun ready. "I don't care what that fucker said, I want to look for Carl and Aiko. We can toss the tech where it needs to be as we go."

"Well, if those are your orders." Orion said with a chuckle, already moving off in the direction his communicator indicated was the coastline. The planet's magnetic field was different from Earth, but it was nothing a few calibrations couldn't fix.

The world moved up over a gradual slope to a hilltop nearby, but in the distance, he could see the Consortium compound. Trust the Consortium brass to be self-absorbed enough to force a white sand beach in their compound on another planet just so they could enjoy it, natural ecology be damned.

"God, I wish we had a way to systematically go through and get rid of those fuckers. So many people have died so they can have a fucking beach house on Eleusis." Fitch tossed a piece of Xander's tech where it showed on the map, but she also looked around for where Carl would go. "He wouldn't stay in the open, that's for damn sure. He would build a fucking good shelter where he could see and not be seen."

"Which is the same kind of place we're looking for." Orion agreed, and looked back at the rest of her squad that moved along with them. Koskei was keeping quiet and watching their rear for any signs from the Consortium compound, but they were all dressed in charcoal greys with no visible lights on their persons. "If I were the one stranded here with a pregnant wife, and I came out of the gate, this would've been the closest I would've stopped even to get a breath. I wouldn't have stopped at all until I got to forest cover. Preferably the other side of a forest somewhere, but we don't have that kind of time."

"We have to find time to leave them a message or a sign or something." Kameron said as she scanned the area. She didn't know how she could leave some kind of message, but there had to be a way. "I can't even imagine what they've had to live through out here."

"A message for them could be a message for the Consortium." Orion cautioned, though he wished they could do exactly that anyway. "Unless we find them alive, all we're going to find is their corpses. Carl's too smart to leave any kind of sign for the Consortium to use to prove they've still got something to hunt out here. I went on survival training with that guy. If he doesn't want to be found, he won't be."

Kameron sighed. "The Consortium isn't going to be looking for shit. But I am. He's our best friend, Orion."

"I'm trying to be reasonable. Doesn't mean I want to find him any less than you do." He moved to take point in front of the rest of the squad just as they were nearing the top of the hill, and though he opened his mouth to say something, his chin just dropped as he got to the top. He waved the rest of the squad onward with him, since he had only stopped because of the view.

On the far side of the hill, the world dropped away like it had been cut by a knife, a wall of smooth cliffs arcing to the east and climbing with the mountains. The world above them was grey and cautious with the morning light, but the sea didn't seem to be. The waves were a rich blue, with flecks and strands sparkling beneath the waves in brilliant shades, as if the aquatic life didn't understand any other color. The sea extended for as far as anyone could see toward the south, but there were small sandbars that cropped up from place to place, rising in small patches of vegetation, stepping stones to the edge of the world.

"Hell of a view." He finally said out loud, taking in the entire image with a deep sigh, still trying to convince himself of the truth of what he was seeing. Another world. Another coastline. Another planet, another sky, almost completely unexplored. Empty. A place where anything was possible.

"No joke." Kameron stared at the water. She didn't say anything as the sea air hit them with a welcome breeze, and she took a deep breath. "I wish Melissa were here with me."

"She will be." He took a deep breath of the breeze and shook his head to snap himself out of his reverie to pay attention. "Alright, let's follow the coast and see what kind of ground we can cover in an hour." He went down the far side of the hill until he got closer to the coastline and took a particular probe out of his pocket. He launched it as far out over the water as he could, to get it into deeper currents, and watched it fall until it hit the water. Once it was under and he flicked the command on his communicator to activate it, he turned and moved on with the rest of them.

Fitch followed after Orion instead of the other way around, since she was still so stunned with everything she saw. It was incredible. "This place can be home to so many people. Why do they have to do this to the people of Earth? Deny them this? Kill so many people just for this? We can live here peacefully."

"That's why. They've got no interest in peace unless it's on their terms." Orion said quietly as they walked, moving as quickly as the tall grasses would allow. He carried his gun at the ready, but there was nothing in the open meadow to shoot. "The rest of the world could fit on this planet with more than enough room to spare. It'd be as easy as opening the door and letting everyone through to do as they do best. Instead, all they want is more control."

"We need a *bunch* of fucking doors. If we give everyone a gun, they wouldn't have any chance to say no." She growled as she shook her head. "Their games keep fucking shit up all of the time. People get angry and blame the Consortium. Or hurt others because the Consortium fucked with them in the first place." Kameron looked over at Orion briefly. "Including one of my best friends."

They walked in silence for a long time after that, all of them spread out across the landscape depositing sensors from time to time where their instruments denoted they should. The hills rolled comfortably onward and upward, until they began angling down again toward an abrupt treeline. It was as though there was some kind of war between the field and the forest, though it was hard to tell which was winning. The difference was so stark and immediate that it made Orion nervous, and not just because the leaves on the forest trees still looked like they were pieces of the night.

Kameron hesitated as well, since she wasn't exactly a fan of the idea of running into a thickness of trees. The Consortium couldn't be the only danger on Eleusis, certainly. There had to be wildlife, and they had no idea what Eleusis was hiding. "I don't know if our guns are big enough if a bear pops out of there."

"Well, they're what we've got, so they'd better be." Orion hesitated at the treeline for a while, watching the interior to see if they could see inside. While they were stopped, he noticed a few tiny animals moving back and forth between the field and the trees, something like mice but longer and skinnier, with longer filaments for tails. They stopped and nibbled on a particular growth of grasses as they went, but they were the only kind of animal he saw as they approached the treeline.

Just inside, though, he saw birds coming back to their nests for the day after a night of hunting, one of them with one of the mouse-like things still in its beak. A few of them had slippery, frog-like creatures in their deep beaks which they then brutally killed by throwing them against the trunk of the tree they were nesting in. Orion just kept moving deeper into the foliage. "Some things never change, even here. Big guy eats the little guy, big guy gets eaten by the bigger guy. It might be comforting, if we knew who the biggest guy on top of the chain was."

"I shudder to think. Earth has some pretty big guys. And there were the dinosaurs before people ever started walking around. I fucking hope Eleusis skipped the dinosaur stage, or is past it. Cuz if not, we could be in a fuckton of trouble."

"According to previous research and initial surveys, no, Eleusis was never dominated by lizards." Koskei broke in, easily the most reserved and most intellectual of the group, which was the only reason he was there. He acted as a coordinator on Logan's behalf even after the Executive Council had been disbanded, but he had worked with Jason to study Eleusis in preparation for the exact kind of expedition they were on.

"The best theories from the scans is that until recently, Eleusis has actually been a great deal hotter than it currently is, which means most of the biodiversity in the planet is still in its lakes and oceans. Only in the past few million years has the water receded enough into the frozen poles to allow continents to be above sea level, except most of it was exposed all at once. The resulting theory states that most animals who live on land are near derivations of sea life. Much of the large herbivores still have at least vestigial gills. Those that have been studied, anyway."

"That was way more explanation than was necessary, but I believe whatever you say." Fitch looked over at the weirdo. "So what should we be looking out for, exactly? You sound like you know what might be lurking around here."

"I talk when I'm nervous. Sue me for trying to make it something useful." Koskei glared at Fitch, but he generally didn't have any problem with his leaders. Things were just very tense, being on the other side of the galaxy and all. "Most of the creatures to be worried about are small carnivores. There are several varieties that hunt in packs and sometimes take on larger predators, but they've only been documented in some of the regions north of here. I don't know if they're coastal or not. Honestly, I focused mostly on the plant life. So don't eat anything unless you show it to me first."

"I'm not that hungry, don't worry." Fitch looked around carefully and she narrowed her eyes on some flowers. "So what about flowers? I would love to take my wife some Eleusis flowers."

"Those should be fine." He looked at them in passing, then raised his gun again and went back to eyeing the surroundings, as he took deep breaths to steady himself. "Just don't let your daughter eat them when they get there."

The forest made the world feel as though it was still nighttime, even as half an hour passed and their communicators indicated that the sun should have risen. The canopy of the forest was incredibly thick, leaving almost no light for the undergrowth, of which there was almost nothing. What little growth there was latched against the sides of the trees, drawing nutrients from them rather than the ground or the sunlight. Orion could see small burrows from time to time as they moved through the darkness, but he only saw things scurrying out of them a few times, and none of them looked dangerous.

"I'm not getting accurate atmospheric readings down here." Koskei said in the same nervous tone as earlier, only worse on account of the continued darkness.

"The foliage is making it worse." Orion said with a look over at Fitch, since he saw the same problems on his own instruments. "Could be an asset for setting up a camp, though. If the vegetation is thick enough to fuck with scanners, it'll be just one more layer of security against getting picked up by the compound down there."

Kameron stuck the flowers in her back pocket so she could carry her gun steadily. She looked up and over at Koskei and then Orion. "It's quieter. Isn't it a bad sign when the animals get quieter?"

Orion nodded and moved slowly through the trees, keeping his gun up at the ready. As they went, there were patches of what looked almost like nesting strung between trees, heavy carpets of moss and fallen logs netted together with patches that smelled like decay. He wasn't sure if there was some kind of patch of mud or tar that had trapped dead animals, but whatever it was, it looked awful, and he moved past it as quickly as possible. There were several such patches as they went, each one as foul-smelling as the last.

"If we're gonna camp here, we're gonna need to keep our distance from these things. These are terrible." Orion made a face and stepped over a little closer to one, just to get a closer look at what it was that made the thing such a stinking pile. "It looks like there's some kind of mud pit at the center." He looked up, and the canopy was a little thinner just above the spot. "Maybe it just rains that much here, turns these spots into bogs, I don't . . ." He recoiled as he heard two silenced gunshots behind him, and fell to the ground from the slippery footing beneath him.

A squelched animal scream came out of the bog the moment after Orion fell, and a wriggling creature came down only a few feet away. It looked as though some kind of barracuda or predatory fish with legs and claws. He looked up at Fitch, breathing heavily, and sighed as the creature continued to thrash on the ground. "Thanks. Didn't see that little fucker."

"As much as I would like to take the credit . . ." Fitch replied nervously, her gun still slanted toward the ground. "Those didn't come from me."

Orion only allowed himself a moment to panic, then started looking around frantically along with everybody else, guns pointed up into the trees to try and figure out who had just saved Orion from getting attacked. The more the seconds dragged on, the more nervous they got, but Orion was glad when they seemed to remember their training and moved back to back to protect each other from an unknown threat.

"You all make a lot of fucking noise, you know that?" A voice none of them thought they'd hear again said from the branches of a tree just above a nearby bog. A piece of the tree seemed to move as they followed the sound, and a huge shape dropped from the branch to the ground without hardly making a sound.

There was a billowing cloak around it that was dotted with moss and mud and stray twigs and leaves. The man beneath the cloak had skin as dark as the world around them, and wore clothes that seemed to be made of some kind of cured black leather. It was easy to see why none of them had seen him. "But it's a good thing you do, because I was headed the other way."

Carl's smile cracked most of his face as he started walking toward them, holstering his gun at his back and putting aside a spear of dark wood.

"No fucking way." Kameron replied just above a whisper as she stood there, frozen. "Please don't tell me I'm looking at some fucking weird ghost of one my best friends." She started moving forward slowly. "Is it really you?"

"I've seen a lot of shit on this planet, but no ghosts." He reached up as he walked and unclipped something holding his cloak around his shoulders, letting it fall to the ground around him. If anything, Carl had only somehow gotten bigger, taller, or maybe it was just the bestial nature of his appearance that gave him that aspect. He picked Kameron up almost without trying in the hug he gave her, and only set her down after nearly crushing the life out of her. Orion wasn't far behind, but Orion was taller than he was, leaving the two men to cling to each other as they took in the fact they were both still alive.

Kameron had tears in her eyes, and she fought them only to avoid getting teased, but she didn't know if she could fight them off completely. "I fucking told them you were still alive! I fucking told . . ." she wiped at her eyes before tears could fall, and then she looked around. "What about Aiko . . .?"

"She's fine. She's at home. They both are." He grinned as he said so, moving quickly to grab his cloak and spear. "Come on. Walk and talk. Did you guys get here through the Twist? When no one came through for weeks afterward, we figured you had all been killed or the Twist had been destroyed or something."

"We couldn't get the fucking thing to work again. It's working now, but we're on a tight timeframe." Fitch looked down at her watch and back up at Carl again. "Aiko had her baby here? Fucking hell. I can't even . . . how the fuck did that go?"

The grunt that came out of him at that question said just about everything that needed to be said about it. "It was a fucking mess. But Aiko is fucking indestructible. And William has been a trooper. Talk about a tough kid." He shook his head. "God, it's weird to be speaking English again. I'm amazed I actually remember it."

"Hey, we've only been gone a year and change. You get fluent in Japanese that fast?" Orion walked on the far side of Carl from Kameron, staring at his friend incredulously in between nervous glances at the forest they passed through.

Carl's response came in quick and flawless Japanese, and he smiled up at the only friend he'd ever had who was taller than him.

"I've had a lot of downtime. We want William to grow up speaking it, so it seemed to make sense."

Orion was still completely in shock at the fact his friend was still alive, and he laughed without taking his eyes off the big man. "You are still a crazy bastard."

"I didn't expect that to change." Kameron said as she gazed at both of her friends. "We are running out of time, though. I hope you don't have a lot of luggage, big guy. Your kid is probably the first real Eleusian, but I'd rather take you back to Earth if that's okay with you."

"Well, that depends." He tried to act cool and indifferent, but he didn't succeed very well. "Do you have hot, running water wherever you're hiding right now?"

"Most of the time, yes. And as of recently, a shit ton of booze." Kameron said with a hopeful smile as she looked up at one of her closest friends, since she couldn't believe he was still alive. "I can't believe that I'm looking at you and you're alive. What's even scarier is that you're someone's fucking dad."

"Yeah, that part is still scarier than . . . well, I was gonna say everything here, but it's not. There are scarier things here than being a parent. Not many, but a few." He took them up a steep incline in the middle of the forest and through a narrow passage between trees that was hidden by a bog on either side. "Be careful how you step in here, and don't touch anything until we're out the other side. I haven't had to actually use any of these traps on humans, but they've done some pretty nasty things to the wildlife."

Carl guided them up the single-file path, which climbed steeply up and away from the bogs and eventually turned into a wooden ladder made of rough-hewn logs. It led up into a house that was constructed entirely in the canopy of the forest, huge logs cut and lashed together in ways that were far from perfect, but appeared to be stable, at least.

The house was a single room, but there were basins of water off to one side, cabinets of food near them, and a bed made of piled furs over in one corner, with a crib beside it. Carl was speaking Japanese on his way up the stairs. "Sweetheart, we have company. The good kind. Even though it took them a long time to get here."

"The good kind?" Aiko responded even before she made herself seen, but when she appeared, she was also dressed in furs and she held a baby that was surprisingly small, since they all expected Carl to have produced some kind of hulk baby. The little boy was beautiful, though, with a lighter skin tone than Carl, but an equally bright smile. Aiko was stunned into silence at the sight of their old friends, her grip on the baby still tight even as a wooden cup slipped from her fingers to fall to the floor. "Kameron? Orion?"

Orion was up the stairs before anyone else, and he grinned down at Aiko before he picked her and the boy up in a hug all at the same time. "God, I cannot believe you survived a year with only this big idiot for company. As soon as we get home, I'm finding you a medal. Holy crap."

"Other than missing electricity, running water, and a few other modern developments, it has actually been a pretty amazing year." Aiko said honestly. "I love Carl, and doing this together . . . well, it proved that we're in this together. We needed each other to survive."

"And we're gonna need to hear all about exactly how you two managed that." He said as he put her down, giving her time to hug Kameron in turn, since Kameron clearly had more reason to be excited about Aiko's survival than Orion did directly. He pulled out his communicator as they had their reunion to check the time. "But right now, we've got exactly two hours before we need to be back through the Twist to Earth. So if you're interested in having some modern conveniences, we need to pack up everything you've got here and we need to move. Fast. Better not to take any chances."

Aiko nodded and looked over at her little boy in her arms before she handed him off to Kameron when Fitch held her arms out for the little boy. "Holy hell, Kass really does have a cousin. You hear that, Carl? Our kids are cousins. And your kid is actually pretty cute."

"Don't say that like you're surprised. He's gorgeous. And his name is William." He said with a grin, but he was already moving to gather up their belongings. He threw down what looked like a spare cloak made from the same black leather as his own but without the moss and twigs for cover. He used it to gather up their spare clothing and some of the things they made for William, throwing everything quickly in a pile as he spoke quickly in Japanese to Aiko. "I can't believe we have to pack all this stuff up now. I was really close to getting us some indoor plumbing."

"We'll be back." Aiko promised as she rushed around as well. They had amassed quite a collection of things they had created, mostly because after few weeks of no sign of help, Aiko hadn't been sure they would ever know any other life other than Eleusis for the rest of their lives. After that wait, they had moved on with their life. For over a year. "No one is going to disturb this while we're gone. No one even knows it's here except us."

"Is it bad that I almost hope someone finds it?" He smiled at her over the growing pile of their belongings between them, and went to tie on the set of knives he had luckily been carrying when they were attacked on Nine. They were considerably worn down after being their primary tools for a year and more, but he would treasure those knives until the day he died for the lives they had helped to save. "I mean, I think they bought it when we faked our death right after getting out here, but it would be pretty great to know that somebody felt like a complete moron when they found out we actually survived out here for this long."

"And gave birth to the first Eleusian without their permission." Aiko said with a smile as she glanced over at Will in Kameron's arms. "Working on number two." She spoke in Japanese, since she didn't know if he wanted his friends to know about their news upon just finding them on Eleusis. "At least I think it's only one in here. I suppose Mercury will tell us."

"However many there are, it's gonna be somebody else delivering them this time. I love you, but I'd rather you had a professional attending you the next time, not me sitting there pissing my pants praying to any god in town that you'll be okay." They finished up with their possessions, at least those they could think to grab. Carl rolled up the bundle tightly and slung it over his shoulder. "Alright," he said in Japanese at first, then had to force himself to switch back to English. "Alright, let's get out of here. I think we've both fallen in love with this planet while we've been here, but I don't feel the need to stick around any longer than absolutely necessary."

"We'll come back, right?" Aiko asked Orion as she took William back from Kameron after Orion hefted one of their bags. "If you have the Twist working, that means we're coming back, right?"

He nodded as they headed back down the ladder, following Carl's lead closely so as to avoid the traps he'd left along the way. "We actually weren't here on a rescue mission. Most people back home have given you up for dead. We're here on reconnaissance. Looking for good places to build a camp and keep out of sight of the Consortium while we get ready for an assault."

Aiko knew realistically people probably thought they were dead, but it didn't feel good to hear it. "Well, I'm glad you stumbled into our area, then." She said softly as she looked down at Will. "Otherwise we would have gone on our merry way populating Eleusis ourselves."

"Well, if we manage what we're about, you can feel free to go right back to populating Eleusis when we're done. You just won't have to worry so much about potentially homicidal neighbors." Orion moved with Aiko near the rear of the group, but he saw Koskei drop back even farther so Aiko and the baby wouldn't be in a vulnerable position while Carl and Kameron led the way back to where Kameron told him the Twist site was located. "Has the Consortium ever even pushed up this far? We picked this area because we figured it would be too far out for their patrols."

"They rarely come out of their campus." Aiko replied as she looked in the direction of the Consortium's compound. "When they do, they come out with prisoners they just let loose. Sometimes cuffed up, sometimes not. We've never seen them enter with prisoners, obviously, but they come out with people sometimes. No one we have ever stumbled into, mostly because . . . well, our best guess is that they get eaten."

"You haven't been able to get to them before that? Bring them up, start putting something together?" He was trying to think as Carl would have thought, but then he checked himself immediately afterward. "No. There would be too many risks in that. Any of them could have been spies or have tracking devices or something. I can see that. I wonder why they just let them loose. They're usually not about keeping blood off their own hands."

Aiko chewed on her bottom lip as she shook her head. "We've seen a couple corpses. They all have numbers tattooed in the middle of their left hand. The numbers seem to be going up, but it's hard to tell what the order is for. But the numbers mean something. My guess is that they are servants. Or a part of a different trial the Consortium is conducting."

"Jason and Xander are gonna want a full report on pretty much everything you guys have seen in the last year." He looked down at her as they walked and laughed. "I imagine that's gonna be a long, *long* report, but you know, the important stuff first." He smiled as they got out of the trees along the side of a mountain in a different place than they entered, facing inland rather than looking out over the sea.

They could see down into a valley between where they stood and a hill beside them that was similarly covered in trees. As Orion stood looking out at the rest of the inland hills of Eleusis, thinking about how an army would maneuver in them, what a settlement would look like, he caught a flash of movement inside the trees a few hundred meters away and at least a hundred meters below them. Watching for a few moments, he saw half a dozen figures moving through the trees, all of them armed, dressed similarly to the way the other team had been when they left hours ago.

"Kam." He said loudly enough to be heard, then pointed down to where he'd seen the other team, walking with the rest of them to a slightly better vantage point to see from. "Looks like the beta squad is circling back."

Kameron looked down and watched the other team for a moment, but when she looked at Aiko again, the woman looked nervous. "Aiko, are you alright?"

"They're being too loud." She said without any explanation, and she looked over at Carl with an expression that could only be described as fear. "How close are we, did you say?"

"Still a kilometer out at least." He said with the same worried expression on his face. His hand was on the spear he carried, hefting it as if he was expecting to use it. "If they keep that up, they're not gonna make it." He was speaking in a low whisper, and moving faster along the open hillside. "Have you got a radio?"

"No, of course not." Orion said as he picked up his pace. "We didn't know what the Consortium would or wouldn't intercept, we're completely on radio wave silence."

Aiko looked even more afraid as she picked up her pace as well, holding William as tightly as she could to her body to both protect him and keep him from jostling too much. "Shoot your gun opposite the group, but into the trees. It will at least give them some time. And start running." With that Aiko just took off, even though she had no idea where the Twist actually was, she just knew what direction they were going and what direction she didn't want to be.

"Why?" Orion said as he ran with them, taking out his gun and taking aim in the direction she had indicated. "What am I shooting at?" He let off a few shots anyway, quiet but still audible for those close by. His shots landed nowhere near the beta squad, but he could hear some delayed cracks as they landed anyway, sounding like the trees or surfaces where they landed were either hollow or . . .

The roar that followed one of the shots was unlike anything he'd ever heard before in his life, and he saw the beta squad stop and react to it before he actually heard the sound. It was as if he had somehow pissed off an entire arm of a Station and all the joints were growling back at him for it at once. Under the foliage he had been shooting at, something winced in pain, and it looked as though the entire patch of forest was shaking and thrashing. "Um, guys, what the fuck is that?"

"The one thing on this planet that will think someone your size is just an appetizer! Run! They are huge and hairy and they don't stop until they eat! Ask questions later!" Aiko wasn't even looking back, she didn't have to look back to know what was back there.

Orion ran, and eventually, so did the people in the beta squad, but he couldn't help looking back over and over again to try and catch any glimpse of what Aiko was talking about. When he saw what he thought was a split second of it, though, he decided that watching where he was going would lead to fewer nightmares, so he turned and made sure to keep himself between Aiko and whatever was behind them. A few times, when he thought he had a clear shot without risking anyone in the beta squad, he let out a few more shots, as did Koskei and Kameron, but all it seemed to do was make the beast recoil for a moment and then redouble its chase.

The morning hadn't actually gotten much brighter in the time they had been on the planet, since the entire sky was overcast and the dimness they experienced beneath the canopy seemed to extend to the entire landscape. The low light didn't allow them to get much of a look at the beast even after the beta squad burst out of the treeline and they all began to converge on the far side of the field where the Twist still stood open. It was clear the alpha squad was going to get there first, which Orion was happy about, but even as he saw Carl and Aiko disappear through it, he didn't feel like celebrating. Instead, he took up a stance beside the Twist off to one side, still on Eleusis. "Get ready to shut it down the second everyone's through! We're not alone over here!"

"How many are there? How did they find you?" Jason was

yelling back at them, though from the way he was looking frantically at Carl and Aiko as well, the question went several ways.

"It's not the Consortium, it's the wildlife." Carl said breathlessly, glaring through the Twist at Orion. "Get in here, you moron! You can't fight these things with guns!"

"Hey, they seem to slow it down well enough." Orion shot back as the beta team came ripping into the field. He only had to wait a few seconds before a monstrosity nearly two stories high came into view behind them, bringing down parts of several trees as it moved. Orion opened fire without even getting a clear look at it, hoping that he hit something important even though he couldn't distinguish one of the beast's body parts from any other in his panic.

Anna, who had already made it through, ahead of some others, turned back around when she noticed that Orion wasn't coming back through and she started shooting her gun through the Twist. The beast was wicked fast, though, and it looked like it was easily catching up with the stragglers. "Orion! Come on! We can't let that thing through!"

Orion completely ignored Anna as she yelled at him, keeping his place on the far side of the Twist as the last of the beta squad stumbled across the terrain toward the Twist. The way the creature moved, it made it look as though part of the forest followed them out onto the open plain, and Orion could only catch the vaguest flash of teeth and claws as it raced after them, nearly the size of the house he'd just barely moved into.

With two of their squad left, he tossed his gun through the Twist and reached out to Carl for the spear he was carrying. Part of the end grazed the edge of the Twist's frame as he tried to bring it through, shearing off the very end of the haft to leave it partly on Earth, but Orion hardly even noticed. "Run, you assholes!" He bounced the spear a few times in his hands just to get accustomed to the weight of it as the creature approached, but he waited until the last possible second of safety to throw it, straight down the creature's throat.

The beast let out a roar of pain and went down, clawing at its own mouth to try and remove the spear, giving the last two runners time to cross the ground and leap through the Twist to safety. Orion was right behind them, stepping backward through it carefully so as not to take his eyes off the creature. Once he was fully through and a few steps back from it, he let out the breath he'd held. As the Twist shut down, the sound of the beast's howling still echoed around the room in the blast of heat that came with the loss of the connection.

"You fucking crazy bastard." Fitch said as she stood there, stunned, not far from where Orion had stumbled back through the Twist and into the safety of Earth. Everyone was stunned, and she was certain that most of the beta squad had shit themselves. "We didn't save one friend for you to fucking die. Don't do that!" She yelled at him, but she wasn't really angry at him. She was angry they had been that close to danger in the first place. Kameron turned her attention to the rest of the people around her. "Don't you assholes know how to walk around without alerting the entire fucking forest? Holy fucking hell."

Several of those on the beta squad clearly weren't accustomed to being berated by a senior officer quite in Kameron's vein, and they looked suitably embarrassed as they worked to catch their breath. Xander and Tatyana had been two of the faster runners in their squad, and they didn't look any happier about their team's performance than Kameron did. "We were checking out one of those damn bogs. Prince thought she saw something in one of them and it turned out to be a Consortium-issue rifle. We were working on retrieving it when we figured out the bog wasn't a bog, it was one of those damn . . . we didn't have any intelligence that there were carnivores that size on the fucking planet. How did early surveillance miss that?"

"Because they look like part of the forest." Carl said as he tried to catch his own breath, looking every bit like some kind of barbarian that had stumbled into the civilized world. "They don't even show up on heat mapping under all the armor they've got. If you're lucky you can see them breathing on thermals, but they spend most of their time in a kind of constant hibernation. Slowed breathing, heart rate, metabolism, the works. Best we can figure, behemoths only need to eat about once a month, if they get a big enough meal. If not, they stay awake until they do, then they go back to sleep."

"Behemoths?" Orion asked as he panted, taking a water bottle from his pack to rehydrate.

"Well," Carl said with a demented smile, "initially I was just calling them big motherfuckers, but you know how it is. Gotta watch the language around the kid."

"Melissa is convinced Kassie's first word is going to be fuck, and I'm okay with that. Just as long as I get to live long enough to fucking hear it!" Kameron yelled at no one in particular. "Goddamn it. I'm going home. We can talk about this shit in a few hours." She didn't wait for anyone to give her permission or to deny her, she just started walking out. "Carl and Aiko, I can find you a place or Jason can do it. I'm fucking glad you're alive."

"That goes both ways, Kam." Carl grinned back at her, since he could understand why she was freaked out. More than a few of the other squad members followed her, clearly rattled by the experience against the behemoth.

"I'll get them set up, Fitch. Thank you." Jason said as she headed out, turning his attention back to Carl and Aiko in amazement. There was no shortage of guilt on his face as he looked them over, since he had, after all, been the one to trap them on Eleusis in the first place. "I'm sorry." He said immediately, since the dust seemed to settle on the room. "I've been waiting over a year for the chance to tell you both that, I just . . . I'm sorry. And I'm equal parts stunned and ecstatic that you're actually still alive."

"Ecstatic? I'm surprised about that, but I'm glad to stun you." Aiko replied as she looked at Jason. She'd definitely increased in confidence after a year on Eleusis, mostly because being around Carl almost exclusively really rubbed off on her, and because seeing so much death and nearly dying however many times (she'd lost count) made it almost impossible for her to be afraid of Jason or care about what he did, what he didn't do, or what he was capable of doing. "I'd studied Eleusis botany for years before going up to Nine. I even got to plant some of my own trees there. I'm sad we had to leave them. And Carl is the strongest man in this universe."

Carl grinned even as he unclipped the cloak he was wearing and tossed it on the floor for later retrieval. "Brains and brawn. We had pretty much everything we needed of both between the two of us. I'm a little offended that everybody's so damn shocked, honestly."

"Oh shut the hell up." Orion was only going to put up with so much bragging from his friend, but he was still grinning as he said it. He was glad to see that not only were they alive, but they seemed like they had really been happy on Eleusis, if not entirely safe. "You look amazing. Both of you. If I'd been hiding out there for over a year, I doubt I'd exactly be running around carving spears."

"You would." Carl said as he took William, allowing Aiko to set down and re-secure some of the bundles of belongings they brought with them. "The place is just . . . I'm pretty sure it's not just me, or us, the place is just . . . better. I don't know. There's something in the atmosphere that she knows a whole lot more about than I do, something in the biology of the place, it's just better. Honestly, I've never felt so good in my life as I have this past year. Working, fighting, just making a life for ourselves every day. Even if it took some bloodshed, you know I don't have much of a problem with that." He ran his hands over the clothes he wore as if reminding himself of their source, and Orion's eyebrows went up a little.

"Is that from one of those things? The behemoths?" They didn't look killable, from what Orion witnessed. A spear down the throat seemed to have only pissed it off.

"I've killed three." Carl said as he nodded. "Two while they were awake and pissed off, one while it was sleeping. Sleeping was a hell of a lot easier." He took off the vest he wore and handed it over, letting Orion feel the heft and weight of it. It was like picking up a set of plated steel armor. "Their hides made signal protection for our home and something to keep us from getting killed by anything not trying too hard. They don't taste too good, but the meat lasts forever if you smoke it right, and there's a hell of a lot of it. Most of that was her idea. I just did the killing work." He smiled down at Aiko again and looked at William, who was taking in the entire scene with wide eyes. Apparently even at a young age, the boy had learned that crying was a bad idea, so shocked as he appeared, he wasn't making any sound.

Aiko smiled at William to reassure him he was safe, since she knew he always looked for cues from his parents about the world around him. Once he smiled back at her, she knew he felt a little better, but she knew William also knew there wasn't a safer place in the world than in his father's arms.

"All of the plants and animals on Eleusis are pure, even if some of them are poisonous, just like here on Earth." She looked around at the dark, cave-like room they were in, not exactly sure where they could possibly be, though it felt like Earth from the feeling of the gravity. "So eating the right things and even breathing the air on Eleusis is better for our bodies. I'm even more convinced now than ever that Carl was made to live there. His body has been functioning better and more efficiently on Eleusis than anywhere else. I've been able to modify his daily intake with just Eleusis herbs, though I suppose I'll have to review new pharmaceutical options again now that we're here." Aiko shook her head. "We have a lot of things you're going to want to know before you send anyone else back there."

Jason nodded, and spoke before Xander could butt in and start interrogating them. "That can wait until after you've had a chance to settle in here and get some rest." He turned his eyes to Xander and Tatyana, speaking in a tone that made it clear he wasn't asking their permission, he was informing them.

"I'm going to bump them to one of the apartments along the southern ridge. Whoever it was slated for can wait a little longer. I'm not going to put them underground after what they've lived through and considering the help they're going to be to us. Reed can go fuck himself if he gets angry about it." He didn't leave any time for either of them to respond as he keyed in a few changes on his ever-present interface, looking back at Aiko. "You remember me telling you back in St. Louis about the six centers we had operational? About the Labyrinth? Up in the Rockies?"

"I remember." She remembered most things, it just seemed like her life was fragmented anymore. Life on Earth. Life in space. Life on Eleusis. "Is that where we are? In the mountains?"

Jason nodded as he worked. "A few of the other sites have been found and destroyed by the Consortium in the meantime, but we've got almost three thousand people here now, and we've had no indications any time recently that the Consortium is even looking for us anywhere near here."

"So this is where your army is stationed?" Carl asked hopefully, since three thousand didn't sound that terrible, so long as it was a military force.

The look on Jason's face answered the question before his words did. "No, we're not primarily combat here. Or anywhere, anymore. Fitch has about forty other trained soldiers like you and Orion here with her, they've been training maybe a hundred more. The midwesterners who just came in add maybe a hundred more out of them who'd be willing to pick up a gun and shoot when push comes to shove."

"Please tell me you're joking." Carl looked back and forth incredulously between Jason and Orion. "Math isn't my best subject, but you're implying that you're planning to assault the Consortium compound with less than three hundred people? That's adorable."

Anna trailed behind the group without saying anything at first but she finally piped in. "It's all we have. We can't move any of the other rebel groups without getting attacked or killed." She was speaking softly, since she was not trying to piss off Orion though she knew she was likely to anyway.

Carl didn't say anything else immediately, in case somebody else had something to offer, but he adjusted the bundles he'd brought on his shoulders and scoffed when only silence answered Anna. "Once I dig through here and get to our notebooks on Consortium personnel movements, you'll know why that idea is absurd. There's no way to lead an attack on that compound, on Eleusis, with less than three hundred people and survive."

"We'll figure all that out later." Orion put a hand on Carl's shoulder to reassure him that no one was going to push for anything against his own expertise. "We were just working on recon for now, like we said. We'll figure out what's needed and do our best to figure out our next move." They stepped out into the crisp air of the spring evening, and Orion smiled at the look on Carl and Aiko's faces. Clearly they had gotten accustomed to the subtropical climate on Eleusis. "Welcome home. At least until we can get you back to your treehouse."

"Earth is nice and all, but you'll like it much better once we can get back to Eleusis." Aiko assured Orion as she glanced back at Anna a few times. It was strange for Anna to trail along like a kicked puppy, and then she disappeared without a word altogether. "What happened to her?"

"She happened to herself." Orion said coldly, clearly not looking to speak on that topic, though they deserved to know at least vaguely what was going on. "She and Logan got back together a few weeks ago out in the midwest district while we were recruiting some of their friends and family. So now we're passing the twins back and forth from one week to the next." He shook his head to dismiss that topic altogether, and pointed at a pair of houses up on the ridge near the entrance to the Labyrinth.

"That's us up there, her and Logan on the end, Mercury's right next to it. I'm crashing on her couch right now in the interest of leaving more space for the midwesterners. This is you guys down here." He went to the other end of the narrow valley, where a set of long and tall row houses were under construction. Jason gave Orion the code for one of the houses, and he led them down to the unit through all the stares of the people gathered around. Some of them were familiar from Nine, some were not, but many were carrying babies. Babies seemed to be the great unifying factor of their community.

Aiko had not thought that she was going to look crazy until people started to stare at them, and she realized she looked vastly different than anyone else. She didn't look like she was from Earth. She didn't look like she was from Orbit. She looked alien. "I was used to people staring at you, my dear . . ." She said to Carl as they walked. "Since you're so large and attractive, but I'm not used to people staring at me."

"You're the queen of the savage Eleusis wilderness. Let them stare all they like." He put one arm around her shoulders as they walked, his other huge arm holding the massive bundle of their belongings over his other shoulder as she carried William. "I've told you before, in that outfit you look like you're about to kick some ass and like it. The warrior woman look suits you." He knew full well that Aiko was far from being a warrior or having any desire to be one, but the simple leather clothing she had managed to make for them from Carl's various kills on Eleusis had been utilitarian in the extreme, which meant that it wasn't quite as modest as most of that worn by the Earth-dwellers staring at them. They both looked wild, but Carl couldn't have cared less.

"Warrior woman." Aiko laughed and shook her head, but she was smiling when she looked up at Carl again. As much of a grudge as she had held against Jason, she wanted to thank him profusely for matching her with her giant husband. He was the best thing that ever happened to her. "I just barely started getting brave enough to kill the mice-thingies."

"Hey, you were savage on those things the last time I looked. The way you swung that pan at them? Terrifying. Completely terrifying." Carl squeezed her shoulder a little more and followed up the stairs as Orion showed them to their abruptly-assigned home.

Walking into it was surreal. He had built every inch of their home on Eleusis himself, and therefore he knew every piece of it. The home they walked into had just completed, but it was furnished with a simple table and two chairs, a kind of padded bench that passed for a couch, and a large bed in the one furnished bedroom up the stairs. He set his bundle down in the middle of the main room as they looked around at the bare white walls and the perfect windows closed against the evening. It seemed so ridiculous, and yet so familiar at the same time. "It's um . . . it's nice." He tried to make it sound like a compliment, but it didn't come out that way.

"It was the most efficient. design we could find to mass produce. There's gonna be hundreds of these things by the time we're done with everything here." Orion said as he shook his head, since he hadn't been involved in the designing and planning stages. "It's not much, but like I said, we all know this place isn't permanent."

Aiko had a strange moment where she wondered if she would rather be back on Eleusis. On Eleusis her life made more sense than what she was staring at. They had a good life back on Eleusis, even if it wasn't easy, but everything they had, they created together. This . . . felt too similar to a prison cell. "It's very clean. No animals rustling about." Aiko didn't put William down anywhere, though she knew already he wouldn't take to the place as well. The noises of Eleusis were all that he had ever known.

Orion clearly hadn't expected their reaction after living on Eleusis away from the world for so long, but he could tell that they needed their space to deal with it, so he left the key to the unit on a table near the door and made his way backward toward it. "I'll talk with some of the supply supervisors and make sure people from the various departments stop by throughout the day. Set you both up with a new communicator, new issue clothing if you want it, and make sure the cabinets are stocked with whatever you need. We don't have a lot, but we try to run a pretty smooth operation. And I'll run by the house now and let Mercury know you're back, in case she hasn't heard already. You can run by the clinic and she'll be glad to set you up with whatever kind of cocktail you need to keep Big Ugly over here running."

"He's not ugly." Aiko said quickly, since she thought Carl was the most attractive man she'd ever seen. Scars and all. "And . . . I think we'll both need to be seen by Mercury. She's still delivering babies, I hope?"

Orion's eyebrows went up, but Carl grinned as Orion ingested Aiko's meaning. Orion laughed afterward, and nodded as he leaned against the door frame. "Yeah, she's still popping 'em out. Of other people. She had her own twins about eight months ago.

You want me to see if she can make a house call later, or would you rather go find her in the clinic once you get settled in?"

"I'd rather not wander around too much if that's alright. If she'd be willing to come to us, that would be great." Aiko said as she smiled over at Carl before she looked back at Orion and shrugged. "I'll take as many babies as he can give me."

"Something tells me he's gonna make you regret saying so." Orion said with a laugh, looking back and forth between them with a shadow on his features that Carl had never seen there before. It had clearly been a very different year for the two of them. "It's good to have you back. Both of you. You go anywhere with the intention of telling anybody any crazy stories about you killing monsters the size of a house, you make sure I'm around to hear it, alright?"

"My word. We'll see you around, brother." Carl promised on Orion's way out the door, then sighed as he looked around at the sterile, blank space. "Yeah, this is gonna take some getting used to." He took one of their blankets out of the bundle and spread it on the floor so William would have a place to crawl, then laid down across one side of it to form a human wall between William and the rest of the room before pulling Aiko down with him. "You feeling alright after all that running?"

Aiko nodded and curled into him easily, even though it meant she had her back to William, but Carl would still keep an eye on him. "We did a lot of running in the last year. Running won't hurt me or the baby." She kissed him soundly before she looked up at the ceiling. "I feel . . . trapped here. This is nothing like . . . home." She turned her attention back to Carl's eyes. When they had first been trapped on Eleusis, they were terrified every moment that they wouldn't survive. Then they decided they would do everything it took to survive. They built a home and a life on Eleusis, and they were happy without modern conveniences or even other people outside of each other. "We were happy with less there than they seem around here. No one looks particularly happy."

"Oh good, that wasn't just me thinking that everybody seems to be walking around looking like somebody kicked their cat." He relaxed a little and shrugged slightly as he kissed her again, glancing up occasionally to look at William, who was fascinated by the colorless walls he'd never seen before. "If they've been trying for over a year to get that thing to work, though, I can understand everybody feeling pretty frustrated. Also explains why they're ready to jump into a plan that's complete suicide. They're bored and irritated enough to be stupid. And if there's stupid drama like people switching spouses going on and who knows what else, yeah, they've been having a crap time of it."

It had been a very long time since his hands had hesitated in wandering over her however they pleased, and just because they were back on Earth, that clearly hadn't changed. "It's not really fair, honestly. I had you for the last year. They didn't. Can't blame people for getting cranky about life when they don't have one of the best parts of living around every day."

Aiko smiled brightly, since she loved hearing how much he cared about her, cared for her, and adored her. It made her feel even more comfortable being crazy about him, since it didn't feel one-sided when he told her how much he loved her in return. "Well, they still don't get to have me even when I'm here. Other than my assistance with plant and/or Eleusis knowledge." She kissed him soundly before she put her hand on his cheek and caressed his cheek with her thumb. "They're going to get sick and tired of seeing us so deliriously happy together, but I love you that much. You're my other half. A much bigger other half, but still."

"I hope they do get sick of us. Mission accomplished, if you ask me." He kissed her again and turned to look with her as William began to explore the plain grey carpeting of the unit, running his fingers across the artificial fibers in confusion. "I'm gonna have some pretty strongly mixed emotions about this place. I'm glad they found us, and I am very, very much looking forward to fucking you senseless under some hot water, but mostly I'm just glad we're somewhere a little safer, for your sake and William's. Even if I do look forward to getting back to our treehouse someday. If we can get to a place where the worst thing we have to worry about every day is one of those behemoths waking up hungry or a mouse getting into your skirts, I'll call that a win for life."

"I remember desperately wanting to get back to our friends, wanting to get back to Earth." Aiko kept kissing him and running her hands along his body, since she liked to touch him just as much as he liked to touch her, and they had gotten really good at driving each other crazy. "Then everything was okay. You did that. You made us a home there. You delivered our baby boy when I thought I couldn't push any more." Aiko kissed him harder. "You are the best thing that has ever happened to me."

"Mmm." He laid back contentedly as he held her, enjoying the fact that they were somewhere they didn't need to listen for every single little noise, even as he wrinkled his nose a little at the smell of fresh paint throughout the place. "Three things need to happen here very, very soon. First, we need to throw open some windows and get this smell out of here. Second, we need to get William's bed set up and get him to sleep. That one's gonna take some doing. Once that's done, we need to lock that door and break this place in. I absolutely refuse to abide in a place where you have not yet screamed my name. Just doesn't seem right."

"You are such a wild man." Aiko laughed, since she didn't actually think he was being that barbaric, and she liked it. Aiko kissed him a few more times. "Alright, if you insist that William needs to be put to bed first . . ." It would not have been the first time they had sex near their son. He was a baby. Aiko didn't care what he saw or heard as an infant as long as he was content and not crying. They were good at keeping William happy and keeping each other happy.

$$17$$

SUMMER

Gwen felt nervous as she stood outside of Liam's house, the house he and his wives were given two months prior, not long after they arrived. Liam's situation had proven a necessity for a house before a lot of others, but most people weren't angry about it. Gwen had been invited over several times, but always at Bree's request.

She needed to end it before he realized she'd caught feelings. Before he called her an idiot for falling for a thrice-married man who just wanted to have fun.

So she asked to see him so she could talk with him briefly and lay things out. He said he had a free morning while the ladies went out to give him a break on his day off. Gwen brought freshly-made donuts hoping it would smooth over the 'I-can't-fuck-you-anymore' news.

Maybe he wouldn't even care.

God, that would be worse.

Gwen knocked on the door loudly so he would hear and tapped her foot nervously on Liam's porch.

Liam's house had originally been two different row houses, but they were combined for the sake of Liam's separate families. He had done some remodeling in the time he'd been there, between managing personnel from the midwest and a few Eleusis recon missions. His wives had unanimously despised the fact that he volunteered for those, but he had gone anyway. Never for more than a few hours at a time, and never for anything particularly dangerous, but he still went.

When he answered the door, he was in boxers and his shaggy hair was damp from his shower. It was far from the first time she'd seen him nearly naked, but it was the first time she'd been anywhere near him when he was by himself. As always, though, he seemed perfectly at ease, and he nodded back into the house.

"Good timing, I just got out of the shower. Come on in."

He was the worst kind of fucking tease. Gwen's eyes raked over him hungrily before she looked up into his eyes again. She desperately wanted to run her hand through his wet hair. Gwen had joined them in the shower once, and the memory burned hot in her mind. Another reason to cut it off. "I brought donuts. I made them myself."

"Well, if I ever say no to that, put a tag on my toe and make sure my eyes are closed." He closed the door behind her once she was through. He was close to her, but he didn't actually reach out to touch her as she slid in through the entryway. He walked with her through the front living room toward the kitchen. "You've never come over with baked goods. If this is the beginning of a new fetish exploration, I want you to know, it gets pretty sticky, but I could get into that."

Gwen shook her head, but he wasn't looking at her, so she spoke up. "No, I, um. No, not a new fetish. I knew today was your day 'off' so to speak, and so I thought I would bring you something instead of letting you resort to oatmeal or something. I won't stay long."

"You won't? That's a shame." When they got to the kitchen and she went to put down the plate of donuts, he moved in behind her casually. He slid one hand around her waist along the front of her blouse as the other moved over her arm. "Do you have somewhere you've gotta be?"

"No, I . . ." Gwen looked down at his hand and up at him again. "It's your day off. And Bree didn't ask me to come here." Why was he touching her without Bree here? Was that wrong? Definitely, it had to be wrong. She wasn't married to the man, and she wasn't invited to be there. "I just kind of needed to talk to you about something."

"Talking. It's probably somewhere in my top ten list of favorite activities, but it's not in the top five." He didn't let go of her and she didn't ask him to stop, so he stayed there beside her as he plucked up one of her donuts and took a bite; his free hand lingering along her waist as they leaned on the counter. "What do we need to talk about?"

Gwen liked his hand where it was, lingering on her waist, but she knew she shouldn't. She chewed on her bottom lip for a minute before she cast her gaze away. Looking at him would only change her mind about what she needed to say. "I don't think I can be involved with you and Bree anymore."

That clearly hadn't been what he was expecting to hear, and though his touch paused, it didn't go away, and his hand was back in motion after he'd had a moment to process his surprise. "That's . . . easily the worst thing I'm gonna hear all day." His hand moved down over her hip to press her a little more against him, and when he didn't feel any resistance or reluctance from her, he only felt more confused. "You never gave us any indication that you weren't interested anymore. What's changed?"

Gwen felt like an idiot, or worse, a *teenager* because she'd somehow developed feelings for the guy that was definitely not available. Three wives was already a task. He didn't need a girlfriend, and he told her from the beginning that it was nothing more between them than anything Bree wanted on her time. Gwen had also spent enough time with his family to know the situation with Margo, and Margo knew about her casual sexual involvement with Bree and Liam. Gwen felt like Margo wanted to stab her every time she showed up to help with the babies or at Bree's request. "I've . . . developed feelings for you."

His touch on her paused again, but eventually resumed, moving up her side as he took in a slow breath. "Feelings." He repeated just to confirm. He brushed off the hand he'd used to pluck the donut, then reached up with it to draw her hair back over her shoulders, tipping her head back just a little to place it closer to his lips, which grazed her temple afterward. "What kind of feelings?"

He was being so gentle and sweet that it made her feel worse about her crush. "The feelings I'm not supposed to have. You made it very clear what this is from the beginning, and I agreed. I'm only involved when Bree invites me. It's not about you and me." Gwen closed her eyes so she wouldn't risk seeing his expression, since she imagined disappointment.

"Usually I don't care about getting involved with someone. But I've spent two months with you and your family. Bree and Rachel are my friends. And watching you with your wives and your children . . ." It made her want more, and she didn't realize she even wanted it or him until it was too late and her feelings were real and not something she could just dismiss. "When I see you, I'm excited to see you. Thinking about you makes me smile, and while I have fun with Bree, I don't . . . I'm not falling for Bree. I'm falling for *you*. Like a pathetic schoolgirl. And it's not supposed to happen, so I need to go back to being *just* the babysitter."

Instead of answering her immediately, he was quiet as he thought over what she said, and eventually moved away from her just a step, to take a chair at the table nearby. He pulled it away from the table and sat down, but then turned her toward him and pulled her by slow, guided motions, down into his lap with one of her legs on either side. They'd been together enough times and knew each other's bodies well enough that it was a simple thing to move her against him, and once he had her, his arms wrapped around her waist to tell her she wasn't going anywhere until he gave her his express permission.

"We talked early on in . . . this . . . about what you wanted, just in general, around here." Once he had her against him, his hands roamed up and down her sides, her waist, her thighs, as he looked up into her eyes to speak candidly. "You're not a schoolgirl. Though you definitely look hot in the uniforms, don't get me wrong." He grinned, since he and Bree and Gwen had definitely played out that scenario before. "But you're not pathetic. You're a woman who's known herself well enough to know what she wants for a long time. I didn't know your feelings on what you wanted were changing."

"I didn't know that they would or could change, really." She admitted, though she seemed thoroughly embarrassed about it. "I'm . . . not even sure . . ." Gwen shook her head. "When I thought about a family with someone, I thought it would just happen, but I didn't think I would want to be a part of a family this way. No offense. Your family is great, I just never . . . not that I think you would even invite me to be a part of it. Clearly, your life is full. You have a beautiful family." A family that she realized she wanted to be a part of, but that she had no right to be a part of.

"I'm sorry." She eventually said as she looked into his eyes. "I want to be around to help, but I can't keep going down this path. I can't fall in love with someone who can't love me back. And it would be wildly unfair to even hope that you could. You have three wives. I just . . . I guess I can't help myself when I'm around you, or when I fall asleep next to you in your bed. I want you. For myself. And that's wrong, I know. I'm sorry."

His hands didn't stop the entire time she spoke, and she clearly had his full attention, his clear grey eyes focused on her through every word. When she apologized, though, she saw him shake his head. "If there's any need for you to apologize, then we're both going to be sorrying back and forth all morning, and that's not how I want to spend my time." His hands moved up her back, cradling her against him in ways that had rocked her senses dozens of times in exactly the same position.

But the touch was warmer, gentler, different than it had been between them before. "Some of those first times we talked, I told you something that I didn't think would change either. I said I wasn't going to go looking to add another wife. My family is pretty crazy as it is, you know that better than most people. But Bree and Rachel have both asked me why I haven't talked to you yet. Yelling at me for not talking to you yet, in Bree's case." He smiled as he remembered the conversation, since it had been fairly funny to him at the time.

"I know how complicated this is, and how strange. But honestly, I never thought I'd run into anyone who . . . clicked . . . with my family. With me, both in spite of and because of my family." His arms closed around her back again as he looked up at her, smiling faintly. "You're a tough one not to love, and I've got no interest in trying not to."

Gwen didn't really know what to say, since she wasn't really expecting to hear what he just said. She opened her mouth and closed it and then repeated the action again before she said anything else. "What? You're . . . falling in love with me too?"

He gave her a brief glare as if to yell at her for being surprised by that, but afterward, he reached up with one hand to caress her cheek, and pulled her down close to a kiss without actually sealing it. "I've been in love with you since just after we moved in here, that one night when I woke up to get a drink in the middle of the night and came back to find you awake."

It had been a very interesting event for both of them, since it was arguably the only time they'd ever done anything without Bree, with Bree sleeping through the entire thing. They hadn't even had sex. He had returned to the bed after getting a drink and found her awake and watching him in the dark. He had slipped into the covers on her side of the bed, and the two of them made out until they had fallen asleep again in each other's arms. There had been no conversation, during or afterward, but he had wanted her to himself ever since.

"You're the best kisser." She whispered, as if she was afraid to actually acknowledge what happened, and that she wanted it to happen again ever since. "That was amazing. We never talked about it, but I've always wanted that to happen again."

"It will." He promised quietly, kissing her so lightly it was both a teasing promise and a clear threat of future encounters. "I haven't been awake that long. If you're interested, we can go upstairs to my room and take a morning nap. From which I'd be more than happy to wake you up."

Gwen nodded, but she didn't want to get off of his lap or get any further away from his lips. She wanted to keep kissing him, except not lightly or teasingly. "I don't want to get married right now." She said quickly to finish the conversation. "I just want to be a part of your life. I want everyone to be okay with it if you want me to be a part of your family." She wanted Margo to like her, or, at least, not look at her with intentions of murder. "And if you want to marry me, you have to propose. You know, eventually. If everyone else agrees to . . . you know, keeping me around."

That made him laugh, but he kissed her again anyway, as his hands moved beneath her blouse to tease her skin. "I have to propose? Wow. So demanding already." His kisses moved down from her lips to her neck, and his hands pressed her against his body. The weather had turned warm in the time they'd been there in the mountains, making short shorts and tight t-shirts the order of the day when it came to Gwen's wardrobe, both of which he enjoyed. "What other demands have you got, exactly? I should know these things going into this."

"No other demands at the moment." She tilted her head back, since she couldn't believe he was actually kissing her and they were alone. "Other than a little bit of time. I know you don't have a lot to spare, but I want to know if we would be good together. If we can even make a good couple. I want to know you better. I want to know if you can look at me the way you look at Margo, Rachel, and Bree and love me like that."

"Time isn't a problem." He assured her, looking up in her eyes with a slightly deflated look, since they both knew what the problem would be. Even so, he avoided talking about Margo with Gwen or even with Rachel and Bree alongside, since he wouldn't allow himself to take sides with one of his wives against or for any of the others. It was a hard line to walk, but it was also a necessary one. "Once some other things get sorted out, we'll have a better idea of how we can go. But so long as you're not going anywhere,

I'm not in a hurry, and I know you've never been in a hurry to have kids of your own. I respect that."

"I'm not ready for my own kids." She said at first, but she realized the others' children would be hers too, if she became part of the family. "I mean, I'm not ready to *produce* my own children. I like yours. And I know Bree is calendar-counting, so you'll have another baby on the way soon anyway." Gwen didn't like even a hint of sadness in his eyes, so she kissed him. Mostly for selfish reasons, but the feeling of his lips captured in hers made her moan softly against his mouth. "You let me know when you have time for me, and I'll be here. We'll figure out if this is really what we want together."

"I'll do that." He leaned back in the chair and brought her with him, his hands held her backside possessively. "Right now, though, the girls are all out for the day, and you're not going anywhere until at least later this afternoon. I hope you didn't make any plans."

"I left my communicator at home." She thought she would be going right home after spilling her feelings to Liam, but she was glad that she wouldn't have any interruptions or anyone calling her to watch their children. "I'm yours for as long as you want me." Gwen kissed him passionately and ground herself into him. "I want you so much."

"Mhm. That sounds like a problem." He grinned as he kissed down her neck again before he stood up with her still on top of him. He wrapped her legs around his waist and moved toward the stairs that led down to the small bedroom that he had claimed as his own. Margo's room was the closest to his own, up on the second floor of the same side of the house, but Rachel and Bree's rooms were in the other half of the home.

The basement room was very simple, with just some of his clothes and belongings that didn't really have their place in the other women's rooms. The bed hadn't even been slept in, since he was coming off the last two nights spent with Bree, and the night to come would be his own to spend either on his own or with whoever he wanted. He put a knee up on the tightly-made bed and pressed her down on it as he kissed her, moaning freely in the empty house, since he didn't have to worry about them being overheard or walked in on by anyone, for a change.

Gwen melted at the sound of his moan, and her hands didn't stop moving over him, since she couldn't believe she had him to herself. She kissed him frantically as her heart pounded in her chest with her excitement, but also her fear that it would only happen once. "You make your bed?" She knew it was a silly question to ask between kisses, but she wasn't expecting a perfectly-made bed.

"Wanted to join the military a few years ago." He said casually as he returned her touches just as frantically. The smile on his face said that he was amused by the casual conversation in the midst of everything, but he clearly wasn't bothered by it. He knelt on the bed with her legs still around him and pulled her shirt up over her torso. "Wanted to be organized, disciplined, thought the bed was a good place to start. Didn't get much further."

"Why not?" She shivered when he tugged her shirt off, since it exposed a lacy blue bra that didn't leave anything to the imagination. He could see her breasts through the fabric, nipples pert and begging for him. Bree expressed how impressed she was with Gwen's taste in undergarments, and she didn't disappoint even when Bree wasn't there. "Just decided the army wasn't for you?"

He shook his head, though it placed his face between her ample breasts at the moment, his lips showing their appreciation of the curves exposed along the blue fabric. "Logan's first wife fell into depression and I mostly took over running the farm. Too busy to worry about going off and killing people." He left her bra on for the time being, but his lips moved down her torso and his fingers tugged at her shorts that might as well have been underwear. "Besides, I don't see myself taking orders real easily. I was gonna try and be an officer."

"I don't like the idea of you rushing off to fight for the Consortium, or anyone, really, but you would probably do well." She shivered as he ran his fingers across her skin after kissing his way down her torso. "I can't believe this is really happening." Gwen whispered as he tugged off her shorts and tossed them aside. Gwen was wearing a matching thong to her bra, pathetic scrap of fabric that it was.

That kind of surprise made him grin, but he left the thong in place as he moved to lie beside her, clearly interested in taking his time. They had the time and the space to do so, and he'd be damned if he wasn't going to take full advantage. "I want to get to know you more. Just as yourself." He kept her on her back as he laid next to her, one hand propping himself up while his other hand teased over her body in a rhythmic caress. His fingers dipped between her legs to tease along the strip of fabric, but smoothed over the rest of her body casually, teasing and waking every one of her nerves. "Right now I'm excited to learn exactly how you like to be fucked when Bree isn't having her fun telling me how she wants to see me fuck you."

Gwen grinned, even though she was feeling a little bit nervous. He was giving his attention only to her and entirely to her, and it was strange and thrilling at the same time. "I love your dirty mouth." She murmured as she slowly turned to face him and she ran her fingers over his exposed body. He had opened the door in his boxers, after all.

Gwen was probably the most feminine of the women in his life, since she was always concerned about being well-dressed and well-kept. Bree was girly, but Gwen kept her fingernails and toenails polished, and never once had she shown up to see Liam and Bree without the silkiest legs and the softest skin that often smelled floral or sweet. Bree always complimented Gwen on the way she smelled. At that moment, her blue-painted nails scratched lightly across his skin while her golden hair fell over her tanned shoulder. The woman didn't even have tan lines. "I'm excited to learn more about you too. Tell me something. Anything."

"Anything is a broad place to start." He laughed and kissed her again, moving his hips against her hand whenever her touch grazed over him, but he wasn't being insistent. "Here's a fun fact for you." He reached up to run his fingers through her hair. "You're the only blonde I've ever slept with." He grinned, since from an Earth-based mentality, that was difficult to believe, but it was the truth. "My man-maker was a brunette, my first long-term girlfriend was a Spanish girl and a total fucking nymphomaniac, I'm lucky I survived that one. After that it's been either Spanish girls or brunettes. Never once slept with a black girl until Rachel, no redheads besides Bree, and no blondes besides you."

"You're gathering quite a collection, aren't you?" She wanted to fucking purr as he ran his fingers through her hair. "So what do you think of blondes now?"

"I'd need to fuck more than just you to form a general opinion. But I've got a pretty high opinion of you, and I'm not interested in a larger sample size when I've got you." He cupped one of her breasts in his huge hand as he kissed her, slowly pushing the strap aside. "What about you? Tell me something about you I don't already know."

Gwen whimpered as he slowly pushed the strap down, but she did want to continue the conversation. She also wanted to have sex. Maybe they could have sex and talk? She wasn't sure she could pull that off. "I've never been in love before. Just the knowledge that I'm falling for you makes me feel even more nervous than the first time I had sex."

"That's something I think I want to hear about." He chuckled and moved his lips down to her newly-exposed breast, just because he knew it drove her crazy. She and Bree had bonded (if it could be called that) over the fact that they were both hypersensitive when it came to their breasts, and it was something he constantly took advantage of. "You're easily one of the best I've ever had or heard of in my life, so I've gotta hear where this all got started."

She gasped as he kissed along her breast, and when he momentarily sucked on her nipple she moaned involuntarily. "One of the best? Really? I'm glad." Gwen took a sharp breath as her puckered nipple was left unattended. "I was fifteen. He was sixteen. My breasts came in quick and he always told me I was beautiful. Even before I had boobs. I always wonder what happened to all the people I left behind when I left home."

"You never told me about that either." His lips lingered along the inner curve of her breasts, but returned to her nipple after his heated breath left it cool. "How you got here, how you got involved with all these assholes." His free hand moved between her legs to tease her over her thong, even though it didn't provide much of a barrier. "I always figured you joined up with some guy and rode him all the way to the mountains."

Gwen tried to laugh, but it was hard to think clearly as he teased her. "I didn't." Her back arched slightly as his mouth tortured her breast. "I ran away from home." She replied between moans until he let up briefly. "It took me two years to find real rebels. Everyone was all talk at home. Wanting to make a difference, but never changing. Even my parents. My mother especially. 'The world is shit, Gwendolyn. Your father was a hero. We should live like he did." Gwen paused and looked up at Liam. God, she loved his eyes. "My father was a Firefighter. My mother was his mistress. He died in a building fire when I was seven."

"Sounds like there wasn't much to run away from." In spite of the dark topic of conversation, his touch didn't stop, but he did move himself up against her to kiss her, grounding her in the moment instead of the past she described. "I'm glad you found this place." He pulled away to look her in the eye, and his hand moved insistently against her core. "I'm glad I met you. That you're a rebellious bitch like the rest of us." He grinned and kissed her again roughly.

Gwen moaned again as he kissed her and her back arched as he teased her core. "I'm glad I met you." She replied between gasps. "You're incredible, Liam. No one pays close enough attention to see you. No one other than the other girls. You have such a big heart." Gwen moaned louder as her hand finally managed to graze his groin. "And a big cock."

He grinned and moved her legs to press her knees together as he pulled her thong down over her legs, unwrapping her slowly so she would be completely exposed to him. "Good thing you get both." He tossed her underwear aside, his hand returning to its ongoing caress of her legs and her ass, pressing her in against him so that she could feel the ready heat of him against her.

Gwen groaned as he pressed against her. "You know . . . eventually . . . we might want to make beautiful kids. Would you still . . . want me if I get fat?"

"There's a difference between fat and pregnant. Trust me, I'm familiar with the difference." He was having a harder time keeping up the conversation with the way she was moving against him, and he didn't mind her knowing it. "And do you really think you're gonna have time to get fat? I've got three kids already and a five-minute bounce-back. You can try to get fat all you want, but you're gonna work off whatever you can get right here on this dick."

"How . . . did you manage that, anyway?" She squirmed against him and made sure she had a firm hold on him so she could stroke him hard. Gwen wanted him just as needy as he was making her.

"How did I manage what?" He asked a little breathlessly, legitimately not sure if there had been context he missed because what she was doing felt too good or if he just hadn't understood what she asked.

"Five minute bounce-back." She slowed her pace on his cock, but she only paused for a moment to lick her lips. Stroking him made her want to put her mouth on him. "I haven't had a chance to taste you, you know."

"Like I've been stopping you." It never came up with Bree, since Bree had a penchant for taking charge with her mouth and taking no prisoners. He moaned as she kissed down his neck, moving out of his reach in her attempt to torment him, though his hands lingered on her sides and on her breasts as she slid down his body. "The bounceback I can't really take credit for. It's just the way I'm built. Been like that since I learned how to jerk off as a kid. There was a long time when I went through a fuckton of socks, let me tell you."

Gwen giggled as she slid down his body, since she knew he would love her even more once she was done with him. She wanted him to want her more. She definitely didn't want to be forgettable. She kissed along his shaft once she got close enough and she circled her tongue around the head. "Mmmmm…"

At first, in what she had seen was typical fashion for him, Liam laid back on the bed and let her do as she liked, groaning under every single touch. Her hands were warm and she clearly had years of experience pleasing people behind every move she made. He leaned up on one elbow, one of his hands tucking her hair back as he looked down at her. "Go slow, baby. I might … oh, fuck, right like that, yeah, exactly like … oh fuck … I might have a hell of a bounceback, but I want you."

She slowed, but she was getting one hell of a high listening to his moans and every time he said 'oh fuck' just like that, she felt like a rockstar. Gwen eventually pulled her mouth away with a pop, since she wanted him too. "I want you too, Liam." She crawled back up his body so she could sit on top of him. "More than anything I've ever wanted."

He definitely became rougher the longer he was teased, she had seen that before, and that moment was no exception. He violently unlatched her bra before he threw it aside and assaulted her exposed breasts with his mouth. Even significantly smaller than him as she was, he made no apologies and pulled no punches when it came to how he threw her around, and from the way his hands gripped her hips, it was clear she'd gotten him good and frantic. "Careful what you wish for." He promised between kisses, groaning as her heat slid closer to him and her knees locked around his waist. "You want me, you get the crazy me along with the rest."

"I want you. Definitely." She didn't hesitate any longer to slide down on top of him, and she certainly wasn't gentle about it. "Fuck!" She normally didn't curse quite like Bree did, but she couldn't help it at that moment. She really did *love* his cock.

He growled loudly as she first took him, but after that, the insistence of the moment turned to a slow burn between them. He had fucked her every which way Bree thought would be hot, but it had never been something simple, something intimate, just between them. He raised his knees between her legs to entwine them with hers, his arms clasped around her back to press her breasts against his chest as she rocked herself on top of him.

The movements of their bodies were small, but the heat of the kisses they shared burned between each and every moan, giving and demanding, begging and receiving all in the same blissful moment. "God, you feel amazing, Gwen." He moaned between kisses.

"So do you." She whimpered as she moved slowly. Gwen watched his eyes and his expressions closer now that she didn't have to worry about anyone else watching her. She touched his cheek tenderly, and while her kisses were hot and passionate, there was more than just lust behind each one. Gwen felt some fear as the moment turned intimate, but it was also incredibly thrilling at the same time. She'd fucked plenty. Making love was definitely new.

The difference was intentional on his part, but feeling it returned was something incredible. He could remember when the same change had come about with each of his wives, the moment he had gone from simply having fun with them to really making love. He relished showing them he cared about their pleasure, their happiness, their life, and wanted to share it as a part of his own. He turned her onto her side to let the two of them thrust equally against each other, in a delicious contest that had them both writhing on the tightly-made covers. Every heightened sensation was shared, every moan echoed between them, every shiver of pleasure was passed back and forth.

Gwen was so wrapped up in the moment, so wrapped up in the unspoken and unexplained dance happening between them that she didn't expect her orgasm when it snuck up and shattered her. She cried out in pleasure as he thrusted, and somehow he moved just the right way that it kept going. "Oh god, Liam . . . Liam . . ." she kept moaning his name like an incantation.

At other times, he had been merciless with her, forcing one orgasm on her after another until she was left shivering in pleasure. But that moment, just like the rest, was different. He kissed her as she came, teasing over her breasts as her body called out his name, begging for more and getting all she could take. When her breathing turned ragged and she couldn't take any more, he laid her flat on her back and drove himself into her hard, shattering her body's resistance down to the tips of her toes as his own orgasm overtook him. He rocked his hips against her in the hypersensitive moment following, both of them drifting in a very different world than any they had ever inhabited together, and of which Liam wanted a hell of a lot more.

Gwen's body was more relaxed than it had been in a very long time, and not once did she have to think about moving out of the way for Bree or worrying what he thought about her behavior, appropriate or not. "That . . . has to be . . . why people fall in love." Making love was intimate, but it was also pure. It didn't come with guilt or expectation. Just a mutual care for the other person.

He let out a satisfied groan of affirmation and a slight nod against her shoulder as his entire body agreed with her, the full weight of him pressed against her. When he was able to speak at all, he rested himself on one hand to look down at her, as he caressed up over her chest to her cheek with the other.

"I started falling in love with you when I figured out just how much you roll with things. Nothing in this world is ever gonna stay the same forever, and anybody who says otherwise is an idiot. I'm gonna change, you're gonna change, and fucked if I know what into. But I started loving you because I knew no matter what happened, there was nothing that could come out of the world you wouldn't be able to roll with and adapt to. Then of course you started helping take care of my kids and I find out you fuck like some kind of pagan sex goddess and yeah, I've been a doomed man for a while now."

Gwen tried to laugh, though she was so spent it was difficult to do much of anything. She did smile up at him, though, and she stared into his eyes for a moment. It was almost laughable that originally the eyes that caught her attention were not his, but his brother's. Logan never once made her feel this giddy or happy, even though she had wanted to see Logan naked. Now she didn't care so much. She wanted Liam. Not Logan.

Logan.

"Shit." She muttered as she thought about her boss and how she promised she wouldn't make a mess of things. Hooking up with his brother, interrupting Liam's family, *falling* for his brother . . . she didn't think Logan would take any of that lightly. "If your brother finds out about us, he'll . . . he already hates me. He basically told me to keep my legs shut if I want to keep my new job. If he finds out I've been sleeping with you, he'll be so angry."

"My brother will keep his nose in his own fucking business." He groaned and moved to lie beside her with another heated kiss. "He arranged my first three marriages, he can fucking well stay out of this one. Even if I haven't proposed yet." He said with a teasing grin. "The people whose opinion I give a shit about regarding my own family are few, and we've already talked about all of them. Logan can be pissed if he wants, but he's not gonna do shit. He doesn't have to know anything until we're engaged, as far as I'm concerned."

"*If* we get to that point." She said cautiously, since she was honestly afraid of not being able to continue some kind of relationship with Liam because of Margo. Maybe the other two wanted her around, but it wasn't a majority rule kind of thing. Was it? Shouldn't all three opinions matter?

Gwen easily and gladly curled close into Liam since she liked the way his body enveloped her own. "I'm already the resident homewrecker. I don't need to wreck yours too."

"You're not wrecking anything right now, except for my perfectly-made bed. Which you can come and wreck any time you fucking please." His hands went back to their previous constant caress, only his touch on her body was rougher than before, much more possessive and thorough since she was bare against him. It kept the warmth they had generated between them humming through every part of her, and his eyes taking in the full sight of her held a promise that he was nowhere near finished.

Gwen cherished his attention and she took every bit of it she could get while it was focused completely on her. Her fingers kept constant movement as well, as though she was memorizing his body with each caress. "Are you excited about the idea of going to Eleusis?"

"I'm less excited now that we're finding out just how many of those fucking behemoths there are over there." Carl's nickname for the creatures had become an official moniker, along with most of the names Carl and Aiko came up with for the wildlife. "But I'm excited to build something for my family, yeah. The war isn't going to be fun for anybody, but after seeing some of those valleys a few clicks away from the Twist, yeah, I'm excited to stake a claim and start growing something. It'll feel like life is back to the way it should be for a change."

"We'll be able to think about life as more than the next ten to fifteen years. How crazy is that?" She replied as she kissed along his jawline. "You're too sexy to die young."

"I'm not gonna be a sexy old man." He warned as she kissed him, though he was smiling under her attention. "I'm gonna be a fucking mean old grump yelling at kids to get the fuck off his lawn and complaining about grandkids making too much noise. Plus, if I get the chance to live that long, I'm gonna be popping some kind of pill until I'm eighty-five to make sure when I go out, I go out fucking happy."

Gwen laughed and went back to kissing him like crazy. "You're not going to be mean. I don't think you're capable of it." She nibbled on his bottom lip and tugged at it playfully with her teeth. "I'm younger than you are. I'll keep you young."

"Oh what, and because I'm a few years older, I'm some old man?" He took playful offense at that, and shoved her onto her back on the bed before he attacked her with rough kisses and the full weight of his body, already getting hard again. "Come on and find grey hair. I fucking dare you. Go ahead and try."

"You're so so *so* old." She replied with a raucous laugh as she bounced on the bed as he hovered over her. Gwen plunged her hands into his hair and tugged a little to bring him closer for inspection. "Oh my god, I think I found one!" Gwen cackled, even though she hadn't found a damn thing. They were far too young for that.

"You lying bitch!" He attacked at her ribs and along the side of her neck where he knew she was most ticklish, not about to tolerate that kind of insult. He never pushed the ticklishness when he'd discovered it accidentally, but he was as merciless about making her laugh as he had been about making her come.

Gwen squirmed even more when he was tickling her vulnerable ticklish spots until eventually her ribs started to ache. "Okay, okay! I lied! I'm sorry!" When he let up even a little, she turned the tables and went after any tickle spots she could find.

"Oh hell no . . ." He had to go on the defensive, since she was smaller than he was and faster, but after a few minutes of both of them screaming at each other and rolling around on the bed, he managed to throw her onto the other side of the bed and throw himself on top of her, pinning her on the pillows with her wrists in his hands and her legs pinned with his own. "See, this is what happens when you try to lie like that and call me old. You get yourself put in a compromising situation."

"I'm not lying about you being old. Der. Older." She qualified the term once she realized he had her truly pinned, but she still wiggled and struggled beneath him. "Three years is a loooooooong time. I mean, you were walking, talking, feeding yourself, probably making trouble before I was even born."

"Oh, I'm sure I was making trouble." He slid himself against her, spreading her legs on the bed with his feet and moving his hard length against her still-sensitive core. "Not this kind of trouble, but some kind of trouble, no doubt." She had seen him jump back and forth between herself and Bree before, taking them one right after the other the way Bree wanted it, but having his attention completely focused on her was a very different experience. His general insatiability was hers alone.

Gwen wasn't expecting to be attacked again so soon, but the surprise and his enthusiasm was exciting all over again. "Bree is much nicer than I am." She finally responded as he teased her. "She shares in bed. I don't want to share."

"Oh, so you're selfish. Good, I'm glad I get to know these things now rather than later." His hands kept hers pinned against the bed, but one of his hands wandered down her body as he moved against her, taking her one slow movement at a time, at a teasing snail's pace. "So you wouldn't want to join in with Bree again if she wanted you to later on?"

He was torturing her and enjoying it. It wasn't fair. "I didn't say that." She continued to squirm, but he had her legs pinned the way he wanted to. "You're stronger than I am. This isn't fair."

"Flip a coin if you want fair. I'm the wrong place to look, if that's what interests you." He didn't let up for a moment, in complete control of her and loving it. "It's like you said, Bree's the nice one. I'm the mean one. Because the night's gonna come when I'm gonna wake you up exactly like this and keep you this way until you can't walk in the morning."

Eventually Gwen stopped wiggling because she knew she could do more damage with her mouth than with any part of her body at the moment. His blissful torture was relentless. "Oh, I think you're overestimating your stamina and underestimating mine. Mr. Bickford."

That kind of challenge wasn't something any of his wives gave him most of the time, and she could tell by the way he moved against her just how much of a turn-on it was. He kissed the back of her shoulder and slammed himself into her hard enough to draw out a moan before he said anything else. "We'll see about that. I do love pleasant surprises."

It was well into the afternoon by the time they gave up trying to outdo each other, and they woke up from their nap to the sound of the rest of his house returning home. Gwen felt a surge of panic as she opened her eyes and felt Liam next to her, since she felt like she was going to get in trouble. "Did . . . did you want me to leave before they got home?" She whispered as they heard Rachel and Bree laughing about something and the sound of three babies who were always babbling.

Liam shook his head sleepily, and ran a hand over his face as he pushed himself up on one arm. "Did it look like I wanted you to leave?" He leaned in to kiss her once before he forced himself to get up. Naps always left him feeling groggy, however well-earned they were. "Clothes would probably be for the best, though. I didn't think they'd be back until tonight. Something must've gotten cut short." He wasn't in a rush or a panic as he got up to pull his boxers back on for the first time all day. The room was in clear disarray, but they left a back window open high up on the wall, so that even though they were in the basement, they had gotten at least a little ventilation.

Gwen was definitely nervous and worried as she dressed quickly, even though he didn't rush. She was afraid of what his family would say when they saw her emerge from his room. "Are you sure? I can wait here and sneak out later if you want me to."

"That's not the way it works with us." He shook his head, since that had been one thing the four of them discussed early on in their marriage. They had to undo his own machinations in dating three women at once, since he didn't want to feel as though he was sneaking around in his own house or that any of his wives had to either.

"The compromise we struck early on," he explained as he pulled his shirt over his head, "was that we wouldn't do anything more than kiss, hold hands, or sit with each other in front of any of the others. In turn, if anyone saw anybody else come out behind closed doors, there wouldn't be any judgment or shaming going on. It's worked pretty well for us and eliminated a lot of potentially awkward situations. Besides, they all know our situation and they know my mind about it. They know where it's heading and what could be happening between here and there."

Liam still kept his voice down, just to keep the conversation private, but once she was dressed, he abruptly picked her up by the waist and sat her on top of his dresser, not for the first time that day. He leaned in and kissed her soundly, his thumbs moving over the playful texture of her bra as he looked her in the eye. "I'm not interested in shame having a place in this family, and you're not here to do any homewrecking or tempting the way you might've had to hide and sneak around with other men. We're seeing how this is going to go between us and with the rest of my family. I'm not ashamed of that or guilty about it, and you don't have to be either."

Gwen nodded, though she still couldn't quite shake the guilt that she felt, even though she really hadn't shown up to be a homewrecker. She had shown up to take herself out of the equation, and now she was in it more than before. She kissed him gently as he held her up on his dresser, and she let out a slow breath. "I'm new at this. A relationship in general, let alone a plural one. I'm sorry."

"Nothing to be sorry about." He kissed her again then slid her off the dresser pressed right up against him. The man never stopped teasing. Ever. And after the day they'd had, her body knew better than ever what kind of havoc the man could wreak on her. "Let's see what happened with them today." He smiled down at her and gave her another minute to get herself situated before they headed out and up the stairs, toward the sound of babbling children.

His three wives were busy, as usual, Rachel and Margo with the children and Bree whirling around the kitchen, pulling out ingredients for a meal. When she heard Liam coming up the stairs, she called out to the rest of the girls. "The monster has awoken, ladies!!"

Rachel finished putting Anders down on the floor with a toy before she went to take a peek toward the stairs. "Did you really sleep all day?" She asked before she could even see him. "I thought you were going to work on the high chairs . . ." Rachel was surprised to see Liam wasn't alone, and she smirked. "Well, now you have no excuse for unfinished high chairs when you had help."

Bree whipped around at that statement, since she wouldn't stand for some stranger in his bed, but she squealed when she saw

Gwen. "Finally! Liam, you take far too long to listen to us. Though if you had planned a day in bed, you should have warned us. We could have gone over to Logan's or Larissa's for dinner."

Margo was the only one who didn't say anything, and she remained on the floor with the children. Chrissy was in her lap while the boys crawled around. She looked queasy at the sight of the perfect blonde at Liam's side, but she only glanced at Liam before she turned her attention away.

"I'll hit the high chairs tonight after the kids go to bed." He promised without lingering on the topic of Gwen beside him coming up the stairs. He went up to Bree first, since she was closest, and gave her a kiss to say hello, before moving to Rachel for the same. "It's quiet enough work, so I shouldn't cause too many meltdowns with it." He moved through the room to get closer to Margo, but clearly she wasn't getting up to say hello and was keeping her attention resolutely focused on the kids, so he didn't push her in a public setting. "How was your day?"

"Anna took us out for a long walk and we picked some berries. We mostly just wanted to get the babies out into the fresh air." Rachel replied as she nodded toward a bucket by the door. It was a smaller bucket than one would have expected from an entire day of berry-picking. "They ate a lot of the berries. So did we." She laughed and looked over at Bree. "Bree said she'd make a pie from the rest."

"I didn't want you to feel left out." Bree beamed at Liam and nodded toward the abandoned donuts. "I imagine you're hungry if you skipped breakfast. And lunch?" Bree looked them both over scandalously before she turned her attention back on her meal prep. "We went to the food storage and Anna managed to get us the steak we brought from the estate. Does that sound like a hearty meal after a marathon?"

"I never say no to steak." He said without actually admitting to any kind of marathon, though his lack of admission was as good as a confession in present company. He looked over at Gwen, standing awkwardly in the middle of all the innuendos, and just smiled, since he could understand how strange it was to be a part of his family, even indirectly. He looked down at Margo afterward, though, as he picked up Beckett to get him away from a hard edge. "Did Anders insist on walking most of the way or did he wimp out after twenty feet like usual?"

Margo looked up at him after a moment and the only thing he

could see in her eyes was hurt. She wasn't even angry at him, even though she wanted to be. She had convinced herself that his time with Gwen was only spent with Bree and that Gwen didn't mean anything to him other than as a friend. Clearly the evidence in front of her had shattered whatever story she had in her head. "He wanted to be held until there was something dangerous to crawl into or climb up." She reached out and ran her fingers through Anders' hair, and he could see the boy's berry-stained lips. "He ate more berries than nearly anyone else. He sure does love to eat."

"Well, he's a growing kid. He'll probably be like that until he hits twenty-five or so. Then maybe he'll cut back to only three meals in a day." He gave her a smile, but it was clearly sedated after the hurt he could see in her eyes. He never completely ruled out the possibility of taking on other wives with any of those he was currently married to, but he knew Margo's mind on the subject. "At least it's warm enough to get them now. It took its sweet time getting that way."

Margo nodded, but she looked away from Liam after that. She had been excited to get home, to go through the evening and get to tomorrow, since it was supposed to be her turn. Now she didn't care. "After dinner I think I'm going to go back to the workshop." It was where she worked on mending and making clothes frequently. "If that's alright."

He nodded his understanding, swaying back and forth with Beckett a little to keep the boy entertained. "Sure. Whatever you need to do. It'll be mostly varnishing fumes around here after bedtime. Right now I'm scheduled to help out with some of the ventilation repair in the Labyrinth tomorrow morning. They said they don't need me on any more Twist missions until they start sending through machinery, but they're still weeks away from that."

"Sure." Margo replied without asking for any further explanation of his time. He could decide whatever he wanted to do as far as his time went. Clearly. "I finished your new shirt last night." She set Chrissy down and went to a black shirt that hung over the back of a chair. She put it there before they left so that he would see it when he came upstairs, but clearly it hadn't been noticed. "I hope it fits right."

"I'm sure it will." In dealing with Beckett, he and Margo ended up around a corner of the living room, mostly out of sight of the kitchen and the other three women in it at the moment, though they clearly weren't quite somewhere private. He took the shirt from her when she brought it back, and held it up to take an approving look. Margo had made more than a few of his clothes, and they always fit him perfectly.

"Thank you." He put Beckett down in the middle of a few toys then turned to Margo, putting a hand on her waist to keep her close, if she would let him. "You've mentioned how busy you were these past few weeks, I didn't know you were going to be able to work on it."

Margo let him keep his hand on her waist until she remembered that he'd spent all day with someone who wasn't even one of his wives, and she stepped out of his touch, but not completely away from him. "You said you were disappointed the other black one got left behind. Of course I wanted to get a new one finished for you." He'd only mentioned missing his black shirt once, but it was enough to encourage her to jump into action. Margo's eyes looked past him and she looked down at the floor again. "Is tomorrow still my turn?"

He could feel the hurt she had intended to convey by asking the question, but he tried not to respond to it by calling her out on it. That never ended well for them in the past. "That was the plan, yeah." He said quietly, glad at the moment that Bree and Rachel had struck up a conversation of their own and involved Gwen. "Nothing changes without all of us being on the same page, Margo. I don't want to get into a fight with all of us together in one place like this, but nothing about this changes what's between you and me."

"Nothing changes?" She nearly started laughing and crying at the same time, even though they were whispering. "Three wives and a girlfriend is different than three wives, Liam." Margo covered her eyes for a moment with her hand, since he said he didn't want to fight. "I didn't agree to be a part of a circus of women, so if you're intending to continue adding women to your collection, then tell me now." She removed her hand so she could look at him again. "Two days. I get two days out of seven and now what? If you end up with four of us, what will you do then? Why do you *need* four women to love? Why can't you just be happy with what you have?"

"It's not about that." He said in a low voice, starting to fight even though he said he didn't want to, since that was the way things always seemed to go with Margo, even outside of marital relationships. "I've never once thought of any of you as not enough for me. Any of you, by yourselves, are more than any man deserves, let alone me. Gwen is here considering being a part of this family, as a whole. Heaven knows she's already done more to take care of the kids than I have in their entire lives. Our family is not a circus."

That part of what she'd said hit him very much the wrong way, since unlike living back in the midwest, he'd actually had the chance to meet and know several other plural families in the mountains. They all did things a little differently, but they were all focused on the well-being and happiness of everyone involved, no matter what. "Our family is our family. We all came into it understanding what this was, and if it changes along the way, that's something we're all going to agree on. She's not even sold on the idea herself, believe me."

"Why didn't you just . . . warn me?" She was having a hard time fighting tears, and her eyes were burning with hurt. "I knew about her and you and Bree, but I didn't think . . . I didn't think you were involved with anyone else. I didn't know our marriage was that open."

"I didn't plan on today." He explained in a slightly more sedated tone. "I didn't invite her over here on her own, on my own. She came over earlier to talk about what was going on. What was going to happen. I told her the same thing we all said to each other when we were all trying different ways of adjusting to this. That we're making this up as we go along."

Margo wiped at a few tears that escaped despite her best efforts, and she refused to look at him again. "I guess we'll have to talk about this some more later. Tomorrow."

"Tomorrow." He agreed, wishing she would at least look at him. "Thank you for the shirt." He tried to salvage some kind of positive from the conversation, whatever there was to be had. "I love it. And you."

"I love you too." She said softly as she forced herself to look up. "That's why this is so hard." Margo wiped at her eyes again and she cleared her throat. "I'm sorry, I need to . . . use the restroom."

Liam didn't try to stop her as she headed away, and took over the children while the other three women spoke in the kitchen and worked on dinner. He could smell the steaks cooking, and it made his mouth water after a day without nourishment and a whole hell of a lot of exercise. "What do you think, baby girl?" He asked Chrissy as she looked up from her bouncer, still not quite crawling, but curious. There was no way the world could be anything but right for her, so long as it had milk, shiny things to play with, and clean diapers. "It's not that complicated for you. Must be nice."

The little girl cooed and giggled at her father as he talked to her, with her adorable round cheeks and eyes that were exactly like Margo's. Rachel appeared as Bree and Gwen continued to work on dinner, and she leaned against the doorway to look over at Liam. "Didn't go very well, huh?"

Liam shook his head without looking up at first, only glancing at Rachel once Chrissy had a toy in her hands. "About as well as expected." He sighed and shook his head as he turned to look at his sons again to make sure they weren't crawling into trouble. "Most of me wonders how long it would have taken for it to get to this point without . . . other things happening. The rest of me is just sad."

"You love her. We love her. Don't count her out until she says she is." Rachel said simply, as if the whole situation wasn't immensely complicated. "Ultimately we all started this for a stable and happy life together. If that's not what she has here with us anymore, then I would hope we can all talk about it and sort it out. Chrissy belongs to all of us, so we're a family regardless. Families work things out."

"Yes, they do." He said hopefully, then pushed himself to his feet and dropped a soft plastic ball on Chrissy's face, which the little girl found momentarily hilarious. "I'm sorry if the homecoming undid anything you and Bree were able to accomplish on your walk. I know you said you planned on talking to her about some things today."

Rachel walked up to him and gave him a hug, and she just held onto him a while. "She talked a lot about her job and how much she loves it." She spoke softly and continued to hold onto him. "She's really good at her job. She talked about how much she loves watching Chrissy learn new things, and she hopes she can have another baby again soon. She said she loves us, all of us, it's just hard sharing you. She was very candid about it."

He held her right back, his hands massaging over her shoulder blades, since that was about as far as he reached. Rachel was the smallest of his wives, to the point where they had been concerned about her during childbirth, but she was also the curviest. "When you and I talked about it early on, I thought eventually she'd turn a corner, decide to go or decide to stay. I didn't think she would continue in this kind of in-between angry for so long. I'm glad you didn't." Of his three wives, Brianne was the only one to immediately and wholeheartedly accept the idea of sharing a man the rest of her life. Rachel had had her own moment of doubt, and he hoped she would be able to help Margo find the same kind of turning point.

Rachel glanced the direction that Margo had gone and she sighed again. "If you ask me for my honest opinion, I think she's still hoping that one day you'll decide she's the best thing that ever happened to you and you'll want a life with only her. Not because she wants to screw everyone else over, but only because she never got into this for the family. She's really only here because of you."

He sighed at that judgment, since he thought the same thing for a long while. "That's not enough." He said eventually, reaching up to caress along her cheek as he held her. "I'm not going anywhere. I'm here for this. For us." By which he meant all of them, even if it was Rachel in particular he was holding. He leaned down and gave her a more lingering kiss than he typically did in public settings, his hands on her waist afterward. "Thanks for talking to her. Maybe it did her some good to say some of the things out loud, I don't know."

Rachel gave him another kiss in return and leaned sideways a little so she could look back into the kitchen where Bree was carefully instructing Gwen on the fine art of pie-crust-making. Bree was a good teacher when she wanted to be, and it made Rachel smile to see them getting along so easily. It was refreshing, since there rarely existed such a moment with Margo.

"Bree adores Gwen. And I think she's pretty funny. All of the babies love her already, Beckett most of all, I think." Rachel smiled and then reached up and ran her fingers along Liam's cheek. "No matter what happens with Margo, I'm not going anywhere. Neither is Bree. For sure. Bree is addicted to you."

"I'm glad you're not going anywhere. Either of you." He turned his face to kiss her fingers, savoring the closeness of the moment, even though the two of them together were typically very private about their relationship. "This family is the most important thing in the world to me, and it would be fundamentally incomplete without you. Over and above the fact that you're the brains of this whole operation." He grinned and kissed her again.

"I love you."

"I love you too, big guy." She smiled and kissed him one more time. "And you're right, I am the brains. Don't you ever forget it." Rachel grabbed his large hand with both of hers. "Come on, let's eat before the steaks go cold. Yours is still bleeding, I'm sure."

"Exactly the way it should be." He headed toward the kitchen with her hand in his, and with Margo still in the bathroom. He slapped both Gwen and Bree on the ass at the same moment as he went to inspect his steak and make sure it was still alive enough for his tastes. "Mmmm. It's good to be a carnivore."

The four of them had as peaceful of a dinner anyone could have with three babies in the next room, and Margo never made a reappearance. Bree left to check on her and to give her some dinner, but she didn't look hopeful when she returned. "She's getting ready to go work on some sewing. She said she feels like a few hours away will settle her." Bree shrugged and went to clear the table. "It's my night with the babies anyway."

Liam nodded to acknowledge that, and took the last bite of his steak with a grateful sigh, reaching out across the table to take her hand and kiss the back of it. "My heartfelt compliments to the chef." He smiled at her and looked back and forth between Gwen and Rachel, settling on Rachel. "Any interesting buzz from your friends or your parents today? It's a no-mission day, the rumor mill must have been churning out *something* interesting."

Rachel shook her head, since she didn't want to talk about the rumor mill. "They said the Consortium is going after some of their own leadership. They're doing some sort of cleansing of leadership, going from station to station. Apparently they intend to do some real reorganization." She chewed on her lip as she looked at Liam again. "I was going to let Logan know, since his ex has family in Orbit leadership. But then I didn't know if he was even talking to her, and besides, there's nothing we can do about it."

"Did they talk about Mercury's parents specifically?" He understood Mercury much better since living in the mountains, mostly because all of his wives had checkups with her, and she was around to talk to while his children had appointments with Barry. "If they're on the chopping block, she deserves to know."

"It sounds like everyone who is anyone is going to be scrutinized. She was part of the rebel force. I would think that her parents would be scrutinized especially." Rachel looked a little fearful.

"I can go tell Logan. Mercury should know, you're right." Gwen volunteered, since she knew she should leave anyway. Gwen didn't like the fact that Margo felt the need to leave her own house just because she was there. "My communicator has probably blown up with messages by now anyway, so I should go. I'll tell Logan to call you for more details."

Liam nodded to let her go if she wanted to go. As she got up, he took her hand and pulled her down into a quick kiss on the cheek. It was a strangely intimate touch, considering every other kind of intimacy they shared that day, and he squeezed her hand afterward. "Be safe. I'll talk to you soon."

Gwen smiled and nodded before she returned the kiss on the cheek. "You know how to reach me." She looked over at Rachel and smiled brighter before she stepped away and went to give Bree a side-hug. "Have a great night, Bickfords."

As Gwen left, Liam was left holding Chrissy on his knee, attempting to eat everything in sight except the baby food he was trying to feed her. He waited until Gwen was out the door before he looked up at the other two with a sigh, though he was still vaguely smiling. "I didn't do the high chairs, but I did get up early this morning and finished varnishing their cribs. It should be fully dried by now, I left them out on the back porch all day. It didn't rain, did it?" By that comment, he clearly wouldn't have known if it had.

"No, it didn't rain, you lovesick puppy." Rachel replied with a laugh. "Come on, let's go work on them. They need to be put back together."

18

Margo didn't know if she would be in the shop alone or not, but she was glad when she arrived and there were only a couple of girls finishing a project. Margo worked quietly as they finished up, and when they left, she turned on the radio. Some fun country music played through the speakers, and Margo was grateful for the temporary reminder of home. She was working on another shirt and pants for Jela, so she had to pause to send him a picture.

These should be done tonight!

The friendship she had developed with Jela was a breath of fresh air in her life. A breath that felt . . . like a great deal more than friendship. He had kissed her goodbye the last time they saw each other. Margo knew it was wrong, but she had enjoyed the kiss enough to ignore that it happened and pretend like they were still just friends. If she ignored it, it wouldn't be real. Somehow.

He didn't answer, but then again, he often didn't. When he did send her messages, they were often pictures of beautiful things he had found around the mountain settlement, things as simple as a sunrise or a completed frame of a house not yet filled in. Sometimes it was an image of his neighbor's children, with whom he was very close, getting into some kind of trouble. He always hoped it would make her smile.

After several minutes of work, she did receive a message from him that was simply a picture of his bedroom, his simple bed in the background with a space made in the closet, complete with an empty hanger and a hastily-scribbled outline for where the clothes she was making would soon be placed. Clearly the fact that she was making something for him had never been far from his mind, and consequently, neither had she.

It was well after most people had left the shop when she finally saw him come in through the double doors. There were one or two people still working in the carpentry portion of the shop far in the distance, since there were still so many homes to be built to demand round-the-clock work, but there were very few others around her. From the look of his sawdust-covered pants and sweat-soaked shirt, he had been working construction from the moment the sun rose until sunset, but had decided to see her anyway.

"I didn't realize you'd be working so late. Isn't today usually your day off?" He asked as he got closer to her, closing the flimsy half-gate behind him with one hand hidden behind his back.

"Usually." She said softly as she held his clothes in her hand. It made her think of the shirt she made Liam, and how he hadn't even noticed it until she gave it to him. "I went out to pick berries with Bree and Rachel. We came back to Liam sleeping with the babysitter."

He was so taken aback by the abruptness of that announcement that he stood with his mouth open for a solid twenty seconds before he recovered. There were years of history and upbringing in that moment, as she had learned to see in all of Jela's reactions. He was baffled by things most people took for granted and took for granted things most people thought were incredibly rare and precious.

Most people, knowing Gwen as everyone did and knowing Liam's plural marriage situation as everyone also did, wouldn't have thought it in the least bit strange Gwen had taken up with the man or he with her. Most people would have acted like it was just the way things were, no matter how understandable or terrible it made the people involved. Not Jela. He was shocked and affronted, almost entirely on her behalf. "You, so he was just . . . what? Why? Why would he even . . ." he couldn't even fully process it to articulate a response.

Margo got up from her workstation and brought the newly made clothes to Jela. She didn't want to talk about Liam, but it was inevitable. "He can do whatever he likes, clearly. Maybe he's bored with the women he has in his life. I don't know what goes through his head anymore."

Instead of taking the clothes from her, his huge hand settled on her wrist as she moved to hold them up against him. His eyes were on her, rather than the clothes she made. "I'm sorry." His sympathy was every bit as heartfelt as her dismissal of the situation wasn't, and he clearly didn't buy it for a moment. "Nothing about that makes any sense. At all."

She could feel the tears building and burning all over again, and this time she didn't fight, so they fell down her cheeks as she looked up into Jela's eyes. "I never wanted to be one of three wives." It was rare she admitted it out loud, but it wasn't a secret the life she was living was not the one she had originally envisioned. "I thought eventually he would make a choice. I thought that if I proved something to him, he would pick me." Margo just shook her head again. "Now he wants to add another person? Why? Why aren't we enough? Why wasn't I enough from the beginning?"

Jela couldn't just let her cry without doing something about it. It wasn't in his nature. He stepped in and pulled her into an impromptu hug, holding her lightly against his chest inside arms she knew were every bit as strong as her husband's, if not stronger. "Liam seems like a good man, the times I've met him." He said quietly, not wanting to speak badly about her husband, however much he disliked the man, "but he also seems like an idiot. I've known people like him all my life. People who don't make a decision because they don't have to, and end up hurting people because they're too busy doing as they please."

Margo remained in Jela's tight embrace and she knew she shouldn't enjoy it, but she did. She felt comfortable there, protected, cherished, even. They had become close friends, and she trusted Jela. "What should I do?"

He didn't respond to her question right away, since he had his own bias about what he thought she should do, and she was well aware of his own opinion on the subject. He tried to think of the right thing to say for a long time without letting go of her, and finally sighed against her hair. "You should do the same thing everyone on this planet ought to do with themselves. You should do what makes you happy."

"That's so complicated." She shook her head, but she didn't back away from his hug. Instead, she actually ran her hand across his chest. Margo looked up at him and stared into his eyes for a moment. "Liam makes me happy sometimes. Having a family makes me happy." She paused as her gaze flicked from his eyes to his lips and back to his eyes again. "Being your friend makes me happy."

His hands moved over her back, trembling a little just from how much he had wanted to hold her that way ever since he met her. It was a desire that had only gotten deeper the more he got to know her. "I'm glad that I can do something to make that happen." His hands moved to her waist hesitantly, his eyes never wavering even if his touch was tentative, fearful of overstepping boundaries that she might or might not want overstepped. "I would consider myself fortunate to be able to do more."

Margo was afraid to open the gate she knew she was standing in front of when it came to Jela. She was afraid to want more, and certainly afraid to let herself develop deeper feelings for someone other than Liam. He had kissed her only once, briefly, and she ran off after that. When he had been in orbit, he was matched with someone who had left him for someone else. She didn't want to be someone who did the leaving, but she knew that things weren't going to get better with Liam. Especially not now with his new blonde girlfriend.

"I'm scared." She replied softly as she looked into his eyes. "If . . . we become more, what if I'm not enough for you either?"

He actually laughed at that, but not because it was funny. He shook his head as his hands moved over her sides, investigating her in subtle, innocent ways that spoke his interest directly to her senses.

"You know me well enough to know that I am a simple man, Margo." Even his English needed work from time to time, but he did as well as he could. She had heard him going off with some of his friends in Swahili, and they seemed to be having a marvelous time, but his English was always deliberate and premeditated. "I've seen enough of what happens when a person tries to lead a complicated life. I'm here to fight the Consortium and build a life that is worth living, not the mess they've left for us here on Earth or the puppet show they live in space. If I could live somewhere, left alone, with the chance to grow old and die with someone I love beside me, I can't imagine what more a person could want from life than that. Anything else is greedy or stupid. I try not to be either."

It was Margo's turn to tremble a little as his hands and touches grew bold the longer she let him touch her. She didn't want him to stop. "What about Chrissy? Could you love her too? And a family, would you want that?"

That made him smile, since she knew the background he had come from. "I grew up in the middle of seven children. I'm not sure I would know how to do anything if there was not some kind of chaos around me. I want as many children as you are interested in having, but family means nothing if the parents are . . . not the first for each other." He stumbled a little over the language again, since she could see him thinking what he wanted to say another way first before translating it as best he could. "I love children, even if they do not always like me. And Chrissy is as beautiful and sweet as her mother. How could I not love her?"

Talking about Chrissy made Margo smile a bit more, but her smile faded quickly. Was she really thinking about this? Talking about this? Margo had been crazy head-over-heels for Liam for as long as she could remember, and when he actually showed interest in her, she thought she was dreaming. It would have been a good life, if things had gone differently.

Margo reached out to run her hands over Jela's arms slowly, her fingers investigating his skin. "Chrissy probably wouldn't live with us." She finally said as the thought twisted in her heart. It hurt, realizing she would have to be separated from the daughter it took so long for her to have. "She will be happier with all of her mothers and her brothers and her father. I can't take her away from the rest of her family full time." Margo lifted up a hand as she looked up at him again, and she ran her fingers over his cheek. She was absolutely terrified of thinking about being with someone else that could hurt her, and she was equally terrified of leaving her life and Liam, since she loved her daughter and Liam. But nothing about her life was getting better. Except when she spent time with Jela. "Can I kiss you?" It was the worst idea, but she wanted it.

The question brought a sad smile to his face, and instead of answering, he leaned down and kissed her first, a warm touch that drew every part of her in against him and told her that nothing else existed for the man in that moment besides her. "You never need to ask me for something like that." He said as the kiss broke, immediately followed by another, and another. "What you need from me, you can have. Now and whenever. No matter what it is."

Margo held tightly to him after he said that, and she continued kissing him until she couldn't easily breathe. She savored each kiss and refused to feel guilty. Liam had never asked her once if his involvement with Gwen made her feel happy or unhappy before he acted. She wasn't using Jela to get back at Liam, but she was not going to feel guilty about having feelings for someone else.

Her face was truly flushed by the time they paused, and their bodies were nearly melded together, so she could feel the kind of effect that the kissing had on him. "Being with you would make me happy." She admitted against his lips, since he told her she should do what makes her happy. "I want this. I want more."

He lifted her easily, casually, and placed her on a cutting counter so she would be at his eye level as he kissed her, leaning into her as she felt every part of him celebrate that kind of desire from her. He was quieter in his kisses and the small moans that escaped him than Liam generally was, but there were plenty of them, and his hands became less and less shy. Eventually when the kiss broke again, he rested his forehead against hers, his hands enveloping most of her sides between them.

"I don't have much." He admitted, not for the first time, since he had always been self-conscious about his own station in the world with relation to Liam's, brother of the governor and easily one of the richest men in the rebellion. "But the cooling in my apartment works, the television has all of the shows you have told me I simply have to watch," he said with a teasing smile, "and the bed is warm. That is about as much as I can offer you."

"If *things* made me happy, I would already be the happiest woman alive." While living on the Bickford estate, Margo had never wanted for anything. Liam made sure they all had what they needed, even if it took time to get whatever they wanted. None of it filled the need she had for attention, love, and care, and those were the things Liam didn't have in unlimited quantities. "I want someone who wants me, only me." She put her hands on his cheeks as their foreheads pressed together. "And not just anyone. I want you."

He took in a deep breath, as if he could hold it and hold onto the moment. His hands moved to press her against him, and he closed his eyes against hers to take in her promise. "You know where to find me." She had only come to his unit once, very early on in their acquaintance, to drop off some pants that had been torn through the knee while working. He hadn't even invited her in, but they had lingered in his doorway, each of them wondering if she would come in or not. "I'm going to go home and . . . clean my entire unit in a panic, since I am afraid it is a mess. But come and find me, when you are ready. I will be there."

Margo kissed him again and then she took a deep breath. When she was ready? She was ready for a lot of things, but not ready for others. She was also a little afraid of intimacy with a man that wasn't Liam, particularly a man that was bigger than Liam. "Are you worried about . . . the physical part? What if I am too small for you?" She wasn't curvy or tall, and Margo knew she was rather plain, except for her eyes. She always got compliments on her eyes.

Jela shook his head with a chuckle. "I'm worried about hurting you, but that's all. I think you are beautiful, Margo. Any other trouble . . . we will find a way to work it out, I'm sure. We can take things slow, however we need." The way they were pressed together against the cutting counter didn't leave much to the imagination, but since they didn't have an audience except for those at a distance, Jela took one of her hands and placed it slowly on his pants without looking away from her gorgeous eyes. "I can be very patient when I have to be, and you are worth all the world's patience."

Margo's cheeks were burning almost as soon as he took her hand and placed it on his pants. She was definitely a closed-doors kind of girl, but it had been a long time since anyone had shown her any interest, and his openness about it was incredibly erotic. She moved her fingers slightly to touch him a little more. "You say all the right things. I hope that I can make you happy. I want to. I want to be what you want."

His huge hand moved up to cup her face in a slow caress. She could feel how rough his hands were, she could catch the scent of sawdust, but she knew the man well enough to know that if he had a vice, it would be working too much. He liked being able to produce things for people, contribute to the creation of someone's home, and he tended to get obsessive about things being done right. "I know this hurts." He said a little more realistically. "I wish there was some way I could change that for you, but I can't. All I can do is promise that it won't happen to you again."

Margo kissed him again after that, since she didn't want to talk about pain, even though the pain was a constant part of her life. She hoped that would change with Jela. "I don't know when I'll have the courage to talk to Liam. I'm going to try my best. I promise." She pulled him into yet another kiss, and it deepened by her tongue tangling with his. It was clear how much she wanted him, that was certain.

That kind of forwardness from her got a moan from him, since clearly that wasn't a side of her he'd seen previously, and his arms tightened around her at the prospect of her leaving. "Take the time you need. I'm not going anywhere."

The more he assured her that he wasn't going anywhere and the more she realized that she didn't have to share him with anyone, the more she wanted to keep holding onto him and kissing him. "I don't have to go home for a while." She finally said between kisses. "Do you want to stay here with me for a bit?"

"Sure. I need to try these on anyway." He smiled and nodded down at the clothes on the counter next to them. Without moving away from her, he untucked the shirt he was wearing and started unbuttoning it. It wasn't the first time she had seen him without a shirt on, but was the first time up close. She was accustomed to being with a bulkier man, but Liam was well muscled mostly out of vanity and personal exercise, his significant physique sculpted on purpose.

Jela, on the other hand, was less well defined but clearly stronger in every respect. His childhood also hadn't left him without his share of scars, each of them with an untold story behind them that her perfectly-formed husband would never understand.

Margo almost reverently ran her fingers over his dark skin and traced a few of his scars. She wanted to ask him about them, but at the same time she didn't want to bring up any potentially painful memories. She looked up into his eyes as her fingers continued to explore his skin. "You're so handsome, Jela."

He seemed slightly self-conscious when her hands ran over his scars, but he certainly didn't move away from her touch. "I'm glad you think so."

She slowly pulled her hand away from him and trembled a little as she put her hand back on his torso. "Can we . . . go back to your place? I don't care about how messy it is." Margo kept feeling guilt creep into her thoughts, but she kept pushing it away. Liam didn't feel guilty about the things he did with Bree and whoever else they invited. She wasn't going to feel guilty for this. Not now.

He was surprised by that offer from her, but clearly from the look on his face, he wasn't going to say no. Not when they had gotten so close in such a short time, and when they were looking their own future fully in the face. "Sure. It's not far." He immediately felt stupid for saying so, since she had been to his place and knew how far away it wasn't. He picked up his older clothes and wrapped them quickly in a bundle under one arm, glancing around the space. "Did you, um, did you need to finish anything else here?"

Margo shook her head as she looked around, but then she looked toward a closet where there was a bunch of clothing stored for anyone who needed it. New, old, clothes recently mended. It was a place where new arrivals could go to get whatever they needed, and a place where people could put clothing they didn't want anymore so it wouldn't be thrown away and go to waste. "Let me clean up a little. I'll meet you there." She said quickly before she kissed him once more. "I'll be right behind you."

He clearly believed her when she said so, and kissed her one more time. "I'm yours." He said between kisses, every part of him promising itself to every part of her. He backed away and walked (with difficulty) toward the nearest exit leaning toward his house.

She dashed to the closet and found a dress she wanted and changed into it quickly before she threw a coat over the top. She grabbed her own clothes and hurried out after she shut down her station. Even if she saw Liam, she wasn't sure she would stop or pause, she wanted to get to Jela. Someone in the world wanted her, and only her. The gravity of that fact drew her in like a moon that couldn't wait to fall.

19

For most of the population of the mountain refuge, child-rearing was one of the last things anyone would imagine their governor doing. The majority of the afternoon, however, he had taken himself away from his duties and declined to drop the children off in the Labyrinth childcare, preferring to take care of them himself. Most of what they needed was already in his house, since Leo and Lynnette were already using most of the things Declan and James required, so the children themselves were really the only things that moved between houses.

For hours, Logan had gone back and forth between sitting on the floor of his living room, running back and forth to the kitchen to get whatever they needed, and frequent trips with James back and forth to be changed. It had been a long day, but a very different kind of day than he generally had, and he was grateful for the change.

James was asleep on his shoulder as he headed across the small yard between their houses toward Mercury's front door. Declan was awake in his other arm, and had been fairly cranky, but he was looking around in fascination at the outside world. He wasn't even sure if anyone was home, but Mercury said she wanted to trade the children again at six, so there he was.

Mercury had picked up Leo and Lynnette from childcare a few hours before, and she just finished feeding them when she heard a knock on the door. Without looking up she knew who it was, so she didn't get up. She just finished changing Leo's diaper.

"It's unlocked." She raised her voice just barely loud enough to be heard. There was a stew cooking on the stove, a fresh dessert on the table, and the house was picturesque. Clean. Organized. Particular. Yet homey, at the same time. Except by the door, it wasn't Logan's shoes, but Orion's spare shoes. It wasn't Logan's jacket on the hook, but one of Orion's. She and Orion weren't even a couple, they weren't seeing each other or sleeping together, they were just friends, but they certainly shared a home.

Logan let himself in and closed the door softly behind him, careful not to wake James as he did. Through something of a balancing act, he managed to set Declan on the floor near his half-sister, then moved to one of the two small bassinets in the living room to lay James down. Only when James was settled did he turn and speak to Mercury, without fully looking at her. "Dec doesn't seem affected, but something about the baby food James had at child care didn't seem to agree with him. He's thrown up a few times this afternoon and seems pretty wiped out. No fever, though, so I'm hoping it passes quickly."

Mercury looked up when Logan mentioned James throwing up since she was instantly concerned. She immediately thought about contacting Barry. "You could have brought them back if you wanted to. That's a lot of mess. Did you have any help?"

He shook his head, but didn't seem concerned. "The house next door never had a rug or any carpet in the living room. Tile floor is easy enough to clean up and disinfect. I set Dec up with something to watch for a minute while I put James through a quick bath, then put him in front of the screen while I got the floor cleaned up. Then did that whole process . . . three more times." He shrugged, since compared to everything else he typically had to deal with, it was nothing. "It's been over an hour since the last one, though, and he's kept down the last few ounces of milk. Fingers crossed."

"Well, even if he gets sick, I'll handle it. Leo and Lynnette have been fine, though Lynnette is refusing to eat any baby food. I don't particularly blame her, it doesn't taste great." Mercury finished up Leo's diaper and tickled along his sides until he was laughing. She smiled down at the miniature version of Orion and leaned in and gave him a kiss on his nose. Neither Leo or Lynnette were biologically hers, but she loved them both. They were sweet babies. "She'll probably want another bottle soon."

"I'll take care of it." He went to pick up Lynnette from crawling under the coffee table. She wasn't happy about being taken away from her furniture toy, but she was entertained by the collar of his coat once he had her in his arms. "What about you? From the reports I've seen, things seem to be settling down at the clinic for the summer. Hopefully that's eased your workload for the time being."

Mercury nodded and picked up Leo so she could go stir the

stew and check on it. She held him on her hip as she looked over the stew carefully so he couldn't touch the hot pot in any way. He was blowing raspberries and Mercury laughed a little at his noises. "Seems like most people are slowing down on having babies. Your doctor from back home and her daughter and a few of their assistants have eased the load considerably. It's allowed me to pick up some research again and be home more often." Mercury glanced back at Logan temporarily, since she had wondered after kicking him out, that maybe part of the deterioration of their marriage came from her spending too much time away. He hadn't ever blamed her for anything, but she knew that somehow something must have gone wrong or that she had done something wrong. "Hopefully my children will know me a little better by having me home."

"I know they're happier being here than down in child care. Ms. Pierce has done an excellent job in setting up the place and she does a fair job of managing the staff and expectations, but whenever I pick them up, they always get very excited when the house comes into sight. I'm sure they're glad to have as much time with you as possible."

He stayed on his side of the room with the other children rather than following her into the kitchen as he might have done at one point. Aside from looking over at her to listen to what she had to say, he mostly kept his eyes on the other children in the room to make sure they were out of mischief and safe. "Is there anything you need from me or Jason to assist in your research? He's fond of telling us how important it is to maintain as much of an information wall as possible, but if you've got something you're working on, I can see if there is anything he can try to crack to assist you."

"I'm still researching CV, as I was working on it before." She stepped away from the stew and put the lid on top, holding Leo with both arms instead. It was unsettling for Logan to see, since her babies would have looked similar to Leo if she had stayed with Orion. In that moment she was as she would have been, except that she and Orion weren't actually together. "I'm working on something for Orion, and looking into my own genetic coding to try and find more information. I'm almost certain I'm some kind of ticking time-bomb. My coding has a lot of similar features to Carl's, only I believe that a lot of it will not be triggered without a specific kind of compound, or my body's stress levels simply haven't reached the level necessary."

She wasn't sure if he was following her, but she couldn't help her explanation anyway. "Regardless, I have enough data for now. Thank you." She walked over to Logan and held out Leo for him to take. "We have too much stew, would you like some?" She had only recently realized she was home a little more often than Anna was, and so Logan was sometimes left alone with the children. She tried to be nice. She wanted to be nice. Mercury still cried over the man, for crying out loud. She still loved him, and she hated that he had that power over her still.

Logan shook his head, but he hoped she wouldn't be angry about it. "I . . . tried my hand at making a casserole, actually. We'll see in a little while if it ends up any good or not." He held the children one in each arm, and was glad that they were still small enough they didn't particularly fight being held. Fighting both of them at once would have been difficult to say the least. "There's a group coming back through the Twist in about an hour, though, and I know Kameron actually took Melissa on this jump with her for once, so I'm sure they'd be grateful to have something waiting for them. If the casserole is edible, I was going to send along some of that as well. They've been gone all day, and those ration bars they take with them are . . . well, I think I'd rather eat Eleusis dirt, honestly."

"It's better than nothing, I suppose." She said about the ration bars and not his casserole, though she didn't know how he would take it. Mercury decided not to clarify. She gave him a polite smile before she walked with him to the door so she could continue her tasks and check on the boys. After she opened the door and he walked out, she stood at the doorway for a moment.

After all this time she didn't know how she was still so angry, but she knew she needed to let go of it. Somehow. "Barry told me that Doctor Weber is moderately trained as a therapist." She crossed her arms as she looked him in the eyes, which was rare. "Our relationship is over, but I was wondering if you could make time to go with me to talk with her. Being this angry is unhealthy, and we have children together. I need to be able to move past this, but I don't think I can do it without having frank conversations and discussions with her and with you."

Anyone else might have been surprised at Mercury's admission of being angry, but Logan knew her better than anyone else. The fact that she was polite and even pleasant at times meant nothing when it came to her true emotional state. He nodded, bouncing Lynnette once to shift her into a better position at his side.

"Med school on Earth typically means being trained as a little of everything, especially when you're the only MD for hundreds of miles. I . . . I'm familiar with Doc Weber's therapy skills. She's very good." He didn't elaborate on his reasons for why he knew how good she was or wasn't, but it wasn't difficult to guess. His first wife had killed herself out of depression, after all, while he was close enough to hear the gunshot. "I'll make whatever time you need me to make. Just let me know."

Her posture relaxed a little bit as soon as he agreed, since she assumed that he wouldn't. She didn't know why she assumed he wouldn't, other than the fact that she wasn't his wife anymore. He didn't need to make time for her if he didn't want to. "Thank you." She said in a tone that was subtly gentler than her previous more polite tone. "I just want to move on. I think we all do, right?"

He didn't answer right away, but she could eventually see small signs of a sigh escaping him as he gave a slight nod. "I hope we all can. Whatever that means." He didn't elaborate as he stood looking back at her, the children in his arms taking in the sight of all the houses nearby and the people moving back and forth. "I was wondering something earlier today that I'd like to ask you, if that's alright." He could feel the eggshells underfoot as he spoke, but he got the question out anyway.

Mercury glanced back at the boys to make sure they were alright, and they seemed to be content. "What were you wondering about?"

He hesitated just a little longer before actually asking, but his curiosity eventually overruled his caution. "The Twist has been working for two months now. For the last month, there's been an open call for volunteers to go on simple reconnaissance or supply missions. I've got a waiting list three hundred names long in my office that we're working through as quickly as possible, to get people acclimated to the Twist procedures and to the general awareness of Eleusis wildlife." He paused, looking her over inquisitively. "You've been working to get to Eleusis your entire life, but your name isn't on that list. Why not?"

She looked at him for a moment before she shook her head and sighed. "You're right. I've worked my entire life to get to Eleusis. I've been studying and training and working as hard as possible since I was old enough to go to medical camp. My parents supported me every step of the way. They celebrated with me while I progressed, and when I was accepted." She met his eyes again but she didn't uncross her arms and she remained there in the doorway. "All that work, and none of it has brought me very much good." She admitted in a way that was probably a little bit hurtful, but it was how she felt. "If we're meant to get to Eleusis, then I'll be glad to go up when we go. If not, then I'm going to enjoy the life I have right here and ask for nothing more."

Logan nodded slowly, since he could understand. He thought she would be excited to go, one of the first to get to the world she had always worked for, but when she put it that way . . . he could see Eleusis being a very double-edged dream. "We will." He said without any other explanation, then started moving toward the stairs to take the children back to Anna's house. "Let me know what Doc Weber says. Good night, Mercury."

"I will send you a message as soon as I hear about her schedule. Have a good night, Logan." She watched him go for just a moment before she turned back and walked into her house. Mercury closed the door and leaned against it for a moment as her eyes burned. She was tired of crying over a man who had hurt her so much. She was tired of letting him have that power over her. It was time to move on. Somehow.

* * * * *

It was more than an hour later when Anna returned, though Logan received updates on his communicator as to the status of the excursion and their success in returning safely. The casserole was a little bland to his taste, but was edible, at least, so he felt it had been a marginal success.

When he heard the door open, he was in the bathroom, utilizing a contraption of his own design that held the children suspended in bouncers in the bathtub so that he could wash them off. They thought it was a hilarious game and he could deal with one of them at a time. He didn't get up to see who entered, since there were only a few people who came into the house unannounced. "Back here." He announced so that whoever it was could hear him.

Anna came back covered in dirt and Eleusis debris but she was smiling, happy, and high from the adventure. "This setup is awesome. Now we just need to get a hose so we can spray them off every time." She came up behind Logan and then hugged him tightly. "Hey, you."

He took a sarcastic sniff, since she had definitely been out and running around on an alien planet all day, but he turned around and kissed her anyway. "Hey yourself." He looked her up and down and laughed, then immediately started undoing the coverall she wore on Eleusis all day to peel her down to nothing. "You're next. What were you doing on Eleusis all day, running laps?"

"We needed to bury some tech to get some underground information, so I was mostly playing in the dirt." She teased as she quickly stepped out of her filthy clothes and stripped down to her underwear, which she eventually took off as well. "Alright." She stepped in the bathtub between her children, who were laughing and reaching out for her since they both wanted to be held. Anna looked at Logan expectantly. "Hit me."

The nozzle for the shower was only warm water, but after the hot day on Eleusis and the dry heat outside in the mountain summer, it wasn't unwelcome. He took the nozzle and sprayed her down from top to bottom, and took the same rag he'd bathed the children with and used it on some of the grimier parts of her body. "I saw that it was a full body count that came back. You guys run into anything more interesting than digging tech ditches?"

"We caught some critters so they can be analyzed, if they're edible, that sort of thing. We didn't bring them back alive, since we didn't know how going from Eleusis to Earth would affect them. We also brought back some vegetation Aiko needed us to get, so there's that. She's developing a survival guide."

"They *are* a survival guide, the pair of them." He was glad to hear they didn't encounter too much trouble, but he was starting to get suspicious about the general lack of trouble. Jason managed to get eyes on some aspects of the Consortium's operation on Eleusis, but even Jason was getting frustrated by the difficulties he faced in doing so. "I was supposed to call in on a meeting earlier talking about the rest of the week's missions, but I was taking care of the kids and I missed it. I expect we'll be sampling for a while, so this probably isn't the last shower you're going to get from me." He grinned and washed some parts of her more thoroughly than they strictly required before moving on, their children laughing all the while and splashing mommy in the tub with them.

They got through the bath rather quickly despite all of Logan's lingering touches, and she was smiling as she stepped out and grabbed a towel. "I think Xander was talking about getting closer to the Consortium compound. Obviously that's more dangerous than catching weird mice and plants, but clearly that's important. We need to know what to plan for if we're going to attack them."

"What we need is to pick up one of these numbered lab rats Carl and Aiko told us about, the ones they play catch and release with once in a while." He wrapped up Leo in a towel, leaving Anna to fend for herself naked with their daughter. "I realize I've been shouted down by pretty much everybody else in terms of actually following through with that plan, but we need to know what the hell they're doing with those people. It could be a way in somewhere for us."

"What if they're chipped or something? I don't know, that could be bringing the Consortium straight into the middle of our haven. I kind of agree with your opposition on this one. If we can find a crack and get into the compound, then maybe we can figure shit out without compromising our safe place." She wrapped the towel haphazardly around her body and then wrapped up Lynnette. "We don't know much of anything about the compound and we need to know more."

"Even if we kept the person on Eleusis for interrogation until we could be sure, it would be useful." He levered his final piece of opposition for his opposition, but didn't press the issue. "I hate the thought that we could be doing all this research while they're just down there laughing at us. I know we don't have any reason to think they even know we're there yet, but still, we don't know. And you know that drives me insane."

He laid Leo down to diaper him, and had to distract the boy just to get him to lie still long enough for the process. "I keep hearing whispers from Renata and some of the others talking about the general opinion of everyone here on what we're doing. No one seems particularly confident that we actually have our shit together. Most days, that includes me."

"I don't fucking care what they think, half of them are too chickenshit to even go to Eleusis and do anything anyway." She rolled her eyes and fought with Lynnette to diaper her as well, which was fairly comical, since Anna was naked as she attempted to wrangle her naked daughter. "How is bitching and moaning going to do anything anyway? What are they going to do, drop out of the resistance and kiss Consortium ass? I mean, what a joke. If they want to give their opinion, they could at least be open about it instead of talking shit behind people's backs."

"It'll come to that eventually." He said with a fair degree of foreboding and morose confidence in what he was predicting. "I'm not looking forward to it and I don't think anybody else is. But if there's no movement soon, if there's no real plan for how to proceed, then people are going to start . . . fragmenting. Going home, becoming liabilities, possibly trying to do things their own way, I have no idea." He shook his head, since he thought resisting the Consortium would be a more straightforward thing, but as always, the world was more complicated. "I'm not saying any time soon, but eventually. We could have some kind of breakthrough in the next week that tips the scales back, I have no idea. We just have to keep doing what we know until we know more."

Anna shook her head again as she grabbed some pajamas for Lynnette and wrangled her daughter into those too. "Attempting to takeover and then defend an alien planet is a little more complicated than taking a bunch of guns and going at it with the Consortium. God. This is further proof that we need more people with real military background, not a bunch of impatient people who just want to get to their dreamland."

"And we're back to the same runaround I always get with the rest of the councillors." His voice sounded defeated, but he wasn't angry at Anna, it was just the same rut he'd already run in so many times he had lost count. "We need military minds, but the only place to *get* military minds is from actual militaries, all of which are in some way either loyal to or controlled by the Consortium. The pod they've managed to put together in Singapore is nothing more than a tiny exception to that rule."

A small rebel government recently managed to take over control of the mostly-deserted territory. Oddly, none of the greater nations of the world seemed to give a shit, since it was a mostly dead region anyway, and there were at most a few thousand people involved. "Every time we try recruiting from within military structures, we end up creating problems for ourselves and giving the Consortium a chance to fu . . . find their way in the back door." Cleaning up his language around the infants was not Logan's strong point. Anna didn't seem to care about censoring herself.

"So what are our options?" She glanced over at Logan once Lynnette was dressed. She placed Lynnette on the floor so she wouldn't roll off the bed. "Just run in guns blazing and hope for the best? We can't do that."

"No, we can't." He didn't have to struggle as much with Leo in order to get pajamas on him, so Logan sat back and watched the boy crawl along the hallway and the doorway leading into their bedroom. "And militarizing our own . . . is going to take too long. Orion and Kameron do their best to teach, and Carl's been a help since he's been back, but besides them . . . we have maybe three dozen real fighters or soldiers in this entire valley. Even if all those who've volunteered for security duties turned out phenomenal, that's just over a hundred, most of them with no real experience. That's just not going to be enough, in this world or on Eleusis."

"We'll find more people somehow. We don't have any other choice." She put on her underwear. "We need to recruit more people, then. We have to do something. We're going to win this war, damn it." He didn't disagree with that as she went after her pajamas. "I saw a casserole in the kitchen. When did you go all domestic on me? It looked good."

"It's edible. Yours are better. If you want some, make sure you put some salt and seasoning on it." He rolled onto the floor to be on the same level with Lynnette as she explored, closing his eyes to keep from having them gouged out by an infant. "I just didn't feel like having soup again for another straight night, so I thought I'd try something different."

"Thank you for making dinner while I played in the mud." Anna finished putting on her skimpy pajamas. "How did the infant-swap go?" She said a little more seriously as she looked at Logan on the floor.

All traces of mirth vanished at that question, and he sighed before answering, as he always did. "James wasn't feeling good, so I cleaned up a few rounds of infant puke this afternoon. That was fun. I don't think it's serious, but Mercury's going to have him looked at tomorrow, I'm sure." He sat up on the floor and leaned against the wall to watch Lynnette and Leo explore. "She and I are going to be seeing Doc Weber at some point. She says she needs a therapist to help her talk through how furious she is with me and to help her move past it."

"Couples therapy?" Even though that wasn't what he said, that was what she heard. "If she wants to talk things out with someone, why can't she go with her boyfriend?" Anna believed that Orion and Mercury were together again, even though they said they weren't.

He glared at her for that comment, since they disagreed on their perception of Orion and Mercury's situation. It was a strange boyfriend to have, in his opinion; an ex-husband who slept on the couch but was supposedly her secret lover? Logan doubted it. "It can't be couples therapy if you're not a couple. I'll be more of a therapy accessory, I imagine. Part punching bag, part witness for the defense."

Anna sighed. "I want everyone to move on too, but therapy . . . I mean, sometimes it doesn't work the way it was intended. What if it makes things worse? Or what if she decides she can't live without you and then starts throwing herself at you?"

Logan actually laughed at the possibilities she mentioned, though he realized she was being entirely serious. "She wants to castrate me, not throw herself at me, baby. That's not going to happen."

"Castrating you is not going to make me happy either. I need that penis, thank you very much." She flopped down on the edge of their bed. "God, it's good to be home. I like going to Eleusis, but I like being here with you and our kids." She smiled at Logan and picked up Leo before she fell back onto the bed. "Once we get settled on Eleusis, things will seem a lot less crazy."

"That's about right." He said with a sigh, watching Lynnette as he rolled his eyes slightly. "Once all our problems are solved, all our problems will be solved."

Anna remained on her back with Leo on top of her as she stared up at the ceiling. "Are you happier being stressed? Is that why you get this way? A little optimism wouldn't kill you."

"Maybe not, but it would definitely kill my reputation." He knew he was being incredibly glass-mostly-empty lately, but her calling him out on it didn't make him feel differently about it. "Back home, I needed to have all the answers. And I think I did a pretty decent job. Ran the farm, learned how to fix the machines, how to work the market, how to keep Liam and Larissa from killing themselves or getting taken advantage of by gold-diggers, all that. I've been the guy who's supposed to have all the answers for a lot of people now for a long time, and I don't. Whatever rose glasses I had, I wore them out a long while ago."

"I'm not saying put on rose glasses. That means not seeing what's really there. I'm saying appreciate the progress we've made and maybe be a little fucking excited about it?" She sat up slowly.

"You haven't even gone. Are you changing your mind about living on Eleusis? I thought we were fighting for this together."

"Of course I haven't changed my mind." He gave her a look once she sat up, just to glare. "I've just been focused on dealing with things here. If I start taking missions, people will perceive me deciding this place isn't worth worrying about, that the people here aren't worth worrying about. Eleusis is all that matters. If we're going to make this rebellion work, people here need to be brought completely on board instead of this only-here-because-we'd-die-otherwise bullshit we get from most of them."

"I just thought I would get a chance to explore some of Eleusis with you. I dug ditches with Oliver and Orion." She looked down at Leo and back at Logan. "I like making plans. I want to make plans with you, Logan."

He decided to let go of his own reticence to go to Eleusis, and moved across the room to pick up Lynnette. "From the scans I've seen of the hills, it doesn't really look like there's any decent farmland near where we've got the Twist. I was sort of hoping there'd be something within decent range of the sea. Have you seen an end to the hills yet in moving inland, or is it all too up and down like that?

"We haven't moved too far from the Twist, but I've been pushing it every time." Anna sat back as she looked over Logan again. "Will you come with me next time? We can go scouting together."

He nodded, since he knew he had been remiss in doing his part for Eleusis. "Yeah, I can do that. Maybe not this next excursion, since I know they're gonna primarily be starting up excavation with the sites they've identified, but before the end of the week." He was familiar with all the plans for Eleusis, even if he wasn't personally involved in executing them.

"If I can tell you a secret . . ." he said with a slight smile, "Xander's been working on a project with Liam in their spare time. They took some of the charge bikes a few of our friends brought from the district and they've been stripping the dangerous tech out of them, masking the rest. Once they do a few more tests to make sure they're undetectable, we'll have a much better chance of outrunning the behemoths if we run across one while it's awake. Not to mention covering more of the countryside on scouting trips."

"No way." She said with clear excitement, since she could

definitely go for a ride on a hoverbike through Eleusis. "That would be *awesome*. I really have to tell . . ." Who was she going to tell? The first person she wanted to tell was Orion, but he rarely said two words to her. "Well, I guess I would tell you, but you already know."

He grinned. "Perks of leadership. I know things." He spun Lynnette around on the floor, which amused her greatly, then looked back up at Anna. "I'm a little sad that dirtbikes would be too loud and too much of a risk. I haven't forgotten how much you, um, *enjoyed* those that one time when we were kids."

"You don't know what you're talking about." She replied innocently. "I rode dirtbikes for the speed and nothing else."

"Sure. The look on your face wasn't speed, it was ecstasy." He chuckled, since he had tried not to make it obvious at the time that he had seen her at all.

"I didn't know you were watching for my o-face." She said with a laugh as she started to bounce Leo. "You were watching me way more often than I ever remember."

"Guilty." He owned up to that much, since that kind of perversion was safe to own up to, given the rest of their history. "I want that on Eleusis." He leaned back, watching Lynnette crawl some more. "I want our kids to ride dirtbikes across it and laugh at each other, break an arm, learn a lesson, all of that. I've never not wanted that. But part of me feels almost guilty about going there. Not just me, all of us. Like we don't deserve it, as a species, given the job we've managed to do to ourselves. Not gonna stop me, though. I see pictures of the place and obviously the Consortium complex is a blight on nature, but eventually the whole place is gonna be suburbs, roads, skyscrapers, parking lots, the whole thing."

"I want it all too, Logan." She put Leo down and moved closer to Logan so she could sit on his lap. "I don't care if humanity doesn't deserve it. I want it anyway. And I'm gonna take it."

That comment made him smile, since he had always treasured that take-charge side of Anna when they were children. Every bad idea anyone had ever had, she had been the first to support, and they usually led to the best times he could remember. "What are you thinking, a beam-by-beam recreation of the estate house, just on a different planet? Copy the furniture, the windows, those fucking lions in the entryway?" He nodded over at Leo, since he had always thought the boy's name worked just as well for a

Bickford as for an Al-Jabbar or a Prince, whatever the boy happened to be at the moment. "Or do we throw that out completely and start over from scratch?"

"We can keep the lions. I say we make at least one wing the exact same, and then shake it up for the rest of the house. I mean, this is Eleusis, after all. We should definitely throw in some new designs and ideas." Anna jumped off of his lap to grab Leo before he put a cord in his mouth, then she moved him to a safer place. She grabbed Lynnette and put her next to her brother before she darted back to Logan and hopped up onto his lap again, this time facing him. "It needs to be a huge house, though. We're gonna fill it with babies."

"We can make that happen. On both counts." He kissed her once she was back in his lap, and only spared a glance for the kids before he kissed her again. Lynnette was watching the two of them, but if their children saw their parents being intimate, Logan couldn't have cared less. Anna's pajamas were so skimpy they might as well not have even been there, which was exactly the way he liked them. "Only took us, what, five months the first time? I'm thinking that's a record waiting to be beaten."

Anna kissed him several more times and wiggled in his lap to get his attention in every way she could. "I love breaking records. It's the best feeling in the world."

"The best? Wow. Way to make a guy feel like he needs to try harder between the sheets." He grasped her backside as she wiggled, then glanced over at the doorway leading out toward the children's room. "Or against that door frame, since the way you're being right now, we're not gonna make it all the way back to the bed once the kids go down."

She grinned as she kissed him harder. "I would love to be fucked in the doorway, Mr. Bickford." Anna thrust her hips against his, since she was all about tempting him. Even if there were kids around. No one, including her children, would ever be confused about how she felt about their father.

Her calling him Mr. Bickford brought up memories of the first few times he'd been with Mercury, but he didn't say as much as he kissed her, enjoying the way she constantly teased, since he knew she was all about following through on the things her body threatened to do to him. "There are times . . . a lot of times, actually, when I feel like kids should come with a light switch. Awake, asleep . . . that would make doorway sex a hell of a lot easier. Along with a lot of other things."

"Where are those bouncer things? Let's just trap them in those and then fuck really hard against the wall. Please?" She begged as she kissed him passionately. "I think your cock agrees with my plan. Just say yes."

He leaned back under the kiss, and knew he wasn't going to say no. He had been irritated with her for being gone so long during the day, but he also missed her, and he was going to make sure she knew it. "Their show should still be queued up on the screen in there. You get him, I'll get her."

* * * * *

Mercury had the boys in bed by the time Orion came through the door, which was unmistakable, since she knew how he walked and how it sounded when he arrived home. She looked up from where she was snuggled up on the couch in her pajamas underneath the blanket he usually used to sleep with.

Mercury's hair was piled in a crazy bun on the top of her head with a few stray red strands framing her face, but otherwise she just looked incredibly comfortable. She had a mug of coffee next to her and a worn book in her hands that had clearly been rebound, since there was no cover nor was there even a visible title on the front or on the spine. She smiled at Orion when he walked in, but she didn't get up to greet him. They still led fairly separate lives, even though they lived together. His schedule was his own, as was hers. "Hey there."

"Hey." He said in mild confusion, since it hadn't been that long since the boys had been put down, and it wasn't out of the question for them to still be awake. "Sorry I'm so late and you had to deal with the boys on your own. There was a tech liability left over on the other side and I had to go back and take care of it." He shook his head in obvious frustration and took a bag off his shoulder to set it aside by the door.

He leaned down and pushed back a flap on the bag, then pulled out a few small fruits people were calling Knotted Pears, from the way their stems grew in a mess before they fell ripe from the trees on Eleusis. He stood up after he got them from the bag and left his boots by the door to cross over to her. "You seemed to like these the last time I brought them home, I figured I'd bring back a late-night snack."

"Thank you." She held out her hand for the fruit, glad he brought more back. Mercury smiled up at him, since she wasn't angry with him at all. "Don't worry about the time. I'm glad you're alright. James wasn't feeling well, so I put the boys down early. I made stew and some bread, you can reheat it. I thought I would get some reading in while I had some downtime. I needed to step away from everything for a bit."

"Looks invigorating." He glanced down at the book, with smaller print than anything he could recall reading for pleasure for himself. As usual, he was wearing a shirt and some light shorts beneath his Eleusis jumpsuit, so when he stripped off the suit in the living room, it was hardly scandalous. He just didn't want to track Eleusis dust through the house. "What is it?" He asked mid-strip.

"It's, um . . ." She hadn't really expected him to ask what she was reading, since normally she was reading research. "A book I picked up from the small library as I was leaving my shift today. It's called *Sins of a Wicked Duke*." She admitted with a blush to her cheeks. "It looked like an interesting way to brush up on Earth's history. It is historical fiction, after all."

The title by itself got a set of scandalized eyebrows from him, and he glanced back and forth between the blush in her cheeks and the text in her hands, a grin slowly spreading across his face. "Sins . . . of a Wicked . . . give me that." He abruptly reached down and took the book from her hands, as he slid down onto the opposite end of the couch in the same motion as he held her place with one finger and started leafing through the book with the rest.

"I . . ." She tried to give some kind of defense after he sniped the book, especially because she was reading over a rather explicit part of the book when he walked in. Clothing had been ripped away, mouths and bodies were tangled . . . "It's not *all* . . . like that." It was a feeble defense, but something was better than nothing.

He grinned at that weak defense and thumbed through the pages, still finding it strange to hold an actual, paper-made book. There were some things a life aboard space stations simply hadn't prepared him for.

"Oh my . . . he *is* a wicked one, isn't he?" He chuckled at the part he'd found, then caught up with where she'd stopped and read for a few paragraphs. "Hm. I see. Well, yes, that would pretty much take care of that. I thought corsets were quite expensive back then. You'd think that would make people pause about ripping them off quite that way." He looked back up at her with a teasing but good-natured grin, since he certainly wasn't meaning to make fun of her.

"On the other hand, I've always heard one of the best parts of a woman's day is getting rid of the bra at the end. Especially if they're as um, how did they put it . . . *full and heaving* . . . as this context seems to describe. I only imagine getting rid of a corset is just *that* much better."

"Probably so. You're very good at putting yourself into the story." She replied with a small laugh, though she was still incredibly embarrassed. "I didn't think you would ask me about the book, it's rather nondescript. I feel incredibly embarrassed."

"Don't be. My sister used to fill up libraries of these things. Probably still does." He handed the book back to her, careful to hold her place for her. "That author's name doesn't ring a bell, but it's a pretty old one. Khadi mostly read colonizing romances about alien planets and how the new settlers have to have as much sex as possible to save the species or they'll all die out." He grinned back over at her and laughed again. "I never knew you read those. Have you always, or is this a fairly recent development?"

"It's not new, but I didn't read them back when we first met. I never would have wasted my time back then, and I should have. I was far too focused on research. This is a nice way to get away from all of that for a while." Mercury grabbed her bookmark and put it aside. "I've had a lot of reasons to want to take a mental break over the last couple of months. And . . . well, to be quite honest, I'm single. It's refreshing to read a little romance."

"I get it." There was no judgment in Orion's eyes whatsoever when it came to her reading preferences, and he nodded his understanding with the same smile on his face. "I've never been big on novels or movies or anything like that, but the single thing is . . . weird for me too. Aside from the six months before getting matched with you, I think this is probably the longest stretch I've been single in my adult life."

"You made out with a bartender before you met me, at least." She was smiling as she said it, but then she looked a little worried. "You don't have to be single, though, just because I am. If you want to bring someone home, just let me know . . . I don't want to be in the way."

He shook his head without hesitation and leaned back into the couch. He moved so he wouldn't sit on a corner of the blanket she was using to get in her way. "I'm really not . . . yeah, no, that's not gonna happen." He smiled a little sadly, but turned a little more toward her as he spoke. The couch was a good one for him because the arms of it were a little removed from the cushions, so rather than having to sleep crumpled up, he just stuck his feet out beneath the armrest and he was actually quite comfortable. The couch itself, however, wasn't actually that wide.

"I went out drinking with Carl a few weeks ago when we were both off duty for a couple days. That one day you came home and I was already passed out on the couch by eighteen hundred." He looked sufficiently embarrassed by that, but it had been a while since then, and the awkwardness of it had mostly worn off.

"He suggested the same thing, that I needed to go . . . do something. Get out there. All that talk never actually works or means anything. I told him I didn't think I could do that anymore. And I really don't. Part of the reason I submitted myself to the match program in the first place was because I wasn't happy with that kind of bouncing around anymore. I wanted something real. I don't think that's the kind of thing a person goes back from once you've crossed that line."

"I agree." She turned toward him as well. Mercury sighed as she looked into Orion's familiar dark eyes. "Do you think we'll ever find someone again? We had something great both times. With each other. With them. I'm beginning to wonder if I have used up all my chances at love."

"I'm pretty sure that's not how it works." His smile was sedated enough to tell her he had asked himself the same question. "But we did have something pretty great. I still think it's possible to have that again. If the universe has any sense of justice, and I've always felt like it does, then we . . ." Orion shook his head, anger tucked away in a corner of his expression that he didn't usually have the kind of temperament to experience or express. "We didn't choose to be in this situation. That was chosen for us by other people. I can't believe in a universe that's going to spend the rest of our lives punishing us for somebody else's choices."

"I hope not." Mercury said sadly as she looked at him, close enough to hug him, but she tried not to appear so weak. "I'm sorry. I didn't mean to bring the conversation down. You didn't get a chance to tell me about your day."

He shrugged, since that was the best descriptor of his day that he could think of. "Not much by way of world-shattering news. I spent most of the day looking at the Consortium compound and theorizing with Kameron about what's going on in there. Identified some of the personnel they've got working there. We saw Vance and Gehrig. That was the first confirmation we've had since Nine that they're still alive."

Mercury seemed to go cold at the mention of the previous director of the Initiative, and all the joking from discovering the romance novel was truly gone. "No one else you recognized?"

"No, they've got . . ." he shook his head, seeming more curious than concerned, because he tended to want to understand first and worry later. "There's this whole . . . category of people who are mostly the ones out moving between buildings. I'm not sure how else to describe them. They're all in the same kind of plain grey uniforms that aren't . . . exactly uniforms. They look pretty comfortable, actually, all grey and loose. Anyway, they all wear this same kind of bulky something or other on their forearms. I don't know if it's a security device or what, but they never talk to each other, they never deviate from the paths, and they never look up. The best we can figure, they're some kind of slave population. They're also the same ones who get tossed outside the fence to fend for themselves, except they don't have the device with them when they get thrown out."

Mercury looked extremely concerned. "They don't talk to each other? They *never* deviate? That's . . . even slaves talk to each other. Historically, they had lives, families, children . . ."

"I'm not sure the Consortium particularly cares about history at this point." He shook his head, since watching the slaves freaked him out whenever they came out, which wasn't often. "Anyway, aside from that, it was just a bunch of sitting around waiting for the rest of the team to do the work. A lot of buried tech to work on geological surveys. One of our drones was left flying when we came back through, so that's why I had to go back and retrieve it. Don't exactly want the Consortium noticing they've got somebody spying on them from a thousand feet over their own heads."

"I wish we could get more information from inside." Mercury wondered about the slaves. "They were experimenting on us as members of the Initiative. I think it would be crazy to believe they would stop doing that when they didn't get all the answers they wanted."

"Or that we were the only group they had running at any given time." He agreed, sinking into the couch a little more with a sigh. He was so tall that between her lounging with the blanket over her and him making himself comfortable, there really wasn't any room between them. "We'll get some answers one of these days. But they're sure to be worse than we expect them to be." He shook his head and immediately changed the subject, since he didn't want to dwell on the Consortium and how woefully unprepared they were to deal with it. "How are the pears, good? They were smaller than the last ones, I didn't know if that impacted the flavor at all."

Mercury had only taken a bite, so she held it out for him to take a taste if he wanted to. They had swapped a lot more than a little spit before, so she didn't mind sharing. "It is a little more tart. But still incredibly delicious."

He leaned over to take it from her and laid back along the arm after the bite, enjoying the richness of it. "I know I'm making it up in my head because it's all new and different, but seriously, everything made on Eleusis tastes better. All of it." He laughed at himself and handed back the fruit if she wanted the rest of it. "I'm sorry I left early this morning, we didn't get a chance to get in a round of combat training. Jason wanted everybody early for a tech briefing on things we already knew." He rolled his eyes, since that surprised no one. "Did you want to go a few rounds now, or are you pretty much done for the night?"

Mercury thought about it for a moment and she shook her head as she took a few more bites of the fruit, and set it aside by her forgotten coffee. "If I work extra hard in the morning, you'll forgive me for saying no tonight, right?"

He laughed and nodded. "This time. Just this once, I'll let it slide. I'm nice like that." He sat up on the couch and scooted to the edge as he looked over at her with a smile. "I'll, um, let you get back to your duke. Seems like a very interesting guy. I think I'll get Eleusis showered off me and do some reading of my own. I've got supply meetings all day tomorrow, so I need my mind prepared for extreme and possibly fatal boredom."

"Oh. Alright." She got up to let him get up, grabbing the Eleusis fruit and her cup of coffee so she could clean up after herself. Prior to breaking up with Logan, Mercury didn't really have pajamas that were appropriate for company, so in the days since, she wore clothing she found at the Shop. She had donated a lot of her scandalous lingerie and took up wearing comfy sweatpants that were cut into shorts and someone's old and worn t-shirt. None of it was Logan's. "I can move into the bedroom so I'm not taking up the couch. Sorry about that."

"You don't have to." He said quickly once he was up on his feet, looking her over in her comfy attire with a smile. "I'm planning on grabbing some of that coffee once I get out, and if you got some, you're not planning on going to sleep for a while either. It would be nice to just kind of . . . be . . . for a little while. Without the prospect of behemoths charging out of the woods or exploding diapers, for a change."

"It is nice." She turned around and looked at him again with a smile after she cleaned up after herself. "It's better with company. I don't know what I would do without you here, Orion. I'm really glad you're here."

"Well, you'd have fewer snacks. And once in a while when the boys are trouble, you'd be a little outnumbered, but I'm pretty sure it's nothing you wouldn't be able to handle. Clearly, since you got them both down and handled tonight." He shrugged. "I'm glad I'm here too, though." He paused afterward, considering what he was going to say before he said it. "I'm glad I'm still a part of your life. That you're part of mine."

"Me too." She agreed without any hesitation, and she stepped up and gave him a hug. Mercury wasn't an overly affectionate person when she and Orion first met, but in the time of getting beaten up by so many different things, she learned affection was one of the things that made all of the pain a little more tolerable. As she hugged him she pressed her cheek to his chest and sighed. "I feel like a lot of this is my fault. I should have fought for the relationship you and I had together. You and I never would have done this to each other."

He put his arms around her shoulders without hesitation or awkwardness to the touch, rubbing along her back as he did. "No, we wouldn't." He'd clearly had the same thought more than a few times. "Everything we had was new, though. Don't get me wrong, I had made my choice and would've stuck with it, but this wasn't your fault. We both . . . I don't know. I believed in the match program to begin with, and even though I didn't want to believe it when it matched you with him, I started to believe it when it seemed like it made you happy. That's all I ever cared about."

"That's because you're a good man. All you ever cared about was making Anna happy too." She eventually leaned back a bit so she could look into his eyes again, and she gave him a gentle smile before she placed her hand on his cheek. "You're the best man I know. Whoever you end up with is going to be lucky she has you."

"There's a hell of a lot of better men than me." He didn't move away from the touch, though, and without really thinking about it, he moved his face to kiss the inside of her wrist. It was such a simple gesture, an easy habit to remember, that it didn't occur to him to feel awkward about it until after he'd already done it.

Mercury was a little stunned he'd kissed her wrist, since she certainly hadn't expected it. She remained still and silent for a moment, and she looked a little panicked. "I don't . . . you don't want anything with me, trust me." She said quickly, though she realized maybe it was only a friendly gesture and she was overreacting. "Not that I'm assuming . . ."

"I didn't mean . . . I mean . . ." He went from slightly panicked to concerned as he processed what she'd said, and he still didn't fully let go of her. "You . . . what are you talking about? You're amazing. Any man or woman on either side of the galaxy would be the luckiest son of a bitch in the world to be with you, and not one of them would ever deserve it. Me included."

She shook her head and looked away, even though she didn't physically move away from him. "I'm . . . broken, Orion. I don't even really know how to fix it, even though I've tried. I . . . I wanted you to teach me how to defend myself because of something that happened on Nine, but I let it happen."

The look on his face wasn't surprised, exactly, but it was cautious. If anything, he only held her more tightly. "Well, you've learned a lot just in a couple months, and you're a hell of a lot stronger than I think anybody's ever given you credit for." He meant the compliment in every sense, but he wasn't sure she would take it as such. "I knew something happened, I just . . . I didn't want to pry. Whatever it was obviously hurt you, and I'm never gonna want to make you relive that, even as a memory."

"I relive it all the time anyway." She admitted very softly in a painful whisper. "I . . ." Mercury was afraid to lose Orion's good opinion of her, but she had to wonder if talking about it with someone other than Logan would help her. Not that she and Logan even really ever talked about it in the first place.

"Logan and I had a very different romantic relationship." Mercury knew for sure Orion didn't want details, but she had to give him some kind of explanation why the Kaplans would have been able to convince her to do anything in the first place. "Logan was very authoritative, and I enjoyed it that way." Mercury hoped explaining it that way would be enough. "The Kaplans had been watching us, I guess. They threatened to expose him as some kind of deviant, and I was worried that people wouldn't trust him if they knew. We were trying to get everyone to work together so we could get out of that place. I couldn't risk . . ."

She was saying everything so fast, but she had to, in order to keep talking. "They said they would expose him unless I . . . joined them. Only it wasn't twenty minutes of hell, it was . . . hours and hours, I can't exactly remember. They drugged me." She said matter-of-factly, and in her mind she could still see the glass in her hand and feel the horror all over again. "It was a mind-controlling drug. It made me *want* to do what they told me to do. It made me . . . Beg . . ." Her voice cracked on that word, because of all the hazy things she remembered, she remembered that the most. Begging.

"When it wore off, I never felt more disgusting in my life, and even after we came back down here to Earth, the effects of the drug made me want it again for a week. I dreamt about them. I had nightmares constantly. Even thinking about it now, the memory is mixed with absolute disgust and horror . . . my brain remembers the way the drug felt . . . The control. There wasn't pain, really. The pain is knowing, knowing what they did, knowing how powerless I was, and knowing that I couldn't escape."

As she spoke, and especially after she was finished with the account, there were shadows of both men's faces in her memory; Logan's anger and killing fury against the Kaplans, and Orion's right in front of her. He wasn't angry, and certainly wasn't angry at her, he just listened patiently until she was finished, though she wasn't looking at him through most of it.

When she did look back up at him, he was staring down at her, and a pair of tears fell from the corners of his eyes to run down his cheeks. "I'm so sorry, Mercury." His grip on her had only gotten tighter as she told the story, as if he could keep the memory of it away by keeping her close. "That . . . I can't imagine that. I don't even know where to start."

Mercury looked at his tears and she felt even more ashamed. "I went to them. I agreed to it. I thought, 'it's just sex'. I thought if I went and gave them what they wanted then they would leave Logan alone. I gave them that power over me in the first place because of the nature of my relationship with Logan." She shook her head and looked down at the floor. "There has to be something wrong with me. If I enjoy the kind of relationship I had, and after what they did. There's something wrong with me. That's how I know you're too good for me."

His hand moved up from her waist to her cheek, and didn't bother being careful about avoiding a brush with any other parts of her on the way. He lifted her chin gently to look at him, his eyes still glassy from her story, but fixed on her perfectly green eyes. "There is nothing wrong with you, Mercury." He said it as firmly and authoritatively, though it was strange to hear Orion in that kind of tone. It gentled the next moment, though, as he shook his head.

"You dedicate all of yourself to everything you do. I had . . . theories . . . about your relationship with him before, but I never once judged you or thought less of you for it. Either of you. People enjoy different things, and that's what makes the world go around. It doesn't make you defective or deviant. You were defending him and they were taking advantage of it. I won't pretend to know what any of it felt like, but I know *you*. And you are amazing. Whatever else they took, they haven't taken that. And they can't. Because it's you."

Now it was Mercury's turn to cry, and the tears slid quickly down her cheeks and she stepped back into Orion again, hoping he would just hold her. His encouraging words didn't heal her, and she knew it would take a lot more time and therapy for her to feel repaired, but she did feel a little better. She felt encouraged, and at least she wasn't alone and he didn't hate her. "I was worried . . . that you would think . . . I am disgusting."

He cocked his head to one side and in that single motion, the Orion she had married was back in her memory in full force, looking at her most of the time as if he didn't quite understand what she was saying. "Well that was uncharacteristically silly of you." He said in a slightly lighter tone. "I've never once thought you were anything close to disgusting. I know you better than that, and I love you more than that. You're not disgusting. You're not broken. You're you."

Mercury looked at him through her tears and couldn't stop herself from leaning in to kiss him. She didn't have any idea if he wanted to kiss her or be kissed, and she knew they were amazing friends. She also knew that she loved him for being exactly who he was, and their relationship hadn't ended on bad terms. Their relationship had changed, but that didn't mean it couldn't change again. If they wanted it to be more, there was nothing stopping them.

He didn't shy away from the kiss, but it took him a little while to kiss her back. Not because he didn't want to, but because it seemed like he was making sure she wasn't just kissing him out of impulse or vulnerability. When it continued, his arms tightened around her back to let her know he wasn't going anywhere, and the kiss deepened quickly. He had been in love with her when they were first matched, even if the beginning of their relationship had been arguably artificial. They had both been open to it and found that the other person was, in many ways, exactly what they needed. If he could be what she needed, as a best friend, as anything else, that wasn't something Orion was capable of walking away from.

Even though he eventually kissed her back, she was worried he might not want what she was hoping for in that moment. Mercury stopped kissing him after a moment and held herself back slightly. "I never stopped caring for you, but if I'm going too far, I'm so sorry. I don't want to lose our friendship over a kiss."

He shook his head, but held her rather than kissing her again, since he was concerned about the same thing. "You're not going too far. And I hope I'm not either." He reached up between them to caress her face, wiping away the remnants of fallen tears. "I admit, in a few months of sleeping on your couch, this is not the first time I've wanted to kiss you."

"Really?" She turned her face into his touch, since it was so strange to feel him touching her face again, but it felt like home at the same time. "I didn't know . . ."

He leaned down to kiss her again rather than letting her finish saying what she did or didn't know. Kissing Orion had always been a very different experience than kissing Logan. Him being so much taller than she was meant that kissing him wasn't a simple tip back of the head or a casual thing. Her head was swept back with every brush of his lips on hers until it was as if her entire body was primed and ready for some force from the sky to come down and take her away in the kiss. When he leaned down into her, her entire body caved in to his, cradled by his arms around her back. It wasn't a simple or a passing touch. It was premeditated and powerful enough to make her feel as though she'd be lifted off her feet at any moment, but never permitted to fall as a result.

Mercury certainly didn't hesitate to kiss him back after a kiss like that. She wrapped her arms around him and held herself close to him as she kissed him back with just as much fervor. When Mercury was with Orion the first time, she had little experience and no desire for sexual exploration. Now her life was very different, and her experience was very different. She kissed differently, she was sure, but she hoped it was better than before.

It was strange for Orion to feel the difference in her, but it wasn't something he minded. In some ways she was more confident, in other ways less. He had to wonder what kind of differences existed in him just as some of them existed in her. When the kiss broke, he leaned his forehead against hers, breathing more heavily than he had before, his hands moving over her sides instead of just holding her. "Yeah." He said with a single breathless chuckle. "Definitely been wanting to do that for a while now."

Mercury laughed softly and kept her forehead pressed to his as she put her hands on his cheeks momentarily. "I know we didn't end up here, but I like it here." She kissed him again after that as her hands wandered tentatively. Mercury had taken several months after the incident with the Kaplans to even open up to intimacy again, but now she didn't have as much of a problem as she did before. She didn't want to have problems with Orion, she wanted to just be with him. Mercury had endured enough problems in her life. Being with Orion had been one thing that had gone right until she had made a decision to pursue things further with Logan. "I'm not going to make another mistake and let you go."

"You're assuming I have any intention of going anywhere." He said with a grin, leaning into her tentative hands with another playful kiss. "You'd be very wrong about that."

She laughed again and kissed him once more before she leaned back slightly. "Do you, um, would you rather sleep in the bed instead of that couch? I've been feeling bad about that for a while."

That made him laugh. "The couch isn't that bad, actually, you shouldn't feel guilty about that. And even the beds we've got around here aren't exactly made for somebody my size." He started walking backward toward the stairs leading up to the bedrooms, though, without taking his hands off her. "Of course, if I steal some of your side, maybe I can make it work."

Mercury followed after him, feeling nervous, but not because she was an inexperienced woman this time. She hoped he wouldn't be disappointed, or something wouldn't go wrong. "I'm nervous." She finally admitted when they made it up to her bedroom. It was a room she hadn't shared with anyone yet, since Logan had been kicked out even before they had unpacked a single box.

He paused just inside the doorway, kicking it softly shut as he leaned back against the wall to draw her in close. "This is usually the part where I say something like 'hey, Nervous, I'm Orion. It's nice to meet you." He ran his hands over her back with a grin before kissing her again, the look on his face much more serious. "If you want to just go to sleep, I'm alright with that, if that's something you want or need. I just want to be with you. However you need that to be."

They hadn't turned on any lights, and though he wasn't familiar with the room, she hoped he felt comfortable in it anyway. Mercury kissed him gently and backed away slowly. "Maybe if I just get undressed and get under the covers? Is that okay?"

She could feel him nod, and he kissed her again to let her know he was still very much into the situation. He let her go, and the room was so completely dark it was almost difficult to follow her or see where anything was laid out. He had seen her bedroom in passing before, of course, so he knew generally where things were, but actually navigating the room was something else entirely. As she stepped away, he took off his shirt and inched in what he thought was the direction of the bed, opening his eyes wider as if that would somehow help him adjust to the complete darkness. "You still sleep on the left?"

"Yes." She quickly took off her pajamas and scurried over to her bed. Once she was under the sheets, she felt a little better. Mercury tried to be more confident about her body, but it was harder now than before. "Do you need me to turn on the light? I don't want you to get hurt stumbling around here."

"No, I think I can find my way." He was encouraged by the sound of her voice, and he dropped his shorts without much more hesitation, kicking them in the same vague direction as his shirt. "Just keep talking, I'll follow the Irish." She could hear the grin in his voice as he teased her, but he was heading in vaguely the right direction.

Mercury laughed a little bit louder. "Really? You'll follow the Irish?" She shook her head as she remained tucked under the sheets. "All the way o'er here, ye tall beastie." She laughed at herself, since she was really pushing her accent.

That got more laughter from him, but he swore under his breath when he did hit his knee against one of her bedposts on his way to her. Still, he slid into the other side of the bed from her, which she could feel more from the sheets than anything she could actually see. "Wow. I'm not sure I khave ever kheard you be kvite so native before. Dis is very sexy." He teased right back in a thicker version of his own accent. Once he was under the covers, though, she could feel him move onto his side in the middle of the bed, his hand searching for hers along the sheet between them.

Mercury giggled and she slid closer to him underneath the covers as well, her hand finding his as he searched. She didn't stop moving closer to him, even though her heart was racing. "We make an interesting pair."

"Interesting isn't the first word that comes to mind." He said as she finally got close enough for him to kiss her, lacing his fingers with hers before running his hand up her arm to her neck. It felt so strange to be back in such a position with her, and yet so normal at the same time. "I'd say excellent, exciting . . ." he kissed her again, a gentler and more lingering than before. "Good. I think the first word I'd go with is good."

"Good." She agreed as she breathed quickly. Mercury kissed him almost frantically, since she was both nervous and eager. "Being with you feels like going home. Like I'm where I'm supposed to be."

Orion groaned under her kisses, the rest of his body moved under the sheets to press against hers. It hadn't been difficult for her to tell the kind of effect she had on him, and it was ten times more obvious when there was nothing between them. "You've been home to me for a long while now." His hand moved down her back and over her backside, refamiliarizing himself with her one piece at a time. "It was a good home we had, for the time we had it." He moved his kisses down her jawline to her neck, holding her tightly in an embrace that was half hug and half promise of more to come. "It still can be."

"It will be." She agreed as she let out a very soft moan while he kissed along her neck. "I like that." Mercury said softly as he continued to tease her skin. She wanted him to know all of the things she liked with the hope he would tell her the same about him.

That was a little more vocal than he was used to Mercury being, but it certainly wasn't something he had a problem with. He kept up the touch when it was clearly getting a reaction, his fingers still scratching over her back. "You remember that one time . . ." he said between kisses, his voice low and whispering near her ear, "when you dug into my back with your nails? You apologized for about twenty minutes afterward but I couldn't talk because I was too busy having the time of my life?" He teased her with another kiss, this time to her lips. "I'm a big fan of that. It lets me know I'm doing something right."

"I'm glad to know that." She said as he told her what he liked, since she definitely wanted to know. "I'm . . . much more adventurous now. Anything you want to try . . ." She didn't sound at all hesitant, since even though she lived the rest of her life orderly, she liked sex to be adventurous. "Really, anything. Except including someone else." She added quickly, even though she didn't think Orion was the type.

"You know, I tried that back in the day," he said it as if he was relating some interesting factoid he'd read that morning rather than talking about his own sexual history, "honestly, I understand how some guys get off on it, but for me, it just kinda feels like a lot of work." He leaned back and drew her in closer, just to feel her breasts against his chest. He had missed them. "And, like we said back at the beginning of all this, I'm a greedy bastard. I've got no interest in sharing. With anybody. The kids get a pass with these," he ran his hand over her chest once before leaning down and giving her cleavage a loving kiss, "but they're the only ones."

A moan escaped Mercury's lips, louder than she intended, but instead of being embarrassed, she decided to just go with it. "I really like anything involving my breasts. They never got less sensitive after the boys were born . . ." She trembled when he ran his hand over her nipples again, and she moaned again. They had been large before she had children, and they definitely stayed that way.

"Hey, what a coincidence. I like anything involving your breasts too." He chuckled beneath her, and his hands roamed enthusiastically the more she described what she liked. He went back to kissing along her shoulder, before his hands slid to her backside to draw her closer to the part of him that wanted her touch most urgently. "One other thing I didn't know about myself is that I really like . . . non-standard places. So when it comes to things I'd like to try, that's definitely on my list."

"You do? That sounds adventurous." Mercury briefly thought about the places she had investigated with Logan at his request, but she didn't want to think about Logan. Now or ever. Eventually Mercury became brave enough to slide her hand down his body, and when she reached his rigid manhood, she stroked him confidently. "You seem very excited."

"Seem?" He said with a gasping laugh, his kisses became more intense the longer she touched him. "No, no, see, that hard cock in your hand? That means I *am* very excited. Nothing *seems* about it." He groaned under her kiss, his hips moving against her grip. He was exactly as he had been in her memory, which was clearer and clearer with every reminder of their time together.

Mercury wanted to laugh, but hearing him talk about his hard cock made her even more aroused. She stroked him harder and followed his groans in order to change her pace. It was such a turn-on to hear him groan and growl. "I like hearing how much you're enjoying this." She kissed along his skin as she continued to torture him. "I remember how it felt. How you felt. It's a good thing I'm not a small woman."

"It is a good thing." He agreed with another growl. He didn't want to think about Logan, and he found it strange that it was even a temptation, since for obvious reasons, he had never once been concerned about women comparing his own size with other men. He had yet to meet a woman he couldn't satisfy and then some. He reached down between their bodies and nudged her knees apart with one of his own. Orion's long fingers found her core with ease and a skill that her body remembered, even if it had been a long time for both of them. "I'm not the only one who *seems* excited."

Mercury gasped as his fingers explored, and she trembled a little as soon as he found the spot that was aching for attention. He had taught her a lot about her own anatomy, once upon a time. Now he was discovering her all over again. "I'm very excited. So very excited."

He loved the sound of her gasp, and the fact that she was being as . . . open . . . with him as she was. His fingers still knew how to tease her, how to elicit all the right reactions from her, even if the way he touched her was very different from Logan. Logan's touch had been the same as his personality, commanding pleasure into her body with every stroke, every caress, and leaving her no choice but to feel what he wanted her to feel.

Orion, on the other hand, was one to entice, to invite her along with him on the ride of her life. The first time they had been together, everything had been so new, they had both been more focused on the experience itself, than each other. Now, all he could do was look up in her eyes as he gripped her backside firmly and moved her directly over him. He wanted her to have all the control in the situation, at least for the time being, but he wasn't feeling particularly patient about it. "I want you, Mercury." His hands raked up her chest to cradle her face, his hips still bucking between her legs. "And I want you to have me. All of me."

She kissed him several times before she moved to do anything else, but then she let go of his hardness and gripped his shoulders with both hands before she threw a leg over him so that she could straddle him. Mercury lowered herself slowly, but once she felt the tip of him at her core, she moved quickly so he could slide into her all at once.

He cried out a little too loudly with two children a few doors away, but he couldn't help himself. Anna had been possibly the most limber and flexible sexual partner he'd ever had, but Mercury was . . . she hadn't been kidding about the fact they were a perfect fit. "Oh, sweet stellar fuck almighty, that's good." His hands gripped her breasts as she adjusted herself on top of him, and his breathing was already ragged as he managed to open his eyes and look up at her again.

Mercury's hair had partially fallen out of the bun on top of her head, but it made her look a little wild as she hovered over him, her red hair still beautiful even in the darkness. She was trembling a little before she moved, but he could see she was already enjoying herself as she started to rock on top of him. "It is so good." She gripped his shoulders tighter as she picked up the pace slightly. "You have a way with your words, Orion." She added with a smile, since she wasn't complaining.

"Words don't cut it with you." His hands made it down to her hips, rocking her against him. Just in a few moments, he could tell she was much, much more skilled with her body than she had been when they were last together. But he certainly didn't look at that kind of change as a bad thing. She knew what she liked and she remembered plenty about what he liked. He had absolutely no complaints. "Actions . . . fucking good actions . . . oh, that's more like it . . ."

Mercury was only encouraged to do more, to do better, whatever she could do every time he said he liked something. She wanted to please him, and while her relationship with Logan was different than anything she could have with Orion, the need to please would never go away. "You can tell me . . . what you like. Anything you like." She said between gasps as she rode him harder and faster.

He was in no condition to tell her much of anything, but when he finally did respond, she could tell he was holding off his own climax by slowing her down, one shaky breath at a time. When he could move, he rocked beneath her one time just because he couldn't stop himself, then pushed himself up so that he was sitting, without ever leaving her. Once he was upright, he took her legs and wrapped them around his waist, then bent his knees beneath her. His arms moved around her back to give him some leverage against her, but it felt like his entire body was enveloping hers, not in some kind of domination of one person over another, but as equals.

It was a different kind of tension between them than it had been a moment before, but the pleasure of it was a slow build, an explosion that was waiting to overtake them both whenever they chose to surrender to it. "This." He said as he kissed her, their hips rocking against each other to bind them ever tighter together. "This is how I want you . . ." he gasped, groaning between every word.

Mercury was moaning louder than she knew she should, but she truly could not stop herself. "Orion . . ." She had to dig her fingers into his shoulders to stop herself from climaxing, since she was so used to holding off until she had been given permission. "Orion . . ." She moaned his name again and she was surprised by the depth of emotions she felt in that moment. Mercury had fallen in love with Logan, but she had never stopped loving Orion, and she felt it again as she allowed herself to feel. Everything felt right, as it should, and she wanted things to stay that way.

"Don't hold back." He said in a breathless plea, not a command, as he rocked inside her. He only gripped her tighter as she fought her climax, taking a little more control over the way they moved so that he could thrust harder. He kissed exactly the spot she pointed out along her neck as he took her over, waiting to feel her lose herself completely.

Even though it wasn't a command, it was good enough for

her, and Mercury didn't fight the orgasm any longer. She cried out as he thrust into her and sent ecstasy through her body, and she leaned back in his arms as the powerful climax rippled through her body. She was moaning his name as the delicious feeling turned her body into a relaxed mess, but she kept her grip firm on his shoulders.

"Mmm." He moaned right back at her as she relaxed, still hard inside her and forcing her orgasm to send heated waves through every part of her with every move. "This right here." He said as he gasped for breath, his heart slamming against her breasts. "This is my favorite." As she leaned back, he leaned down to kiss over her collarbone, sucking hard enough to leave a mark on her to remember him by in the morning. "That moment when you've let go of gravity for a minute and you're all mine. This is my favorite."

Mercury didn't know why, but telling her that something was his favorite touched her, and she wanted to cry happy tears for the kindness and the warmth she felt because of him. She instead rocked her hips against his in hopes of giving him the same pleasure he gave her. "More than a minute." She said softly. "I'm yours for more than a minute."

He didn't fight her or try to take control back as she leveraged herself against him, and he leaned back on his hands to let her do as she pleased. After an orgasm like the one she'd had, though, it didn't take him long to follow. When she finally showed him mercy, he was panting for breath and clutching to her like she was the last stable thing in the universe. "Holy . . . fucking . . . hooo . . ." Orion couldn't catch his breath as he kissed along her shoulder, still shuddering against her as he gasped. "That . . . I . . . we . . . are gonna need to do . . . a fucking lot of that."

Mercury laughed a little, but she was still recovering from her orgasm, so she just collapsed into him, pressing her ample breasts into his chest. "I'm not tiny, but I'm still limber." It was her explanation for what she did to him to keep him going longer, and she was proud of the fact that she could please him that much. Not that she liked comparing herself to Anna, but she knew Anna's reputation and hers was nowhere near it. "I'll do whatever it takes . . . to please you, Orion."

He wasn't sure he was a fan of the tone of that, but he understood what was behind it, and he reached up to run his fingers through the wisps of hair that had escaped along the back of her neck. "That street runs both ways, baby. And you please me plenty just by being you. That's all I want."

She smiled as her hands let go of his shoulders. Mercury wrapped her arms around his neck and laid down on top of him. "I like it when you call me baby." Mercury kissed him again and ran her fingers across his cheek. "I still love you, you know. I still love you a lot. I never stopped. It just changed for a little while, but I love you."

"I never stopped loving you either." He settled back on the pillow on his side of the bed, since he could almost fit entirely on it if he was laying diagonally. "I'm gonna be spending a lot of time showing you exactly how much. I'm thorough like that." He groaned as the necessity of their position pulled them apart, but they didn't put any distance between them as they settled in beneath the covers. "You still prefer to sleep naked?"

"Mhm." She settled against him, using Orion as a pillow, since he was the best kind of pillow. He had his arms around her, and she felt secure and safe. "Sometimes I have nightmares." She said softly, though she wondered if he ever heard her wake up from one before. Mercury had only a couple since Logan left. "But maybe I won't if you keep holding me like this."

"If you do, I'll be here." He promised without hesitation or judgment. "If I'm not here, there's one of four reasons. I'm either handling one of the boys, in the bathroom, on the floor because I fell off the bed, or I've already woken you up in the most pleasant way I can devise. Otherwise, I'm going to be here all night, every night."

Mercury held him tighter as he promised he would be there for her. "You're amazing, Orion." She replied softly, and her eyes closed as sleep threatened to take over. "I love you." She repeated, since she wanted him to know that she was all in, and she wasn't looking back. There was no reason to look anywhere else except forward with Orion.

He kissed her cheek softly, his heart still pounding too hard in his chest to allow him to fall asleep right away, though it wouldn't take him long. He pulled the blanket up over them both, tucking it in around her tightly to make sure she didn't get cold. It was good to sleep in a real bed again, but nothing trumped the fact that it was Mercury's. "Sweet dreams, baby."

20

It was going to be one of the worst days of her life, but Margo knew she had to get through it to get to the other side. When she got home after being with Jela, it was early enough that everyone was still sleeping. She took a shower and went to bed, and the next day went without incident, except she barely talked to Liam, only to tell him she needed space. The following day, she had lunch with Jela and knew what she needed to do.

She had been dreading it all day, but she sent a message to Liam asking if they could have a private conversation away from the house. The message she had received back had been a vague acceptance, together with a mention that he would be down in a mechanical bay of the Labyrinth.

When she got to him, it was clear he had been working the entire day and possibly the one before, since she hadn't actually seen him, even though it was supposed to be her time with her husband. He was still working when she came in, and he didn't see her because of the angle he had to contort himself inside of the massive tunneling machine built from scraps.

She had seen him a thousand times in the hangar of their estate, working on the machines when they broke down, sometimes taking them apart and putting them back together just to see if he could find a better way to do it. It was Liam at his most common, though he looked less greasy at that moment than he usually did. Dirty, sure, and plenty sweaty, but he seemed to be doing more with the electrical work than the actual engine parts.

"Liam?" She asked gently as she got as close to the machine, since she didn't want to scare him and watch him get electrocuted. "This looks like a bad time." Every time would be a bad time for the conversation she needed to have.

"No, it's a fine time." He said in a sedated tone that she knew well enough to know was as close to depressed as Liam generally got. "Give me a minute, let me finish up with this circuit and I'll be down." He finished his work, then climbed down the machine carefully to get to the floor, all without looking at her directly.

"Sorry about the location." He grabbed a rag from nearby and wiped off his hands. "I would've chosen some romantic overlook up on the ridge, but despite what movies try to tell us, I don't really think that's a great place for a guy to hear that his wife is leaving him for another man. Tends to ruin the place permanently with bad memories." His tone wasn't angry, he was just stating facts. She had been away from the house completely for a night, and the nights that were supposed to be theirs, she had purposefully kept her distance anyway. He wasn't an idiot.

Even if he didn't intend to be hurtful, it was anyway, but she knew it was hurtful because the entire situation was painful no matter what. "I didn't know you knew about him. Not that I was trying to keep something a secret. I just refused to acknowledge my feelings otherwise until I saw Gwen. I'm sorry."

He shook his head and focused on the rag even though his hands were clean. "Costanza saw you with him at lunch. She told Rachel a little while ago, Rachel told me." The way he said it, it was just the way things worked in the world, but he eventually dropped the rag with a sigh.

"I don't think I've ever met the guy, but Connie seemed to know him. Said she was surprised, since he usually seemed like a pretty decent type. I told her it was a little more complicated than that." He finally looked up at her, and the sadness in his eyes was a little bit like trying to watch a rainforest build a sand dune. It wasn't a natural emotion for her husband, and it had never lingered for very long, with the exception of his brother's presumed death.

"Well, you shouldn't have had to hear it from Rachel or Connie, you should have heard it from me. Sooner than this." She said just as sadly, since she didn't want to cause him pain or see him sad because of her. "I can't do this, Liam." Margo's voice broke, but she knew she didn't have the right to be sad. She was the one breaking them up. "I'm not happy being one of three, certainly not one of four. I should have never agreed to it, if I didn't think I could do it, but god, Liam . . . I love you, I do, and I just . . . I should have let go, and I didn't."

He wasn't sure what to say about that, since it felt like there was nothing he could do or say that would make any difference. "You said it was going to take time." He said gently, his hands tucked into his pockets so that he wouldn't fidget with them endlessly. "Time to get used to how things go, time to settle in and . . . I thought with us getting out here, getting our own home, getting ready to go to Eleusis . . . I thought that was the kind of time you were thinking about." He stopped himself before he kept going, since obviously that wasn't the case. "I love you too, Margo. We promised each other that love was all that would matter." He said even more quietly. "Don't do this."

"It's not all that matters." She was already crying and she hated it, because she wasn't trying to make him feel bad. "Time isn't going to change the fact that I can't handle living this way, no matter if it's here, back home, or on Eleusis." Margo watched him carefully, but she didn't know how he was going to react. In anger and sadness or just sadness, she didn't know. "I can't keep wanting more and knowing I'm not going to get it. I can't be one of four, Liam. I won't do it. If this is the life that makes you happy, then you can have it. I'm tired of feeling like a piece of who I want to be. I'm not happy. I haven't been happy with this. I can't do it."

She could feel him give up on the possibility as she watched him, hopelessness about their situation replacing the sadness in his eyes, since certainty was only more depressing, given the circumstances. "What about Chrissy?" He asked almost sharply, since Chrissy at least had been something that he thought would help tie the two of them together. "From what I hear, this guy's never had kids. He's not gonna know what to do with her. At all."

"He'll learn. We all had to learn, and he will too." She never took her eyes off Liam. "But I also don't want to take her away from you, or her brothers, or Rachel and Bree. I . . . I don't want to punish her and take her away from her family. I don't know if she should spend most of her time with me when most of her family is you, the girls and her brothers."

His reaction to that bit of confusion on her part, at least outwardly, was not what she had been anticipating from him at the moment. He gave her a confused look as though she was some kind of stranger speaking a dialect he didn't quite understand, but eventually he just shook his head and dismissed it. "Work that out with Bree and Rachel, then. You're her mother and so are they. You can decide what's best between you."

She could hear notes of disappointment in his voice as he said so, but clearly since he had heard about her and Jela before that conversation, he'd had some time to prepare himself for it, however inadequately. "I didn't choose this life. Not at first, anyway." He took a breath, needing to get it off his chest. "If I had it to look back on, I don't know what I would change. I never meant to hurt you by accepting this when Logan sprang it on us, and I didn't mean to hurt you even more by embracing it when it turned into a life that seemed to work."

"I didn't mean to hurt you either." She was still crying, but she wasn't looking for sympathy. "When Logan came to me, I . . . I agreed because I wanted to be with you. I guess I thought before it all happened that maybe you and I would still work out, and . . . well, I was wrong. I was wrong to think that this life could make me happy, even if you're one of the most amazing men on this earth." She wiped at her eyes and looked down at the ground. "Obviously you and I want different things."

They stayed locked in that moment for what felt like their own personal eternity, since they both knew it was the last moment that would belong to the two of them together. He couldn't even open his mouth to speak, but it took more than a few deep breaths to work the words up from where they were caught in his throat.

"I want you to be happy." He finally said in the same soft voice. "That much is never going to change. I hope you're happy. With him. Wherever. I'm never going to stop wanting that for you."

Margo cried harder, and while she knew that the situation was painful, she went up to Liam and hugged him anyway. It wasn't as though they were separating because he abused her or she hated him, even though technically she had cheated on him. She still loved him, she just couldn't be with him the way things were. Margo didn't care if he was dirty or anything else, she just wanted to hug him.

"I want you to be happy too, I don't know what kind of life I'll have without Liam Bickford in it." She said between her tears. So much of her life was spent wanting and loving Liam that she truly didn't know how happy her life with Jela would be, but she had hope and the promise of something more.

It was hard to hold onto her at that point, but he eventually did wrap his arms around her, for what he imagined might be the last time. He put a hand along the back of her neck the way he always had to hold onto her, as he let out shuddering sighs against her hair. "Whatever it is, be safe, Margo."

Margo held onto him probably too long before she finally let go and backed away from him. She looked up at him, even though it was hard to do so. "I'm sorry." She said again, since she knew it was her mistake from the beginning for letting herself get involved in something she knew wasn't the lifestyle that she wanted. "I hope you're happy too." She waited until he met her eyes and she looked into his for just a moment before she turned to walk out and away. Her heart was breaking, but she knew it was right. The only reason she could ever convince herself to leave Liam was knowing that it was what she needed to do.

Liam stood in the shop and watched her go until her slight frame slipped out of sight around a corner. They'd had a family. They'd had a good family. They worked together, they made each other happy. They . . . he broke off in his thoughts as he watched her leave all over again in the recently-seared memories. He had never once in his life been unable to give a woman what she wanted. For the first time . . . the first time . . .

He had already cracked the massive wrench through two nearby machines and a support handrail before he even knew what he was doing, but he stopped himself afterward. He tossed the wrench to the ground with a heavy clang as he leaned on the pieces of the support rail that were left and let the stinging fade from his hand. When a few other guys from the workshop nearby came running to investigate, he just barked at them. "Everything's fucking great, get back to work! You never seen a broken rail before? Fuck you, and fuck off!" He snarled at them until they left him alone, and he hung his head afterward.

Liam had work to do. Even if one of the knots tying his family together had fallen apart, he still had work to do. There was a future to be had, and he meant to have it. If that had to be on slightly different terms, well then, so be it. What Margo wanted was more important than anything else. He went to a different station and picked out welding materials to fix the damage he'd done first, but there was still much more to do. Keep working. Keep busy. That was the secret. At least, that was what he told himself as tears slipped down from beneath the welding mask to evaporate before they hit the floor.

When Liam came home at the end of the day, he came home to a quiet house, but there were still baby items around the front room, there were plates on the table, food recently cooked, and Rachel and Bree were sitting quietly by the table. The children were either sleeping or elsewhere, but the cleaned up state of the house said that the children were elsewhere.

Apparently the two women were in deep discussion when he came in, but they both looked toward the door and got up when he stepped inside. Neither of them knew what to do, if he would want space or not, but together they approached him and hugged him on both sides as he stood at the door anyway.

"We were worried about you." Rachel said from one side as she looked up at him. "You're usually not out so late."

"We took the kids to childcare." Bree explained, since she didn't want him to worry about anything. They rarely used the child care services Logan had implemented, but today Bree and Rachel both agreed they wanted to focus on Liam. Their family had taken a hit and suffered some damage, and they needed to refocus on each other. "It's just us tonight."

He put an arm around them both, glad to have them close. The fact that they had worried about him only brought the events of the day surging forward in his memory. "I had work to do." He said in a quiet tone of apology, still holding them tightly. "Sorry if I still smell like oil. I had an engine blow up next to me. I showered at the shop and I think I got most of it." He was more sedated than either of them had ever seen him as he let them go to look back and forth between them. "I told her to come by and talk about Chrissy with the two of you. Did she?"

"She came by." Rachel said by way of information, since she knew Bree would be much more outwardly emotional about it, so she didn't really want to let Bree talk. Trying to stop Bree from doing what she wanted was like trying to stop a waterfall, though. "We discussed how it should be handled."

"And we told her that she's not going to take our daughter away." Bree said sharply, though she softened her tone when Rachel glared at her. "We settled on a schedule." She said a little more sedately. "Chrissy will spend most of the time home here with us. She'll spend two days, *maybe* three with Margo. She seemed to agree that most of Chrissy's time should be with us. Which is both infuriating and a little insulting, but she can do whatever she damn well pleases, I guess. We're not going to let the rest of our family fall apart."

He took Bree's hand and squeezed it, since he had felt exactly the same way when Margo hadn't fought to have her daughter, their daughter, with her. "As long as you've got it worked out, that's the main thing." Once he let go of Bree's hand, he reached up to rub at his forehead. When he looked back at them both he pulled them back in close, one arm around Bree's waist and the other around Rachel's shoulders, since she was that much shorter than he was. "I love you." He said to both of them at once, just holding them there for a while. "It's been a long day, and I'll be a lot less prone to breaking things after getting some sleep."

"We'll come with you." Rachel volunteered as they let him go, but it was obvious that they didn't want to let him go.

"We don't want you to break anything important. Like your leg. Or your neck." Bree said as she moved to kiss his cheek. "Let us take care of you, we want to tuck you in and all that gooey stuff."

He gave them both a look as they went through the house, but most of the lights were already off and he had locked the door behind him on his way in. He went down the stairs with a glance up in the other direction, since it was strange that there weren't any children in the house for the first time he could remember. Still, he plodded down the stairs and took off the spare clothes he had worn to the workshop that day. His wives had already gotten into their pajamas for their late-night chat, after all.

He didn't bother shutting the door behind him before he crawled onto the bed, pulling back the tightly-tucked corners of his sheets to make room for himself. It had been a hell of a day, and he had mixed feelings about it being over. He would have to wake up the next morning and still not be married to Margo anymore. His family would still be fundamentally different than he had started with. Of all the things he knew would change when they decided as a family to join Logan against the Consortium, that hadn't been a possibility he had considered.

Both of his wives moved around him to put away his dirty clothes and to help him get comfortable, and once he was settled, they both crawled in with him, one on each side. Rachel and Bree cuddled close to him and held tightly to him as they all laid on the bed together.

"My parents used to tell me that life was always going to be full of hard times." Rachel said as soon as the lights were off. "But they said not to let discouragement hold me back, because if you do, the hard times will stay and the good times will never come." She kissed Liam's cheek lightly. "The good times will come back for us, Liam."

Bree kissed his neck instead of his cheek and she just rested her head against his chest. "She always knows what to say. I'll just leave it at that."

Bree's comment got the tiniest, unenthusiastic laugh from him, but he put an arm around them both and ran his hands over their backs as they held themselves to him. The day had hurt, and when they said they were going to tuck him in, he had thought they were joking, but he was grateful for them being there with him.

"We'll be alright." He finally responded, holding tighter to the both of them in the process. He wasn't sure if he managed to convince either of them, but he was doing a better job of convincing himself as the hours went on following Margo's departure. He just had to figure out how the world worked when he had lost a third of it.

* * * * *

Logan passed the Twist room on his way to the child care center, and looked through to see Jason, hard at work as ever. There were a number of other scientists analyzing samples that had been brought back through the portal for various properties they believed were important. Anna had gone on an overnight mission through the aperture a few hours before, and it hadn't been the kind of outing that would really allow them to do much by way of exploring or sightseeing, so they decided that Logan wouldn't accompany her. It was going to be several more hours yet before she came home, but he checked in on their status anyway and sent a message to her communicator that he hoped would get her excited about the prospect, even if she was busy.

It was impressive to see the transformation that had taken place in the area known as the child care center in the preceding few months. Gwen had taken on the project and run with it once given the manpower to do so, converting a wide, open space into several smaller play areas for children of various sizes; with a hallway that led to dozens of tiny, remodeled sleeping rooms where children could rest monitored and undisturbed. The place was always loud and chaotic, but there were people in each of the small pods seeing to the needs of the children, and Logan could appreciate the way everything worked in its component pieces.

"Hey, Connie." He stepped in through the check-in counter, where all parents had to sign in or out their children. "I'm not here for the kids, I'm here for your boss, is she around?"

Connie looked back to see if she could see Gwen, but her boss was missing at the moment. "I know she was with your brother's kids, so maybe she's doing a diaper change or something. Hold a sec." Connie skipped away and found Gwen, who was indeed tending to all three of Liam's kids at once, systematically going through diaper changes to make sure they were dry and happy. Connie switched places with her once she informed Gwen about Logan, and within a few minutes Gwen made her way up to the front.

"Mr. President." She said with an easy smile, even though he rarely smiled back. "Is there something I can do for you?"

"Yes. Leave Connie in charge for a few minutes." He nodded toward the exit, of which there was only one, in the interest of minimizing the possibility of runaway toddlers. "Need to talk to you."

Gwen looked mildly confused, but then she yelled back to Connie that she was going to step out a minute and then she went out after Logan through the exit. "Is everything alright?" She immediately asked, since she was just as worried about his kids as she was about a lot of children she tended to. Leo and Lynnette were in the center being cared for, but James and Declan were not.

He walked in silence for a little while, hands swinging at his sides and no expression on his face, as always. He waited until they got farther out from the child care center into some of the emptier parts of the upper Labyrinth floors before he said anything.

"Two things we need to talk about." He began without looking at her. "First off, it was decided earlier today that you, or a representative you designate, should sit in on all council planning meetings from now on. Don't worry, they're just every single day at one in the afternoon until we get done arguing with each other." His tone didn't sound joking, but didn't sound harsh either. It was one of his more disconcerting middle grounds. "Someone made the excellent point that you are the person best qualified to make sure the interests of roughly a tenth of our total population are represented in any planning. Just because the rugrats are still monosyllabic doesn't mean their needs shouldn't be taken into account."

"I, um . . . sure, I can go to council planning meetings. I would think that my skills are better served taking care of the children, but I get it. Sure, I'll be there." She watched him carefully, since she was always trying to figure him out. "That one was easy. What are you going to say next?"

He stopped walking before he continued, in a hallway where they hadn't seen anyone for a few minutes. "Margo left Liam." The words were just as neutral from him as everything else, but the look he gave her afterward wasn't. "She seemed under the impression he was going to add a fourth wife to his family and it appeared to be the last straw for her already-strained patience. She moved in with one of the construction workers on the east ridge a few hours ago."

"Oh my god." Gwen said softly, except there was far more behind it than Logan would understand. She immediately felt nauseous as her stomach twisted in knots. "I . . ." She really was a homewrecker. Not only with couples that were shit to begin with, but good people with good families, people that loved each other. "Fuck." She finally glanced back toward the center. She had wondered why Liam's children were there when she arrived, but she didn't think too much about it. She certainly didn't think it was because Margo left. "Wow, um, did you talk to him? Is he okay?"

The look on Logan's face was actually readable for once as he looked back at her. He was surprised. Which meant he had thought she knew already. "Well, his wife just left him for another guy, that tends to fuck a person up. He stopped by to keep me in the loop on his way out of the machine shop and he's home now, I'm assuming. Rachel and Bree are bound to be pissed about it, but I'm sure they'll take good care of him."

"I'm sure they will." She agreed, but she didn't look at Logan again, since looking at his face made her feel guilty. So much guilt. If he knew it was her fault, she wasn't sure what he would do to her. Try to get her exiled? He would be furious. Her voice trembled a little with both fear and sadness. "I'm really sorry to hear that. I really am. We, um, we'll take good care of his children here, of course."

"Yeah, that part I wasn't worried about." He said in the same mostly-surprised tone. "You actually care." He looked her up and down as if she was a stranger instead of the person who'd been trying to flirt her way into his pants for the past year and a half. "I've seen you run through two dozen marriages at least and this is the first one I can remember you actually seem like you cared about."

"Thank you for making me seem like some kind of heartless succubus." She said softly and with a little edge, but she was trying not to be obvious that she cared *that* much, even though her heart was breaking. Also, he didn't know for certain she was involved in this one, which made his accusation even worse. "The men I've slept with were in relationships that were crumbling at their feet, and they didn't care about salvaging them. I flirt, they come running. Liam loves Margo." She said respectfully and a little reverently. "He loves her a lot. This is different."

It was Logan's turn for his voice to get softer, and he didn't look away from her as he spoke. "I should never have roped Margo into marrying him in the first place. I didn't know her well enough at the time to know that." He shook his head with a sigh, and looked just a little bit like Liam, when he was speaking like a human being instead of an authoritarian governor.

"None of the three of them were exactly excited about the idea of sharing the guy right from the start. Maybe Bree, but Bree is that fucked up in the head, she'd have been excited no matter what kind of kink was on the table. But they all said they could adjust to it, make it work. I thought that was what mattered. If you were involved with Liam, and believe me, I don't want to know if you were, then you didn't break anything that wasn't already coming apart. It's the same MO as you've had the whole time you've been here, it just . . . hurts more. Because they do love each other. It's just not a relationship that was going to last. He might've been in denial about that, but Larissa and I certainly haven't been these past few months."

Gwen just shook her head, since she wasn't about to admit the depth of her involvement with his brother. She wasn't going to admit that she loved Liam. She didn't want to say she had been the final straw in his brother's marriage, even if what Logan said was true. "I'm not involved with your brother." She lied, to a degree, because she was involved, but she wasn't going to be again. She wasn't going to make anything worse for Liam and his remaining two wives, since clearly she'd done enough damage. "You can't blame yourself for the choices other people made." Gwen said to relieve some of the guilt off of Logan's shoulders. "You arranged it, but they agreed. It's not your fault that it didn't work."

"That's the great thing about guilt. Spreads on nice and thick and there's always enough for everybody to share." He sighed and almost rolled his eyes. "Sorry, I forget sometimes that you're west coast and not country. That analogy might've been a little too much barnyard and not enough beach house for you."

He started to move back down the hall the way they'd come, nothing about his tone or his manner intimidating or blaming her in any way. For once. "Anyway, I just thought you should know. I don't think the general rumor mill has anything about you and him spinning through it, but my rumor mill is private, so I tend to get more detail than most. Or than I would like, most of the time."

"I would think you would know by now that rumors aren't always true." She said as he started to move away from her. "And I'm not just some bimbo, you know. I'm a person." Gwen didn't know why her eyes were burning, but she turned away from him anyway. She cared too much about what Logan and Liam thought, and she didn't want to care. She wasn't sure how both Bickford men had made her care about them in one way or another, and she was starting to remember why she steered away from any kind of permanent friendship or relationship. They were too painful.

He stopped when she snapped at him, and they weren't quite out of their private hallway when he did it. "I'm aware of that." He said to her back, since she wasn't looking at him. "And you're right, most rumors aren't true. I've heard some pretty creative ones about you that I know aren't true, for example. Just like I know you've heard some pretty creative ones about me that you may or may not know aren't true. People like us make things work, whether other people like our methods or not. If I thought you were just some dumb bimbo, I'd never trust you with my children, let alone everybody else's. I made an assumption about you and Liam when I heard about Margo. I'm sorry for that. That was me looking around for a reason and not looking in the right place. Hopefully you can forgive me on that."

Gwen paused when he responded to her, but she kept going after he asked for her forgiveness. He didn't need to be asking for her forgiveness, since he was right, and she was a liar. She broke up Liam's marriage, and she was as terrible as he always thought she was, even if he trusted her with his kids. "You don't need my forgiveness, Logan." She paused at the doorway back into the childcare center. "Have a nice rest of your day."

Logan was even more confused by that, but Gwen had always been back and forth about allowing other people to really understand what she was thinking. He didn't expect that to change any time soon. He just shook his head and went back to his office. There was no point going home if Anna wasn't there and the kids were being looked after. If he could get a few hours' sleep before the Eleusis mission came back in the morning, it would do him some good.

* * * * *

Xander leaned back on the steep hillside, his boots planted wide in front of him with Tatyana sitting with her back and backside pressed against his lap. It wasn't his favorite position to have her in, but it was in the top ten, at least. They were watching past a small cluster of cover trees at the compound in the distance, winding down its activities with the end of a Eleusis day.

There were fewer slaves moving back and forth between buildings as the sun crept lower in the sky behind them, casting the entire compound in a golden glow it didn't deserve. "You think they've gone so far as to actually tunnel between buildings? It would make sense, if they're building the whole place from the bottom up. And if they're as paranoid as they seem to be about leaving their precious walls. What's the point of going to a planet across the galaxy if you're not actually stepping out and exploring it beyond your own front yard?"

"Because they don't have enough people to do the hard work for them." She said bitterly as she shook her head, since anything and everything about the Consortium infuriated her. "They're waiting for the right opportunity to bring more slaves up here to die for them."

"It doesn't seem to me like there's much stopping them." He looked around at the vast nothing of Eleusis waiting for the Consortium to trample over it. He was just as infuriated with them as Tatyana was, but he was trying to understand their angle a little more. "I'm starting to think the only way we're gonna know is if Bickford is actually . . . right." He hated saying it out loud, even hypothetically, since he'd been one of the biggest opponents of Logan's plan from the beginning.

"We need to know why they're releasing their slaves to die in the wilderness. We've tracked two dozen of them in the past two months and no two of them go the same place or die the same way. They all just wander until they either run into something vicious, get poisoned, or simply starve to death because they won't eat. The only thing any of the fuckers have in common is that they don't come near the behemoth nests." They had learned, in their time on Eleusis, that their section of the hills was the only one thoroughly wooded enough to provide a lair for the behemoths for a dozen kilometers around. Apparently the slaves knew enough about the surroundings to avoid the place, if not much more than that. "They're the only way in I've seen yet, short of nuking the whole damn compound site and possibly turning the Twist into a black hole that kills all of us in the process."

"The only way we're going to find out what's in there is if we tunnel our own way in there or if we send someone knocking, asking to get captured, and give them a camera or something." Clearly that idea was ludicrous, but she didn't know how they could get in. "We could potentially set up a camera to capture the gate at all times and attempt to intercept someone after they have been released. However, we would have to get dangerously close to the compound."

"Dangerously close to anything doesn't bother me." He said thoughtfully, leaning back on one hand while his other was resting casually along the front of her shirt to hold her back against him, not confining her, exactly, just teasing her absently. "I could rig up a scanner to go along with the camera, to look for any kinds of electrical implants or transmitters while we're watching the gate. It'd be risky, since you can't always pick up anything and everything, but it'd be worth a try."

"I think we are going to have to take some risks." Tatyana finally said as she gladly leaned back into Xander. "We have been taking things too slow. People are starting to believe we'll never actually bring them here. We can't lose people to disbelief, we don't have enough as it is."

Xander took a deep breath as he considered the problem, since it was much easier to work things out with Tatyana than with the rest of the impulsive and defensive cowards on the so-called council. "What if we put the Twist down somewhere else here? Somewhere close enough that we can still get ground support to the compound when we need to attack, but where by the time the Consortium notices us, it'll be too late? We can start deflecting construction efforts to build our own base here the way we should've this whole time. Get people moving here, really living here. Being halfway across the galaxy would be a pretty huge reason for people to be on board with things, I would think. Bring a construction crew first to get a wall constructed, start building houses . . ." He shook his head, defeating his own point. "Or it'll take too long and they'll be all over us before we can even get moved in."

"Before we start building, we need to get more information about the compound. Which means getting closer to it and taking some risks. If we get spotted, we shut the damn thing down, since they can't pinpoint us from the compound. Though they will redouble their efforts to find us. We do that for a couple of weeks and then put it to the people to decide what to do. Councils, meetings, all that shit is the Consortium's way. I want to hear what everyone has to say. We all have equal skin in the game."

"More doing and less talking. I can always get behind that kind of plan." He agreed with a few more fond caresses.

She leaned back into him again as she looked out at Eleusis. "What do you want to put out there?"

"Put out where, exactly?" Eleusis was a big place, and he'd had plans for most of it for a very long time. "Here where the Consortium claimed their own turf? Not a damn thing. All I'm gonna put here is a crater the size of one of their space stations as a cautionary tale for future generations not to make the same mistakes the Consortium did."

Tatyana laughed at that. "I meant what do you want to add personally to Eleusis? Do you want to build your own house here? What do you see for yourself?"

He shook his head behind her, his fingers trailing lazily up over her neck and down along her breasts as they sat alone for a while. She told him never to hesitate about touching her or being with her in the ways he wanted to be, and he hadn't needed to be told twice. "I've been asking myself something like that ever since we actually got that fucking Twist working. I still don't honestly know." He reached up to give her a sincere caress along her cheek, gentler than the majority of touches that passed between them, but his tone was just as heartfelt.

"You were with Jason long enough for him to trust you in ways he and I never trust anybody. Especially him. So you already know he and I are both fully immune to Earth's problem. And you were tested for immunity markers. And of course you know I know that because I'm a nosy bastard." He looked out over Eleusis and chuckled. "This place is amazing, don't get me wrong, and I look forward to spending a lot of time here. But if we're two of the .001% of the population who have a long and eminently fuckable life possible back on Earth, it might be fun to work on getting the rest of the population transplanted here who want to be here and then just hang out on Earth and claim a few dozen countries' worth of territory. It has been a while since Australia had a king or queen. Might be worth reinstituting that."

"I don't know how they feel about Russians." She turned toward him. "Are you saying you want to fuck me even if I get old and wrinkly?" Tatyana had never thought of herself as old. She had never been that optimistic about her own life expectancy as a rebel.

He gave her a strange look when she asked that question, but it was a look she knew. It hid something. Something he didn't mind other people knowing he was hiding, but still, something he was hiding nonetheless. "You're not going to get old and wrinkly."

"You're probably right." She said without pressing the issue, since she didn't want to hear at the moment he thought she was going to die young, and she knew he would reveal his secrets whenever he felt secure to do so. Trying to push Xander into anything was usually not worth the effort. "Still. You're right. Earth is nice."

He shook his head again, since she misunderstood his meaning. He didn't blame her. "How old are you now, twenty-three?"

"Yes. You *are* nosy, aren't you?" Tatyana replied with a laugh. Obviously she'd never discussed her age, but he knew.

He nodded his acknowledgment, both of the fact that he was right and the fact that he was nosy, but he wasn't finished. "And how old am I? Or, if you prefer to start with something you're slightly more likely to think you know, how old is Jason?"

"Jason is twenty-eight. He told me to rub it in my face that he has years of experience on me." She seemed amused by the words and not angered, clearly she didn't exactly agree with Jason's assessment of the worth of his age.

"Jason is a liar." He said without any anger or venom to the statement. "But we've all had to be, so I can't really fault him for it, and neither should you." He spoke gently, but he let her go afterward and pushed her slightly so that she would turn around to face him. "You already know I'm the oldest of the Montgomery brothers." He stated the obvious, since she had known that ever since Jason had dropped the 'clone' bombshell on her during their relationship. "How old am I?"

She wasn't sure how to answer now that he said Jason was a liar. "Thirty? Thirty-three?" He looked older than Jason, but only marginally. She thought he looked a little older because he looked healthier.

His look seemed mildly amused by her guess, but somehow . . . understanding, as well, though there was no immediate indication of what it was he was hiding. He looked down at the space between them briefly as though looking for something explosive or gauging Tatyana's ability to attack him from her current placement. But there was no situation in which the tiny woman wasn't lethal, so he quickly gave up the effort.

"This coming October, I will be ninety-six years old." He said in a low voice, even though none of their companions were anywhere nearby. "This past January, Jason turned eighty-nine."

"You are not." The shock in her voice turned quickly into accusation. He was trying to play her for a fool, but she wasn't sure why. "That's not possible. Even CV-free, most space-dwellers only live to sixty or so."

"CV-free. Not CV-immune." He corrected gently, and nothing in his eyes was telling a joke. "And anyone born in orbit who is CV-immune will still die in their natural course. Same as I imagine people will here, as amazing as the place is." He glanced away from her in the direction their comrades had gone. "Maybe not Carl, but my understanding is that Mercury hasn't quite finished her genetic workup on him yet, so we're not sure what the Consortium packed into his coding."

He looked back at Tatyana to watch her process the information and take note of her reactions. "Most of the world, most of the universe, thinks CV leaves humans with two options; either die young, or evacuate the planet and lead a natural life. The people who created me and my brothers were trying, mostly, to create a third option. Design a person who isn't just immune to CV, but actually benefits from it."

"If you benefit from it, then won't leaving Earth harm you? There's no CV here or in space." She looked him up and down, as if seeing him clearly for the first time. "What does that mean, you won't die or age unless someone puts a bullet in you?"

"You keep saying 'you' like I'm the only one we're talking about here." He reminded her gently, but forcefully. "Immunes die on Earth because the Consortium has been killing them since my brothers and I were born. Eventually, an opportunity always manages to present itself, if the people in question don't know what's happening to them. Any kind of genetic test when they're young and the Consortium hears about it. Which is the whole reason your parents were drafted to the Initiative in the first place. For over a century, they've been riding the line between killing every Immune they could find and leaving just enough of us alive to provide fodder for the next generation. They kill us as children if they can, adults if they're notified late, and old people if they're only notified because rumors start to fly about some miraculous person who never seems to get any older."

Xander knew it was a lot to take in, but he cared about Tatyana, and her genes had the same Immune markers as he did. She deserved to know. "I met a guy once who told me he was a hundred and sixty. I had no reason to disbelieve him. He looked old, fairly grey, a little bit wrinkly, but still strong. Lived in a crazy holographic cave in the Pyrenees. Beautiful place, just a fuck-ton of traps to discourage guests. He was killed the year after I met him. But he's the oldest person I've ever heard of. The longest one of us to survive."

Tatyana cursed in Russian and shook her head. "So . . . if you and I had a child, what would happen?" Her expression changed momentarily and there was a flicker of pain at the mention before she hid her pain away quickly.

It wasn't quite the follow-up question he had expected, but he was sure she had her reasons for asking it. "They would live as long as we will. Provided, like you said, nobody puts a bullet through their skull. That's part of the reason the Consortium works so hard to weed out the Immune for the most part. Those traits are dominant. Any kid you and I had would be Immune, no question."

"I see." She said cautiously before she turned her attention away from him. "Well, it's good to know I'll have a long life if we survive this thing, I suppose." Tatyana looked out at Eleusis again and sighed. "I was pregnant once. I was angry about it for a long time, and then when I lost the baby, I felt terrible for not wanting it in the first place. It was part of the reason why your brother and I didn't last. One reason among many."

He didn't hide the fact that he was surprised by that, but he had been surprised about Jason having a child with his new wife as well, so it stood to reason he would have possibly tried it before. "I'm sorry you lost that." His hand moved up to her neck again, cautiously, since he had given her a fair amount to process. "It's a good reason to survive, I think."

"Maybe." She leaned into his touch a little more. Tatyana had never spoken about her unborn child to anyone other than Jason. "It was one of the few things he couldn't solve. There was nothing wrong that the doctors could find. The baby just didn't make it. Of course when the Consortium received notification about the genetic information of the baby, he and I were long gone so we wouldn't be discovered." She just shook her head. "No kid needs a mother like me. Especially when I didn't want it in the first place. I just want to do what I'm here to do. Life after that is a bonus."

"Then we can worry about who may or may not need a mother exactly like you once life is a bonus." He agreed before pulling her into a quiet kiss. "For right now, I just wanted you to know. There's a lot of life ahead of you, ahead of us, if we manage to pull this off. Which is all the more reason to take the right risks, if you ask me."

Tatyana was quiet again as she kissed him several more times, and she ran her fingers slowly over his full beard. "Why didn't Jason ever say anything about it?"

Xander's face showed real pain at that question. It wasn't strange for her to see him actually affected by things, but it was incredibly strange to see him affected by anything regarding Jason. Even so, there was real pity in his eyes as he looked back at her.

"Because he prefers to pretend he's only in his twenties. Everything I'm guessing he told you about his life is true, the way I'm guessing he told it. He was taken from the lab that created us when he was five. He escaped, he wandered off the radar for a while, eventually shacked up with some lonely woman who had a thing for young men. Stayed with her until his body began to recover from what the Consortium did to him, then came and found me. Spent long enough with me to know he hated me, which didn't take long, then went to Russia, and you mostly know the rest." He sighed, since he didn't like spilling his brother's secrets, but Tatyana did need the full story. "He escaped fully from the Consortium's tracking twenty-some years ago. So in the parts of his life that he counts as his own, he's in his twenties."

"I wonder if he'll change his mind again if things continue to go south with his wife." She said with an edge that said that she was irritated with Jason, but clearly she didn't care about having him. Not now that she had Xander. Tatyana l went back to kissing Xander for a moment before she said anything else. "Thank you for telling me the truth. I also wanted to talk to you about something else. Someone else, really." She paused and then looked into his eyes. "Mercury Bickford. Finnegan. Whatever the hell she is now. Her parents are looking for her, I've discovered a few notices floating through rebel information. What do we do about it?"

That was more news he hadn't expected. "He's the governor of Six, for fuck's sake. He sits on the Board. He managed to get a legitimate contact connected to us? Is he trying to draw us out of hiding or is he turning rebel himself?"

"I don't know. I know he's under 'review', so maybe he thinks he needs to reach out before he's discovered. Hell if I know." Tatyana tried to reason it out for herself. "Her own history is quite . . . interesting. She was created by a doctor who was later an Eleusis researcher, at her parents' request and commission, and she's also flagged as CV-immune, though nothing was ever done about it. Also, she was supposed to leave Nine before we were 'shipped' to Eleusis. She was never supposed to die with the rest of us. I saw the orders."

Xander considered the various possibilities behind that, but the consideration didn't take him long. "That means they either wanted her for a lab rat or her father managed to pull that string and keep her safe. Either way, there's something about her they still want. Whether it's just her parents or the Consortium researchers." He wasn't entirely sure what that would be, but he didn't question things he didn't understand. He saved the questions until he had more answers to narrow them down.

"We need to push back on that message and see if they're serious about finding their daughter. If they prove they are, and they're cooperative, they'll assist Jason in his consolidate-and-equip operation he's been working on for months. If not, they don't get to talk to their daughter."

"I'll talk to Jason about it when we get back. He's been a little checked out with everything going on here, I've been taking over the rebel communications. We'll see what he can do. If we have to use her as leverage, so be it. We need a leg up somewhere." Tatyana was all about the greater good, and one person being offered up was nothing if they could save everyone else. Especially if Mercury was that valuable to her parents and the Consortium. "We just have to make sure Logan doesn't find out."

Xander rolled his eyes, since he could rarely stand Logan. "He'd lose whatever shit can squeeze past whatever it is he's got shoved up his ass this week. I'm certainly not gonna talk to him about it. If they're helpful, we'll have good news for his ex. If not, we'll have no more news for her than we did before. Pretty simple."

"Nothing is simple anymore." She kissed him a few more times. "Come on, let's get moving. No use sitting around too long."

* * * * *

It wasn't often Anna heard anybody knocking on the front door of her house. It was even more rare for her to hear someone knocking when she herself was on the outside of it, but that was the sound she heard as she came around the last corner in sight of it. Nobody was home, as far as she knew, since Logan had taken the kids to child care earlier that day and he himself was down in the Shop conducting inspections. It all sounded like the kind of thing that would be boring even with coffee.

On her front porch, as she stepped up, was Oliver, a face she hadn't seen often since they'd reached the mountains. He was dressed in black nursing scrubs, as he'd been the entire time she'd known him, a testament both to his usual occupation and his morbid sense of humor about it. He had some kind of pot by the handle at his side, from which she could see steam still slowly escaping.

"Uh, hello, Oliver." Anna said warmly as she approached her own house, but she hoped she wouldn't startle him into spilling whatever he was carrying. "Logan's not home, he's overseeing something boring. I just got back from Eleusis. What's up?" She hurried toward her house, surprised to see a friend, but always glad to see one.

"Oh, hey." He did a double take between her and the door, then moved out of the way so she could get into her own house. "Sorry, I thought you and the rest of the team had been back a bit already and thought I'd drop by." He hefted the pot in his hand, from which she could smell an assortment of powerful spices, none of them natural to the Americas. "Special delivery from Mr.

and Mrs. Ahmadi. I'm told that there was something of an altercation between Mrs. Ahmadi and some kind of ferocious beast the other day on Eleusis, which you resolved with what I can only imagine was extreme prejudice. She's not yet able to walk on her own, but she did want to cook as a beginning of her gratitude."

"Oh, that's nice of her." She opened the door for him so he could set the pot down. She immediately went to his side so she could open it and get a good sniff. "Yeah, the thing that attacked her is good and dead. I have a couple of gashes myself, but only because it swiped at me a few times. I hate things with fucking claws." Anna moved to get some bowls. "Do you want to sit down and eat with me? I'm starving."

"Well, I . . ." he shrugged and nodded his acceptance. "I suppose it was something of a tag-team effort. You killed the big thing that tried killing her, and I've been pouring antibiotic agents on every scratch she has for the past twenty-four hours. Your save might have been a great deal sexier, but I think mine still deserves soup."

"Definitely. You definitely deserve soup." Anna grabbed a loaf of bread, served him up a bowl and set it down before he had any chance to back out or sit elsewhere except for right next to her. "Your day doesn't sound nearly as exciting as when you came with us on Eleusis the last time."

"Yes, well, that particular type of excitement included me falling headfirst down a blind embankment and giving you a run of stitches, if I recall?" He cleared his throat, since it had been the tiniest bit awkward due to the placement of Anna's injury, but he was a medical professional. He could handle a little awkwardness. "How, um, how has the bum healed up, by the way? There's really no polite or decent way to inquire about someone's ass, I realize, but that was the best I could do on short notice."

"My ass is unstoppable." She laughed as she ripped up a piece of bread to soak up some of the soup. "It's healing up just fine. I've had stitches a million other places, and my ass was bound to suffer sometime. You were very patient with my whining."

That made him laugh as he took some of the bread. "Believe it or not, that wasn't the first time a woman's whined while I've had her ass in my hands. The other times I wasn't stitching it, but you get the general impression. It was nothing new for me." His eyes shot wide in momentary shock at the spice of his first bite, but he recovered fairly quickly with only a small cough. "That kind of kick, on the other hand, leaves quite an impression."

"No joke." She let out a cough of her own, followed by a laugh. "It's good, though." Anna looked over at him and pushed more bread in his direction. "I did swipe some cheese, maybe that'll help tone it down." She got up and rushed to their small refrigerator and brought back the cheese. "I'm sorry to hear you've had whining women. You seem like you can handle an ass just fine."

"I've handled my fair share." He was grateful for the cheese, which did actually help, and the rest of the soup was less of a shock once he knew what he was getting into. "I never, um, picked up quite the legendary status for it that some have in their lives, of course." He grinned over at her, since it wasn't the first time someone from back home had teased her openly about being the district slut.

Living without her reputation for so long had been a change of pace on Nine and in the mountains, but it was a change of pace that had not continued once most of her childhood friends and acquaintances were back in town. Especially when she got back together with Logan. "In all candor, I'm just happy to be more or less out of my usual job up here. Stitching asses, particularly one as easily patched as yours, is far more pleasant work than cleaning them all day long for those who can no longer do so for themselves."

"I would imagine it is definitely an improvement." She laughed as she nibbled on another piece of bread. "I embrace my legendary status, thank you very much. I worked hard on building that. There was a lot of cock involved." She replied with another laugh, since there was no reason to be gentle about it. She was a reformed slut, and she knew it, along with everyone else. One of the few men she never slept with before was Logan, and now she had him too.

"Wasn't intended as an insult. Of all the things your reputation has claimed for you, an unstoppable work ethic when it comes to sex has always been near the top of every list of emphasis." He chuckled as he ate, finding the conversation strange, but at the same time, refreshing. It wasn't often that he found someone quite as comfortable stating the blazing obvious as she was. "When we're finished with the soup, I'll need to have a look at your stitches. I assume if there had been any trouble with them, you'd have told me, so I'm going to assume it hasn't been bothering you?"

"You're really here for a medical visit? You're a tricky one, aren't you? You bring me soup, you chat me up with your cute accent, then you tell me you have to check my injury? Talk about left field." She teased as she looked over at him. "I haven't had much pain. I mean, I expected some. My butt got sliced. But yeah, you can look at the stitches."

"Soup and chatting first. You can strip later." He smiled over at her, since for him, her teasing was refreshing. On the whole, he'd felt like something of a leper around the mountain stronghold. He understood it, of course. No one wanted to hang around by choice with a man who watched people die professionally, even if he was just working as a general duty nurse at the moment. Anna was one of the few people who didn't treat him that way, along with the rest of her family. "Have there been any new developments with Eleusis? I'm scheduled to go back next week on a visit, but Xander didn't tell me much. Only they imagined there was an increased risk of them needing a medic. Which did not engender enthusiasm on my part."

"No, no new developments that I know about. We generally go, investigate a new area, plant tech and whatever else, and come back home. I think they're intending to send a team for a longer stretch, so that's probably why they need a medic with them. If a team is going to stay for a few days, you never know what can happen." She didn't automatically assume she was going to be on said team, but she liked to try and be involved with Eleusis as often as she could. "We are trying to figure out what's going on inside the Consortium compound too. It would be good if we could get in there and do some serious recon. Mostly so we can fucking clean out the place. All of the high leadership with the Consortium has a vacation home in that compound."

Oliver looked almost as nervous about that prospect as everyone else to whom she had mentioned it, but he eventually shook his head with a low whistle. "I *have* always had a soft spot for beach-front property. Don't really have much of that worth having back in Britain." He gave her a nervous smile and took a drink to clear out the most recent assault of the soup's spices on his senses.

"Getting into the compound and cleaning house is all well and good, but the trick is going to be somehow shutting off the Twist on their side. To do that, we'd have to get into Prime. Or wherever it is now, if they've moved it. If we can cut off their supply line somehow, great. If not, anything we do inside their compound is asking to get steamrolled as soon as they can send troops through."

"We'll see what the plan ends up being. That's beyond my paygrade now. I don't usually go to the meetings, I just go to Eleusis and do what I'm told." She smiled over at him and then finished off her soup. "I also have a secret stash of chocolate. Do you want some?"

"Wow." He said with a slow grin, looking her up and down. "You must've enjoyed getting your ass sewn up a little more than I thought if you're of a mind to share chocolate. I'll not say no to that."

"Oh, don't flatter yourself. I just like company." She said with an easy smile as she ran off to get some of her hidden stash and she came back out with a few pieces for them to share. Each was individually wrapped in shiny paper as she set them on the table. "Alright, I'm gonna eat one of these and let you check my ass, but only because you're a medical professional." Anna replied with a grin as she opened one of the candies.

"Only because? Now you're hurting my feelings." He took one of the offered candies and unwrapped it, but nodded at her shorts afterward. "Drop 'em. Panties too, if you're in the habit of wearing such things." Which he doubted.

"Not usually." Anna moved so her backside was facing Oliver before she pulled down her pants. No surprises about the lack of underwear. There was a bandage over the stitches, just because she didn't want them to get irritated or infected. That would be bad. "Is it going to be a good-looking ass scar?"

He took the bandage she'd put in place off slowly, which only meant the tape had that much longer to make her skin sting in ways that were mostly reminiscent of having been thoroughly slapped. His hand lingered along her hip to hold her in place as he inspected her thoroughly. "It's not quite a lightning bolt, but if I was laying on my back looking at it, that's the shape I'd guess."

He ran a thumb over them, and it didn't hurt, exactly, her skin was just more sensitive as it was in the process of healing. She heard him reach into his pocket and pull out a small pair of scissors. "Hold still. They look ready to come out." He reached up like he was about to start, then pulled his hand back and slapped the uninjured half of her ass fairly hard before she felt him get to work on her stitches. "Didn't want the other side of you to feel left out of all the fun."

Anna yelped in surprise, since she really wasn't expecting the slap."You are a dirty nurse, do you know that?" She laughed afterward, though, since it was pretty funny. "You should not take advantage of a woman with her pants down, you know. That's not nice."

"Wouldn't have been as funny if your pants had still been on." He clipped at her stitches with a deft hand, but highlighted exactly how deft his hands were as they rested directly on her ass. Once he was finished with them, he didn't immediately pull away, instead running the pad of his thumb down the length of the cut to inspect it. It still stung a little with pain, but so did the slap on the opposite side. "Yeah, I'd go with a lightning bolt if I had to choose. Maybe pitchfork from the way it sort of frays right down here at the end. I suppose it would depend on my mood at the time. We'll see what it looks like when it's completely healed in a few days."

"Well, take a good look. You're only getting one more gaze at the legendary ass when you give me a clean bill of health." Anna straightened up a little bit. "I need to avoid getting my ass cut open again. That hurt."

"I'll bet it did." He checked it over one more time, just to make sure there was nothing going wrong with the wound itself, but everything seemed to be in order. "You know, I could just sit here and say that you have to keep your pants off. You know, for medical reasons."

Anna laughed and pulled up her pants. "There's no medical reason for me to keep my pants off, Doc Oliver." She shook her head. "You're just a dirty scoundrel who is trying to discover what rumors are true and which are false."

"Oh no. I have no doubts whatsoever about which rumors are true." He chuckled as he sipped at his drink and took one more piece of chocolate while she was busy with her shorts. "And if you have any trouble with my tableside manner, then you may feel free to report me to the ethics board that issued my license. Oh, wait . . ." he grinned over at her as he unwrapped the chocolate.

She turned around and snatched the chocolate straight out of his hand for that comment. "That's for smacking my ass, Doc." Anna popped the chocolate in her mouth and grinned at him. "I don't take abuse from anyone."

"Please. That ass has taken far worse than a slap before and done it for fun." He got up when she took back the chocolate, and leaned across her to pick up her finished bowl of soup to take their dishes to the sink. "If you go on that extended shot to Eleusis, chances are I'll be stitching up some other parts of you pretty soon. You take more risks than anybody I've seen over there."

"If you could see everywhere, you would see the scars I already have. I take a lot of risks, but sometimes it's necessary. Not always, I will say, but things are more fun if you take a risk." She shrugged and followed him to the sink, since he certainly didn't need to do her dishes. "I want to go, but I don't know if Logan would want me to go. He thinks I go too much as it is."

"Well you know why they keep sending you back." When she approached the sink, he moved to get in her way, dancing back and forth as he rinsed out both bowls and washed off both spoons. "You keep noticing things other people on those outings don't. Everybody else they pick is always mission-obsessed, looking for exactly what they're told to see. You're the one that stops people before they step into a toe-biter hole because they weren't looking. You're the one who smells a behemoth nest at fifty meters and makes sure everybody avoids it. You've saved the whole team a dozen times I can think of without even trying. So yeah, they're gonna keep sending you back as often as they possibly can. They've got a vested interest in keeping people alive."

"It's all that sneaking around I used to do. Gotta pay attention to the small shit, or you're gonna get busted." She said with a laugh before she washed out another dish and put it on the towel to be dried, but her smile faded slightly. "I'm not interested in dying to get to Eleusis, clearly. But I get frustrated with the slow progress. Logan says we have to be extra careful, but people are getting angry. We've been here for over a year, going on two. This isn't the life anyone wants, and there are a lot of people who want to leave if we're not really going to get to Eleusis and stay there."

"Yes, I've heard . . . plenty of that." He said a little ominously, then finished his dishes and turned around to face her, leaning against the sink. He was significantly taller than she was, but not quite as tall as Logan, so he didn't seem quite as far out of reach. "I've actually, um, well, that's awkward, but still. You should, um, you should tell Logan that the number of people wanting to leave here and just . . . go try to live a normal life somewhere else . . . is growing. Pretty quickly. I haven't been sent with a message or anything, but it's not going to take long. Another few months, maybe. At most. Unless things start moving faster."

"Things *will* move faster." She said with as much assurance as she possibly could, since she wanted people to know that she was doing her part. "If people are electing you as some kind of messenger, then I hope you'll help me convince Logan and everyone else to move faster. We can't keep tiptoeing around the Consortium."

"See, I'm in a strange position. I think moving faster would be preferable, but I also understand the need to tiptoe. The Consortium is . . . well, necessary to fuck with, but not to be fucked with, at the same time." He shook his head. "Because the other half of my message, if I can be said to have one, is that most of the people I've spoken to are . . . very . . . worried . . . about killing innocent people. Collateral damage. Word of the slaves in the compound has gotten out, so no one is a fan of Xander's strategy of nuking the place from above. Same goes with Prime. Millions of people live there, not all of them demons."

"I know." Anna said gently, since she knew Oliver's own family had been collateral damage she still felt responsible for. "Orion's parents are up there somewhere, and his sister. That is Leo's family. I don't want to start shooting blindly, but I also don't know how we're going to get anywhere without using force. No matter what, we don't have the upper hand. So what do we do? We can't go faster without some people dying. That's . . . I just don't know how it is avoidable. I hate it, but I don't know. It's hard to feel generous about the Consortium when they were using us as lab rats. I mean, they were going to fucking shoot me off in a defective ship, pregnant, and watch me burn. It doesn't make me want to play nice."

"Oh no, I . . . understand that. I'm not interested in playing nice with them. I'm just . . . only interested in being cruel to the right people, I suppose. I know that's not realistic and I know there are going to be unintended casualties. I . . . hope we can keep them to a minimum." Oliver shook his head and sighed, since he knew how stupid he sounded. "If I knew of a way to get in and sabotage them to make it easier, to weaken the right people, I'd be first in line. But I don't. My one talent in life is stitching up women's asses."

"You're far more talented than that. Give yourself some

credit." She replied softly before she looked at him with a sad expression. "I feel terrible every time I think of the lives that have been lost that should not have been. I'm sorry, Oliver."

"What's past is past." He said in a tone that clearly hadn't placed anything too firmly in the past yet. "At least here I'm working to set it right. I'd rather be doing that than anything else."

Anna nodded and watched him for a moment before she turned away. She didn't know how to help him, since she was part of the reason why his wife and unborn baby had been killed. The guilt was terrible sometimes, but there was nothing that she could do. They were gone. "Do you, um, want to take home some of the soup? It's equally yours."

"No, it's unequivocally yours. You handled it much better than I did. You go on and keep it. Thank you for sharing." He was about to move away, since he understood the invitation to leave quite clearly in her offer, but he stopped, looking down at her with a quiet smile on his face. "A lot more lives are going to be permitted to exist because of you than have been ended by anything that's happened. The future is always more powerful than the past. It's not worth dwelling on." He gave her more of a smile, then tapped along her hip near where her cut was along her backside before he drew himself away. "I'll be back in a few days to get another look at that. You can say last, but I'm not willing to be quite that absolute about it yet myself."

Anna raised an eyebrow as he said that and moved away from her, since she found it confusing. Anna was with Logan, and he knew that. Was he saying that he was interested in her anyway? She grabbed the last piece of chocolate off the table and followed him to the door before she grabbed his hand gently and put the chocolate inside his hand. Anna knew she and Logan were working on things, but she didn't know what it meant, exactly.

She and Logan were in a weird limbo, loving each other, but not reunited spouses. Did it mean they were *only* seeing each other? Did it mean that they were trying to figure everything out in a casual situation? It didn't feel casual, but she didn't know for sure. She knew that they weren't 'married' because neither of them wanted to get married again until they were absolutely sure they wanted to be together and nothing else. So if they weren't married, what were they? Why did some attention from Oliver have her spinning? "I'm still sorry. You never deserved what happened to you. I wish there was something I could do."

He took the chocolate, but he took her hand more than he took the chocolate she had placed in his fingers, as he smiled down at her. "Chocolate is always a good start. So is good company." He spun the chocolate through his fingers a few times as he held onto her hand loosely. "Besides, I'm the nurse here, I'm rather accustomed to making sure others around me have what they need. So it's really me who should be asking you what it is you need right now."

"Does anyone ever ask you what you need?" She asked genuinely, since she was concerned he was a man working his life away without actually living it. They were fighting for the right to keep living their lives, and he needed a reason just as much as anyone else. "Everyone needs someone to look out for them."

"Someone did ask me the other day, actually. Which is why they're working on making me a new pair of scrubs down at the shop." He grinned back, leaning near the door. "I need this rebellion to win. I need it to destroy the Consortium that destroyed my family and billions of other lives. That's my need. If that happens, then everything else is about details. And I can work with details."

"Alright." She squeezed his hand once. "I'm here for you. Even if I'm the one person you probably don't want around, I'm here for whatever you might need." Anna let go of his hand after that, since it was a little awkward, but he was her friend. Wasn't he?

His face darkened completely at that, and he shook his head. "There is one person and only one person in this world I despise being around. And I promise, you are not that person." His smile returned to his face just to reassure her, but then he turned around and headed off her porch, back in the direction of his own apartment in the distance.

* * * * *

When he got to his unit, Oliver sighed and leaned back against his door for a full ten minutes before he was able to move. He went through the simple living room into the kitchen, where he left his small personal device on the counter. All of their devices had been put through every ringer known to man upon arrival, of course, and they had been assured (threatened) that every communication they attempted to make would be monitored.

427

The method he used, though, he wasn't sure the technological geniuses on the council would be aware of. The communication method was under such an old protocol that he doubted anyone was bothering to monitor it any longer. The ancient nature of the program involved was both its strength in being undetectable and its security to him, since he knew only the information he placed within the message would be conveyed. It was simply too basic to do anything like track his location.

Doctor,

This is my notice to you that I will no longer be supplying you information on the Prince family. You lied to me when you promised revenge for my family. That is not something I will tolerate.

He didn't have to sign the communication. She would know who he was by the return electronic address. He didn't feel the need to give her any more information about his thoughts or his decision as possible. He had wasted too much time and done too much wrong already.

21

Ever since the Twist became operational, Jason had, to everyone's surprise, spent much more time away from the Twist itself. He was still connected to it whenever it was active, but more and more, he had permitted Xander and Tatyana to take over the tasks of monitoring and maintaining the device he had once thought would always be his alone. They were the ones to make it work in the first place, and Jason had to admit that it made sense for them to be the ones who did the most work as a result.

Their work allowed him to spend most of his time watching the Consortium, navigating their systems and making certain he remained a few steps ahead of their security capabilities. In a twist that he seemed thoroughly amused about, even though no one else seemed to get the joke, he actually wrote some pieces of the Consortium's own security programming. He had them installed in their systems, giving him a permanent back door, so long as the code remained active.

Jason had taken to working mostly at home, especially over the warmer months of the spring and summer. Even while he was at home, though, it was apparent to him how things in the mountains were changing. Every time a mission went to Eleusis for more research and reconnaissance, he felt people's faith in the project falter. More and more, people were clamoring for some kind of action, something other than just another day in the mountains.

But all the leadership had to tell their people was that they didn't know enough, that they couldn't expose their position or their potential to the Consortium without being sure. People seemed to understand the desire to stay alive, but they still called for action. Jason couldn't say he disagreed with them. The summer came and started to go again, and in his mind, they were no closer to truly moving against the Consortium.

For him personally, on the other hand, the means by which

the three of them worked as a family slowly changed. The more he was home, the more he watched Bekah, and the more Jessie was able to go out and take care of her own business. Usually she would come home and Jason would be sitting back in a hard plastic chair with his feet up on a stool, holograms all around him for use in his actual work, other holograms scattered around the legs of his chair as toys for their daughter. She had learned quickly that they weren't actually substantial, but she still batted them around and spun them and occasionally tried to chew on them as she stood awkwardly bracing herself on one leg of his chair.

Jason was laughing for once as Jessie came in through the door, in his usual position, then nodded down at Bekah on the carpet where she'd plopped down from the chair leg. "I programmed one of her stars as a quiet siren. I may not have been very clear about my definition of quiet. Shocked her pretty bad, but she laughed about it after a while. We missed you."

Jessie gave him a small smile and came in with a casserole wrapped up in a small pan. She was in charge of food supply again, so she sometimes spent time in a unit that was designated for food preparation. There were some families who needed assistance due to the nature of their jobs, so she was often making meals from the supplies to take to those who didn't have the chance to prepare things for themselves. Otherwise, she was in charge of what came in and went out for food supplies. "I brought home a meal that wasn't needed. It's still warm."

"Sounds delicious." He worked on closing up his tasks, bits and pieces of the code he worked on disappearing one by one. She could still see several frames that looked like surveillance, a few locales on Eleusis as well as some places with cold corridors that were obviously in orbit. Even when all his own work was closed down, he left those running, just to keep an eye on things. He got up carefully, making sure Bekah was fairly stable against his chair. "Pretty busy day?"

"Yes, pretty busy. Usually when a group comes back from Eleusis, we take food to them unless they say otherwise." Jessie put down the casserole dish. She spooned some chicken casserole onto a plate for Jason and grabbed a loaf of bread from the countertop. "What about your day?"

"Not bad, all things considered. I finally managed to narrow down some blind spots in their surveillance." He slid into his seat at the table with another glance back at Bekah. "I think she's getting another tooth, she's been pretty cranky whenever she's biting on something. But she helped me bring down a supply drone carrying a food shipment up from Brazil to the Republic of Texas. I scrambled it and redirected it to our friends out in Baja. So I call that a pretty good afternoon's work."

"That is good work." Jessie agreed as she plated her own food and set it down on the table as well. She skipped the bread for herself. Jason was skin and bones, and she was not, after all. Even though she'd lost a lot of weight since Rebekah had been born, mostly due to not eating a lot and working often. "I think you're going to need to exploit those blind spots sooner than later. I heard some ladies today talking about where they're going to move from here." Jessie pulled the high chair up to the table and put together a small bowl of food for Bekah.

Jason's good mood dimmed, but it wasn't as though it was the first time he'd heard it. "People need to be just a little more patient. When things get moving, they'll get their fill and more of action and chaos. They should enjoy this kind of peace and safety while it lasts."

"Telling them what they should want isn't going to make any difference, unfortunately." Jessie was still moving around and she put Bekah in the high chair without pausing once. "Hopefully they have more patience than it sounds."

"I hope so." He got up while she was strapping Bekah in her seat, and went to a cupboard to take out a small vase with small, brilliantly-blue flowers in it that had nothing to do with Earth. He brought home the occasional gift for her from Eleusis on the few excursions he joined, and one look at the flower petals told her they were nothing the Rockies would ever produce, even in summer.

He put them on the table out of Bekah's reach, then scooted his chair closer to Bekah's so he could help her with her dinner. "It'll be at least late fall before we're able to proceed with anything. It'll take that long to have suitable shelters and barricades in place. Not much point in moving before we have those kinds of things to pin the Consortium in and fall back on."

"I'm not saying I disagree. Only what I hear." Jessie pulled the flowers closer to admire them before she smelled them. "These are beautiful, thank you."

"They reminded me of you." He smiled over at her and spooned up a small bit of food for Bekah to try, which didn't succeed on the first try, as usual, but be had more luck on the second. "That one blouse you wore last week with all the shades of blue. Just made me think of that."

"You remember what I wore last week?" She asked curiously as she finally sat down to eat a little bit. Her feet were killing her, but she rarely complained about it. Jessie smiled at Jason after a bite. "I don't think *I* remember what I wore last week."

"It made an impression." He smiled over the table at her as he took a first bite himself between feeding Bekah. "Anyway, there's a whole patch of these flowers about two kilometers east of where we've got the Twist focused. Bunch of downed trees in the middle of a meadow with all these flowers growing up from what used to be the roots. Beautiful place." He beckoned over a small piece of interface from across the room, and flicked through the images until he found the one he was looking for, which showed the meadow in an explosion of blue among the damp gold of the tall grass that covered most of Eleusis' surface. "And nothing tried to kill anybody there, so, you know, fond memories."

"Wow." Jessie said with a continued smile as she looked over the images. "That is really beautiful." She looked back over at him and reached out to run a hand along the top of his. Things were back and forth between them, since sometimes things were getting better, and sometimes they took a step back. It was still a rebuilding time. "I'm glad you thought of me."

"I didn't get any pictures of it, but if you climb a tree on the north side, you can see the sea off in the distance." He pointed out the place and set the image to the side of the table to give Bekah another bite of the food. "It's the nicest spot I've seen yet for a house, I think."

"This is where you want to put a house?" She looked at the image a little closer and she swiped at it to turn it every which way. "You better put a lot of rooms in this house. But keep the flowers."

"A lot of rooms?" He asked with a smile, flicking the image to superimpose a blueprint of a home on the landscape where he imagined it. It was settled back into the trees, but essentially made the entire meadow into a kind of front yard with the spray of blue flowers as a centerpiece with a path of stones laid out around it. Clearly the idea was more than a passing fancy. It was a more substantial house than the one they currently lived in, though nothing approaching the palatial dimensions of the Bickford estate. "How many rooms were you thinking?"

"At least five or six." She looked over at Jason with Bekah and she paused in her meal to watch them for just a moment. Jessie and Jason had their problems, but she never once wanted to leave him for someone else. Even if she wondered if that made her a little bit pathetic, considering what they had been through. "I'm not getting any younger. And we're doing well, working on things."

"I think so." He agreed, returning the caress as she reached out for him. "I've been trying to be around more. To keep this, the two of you, first above everything else. I hope that's been something that actually . . . comes across?" They were still fairly hesitant with each other, and it was something very new for Jason, because he was accustomed to being the one who set the terms of the relationships he had or walked away from them. He had no desire to walk away from Jessie, and that meant the two of them figuring out how things were going to work together.

"Yes, it comes across." She smiled and moved close enough so she could kiss his cheek. "It's been great having you home more. I know Bekah likes it too." Jessie looked over at their daughter and back at Jason. "Maybe . . . do you want to sleep in the bedroom tonight?"

"I'd like that." He had been sleeping in *a* bedroom the entire time they'd been in the house, but it had been a long time since he'd been particularly welcome in *the* bedroom with Jessie. He put an arm around her waist to pull her down to sit in his lap as he fed their daughter, his hand moving over her side to hold her close. He wasn't going to give up the chance to hold onto her if one was presenting itself. "I miss you. Especially at night."

"I miss you too." She said softly as she looked at the flowers again. "It's not that I've been trying to punish you or anything, I didn't want to complicate things. If we weren't going to work, and I think we will . . . that kind of intimacy just makes things worse." She wasn't saying that they needed to have sex or anything, but intimacy in general had been hard for her with Jason since she didn't know what to think about him for a long time.

"I'm scared I'm going to end up alone and bitter like my mother, and I don't want that." The longer she sat on his lap the more he realized how much weight she'd lost and how much effort it was taking her to hide the change in her body. Clearly she'd been doing more than just exercising a lot with her work.

It had been a long time since he'd had a chance to touch her that way, and her clothing was still the same as she'd had the entire time she was pregnant with Bekah, so it was all exceptionally loose on her. She didn't miss the mild surprise in his expression as his hand explored her waist. "I've never met your mother in person, but I already know you're nothing like her." He gave her a quiet glare, though clearly he wasn't angry.

"The woman has been . . . vocal . . . on the net about your sister's relationship. And she's been . . . obnoxiously silent about any kind of criticism of the Consortium following the fall of Nine." He smiled a little after that as his hand moved down along her spine. "You are neither obnoxious nor silent, and I love you that way."

"I'm glad you're okay with me the way I am." She felt self-conscious as usual as his hand roamed her body, since it had been a while since he'd really touched her at all, other than holding hands, kissing, and cuddling. "I want to be a wife you're proud of, but mostly because I am not going to keep my mouth shut and I don't want to accept anything less than a happy life. Not after everything we've gone through. After everything *I've* gone through."

"I am proud of you." He said quickly, since he always had been, even when she hadn't thought he had a reason to be. "I'm proud to be with you. To be Bekah's dad. I wouldn't want either of you, or the other five or six still waiting in the future," he said with a quiet smile, "to accept anything less than a happy life. You're better than that."

Jessie leaned into him a little bit more and she wasn't looking at him when she spoke next. "What did you think our life would be like when you picked me?"

He pulled a few of Bekah's toy holograms closer and hovered them around the girl's head so she would be entertained, then turned his attention fully on Jessie. How long had she been losing weight, exactly? His arms remembered there being a great deal more of his wife the last time he'd held her this way.

"I thought our life would be . . . chaos, for a while, but not because of you. Just because of the war. I thought we would get away from the Consortium, live on our own out here for a while, fight the fight to take down the Consortium, then retire to Eleusis. I imagined . . ." he leaned back in his chair and grew bold in the ways he touched her, closer to the way he touched her when they first got married.

"I never imagined things would be perfect, but I knew the cause of most of our problems would be my secrets and the fact that I'm a difficult person to get along with most of the time. I imagined going to bed with you every night, being glad to wake up next to you every morning, and a whole lot of nights with gasping and grasping aplenty between sunset and sunrise. I imagined you with a smile on your face that I was at least partially responsible for."

Jessie wasn't really sure what to say to that or to his bolder touches, so she sat there and let him touch her however he wanted. "I don't think you're difficult to get along with." She finally said, though she was speaking softly. "I know I can be difficult. I was worse before." Worse before, when she was less broken. When she had more spitfire and attitude. "I know why you would say that, but I love so many things about you, it doesn't seem like you are difficult."

"You weren't more difficult before." His smile was a little easier after a comment like that. "I've always gotten fired up about all the wrong things in life, it seems like. So I was glad to be with someone who was passionate about life. I still am." He reached up to caress along her jawline and her neck, and even that part of her was changed without him noticing. "I still see it from you once in a while, but mostly when you don't know I'm watching. Heaven help anyone who messes with the way you run the storehouse. I feel sorry for the idiots who try."

"I'm just bossy and I need a place to channel it." Jessie replied with a small smile before she turned her attention back toward the fact that he hadn't really eaten much before she interrupted him. "I don't want your meal to get cold. You should eat." She moved to slide off of his lap so that he could get back to it. Rebekah had already made a bit of a mess, but neither of them minded. It was fun to watch their daughter explore, even when it was food.

He pulled her back into his lap when she went to get up, so she knew he wanted her there with him. "It's a good meal. But it's not as good as you." His hands moved over her sides, and he leaned in to kiss the side of her neck along her collarbone, sighing against her skin afterward in contentment.

Jessie shivered a little as he kissed along her neck, and she definitely didn't want him to stop. "I wanted you to come into our bed so many times. I hate sleeping alone."

"So do I, now." He kissed her again, moving up along her neck in ways he knew she liked, even though the feel of her in his hands was very different. "Before I met you, I always thought I slept better alone. Now . . . not at all." He pulled away to look up in her eyes. "I've wanted you every day and night since we met. That's never changed."

"I still find that hard to believe." She replied honestly as she glanced over at Rebekah before she looked at Jason again. "I'm very different from your previous girlfriend . . . I always will be."

"And I'm grateful for that every single day." It wasn't the first time he said so, but he felt like he was always going to have to say it at least one more time. "I don't want you to be her. Or anyone but yourself. Just like I hope you don't want me to be like Xander or any of our other brothers."

Jessie shook her head quickly. "I don't want you to be Xander or anyone else. I love *you*." She turned in his lap so she could face him completely, and she kissed him warmly. It had been some time since she had kissed him so openly. "I love you. I miss you so much. I'm tired of feeling so fractured. Our family is the only thing that's worth anything in this place."

"Here or anywhere else." He agreed, kissing her back hungrily. She was close enough to him on his lap that it was no secret just how much he missed her, but Bekah was beginning to fuss. "Please tell me you don't have anywhere else to go tonight?"

Jessie shook her head and leaned back so she could back away again, since she didn't want to push anything. "I don't have anywhere else to be. I'll take care of her, you've been with her all afternoon."

"That's not what I meant. I'm just hoping she goes to sleep early." He let her go that time, and turned back to his food with a vengeance. Once she had her father feeding her again, Bekah seemed a little more entertained, but Jason's eyes were still on Jessie. "You've been on your feet most of the afternoon while I've been rolling around on the floor with this little diva playing with light. You'll definitely be off your feet once she goes to sleep, but even before that, you should relax. I can take care of you while she gets her daily dose of cartoons."

"I don't need to do that. Even though I do need a shower at least. I don't want to disgust you as soon as you see me naked for the first time in a long time." Jessie didn't go back to her meal, and instead she went and dumped the rest before cleaning up the dishes. "It will just be a quick shower."

"You never disgusted me." He said quickly, since feeling the change in her and seeing her throw away food was starting to spin wheels in his mind that frightened him on her behalf. "It's not an emotion I've ever once registered in your direction."

"Never? Not at all?" She found that surprising, especially considering the state she was in after being tortured. "I never thought you were taking pity on me or anything, but I always thought we were more of a 'personality' driven couple than a physically driven one."

He glanced down at himself before he said anything, and didn't look her over at all. "In . . . the case of my particular physicality and your own drive on the subject, I can understand why that would be the case." He finally did look her over as she stood near the sink with her plate still in hand, and he paused only to slip another bite into Bekah's mouth while she was distracted with her luminescent toys.

"You've never believed me when I told you I thought you were beautiful. Not at first, because we had barely met, then not later because you thought it was impossible that I could be attracted to Tatyana, who by the way, *was* more of an attraction of personality and principles than a physical attraction, and then later when you got farther along in your pregnancy . . ." he had gotten angry with her once when she was late in term with Bekah, over her lack of belief when he told her he was still very much attracted to her. It had been part of the beginning of the wedge that had only gotten wider between them since.

"I've wished . . . more times than I can easily remember, that I knew how to convey to you how attracted I am to you, and have been for the entire course of our relationship. If I believed in a god, a way to show you that and have you believe me would be first on my list of things to ask for. Followed by world peace and the destruction of the Consortium, though those two things go pretty closely hand in hand. I love you, Jess. I've always wanted you. That hasn't changed. At all."

"I love you too." She looked back at him as she finished up her task with the dishes. "I couldn't figure out what I had done or didn't do when things started falling apart. Intimacy was one of the first things to go, and I assumed I had a lot to do with that. I know you were busy. Everyone is busy. Not everyone's marriage was falling apart like ours, though."

"It was nothing you did or didn't do." It felt like it had been so long since they actually talked openly about their relationship, but it was a kind of awkward he wanted to work through. "It was my fault, not yours. I felt like we had to have the Twist active to move forward, to keep momentum, but of course even now that it's open, almost nothing has changed except possibility. I was obsessive, and I was an idiot for it."

"Things might have been different if I had responded differently." Jessie was still clearly feeling as though she was at fault, partially, for the decline of their relationship. "I've never looked like Mercury or even Anna. I wondered if I did, if you would want to be home more."

He looked across the room at her in silence for a moment, then gave Bekah another bite of what was on her plate. Without saying anything, he crossed the room to where she was standing near the sink and spun her around into a hard kiss, pressing her between him and the countertop tightly. He wasn't a violent person in general and had never been particularly harsh with her in the bedroom unless it was something she asked for. The touch wasn't angry, but it was forceful. It left nothing to the imagination when it came to how much he wanted her or how much he wanted to be with her.

"I'm looking at you." His hands grasped at her sides tightly. "I'm not looking at anyone or so much as thinking about anyone else. When I've been lonely and missing you at nights these past months, it's your picture that's in my mind. Nobody else's. Now or ever."

Jessie didn't respond immediately, but when she kissed him back, it was just as hungry and needy as his kiss. "I don't want to lose you." Her voice cracked as she talked again, and her kisses went back to tentative. She really was afraid she would end up alone, and he and Bekah were her entire world. "I need you, Jason."

"I'm not going anywhere." He promised with another passionate kiss, bending her backward a little over the counter as he held her. "I didn't know . . ." he took a quick breath when the kiss broke, his hands moving up over her to caress along her jawline. "When I first picked you out, toyed with the matching system to make sure we were together, I had no idea what we would be. I knew I wanted you, and I knew I had hopes of what we would be together. From your history, I thought you would be an incredible friend and partner in all this, and you have been every step of the way. But I didn't . . . I lived for a very long time without considering the fact that people loving each other was even possible, let alone feeling it for myself. I never understood it. I still feel like I'm learning, most of the time. But I know there's nothing I wouldn't do for you. I know I want to tear the Consortium out of the sky just because there's a possibility of them hurting you or Bekah. My vendetta against them used to be personal. Now I just want my family safe. And you will be safe, if my life or death has anything to say about it. You're not going to lose me. You're the reason my world keeps spinning."

It felt good to hear she meant so much to him, because he meant that much to her. Jessie kissed him back passionately, since it made her happy to hear she was the reason he believed in love. He was the reason she believed in love too. Even though it had been a lot harder than sleeping around with her sister's husband, it was better. Real. Tears slid down Jessie's cheeks, but she ignored them as she held tighter to him. She knew her mentality wouldn't be fixed overnight, but she felt confident in the moment, and she wanted their relationship to get better and stronger. "I love you so much." She said against his lips. "You're my world. You and Bekah both. But mostly you."

So long as Bekah was quiet and distracted in her high chair, Jason felt no need whatsoever to move away from where he was. His arms wrapped around the small of Jessie's back to hold her against him almost tight enough to crack her spine, and he groaned under the kiss that followed. She could feel his hands tremble a little as they moved over her, his caution and anxiety over the encounter a far cry from the brash confidence he'd had when they first met. Neither of them had had anything to lose when they chose each other. Now they had each other to lose, and it was too much to risk for any reason.

Jessie continued kissing him as he held tighter, since she didn't ever feel threatened by Jason, even though his anger and his outbursts at times had caused her to distance herself. Only because she knew what he was capable of, not that he ever hurt her. "Maybe . . . we can take Bekah to the childcare center?"

Jason smiled under the next kiss after that suggestion, and nodded with his nose against hers. "That's easily the best suggestion I think I've heard all year." He kissed her again before taking a half step back. "I'll get her things together and take her up. You said you wanted to get a shower."

Jessie nodded and stood there against the counter even though he had taken a step back. She watched him for a moment and stepped up into him again with another kiss. "I'll be waiting for you, alright?"

"Then I won't be long." He promised, cleaning off their daughter before scooping her up in one arm and heading for the little girl's bedroom to gather some of her things for the night. It had been a long time since Jessie had seen him smiling quite that way, and Bekah responded to it, since daddy looked funny when he was happy.

Getting outside was always a treat for Bekah, which made Jason feel mildly guilty, since most of her young life had been spent not just indoors, but underground. He knew a little too much about the impact the environment could have on a child's psychology, so he walked at a fairly sedate pace along the path leading from his house up to the entrance to the Labyrinth.

As he got closer, though, he saw Xander and Tatyana coming out of it, and increased his pace a little. Anything he could do to spend fewer moments around his brother and ex-lover, he would do. "Evening." He didn't want to completely blow them off. He still had to work with the two of them, after all.

"How's my favorite niece?" Xander asked in amusement, looking Bekah over with a legitimate smile on his face. Seeing Jason with a child had taken some getting used to, but after talking through the possibility of the future with Tatyana, he felt a little more optimistic about the choices his deformed little brother made.

"She's your only niece. And the sooner I can teach her to roll her eyes at your terrible attempts at humor, the better." Jason didn't move away from them as they stood off to the side of the path, since technically Xander was . . . well, there was really no common word for a father's clone, but uncle would do well enough. "What do you want?"

Xander's eyes narrowed. "Why do I have to . . ."

"You only talk to me when you want something, even to see Bekah. What's happened?" Jason had somewhere very important to be, and he wasn't going to be derailed by small talk.

Xander's jaw took on a tight set that confirmed for Jason that he'd been right. The bigger man shook his head before he continued, looking back at Bekah instead of her father.

"We just got word a few minutes ago that the Consortium's Earthside base outside of Algiers has been overrun and gutted by 'rebels,'" he used visible air quotes, which seemed to amuse Bekah to no end, "who have now supposedly disappeared. Surveillance, weapons tracking on what was stolen, none of it is working. And none of your toys are able to find anything to reconstruct to follow whoever did it."

He looked back at Jason after tapping Bekah's forehead to make the girl laugh, the look on his face a great deal more serious. "Only one person any of us know who's ever been able to hold a candle to that tech brain of yours, brother. And she's the only bitch I've ever known who's crazy enough to take on Algiers by herself." He glanced quickly over to Tatyana with a smile. "Present company excluded."

Tatyana smiled over at Xander and turned her attention back to Jason as well. "Eventually she's going to realize that she can't do this alone, just as we know that we can't. Have you heard from her?"

"No." Any trace of his good mood was shattered by that kind of news, and his mind spun through his near-perfect memory to think back to the last inventory of armaments he'd seen from Algiers. "Fucking hell, Algiers . . . If she blitzed that place and somehow made off with even half of that weaponry, she's got . . . she's got everything. She's got As, Hs, EMPs, harmonics, rails . . . not to mention truckloads of . . ." he shook his head in disbelief. "There's no way she has enough people to pull off a job like that. We took out most of her followers last year! Where did she get the manpower to pull out something like this?"

"Probably the same way we did." Tatyana replied as she turned her attention to Jason's baby temporarily. It was always difficult for her to see him with a baby, knowing what she knew and what she went through. "We need that stuff, if she has all of that. That's the only way we're going to get anywhere with the Consortium."

"If she has all of that, she just jumped over all three of us to the top of the Consortium's most-wanted list." Jason held Bekah in front of him facing out, though it was just as uncomfortable for him to be around Tatyana with a baby as it was for her. "And we're just barely below the Consortium itself when it comes to people she'd love to wipe off the face of the Earth. Only difference is, now she could actually do it."

"She's not going to wipe us out." Tatyana said as though Jason was being absolutely ridiculous, because he was. "We're still on the same side of all of this. We just approached it differently. She needs us, and we need her. Let us know if she reaches out to you."

Jason looked back and forth at the two of them incredulously. "Neither of you is that stupid." It sounded like a statement of fact, but behind it was a desperation for them to remember that fact. "She is unhinged. Now thermonuclear-level unhinged. She attacked us on Nine, if you'll recall, and jeopardized our entire operation in the process. You got shot fighting her!" He nodded down to Tatyana's leg. "She is insane. Clinically, not hyperbolically. I wouldn't trust her with a sharp knife, let alone the firepower to end human civilization."

"We don't have a choice if she has the control and the firepower we need, Jason. Not to mention the trained fighters. What would you have us do, send out a bunch of farmers with their pitchforks? We need more and better weapons, and we need more people. Crazy or not, we need her."

"Then you're replacing the Alperts with Carmina. And frankly, I'd rather be ruled by the Alperts." Jason shot back with the same incredulity. "If living with these refugees and doing something else with my life besides obsessing about the fight has taught me one thing, it's that farmers with pitchforks are the only assholes qualified to run anything. However much you two hate Logan, he's the only one who cares about people. That includes me. And it sure as hell includes Carmina. She can't be trusted, and we need someone we can't trust right now like we need one of her hydrogen bombs dropped on top of the Twist."

"We need the upper hand, and we need to finish this." Tatyana said sharply before she sighed. "We just wanted to let you know what happened, not start an argument. You have your job, we have ours. Now, I'm going to go back to my unit. I'm not going to argue any longer."

"You . . ." Jason looked at both of them in frustration, then shouldered his way past his brother, who was only staying silent because he knew he wasn't going to change his mind. Jason made his way through the Labyrinth without any trouble to drop off his daughter, thanking Gwen quickly for watching her and giving the little girl a goodbye kiss as he planned to pick her up in the morning.

He didn't head back to the house as quickly as he had originally thought he would, just because he wanted to make sure he put all thoughts of Carmina out of his mind. The woman and her insanity had no place in his life or that of anyone else who was attempting to live a life of sanity, however improbable that was in the world. He eventually got home and locked the door behind him, locking out the entire world besides Jessie, as far as he was concerned. Nothing else mattered.

"Jason?" Jessie asked softly from the bedroom, since she thought he would be back sooner. She peeked out of the room wearing a bathrobe and her expression relaxed when she saw him standing by the door. Her hair was in two braids because it was still wet, but a smile returned to her lips when she saw him. "I was worried. Is everything okay?"

He returned the smile as he kicked off his shoes and headed up the wide stairs toward her. "Just a line to drop off and pick up kids." Which was true, there had been, even if it wasn't the full reason he was late. "Good shower?" He asked as he got up to her and took his time on the last step, leaning in to leave a kiss deep in the cleavage that was partly exposed by the bathrobe before he finished climbing the stairs up to her lips.

"It's nice to feel clean again, if that's what you're asking." Jessie replied with a short-lived laugh, since his hands started to wander and his kisses were so intense she was dazed by them. "It would have been a better shower with you there."

"Mmm. We'll have to make sure to use up the rest of the hot water later." He threatened with a quiet growl against her lips. "Of course, that means I have to make a mess of you again first."

Jessie whimpered against his lips as he kept kissing her. He really knew how to kiss, and he knew what she liked. She had missed it and missed him so much. Jessie wrapped her arms around his neck and ran her fingers through his hair at the base of his head. "You're such an amazing kisser. I missed your kisses." She pressed herself into him even more and it wasn't hard for him to see she was entirely bare underneath the robe, clearly waiting for him to come home.

He stayed there with her in the upstairs hallway of their home as the kisses flared between them, his hands wandering as they pleased over her robe just to savor the feeling of her. As soon as he touched her skin, it would be a frenzy. He wanted to cherish her and the chance he had to be with her, along with the somehow-scandalous feeling of being out in the open in the hallway. It was their own house and no one else would be walking through any of the doors, but it still felt good to be so open with her.

He put his arms up when she drew his shirt up over his head and tossed it aside, always a little self-conscious about the mess life had made of him, but too focused on Jessie to care. "I missed these." He ran his hands up over her breasts, but then grinned as his hands moved to her back to tug on her braids, since he missed all of her. He tugged on her hair just enough to tilt her head back a little to let him attack her neck. "You haven't done these in a long while. I have some very fond memories of these braids from early on."

Jessie could only moan in response as he kissed along her neck and teased her breasts, especially at once. "Every part of me missed you, Jason." She said his name with the same needy tone he could feel in her kisses and her touch. Her hands wandered along his exposed body as if she was memorizing him all over again. Jessie didn't pause at the scars, they were just a part of him. She just wanted him. Her husband.

They didn't have far to walk back to get to the bedroom they were supposed to share but never had. He'd been in the room often enough to get his clothes and put away the wash when he was home, so it wasn't as though he was completely new to the place. Even so, as he pulled her back toward the bed and tossed her down on her back to assault her, it was definitely a new place and what felt like a very new experience. He groaned as her hands tugged off his pants, which were nothing more than simple shorts, since he'd been home all day to begin with. They didn't provide much of a barrier between her and the part of him that ached the most.

Jessie was more comfortable with getting him naked than getting herself naked. Jessie didn't try to get out of her robe as she pulled his shorts away quickly so she could touch him and run her hands along his stiff manhood. "I missed this too."

He groaned even louder when she took him in hand, and it was all he could do to keep himself restrained for the time being. It had been a very, very long time, and he had never had a habit of pleasing himself on a regular basis. The way he had her on the bed, his hand had easiest access to her leg, and he slid it up beneath the robe to get a hand on her as well. His fingers had forgotten nothing in the time they had been apart.

Jessie moaned louder as soon as he touched her, and she

arched her body into his hand, since she obviously didn't want him to stop. "You . . . haven't forgotten . . ."

"It's you." He said breathlessly, holding nothing back as he watched her eyes widen. "Anything about you . . . is nothing I'm ever letting go. Fuck, Jess . . ." he moaned against her lips as she stroked him, every part of him shivering. There were times when he thought he would have to go the rest of his life without touching her. But every caress and every heated breath of hers on his skin was erasing those moments of doubt from his mind.

"I love . . . how you touch me." She continued to squirm as his fingers teased her clit. Jessie was becoming less and less concerned with him seeing her naked the more that he distracted her by touching her in all the right ways. "I love listening . . . to you say things . . . like that."

The more she moaned and the more he could feel her own inhibitions fall apart, the more frantic Jason became. He pulled his touch away from her only long enough to nearly rip the knot out of her bathrobe and shove the fabric aside, his touch roaming over her bare skin as he kissed her deeply. He moved in to press the full length of their bodies against each other, facing each other on their sides as they writhed together. It was a warmer world, a happier world, when he had Jessie with him.

She shivered as soon as she was fully exposed, but she tried not to think about it as she pushed aside her robe and moved closer to him. "I should let you know . . ." She said between gasps. "If we do this . . ." She didn't know why she said 'if', since she didn't think there was any going back now, but she said it anyway. "I might get pregnant . . . it's . . . the right time . . ."

"Good." He said without any hesitation, pulling one of her legs across his waist to put himself closer to her core. His hands were grasping at her backside to drive himself closer to her. "I want you. I want our family. I want this. More than I've wanted anything in my fucking life."

"I want you too. More than anything else." The way she said it was almost a plea, a plea that had so much behind it, a need for him, and a hope things wouldn't go bad again, even though she was well aware there might always be problems. No couple was perfect, after all. Her leg hooked tighter around him and she pushed herself the rest of the way to him so her heat was pressed against him, clearly waiting for him to take control. "I love you, Jason. I want everything to be okay again."

He moved the rest of the way on top of her and pushed her knees wide before he slid inside her. He cried out when she had him, his eyes closing involuntarily under the assault of pleasure, but there was no hesitation in him when it came to pleasing her. When they had first gotten together, they had been wild and fiery, demanding from each other the kind of satisfaction they had never gotten anywhere else. The way he moved against her brought the memory of those first days with a vengeance. He had been too long without her, too long away from her, to hold himself back when it came to finally being with her again.

Jessie cried out as well when he was inside of her, and both of her legs wrapped tightly around him as he drove into her. It was incredible, and she wondered how she had gone so long without his touch, and not much teasing had been required. They were both instantly ready to ignite with each other. He hadn't been with anyone else and neither had she, and clearly both of them had been needy without each other. "Oh, Jason . . ."

He slammed himself into her until her head was hanging off the side of the bed beneath him, something from their past that had been a favorite position of hers. His hands raked up over her breasts as his hips rocked into her. He needed her, he needed every moan, every gasp of pleasure that came from her, like he needed to breathe. Nothing else was more important than that moment. Nothing else in any world could ever be important enough to take him away from her. Never again.

"Fuck, I love you, Jess." He gave a breathless half-laugh as he reached up to caress along her neck, still shuddering with pleasure.

"Mmmm." She replied at first, both from the touch on her neck and his words, but eventually she smiled at him. "I love you too." Jessie yanked him into several more kisses before she said anything else. "I've never loved anyone the way I love you."

"This isn't going to happen again." He promised with a kiss to the inside of her breasts as he moved her onto her back again, just so he could worship her as he pleased. "Don't get me wrong, I'm finding I love make-up sex as much as the next guy, but I'm not going to let it get to that point again. I can't be without you the way I have been. Not again."

Jessie reached out to run her hand along his cheek and her eyes studied him for a moment. She knew that he was being completely genuine in his words. She had no reason to believe he wasn't ever genuine with her, but the worry was still there in the back of her mind. "I can't be without you either. It was so hard. I didn't want it to be that way, I just needed to know we were going to work through our problems."

"I . . . will work through . . . fucking string theory, if it means I get to come back to this bed and this body every single night." He ran his hand over her roughly, grinning when she shivered at his touch on her breasts. "Those are still on high alert from having Bekah, I see."

"I think they're stuck on high alert." Jessie said with an exhausted laugh as she looked at him. "I love looking at you. I missed this so much." She pulled him back into a kiss, since she needed all of his kisses. "I love you so much. I can't say it enough."

"I love you too." He kissed down from her lips to her sensitive breasts, teasing her nipples with his tongue. "And I love all of you." He said with another look over the entirety of her, unspoken meaning behind his eyes as he took in her somewhat diminished frame. "I knew you lost weight after Bekah was born, but I didn't realize it had been this much."

Jessie wasn't feeling nearly as relaxed as soon as he said anything about her size, and she tensed up after his comment. "I wanted . . . I wanted to be beautiful for you. I wasn't keeping your attention before, and I wanted to fix it."

He kissed her heatedly as he felt her tense up, until she began to relax again. "I thought you were gorgeous the day we met. I thought you were gorgeous the entire way through your pregnancy. My attention was elsewhere because I'm an obsessive asshole, not because I've ever once not been attracted to you." He rained kisses over her neck and breasts, holding her tightly against him to allow no space whatsoever between them.

She couldn't really think as long as he continued that kind of attention, and it had her wanting him all over again. "I hope that it's okay that I look different now, then, if you liked me how I was before."

"I like *you*." He added another kiss to her breasts, then leaned back to look in her eyes. "Every kind of you, at all times. I don't want you to think you've got to do something to make that happen. Because you don't."

Jessie ran her fingers through his hair, but she didn't say anything right away. "Are you sure? I'm not trying to gain weight back, it's just . . . I don't think I can keep this up if I end up getting pregnant, and . . . I really fucking miss chocolate."

That made him laugh, and he turned his face to kiss the inside of her wrist. "I will personally make sure we get this house better stocked with chocolate. Though I may have to do some sexual favors for the head of the storehouse to make it happen." His kisses started moving lower along her breasts as an obvious threat. "I hope you don't mind. It's for a good cause, of course."

"How scandalous." Her body arched as he kissed along her breasts. "Well, if you do this to her, she might give you everything you ask for. You're amazing with your mouth."

"*Everything* I ask for?" He chuckled, and his hands moved down over her thighs to push them apart. "I'm a pretty demanding guy. That might end up being a lot."

"A lot?" She asked breathily as he kept moving down her body. "I'll . . . do my best."

* * * * *

When they went to bed, he had left his pants and his communicator out in the hall, and he'd had no reason whatsoever to give them a second thought since. It had been hours . . . glorious, well-spent hours, over the course of which they had thoroughly exhausted each other, and so when he heard his communicator going off in the hallway outside the bedroom, he groaned in his sleep and lifted his head only enough to glare at the doorway. He looked over at Jessie, but she was a heavy sleeper. It was a fact he was grateful for, since it meant she never had an ongoing reason to dread who might be waking her up and for what reason.

He kissed her bare shoulder as he got up, sliding reluctantly off the bed. He closed the door softly behind him before he picked up the communicator. No one who had the ability to call his device would be insignificant, or would be doing so frivolously, so he answered it and held it to his ear. "Whoever this is, couldn't whatever this is wait until it's fucking daylight?"

"Is it not daylight there?" Carmina's voice rang through all too clearly, and she sounded smug for every second she ever spoke. "I thought you would be glad to get my call, White."

He had been mostly asleep when he picked up the phone, but that voice out of all the voices in the world had him brutally awake. He stared into the darkness for a moment in the silence, just to make sure he wasn't having a bad dream. "The last conversation we had contained a promise of a slow and painful death if I ever see you again. I'm not sure how that would lead you to think I'd be happy to get your call, even with thought processes as deranged as yours."

"You need me more than you need to kill me." She said simply before she continued. "We need each other. I'm sure you have heard by now what we have done."

"Speaking of 'we'," he cleared his throat and tapped out a simple command on his communicator to begin attempting to trace her location. It was a long shot, since Carmina was very nearly as proficient with programming as he was, but he had to try. "Who are these new friends of yours, exactly? We killed the last few batches of friends you managed to make, as I recall."

"Why are you trying to trace me, White?" Carmina replied with an amused tone, since she thought he was being cute. "They're rebels, just like you and me. We always make new friends, don't we? You have new friends too, don't be surprised that I do too. Except mine aren't farmers."

He didn't know or care why Carmina knew about the midwesterners. He knew it had made news that an entire district had more or less emptied itself without a trace overnight, but there had been nothing to lead back to their refuge, so Jason wasn't concerned about being followed. "No, yours are now the squad that managed to plant themselves at the top of the Consortium's most-wanted list. Every tool they have has been tasked to find you instead of finding us. Again, it's quite the imaginative leap on your part to think we would want to be associated with that."

"You need us, and we need you." Carmina said simply, since whatever he had against her wasn't more important than overthrowing the Consortium and taking over Eleusis. "We have the skills and the weapons. You have the numbers. We need to work together, White."

"*We* are nothing, Carmina." He answered in a harsh whisper, not wanting to take the chance that Jess was awake and listening. "And as far as I am concerned, the only thing you need to do by way of a service to humanity is find the tallest cliff in your neighborhood and jump off it. You are not welcome here. And if I see you again, I will kill you."

"You can try." She shook her head, even though he couldn't see her. "If this is your decision, then it looks as though I need to make other arrangements." Carmina replied in a pinched tone.

"Say hello to your wife for me."

He hated the fact that Carmina had the kind of hold over him that elicited a response, but rage was the only thing he could feel at a comment like that, especially with the kind of night he had passed with Jess. "The only other arrangements you need to make are with . . ."

"That's enough, Jason." A third voice broke onto the line Jason hadn't been expecting, and the rage he felt increased exponentially. "We'll take it from here." Xander's voice was calm and even, though Jason could hear the disappointment in it. "My brother is justified in his personal opinion of you, Carmina. Heaven knows mine isn't too far behind it. But in this matter, he is not authorized to speak for the council. Tatyana, Bickford, Reed, Haley and I will speak with you to negotiate the terms of annexing your people and your resources."

Jason wanted to respond, to tell Xander one more time that he wasn't that stupid, that she couldn't be trusted, that she was just as bad as the Consortium. But if Xander had gone so far as to tap his communicator, he was serious, and by then, he had the rest of the council on his side. So Jason remained quiet. He had already shown there was a division of opinion on the council by rejecting her out of hand and being overruled. Nothing more he could say would be helpful.

"Wonderful." Carmina said with a renewed, pleased tone and her smile was audible. "I don't presently care about your opinion of me, as long as we work toward our common goal. If you want to kill me, at least wait until the Consortium is destroyed."

Jason hung up the phone, since he had clearly been cut out of communications and he didn't want to hear the plans his brother made with the person he hated most. He sat on their stairs for a long time, staring into the dark silence of his home and allowing his mind free rein to move through the situation in front of him. He needed to be rational about it, to make sure the decision he made was a logical one. But the more he thought about it, the more he came back to exactly the same answer. A half an hour, he stayed there on the step in contemplation, before he got up, went to the kitchen to get a drink, and headed back up the stairs, tossing his communicator on his discarded pants as he went.

He stood at the foot of the bed for a moment to look at Jess asleep, her hair splayed out over the thin sheets, a single paper-thin blanket covering her delicious curves. Eventually, he moved into the bed with her, sliding under the sheet to begin waking her up with a kiss along her breasts. It had been a few hours since they had fallen asleep in mutually-imposed exhaustion, and he warned her that being woken up in the middle of the night was a possibility.

Jessie moaned softly as he began his attack on her breasts, but she didn't open her eyes. "Mmmm . . . are you awake already?" She mumbled with a laugh, though she still refused to open her eyes. "I thought I wore you out."

"Only temporarily." He said with a smile, laying his head on her chest as the rest of him moved to press itself along the full length of her body. She could feel that just the slight action of getting in bed with her and feeling her warmth already had him hard again, but he wasn't attacking her quite as insistently as he had in times past. "I need to ask you something." He spoke against her tender skin, before moving so he could look her in the eye, even sleepy as she was. "Nothing's wrong, and there's nothing we have to do tonight, but all the same, I wanted to ask you now."

"Okay?" She replied with concern, since he had woken her up, and if it was only to ask her something, then she assumed it was serious. "You can ask me anything."

His caresses continued with no less heat than earlier in the evening, wandering over her and drawing her into him with every touch. "If we were to leave here, leave the mountains, leave the resistance . . . not stop working to help it but just . . . be elsewhere ourselves, take Bekah somewhere else to live, somewhere we'd be on our own, where would you want to live?"

Jessie wasn't sure what to say at first, since she didn't ever expect Jason would want to leave the resistance. It was his whole life, wasn't it? He had worked so hard. "I . . . I always thought living by the ocean would be nice. All of the best wines come from grapes that are grown in much milder weather. Out where California used to be."

He nodded and kissed her afterward, glad she had actually given him an answer instead of pushing with more questions. "I've been to a lot of places in the world, but that isn't one of them. It'll be a new adventure." He ran his hands up and down her back to massage along her spine. "We'll talk more about it in the morning. I promise everything is alright."

"Okay." She spoke softly before she returned a few of his kisses. "I'm with you, Jason. No matter what you want to do or where you want to go. We don't need the rest of the world to live a good life, you, Rebekah, and I."

"Don't forget the triplets I just got done knocking you up with." He said with a quiet smile and another kiss that drew her on top of him. "And I'm gonna make it quadruplets by morning."

"That's a lot of babies." She teased as she kissed him back gladly, since she was always glad for his lips on hers. "I'll have as many babies as you want to give me. My mother said I would end up an old maid. I'm glad I won't."

"No, you won't." He moved his hips beneath her to get a little more comfortable, but it was clear he wasn't going to be letting her go back to sleep any time soon. "We won't have the luxury of dropping off our kids at child care where we're going. But wherever it is, it'll be quiet and it'll be ours. That's enough for me."

"A lot of people have lived their lives a long time without childcare. We'll make do." She promised as she kissed him harder, since she didn't know what prompted his desire to move, but she didn't want to question it. Jason was the most important person in her life, other than their daughter. If he wanted to run, she would run with him. No matter what.

22

"No!" Orion screamed over the mass of people all around him, some of them more deserving of his wrath than others. "It's a simple instruction, people! Aim for the target, pull the trigger. Aim, fire. Very, *very* simple sequence of events. It's about precision, it's about control, and it's about *listening to my fucking directions!*" He screamed as loud as he could, which was quite loud, when he put his mind to it.

"When we're in the middle of a fight, you're going to be hearing a lot of very, very simple directions. You need to learn to follow the ones that are going to keep you alive and keep the other guy from staying alive. That means doing what I fucking tell you! Now!" He barked without waiting for any questions or any other expressions of concern. He didn't have time or patience to hear it.

"Center target high. Hit!" He waited a few seconds for the hail of several dozen bullets to die down, since some people were more certain of their aim than others. "Left low. Hit!" He continued through dozens of iterations, training all of those near him to listen immediately and do as they were told. They all still had a long way to go, but most of them at least hit somewhere near the target. He could live with that for the time being.

Anna was moving throughout the trainees while Orion barked at them, and every time he yelled at someone in specific, she knew it was her job to go to that person and correct them. She went up to a young man who was probably barely of marriageable age, and she grabbed his arm. She corrected his aim and glared at him. "Focus. You can do it if you just focus."

"I'm trying!" The boy was clearly space-born and bred from the way he responded to authority, skinny and visibly weak, but he was trying. "My hands shake when I'm nervous. I can't stop it."

"Sure you can." She held his arm in place. "Okay, I want you to watch the target. Don't worry about your gun, just look down the barrel and when I say shoot, just pull the trigger. No hesitation. Agreed?"

"Okay. I can do that." He watched one target while everyone else around him was turning and shooting when Orion said to do so, trying to focus on just the center of the target and nothing else. "Just the target. Just the . . . just the target." He had to talk to himself to keep his focus, but every time the guns around him went off, he flinched, though he did his best to keep his eyes on the target like she'd said.

"What if you think of it as a giant tit, does that help?" She replied with a smile. "I mean, you wouldn't want to miss one of those, right?"

"Well I wouldn't want to *shoot* it if it was a tit." He said with an unconscious glance down at her own.

"No, but your aim should probably be on point. I mean, heaven forbid you miss the nipple. You need to be able to find that thing." She replied with a smirk. "Shoot."

He hurried to obey, and was too distracted by her question to worry about being nervous, so when he shot the tit-target, his shot was much closer to actually hitting the center, though he was still off from the bullseye by several concentric rings of color.

"Hey, improvement." She said with a laugh as she gave the kid's arm a squeeze of encouragement. "Again. Shoot again."

Orion kept up his instruction over and aside from the individual coaches who were walking around, until the practice targets were so completely shredded by bullet holes that they were unrecognizable. "Again!" He called out after the last shot, watching those in particular who had needed personal attention during that session of practice. "Now drop your weapons and surrender!" He barked in the same authoritative voice.

Out of the four dozen recruits training, a handful of them actually complied, dropping their guns to the ground with their hands in the air. The rest either just looked confused or annoyed. Orion was grinning maliciously at those who had followed his command, noting their faces for the future. "If any commander, any enemy, any other human being on any planet tries to give you an order like that, you tell them you are under sacred obligation to tell them to go fuck themselves, is that understood?"

There was a general chorus of agreement at that, though nothing as standardized or disciplined as a true military would have been. Orion had to work with what he had. "Now, drop your weapons and surrender. That's an order."

The chorus was much more united at that command, and everyone's grip only tightened on their weapons. "Go fuck yourself, Sir!"

"That's more like it." He grinned around at everyone and nodded back in the direction of the residential blocks. "We reconvene at 0900 tomorrow. Dismissed."

Anna gave her current student a pat on the back and told him to get some rest before she moved along to check on the rest of the people she had helped. All of them seemed more or less happy with the fact that they were a little better than the day before, so she gave them each a little bit of encouragement before they went on their way. She and Orion weren't friends, but Anna was always trying to get some kind of their friendship back. She missed him in a lot of ways, but she knew she deserved to miss him. She had been the one to destroy it. "Great job as usual. Sir." She gave him a small smile, though she knew he wasn't likely to return it.

"Thank you, Sergeant. It is a good job." He replied without any emotion in his voice, focusing instead on the gun in his hand that one of the trainees handed him. "Next week I want you and Ben to start running this batch through contained-space drills. Make sure they know how to clear out a building and secure it, start gearing them up for some of the situations we're more likely to encounter as we go along than hanging targets. Put Ben in charge of team leadership so you can focus on keeping them on their toes."

"Sure. Whatever you need." She said with a polite smile, even though he wasn't looking at her. Anna sighed as she wondered if he would ever actually look at her again. "How, um, how were the kids last night?" She had taken care of Logan's boys and while she had no problem with that, she often wondered about her own kids whenever they were away.

"Not too terrible." He finished up with the gun, though he still didn't look at her. "Lynnette didn't sleep very well, I was up with her a few times, but she settled down every time I picked her up, so she was fine. Leo was down like a rock the whole night. No surprise there. Mercury took them down to child care on her way to the clinic this morning."

"Okay. Good to know." She watched him for a moment longer but then looked down at her hands. "Well, I'm going to go check and see if I'm needed anywhere else. Let me know if you need me to assist with anything."

"Are you going to be at the meeting Xander and Tatyana called later?" He asked in a tone that said he knew what it was about, even though the invitation had been purposefully scant on details or purpose. "If not, you should be."

"I don't know, they didn't ask me to be there." Anna looked over at Orion again. "I heard about the meeting, but I'm not in charge of anything around here. I just run around with a gun." She gave him a small smile, even though he still wasn't looking. "I attempt to follow orders of people higher up than me, you know how that goes."

"Show up anyway. The more people with an iota of common sense who can attend, the better, as far as I'm concerned. They have decided that's not an important qualifier for leadership." He glanced over at her once and shook his head. "Talk to Logan and come anyway. Nobody's gonna say shit about you being there. And prepare for an avalanche of stupid."

"If you think I should be there, I'll be there." She continued to watch him with an ache in her chest. Anna really did miss him. It was hard, especially when she and Logan were in a weird, unknown place, and she didn't know what to think about that either. When she and Logan were together, it was good, but they both struggled with knowing what they wanted on a permanent basis. Especially because she knew he missed Mercury just like she missed Orion. On too many occasions she wondered about how the matching system might have known her better than herself. Or simply that she and Logan had changed too much. "Thanks for the heads up."

Whatever confusion she was feeling in her own situation, she didn't get so much as a whiff of it from Orion. But then again, she never had, even when he was with her. He just nodded to acknowledge what she said, and moved away from her as coldly as though they hadn't shared any kind of history, much less one as intimate as theirs had been. "You're welcome. Finish up here, get the rest of the guns back into the armory and I'll see you at the meeting."

Before the meeting, Orion got a message from Mercury asking if he would meet her at the clinic, since she had some news that she needed to share with him. She assured him it wasn't anything to worry about, even though she was sure he would worry anyway.

Mercury worked alongside Barry in the clinic all morning, and she was laughing at something he said when she saw Orion come through the door. She was still smiling when she approached, and she went up to him to hug him and give him a warm kiss. "Thank you for coming. I know you're busy today."

"Oh good, so my act of being busy and important-looking is actually working. Phew. That's a relief." He returned the kiss with a grin of his own, threatening to get just a little bit scandalous out in public as they were, though he restrained himself. "I like this kind of busy, though. Better than watching a bunch of people figure out that a gun shoots straight for the seventeenth time like it's a revelation."

She laughed and shook her head before she kissed him once more and looked back at Barry. "Is it okay if I sneak away for a little while? A half hour or so?"

"Yeah, go ahead, I think we're fine here. Sierra's coming in pretty soon, I think, so if you need to take longer, that's fine too. I'll hold the place down." Barry was smiling as usual, since he already knew the news Mercury had to share with Orion, and things at the clinic were genuinely good for the first time since they came down from Nine. Babies had slowed way, way down, and having extra help had made his life a great deal more livable. He certainly didn't mind helping Mercury whenever she needed it, seeing as she had helped him out thousands of times.

Mercury grabbed Orion's hand and led him out into the warm sunshine as quickly as she could, since she always wanted to be outside whenever she could. She could never get a tan, but the sun felt great on her skin anyway. Well, before she was burned to a crisp, it felt great.

"So, um, I have news. Like I said." She looked up at Orion as their pace slowed a little so they could walk leisurely. "I'm pregnant." She said it quickly, like ripping off a bandage, since she had no idea how he would feel about the news. "Twins, too. Twin girls." It really was amazing how much information women could get early on, whereas Mercury knew there was once a time in history where predicting babies was just a guessing game.

Orion knew they clearly hadn't been doing anything to prevent that from happening, but he was clearly shocked that it had happened so fast. "Seriously? Twins? Already?" He grinned and leaned down to kiss her, picking her up by the waist to press her against him and swing her around once in a way not many men in the mountains were big enough to accomplish. "Good god, those ovaries of yours are on overdrive. You can't miss."

Mercury laughed mostly in relief, since she was worried that he would be unhappy about it. "I think they just wanted a piece of you and took two instead." She kissed him several times and hugged herself tightly to him as he held onto her. "I'm glad you aren't upset. I didn't know how you would feel, since . . . I don't really know what we're doing or where we're going. I have no interest in being with anyone else."

"Neither do I." They were walking over a construction site that had mostly been abandoned in favor of other projects, leaving a frame of a house mostly-finished with some spare lumber sitting around and a few bare walls beginning to gray with discoloration. He picked her up in another kiss and set her down on a lumber pile just above him with her back against a barely-finished wall so that she could be more on his level. He kissed her repeatedly, his hands moving over her sides as if to introduce themselves to the children he knew were growing inside her. "All I want is you. How are you feeling?"

"I'm alright. Tired, I suppose. The female body isn't really meant to reproduce so quickly after already having children, but I'm not upset it happened. I'm surprised, really. I didn't think it would happen so fast. But I smile every time I think of you with more children, since you are such an amazing father."

"Babies just like the difference in perspective of being high off the ground. I have kind of a corner on that market." He kissed her again deeply as the knowledge settled into him. It felt very different, finding out he was going to be a father from the woman he truly and unreservedly wanted to be with, rather than all the conflict of the previous time. Of course, Anna had been carrying another man's child at the same time before, so that complicated any situation. "I love you. But you're probably gonna want to get used to the whole . . . being tired thing." He grinned mischievously. "I've sort of . . . got a . . . thing."

"You've got a thing?" Mercury replied with another laugh at his curious grin. "You've got a thing . . . for pregnant women?" She was smiling as she asked, since in her previous life with Logan, she'd completed a lot of research about sexuality. That included all sorts of sexual fetishes. Mercury didn't seem at all disgusted by the possible revelation, but she did think it was amusing and surprising.

"I do." He admitted with a laugh of his own. "It, um, yeah, I do. I'm not really sure if it's something along the lines of damage-already-done, but I'm not gonna go digging around in my own brain to find out. One way or another, it's very much a thing of mine. You'll see. It gets bad. Like, you're gonna have to start shutting me down if you want to get any sleep bad."

Mercury giggled again. "That is so funny. You are adorable. And clearly horny at the same time." She kissed him a few more times from the perch he'd put her on. "I just barely found out and I'm already trying to think of names. They're going to be the most beautiful girls in existence."

"They'll be their mother's daughters, then." His hands wandered over her in ways that weren't really expected in public, but he'd always thought she looked sexy in scrubs. A fact that he attributed to watching too many television dramas about hospitals and hot nurses growing up. "How far into their profiling have you gotten? Do you know anything about their genetics? Their actual phenotypes? You called Leo pretty much the second we found out he existed, I was just curious what you know about the girls already."

"Well, they don't have the markers for the continual growth. I knew you'd be worried about that, so I checked. And they're CV-immune, and Leo isn't. Also, one has dark eyes and the other has green." She said with a grin. "Though we probably won't see that actually develop until they get closer to the age of one."

"Not identical then. Good." He couldn't stop kissing her as he digested the news, his arms wound tight around her back to hold her against him as if he could cradle the two little girls already. "I've always had this tiny little paranoia in the back of my brain that I'd have twin girls and never be able to tell them apart. I dated a set of twins for a little while back on Three. The world doesn't need more of that kind of crazy. Fraternal is better."

"I'm sure they'll be glad to have some differences as well, as they grow up." Mercury felt happier and lighter the more he held onto her and kissed her, since his support was an incredible buoy when she felt concerned previously. "No red hair, I'm sad to say. Your dominant genes win out this time."

He pouted a little, but he had more or less expected that. "I suppose that shouldn't be surprising. I'm pretty dark, I tend to override most things." He shrugged and ran his fingers over her back again, then tugged at her braid once playfully. "Maybe they'll get your curls at least. I've never actually had my hair long enough to know if it's curly or not, so maybe they'll pop out with some dark ringlets going on. And whether they've got the continual growth disorder or not, they're both still gonna be Amazons. I don't think the two of us leave them much choice about that."

"That's true. They will be tall girls." She jabbed at his side playfully as soon as he tugged at her braid, since she was never more playful than she was when she was with Orion. "Will their ribs be a weak spot for them like it is for you, though? That is a serious question."

"Hey, hey, hey." He moved quickly to grab both her wrists and hold them behind her back as he kissed her again, in what he had assured her in the past was purely self-defense. "No need to sully a joyous moment with an act of war. But yeah, that's probably genetic."

Mercury laughed against his lips again and kissed him several more times. "I love you, Orion." She replied before she nipped at his bottom lip playfully with her teeth. "I can't wait to see our family grow."

A moan escaped him at her touch, and he released her arms so he could run his hands over her. He didn't usually get her quite as playful out of doors, and it was something he planned to savor. "Even if it means we're gonna be *horribly* outnumbered. But I'm alright with that. The boys will be what, a little over one and a half? Practically independent."

"Practically." Mercury said with yet another laugh between kisses, especially because his moans always encouraged her. "If my ex-husband had one brilliant idea, it was to set up that childcare center. Not that I'll be entirely dependent on that, but it is good to know it is there and people can help us. Otherwise I'm not sure what our options are. Abstinence? Contraceptive items are heavily tracked here on Earth. It would be dangerous to even try and look for any."

"Abstinence?" He acted incredibly confused. "I'm sorry, I'm not familiar with that word. Must be an Irish thing." He shook his head and kissed her again. "No, when the time comes that we put up the white flag, I'll just have to have a conversation with Barry or Doc Weber about putting a closed sign on the pipes."

Mercury smiled at him and kissed him several more times. "We'll worry about that later. I was an only child who always wanted siblings. I'm glad my children have that. Even though our situation is . . . stranger than most."

"I'm comfortable with strange." His voice was a little breathless under the lingering kisses, and the way his hands gripped her sides, he clearly had no intention of going anywhere any time soon. "That was mean of you, to tell Barry you only needed a half hour." He mumbled as he kissed her again, his lips moving down to her neck. "He's gonna be mad when you take a lot longer than that to come back."

"He said I could take longer." She countered and tilted her head back slightly as he kissed his way down her neck. She really liked it when he did that. Mercury attempted to be braver about public places, but this was definitely more public than she had yet explored. She was starting to learn, though, that people really didn't care much about what other people did, so long as it didn't interfere with anything else. No one was working on the unfinished house, so she was fairly certain they weren't bothering anyone. "Do you want to stay here?"

He hadn't really thought about that possibility, since they were still close to the clinic and there were people coming and going in various directions around them. But the unfinished house did have a finished foundation that was tempting, just down a set of steps. "Let's see what kind of basement they started in this place." He reluctantly stepped back from her and walked over the unfinished base of the house toward a set of poured cement steps.

Mercury was feeling very adventurous as she followed him down into the basement, cooler and dark, except for the daylight coming in from the stairway. "No one is going to see us here."

The place was abandoned, but it had been built in the early spring, and nature hadn't had a chance to come back in and get a foothold on it just yet. It wasn't particularly comfortable-looking, but it was private. In one corner there was a piece of the foundation where the excavators had stopped, since the bare stone of the mountains was exposed in a smooth shelf, brighter in the darkness than its surroundings because of the tiny flecks of mica that caught the sunlight. He made his way over the abandoned boards and discarded materials with Mercury's hand in his, glancing back up at the break in the boards above the carved steps as if someone was going to follow them down into the dark. Given how crazy some of the people around the haven tended to be, he was a little surprised no one else was already there for some other sordid purpose. "They might hear us, though." He leaned back on the shelf, pulling her in between his legs to kiss her roughly. "I'm not in the habit of being quiet with you. That'll be a challenge."

"Do you care if anyone hears?" Mercury said as her lips tangled with his in a passionate kiss, happy to kiss him whenever she got the chance. Even in a mostly-public place. "It's not like we will get in trouble."

He was more amazed with every passing day at just how . . . brazen . . . Mercury became in the time they had been separated. More than that, she was adventurous in ways that still never managed to diminish her inherent dignity and poise with which she always carried herself. He wasn't sure how that kind of balance worked, but he appreciated and enjoyed it every chance he got. She hadn't been joking when she'd told him that she liked things to be . . . a little unorthodox. "No, I really don't." He assured her with another kiss.

His long fingers raked up over her chest to take her breasts in his huge hands, but then he spun her around, holding her back against him as he kissed her exposed neck and his hands loosened her scrubs. His knees were spread wide behind her, but he was wearing his usual, loose-fitting work pants and a simple t-shirt. He guided one of her hands back to the straining bulge in his pants as he tugged her scrubs and panties down out of his way, clearly intending to take the hard seat of the stone for himself rather than throwing her down on it.

Mercury enjoyed how commanding he was with his actions, she knew he knew she liked it, even though she knew it didn't come naturally to him to behave that way. They both couldn't help what they liked. He kissed and touched her in all of the right places, and she was already squirming a little bit on top of him, which didn't make things any easier on either of them.

Sometimes Mercury couldn't believe the things she wanted to do, the things she was willing to do, when she looked back at the woman she had known herself to be when she first met Orion. That Mercury was long gone. This one was a better version, she thought, and she was happy to be back with Orion again. They were good together, and she was grateful he could give her a second chance after everything that happened.

Scandalous as the moment was and open as they both felt the entire time, Orion couldn't devote much of his brain to anything besides Mercury. The height difference between them allowed him to kiss her as she leaned back into him, one of his hands between her legs to tease her as they rocked against each other. He found himself, more and more often, feeling the way he'd felt when they had first been matched. He couldn't believe she was his. Every move she made was elegant and sexy, and he constantly asked himself how he deserved her. All he wanted was to deserve her. All he wanted was to be enough for her, to support her, to take care of her. That included taking care of her in a dark basement when they might get caught.

Once they had well and truly made a mess of each other, Mercury was still sitting on Orion's lap, except once they were finished with each other, she turned around to face him. She was still kissing him when both of their communicators went off at once, and she reached into his pants to see that a previously scheduled meeting had been moved up and attendance was strongly encouraged. Mercury didn't even need to look at her own communicator, and she really didn't want to, since the blanket message was from Logan. "Why would he tell me to be there? I'm just a doctor."

He looked over the invitation and shrugged. "They've got Pierce on here too, so if she needs to be there, you absolutely need to be there." He shook his head and put the communicator back in his pocket, though he was glad she was so familiar with him that she could take his things as if they were her own. "We should get going. If they moved up the meeting, then something's changed."

"Hm." She replied simply before she kissed him again, since she didn't really want to leave, especially because Logan sent them a message. "I want to stay here with you."

"It's always a good thing to find out we want the same things." He grinned and kissed her again, his hands caressed her neck as he held her close. "One of them should be named Claire." He said as his hands moved down over her waist. "Or some derivation of it. Does your mother have a middle name you could pass on?"

"Claire is a pretty name. I've always liked it." She thought about her parents briefly, and the sting of missing them was sharp in her chest. "Fiona is her middle name." Mercury ran her hands along his arms as he held onto her waist. "Should one of them be named after your mother? Or your sister?"

"I always did think Khadijah was a pretty name. But I'm fairly sure my sister would pummel me within an inch of my life if she found out I had used it for my own daughter." He smiled sadly, since they both generally felt the same way about the possibility of seeing their family again. "If we go with Fiona for the one with the Irish in her eyes, we could go with Farida or Fariha for the other. Or Farrah. I grew up with a Farrah. Nice girl."

"Farrah is a pretty name." She agreed as she kissed him gently. "Fiona and Farrah. So pretty. I like it."

"Alright, then." Whatever of the mood between them had been removed or tainted by their summons to a meeting was back, and he couldn't have cared less about anything happening out in the rest of the world. It was his family, and it was all that mattered. "I love you, Mercury. It's going to be an amazing life, wherever we end up living it."

Mercury gave him a small smile, wrapped her arms around his neck, and kissed him several more times before she responded. "I love you too, Orion. It is going to be an amazing life. I'm sorry it took so many detours to get here, but I'm happy we're here. Together."

By the time the two of them got themselves cleaned up and down to the Labyrinth, they were some of the last to arrive. Logan was already present, off to one side speaking with Koskei and Renata in low tones. Orion promptly ignored the man and went to the other side of the room to find seats for himself and Mercury.

Gwen was nearby, talking with Jason and Jessie about something with polite smiles all around. Reading the room was as easy as reading a book. Half the faces present were drawn and nervous about something they knew, the other half were looking around and nervous about the things they didn't know yet. Reed and Haley were there as well, noticeably older than everyone else and clearly nervous about the contents of the meeting, but restraining themselves. Xander and Tatyana were not yet present, which Orion thought was especially odd, since they had been the ones to lead most meetings in the first place.

Anna was one of the last to arrive, mostly because she hadn't even noticed the message from Logan. She had been busy helping a family move into a finished house. She looked around quickly, noticed Orion and Mercury together and found a seat as far from them as she could get. They both hated her for one reason or another. She did notice Logan, though, and she gave him a small smile once he met her eyes momentarily. The meeting looked much too official to concern itself with good news.

Logan was glad to see her there, and when he finally went to sit down, it was near her instead of in any kind of position of authority in the room. He was there representing the people's interests as a whole, but clearly he hadn't been the one to organize the assembly despite having sent the message. "I'm glad you made it." He took her hand under the table as he settled into his seat with a sigh.

"Thank you, everyone, for coming." Xander got started once he finally strode in, glancing around the room at everyone before nodding for Koskei to close the door and secure the room. None of them needed their present topic of conversation getting anywhere besides that room for the time being.

"By now some of you have heard about what took place yesterday in Algiers. One of the Consortium's most extensive weapons depots in the world was raided and plundered down to the last bullet, and not by us." He looked around again to see who already knew and who didn't, and then went on. "Since the news of the raid came out, Carmina has contacted us and claimed personal responsibility for what happened. She claims that her new team has been recruited from various African and southern-European militaries, and has offered herself and her new resources to the resistance. We are meeting today to discuss the terms under which the negotiation for her acceptance ought to be conducted."

"How about starting with the fact that they shouldn't be conducted at all?" Jason spoke up almost before Xander was finished speaking, clearly setting himself in opposition to the more mature-looking man. "An allied psychopath is still a psychopath."

"Very few people here have a clean reputation." Tatyana said calmly as she leveled a glare at Jason and looked around the room. "Even with the influx of Midwesterners and with all the training conducted, we still need the trained fighters she has, and the weapons. In short, we need what she has, even if we don't need her."

"And if she's just negotiating to get us to open the door for her?" Carl spoke up, sitting next to Kameron and Ben, all of them with deeply concerned looks on their faces, as the current security personnel leadership. "I helped out on task forces chasing her, *and* you," he tossed at Tatyana specifically, "across most of the world trying to lock you down. I've read the case files on the shit you've both done, and you're damn right nobody here is clean. But just because somebody might be beneficial in a fight doesn't mean you invite them to come and share an apartment. Besides, *you* were the ones who ostracized her and her ideals in the first place. You think she's just gonna waltz back in all humble and contrite? If she wants to come back, it's so she can clear out our own operation and make sure she's the only rebel business left."

"We're running out of choices." Tatyana said impatiently as she looked around the room at every face for just a moment. "People are preparing to leave as we speak. Even if they don't, we still don't have enough people. So what are our options? Attempt to recruit some more? Spend more time training while the Consortium is still attempting to trail us at every moment? We don't have time. What people we have are too spread out across the world to centralize. We don't have the resources. We don't have the people."

There was a silence around the room since there were a lot of things at stake, namely all of their lives, first and foremost. They really didn't have a lot of options.

Mercury wasn't used to being in such meetings since the fall of the Initiative on Nine, and so she nearly raised her hand to speak, but then thought against it. "We have a working Twist." She spoke into the looming silence, her tone matter-of-fact as ever. "I'm confused why we have only utilized it to investigate Eleusis. I realize that getting to Eleusis is our primary goal, but the Twist is capable of more than that, isn't it?"

Everyone turned and gave Mercury a look she had gotten accustomed to seeing from others her entire life, a kind of confused and slightly condescending expression on most faces as they wondered what the odd-mannered doctor was even talking about. The only earnestly curious face in the crowd was Logan, but she wasn't looking at him. Xander was the one who answered, a confused half-smile on his face as he wondered if Mercury had somehow not understood what they were actually talking about. "The Twist isn't a weapon, and just because it can get us to Eleusis doesn't mean it evens the odds for us once we're there. We've talked about weaponizing it in some respects to slice and dice through defenses and communications for the Consortium compound prior to an assault, but the kind of maelstrom that we saw on Nine from the destruction of the larger gateway, that's not really something that's gonna do much good compared to the transportation capabilities it gives us in actually reaching Eleusis itself."

"I did not mean to use it as a weapon, but thank you for

informing me about its capabilities." She said with her own amused smile, since she knew he thought she was stupid, at least when it came to matters at hand. She hated it when people thought she was simple-minded. "I meant, which apparently I did not clearly convey, why can we not use it for transportation from place-to-place here on Earth? Why, if we need more recruits, are we simply using the Twist to go back and forth to Eleusis? Can it not be recalibrated to take you to any destination you want?"

The silence that followed in the room was of a very different character than the one preceding it, and even Xander was left with his head slightly to one side as if he was listening to something, though he was still staring at Mercury. A few people actually laughed, mostly at themselves, but soon most of the heads in the room turned toward Xander and Jason, whose eyes were getting progressively wider as they looked at each other. Never in anyone's experience had the two men looked more like the same person, and the lightning-fast conversation between them quickly killed the low buzz in the rest of the room.

"That would completely cut out the-"

"Not to mention the scrambling algorithm."

"Wouldn't have to plot around the orbital matrix."

"Or just recalibrate it into the targeting for the stations."

"Stabilizing would be a fucking kid's game comparatively."

"Only problem is the-"

"No, it wouldn't, you could just bypass the temporal-"

"But then you'd have to-"

"So what? It's still easier than the field maintenance."

They went back and forth in the same way for so long that it appeared they were on the verge of completely forgetting there were other people in the conversation, which left Orion to lean forward eventually and bang his hand on the table once to get the men's attention. "So I'm guessing that's a yes, then?"

Neither of them looked happy about being interrupted, but they did at least have the decency to look the slightest bit embarrassed about getting caught up in their own heads for a moment.

"Yes." Jason answered, nodding at Mercury. "Theoretically, it should actually be a metric fuckload easier than getting to Eleusis, since there are so many fewer variables to work with. If anything, restraining the power of the device is going to be the hard part, since it's designed for interstellar work, not . . . local . . . so to speak. But it should be possible."

"So, then all the other rebels." Anna piped up, since it was exciting to find out that maybe they weren't as fucked over as they thought. Hats off to Mercury, even though she wasn't about to say it. "We can bring them all here. Then we could have the numbers and the skills."

Everyone could see Reed almost shrink in his seat at the thought of so many people piling into the facility, but he didn't say anything against the idea, since it was what everyone had wanted from the very beginning.

On the side of the room, Koskei was working on a tablet whose display was visible along one wall, ever the secretary, pulling up statistics and numbers from the various cells that they had networked together all over the world. "We don't have the space to house everyone here, even if we were to open up the entire Labyrinth, which I know wouldn't be safe, so don't say anything, Reed."

He kept working as he looked at the numbers accumulating from all over, and shook his head. "But if we were to get everyone here in one place, the military presence alone would be well above four thousand. That's more than enough to take on the Consortium compound and perhaps enough to begin the kind of targeted assaults on the greater Stations that we've talked about. Certainly enough to start going after the other Consortium armories. Brisbane, the facilities in Kyoto they don't want the rest of the world knowing about, Miami, Buenos Aires, all of them. Possibly all at the same time."

"And all so quickly they wouldn't even know what hit them." Logan finally piped up, since the possibility of the Twist working elsewhere on Earth opened a lot of doors. "Why hasn't the Consortium already done this, if it's a possibility?"

"Two possibilities." Orion shot back, not actually fond of Logan in the slightest, but not about to start a personal fight in the middle of a business meeting. "Either none of them were smart enough to think of it, just like none of the rest of us were," he squeezed Mercury's hand on her own knee as he said it, "or they haven't used the tech that way because they don't want the world believing they actually have it. Most people don't. That's the biggest criticism we've heard since Nine got blown to hell, right? That us rebels are just making up this fairy tale technology to try and make the Consortium look like the bad guy? They've painted themselves into a corner they can't publicly get out of."

"This sounds like our best shot." Kameron spoke up and looked around the room. "No one wants to work with the crazy-pants bitch that tried to kill us, but if she's not with us, she's against us, and we need more people with us. It fucking sucks, but I think we have to bring her and her people here. Now we can do it whenever we want, depending on when the Twist can bring them here. We'll just need to keep a security team on the Twist at all times, twenty-four hours. We can even keep someone on crazy-pants, if that's what needs to happen."

"She already knows the terms of her acceptance are not going to be favorable to her. Or pleasant." Xander said in an attempt to reassure everyone present, even if it didn't work. "We're all going to need a little time to contemplate all the potential for the Twist, now that we've all been violently removed from the boxes we were clearly obsessed with thinking inside of." He nodded back to Mercury. "Thank you for speaking up, Doctor. If any of this works, I'm pretty sure everyone in this room is going to look back at you as the responsible party for winning the war."

"I don't think so. I'm not the one carrying a gun in my hand, or risking my life." Mercury sat back in her chair, since she didn't have anything else to say. "I want a chance to live the life I want. Just like everyone else here."

"Can I make a suggestion?" Reed finally piped up, looking around the room at everyone who was already settling back in their chairs in irritation. "I realize whatever you decide is going to be what goes, that's just how things have ended up, and frankly, I don't care that much. But if we can use the Twist to transport people here who want to fight and want to be standing by the door when people do draw guns, like the good doctor said, can't we also transport people away from here who don't? Tons of people here want to leave, like you said. Having the Twist here makes us a target. That's what the Consortium wants most. If we can transport the non-combatants somewhere else, then we can turn this whole place into a barracks. Keep it the center of the fight and keep the ones who shouldn't be getting shot at out of sight. Then we'd have the room for that bitch and her people and whoever else wants a piece of the action."

"We can get babies out of here." Gwen replied after that, though she usually kept quiet in the meetings, ever since Logan had asked her to attend several. "Babies and mothers and other people who wouldn't survive two seconds trying to take down the Consortium. We have families here." Gwen looked around briefly. "If they believe the Midwest district is already cleared out and I'm sure they've already investigated the place, can't we take the children back there? The Bickford Estate is massive and a single place we can protect and keep the children together. It's more than enough space."

"So long as you don't go out of doors." Logan interjected quickly. "Once you got there, you'd have to stay inside, otherwise they'd be sure to pick up movement eventually if they're watching. But it's also got bomb shelters and basements where you could keep most of the operation." He looked around the room at a few surprised faces, especially those who had already seen the above-ground version of the estate. "My ancestors were a little insane. And apparently pretty adept at foresight."

"It's as good a place as any." Xander agreed, though he had never seen the place himself. "We could make sure to supply you from here . . . hell, we can make sure to supply it from wherever we want, if this works."

"We'll need to somehow conduct a census of those who want to stay and those who want to go." Jason said quietly, mostly to Koskei, since he was the one actually taking notes and working to keep things organized. "And we'll need to do it without either inciting a panic or encouraging some kind of sedition."

"Renata and I can take care of that." Koskei said with a friendly grin. It was rare to see the older man legitimately excited, but he looked like most of them felt, both nervous and a little bit giddy all mixed into one. "Nobody takes us completely seriously anyway, so it'll be easy to get answers out of people. At least enough to get an idea of who's interested in going where."

"Can I talk to my staff?" Gwen asked after Jason moved on without even acknowledging her or what she said. "I need to make sure we can get as much staff there as possible. Especially because this is going to possibly be long-term care for hundreds of infants, some without their parents. Potentially ever again."

That question had several people in the room looking at each other, and on opposite ends of the room, Orion and Logan both looked first at the woman they were presently with, and then to the woman to whom they had been matched. Their children were shared between the four of them, on various occasions, but of the four of them, there were some very obvious distinctions as to who would be involved in the fighting and who would not.

Xander saw the looks down the table, but ignored them. Questions of who would be changing whose diapers in what time zone were so inconsequential to him that he very nearly laughed. "Just ask your staff if any of them would rather be carrying a gun than mixing a bottle, and if they're content signing on to do the work long-term. Even if we can be everywhere at once, we don't know how long it's going to take to fight and win this war." No other option was available, in his mind, besides victory. Even if it involved the sacrifice of everyone who joined the resistance, the Consortium's stranglehold on the world needed to end.

"If you end up losing a few people, I'm sure we'll be able to recruit some more from those who are interested in getting away from the fight. Can you have those conversations sorted out in three days?" Now that they had some idea of what they were going to do, Xander needed to establish timelines. Things needed to move. The faster the better.

"Yes, I can have the conversations sorted out in three days." She mimicked with a little bit of edge to her voice, because she could tell he cared less about the children than about the fight. "You know, some people are only going into this fight because of those children in the first place. You shouldn't be so dismissive."

Xander glared over at Gwen and shook his head, since it was one of the stupidest things he thought he'd ever heard. "People can get into this fight for whatever reason they feel like. I couldn't care less. What I care about is that they show up, and they can't do that while they're chasing their kids around. So yeah, I'm gonna dismiss the kids so they can get out of the fucking way when the shit hits the fan."

"They'll need their own security complement too." Orion said once Xander appeared to be finished with his tirade. "And yeah, that's gonna take guns away from the assault, but there's no way any parent is gonna let their kids go off to the midwest without it. Not just a few, either, something substantial."

"I'll head it up." Kameron volunteered after Orion spoke up, which probably surprised a few of the people around the table. Kameron was one of the best they had, and she knew it, but she also had to think of her baby and her wife. She wouldn't leave them, and she could protect them. "I'm not going to allow subpar security for infants that can't protect themselves."

"You . . ." Xander sighed, but he knew from past experience

that there was no point arguing with Kameron when she got her mind set on something. "Fine. Head it up and make everybody feel better. In the meantime, the grownups need to decide how to handle Carmina."

"Well, she broke away from you before and took a few hundred fighters with her, so it doesn't appear you're the most qualified person to manage that relationship." Logan's tone was cold without being particularly cruel as he looked over at Xander, but he continued without waiting for a response, looking over at Tatyana. "If she's coming back with malicious intent, how will she go about doing harm when she gets here?"

Tatyana glanced over at Jason and sighed before she looked at Logan again. "She's . . ." Tatyana rarely struggled with her English, but sometimes the right word escaped her. "If she does not come here ready to shoot us, which I do not believe she will, she will find . . . sneakier ways to attack. Though at this time, I do not believe that she is interested in attacking us. She hates the Consortium most of all."

"What kind of interest does she have in actually overseeing things once the dust settles?" Koskei asked from the side of the room, looking more nervous than most, non-combatant as he typically was. "I mean, if she's wanting back in, then she's looking to play a longer game."

"Ultimately she's always wanted a position of power." That kind of phrase, Tatyana had no trouble forming. "That's why she plays the game that she does. It will just be our responsibility to kill her before she gets there. I'm sure she's promised a lot of things to her followers. Promises she can't keep. We just need to use her until her purpose is complete. I promise you she is saying the same thing about us."

"You thought you had her under control the last time." Jason shot the accusation across the room at Tatyana, though his voice softened quickly afterward. "We all did. And she still took half our fighters with her when she defected. She knows she has the upper hand now. There's nothing stopping her from doing even worse the moment her people arrive here near the Twist. She knows how to operate it better than we probably do, since that was what she wanted when she attacked Nine in the first place. My research."

That was a bit of information he had never shared with anyone else, and some of the stares he got from around the table showed it. Carl was the one to answer, when the silence lingered. "If she wants to get to Eleusis so bad, why don't we let her?" He asked with a shrug. "Make it part of the terms of her acceptance. She herself goes through the Twist immediately upon arrival, along with whoever she asks to be given a position of military leadership. We send a corresponding group, and together we make up a permanent harrying force on Eleusis itself, coordinating attacks, commanding the assault on the compound itself."

"She might go for that." Xander looked over at Tatyana. "It would give her a command position in a place where she can't control the Twist. And most of the heavy armaments she stole won't be able to make the trip anyway, so she'd have to leave them behind with us. Then when the time comes . . ."

"Friendly fire." Orion filled in the blanks, since he could tell where the man's mind was going. "I don't disagree with the idea of killing her, but that seems like a particularly shitty way to do it."

"And you can think of a nice way to kill somebody?" Jason said with a condescending look. "Please, enlighten us as to the sort of kind, merciful death a woman like Carmina deserves."

"Not much better or worse than the rest of us, I expect, by the time this is all over." Orion didn't seem bothered by Jason's disapproval, but he didn't force the issue.

"So we agree about what needs to be done." Tatyana eventually said, since it sounded like people were willing to bring in Carmina and her people, mostly because they needed her as much as she needed them. "We'll bring her here."

"You can keep thinking we agree if it makes you feel better." Jason said without pushing the matter himself either. He would be overruled, and that wasn't something he was interested in sitting through. "If there's nothing else, I'm going to get to work on the localized protocols for Twist operations, as well as a metric ton of safeguards to keep Carmina and her people from trying to access the Twist. Which you know they will, the first chance they get."

Xander nodded, since he agreed with Jason on that aspect of the impending future, if nothing else. "Does anyone else have any business for the council at large?"

No one piped up immediately and everyone looked around the room at each other, since the meeting had given them all a lot to digest. As soon as people started to get up to leave, Gwen got up and walked over to where Anna and Logan were sitting together. "I hope it was okay for me to volunteer your home. It looked safe, and large, and we wouldn't need to scout out another area. I figured it would be the best place on such short notice."

"No, you were right to think of it." Logan reassured her as he got up. "I worry about it being under surveillance or otherwise occupied, but Kameron will take care of that before final plans are laid in. It's got room for everyone that would go, and then some. I think the place was designed to sleep something like five hundred people comfortably, not including the shelters and bunkers. In beds. So I'm not worried."

"Five hundred people. Talk about a lot of Bickfords running around." Gwen said as she shook her head. She constantly looked nervous every time she was around Logan anymore. She hadn't seen or spoken to Liam except when she took care of his children, and she kept her distance from the rest of his family unless she was spoken to. She had seen Margo with her new . . . boyfriend or husband or whatever, and Margo looked happy, but she knew Liam and Rachel and Bree still had to be hurting. "I don't know what you think your brother will do, but it's still just as much his as yours, so hopefully he doesn't mind either. His wives can run the house better than I can."

"I'm sure they'll decide to go with those who are with you." Logan hadn't thought about what Liam would want for the house either, but once Gwen mentioned it, he was fairly sure what his brother would do. "He'll be there too, I imagine. I think his days of considering actual military service are over. I'll talk to him tonight and find out, unless you see him before I do." He gave a wave to Koskei as the man made his way out, just to let him know that he didn't need anything more for the time being. "He said something the other day about sending you flowers, but he hadn't heard anything more from you at the time."

"Sending me flowers?" Gwen asked in confusion, since she hadn't seen any flowers and didn't expect to see any, especially since she was keeping her distance. Even Bree had kept conversation between them at a minimum after Gwen stopped replying to personal messages. "I don't expect flowers or that I'll see him any time before you do, unless I'm taking care of his children. I just wondered how he would feel about it." She stepped back so she could let Logan and Anna get going. "Sounds like we all have a lot to do."

"Yeah it does." Logan agreed, moving on past her with Anna to head back toward his office with his head still swimming.

They walked in silence at first for a while, but Logan broke the quiet as they finally got into his office. "The kids will be safe back at the estate." He said without looking over at her. "Pretty much as soon as we settled on that plan, I knew you weren't leaving. And neither am I. But Danny and Emily and Ginny will be there, at least."

Anna nodded at first and she looked down at the floor for a moment before she finally looked up at Logan. "I don't know what Ben will do. Or Cory. But I imagine Larissa will want to go back. It's safer for her there, certainly now that she's halfway through her pregnancy." She paused before she moved a little bit closer to Logan. "Do you want me to go back?"

"If you do and something goes south in the fight, you'll blame yourself." He shrugged, since blame wasn't avoidable in his mind. "If you stay here and something happens there, you'll still blame yourself. There's no right choice, in my mind. For me, I need to stay and lead. Fight. I want to see this thing through and I want to make sure the Montgomeries and fucking Carmina don't get the chance to turn the whole operation into replacing the Consortium with something worse. That's what I need to do. You've always been more . . . versatile." He meant it as a compliment, but he wasn't sure if it came off as one or not. "I know better than to try and say I want you safe and expect that to sway what you want. You need to be where you think you can do the most good."

Anna looked conflicted, since she didn't like sending her children away, but she knew they would be well cared for with her family. "I never thought my life would be a fight." She eventually replied in a whisper, since the life she had imagined with Logan was the life of a farmer's wife on the Bickford Estate. "But if you're in it, I'm in it. Otherwise what are we doing? We're fighting for the future. I would really like to go to Eleusis and do that."

"It's a far cry from what we originally thought we were going there to do." He slumped into his chair and pulled her with him, since he wanted to be close to her in the wake of everything. "There's a lot I never imagined. But what I want hasn't changed. Eventually, this is going to end. And all I want on the other side is a cold beer, a warm sun, fertile ground, and you."

"God, that all sounds amazing. Especially the beer and the sun. And you." Anna easily moved into his lap and kissed his cheek and down his neck. "We're too young to not come out of this with the best fucking future we could ever want." She took a deep breath of the scent of him as she kissed along his skin. "I still want everything we wanted together. Someday, I'm going to be a farmer's wife, damn it."

"Hey, I'm still a farmer." He said defensively, giving her a brief glare. "I got that whole north patch of potatoes planted at the beginning of the summer. Just because I haven't had two seconds to work it myself all summer doesn't mean it's not growing." He had needed some way to get away from his work and do something that reminded him of himself for a while, so he made a potato patch. Renata and Koskei mostly kept it up, since they both discovered they actually liked the work.

"Uh huh." Anna said with a laugh as she pressed her forehead to his. "Am I your wife yet?" She asked tentatively, since they had both thoroughly avoided labels and titles ever since everything that happened after they went home. "I know we both still feel . . . unsure. Don't we? Do you? I know that I love you, and I want a future with you . . . but I don't know if we know each other well enough yet. We both changed so much."

"We have. And we haven't." He admitted with a brief kiss, clearly agreeing that there was a reason why they had avoided any kinds of labels in the months they'd been together. "I want to believe that I can be the husband you wanted. The one you want now. I try to be. But I'm someone else too. We fight a hell of a lot more than I ever once in my life imagined we would, especially after things seemed to get off to such an amazing start the first time we were married. But time and kids change that in some ways, I suppose."

"It's not only kids. We both are headstrong. Which is not a bad thing, it just causes problems sometimes." Anna kissed him back harder. "It's my fault more than yours. I'm a downright bitch sometimes."

"You don't get to hog anything in this relationship, woman." He corrected with another kiss. "Not the blankets, not the hot water, and not the blame. I've been more than my fair share of a bastard." He sighed as he caressed casually up over her torso to her neck, leaning back in his chair to look up in her eyes.

"We've just got some things to work out. We've been jerked back and forth by the Consortium too many times already, and it's ripped to shreds more than I try to think about. I want to live in a world where peace is possible. That's the only world where you and I are going to be able to look at the future long-term and figure out what it is we want. But I want to take that look with you. See if this farmer turned asshole can turn farmer again and be the guy who makes you happy."

Anna kissed him several more times before she wrapped her arms around him and hugged him tightly. "We'll get through this and once it's all over, we'll start again. Without all of the nightmarish stress of trying to stay alive." She pressed her forehead to his as she hugged him for a long time. "I love you. And I love that you love me, even if I'm crazy."

"I tend to like your crazy." He ran his hands over her freely, enjoying having her close, even though he knew they both had a lot to do. "Your crazy is also going to be our best chance of outthinking Carmina when she gets here. From what I've heard of her, she's pretty much got everybody else's number. But I've never known a single person in my life you couldn't crack given time and effort. Just be careful, now and however far this show goes down the fucking rabbit hole."

"I will . . . be as careful as I usually am." She teased as she gave him one more kiss. "Okay, well, I know you have work to do, and I want to go pick up the kids. I want to spend time with them before I know I have to send them away."

"I'll try to be home early tonight, but after that meeting, I'm going to have Jason arrange a call with the other civic leaders of the larger holds. We've got a lot to talk about and Xander's right about wanting things to move quickly. We've been here almost two years. That's plenty long enough for anyone, I think."

"It is. Time to get things moving." Anna agreed before she caressed his face and then slid off of his lap. "Well, try not to stay out too late. If you do, then you're obligated to wake me up with all sorts of scandalous kisses when you get home."

"Finally, an obligation I can look forward to." He grinned at her on her way out the door, since he could imagine himself doing exactly that when he got home. "I love you." He said somberly, but still with a smile on his face. "I'll see you later. Waking or otherwise."

"I love you, Logan Bickford!" She yelled so anyone nearby could hear her, and she giggled as she continued on her way out. Even in the hardest of times, it was a little lighter when she and Logan were on the same side.

23

Jessie was waiting impatiently for Jason to return from the meeting, mostly because she knew the cause of the meeting and she didn't know what would happen. She felt sick even thinking about Carmina after Jason told her Carmina was in contact with Xander. As soon as she heard the door open, she popped up from her chair and immediately rushed to it. "Jason?"

He closed the door unhurriedly behind him, and the look on his face told her everything she needed to know about how things had gone. About as well as he had expected them to. "It became more complicated, but in good ways." He pulled her into a conciliatory kiss.

"Mercury had the common sense idea the rest of us have been too stupid to think of. Using the Twist to bridge places here on Earth. We can be everywhere we need to be, bring in everyone, Carmina's people, Elijah's people, Medina, everybody. They're going to use it to bridge back to the Bickford estate, use it as a shelter for the children and whoever wants to go along to guard the kids. Other noncombatants will go elsewhere, I expect. The weaponized part of the population will stay here in the mountains. They're going to do a deal with Carmina for her resources, but require her to be sent through to Eleusis with her main commanders. Try to minimize the risk here." He shook his head. "I still don't trust it. But no one else seemed to see it that way."

"So what are we going to do?" She held onto him as though he was her lifeline, and he was. "Are we still going to leave?"

"I hadn't considered that anyone would suggest consolidating, and I thought we were going to have to go by road to get to the West Coast." He shook his head. "But I've been doing the math in my head all the way back from the Labyrinth, and I'm almost completely certain I can make the Twist work . . . wherever we want, here on Earth. Honestly, anywhere in the solar system is going to be like basic algebra against quantum mechanics when compared to getting to Eleusis."

He squeezed her hands and sighed, and she could tell that his brain was running away with him. He could function that way almost indefinitely if someone was supporting him, but if he was working through problems alone, he tended to burn himself out in short order. "We can either go with the rest of the non-combatants back to the midwest and hole up in the Bickford mansion, or we can go ahead with our original ideas for the coast. I'm leaning . . . very much toward the coast." He said with a sigh. "I don't want her even knowing where you are for certain, let alone have any excuse to get to you."

"They still need you." She replied softly, since she knew if Jason disappeared, then it would be a hard loss on the rebels. Even if most people didn't particularly like him. "I don't want to go back to the Midwest, I spent my entire life there. I don't want to stay here, if she's coming here. But they do still need you."

"It doesn't matter where I am." He actually smiled quietly at that phrase, odd as the expression looked. "Anybody who takes one look at me already knows I'm not gonna be of much use in the fight itself. The work I need to do, I can do from the coast just as easily as I can do it from here. All that matters is keeping you and Bekah safe."

Jessie nodded, since she did agree that their family was priority over everything else. Even Eleusis. "We are ready to leave whenever you want to leave. As long as it's all of us together."

He kissed her and held her for a while to stop his head from spinning. "I have a lot of work to do down at the Twist. Xander gave Gwen three days to get the child care operation in order to see who's coming and who's going, so I gather he wants to start really moving people by then. Which means that's how long I have to get it working correctly for local trips. Once I do, we'll be on the first hop out of here." He kissed her again, his hands on her hips as he sighed. "Start looking for places out west for us. Money isn't something I'm worried about, so long as it's a place we can lie low and where we'll have more or less what we need. And I'm sure you'll have your work cut out for you finding a replacement to run the warehouse for you."

"I'll do my best to help them find a replacement, but I'm not going to stress out over it. I'm more concerned about getting our life packed up again so that we can move." She kissed him a few more times, since she was grateful for his concern and his willingness to sacrifice everything to go away with her. "Thank you for doing this for us. I don't think I could be here with her."

He just held her, since he felt primarily responsible for what happened to her back on Nine, even if it had been Carmina executing the cruelty herself. "I meant what I said before, and she knows it." He promised. "I am going to kill that woman slowly, unless the Consortium beats me to it. She might help us win this war, but she's not going to survive the end of it."

Jessie's grip on Jason tightened, since she l was battling anxiety about being anywhere near the woman who had tortured her. She was definitely going to need to go see one of the doctors in the clinic, or she might end up having a full-on anxiety attack, and Jason didn't need to deal with that right now. "You go do what you need to do. Bekah is in the care center, so I'll keep packing." He promised her that he would take care of her, and she believed him. She trusted him. She hoped he knew that.

* * * * *

Xander was still mostly in shock when Jason finished speaking, the lights from the Twist array nearby casting shadows on his already-darkened face. It was just him and his brother and Tatyana in the room finishing the calibrations for the Twist, but none of them were saying anything at the moment as Jason waited for their reaction.

"You've always been a fucking coward." Xander eventually said, shaking his head as he went back to the control panel to check over the most recent diagnostics. "You were when you first found me and you still are now. I don't know why I expected that to change."

"Strangely, I find that I don't mind being a coward in this instance, Alexander." Jason said in a calm voice, which was more than Tatyana generally heard from him when he addressed his eldest brother. "Discretion is the better part of valor. I'm sure I read that somewhere once."

He went back to the controls near his brother and flicked a certain part of the display to showcase some of the new functionality he had built into the system over the preceding few days. "There's a safeguard here in case Carmina or one of her lackeys tries anything. It will lock out local control of the Twist completely and will re-route it to me out on the coast. There's nothing here she can threaten me with. So if she tries to go somewhere she shouldn't or tries to countermand your orders, I can shut it down wherever I am."

Tatyana was silent for longer than she knew she should be. "I have to admit, I never thought anyone would be more important to you than Eleusis."

Jason didn't look at her as he worked, since it was awkward to have that particular kind of conversation with his brother and her current lover standing nearby. "You of all people should have known me better than to think that would never happen." He turned and gave her a single glare as he moved to a different console. "The place doesn't mean anything by itself. The people who fill a place make it what it is. I want the people I love to survive this and make the world a place worth living in."

"Hm." She said without any elaboration and turned her attention to the Twist. "Hopefully your children are CV-immune. If we all go down in this, you'll end up watching your family die before you do."

Jason's head snapped up at that, but then he turned his glare on Xander before continuing his work. "Revelations from a man who once told me that each person's secrets were their own to tell. Fucking typical."

"Our secrets are the same secrets when it comes to the capabilities of our genetic code, *brother.*" Xander shot back without even acknowledging the glare. "Everything is in order here. In the strange event that I need you, I expect you to be reachable."

"Nothing is unreachable so long as you don't fuck up our possession of this." Jason nodded at the Twist itself, still glaring at Xander. "We've said for a long time now that we fight this war in our own ways and on our own terms. That's what I'm doing. If you've got anything else you want to say to me, now's the time, so you might as well get it out of the way."

Tatyana turned her attention back to Jason momentarily and then, in a moment that was out of character, she walked over to him and pulled him in a hug. "I don't think you should go. But we can't stop you." She stepped back and looked as cold as ever after the hug. "I suppose this is goodbye."

He was surprised by the hug, but he knew Tatyana better than to believe the perfectly-frozen exterior she showed the world went completely through her. She was almost entirely consumed by the ice she had become, but it wasn't the core of who she was. He never doubted she cared about him in her own way, that way just wasn't what he needed. "For now, it is." The two of them had chosen the goodbye every bit as much as he had, and if they were surprised by his choice, it only went to show how little regard they had for him in the first place. Not that he was surprised.

He checked the time and set in the last of the coordinates for the destination he and Jess picked out. He hoped her own goodbyes hadn't taken very long, since he hadn't felt the need to make any himself. He had been all morning running tests on the Twist to make sure the local destinations actually worked, and he was pleased to say that they did, without any of the glitches or inconsistencies that continued to plague their travels to Eleusis.

When Jessie got into the room with Bekah, he was setting the last few boxes in place on the floor at a safe distance from the Twist prior to activating it. A simple electric motorcycle was parked near the boxes, with a narrow modified sidecar behind it and a long, narrow trailer behind for their belongings. He set down the last box he'd brought in from the cart in the hallway and smiled over at her in the doorway. "Are you ready?"

"As ready as I can be." Jessie held Bekah close, even though the little girl was fascinated with everything around her. Jessie looked at Xander and Tatyana as Jessie took her place at a safe distance until Jason told her it was okay to get closer. "We're taking your cute niece, so goodbye for now." Jessie took Bekah's chubby hand to wave at Xander. She didn't care to say goodbye to Tatyana.

Xander did actually go over to say goodbye to the little girl as Jason activated the Twist behind him, the usual fury of light and heat washing over the room and sending the little girl's inquisitive eyes wide in amazement. "Take good care of her. She's one of a kind, even if her father isn't." He shook the little girl's hand, but didn't get any direct attention from her given everything else going on. He looked at Jessie instead, the same serious intensity in his eyes as she saw so often in her husband's, except that Xander's lacked the lingering touch of insanity she saw too much of in Jason. "Take good care of him too. He tends to need a lot of looking after."

"I will. He's my whole world. I'm not going to let anything happen to him, if I can help it." Jessie promised as she looked past Xander at Jason. "Try not to be too mad at him for this. He's doing it for me."

"I know why he's doing it." He snapped, a little too much like Jason in that respect. "But I'm not going to grudge somebody an attempt to live a halfway normal life. It's arguably the only sane choice in this world. Good thing sanity isn't something I'm afflicted with." He stepped back once the Twist solidified the connection and salt air began coming through, infusing the room with the feeling of a beach nearby and a bright ocean just beyond. The sunlight streaming through the Twist was almost blinding in the artificially-lit underground room, but Xander's eyes adjusted fairly quickly, and he even helped Jason move his belongings through to the patch of nowhere just on the other side.

The work went quickly, and in just a few minutes, the motorbike, sidecar, and trailer were assembled on the uncultivated ground. A road was visible in the distance through some trees, but there was no visible traffic on it. Looking the other way from the road, the land sloped down toward the cliffs overlooking the endless ocean, seagulls crying in a chorus of their own devising as Jason went back through the Twist to get a final box from the mountains. "I'll get you final safe coordinates for our basement once we're settled in and I've had the chance to secure the place." He promised as he looked back and forth between Xander and Tatyana.

Neither of them seemed to give him much reassurance or support after he spoke, but Jessie had ventured closer with Bekah, still in awe over what she saw. The Twist was very real and it worked, and it was . . . amazing. "You are amazing." She said to Jason when she was close enough that he could hear her. "I can't believe you work on something this advanced. And amazing. You're amazing."

He smiled quietly but held onto her hand as he led her over to it. For him, at least, the appearance of the Twist itself had become very much a kind of anticlimax whenever it was open. It appeared to be a doorway that happened to look out on another place in the world, nothing more. He understood how much of a wonder it was, and he understood more about how it worked than anyone alive (with two exceptions he could think of), but it was still nothing more than a door.

He stepped through before her and didn't let go of her hand as she followed, pulling Bekah through quickly so that she spent as little time within the doorway itself as possible. He smiled but took a few steps through the grass to get away from it before he looked back at Tatyana and Xander on the other side. "Be safe. Both of you." He knew how unlikely it was for them to follow his advice in any way, but it was the closest he could get to telling them that he cared about them.

"You too, Brother." Xander said flatly, nodding once before the Twist disappeared in a blink. It left nothing behind but a small scar in the landscape where it had sliced through the ground. It was an unsettling thing to look at, since things had been sheared off at a molecular level, and there was a chunk missing from a stone that was as smooth as glass where the Twist had recently closed.

"Alright, then." Jason smiled over at Jess and pulled her into a kiss as he turned toward the bike waiting for them. "Let's go home."

On the other side, Tatyana stared even after the Twist closed, but she shook her head after a moment before she looked over at Xander. "I never really thought he would go. I thought he would be more dedicated to the cause, but that was always an argument we had."

"It's not about his dedication." Xander went to reconfigure the Twist. The kind of power they had in front of them after the morning's experiments was still thrumming through his mind, the ability to gather anyone from anywhere, to be anywhere they needed to be at any time . . . he had to stop himself from getting ahead of himself, and it was a battle he was losing.

"He's as dedicated to this war as anyone I've ever known. He's just also dedicated to surviving it. Which is never something I've completely understood, especially coming from him. If anybody on this godforsaken planet should want his life to be over as quickly and meaningfully as possible, I would've thought it'd be Jason." He sighed once the coordinates were in, since it was so much easier than any navigation to Eleusis. "I'm not looking forward to this."

Tatyana grabbed their guns, walked over to him, and handed one to him before he could finish what he was doing. "No one is looking forward to this, except for her, maybe. Better safe than sorry. Keep your gun ready."

He cocked the gun in his hand and hit the last command to engage the Twist before he backed up toward the door. He hit a button near the door to call Kameron, since she was the one on call for security. "You want to get your detail down here to play the welcome committee?"

"Sure thing, Xan." Kameron responded immediately, since she was always on top of things when she was on call. "On our way."

Xander and Tatyana stayed behind the barriers erected to protect those in the room from the blast of the Twist's activation. They hadn't given Carmina any warning, but they coordinated with her where the portal would open and roughly when so she would be ready. Xander wondered if any of them were really ready for the consequences of what they were all about to accept.

It had been bright and sunny where Jason and Jess disappeared, but there was nothing but darkness visible through the Twist where it opened for Carmina's people. Even the lights from the room around them seemed to be an intrusion on the other side of the portal. Xander held his gun lowered at his side, but ready if it became necessary. "Knock knock." He called through the aperture.

They heard some confused voices but it wasn't long before Carmina herself was the first face they saw. She had a few more scars along her face, a fresh one or two, but she was smiling as she looked through the Twist. "Well, well, well." She had her own warriors behind her who also had guns at the ready, but she just walked through. "This is exactly what I was hoping for."

"A cold welcome designed to minimize potential casualties and a few dozen fighters out in the hallway in case there are shots fired?" Xander said in a condescending response. "You have strange hopes."

"A working Twist and people at the ready with guns." She looked around the room. "Jason didn't want to say hello?"

"If he had, he would've done so with a gun of his own." Xander took a few steps closer to her, testing out whether he was going to be attacked or not. Better to know sooner than later. "He and his family have chosen to do their work to further the war elsewhere."

"I see. Well, you made the right choice. Now this is a war you and I can win together." Carmina looked back at her group of fighters and back at Xander. The people behind her were not kind people. That was easy to see. "Now, are you going to let us through or just keep your guns on us?"

Xander nodded slowly, since it seemed, for the time being, as though she was actually going to keep her word. It surprised him, but he supposed it shouldn't have. "Betray the deal we've made, and this rebellion will crumble in pieces, Carmina. I'm here to give my life to it, and I believed once that you were willing to do the same. Don't make any of us regret believing it again."

"We're on the same page now. That's all I ever wanted, Xander." Carmina said with a continued smile as she gave a nod to her warriors and they started to come through the Twist. "I love this thing. No wonder the Consortium is fighting so hard to keep it a secret. Now, how about you show us to our rooms?"

Kameron, at the back of the room, glared at the newcomer. Kam wasn't a fucking psycho like the woman across the room, but she had absolutely no problems with putting a bullet where it belonged. "You don't run things in this place, lady. You fucking ask him nicely. We have goddamn manners around here."

As usual, Kameron made Xander smile, and he nodded back over his shoulder at the woman as he holstered his gun. "That's Fitch. Commander Fitch, to you. You report to her. So aside from asking me nicely, I'd advise that you ask her nicely too."

"Manners." Kameron reminded the newcomers before she nodded toward the door, but she didn't holster her gun. Especially not when some of the men looked her over. She knew what their raking gazes meant, but just because they were bigger than her didn't mean jack shit. "Keep your eyes forward, assholes. None of this is up for grabs."

The soldiers still eyed her as they marched past her, led away by some of her own people. All of them were armed with two or three guns of their own, but there were entire crates and wired racks of arms in the dark warehouse behind them. There seemed to be an endless stream of them coming through the Twist single-file, each one of them looking around the room in amazement that they really had traveled somewhere entirely different through what seemed to be nothing more than a door in midair.

One of the men who came through after Carmina made his way past her to approach Kameron. When he spoke, his accent was vaguely French, his skin a midnight shade that, together with the white-ink tattoos around one ear, marked him as a member of a particularly vicious rebel sect that she and Orion had hunted for the Consortium in a previous life.

So *that* was where Carmina had gotten some of her fighters.

"We have some artillery and resources that are not going to fit through this tiny doorway. We'll have to discuss how to transport some of them. Commander." He handed her a tablet that showed a digital list of 'resources', and there was a significant number of them that hadn't been on the initial inventory list. Not the least of which was a full flight of four dozen ETS Ascenders. And the battleship to carry them. That particular event hadn't been discussed by anyone, and the smile on the man's face knew it. "Francis Martineau, Armory Overseer."

"Well, nice to meet you. Thanks for this." Kameron said as she held up the tablet. "Good to know that when you lie, at least you try to make it up by giving us better shit than what you said in the first place."

"Yes, well, we couldn't be entirely sure the bunch of you would come to your senses and choose to help us, could we? Full disclosure is almost always a bad idea, especially when it comes to weapons." He stood casually, with his hands behind his back, but the look in his eyes was one that it was difficult for a true soldier to see.

The man didn't even look at her with the same leer or knowing grin as the rest of his companions. When he saw her, he didn't even see a living person. Eyes as cold as his saw nothing worth empathy, since it was a capacity that was lacking in every mannerism and every word that dropped from his lips. He was tolerating her presence until he had an excuse to kill something. The same look existed in Xander's eyes, in Tatyana's, even in Jason's sometimes. But with Carmina and some of her people, the look was particularly strong.

"Do you have orders for me, Commander, or shall I join the others in being led to our new barracks?"

"I don't have orders for you right now. I don't know if I fucking trust you to do what you're told. Just go with your friends and I'll figure out what to do with you by morning." Kameron said with obvious disgust, since she didn't have any compassion or caring for someone who was clearly living to kill. She had more at stake than that. She cared more than that.

"Aye, Sir." He said with an obedient nod, then moved off down the corridor in line with the rest of his comrades, hands behind his back, as cool and collected as if he were taking a leisurely stroll.

Eventually five of them were left in the control room of the Twist in a continuing standoff, Xander and Tatyana still eyeing Carmina distrustfully on one side of the room while Kameron and

Carl waited on the other, watching her with even less fondness. "Is that all of them, or should we expect to receive more 'guests' later on once you've settled in here?" Xander hadn't been counting as her people filed in, but he wanted to see how Carmina reacted to the question. Not that the woman was in the habit of giving much away.

"There are more that wish to come. I couldn't promise them I could get them here, but you're going to want them here if you actually intend to win this thing." Carmina started to move slowly toward Xander, but mostly toward the door. "I intend to win this."

"We all do." Xander said without backing away. He would never again trust the woman in front of him, but he did believe she wanted at least a few of the same things he did. "There's going to be a lot of shifting around in the next few days. Once we can get all of our resources allocated where they belong, including you, we'll discuss our next steps. In the meantime, I want you and your top command staff ready for a briefing in the morning, once you've gotten over your jet lag."

24

"This doesn't change anything for me, Logan." Anna said sternly as she attempted not to raise her voice from where she sat at their table. His boys were asleep in their cribs, and Anna was working on some kind of snack. Stress made her hungry, and recently, she knew she would be fifty pounds heavier if she wasn't doing the damn running routine Orion had established. "I still want to go to Eleusis. I can defend myself against some psychotic bitch."

"Psychotic bitch, I'm not worried about. I've seen Carmina, and you can take her." Logan was doing his best to help with the snack and get things cleaned up from the mess the boys had made, but there was a lot of mess, and it was slow going. "Psychotic bitch and twenty of her closest friends, yeah, that I'm worried about. You can't defend yourself against somebody suddenly deciding it's in their best interests to shoot you in the fucking back."

"Do you really think she's going to do that? Isn't this what she wanted? A revolution? Why would she kill us now? That seems like an incredible waste when she finally gets what she wants. Before she was mad at Gordon . . . Jason . . . whatever for taking his sweet ass time. This is different."

"Right. This *is* different. Now we've actually got the shot we need to take down the Consortium. Before, she got impatient about not moving fast enough, and she killed forty people on her way out. Now she's got a hell of a lot more people following her, a hell of a lot better artillery, and the power to do as she pleases. She cut a deal because Xander and Tatyana were desperate enough to give her one, and she did it to get through the Twist to the other side of the galaxy. No other reason. As soon as she's got herself and whoever she thinks necessary through to the other side, she's going to cut ties and go balls-first at the Consortium, fuck the consequences."

Anna sighed heavily, since she understood Logan's concern,

but she was just as invested in everyone else when it came to going and getting shit done. "So what are you saying? You want me to stay?"

"I want you to be involved in some other detail besides the one that's completely insane." He finished with the mess and went to wash his hands. "There's a dozen other details right now working on inspecting and escorting all the different cells to where they're going so we can get things sorted out and out of harm's way. You could do just as much work or more with any one of them without going back to Eleusis with the psychopaths."

"Logan, I've been training and working toward going back to Eleusis. I've worked my ass off doing recon. I'm going back to Eleusis." Her tone would not be swayed. "I understand your feelings behind this, but I want to be a part of this. All the hell we have endured has been because of the Consortium. I want to be there with my fucking gun this time."

Logan knew that tone, and he knew Anna better than to think the realm of possibility included her changing her mind once she had taken up that kind of stance.

"Great." He eventually said without looking over at her, throwing down the rag he'd used in the sink before he started to move off toward their rooms. "Right, Anna. You're gonna do what you want. Like the consequences don't affect anybody else on the planet. You go ahead and do that, and when it suits you, the rest of us will still be right here waiting. You know, if you feel like admitting that what anybody else wants matters."

"Logan." She pleaded as he moved off toward their room, but she didn't know why she was calling after him. He wouldn't change his mind either, and he wouldn't change hers. "Come on, I don't want to argue about this. We're supposed to be supporting each other!"

"Yeah. We are." He stopped and turned around to look back at her down the hallway, but didn't come back toward her. "We're supposed to be listening to each other when there's a valid concern and taking each other's feelings into account. There will be plenty of opportunities for you to kick ass on Eleusis like you've trained to do. This war is not going to be over quickly. Not with the Consortium's hooks in every fucking country on Earth. All you're doing by going over there with Carmina is getting yourself unnecessarily in harm's way. It's not a matter of 'if' with her, it's a question of when."

"And you're so used to being in charge that you don't really want to have a discussion, you just want me to do what you think is best and be happy about it." She snapped back. "I don't just fall in line, Logan. Living life every fucking day out here is a risk. This is more risk. I get that. But we don't know anything about her no matter what we do. She could have led the Consortium straight to us for all we know, and then if they show up tomorrow, what will it fucking matter? The whole thing is a crapshoot!"

"Yeah, the whole thing is. But your part in it doesn't have to be." He didn't contradict what she said about him, since he knew she was right, both about him and about herself. "And if she did sell us out to the Consortium, or if somebody else does, then you being here would help us sort that out. But that's my job, so yeah, I'm biased." He was past being actively angry at her or fighting about it, since he knew how pointless it was and he wasn't going to push her even farther.

"Fine. I'll think about it, I guess. But I'm not staying here to do it." Anna glared at him, since he was the first to walk away from the argument. "You go take a nap or some shit, whatever you were planning on doing when you decided to walk away from our conversation. I'm going out."

"Of course you are." He said dismissively as he turned back toward the bedroom. "I'm gonna take the boys down to child care when they wake up and I'll be in the Labyrinth the rest of the night if you need me."

* * * * *

When Logan arrived at childcare hours later, Gwen was working the front desk, but clearly at the end of her shift, since she had her bag and her things up on the desk as though she was ready to bolt. She gave Logan a polite smile when he walked in, though, and she tapped out a few more things on her tablet. "Well, if it isn't three Bickford boys." She replied with a polite smile as she looked Logan in the eye, even though he didn't look like he was in a good mood. "Are Dec and James having a sleepover here today?"

"Yeah, they are." His tone was restrained as he handed over the boys, but he gave each of the boys a kiss as the attendants near the front desk took them over and distracted them from the handoff with toys. The boys had gotten to know most of the

491

attendants and trusted them, and Logan was glad that they didn't put up too much of a fight being left at child care. Even so, it was a little painful sometimes to see how easily they left him. "Mercury will probably be along to get them in the morning whenever she can."

"Alright. I'll put that information in so they know who to look for." Gwen typed a few more notes on her tablet. The boys were gone with other members of Gwen's staff, and she looked smooth even if she was actually stressed. "You look like you need a drink just as much as I do." She swiped across the screen a few times and looked up at Logan briefly. "I'm seriously debating on breaking into your brother's secret stash. That's what he gets for giving me the code."

"Liam does his own fair share of drinking these days. I'm not sure his stash is going to hold out much longer." He finished his entries regarding his handoff of the kids, watching her as she finished her work and edged her way out of the center. "Mine, on the other hand, is pretty well intact. Under normal circumstances, I try not to be a complete drunk at all times." The look on his face and the barely-repressed swearing she could hear in his pauses and hesitations told her that whatever was going on, it wasn't normal circumstances.

"Well, heck, why aren't we raiding your stash?" Gwen glanced back, clearly waiting for someone to take her spot at the front. "My full staff is going to dwindle as we head back to your estate. I've only got about half my staff willing to go. Which is better than nothing, I suppose."

"Half your staff should be enough, though, given that most people are electing to go to the Thailand location or the Ghana station." He said in the same business-like tone she'd grown accustomed to. He continued once someone relieved her, walking with her as if they had arranged some kind of business meeting beforehand. "I realize it'll be full-time childcare rather than drop-offs and pickups like here, but it should still be enough. Most of the people leaving are taking their kids with them."

"I hope everything will work out. I know Mercury said she would handle the four kids as much as she could on her own, but who knows how long this will last. I'll do my best to help her. I suppose your sister and sisters-in-law will help too."

"They've got their own to worry about, but I'm sure they'll help out as much as they can, all of them." He only found out that

Mercury was going back to the midwest by seeing her name on the rolls of the hasty census, but it wasn't as though he had expected her to discuss the decision with him first. "You've done amazing things with the child care center in the first place, and I'm sure you'll do amazing things out in the midwest too. You did say you liked my house."

"I do like your house." She agreed though she didn't look over at Logan again. It sucked to look at him and see Liam's face, even if they didn't look exactly the same. "Taking care of kids and fucking are the only two things I'm good at. Might as well stick with the one that does the most good when all hell breaks loose."

"Not true." He said as they walked, his complete aggravation with the world dimming slightly as he glanced over at her. "You're also good at cooking. I've had it before. And you're good at management, which I honestly wasn't sure would be the case or not when I designated you in your position. But I hear nothing but good things from everyone about the center, including from the people who work there."

"I'm glad people like it." Her shoulders slumped somewhat as they walked, since she was clearly tired and stressed. "I didn't want to let you down."

"You haven't. Ever, that I can remember." The child care center wasn't far from his office, since he wanted to be close to his children in case he was needed. "Most of the leadership seems obsessed with vodka or rum, but I prefer to stick to whiskey. Only thing I've ever heard about from California is wine, but I've never been a fan. If you're alright with the whiskey, though, I've got two glasses."

"I'm not picky." Gwen set her bag down at his desk and sat in his chair since he was going to get the whiskey. "So this is the view from Governor Bickford's side. I think I know why you like it so much. Nice chair, too."

"Came with the office." He gave her a less-than-serious glare for sitting in his chair and making herself comfortable, then went to the other end of the room past the long couch to a safe that was recessed into the wall. There weren't many things he had to lock up, but some of the more sensitive information about the people of the rebellion was safeguarded, especially things only Logan was privy to. The bottle was fairly hefty, but from the clink of glass inside as he took it out, it clearly had friends not yet tapped. "And I'm not sure why you like the view so much. I always thought the lighting in here left things looking pretty dismal in general." It was true that part of the lighting in the ceiling was in need of replacing, and it left the room a little darker than most of the corridors, even if it was still easy enough to see.

"I figured you liked it that way. Made you seem a little more serious and a lot more ominous." She spun around in his chair once. Clearly stepping away from leadership lessened her stress, since being away from work made her a little lighter already. "Into the dungeon with Governor Bickford." She said in a voice as deep as she could manage before she laughed.

"Sorry, I left my manacles and torture implements in my other dungeon." The look on his face was more serious than it should have been, but that was because he really had left behind quite a few implements of that bent in a very different place. It felt like a life ago, even if he knew it hadn't been all that long in the grand scheme of time. He went to her side of the desk and nudged her chair aside with a knee to reach past her leg into a drawer. The two glasses he pulled out were plain and slightly chipped, but plenty serviceable, and they didn't matter as much as the drinks he poured.

Gwen made no move to get up from the chair but she did reach out and take the glass once he had poured it. "You know, according to laws before the crisis, I'm barely old enough to drink this. But man is it good." She took a gulp larger than she should, but clearly her day had been that long. The burn felt great, but she knew she would pay for it later. "So are those rumors really true, Gov'ner?" She replied with a raised eyebrow as she looked him over. "I heard you were previously an owner of a sex toy shop."

He rolled his eyes and kicked back his own glass, obviously with less difficulty than she had. He had more practice, especially after the last few months. "I ran a farm, not a sex shop. My family does have some stock in some European sex shop chain, though, I remember that from some early accountant reports. I don't think that really qualifies."

"Well, that's boring." She tipped back her glass to finish off the rest. It burned, and she winced, but she didn't complain. "And here I thought you might be able to hook me up. Every girl needs a few good dildos."

"Every girl?" He moved around to the other side of the desk and poured two more glasses, then took his with him over to the couch to relax as he looked over at her. "I suppose I get that, seeing as you're about to head to the midwest. The gender ratio isn't really going to be in your favor. I've heard through the grapevine that one of the families who came out with us brought a lot with her, but she may have sold out of them by now. If I had known while we were on our way back here I could've made sure she gave you the friend discount."

"Damn." Gwen spun around in his chair slowly so she wouldn't spill her drink as she nursed the second one slowly. She didn't want to get smashed in front of Logan Bickford. That would only make her life worse. He was her boss and he was Liam's brother. She didn't want either of them to dislike her, even though she hadn't talked to Liam in a while. "I hung up my hooker boots. Flip-flops? I don't own boots. Hooker sneakers. Whatever. Guess I'll have to do it the old fashioned way. I've been closed for a while. Not that anyone was paying me in the first place."

"Seriously?" He was legitimately surprised by that, enough to distract him from the reason he had intended to drink in the first place. "I have a very hard time imagining you celibate. It's like trying to picture Tatyana giggling. It just doesn't work. And my vote would be for Hooker Flip Flops. You know, expose as much as possible in the interests of professional appeal."

Gwen glared with obvious offense. "Yes, really. Is it that hard to believe? Maybe I didn't want to be a homewrecker anymore. Except I'm wondering if that's the only way I know how to live."

"You know single people exist, right?" He said with no less amusement in his voice. "People who aren't married to anyone at the moment and whose homes you might make a mess out of but not actually wreck? Most single people go after other single people. I'm just asking because I'm not sure if that's an approach you've tried."

"Very funny." She glared at him and took another sip. Gwen was a lightweight and she knew it. "There are far fewer single people around here than otherwise. I *used* to think that as long as I wanted a man and he wanted me, that was all that mattered. I mean, hot attracts hot. I even wanted you on multiple occasions, but you turned out to be way too mean." She teased weakly as she turned her attention back to her drink.

"I am way too mean, you're right about that." He took another sip of his drink and set it aside on a small table, preferring to relax rather than drink too quickly for the time being. "When we first got here I figured you were tossing your tits in my direction every now and then because you were still working out your daddy issues."

"You're not that much older than me. Even if you act like it." Gwen rolled her eyes at him and finished her drink in a flourish before she looked at him again. It wasn't fair. She missed Liam so much, and now she was staring at someone who looked so much like him. It made her insides ache. Once there was a time that she liked Liam because he looked so much like Logan, but she definitely didn't have feelings for the brooding, grumpy governor. She was in love with Liam, and she couldn't have him. "I threw my tits at you because you're attractive."

"Ah, so you're not denying the tit-throwing." He said with a chuckle so brief it barely existed. "At the time, I'm sure it was also because I was married and therefore theoretically unavailable. So I can hardly fault you for lumping me into the mean old man category now that some things have changed."

"I did not say old. And Mercury and Anna are hot. I would have been up for a ménage a trois." She said with a suggestive smirk before she laughed and got up with her glass so he could fill her up again. Flirting with Logan made her miss Liam just a little less, sad as it was. "Refill please, Gov'ner."

"Californian with a Cockney accent. I admit, not something I thought I'd ever live to see." He took the bottle from the same small table where he'd set down his drink, but held it after he unstoppered it, looking up at her with the same half-amused expression as had been on his face for most of the conversation. "Ask nicer."

"Nicer? I said please." She worked up a pout and tried to look more pathetic with puppy dog eyes. "Pretty please with a cherry on top?"

His look turned slightly more amused, but the bottle still didn't move. "You can do better than that."

"Do you want me to beg?" She raised an eyebrow but she moved a bit closer to him and went to the floor in front of him to her knees. "Please, oh please, Mr. Bickford, can I have some more?"

He looked down at her for a moment as she knelt between his knees, then reached over and took her glass to refill it for her. He gave himself another splash as well before restoppering the bottle, and then put it back on the table and took a sip. "Better."

"You're very possessive of your booze, Governor." She

smirked up at him and again thought of Liam, but as soon as she had her refill, she got up off the floor.

"I can be." He watched her the whole way up, then set his glass aside again. "One of my many vices. I started a collection."

"Well, if you ever want to gift a bottle to me, I won't say no." She said with a teasing smile as she sat on the edge of his desk with her legs dangling over as she drank. Even if Gwen had hung up her hooker flip flops, she was always in short cutoff shorts and some kind of top that revealed some part of her cleavage. It was still summer, after all. "I should slow down on these or I'll have to sleep on your desk."

"You know there's a couch right here." He looked down at himself and the two cushions beside him. It was a pretty long couch, even if it was just as plain as everything else in the Labyrinth. "It's pretty comfortable, I've passed out on it a few times myself. Not drunk, just . . . in need of a place without chaos."

"It's the nice thing about having a place that is entirely your own, right? No one can mess up a place that is yours. I like going back to my unit where there are no babies and no toys and no damn Legos." She laughed and hopped off of the desk and sat down next to him on the couch at his half invitation. He didn't say where she was or was not allowed.

"Where the door locks and you're the only one who has a key." He chimed in to agree, slouching back on the couch to relax with his head resting against the low back. "I thought Eleusis would be like this, actually." He sighed, tipping back another sip of his drink as he looked up at the ceiling. "Maybe it still will be, I have no idea. Just someplace you can get away from everything else going on."

"I haven't been." Gwen tipped back her glass and hissed at the burn before she rested her head on the couch too. She was hoping she was drunk enough it wouldn't burn so much. "I'm kind of afraid to go. Doesn't that sound ridiculous? There's nothing there for me. No one. No future here or there. It's my own fault, but I ran away from my family, I never get into relationships, and I'm afraid of the future. So ridiculous."

"There's nothing ridiculous about that." It was easily the most relaxed she'd ever seen Logan, but in some ways, it was also the most depressed she'd ever seen him. She could feel the darkness of his office differently after the way he had described it, something calmer, cooler, more peaceful. One thing in his life that he could control. Being in the middle of it had him much more relaxed.

"I mean, the never getting into relationships part, yeah, you should probably get to work on that. When you eventually have kids of your own, you're gonna be supermother, and I wouldn't have had to deal with the quantity of marriage problems I've dealt with on your account if you didn't fuck like some kind of ancient Sumerian sex goddess. So whoever you do end up in a relationship with is gonna be a lucky guy, no matter what kind of baggage you're bringing with you. And in spite of all the crazy I've had to deal with because of you, people love you. Because their kids love you. So you're not really as alone as you think you are. You've got people."

"Liking someone because they take care of your kids and genuinely liking someone for who they are, those are two very different things. People like what I do for them, but they don't like me. Unless they've slept with me. Most of those people like my vagina at least." She turned her head to the side and looked at him. "People either like you or hate you. It's not a bad thing, but the people who hate you are dumb. They're not paying attention. You are an asshole most of the time because you care. As backwards as it sounds. You have a big heart, and you can't hide it from me."

"Most of the time, that's why I'm an asshole. The rest of the time, it's just fun." He agreed without looking at her. He took another sip of his drink and gave a slight groan, since the buzz of it was starting to settle into him, helping to take the edge off one of his least favorite days in recent memory. He turned to look back at her without moving any closer, pausing only for a brief moment to consider how strange it was that Gwen, of all people, had turned into his drinking companion on that night, but upon buzzed reflection, it wasn't actually that strange. If he had to list his ten closest friends in the world, he would have been forced to include Gwen on the list.

"So who are you, then, when you're not doing things for other people? What's back in that unit of yours that you keep completely to yourself? Other than the world's most impressive collection of short shorts and a surprising lack of sex toys."

Gwen laughed and she got up slowly from the couch. She went to her bag and opened it up and pulled a few things out. When she walked back over to him, she held out a couple different items that looked like personal journals. When he opened up one of them, there were sketches of cute little scenes and a few sentences underneath. It was a children's book. That she had written and illustrated. "As soon as I can get my hands on some colored pencils, I'll fill in the pictures." She flipped a few of the pages for him even though he was fully capable of doing so. "This is Dec's favorite. He likes looking at all the farm animals and he laughs at the noises I make."

She finally got what seemed like a truly legitimate smile from him as he looked at the children's book, and he took the book from her to leaf through it on his own, though he gave her a quizzical look at her mention of Dec laughing. "Noises, huh?"

Gwen rolled her eyes at him and reached out to snatch the book back. "Not sex noises. I'm not trying to fuck up people's babies."

He held the book away so she couldn't take it from him, and kept looking through the images and the captions. Everything about it was contained and simple, nothing about wars or other planets, just a home and the children inside it. It was refreshing, to say the least.

"These are really good, Gwen. No bullshit. I didn't know you were an artist." He finally handed the book back to her when he was finished with it, then relaxed against the couch again. "I would've put you to work doing something else if I had been aware of that."

"I don't usually share it with people." She admitted as she looked down at her work. "Babies like to be read to, and it's fun to make up the stories. I can do it on my own, draw the pictures at my leisure. Just kind of check out of the world."

"I used to read a lot when I was younger." He said in a faraway voice, before he reached his arms back and stretched, since he was feeling quite relaxed. "Liked school, just had too much shit to do to let myself waste time or check out. And if you check out of the world while you're driving a combine, you end up driving over the next guy's field. That's a problem." He chuckled and looked her over again. "First publishing house anybody sets up on Eleusis, you should definitely have first dibs. Get some of them out in the world."

"I'll keep that in mind." She said with a laugh before she looked at her empty glass. "What else do you have hiding in your alcohol stash?"

He looked back at the safe, which he had left open, since he trusted Gwen and imagined there might be a need for another bottle. "Diego gave me a bottle of some truly great tequila I've never had the courage to finish off. Other than that, there's some moonshine tucked into the back, but it's not that great without ice. See for yourself. I don't have too many dangerous secrets in there."

Gwen went looking and grabbed the tequila, since she didn't want to test out any moonshine. She uncorked the bottle and poured herself too much. "What did booze taste like up there?"

"They had this shit called Shine that was actually really good. But they said you can't really make it right here on Earth. Something about the low gravity. It was pretty sweet, but it would kick your ass in a hurry." He tipped back the rest of his whiskey, but didn't ask for any tequila in replacement, preferring to watch her drink for a moment. "Hopefully you'll get to try it sometime. Things in space are . . . pretty different. All around."

"I don't think I want to spend any time up there after what I've heard." She replied with a laugh before she zigzagged her way back to the couch. "You're right, this is *really* good tequila." She spilled some on her hand and she licked it up just to make sure she didn't lose any. "I'm going to have a hangover from hell after this."

"You just have to remember to hydrate later." He turned his head to look her over, relaxed enough for his eyes to linger on her a little more than he otherwise might have. "There's not that much of you all told, you'll be fine."

"There's enough of me, thank you very much. I haven't had any complaints." She looked him over as well, but she continued to think of Liam. She wondered if she would ever stop missing Liam. "Hydrate. We'll see if I remember."

"Amateur." He laughed at her once and reached across her to take the tequila bottle out of her hand. It shifted him a little on the couch until they were shoulder to shoulder, but he didn't move away afterward as he took a swig straight from it. "Mmm. Back home, I always thought this was what it tasted like to do something stupid."

"What, drink straight from the bottle?" She grabbed his hand and then drank from the bottle as he held it. "Nah, it's fun. And it means I'm not on my knees begging."

"Maybe I should make you get back down there if you want more." He pulled the bottle away from her, though it tugged her against him from the way she was still holding onto it, and him. "I kinda liked you down there."

"That's cuz you're mean and you want me to beg for my booze." Gwen looked away from his face and down at the solid body she was pressed against. She licked her lips slowly as she thought about what she could do between his legs. "Don't put me too close to danger unless you want to get burned. I told you, I've not been close with a man in a while."

"I've got a policy against women too drunk to know better." He clearly wasn't anywhere near as buzzed as she was, but he wasn't pushing her away either. "I'm not saying it's my favorite policy right this second," he looked down to examine the parts of her that her clothes were designed to showcase, and let out a sigh, "but it is a policy. Usually it is, anyway."

"I'm not too drunk to know better." She slowly ran a hand tentatively along his chest and down his side. "I didn't know you were interested."

He didn't push her touch away, which was more than she could say for any of her advances on the man in the entire time she'd known him. Throwing her tits at him had only partly been a euphemism. "I didn't know you still were." He knew she was a career flirt, so he hadn't been surprised when that aspect of her relationship with him had never gone away, but actually doing anything about it was a very different question altogether. "My own interest is . . . complicated."

"Complicated." Gwen repeated as she moved her hand to slide underneath his shirt so she could touch his skin. "What kind of complicated? Do we get to be naked in this kind of complicated?"

Logan didn't stop her, but he did close his eyes for a minute just to enjoy her exploration. Everything outside of the room was complicated, but everything inside that room was as simple as the alcohol in both their bodies. It was easy, it was light, and it was . . . freeing. There was no past with Gwen, no history to deal with in every single gesture and every conversation. More than that, there would be no future with them. He didn't think for a moment that she was after such a thing from him, and she knew him well enough to know that his own situation was so complicated that he certainly wasn't about to go looking to make it worse.

"Go lock the door." He said as her fingertips raked lightly down his chest. "And turn out the first light. Not the second one. Then come back."

Gwen savored touching his muscles for a moment longer before she got up and did exactly as he said. She had no reason not to, after all. Once the office was darker and she was standing in front of him again, she ran her hand through her hair. "What next?"

He wondered, briefly, if some whisper of his own proclivities had made its way to Gwen, but whether it had or not, she was doing precisely as she was told, and that was enough for him for the time being. He could feel the world settle into place a little, as if it had been ever so slightly off its axis and was being righted again. He kicked off his shoes while she was busy locking the door, and he looked every bit as relaxed as he had the moment before. There was nothing relaxed about the way he was looking her over, though. "Shirt and shorts. Leave whatever's underneath, if there's anything to be left."

"I'm a classy girl. I usually wear underwear." She smiled as she kicked off her shoes. She tugged her shirt over her head and tossed it aside and pushed down her shorts and stepped out of them before she kicked them away. She was left in a skimpy black bra and underwear.

He looked her over slowly as his eyes adjusted in the dim light, then threw what little caution he had left out the window. He sat up and pulled off his shirt, tossing it aside on the floor, then leaned forward on his knees as he looked her up and down. "Would you call me a friend, Gwen?"

Gwen liked the way he looked over her hungrily, but she didn't want to admit to herself why, even though she knew why. Liam had a similar look when he looked her over, and it drove her crazy. "Yeah, I would say we're friends. Would you call me a friend?"

"Yeah, I think I would." She knew him well enough to tell that he was a little surprised by the revelation, but that didn't make it any less true. After looking her up and down a few more times, he reached out and hooked the waist of her panties, drawing her in against him until she was straddling his lap and he could relax against the back of the couch again to look up at her. "Fair warning, though, I don't typically fuck my friends the way I'm about to fuck you."

Gwen groaned at hearing the words come out of his mouth, and her pulse picked up along with her breathing. Somewhere in the back of her mind she was telling herself it was a terrible idea, because she had just told him that she didn't want to be a homewrecker anymore. She also thought about the fact that Liam would never want to see her again if she slept with his brother.

It made her pause, but her own words echoed a little too loudly in her mind. She was only good at a few things. More distance from Liam was better for him and his family. Even though she missed him so much it hurt down to her soul.

"I guess we're just *really* good friends." She leaned into him a little, but her hand wandered down so she could investigate the best part of him.

The pants he wore to work were comfortable enough for her to feel the kind of effect she'd had on him, even though she really hadn't done much except to do as she was told. He didn't make any move to stop her investigation, and moved his hands up over her legs slowly to investigate her in turn. For all she had attempted to throw herself at him earlier in their acquaintance, he had never actually touched her on purpose, so it was a very new kind of exploration. The differences between him and his brother were apparent in the restraint Logan showed in the study of his fingertips, but the touch quickly turned slightly . . . rougher, massaging along her legs and backside and up her back to take a firm hold of her.

"You'd better not be fragile." He said almost in a threat, his hips moving slightly to rock against her touch.

The more he touched her the more she needed him to keep touching her, since being desired was something that was a part of her and she had denied it for too long. She rocked against him as well, and leaned in enough to nibble along his neck. "I'm not." She growled in a heated whisper. "You can do whatever you want to me, and I can do whatever you ask."

From what he knew about her, he knew she wasn't bluffing, and he groaned a little under the heat of that kind of certainty. The alcohol was more or less forgotten nearby, but one of his hands left hers long enough to grab a glass (he wasn't sure if it was his or hers at that point) and take a sip of what was left inside. He let it sting his lips and burn his tongue before he took her by the back of the neck and pulled her into a kiss that was both violent and demanding, showing her no mercy until the rest of her body was forced into responding of its own accord.

Gwen moaned loudly as he kissed her violently, since some parts of her mind were thinking of Liam and she wanted him so badly that a lookalike was giving her the ease she had been looking for. The sting of the alcohol in the kiss made it that much more dangerous and violent, but she didn't care. She squirmed on his lap as her lips assaulted him in a similar fashion, and there was need behind it that she was sure he noticed. It had been a while, and she was only human.

When the kiss finally broke, it was clear neither of them were playing around any longer. The violence in his touch didn't stop when his lips left hers, and his kiss along her neck was rough in all the right places. His hands gripped her ass to grind her against him before his arms wrapped around her tightly enough to pop her back, but it didn't stop either of them.

His well-muscled chest was like cut glass against her own, and when he did release her momentarily, it was only so he could shove his pants out from under her and push them to the floor, leaving him fully exposed to her. Once he was bare, he reached down between them to slide his hand into her panties, watching her face so he could see the look in her eyes as his fingers slid against her. "Just think of me as your personal sex toy for the moment." He said with a smile as his fingers teased her aching clit.

"So much better than a sex toy." She moaned as his fingers worked magic she had missed. There was a reason she was a slut. It felt so fucking good. Gwen was biting down hard on her lip as he touched her in all the right places. "Goddamn it has been too long . . . that is so good . . ."

"Like I said. You and celibacy don't seem to belong in the same breath." There was nothing teasing about his touch, no playfulness, no testing or hesitation. He wanted to please her, and that was that. She'd been with men who wanted nothing more than to get in her pants, who were fixated on her because she was gorgeous, who just wanted to touch her, and on the other hand, she had been with Liam, who wanted to be *with* her. Someone who wanted to please her before he even did anything about himself was . . . a little different.

Even so, she could tell Logan was enjoying himself by virtue of how much she was enjoying herself, and the look in his eyes didn't permit her to look away. He wanted to see it. He wanted to hear exactly what he was doing to her. He reached up and unclasped her bra, tugged it off with his free hand and tossed it aside. "You should not be going without. Ever."

"I really shouldn't." She agreed wholeheartedly. When her bra went flying, she felt even better, since being naked was easily her preferred state. He'd get the panties off eventually. "Fucking hell, your fingers sure know . . . what they're doing." The tension continued to build inside her, but she knew she wouldn't last long. She'd been too long without.

"They fucking should." He assured her with a grin, taking one of her hands and placing it behind her on his knee, before reaching around her back to do the same with the other. It forced her to arch her back on top of him, and gave his mouth perfect access to her breasts as his hand continued to push her. "Don't hold back." He said as he started to get a taste of her. "Now or in anything else. Don't hold back, don't hold out, and don't stop until I give you fucking permission."

"Fuck." She hissed as he ran his warm tongue across her nipple and teased her breast, which made her even crazier. "I won't fucking hold back. Sir." Gwen couldn't if she tried at this point, since her whole body needed everything he was giving her, including his cock. All it took was a couple more teasing fingers and his teeth scraping her nipple and she was already orgasming for the first time, though she knew it wouldn't be the last.

He drew back to watch her, smiling in satisfaction at the way her entire body shuddered under his touch. It was the ultimate control, for Logan, to be able to give someone that kind of ecstasy, to be able to, in every sense, hold a person in his hands and change that moment of their lives. Gwen felt different from anyone else he'd ever been with, but every woman was unique, and they all worked in their own way. He teased out every aftershock of the orgasm he could, feeling out exactly what her body could and couldn't take from him as he watched her. "Feeling a little better about life?"

"Mhm." She relaxed on top of him, since she was halfway holding herself up and he was halfway holding her too. Gwen groaned again and almost purred like a cat. "But I want more."

"I'd be disappointed if you didn't." He grinned up at her and kissed her again, just as violently as the first time, then moved to half-drop, half-throw her down on the unoccupied half of the couch. Once she was down, he pulled her panties off one-handed and threw them aside as he moved to get up, letting her stretch out languidly across the entire couch. "I want to know your favorite." He stood next to the couch, one hand down to trail over her body lightly. "I don't do anything half-ass, including temporary escapes from the world."

"Hmmm . . ." Gwen said as she looked up at him and over his body. She wished he was Liam, but she was feeling too good and too buzzed to care about much at the moment. "My favorite . . . well, I like rough. And I like *deep* penetration. Upside down, on top, sitting and on top . . . it's hard to choose."

"I like a girl who likes variety." He laughed as he looked her over, running his hand roughly over her breasts to keep the buzz in her body flowing freely. Once it was clear she was starting to recover, he picked her up and spun her until she was on her knees on the couch cushions, facing the wall. His hands took hold of her backside slowly as he nudged her knees wider apart and let her feel the heat of him stroking her still-sensitive core. When he was good and close, his hands ran up her spine to her shoulders in a warm massage, before one of his hands wove in her hair. "I'm pretty sure I heard you say rough. Let me hear you say it again."

"Mmmm. You're bossy, aren't you? I don't mind, though, Governor." She replied with a smirk he could hear, since Gwen was a very adventurous woman. She liked men, women, and just about anything she could handle. "I said rough. I like being roughly fucked, Logan."

"Remember you said that twice." He almost growled before he moved back and slid inside her, one slow inch at a time. The growl in him only deepened as he filled her completely, his grip on her hair forcing her to arch her back until she had every bit of him. "Fucking god, that's . . ." He devolved into more groans as he pressed himself fully into her, and became incapable of speech as he drew back to slam into her hard. Part of the reason he had consistently said no to her and avoided any kind of reaction to her advances had been that he knew he wouldn't be able to resist her at all if he gave in, and he hadn't been wrong. When she said rough, he hoped she meant it, since that was exactly what he gave her.

Gwen gave back as much as she could, even with him gripping her hair and controlling her. Her core gripped his cock tightly, and apparently she knew what to do with all the muscles that no one could see.

Thoughts of Anna ran through his mind more frequently than he wanted to admit, just because he knew part of the reason why he'd been attracted to Gwen in the first place rested in her similarities to Anna. She had something to prove, she was incredible at what she did, and every nerve in his body was becoming more and more convinced of exactly how good the woman was. She hadn't been lying about liking it rough, judging by the sounds that escaped her every time he slammed into her. He didn't want it to be over quickly, even if it was clearly just the first round of many given both their mental states, but she wasn't the only one with something to prove.

The longer it took Logan, the more Gwen tried every trick in her book to get him closer, since she desperately wanted him crying out her name. She wanted to know that she could unravel the man that seemed impossible to unravel, especially because she'd fantasized about it long before she even knew Liam existed. Whenever she thought about Liam there was a sting in her chest, but she pushed the thoughts aside quickly. Liam wasn't hers. Never would be. Logan wasn't either, but for that moment, he was. "I'm gonna . . . get your number . . . and crack you, Logan Bickford."

He pulled her back against him after her threat, yanking her up by the hair until her back was pressed against his chest. "We'll see." He groaned violently against her ear. One of his hands reached up to take her by the throat while the other held onto her hips as he kept her from taking too much control. His hand eventually crept down between her legs to resume his torment mercilessly. "You can figure my number out, but it's good to have yours."

Gwen growled loudly as soon as his fingers tortured her clit, and her body couldn't help but buck against him no matter how he tried to control her. Her moans got louder the more he teased her until she was climaxing against his cock. She was caught by surprise with the violent orgasm, but it felt incredible.

He actually cackled behind her as he felt her body cry out in pleasure, but he was ruthless as she collapsed in front of him against the back of the couch. He didn't let go of her or leave her to come down from the orgasm in peace. If anything, his movements inside her only got wilder, harder, but a frenzy later, he was crying out himself, holding onto her so tightly her hips were sure to have bruises.

Gwen moved every way she could to make his orgasm last before she just collapsed. "Fuck." She panted as he remained pressed inside of her. "So . . . good . . ."

He groaned with her as she fell face-first onto the couch, and laid himself flat against her back as he ground his hips into her to savor the last of his orgasm. He kissed the back of her neck as he laid most of his weight on top of her, savoring her racing pulse as he felt it against his lips. He had her well and truly captive, his strong arms holding her on both sides as he continued to set her nerves on fire. "You . . . never quit. I like that."

"Ditto." She replied with another satisfied groan since her body felt like putty. "As soon as . . . my body recovers . . . I want to do that again."

"I'm not gonna give you that much of a break." He said with a kiss to her shoulder, before he pushed himself off her slowly and fell back against the other arm of the couch. "Come here and give me that ass back." He knew he was being flippant and demanding, only one of which he'd ever been at any given time, but it felt good to be both, if only for a little while.

Gwen laughed and fell back against Logan and rested her head against his chest. Cuddling was a reward for awesome sex. She convinced herself it had nothing to do with missing Liam. Logan's chest was warm and full and his touch and heartbeat meant company that wanted her around for the moment. "Good thing you're warm. It's cold in here."

"I can see that." He said as his hand brushed over her nipple, his arm resting casually over her chest just to keep touching her as they caught their breath. "You're every bit as good and better than rumors say you are, by the way. Part vixen, part vacuum, is I think how I heard you described best."

"Part vacuum?" She replied with a laugh but she shivered as his fingers played with her nipple. "I don't think we got to that part yet."

"No, but we will." He said with a hefty amount of self-assurance, his fingers tracing lazy paths all over her body. "This is not the night I was planning on having." He admitted, though it did nothing to stop his caresses from going lower and moving along her inner thigh to tease her. "But it's going to be a very long night. Hope you managed to get some rest sometime earlier today, because you're not going to get any here."

"This was not the night I planned on having either." She agreed, since she didn't want him to think that she somehow planned on seducing him. "But maybe it's the one I needed. I'm okay with a long night in here with you." Gwen said softly. "It means not being pathetically alone for a day."

"In your defense, the alone part would be slightly less pathetic if you had something at home to play with besides your own fingers. I can already tell you're one of those rare girls who needs something stiff between her legs to really get done right." His fingers teased along the still-sensitive parts of her as he chuckled against her hair. "But you're not pathetic." He kissed her neck. It wasn't the lingering, emotional kiss of a lover, the kind of touch she'd gotten from his brother during the single day she'd spent with him, but it was supportive nonetheless. "You've got some strange taste in men, but if that's the worst thing you can be accused of, you're doing a hell of a lot better than most of us. Friends don't let friends throw pity parties."

"Just sex parties." She replied with a renewed laugh and she squirmed a little bit on top of him so she could touch him. "The best kind of party. Especially with a cock like yours."

"I'm glad you like it." He groaned a little at the way she squirmed, and she could already feel him starting to respond to her again. One more thing to remind her of Liam. Both men were nearly indefatigable. "It likes you too, clearly. I've gotta say, the size you are, I thought you'd have more of a problem taking it, but I should've known better than to doubt you."

Both men were not exactly the same, but Gwen was thinking more and more of Liam, and part of her was shocked that she didn't cry out his name instead of Logan's in the middle of her orgasms. "We need more tequila. And then I need more of you."

* * * * *

"Here's what's *not* going to happen." Carl said in a growl, pausing momentarily where he was walking through the underbrush to look back at Carmina and a few of the others in the squad with her. There were almost two dozen of them all told, and however talented Carl had to admit they were as soldiers, every one of them was an asshole.

"What's *not* going to happen is anybody here listening to a fucking word you say when it comes to what we're doing and how we're doing it. What *is* going to happen is that we're going to follow the trail I lead, because that's the whole fucking reason we're here in the first place, and the reason why I'm the one in the Alpha slot on this mission. And you're gonna keep your fucking mouth shut about it because you know exactly shit about this place. You're here to learn and to be slightly useful in case anything requires shooting. That's where your job description stops. Is that in any way unclear, Sweetheart?" Carl had just about enough of the woman and her endless second-guessing after only twenty minutes. He couldn't imagine having to spend days and possibly years dealing with her as she hung around and the war dragged on.

"We're here for the shooting part and you're here to see the scenery." Carmina growled back at Carl, since she was frustrated with his leadership methods. "You're not being *unclear*, you're being too cautious."

"Good, so it's clear, then." Carl didn't care what she thought of how he was approaching things, obviously, and he gave her a dismissive nod before he turned to head back to the front of the outfit. He strode through the trees in a direction that would allow them to circle back around the entire Eleusis compound to get a better look at parts of the Consortium's operation the mountain rebels hadn't yet been able to see. Carl had seen it plenty of times, but seeing it in person was always a very different thing. "Take six of your people and set out a pair on both our flanks and one hanging back, quarter click intervals. We've got about three clicks to go, and if anything starts coming at us sideways, we'll be glad of the cover fire." Mostly he just wanted to get rid of as many of Carmina's people as possible, but he assumed that had been implied in the order.

Carmina started pointing at people to get them to organize the way she wanted them to organize, and while they did follow Carl's order, Carmina didn't look at all happy about it. It was the last scouting mission before shit started to get real, so Kameron was with Carl for one last time before she headed up the group going to the Bickford property. She didn't know if she would ever get the chance to see Eleusis again, so she wanted one more trip. Kameron shook her head as Carmina stormed off with her fighters. "If we can't kill her yet, you would think we could at least tranquilize her."

"Oh, I've had fantasies involving muzzles and rooms with no windows, believe me." He glared off after Carmina but continued moving forward anyway, keeping his eyes out for anything of the Consortium's they might have placed in the area between that morning and the last time he'd been there. "Right now I'm hoping they completely ignore my safety briefing and one of them decides to poke a Behemoth with a stick. Make all of our lives a lot easier."

"Mostly." Kameron agreed as her own eyes scanned the area, but she was glad to see it seemed quiet. "I can't believe this is my last time coming back here for a while."

"You'll be back." Carl said with a shove to her shoulder as they walked, ducking under branches and pointing back at the rest of Carmina's goons from time to time just to point out various things they shouldn't be stepping in if they wanted to keep their feet. "Have you even told Melissa you're going yet? You've been running the leash and collar show with Psychobitch for the past few days pretty solid."

"No, I haven't told her. She assumes she's going to the Bickford estate without me, which is why she's mad at me and not talking to me very much." Kameron actually looked slightly amused by it. "I can't blame her for assuming, and I truly have not had time since the arrival of the Death Crew to sit down with her and spend more than an hour with her. Kassie has been sick. It's just been rough. I'm trying to make a romantic moment out of it, but I should know better."

"Well, take her back some flowers this time. Or, you know, the severed head of your enemies. Women love that." He grinned down at his friend as they moved through the trees, both of them alert for any sign of danger, but much more comfortable on Eleusis than they had been months before when doing their initial reconnaissance missions. "You're off rotation after this one and I get the lovely duty of trying to follow up on what you've done here. Way to make my job easier. You could've slacked off just a *little* as a commander. You know, just out of consideration."

"Nah. I'm tiny compared to you. You know what they say about size, I had to compensate somehow." She smirked at him and looked around and back at Carmina's people once, which erased her smile temporarily. "Xander is still pissed as fuck that I'm sitting it out. I don't fucking want to, I want to be here. I've spent my life training to fight and fly. Just like you and Orion. Even though he still thinks I can't fly a shuttle worth shit." She shrugged, since it was mostly true. "I have to make a big gesture. Melissa needs to know I'm in this with her until I'm fucking dead, or I'm worried she'll think it's not worth sticking around."

"You need to stop underestimating that woman. She loves you like an Eleusis rat loves peanut butter." It had been one of the more amusing discoveries they had made upon first doing recon missions on Eleusis after his return to Earth. Eleusis rats weren't carnivorous and weren't proper rats, but the moment someone had taken out a peanut butter sandwich to eat for lunch, they had been swarmed with hundreds of the creatures crawling up out of tiny borrows for acres around. It had been a tense but ultimately entertaining lunch.

"Even if you were staying here and she was going with Kassie, she'd still stick with you. But you're a better person for going." He gave her a subdued smile. "Aiko and I both have bones to pick with the Consortium on a very personal level. When we breach those walls," he nodded off in the distance at the compound visible through the cleft in the hills, "I plan to be the one ringing the doorbell. But I'm aware that fact does not make me a better person."

"You're doing what you need to do, and Aiko is going to be here with you. That's different." She sighed as she kept her eye out for any danger. "I'm not underestimating her. I just know that we love each other differently. I would be less without her, but she's stronger than I am. She doesn't need me like I need her."

"More things I don't agree with. We've got a lot of those." He heard an innocuous-sounding beep from his pocket as he walked and stopped immediately, falling back against the trunk of a tree to not be out in the open as he checked it. Many of those behind him did likewise because they were startled, but Carl didn't correct them. The hills around them went for hundreds of meters over their heads in soft vertical pillars with rocky cores that defined the landscape for dozens of kilometers out even over the sea nearby. It was an easy place for someone to get snuck up on.

He pulled his communicator out of his pocket to check it and swore a few times in Japanese before he looked up at everybody. "Drone launch! Topographical survey and slave-tracking. Twelve minutes to the sweep! We've got that long to get out of sight." It wasn't the first time it had happened and Carl imagined it wouldn't be the last. He was glad they had a warning, and that the sweeps never went as far out as the home he'd built with Aiko.

"Anna, take Masterson and go warn the left flank. Valencia, you and Rumfeld take the rear, Kam and I will get the right. You've got your own surveys, fucking use them and get underground." He was already off and running before he was done giving orders, and everyone scattered quickly, frantically checking their personal units to tell them where some kind of shelter could be found.

Kameron followed after Carl so they could find a place to hide from the drones, and she looked back to see if she could see Anna run off, but Anna was already gone. "Now where am I supposed to hide a big-ass knucklehead like you?!" Kameron yelled at her friend, since Carl was one of her best friends and always would be. "I'm gonna need a really big hole in the ground!"

"Oh, shut it, we passed an overhang about two hundred meters back that's big enough for ten of us. I want to see if those assholes were paying attention." He yelled back over his shoulder at her, then yelled to alert the flank guards that Carmina sent out before he took off at a sprint toward the overhang. For a man as huge as he was, he shouldn't have been able to move as fast as he did. Physics on Earth seemed to agree on that, but on Eleusis, it was like there was nothing he couldn't do. "Come on, keep up!" He yelled playfully back at her, even though he was checking the countdown on his communicator at the same time.

"Keep up?! You're as bad as those fucking Behemoths! Your legs are like three times the size of mine!" Kameron was fast, but she was still having a hard time keeping up with Carl. She didn't think she could for much longer. "Can I ride on your back like you're my horse?"

At first he was going to throw some kind of mean comment back at her, but he seemed to reconsider and stopped for a second to shoulder-check her right in the waist, picking her clear up onto his shoulder like she was some kind of toddler. The whole time, he barely even had to stop running. "That's all the pony ride you get. Can't keep track of a cave. What's wrong with you?" He did his best to keep from slamming her into any branches as he ran, but he still hit a few low-hanging intruders along the way.

Kameron groaned every time she got smacked, but she still thought it was fun to be carried by the massive man she called her friend. "This is nice. Minus the trees. Watch where you're going!"

Anna could hear Kameron and Carl yelling at each other as they ran, but she kept her eyes on her own path back toward a different set of caves she had seen during previous recon missions. She didn't yell, except to give directions, but she ran her ass off. "I am not about to get picked up by a fucking drone . . . not when we're this close."

Oliver was running right behind her, with a heavy medical kit strapped to his back that was the best shot they could take at being prepared for all eventualities. Warning Carmina hadn't been quite as unpleasant as he thought it would be, since she obeyed and ran off on her own fairly quickly to find some kind of cover, but that still left him and Anna running for their lives. "Wait, back at these?" He called ahead to her, though she was leading the way and there wasn't much he could do about it. "These are the ones that are barely . . . oh bloody hell . . ." They didn't have time to be picky, so he saved his breath and ran as fast as he could.

He had been with her on the recon mission where she found the caves in the first place, but calling them caves at all was being incredibly generous. The hill sloped up sharply and actually turned slightly concave at one point in the curvature that was actually facing the Consortium compound. There was a system of slits and holes in the side of the rock that made it look like some kind of natural missile silo. The hole that was most easily accessible was barely wide enough for Oliver to have stretched his arms out in front of his body, and was just barely tall enough for them to slide themselves in feet-first with the stone just a foot above their heads.

It was a hell of a tight fit, but if they didn't want to get picked up by the Consortium, hiding inside the rock was their best bet.

Once he climbed in, rather ungracefully and with no shortage of whispered cursing and bashing of knees and elbows, he pulled his medical pack in against the mouth of the cave in front of them, leaving them both the tiniest of slits on either side of it to see through. Thankfully, the cave was more than deep enough to accommodate them both, curving initially down from the exterior and then just as slightly upward into the stone heart of the hill.

"Prince and Masterson secure, Sir." Oliver radioed in, still speaking quietly as the rest of their team began reporting in as well.

Anna curled up as much as she could no matter how uncomfortable they might be, since her heart was racing and she was incredibly paranoid about being spotted. She for sure did not want to get picked up by the Consortium. Not when she had shit to do. Not when she needed to get back home and talk to Logan. Not when she had so much else to do. "Fucking drones. At least we got in here."

"Sure. Put the claustrophobic fellow in a tight little hole in the ground and tell him his life's in danger. Something to be grateful for." He chuckled and smiled over at her, shaking his head. "I'm not actually claustrophobic, but if I were on the edge at all, this fit would be enough to push a bloke over, I would think." He turned onto his back to look at the ceiling, and shook his head before he turned back onto his stomach to look out the holes.

Drone launching in thirty seconds. Carl was saying over their closed-circuit radio. *Jason is reporting that drone survey activity may take as long as two to three hours. Hopefully you all found caves big enough to take a piss without pissing off everybody who you're in there with.*

"Two to three hours? Dear god almighty." Anna growled and sighed loudly before she moved to get as comfortable as possible. "I hope you're a good storyteller. That's a fucking long time to be stuck in this teeny tiny cave."

"Generally if I'm telling somebody a story it's because I've got a book open and they're dying. Neither of those really apply in this instance." He shifted his pack around just a little, since if they were going to be stuck in a hole for hours, they might as well be comfortable. He laid out an emergency blanket he had in the pack and began working his way out of his boots and jumpsuit, since if they were going to be there for a while, he figured he might as well be lying on padding rather than rocky ground that was trying to kill him. "There, move the, alright, right, lift the ass there, and . . . there you go, that's for your half. Wonderful thing, this blanket. I've had this with me for as long as I can remember. Never had to use it but maybe two other times, and that was just because it got that fucking cold."

"Thank god it's not cold. That's the last thing we need on top of being stuck here." Anna got out of her own jumpsuit so she could be comfy as well, and she was glad to get the boots off. They were heavy. "Thanks. Might as well get comfortable, right?"

"No reason not to." Not much light got into the chamber past his pack blocking the mouth of it, but it was the middle of the morning and a typically clear sky outside. Even so, living under blue Eleusis sunlight always felt like it left everything half a dream, even in the shadows it cast. "How's the ass, by the way? I never did get a chance to come by and get a look at it after I took the stitches out."

"Really? You're asking me about my ass?" She replied with an incredulous laugh but shook her head. "It hasn't been bothering me, so I assume it's not infected or anything."

"Oh, what, you've got something better to talk about while we're stuck here for hours? What would that be?" He was clearly nervous about their situation from the way he was anxiously looking back and forth between her and the tiny slit of light he could see the rest of the world through.

"We're okay." She assured him, even though she was nervous herself, but she was fairly certain they were in a safe location. "Even if someone comes at us, they'll be dead before they see us. I'm a good shot."

"I know that, but even a corpse becomes a liability out here." They'd had conversations about it in security briefings before, but it was still a relevant problem in his brain. "A corpse means something killed it, and a gunshot wound means somebody else's gun, and that means questions, and that means they find us. So yeah, I'm glad you're a good shot and I definitely prefer their corpses to ours, I just . . . get nervous." He shook his head and sighed, turning away from the opening to force himself not to keep too much of an eye out. His pack was camouflaged already and the cave had vegetation growing mostly across the front of it anyway. There was nothing to worry about.

"Let's talk about something else. Or sleep. We're doing everything we can do to protect ourselves by hiding here. We can't do anything else."

"Good. Talk more about the futility of action. That'll help." He smiled over at her and relaxed on his side with one arm beneath his head. "I'll work on not being a nervous talker, but no promises. I'm also a little worried about possibly not being able to help anyone else in the squad if they're injured. But I'm good here."

"Hey, I lucked out. I got the medic to take care of me and he's a nervous talker with a sexy accent." She smiled at him and turned onto her side to face him. "Talk all you want."

By contrast, he was actually quiet after that, but he did laugh as he attempted to relax, permitting himself one more look out into the clear and empty morning. "Is it bad that I'm not actually that upset about being locked in somewhere for a while? Ever since you came back from the dead and brought us all in on this thing, it's been non-stop. Not that I mind most of the time. But it's nice to have a break for a while. Even under the circumstances."

"I'm sorry." Anna said softly as her smile faded away. "It seems like my life just keeps turning yours upside down."

"No, no, I like my life upside down." He reassured her with a smile and a brief touch to her arm. It was too easy, since they were well within each other's reach. "It's better than my life ever was right side up. This way I'm . . . doing something. Something that matters."

"Your whole life's work is something that matters. You don't give yourself enough credit." She gave him a small smile and returned the touch to his arm. "You're amazing."

"My life's work is death's work." He gave another laugh, and she could see him glance down to her hand on his arm in the dim light filtering through to them. He was surprised she was touching him at all by choice, but he certainly wasn't trying to brush her off. "I like the work I do here, though. Well, here and back in the mountains. Kind of weird how this place still feels like there, even if I know it's not. Like this whole place is some kind of wonderland that's hidden beneath the Labyrinth back on Earth instead of being a few stars away." He was already lying on his side, but he took her hand as she started to pull it away from his arm. "I prefer to work for the living."

Anna was surprised he took her hand, but she held onto his for a little while afterward. "What's, um, do you hold everyone's hand?" She replied a little nervously.

"No, and, though this may come as a surprise to you, I also don't follow up on people's asses quite as intensely as I do yours." He didn't let go of her, smiling quietly in the darkness. "I'm sorry, apparently I was being more subtle about my interest than I intended to be."

Anna laughed softly and looked down at his hand holding hers again. She knew she should feel guilty about holding anyone's hand, but it felt nice. Especially at such a nervous time. "I didn't really realize you were interested." She slowly looked up and gave him another small smile. "I'm seriously fucked up. I don't know who would want to deal with it. I left my first husband for my Match, I left my second husband for my first husband, and now I don't know what the hell is going on with Logan and I. It feels like we're constantly at cross-purposes but we want the same end goal. We disagree more than we agree, except we agree, currently, that we're not at a place to remarry. I am a ridiculous mess."

"That is true." He responded with a shrug, then chuckled as she gave him a glare. "Oh, what, I'm not supposed to agree with you? No, that's not how that works at all. I mean, I don't *entirely* agree with you. Your situation is a mess, your history is rather convoluted, but you, as a person, I've never considered *you* to be a mess. Not that I suppose I'd call you the most orderly person on the planet either, but you get my meaning. And besides, neither am I."

She laughed and shook her head. "So you've been interested in a mess with one ex, one potential husband, and kids with different fathers? I'm not that hot."

"You are, actually." He contradicted her immediately. "More importantly, I believe you might be the single bravest person I've ever encountered, which is why I've heard more than a few people call you reckless. They simply have their bar set too low on courage, in my opinion."

The compliment made Anna smile a little brighter. "I'm going to look at it that way. Their bar of courage is too low. Reckless just doesn't sound right." She gripped his hand a little tighter. "I really like you. You're easy to talk to. And look at. And listen to." She added with a continued smile. "You deserve happiness more than most people I know."

She could tell from the look on his face that he didn't agree with her when she said so, and he took a slow breath as he shook his head. "I'm . . . I've never been much for faith, but in my job, it's difficult sometimes not to be a believer. I am, however, of the hope that we don't all get what we deserve in this life. I wouldn't merit much if that were the case."

"How can you say that?" Anna looked at him incredulously, since she thought he was one of the most selfless people she knew. "You were the only reason my dad lived comfortably at the end of his life. He lived as long as he did because you helped him. I probably never would have seen him again if it weren't for all that you did." She grabbed his hand with both of hers instead of the one hand. "You listened to me and comforted me when you didn't even know me. You're so kind and generous, and of all the people, I deserve it least."

"You deserve it more." He contradicted again almost harshly, if harsh was even possible in his smooth accent. "The people here in the mountains don't understand you or your family, I don't think. You even forget things about yourselves sometimes. But you, more than anyone else I think I've ever met, just want to be happy. There's no sin in that, and no shame, even though everyone here seems to be hell bent on jamming some in where it doesn't belong. People criticize you for that and I think even you get on yourself for it once in a while, but being happy is not a terrorist action. It's what everyone wants. Some of us just admit it more freely than others. Unraveling the Consortium, opening the gate between Earth and Eleusis for colonization and a longer, unrestricted life for everyone, for your family, for your children, that's what happiness seems to mean to you. You should let nothing get in the way of that. Too many things get in the way without our permission anyway, there's no sense in going on the search for things like regret and guilt to hold us down from it as well."

"Easier said than done." She replied softly before she took a deep breath and laid her head on her arm even as she held his hand with hers. "I want to be happy, but I want the people I'm with to be happy too. I fucked everything up with Orion. If I died today, I don't know if he would care. I miss being his friend, and I just . . . miss him so much. Logan and I . . . some days we work amazingly well. Other days, it's like we're speaking in two different languages and neither of us will budge. It wasn't like that before, but we were different people before. Either way, I just . . . don't fucking know what to do with my life. I've lost both my best friends since the Initiative. I don't know what to do except this. Get to Eleusis. Destroy the Consortium. Have a life *after*. Somehow. That's all I can think about anymore."

"That's all it should be." He agreed with a sigh. "That's all that's going to matter in the end. That's all that *ever* matters in the end. Being where we want to be and being happy with the people we're with. Doing what we can for others, finding joy in life everywhere and every time we can. I've listened to enough dying people to know they're not fucking with the rest of us when they keep telling us not to waste our time."

"What about you? What do you want? What would make you happy?" She slid a little bit closer to him while still laying on her side. "I think it's important for you to be happy too."

There was a conflict in his eyes as he thought about her question, but since she had moved closer, he moved his hand to her waist to rest over the thin shorts she'd worn under her jumpsuit for comfort. "What I want is complicated." He admitted with a short and morbid laugh. "I have the unenviable conundrum of being a man of peace and medicine who has dreams every night that revolve around revenge. Even if given the chance for it, I'd be rubbish at it, so I choose to focus on peace and medicine."

"I'm pretty good at revenge." Anna admitted as she slid a little bit closer still. "Maybe I can help you with your revenge. I've made a lot of people cry. I've shaved off hair and eyebrows. I even let a bunch of cows loose."

He always squinted a little when he laughed, and that was no exception, even though he was trying to keep his voice to a whisper so they could keep from being discovered. "Cows? What could somebody have done to piss you off so much that cows had to get involved?"

"Well, someone who wanted action and who I didn't want similarly, went around town telling people I moan like a cow and that I'm diseased from getting frisky with farm animals. So I went to his farm, stole all of the tires off of his truck and let his cows loose. I even took one as a souvenir. She was such a good cow. Best milk." She smirked and reached out to touch the side of his face gently. "You have a cute laugh."

He laughed again once she was finished with the story, but turned his face into her hand a little to kiss her fingertips before he looked back at her. "Remind me not to piss you off. I don't have any cows, personally, but given your talent for creativity, I'm sure you'd make do with what's available."

Anna laughed as well, even though she attempted to keep it down though she wasn't really concerned they would get noticed. She felt the rush of getting close to someone new, and while she knew she shouldn't, she liked it anyway. There were pros and cons to both being in a relationship and being without one. She was in relationship limbo and she and Logan both knew it. "Damn right I would."

He moved himself closer to the center of their small cave, which placed the height of him against her over the tiny gap between their coveralls on the unforgiving ground. It was far from the most comfortable place that he could have wished to have such an encounter with Anna, but he certainly wasn't going to pull away. He had expected her to brush him off because she was still working things out with Logan, but that was one more thing he wasn't going to bring up.

"I'm not sure I've ever enjoyed having my life in jeopardy quite as much as I do at this particular moment. That's quite a first for me." His free hand moved from her hips up her side and along her back as he held her in close, and the arm he'd been using to support his head went flat along the ground to support hers instead as he gathered her against him. "I must remember to get into life-threatening situations more often in the future."

Anna felt a sting of guilt as she easily moved flush against Oliver, but she ignored it in favor going the rest of the way and pressing her lips to Oliver's. Anna wasn't married. She and Logan had talked extensively about how they didn't know how they felt about each other and the future. They talked about what they hoped for, but she wasn't nearly convinced that the current versions of themselves could be what each other needed. Even now. Anna loved Logan. She still loved Orion, and she missed him terribly. She was so fucked up it was ridiculous, especially because kissing Oliver felt good too.

He was immediately different from any other man she'd ever been with, because his kisses were patient while still being greedy. Every man she'd been with before Logan had been in a hurry with her, usually too excited she was with them to take their time and really focus on doing anything right. Orion and Logan had been the first to approach her like a true person, focused on her own enjoyment and on the long-term possibilities between them. Oliver's touch was something else entirely, savoring the novelty of having her against him while also declining to rush headlong into anything. His hands took full advantage of the thin shirt beneath her jumpsuit to scratch over her back and flow over her completely. "He did say hours in here, right?" He confirmed between kisses. "I didn't just imagine that in a phenomenal leap of wishful thinking?"

"Two to three hours." She replied between her own kisses, and while her kisses and touches had been hesitant, she was definitely getting into it now, and she was becoming more needy between kisses. "Maybe more. Who knows."

"That's true. These things do take time." His voice sounded perfectly casual and light even when discussing enemy surveys of the area, but there was nothing light or casual about his touch. His fingers scratched up over her back beneath her shirt as he adjusted himself a little beneath her. The closer she got, the more uncomfortable his shorts became. "This is . . . infinitely better than the best-case-scenario I had in mind when they first started yelling about a drone survey."

Anna laughed and kissed him even harder. "Seriously, you could say anything and it would sound sexy coming out of your mouth." She moved from his lips to kiss along his jaw and nibble on his neck. "I'm sure you get that a lot." Anna didn't know his sex life or who he was with, but she assumed he was with other women since his wife. Maybe not. She had no idea.

"Well, the last time I tried to seduce anyone, it was back home, so the accent didn't have quite the same effect." He chuckled against her lips when she returned to them, then rolled her on top of him so he could kiss along her neck. He did nothing to hide or hold himself back from her, so as she moved on top of him, there was nothing about his excitement left to her imagination. "Don't be surprised in the future if I show up and just start reading straight out of the dictionary for you. I'm not above exploiting weaknesses where I find them."

"You just made the dictionary sound sexy." She replied with another laugh as she ran her fingers slowly through his hair, each kiss more heated than the last. "No one since you left home? That's . . . a long time."

"It has been a while." He agreed with another groan, rolling her back to one side to press her against the floor of their tiny universe to kiss the breath out of her. His was a very different kind of body to wrap herself around than the two she'd spent the most time with in recent years, but there was an art and tenderness to his kisses that patiently ignited everything inside her one piece at a time. He moved down her body so his lips could follow down along her collarbone, and continued moving lower as his hands pushed up her shirt to get it out of his way.

She easily pulled her shirt over her head and tossed it aside, and when his hands moved across her skin she shivered. He was different from Orion or Logan, but in that moment, she was grateful for the difference. "I'm not the only one getting naked, I hope you know."

"No, but you're the most fun to get that way." He grinned as his lips returned to her chest, teasing her hungrily the more naked she got. Stabs of guilt were trying to work themselves up from the back of his mind, but he shot each of them down before they could take his attention away from the woman beneath him. He had too many reasons to be guilty and not enough reasons to excuse himself in enjoying the present.

There wasn't much room for him while he was on top of her, but he reached along his own back and pulled his shirt up to let her pull it the rest of the way over his head. His hair went a little wild in the process, but he pushed it back mostly out of his eyes afterward before looking down to watch her take in the sight of him. He was stronger than he looked, she could feel it in his touches already, but he had much less by way of physique than either of her husbands.

"I hope to see you under the sunlight sometime." He said with another kiss to the inside of her breasts before moving his kiss back up to her lips. "I've always thought you were beautiful. Even before I knew you were still alive."

"That's not creepy at all." She teased as she shivered again from his exploratory kisses. Anna wasn't sure how familiar he was with women that had tattoos, but she had enough artwork for his perusal as soon as her shirt was off. Anna ran her hands along his back and along his chest whenever he lifted up enough to allow her to do so. "Your accent is sexy but so are you." Anna kissed him sharply and attempted to wiggle out of her pants so she could hook a leg around him. "We can do this again if you want to. Sunlight or not."

That got a chuckle out of him, but he worked his way down her body with his kisses to help her with her shorts. The cave went on for a few more body-lengths deeper into the hillside, but got narrower as it went on, so he didn't go too far into the darkness. "You've not had me for the first time yet. We'll see if you're interested in a repeat performance." He took her shorts and tossed them back up at her face to mess with her, but his own shorts followed after a moment, before he started working his way up the inside of her thighs with his kisses.

Anna tossed her shorts aside with her shirt, but she gasped softly a few times as he moved closer to her core. "Well, if you're headed where I think you are, then you're already winning points, let me tell you. Most men . . . just want to stick it in."

"I'm interested in as many points as I can get." He said right up against her inner thigh, before his fingers and his tongue took a taste in ways that proved even more than the accent that the man was European. There were no inhibitions from him at all about anything he wanted to do, and the absolute ease with which he performed left most of the men she'd ever been with in the dust. Clearly the man's people-pleasing nature was not left behind in his professional life.

After losing her mind at least twice, maybe three times, Anna was unable to move without feeling like her whole body was over-relaxed muscles and bones. She was still moaning and groaning when he hovered over her and smiled down at her, and she grinned back at him. "Holy hell, that was fucking awesome."

"I have a few talents in life. I make use of them as often as possible." He grinned and leaned down to kiss her neck a few times before rolling to lie beside her with an arm behind her shoulders as a pillow.

How's everybody doing out there? Carl's voice came over the radio for the first time since they'd found the hole in the first place. Other groups began to radio in, none of them sounding particularly concerned about their situation, besides a few complaints about tight quarters.

Oliver looked over at Anna with a grin, since she was closer to the communicator. "Oh I think that's for you right now, love."

Anna gave him a playful glare before she rolled slightly to grab the communicator and to show off her ass a little in the process. "We're good here. No complaints." She replied before she realized she hadn't identified herself. "Oh. This is Anna."

There was more of a pause after her response than there should have been, but it was hard to tell from Carl's voice whether he suspected anything or not. *Yeah, I figured that out, thanks. The Montgomeries have gotten into the flyover data, so they're actually co-opting it for our own sake this time. Which should cut out the need for a few more of these kinds of surveys later. Should still be another couple hours, though. Back to your books, everybody.*

"No complaints, eh?" Oliver moved in closer and kissed the back of her shoulder before slapping the ass she had presented for his inspection.

Anna laughed loudly at the slap on the ass and she turned to look back at him. "What, would you prefer I tell him I'm dazed out of my mind because you have a fucking insane tongue? I can call him back and let him know."

"Not a chance. Then he'd stop assigning me with you all the time on these outings. If there's a chance of us getting trapped like this again sometime, it's a chance I plan to take." He grinned at her and teased a nipple again, clearly not finished with her by a long shot. "Besides, if any of the rest of them ended up anywhere nearby, or if these caves echo through the hill to somebody else's spot, then they're already quite well-informed of your dazed status."

"I'm not quiet." She said without shame as he continued to kiss along her body. "It's not my turn anymore." Anna sat up slightly, as much as the cave would allow. "You didn't get naked for no reason."

"No, I did not." He laid back as she sat up and turned more toward him, though he couldn't resist her breasts when they were right in front of him. "You're a very good reason to get naked."

Anna crawled over him and pushed him back into the ground padded with the blanket and laid flush on top of him before she reached down to run her hand along the length of him. The slight break had taken a toll, but she was going to work hard to bring him back to where she wanted him to be. "I would say that I would suck your cock until you're moaning my name, but I want to feel you inside of me more than in my mouth."

It was obvious to her exactly how long it had been since he'd been with anyone, since even her lightest touch had him squirming and groaning beneath her. "I do like your priorities." He agreed breathlessly, fighting the urge to grab her and rush things so he could lie back and enjoy what she was doing to him. "I want you too. Especially after . . . well, all that. I like a woman who doesn't hold back."

"Then you'll really like me. Because I don't. Ever." Anna kissed his lips roughly before she stroked him a few more times and let go so she could slide him inside of her slowly. Having sex was a fucking amazing way to not freak out about essentially being trapped in a cave.

She'd been all over her district when she was younger, worked her way through nearly her entire school class with the exception of the Bickford twins and a couple others, and she had all manner of experience with Orion and Logan themselves. But Oliver was the first man she'd been with who was in any way significantly older than she was, even if it was only ten years. Those ten years, though, made a big difference in the man she had beneath her. He held her differently, he touched her differently, and he was in no hurry to be finished.

He figured out very quickly just how rough she liked things, and he responded to that as well as he could with the way she had him pinned down. Her name came easily to his lips as she rocked against him, even with his eyes half-lidded. She could almost see the thousand times she had already run through his imagination on his face, but his hands gripped the reality of her to savor every movement. "Holy fuck, woman . . . sweet . . ."

Anna loved those words. Oh how she loved to hear it when she was able to make a man curse and worship her at the same time, and it only encouraged her to do absolutely everything she could to blow his mind. "You like that, huh?" She replied with a smug grin before she changed it up a little bit. Even though he was a patient lover, sometimes she was not. "I want to know more about what you like sometime."

He couldn't talk or think to answer at the moment, and she could tell he was starting to lose what little control he had over himself as he started getting louder. He was good at many things, but holding himself back under what she was doing to him wasn't one of them. His hands latched onto her hips as he gasped. "You . . . I'm . . . holy shit, I'm . . . you're . . ." he lost himself in a hurry, and if there was anybody outside the cave or in the vicinity, they knew her name and they knew exactly what just happened.

Anna smiled and laid herself against him as soon as he came, since she liked hearing his pulse race because of her. She covered him in kisses as he continued to groan with every strategic wiggle of her hips. "I like the way my name sounds when you moan. So fucking sexy."

It was a long, shuddering time before Oliver gave a last groan and acknowledged what she'd said at all, collapsing back onto their jumpsuits as he tried to breathe. "You . . . You . . You are not human." He finally gave a shuddering laugh and moved his hands over her to try and get a grip on her.

She giggled and curled into him, since she definitely enjoyed cuddling afterward, especially with Oliver. He had already been a comfort for her in hard times. "I'm going to take that as a compliment."

"It was intended as one. Terribly sorry if that didn't come across." He was staring up at the ceiling of the shallow cave just beyond Anna's wild hair, sighing out in satisfaction. "God, I'm fairly sure I've not been fucked like that since nursing school. And that was by one of the Attendings."

"Wow, an Attending, huh?" She said with a smile as she ran her hand through her hair and then through his before she kissed him again. "Aren't you a bad little student."

"Oh, I was rubbish at school. Never studied, repeated classes, nearly got kicked right the way out of the program, it was a disgrace. That Attending is likely the only reason I made it at all." He clearly wasn't thinking about the Attending at the moment, though, whoever she'd been, as he looked Anna over with a greedy expression. "You make it into an art form. I'm not sure I've even got the language for it, and that was only my first encounter with your otherworldly abilities."

"Your language for it was eloquent enough with the noise you made." She kept running her hands over him before she kissed along his jaw and remained silent for a minute. "What, um. . . I don't care about labels, but is this . . . something you wanted at the moment? Or like, you know, on a regular basis? I don't know what you're hoping for… Like I said, my life is super fucked right now. I don't know where I stand with Logan or anything in my life, honestly. I don't want to lose a friend over this, but I am kind of okay with being friends who fuck . . . if you are okay with that."

"I'm alright with that." He assured her with a caress along her jawline. "I care about you. I've got no intention of losing that between us because of anything else. And it wasn't my intention to complicate your life even more than it already is. You've got quite a plate full of . . . well, complications. As I said, I think you may have broken the part of my brain that contains words."

Anna laughed again and kissed him harder once they had clarified whatever the hell was going on between them. She couldn't manage the relationship she was trying to have with Logan, let alone anyone else. Maybe she couldn't manage a relationship ever again, at this rate. She'd always been shit with them in the first place. "You let me know when I can break your brain again. I want more of you."

He joined her laugh, but turned her over on top of him so that he could be most of her cushion, and returned to running his hands over every part of her. "I read a theory once in a journal of sexual health that the male refractory period actually has an evolutionary imperative behind it. It exists so we can please our women more adequately while our bodies are recovering from you. It's as good a theory as any I've ever heard."

"Huh. Interesting study." She said with a smile, though she hated that his random medical fact made her think of basically any time she was around Mercury. Anna kissed him again to chase away any other thoughts. "My body is yours to explore."

* * * * *

"This cave should have a name." Oliver said hours later, lying beneath her as she laid on top of him with one of her cheeks pressed to his, facing the same wall. Their bodies were mostly recovered from their last round of enjoyment, but Oliver was

527

tracing in the dirt wall of the cave with a knife from his jumpsuit. He hadn't gone for paired initials inside a heart, at least, but he had drawn a terrible, horrible rendition of a woman with her mouth open screaming in pleasure that he swore looked just like her. "Glory hole is a bit too on the nose and low-hanging fruit. We can do better than that."

"You can be so crass when you want to. I love it." She laughed and watched him draw with the knife. "Cave of wonders?" She teased, but she was pretty proud of the damage she had done to Oliver. She had him good and fucked.

"Wonders, Twoders, Threeders, I think fiveders or sixders for you, that last round, unless I'm guessing wrong." He gave her a sarcastic look sideways and started drawing tick marks in the wall next to her face, crossing off for every batch of five. "I really should have been keeping track. Very negligent of me."

"Very. You should be punished." She replied teasingly as she ran her hands over everything she could reach. "You're going to keep in touch with me even when we go back, right?"

He looked over at her and grabbed her by one breast before kissing her once. "Why do you keep asking me questions like that as if I'm going to just dump you off somewhere after we leave this cave? No, I'm not going to keep in touch with you when we go back. I'm first going to go back to my unit, tidy the place up a bit, maybe run a load or two down to the laundry, *then* get you a text to let you know I need your help with something. The something being my bed which you'll be helping me demolish in short order."

Anna kissed him several times before she said anything else. "I like that idea a lot. A whole lot."

"I told you that I wasn't going to complicate things for you." He assured her as his caresses moved casually over her bare skin, as if he owned every part of her. In that moment, he did, even if that ownership wouldn't last. "That means I'm not going to be dramatic about this. I want you even more now than I did three hours ago, I can tell you that. And I imagine once I've had you on a decent mattress or in a hot shower, that's only going to get worse. I'm not the sort of person who looks at things only in the extreme short term."

"I'm not either, usually. Not anymore." She said softly before she kissed him again. Anna knew she didn't need to prove what she was saying, since she had Orion's last name inked into her skin. She missed Orion more and more but she had ruined that for good. Anna also missed Logan. *Her* Logan. The version of Logan that didn't really exist anymore. Maybe she thought that her happiness could only come from Orion or Logan but now she wondered if she had looked in the wrong place. Maybe it was supposed to be Oliver? Maybe it was no one. Fucked if she knew anything for sure. "I'm not attached to anyone at the moment. Maybe you and I could have a future together. If you think you could want that someday."

"Hm. Let me think." He laid his head back on the floor of the cave again and looked up at the ceiling with an expression of deep seriousness. "Well, on the one hand, you're incredibly hot, but on the other hand, you're incredible in bed. On the first hand, you're a badass bitch who takes no shit from anyone, on the other hand, you're an excellent mother who loves her kids to pieces. On the first hand, you're incredibly smart and good at everything you've ever done, including me, but, on the other hand, you're just . . . fucking incredible." His look of consternation was so thorough it might have been heartfelt. "It's troubling to think about. I'll have to weigh the positives and negatives pretty seriously as I think about that."

"Those are a lot of nice things you just said at once." Anna melted a little bit more on the inside, since he said a lot that she hadn't felt very confident about in recent months. "I do love my kids to pieces. I don't feel very smart most of the time, but I try to be." She replied softly. "You are so good with kids. You would be a great dad." Anna didn't know what she was really contemplating, but her world didn't make sense. Eleusis felt different without Orion and Earth felt different without Logan. It felt like she was trying to invent an alternate reality since she knew any reality with Orion or Logan was fucked.

"They tried to recruit me to go back to the Bickford estate with the children. I decided to decline." He grinned as his hand roamed down over her ass. "Didn't want to be too far away from . . . all this."

"You declined for *me?*" She didn't mind his touch on her ass, but she was surprised that he would decline safety to be around her. Especially prior to their sexual exploits. "Wow. I . . . I didn't realize . . ."

"I also wanted to be where I could do the most good. But yes, mostly for you." He kissed her roughly and ran his hands over his face to push his hair out of his eyes. "So far it's turned out to be one of the better decisions of my misbegotten life."

Anna kissed him in return and ran her fingers through his hair as she smiled at him. "Thanks. For wanting to be here with me and for wanting to do the most good. I told you you're too good for me."

"And I told you you're wrong." She could feel him kiss his way down her neck to continue the frenzy they'd started, but as he did, one of their communicators chimed near the pack to indicate a message.

Anna whined softly but reached for the communicator even though she wanted to ignore it. "Some people have the worst timing." She replied quietly as she grabbed the communicator and swiped it on so she could see the message.

Drone survey complete. Ground movement detected near the compound fence. 6, maybe 8 on foot. Stay as silent as possible and wait for orders. Do not engage.

Anna turned the communicator toward Oliver and nodded toward their clothes. If they were going to have to run, she preferred not to be naked. Not that it would be the first time she was running away from something or someone while naked. "Let's get ready to move." She whispered, but she followed it with a kiss.

He looked more nervous than she did at the message on her communicator, but he got moving. The act of getting dressed in such a confined space made for comedy, though, and he couldn't fully stifle some of the laughter that escaped him every time his crotch came in contact with her ass in tight quarters.

With a great deal of trial and comedy, they managed to get themselves back into their jumpsuits. Oliver gave a whimper for Anna's benefit at the sight of her all covered up again, but they quickly turned their attention back to the small slits leading out onto the rest of the new world. "There's no way they spotted us here." He whispered in her ear, both of them looking through the same slit between the rock and his pack just because it gave him an excuse to be more or less on top of her again.

Anna reached out to touch him at every opportunity, especially because he was whispering in her ear in his sexy accent. "They're close to us. Even if they didn't spot us. But we'll be okay."

He chuckled in her ear as she touched him, and he continued his own torments through a convenient zipper built into her jumpsuit. Soon, though, his touch stopped mid-stroke, and withdrew from her jumpsuit completely as they watched what was coming near their hiding place.

A squad of half a dozen Consortium soldiers walked with guns drawn, their clear helmets catching stray strands of sunlight as they watched the landscape. They were armored in ways that neither Oliver nor Anna had ever seen before, in white and silver clothing that was clearly designed to withstand anything. "Negative on contact one." They said as they swept the area with a few handheld instruments, some of them pointed straight at Oliver and Anna. "Proceeding to the second contact tower, run a recheck on your thermals. We're getting nothing on the ground here, even traces."

Anna put her communicator up so that she could record what she saw. Any footage could be analyzed later. She was comforted hearing they were getting nothing even while pointing their equipment straight at her. At least they knew the cave was a good hiding place. "They didn't see us."

The group passed them by, but Oliver couldn't quite shake the anxiety their presence had produced. Even when they were a few minutes gone and Anna had long since stopped recording, Oliver shook his head as he looked down at her. "I feel like there's still more out there."

Their communicator clicked on immediately after Oliver's whisper, to the sound of a chuckling voice that didn't belong to any of the squad they'd come in with.

Smart nurse.

The accent was vaguely French, becoming more distinct the longer he spoke.

You get points both for observation and for making a woman scream. The two go hand in hand, in my experience.

Anna's blood went cold at the sound of a foreigner's voice on her communicator, especially because they hadn't been talking to anyone. She looked at the communicator and then typed an SOS even if the communicator was hacked. She moved close enough to Oliver to whisper into his ear. "When I go, run, and keep up with me. If they know we are here, I'm not going to be fucking trapped in this cave."

Good girl.

The voice on the communicator said with a growl.

I love it when they run.

"I'm right behind you." Oliver promised, ignoring the fact that they were clearly being overheard as he slipped his arms into his pack awkwardly, getting ready to move. He hesitated only for a moment, then shoved himself out of the opening to roll down the terrain onto his feet, immediately breaking into a run in the opposite direction from where the patrol had disappeared.

Anna knew the terrain and she was running at full pace but also keeping track of Oliver as soon as they were out. She wasn't about to lose him, not after what happened. She had her gun out and ready but she had no idea what they might run into.

As they ran, there was no sign of anyone running after them, but after only a few minutes, there was a muffled sound of two gunshots far behind them. Anna heard Oliver groan in pain near her, and one of the bullets grazed the side of her calf. Oliver turned as he fell, and once he came to a stop on the ground, he turned and fired back into the trees. The first few shots seemed to hit nothing but air, but on the fourth, a suspiciously-mobile bush fell to one side with a grunt. Oliver got up and kept running, since he didn't want to stick around to see anything about who or what was following them.

"Are you okay?" Anna yelled back as her leg felt like it was on fire. "We aren't that far!!"

"Still right behind you!" He yelled right back, glancing behind him every once in a while to make sure the disguised bush that followed them stayed down. More of their people gathered at the Twist and frantically jumped through, but there didn't seem to be any Consortium patrols heading toward them. He tripped when they were close, though, and went down holding tightly to his ankle, still trying to crawl toward the Twist. "Go!"

Anna refused to leave him behind, and instead of going forward, she ran back for him, helping him up even though she was smaller than he was. She was stronger than she looked. "I'm not leaving you here. You're insane to think I would."

Most of the group had already gotten through the Twist by the time she went to drag Oliver through, but Carl was running back toward the two of them when Anna's communicator went off again with the same French accent.

Freeze where you are, unless you want three bullets. One for each of your foreheads.

The man was clearly breathing heavily, so Oliver seemed to have actually hit his mark.

The stand of trees to your left, Ms. Prince. Look up.

Anna didn't look up but she didn't move. "Look, just let them go. You don't need three bodies, do you? Just one."

"I've got no interest in any of you." The voice moved a few steps away from the trees he'd used as cover, though he was still out of range, and no one was drawing a gun on the man in the first place. None of them had time in their mad dash to get back to the Twist. The man was covered from head to toe in Eleusis camouflage, but his helmet had the face of a Behemoth on it. As much of a mess as he was, he looked like he could have been one of their young if he moved the right way. "I want you to take a message back to Jason and Alex for me. Do you think you can do that, in exchange for your lives?"

"Yes." Anna said without hesitation, since she definitely wanted to get away with her life. "Whatever the fuck you want. Just say what you need to say."

"Please tell them that Henri sends his best regards, and I look forward to their next visit." They could hear the man smiling behind the mask he wore, and he took a few steps back dismissively, with one gun still pointed on the group of them. "I would pass along a message from Charles as well, but he's said nothing coherent for years, so that would be pointless."

"Henri. Charles. Got it. Anything else?" She finally looked over at the freak with a mask, and she moved a little closer to Oliver. "Since you're making quite a trade."

"Not if you knew the full story." He laughed again and put down his gun once he was back behind cover. "Your miserable little lives are worth imagining the look on their faces. Go in peace, little one. This war is just getting started, and I am sure I will see you again."

Anna didn't have to be told twice and she helped Oliver through the Twist even though Carl was there. "Fucking Hell. How did he find us? We were holed up in the tiny fucking cave!"

Those on the other side of the Twist wasted no time in closing it, but the floor of the control room was littered with bodies as Anna and Oliver struggled out of their jumpsuits to tend to their wounds. Carl was one of the few who didn't appear injured, along with Kameron, which left both of them to move between those who had come back through to make sure nothing was life-threatening.

"Fucker was taunting the two of us the whole time we were in there." Carl was incensed and barely-restrained as he went from person to person, giving some of them with superficial bullet wounds nothing more than a passing glance. "He knew we were there the whole time, but the patrol squad walked right past us without doing shit. If he's working for the Consortium, he's got a fucking strange way of doing it."

"He wanted us to get back here." Anna said as she glanced back at the shell of the Twist before she was down to her thin clothing underneath so she could look at her still-bleeding leg. It was far from the worst she'd ever endured. "If he has some kind of vendetta with Jason and Xander, we're more fucked than we realized."

"In any event, they know we can get there. Or at least he does." Oliver said as he scooted himself closer to take her leg and begin tending to it. The bullet had gone straight through the side of her calf, so it was mostly just superficial and it would hurt for some time. The exit wound needed stitching. He was into the bag he'd carried in just a few seconds and stabbed her leg to numb it without asking permission. He dove in to work on stitches. "So we have to consider whatever element of surprise we thought we had to be gone. Lucky us."

Anna only winced as Oliver went to work, but she kept her attention on Carl and Kameron. "So things just got ten times more dangerous. Great."

"Just what we all wanted, I know." Carl said with a sigh and a slight wince. He looked down at himself after he winced, and winced again at some small pain in his ribs. He felt along his back as high up as he could reach, until his fingers came across a bullet wound. Instead of going looking for medical attention, though, he reached down into Oliver's medical kit and picked up a single-use scalpel. After a little feeling out along his ribs, he gritted his teeth and made a short incision along one, still standing, then finally gave an actual grunt of pain as he fiddled with the bullet that was lodged behind them. Eventually it popped out, and he went back to the nurse kit to grab some gauze to hold over the self-inflicted surgical wound.

"Once you're patched up, get up to Xander and make your report to him. You're the only one whose questions the bastard in the mask even answered. He should be on his way here now, he was notified of the attack."

Anna stared at Carl as he cut himself open but looked away when he went fishing for a bullet. The man was a fucking freak and she wasn't about to watch him. When Xander finally arrived, Oliver was pretty much done with her leg and ready to move on to someone else's bleeding injury. Anna hopped her way to a chair and glared at Xander. "Do you have some psycho friends with the Consortium that you could have fucking warned us about?"

Xander glared right back, but was mostly concerned about the non-lethal bloodbath he was seeing all around the room. "Do I look like I have anyone in the Consortium I would consider a friend? What are you fucking talking about? What happened?"

"Some psychopath in a Behemoth mask called himself Henri. Stupid fucking French accent and all. He was apparently stalking us during the drone scan. He said to let you know he looks forward to the next visit. And he said something about some guy named Charles who is deranged or something."

Anna had seen Xander angry several times in the fairly short time she'd known the man, but she'd never seen him look actually and truly surprised, let alone speechless. He had to grip the console near him as he looked over at Anna to ingest the news, but he didn't ask her to repeat it. Hearing it again wouldn't change what she'd said. The blood drained from his face as he looked back at her, and he attempted a slow breath before he spoke. "Did you see Charles? Or was Henri just out there by himself?" When Xander said it, there was no French accent, but clearly he still intended the same person.

"I didn't see anyone else. Hell, we didn't really even see this guy, except when he had a gun at our fucking heads. Somehow he tapped our communicators."

"Yeah, Charles taught him that trick when he was a kid. Henri always thought it was hilarious." Xander was slowly recovering from shock, and he blinked a few times before he sighed. He kept his eyes closed as if that would help him think through the information he'd received. "And you have seen him before, or at least somebody who looks a lot like him and Charles both. Two people, as a matter of fact." He looked up at Anna as Carl groaned his understanding and shook his head.

"I thought the bunch of you got kidnapped and tortured by the Consortium when you were kids?" Carl couldn't believe what he was hearing. "If the Consortium's got a you and maybe a Jason working for them, then how are we supposed to outmaneuver that?"

"Some of us took to torture better than others." Xander shot back without acknowledging the larger man's other question at all.

"Fucking hell." Kameron shook her head and stared at

Xander. "You need to get this fucking sorted with Jason and figure out a new game plan with Carl. The spot for the Twist needs to be moved, or else there are going to be people waiting at the spot we just left." She glanced over at Carl and shook her head again. "I need to focus on getting the children out of this place, especially if our location might now be compromised. Looks like our time here is truly up."

Xander was still reeling from the message, but he nodded up to Carl anyway. "Get your people patched up and then we'll talk about next steps. Nobody goes near the Twist for Eleusis purposes until we've regrouped. Earth transports only." Those orders were for the operators standing nearby, all of whom nodded eagerly. None of them were excited for another possibility of screaming and gunfire coming back at them. "If any of you see Henri again, run. It's what he'll want you to do, but it's the best option you'll have. Don't shoot, don't talk, don't do anything. Just run."

"He did seem to get off on it." Anna replied as she got herself up onto her good leg. "Are all of you crazy in one way or another? Sure seems that way."

The angry Xander she had gotten to know was back in a flash at that question, and his glare was in full force no matter how surprised he was. "Walk a mile first, Princess. You don't know shit about crazy yet."

"Hm." It was her only reply before she tossed back the compromised communicator, since she didn't want it anywhere near her. "Maybe you two can chit chat if you're so inclined." She went to grab her bag from where she'd left it and glanced back at Oliver who was still helping someone. "Thanks for fixing me up, Oliver."

"My pleasure." He said with a hiss of pain of his own, though his own wound was superficial compared to some of the others he treated. "It's not as though any of us went over there with the intention of getting shot, so fixing you up seemed like the thing to do at the time." He gave her a quick smile that could have been misconstrued as merely polite by most of those watching, but he mostly kept his eyes on his work. "I'll be seeing you pretty soon for another of these sessions, I expect."

"Definitely." Anna said with a nod as she picked up her personal communicator, though she was a little hesitant to do so. "See you soon. You have to make sure my leg isn't infected." She watched him for a moment longer before she headed out and didn't look back, even though she wanted to. Bullet wound or not, she wanted to see Oliver again. "Carl, let me know what our next move is when X figures something out."

"I will. Are you sure you're good to walk?" Carl said with a perfectly straight face, looking down at her with a full pad of gauze slowly soaking through where it was taped against his ribs.

"Are *you*?" She said with a nod toward his bloody gauze. "My leg isn't bleeding nearly as bad as you are."

"I've had worse to worry about. I'm used to it." He nodded at her leg and then at the door. "I'll keep you posted on next steps. Take it easy for a while with that leg." The look he gave her didn't give much of an indication of his opinion of her one way or another, but there was the slightest of glares behind it. Maybe he did know. "Make sure you tell Logan about Behemoth-face and the fact that we've got more Montgomeries to worry about. If you see him."

"I will." She watched him for a moment longer and kept moving. So many times she wanted to ask about Orion, but she didn't have the right to know. She had asked in the past and gotten nothing, and she knew she looked pathetic, but she still loved Orion. Now she was going home to a likely empty house, and she had no idea if Logan would still be mad at her or not. Everything had been complicated enough before. The day had made things a thousand times worse, and it wasn't even noon.

25

It was anybody's guess how long it would take Melissa to find out about what had happened on Eleusis, since news of the attack was spreading quickly through the community. The answer came in the form of Melissa running full tilt up along the path from their house to the Labyrinth, meeting Kameron and Carl roughly halfway. She stopped sprinting when she saw the two of them walking together, just to get a look at them and catch her breath, then started running again at the same breakneck pace.

"You said it was just a survey!" She figured if Kameron was well enough to walk, she was well enough to get yelled at. As she got closer, it became clear she also thought Kameron must have been well enough to tackle as well, since she hit the smaller woman going full speed and took them both to the ground with her arms wrapped around her neck. The tackle sent them rolling down a slight incline just off the path, but Melissa was less concerned about the fact that Kam might have been injured than she was about the fact that she was still alive.

Kameron didn't know if she should laugh or not, since she didn't want to make Melissa angrier, but she wrapped her arms around Melissa and ran her fingers through her wife's hair. She hadn't been injured, but getting that close to being taken wasn't a good feeling either. "It was a survey, but the Consortium sent out drones. We thought we were in the clear, turns out we weren't." Kameron kissed Melissa and let out a sigh. "I'm sorry I made you worry. It won't happen again."

"The hell it won't!" She kissed Kam back hard, still breathing heavy from her run and from the panic when she heard about the attack. After the kiss, she drew back and hit her on the arm as hard as she could. It wasn't much, with an accompanying glare through the blonde hair that was hanging partly in her face. "Every time something happens, it's going to feel like this! Every time!" Every word was punctuated with another hit, but soon she settled with her hands gripping at Kameron's jumpsuit. "And it's not like I can even help, or I'll even know! I mean you're . . . you're all the . . ."

Kameron took the abuse without complaint, mostly because she knew she deserved it for all of the times that she'd made Melissa worry or scared. She knew the life she was trained for was hell on her wife, which was why she didn't want to do it to Melissa anymore. She didn't want to lose Melissa. "I'm not going back." She said softly as she moved one of her hands to caress along Melissa's face and to push a few beautiful strands of hair out of the way. "That was my last trip to Eleusis."

Melissa's mood went from angry and panicked to confused so quickly it would've made a person's head spin. She was visibly taken aback, but then she cocked her head to one side without loosening her grip on Kameron's jumpsuit. "Wait, what? Last trip? What are you talking about? You're the commander for the whole force."

"Carl can take it over from here. I'm going with you and Kass to the Bickford Estate. I don't get to sit on my ass, since we'll have our own security I have to manage, but I told them as soon as they decided to send the kids away that I wasn't going to let you go without me." Kameron ran her thumb underneath Melissa's bottom lip and sighed. "You're more important to me than anything else in the world. I don't want to lose you or our life together. Eleusis isn't worth that."

Melissa's life and personality were written out on her skin for the entire world to see, but her thoughts were also constantly written right across her face, and that moment was no different. Kam could see the slow twist of her features as they moved from confused to overwhelmed, and the next attack that came was of Melissa's lips on hers and her legs latching around Kam's as Melissa's momentum sent them rolling farther down the hill under the sunlight. "I love you." She said through tears, without even looking around to see if they were safe wherever they had landed. All that mattered was holding onto Kam. "I love you so much."

Kameron hadn't expected tears, though she had hoped, certainly, Melissa would be happy. She had never loved anyone as much as she loved the tattooed woman on top of her. Kameon held on tightly and kissed her back just as fervently, even though she was wiping away Melissa's tears at the same time. "I love you too." She felt like her heart was going to explode as she realized more and more how happy she was making Melissa by going with her and their daughter. "I'm sorry that I've made you worry as much as I have. You're the best thing that has ever happened to me."

"I always worry about you." Melissa said through tears as she buried her face in Kam's shoulder, every part of her body adjusting and readjusting itself to latch onto her tightly at every point. "You're going to get to Eleusis." She eventually promised when she drew back to look Kam in the eye, reaching up to caress her cheek between kisses. "You deserve it more than anybody I know. We'll build the house you told me about there. I'll do naughty tattoos for people until I'm a dirty, wrinkled old woman giving terrible advice to our grandchildren."

Kameron smiled and kissed Melissa several more times before she allowed herself to say anything. She didn't know why she always had a fear of Melissa leaving her for someone else, someone better, but she hoped she wouldn't always worry about her wife leaving her. At that moment, she felt pretty confident about Melissa wanting to stick around. "Don't cry." She finally replied softly as she continued wiping away Melissa's tears. "I didn't mean to make you cry." Kameron kissed Melissa again and held her even tighter, one hand firmly on Melissa's ass while the other was far more comforting by wiping at tears. "If we get to Eleusis, then that's great. If not, I'll die happy as long as you're mine when I go."

* * * * *

The days following the attack on Eleusis were chaotic and disconnected for most of the people in the mountains, though everyone quickly learned they had someone to report through and those reports were expected in a timely fashion. Several groups returned to various parts of the globe where they were most comfortable, joining up with rebel forces in different states of readiness for a fight.

Non-combatants were exchanged for volunteer soldiers with every gate opening, and the Shop was slowly converted from a gathering place of artisans to a storehouse and barracks for the incoming fighters. Groups of rebels as small as half a dozen people were brought in from every part of the globe by the magic of the Twist, leaving everyone who passed through it in awe as they took in the enormity of the safety that had been provided to them. Bases were abandoned, and the nature of the world changed, one person at a time.

Liam had requested early on that he and a few others be permitted through the Twist back to his own estate first in order to make some initial preparations, and they had been one of the first groups through. There had been a lot to do in order to make the place livable again, let alone making it secure and comfortable for hundreds of people.

At the appointed time, he made his way down the hall toward the grand entryway with a baby monitor in his hand, looking over the sleeping infants through the camera on a swivel in their room. With Rachel on one side and Bree on the other, he felt invincible, as usual, but he was still nervous about their situation. A lot was happening all at the same time, and there wasn't much peace to be had about it.

"You're sure the northeast wing will hold that many people?" He asked Rachel, their clasped hands swinging casually between them as they walked.

"Are you sure you want to ask me if I'm sure for the hundredth time?" Rachel teased as she squeezed his hand and gave him a reassuring kiss on the cheek. "I'm sure. I've double and triple checked capacities as well as comfort levels. Everyone will be comfortable but close without feeling claustrophobic. We'll be fine."

"That is probably pushing a hundred by now, isn't it?" Liam wasn't sure why he felt so protective over his estate, since he'd just left it months before to join the cause without much hesitation. Coming back to continue supporting the cause felt harder than leaving ever had. "Alright. Time to see what this house can really do." It was the first time in history Liam knew the entire place would actually be utilized. He wished his parents were alive to see it.

He squeezed Rachel's hand once before he let go to take out his communicator and make a call, even though Larissa was in the same house with him. It was easier than shouting and running down endless hallways to find her. "Rissa, where's that binder with the assignments, have you got it? I'm about to call Xander and have him start sending people through."

"I have it. Cory and I are going to work on handing out assignments because I'm not giving this thing over. I worked too hard on it." Cory came back with her to the Estate to help her get re-settled, but he was going to go back through the Twist to help Anna, and Larissa was still broken up about it. She wanted to spend every second with him, especially because she knew that it wasn't likely he would be home before their baby was born. "And neither of you are going to make me sit down. I'm not THAT pregnant."

"Have you looked down at yourself lately?" He smiled against the communicator, but only because he knew she was somewhere else in the house and therefore incapable of beating him up at the moment. "It's like you're smuggling sports equipment. Seriously, woman, chairs were made for using."

"Good god, do you talk to your wives like that when they're pregnant? You're lucky I can't kick you in the nuts right now." Larissa said with a glare down at the communicator before she looked over at Cory. "I don't look that bad, do I?"

"No, you really don't." Cory said with a glare of his own at the communicator and he leaned in to kiss her once before he continued on his way with a table that needed to go to a different room. "I actually expected much worse by now. I guess I didn't hit you with twins after all. Shame." He smiled back at her and backed into the room he'd headed for to get the table in its designated place.

"My brothers are twins. I don't need to be cursed with twins." Larissa ran her hand over her bump while she held the binder in her other arm. Each minute was one minute closer to having to watch Cory leave her for the first time, and she hated it, but it was consuming her every thought. "Do you want to know? Before . . . before you go back? Mercury will be here, she can probably tell me . . ."

Cory shook his head, but he was smiling as he came back out of the room toward her. He had gotten taller in the time she'd been dating him, just as she had, and he was actually taller than Ben, though he wisely made sure not to make a big deal out of it. He stepped up close to her and ran both hands up her body from her waist to her cheeks before he kissed her. "Obsessing about it will help keep my mind off other things. Keep me spinning in the same circle back and forth, you know how I am." He kissed her again and let his hands rest on either side of her bump. "I still say it's a girl, but I've got exactly nothing to base that on. Just hoping there can be more of her mother in the world."

"You have got to be the sweetest man in the world, Cory

Prince." Larissa replied with a smile before she kissed him back. Without Anna and Logan putting the two of them together, Larissa was certain she would not have found herself a better man. She didn't know why she never thought about Cory before it was suggested to her. Larissa kissed him a few more times before she took one of his hands. "I want to make time stop so you don't have to go."

"If time stopped, I'm pretty sure you'd want it to get on its way again before too long." He poked her belly one more time between kisses, but he was grinning anyway, until he settled back into the inevitability of the day. "The more of us fight, the faster this is going to be over. That's the way I'm looking at it. I want to earn our place on the other side of the galaxy. Once that's done, you know I'll be more than happy to hang up my rifle and only take it out again for squirrels for the rest of my life."

Larissa responded with several more kisses. "I don't want to lose you." They were newlyweds, after all, and not having Cory around was going to kill her. "You're leaving me here with Liam. And you better not go after some pretty warrior woman somewhere."

That made him roll his eyes. "Please. Like I'd even know what to do with anybody else." It was a strange thing for people from Earth in general, but he cherished the simplicity of his own history and Larissa's. "You're the only woman I'm ever going to want. Warrior women need not apply."

She pressed her forehead to his and her pulse kicked up, which had their baby kicking Cory's hands on her baby bump. Larissa smiled and wrapped her arms around Cory's neck. "This baby loves you almost as much as I do. I want to tie you up and make you stay."

"You can tie me up any time you like, when I get back." He promised with another kiss, resting his forehead against hers afterward. "I love you too. Both of you. It doesn't feel like we've had very much time together, all things considered, but I plan to have a whole lot more."

"We haven't. But I want more." Larissa ran her fingers along Cory's cheeks and she kissed him several more times. They both couldn't stop kissing. Clearly she did not want him going anywhere. "I love you, Cor."

"Aw." Bree said as they rounded a corner and finally met up with Larissa. "Look at them, Liam. They're so cute!!"

He gave Bree a look that was noncommittal on cuteness at best. "I'm already inviting over a few hundred houseguests, let's not push my gag reflex any further today, alright?" He was still smiling as he said it, though, and he nodded at Cory once it appeared he was finished with Liam's sister for the time being. "Are you about ready?"

"No, probably not." Cory admitted, then sighed and turned to go with Liam and his wives, Larissa's hand still held tightly in his. "But yes, about as ready as I'm likely to get."

"Alright then." Liam lifted the communicator to his face again and headed back down the hall the way they'd come. "Alright, Labyrinth, central hall is ready to receive, markers are in place, good for touchdown."

Gwen and a team of her employees led the front of the first group headed out to the Bickford Estate, since they needed to bring supplies ahead of the babies and get everything in place before the babies were brought over. She was nervous about the entire thing, not because she was about to go through some crazy portal, but because she was going into Liam's house on the other side. Logan's too, obviously. She didn't want to think about that either.

Every time he saw Gwen, it tugged at Liam's heart, but that time, at least, he appeared to be ready for the first sight of her. As she came through with a few bags of supplies, he was standing next to Larissa, who was explaining that everyone had been given room assignments and that rooms had been labeled and categorized. Liam took a small slip of paper from Larissa and stepped up to hand it to Gwen personally, as his wives and his sister handed out similar instructions and directions to everyone else moving through the portal.

"I set aside your room myself." He said quietly, though it was strange to think it was one of the first things either of them had said to the other in a long time. "You'll want to go ahead and get the rest of your things settled before you go up there, though."

Gwen was confused by his directions since she wasn't hearing similar instructions given to everyone else, but she nodded as she kept one hand on a bag of supplies and she had a heavy backpack on her back. "Thanks." She stared intently at the piece of paper before she allowed herself to look up at him. God, it hurt to look at him. She missed him so much. "Must be nice to be back home, right? I mean, for you." This wasn't her home and never would be, not really. Gwen was not a Bickford.

"Weird is more the word of the day than good, I think. But I hope it'll be good by the time all's said and done." He shrugged, seeming to care less about the experience of living at home than what was on her paper. "Anyway, you've been here before, which is more than most people, so make yourself at home."

"Thanks. Again." She glanced back down at the paper and started to walk past him. "It's good to see you." It was all she could say without telling him she missed him, which would be inappropriate. 'Good to see you' was nice enough without sounding pathetic, anyway.

"It's good to see you too." He said without looking away afterward, and he even gave her a quiet smile as people filtered in past them, moving under the able direction of the three ladies of the house. "I'm glad you're here, as opposed to . . . well, pretty much anywhere else on the planet."

Gwen laughed softly, but she was glad to be in the same place as Liam too, even if it was also incredibly painful. "I am a pretty good babysitter." She replied with a nod, even though she knew that wasn't what he meant.

He gave her a look that made it feel, just for a moment, that no time whatsoever had passed since the day they had spent together. As if she hadn't avoided him for months. "Among other things."

"Hm." She gave in reply to that, but she knew he didn't have time to chit chat. "I'll see you around, I'm sure. I better get these supplies where they need to go." Gwen didn't pause to see if he would say anything else, since she was too afraid that she would say something she shouldn't. She still needed to keep her distance from Liam. Hours of work would distract her, she hoped.

One of the later arrivals to the house was far from a stranger to the place, but Liam and his wives were still in the grand entry hall directing traffic when she arrived. Liam hadn't paid attention to the Twist itself as the last few people came through from that round of settlement, but when he saw the slight frame and brown hair, he did a quick doubletake and looked up. Unlike Gwen, he hadn't taken the time to steel himself against seeing Margo again, but he took a deep breath and tried to will himself to look calmer than he felt. Especially since she was holding Chrissy and had Jela right behind her carrying what appeared to be their luggage.

Margo didn't know if she should say anything, but she thought it was better if she did, so she just gave Liam a polite smile. She didn't want him to think she had any reason to be angry, since she didn't. Even if he did. "Hi, Liam." She said softly, but Chrissy wasn't quiet as she giggled and held out her arms for her father. He was the fun person in her life, after all.

Liam just nodded, since saying her name still hurt too much, but he took Chrissy from her briefly, since the little girl was excited to see him. "Hey there, Princess. Are you happy to be back in your palace?" He kissed the little girl's cheek and swung her back and forth as he talked to Margo. "I had them carve off part of your wing, including your old room. There's other rooms down there too, of course, but go ahead and take your pick. We'll probably have to give out whatever you decide not to use, but go on and get in there first and see what suits you."

"You didn't have to do that. But thank you." Margo glanced back at Jela and at Liam again. She had loved Liam for so long that it was impossible not to love him now, and she missed him, but she was happy with Jela. They were good together, and their relationship was exactly what she wanted out of a relationship. "I better go decide on something. Thanks for being so nice about this."

He kissed Chrissy again and handed her back to Margo, since it was her day to keep their daughter. He purposefully didn't look around to see what Brianne and Rachel's expressions looked like at the moment, since he could imagine it perfectly well without needing to verify it by sight. He gave Jela only a single look before he turned away and made himself busy. The less he had to interact with Margo, the better, even though they were going to be in the same house. Again.

Gwen was part of the first wave, so she was able to get the main nursery fully stocked before any of the babies whose parents weren't staying had arrived. When the work was done, she eventually wandered up to the room that she had been assigned. Maybe she could get a nap before she was really needed.

When she first turned on the lights in the room, it was easy to wonder if she had somehow taken a wrong turn and ended up in a different house altogether. Everything about the residence had been stripped down and allocated where it would do the most good, but her room was . . . regal. There was an ornate woven rug covering most of the Estate's rich hardwood floors, and the furniture surrounding her in the room was all clearly handmade and hand-polished.

On one side of the room, there was a fine woven curtain drawn back inside the opening between the room and its accompanying bathroom, which was inlaid with marble tile and embellishments at every opportunity, not to mention three showerheads in an open shower surrounded by a crystal block. The king-size bed was turned down with crimson sheets and a thick, embroidered comforter, and the pillows looked like the most comfortable objects ever designed by humankind.

On the bed, on the sheets that had been bared by the turned-down comforter, was a scattering of pink rose petals surrounding a short note. Liam never had been one for long speeches or using more words than absolutely necessary.

This is where I wanted you, before things went south. This was the room I wanted to be yours. Ours.

I still want that. I'm hoping that you do too.

You can find where my room is. If you don't come find me, I'll come find you. If only to talk about all this once and for all.

P.S. I thought you'd like the robe on the table. And there's chocolate in the nightstand.

Gwen was too stunned to do anything but stare as she looked at the rose petals, the nicest room she'd ever seen, and the note. It thrilled her and it made her feel sick at the same time. She ruined his family. She'd slept with his brother. Liam should want nothing to do with her. The first thing she could force herself to do was go for the chocolate, and she ate a few pieces before she pulled her communicator out of her pocket. She still had his contact.

We need to talk about this. I'm not going to your room.

It was almost fifteen minutes before he answered her, but that didn't mean anything, did it? The whole house was buzzing with activity. Everybody was busy. *I'll be there soon. Are you in your room?*

Yes. I'm in here. I've never seen anything like this.

I must've forgotten it on the guided tour. He texted back quickly, though nothing followed it.

It was almost another full fifteen minutes before he actually arrived, but it was just that big a house, and there was a lot of ground to cover to get anywhere. He actually knocked when he got there, even though it was his own house. Was that normal? Did knocking mean something? There were too many questions after too much silence permitted between them.

Gwen stared at the door for a moment before she finally

convinced herself to open it. Her hair was down for once, since she had intended to relax in her room before she realized she was in some kind of suite for royalty.

"Um, hi. We really need to talk about this room. I can't stay here. I . . . and the note . . ."

"Yes you can." He said without moving inside the room, since he hadn't been invited. "Is something wrong with it?"

"No, it is gorgeous, but I think it's better for Bree or Rachel... this isn't for me. We haven't even really talked in months, Liam. I can't." She picked up her bag she'd dropped at the door and pulled her hair back. "Someone else should have this room."

"Rachel prefers to be down near the front door, because she likes to be able to see everybody coming and going, keep track of things. Plus, it's the best view of the sunrise. She likes to wake up with the light most days." He smiled as he stayed in the doorway, physically preventing her from leaving. "Bree prefers the far west wing, at first because it reminds her of a television show she liked, but eventually because she turned her room there into . . . well, her own playroom. You can imagine what Bree would make out of it. Now she's got it the way she likes it, so she wants to keep it." He looked up and around the room with a slight sigh.

"To my knowledge, nobody's ever actually lived in this room, except maybe spending a night here and there. The original plans call it the Queen's room, just in case the Bickfords had royal visitors." He nodded toward the far side of the room away from the bathroom. "But there's a hidden door behind the vanity there that leads straight down to the suite right below us, which is where we're setting up a major living room as the childrens' playroom. Behind those are the sleeping rooms where you've been most of the afternoon. The secret staircase lets you get back and forth as quick as you please, and it lets you live the way I'd have you living if it was left up to me."

Gwen looked around at every secret passage as they were pointed out and eventually she looked back up at Liam. "You have to stop this. I can't be your wife." She ran a hand through her blonde hair. "I fucked up your life. Margo left because of me. I caused your whole family so much pain, and I'm not fucking doing that again."

"Margo left because Margo didn't want a plural family." Liam corrected gently, though Gwen could see that it was still hard for him to talk about. "She had been pulling away almost since the day we got married. Bree knew it, Rachel knew it, even Margo knew it. We kept trying different things, different arrangements, different situations, nothing helped. No matter what had happened or hadn't happened between you and me, Margo wasn't happy." He let out a stifled sigh, and tried to shrug, but he couldn't look that lackadaisical about someone he cared about. "It was a matter of time. Not something you caused."

"Maybe." She shook her head and looked down at the floor. "I slept with Logan." Gwen took a deep breath, but she knew it would prove how worthless she was. "We got wasted and I just . . . I missed you and I got tired of being so lonely and I don't know what his fucking deal is, but it was more than once."

That clearly shocked Liam, since his eyebrows went wide and he had to shake his head. "Um . . . wow. Okay, wasn't expecting that." He looked a little dazed for a few more moments, but he didn't move away from her. "Are you still . . . I mean, are you and him together? I've never really seen the two of you . . ."

"Together? God, no. He's not my type." She sighed as she looked up at Liam. "He was as close as I could get to you. Terrible as that is to actually admit."

He shook his head again. "I'm the last person on this planet to call anything terrible. Honestly I'm still just kind of in shock. Not because of you, I'm just . . ." he actually smiled again, odd as it looked. "Usually I'm the Bickford twin women fuck because they can't get to Logan. Kinda weird to feel it the other way around."

Gwen felt so ashamed, since she knew he wouldn't want anything to do with her now, not even as a friend. Not that she could handle a friendship either. "It has been the worst without you. I hate it. I miss you all the time."

"Then stop." He said simply, though it had the same kind of force behind it as everything else he'd done with her before Margo had left him. "I told you months ago, before . . . all of that happened, that I want you to be a part of this family. Nothing about that has changed. Hell, Anders and Beck come home from child care talking about you now. They know you. They look forward to seeing you. And so do I." He sighed as he looked her over, and stepped a little farther into the room, even though he hadn't really been invited. "I miss you too. I miss thinking about what the family would be like with you in it. If you don't mind me skipping to the ending, it works. It's happy. It's the kind of family

I want. And I want it with you."

Gwen's eyes filled with tears since she still wanted it too, she just didn't think she would ever really get the chance. "Even after what I just told you about Logan? You still want me around?"

"If you tell me there's nothing between the two of you that way, then I believe you." He took a few steps closer to her, since he had half expected to be sent packing the minute he stepped through the door. "And hell yes, I want you around. I've wanted you around since damn near the minute I met you."

Gwen stared at him for a moment with tears sliding down her cheeks before she rushed the rest of the way into Liam's broad chest and wrapped her arms around him. She had missed him so desperately she just wanted to touch him and see for herself she wasn't imagining what was coming out of his mouth. This was real, wasn't it? He was really telling her he still wanted her? Was he really telling her she hadn't destroyed his family?

She actually pushed him a step back on contact, but he took a few more backward as he put his arms around her back, eventually falling back onto one of the several plush couches in the room. He sank into it almost comically as he landed since it was that soft, but he pulled her completely into his lap with a groan of pleasure just to have her close again. "So you'll keep the room, then?" He asked tentatively, smiling as his hands moved over her back.

Gwen was still crying as she nodded slowly, since she just wanted to sit there in his lap with his arms around her. "If I get to share it with you." She said softly, since she desperately wanted to share anything and everything with Liam. "I missed you so much."

He kissed her neck as he held her, sighing into her shirt afterward as she clutched him tightly. "I missed you too." He drew back eventually to kiss her through the tears coming down her face, and reached up to smooth them away with his rough touch. "And no, before you clarify, this still doesn't count as your proposal. I've got a whole different plan for that."

"You do, do you?" Gwen replied with a laugh before she kissed him several more times, each time more desperate than the last, since she had missed him that much. Never before had she missed someone like she had missed Liam. "I guess I can wait for that."

His own touch grew more heated in tune with her kisses, and he laid back against the plush back of the couch l to bring her down against him. They had both dressed for the late summer, in shorts and t-shirts that had seen their fair share of dust from moving everything into the abandoned house, but even dressed so simply, she was still one of the sexiest things he'd ever seen. "You mean there are things you *can't* wait for? That doesn't sound like you."

"You're right, I'm not impatient at all." Gwen said sarcastically, since he had teased her before about being impatient. Her hands were all over the place, re-memorizing everything about him, his hair, his face, the way his stubble scratched against her fingertips. She kissed him everywhere she could reach as her hands moved down over his arms slowly. "I can't wait to be your wife. I can't wait to be a part of your family. I can't wait to have your babies." She kissed his lips again, harder than before. A dam of emotion had burst after holding back so long. "I love you, Liam. I love you so much."

Any talk of babies was something very new from her, and it startled him a little to hear it, but he certainly didn't stop kissing her. His fingers moved through her hair as she explored him, his lips proving to her exactly how much he meant what he had come to say. "I love you too, Gwen." His hands moved down over her body just as roughly as she remembered, until they settled along her waist and he gave her a slightly quizzical look. "I thought you said you didn't want babies of your own yet?"

"I didn't say I wanted them *now*." She said quickly before she kissed him again. "I still can't wait to contribute to your growing brood. I haven't talked to Bree in a long time. . . Did you get her pregnant yet?"

That made him laugh, but he didn't stop kissing her. It was a testament to him of just how incredible Gwen was and how perfect she was both for him and for his family that she was capable of asking him whether he got another woman pregnant while she herself was busy kissing him. "We think she is now, yeah, but she didn't want to get tested in the middle of the chaos. She'll have Mercury or Doc Weber give her a workup once the dust settles here. We went at it pretty hard a few weeks ago on her week, same way we did when she got hit up with Anders. So yeah, she thinks she is."

"That will make her happy." She said with a smile before she kissed him passionately. "I'm not going to take my birth control again when it is supposed to renew, not if we're going to get married. That way it'll just happen whenever it should." She scared herself a little, talking about babies that could be her own, but she tried not to focus on it. "Not that you need any more kids."

"I need more *you*." He said with a deepened kiss of his own, his hands moving down her spine as he was forced to adjust himself beneath her due to pressures in his pants that hadn't existed when they were talking a few minutes before. "And I love my kids. I didn't get started on the alphabet just because I like the first few letters. There's a long way to go yet." He chuckled and drew her down against him with one hand raking up her body to the side of her neck. "But only stop taking it if it's what you want. The only thing I'm ever planning on pushing you into is a wall when we're both very naked."

"That sounds amazing." She shivered as his hand ran over her body, and she knew it was because of how intensely she felt for him. He knew what to do with his hands and everything else, certainly, but her emotions made every touch and every kiss that much more intense. "Can you stay here for a little while?"

"It's my house. I can stay wherever the fuck I want." He grinned under the kiss, but he got up beneath her under the kiss that followed, and swung her in the air effortlessly until he was carrying her threshold-style across the carpet. "That includes right here."

He carried her over to the slightly-raised platform the bed was resting on, then unceremoniously dropped her on top of the petal-covered sheet before he leaned down and kissed her. He kicked off his sandals and moved to cover her completely with the bulk of him, every bit as hungry to hold her as she was to hold onto him.

Gwen laughed as he carried her across the room, and she laughed even harder when she landed on her ass on the bed, especially since it wasn't the most graceful landing and flower petals went flying. When he leaned in to kiss her, she grabbed onto his shirt and pulled him closer, since she wanted him as close as he could possibly get. "I can't believe this is real." She said between kisses, since she thought she would spend the rest of her life without Liam. "But you're really here. You're really kissing me. This isn't a dream, right?"

"No, not a dream." He assured her as he moved to kick aside the huge and ornate comforter so he could stretch out with her on the bared sheets, petals or no petals. "The dream comes later when I molest you in your sleep and you wake up already halfway to screaming my name."

"That sounds amazing." Gwen mused as she tugged at his shirt, since she wanted it off so she could touch his skin. He was so different from his brother, even though they looked similar. Logan would never compare to Liam. "You should keep telling me all sorts of dirty things you're going to do. I want them all."

"I'm really more of a show kinda guy." He held himself up so she could tug his shirt off, but the action made every muscle in his torso flex at once in the process, which only made her situation even worse. He wasn't far behind in retaliating once she had his shirt off, burying his kisses in the cleavage her shirt showed off for his enjoyment. Clearly he wasn't interested in teasing her or wasting any time in having her all to himself again. "Besides, showing is more fun."

"Way . . . more fun." She replied haltingly, since having his face in her cleavage while she explored his bare chest was frying her brain. "You really did miss me?"

"You think I was lying?" He drew back enough to give her a sarcastic look, then proceeded to pull her shirt off almost violently before he unhooked her bra and snapped it straight over her arms at a mirror across the room so hard there was a chance of it actually cracking the glass. His assault on her resumed once she was bare, clearly much more interested in showing her how much he had missed her rather than telling her.

Gwen was putty in his hands as soon as his hands and mouth were all over her, especially because he knew everything he needed to know about her. He touched her in all the right places in all the right ways. He was that good of a lover, but she knew it was more than that. It was because he *wanted* to know everything about her, and he wanted to make her happy. Gwen was glad Liam was it for her, since he ruined just about everyone else in the world for her, at least while sober. Apparently when she was drunk she was a different story altogether, and a mess who made stupid decisions during heartbreak. Gwen was already tense from the first kiss they shared, and she knew she wouldn't last long with his wild attention all over her body. "Liam . . ." She moaned his name, and it felt so good to do so.

He moaned again at the sound of his name on her lips, and moved hastily to remove what little clothing the two of them still wore. He needed her, needed the world to be the right kind of place again with her in it, and with him. Once their clothes were thrown around the room, he paused above her, one hand moving up her legs over the entirety of her to cherish the feel of her. When he leaned over her again, the look on his face was serious, but the thoughts behind his eyes were completely focused on her. His kiss was as possessive as it was demanding, and the touch of his hands on the rest of her body was no different as he pressed himself into her. "I'm yours, Gwen." He promised solemnly, even as his fingertips raked up over one of her breasts under his kisses. "And I'm not letting you go again."

Gwen gasped softly as his fingertips slid over her sensitive breasts, and she wrapped a leg around his waist to beckon him closer. "I'm not going anywhere. I promise." She replied before she kissed him again. "I'm yours too, Liam. Only and completely yours."

They both knew better than to think the promise was going to be a simple or easy one to keep, but the chaos of the world outside that room ceased to matter the moment their bodies began to echo the promise they made. There was so much to do, so much to prepare for, two worlds waiting on the edge of a war that only a handful of people even knew was coming.

But as important as Liam knew all of that was, nothing was more important than his family. His wives came first. His children came before the world, and that room, that moment, that promise with Gwen came before any war. It mattered more, to him, than any success or failure anywhere else in the universe. He lost himself in Gwen completely, and gave her everything that he had to give in that moment. She was the only world that mattered, and hers was the only name on his lips in the moans and growls that followed.

By the time the frenzy ended and they settled into holding each other on the giant bed, Gwen was quiet with her thoughts even though her heart raced in her chest. "This is the first time I feel like I have a home. With you." She finally admitted softly, since she never felt safer or warmer than in that moment, at his side, with his arms around her. "A home and a real family. I didn't know it was even possible to find something like that in this kind of world."

"Anything is possible." He said with the tone of a man who believed it, and she knew him well enough to know he really did. Liam didn't know the meaning of despair. Things either worked or they could be fixed. His grip around her shoulders tightened to pull her into a warm, lingering kiss. "And this is your home. I have no idea where we're going from here, or when, or if we're just going to ride out the rest of the war from here until we can go to Eleusis, but this is ours, and always will be. Wherever I am, you're gonna have a home. I'll make sure of that."

"I love you so much." She repeated as she kissed him several more times. "You are amazing, Liam Bickford." Gwen smiled at him and jabbed playfully at his ribs. "And you make me deliriously happy."

"I'm comfortable with delirious." He grabbed her hand and forced it back onto the bed, since he was both viciously ticklish and vicious in defense when tickled. "And you better watch yourself. I *will* fight back when provoked. Do not test me." He attempted to appear deadly serious in his glare, but his face, unlike Logan's, seemed incapable of such seriousness.

"Do not test you, huh?" She struggled to free her hand, but he was obviously a lot stronger than she was. Gwen showered him with kisses in order to distract him. "Thank you for giving me another chance."

"Thank you for saying yes." He fired back with a kiss of his own as he moved to get a little more comfortable against the ridiculously-plush pillows. "Come on. It's been a long day for all of us, and I need some sleep to recover from you before you destroy me all over again."

"You can stay?" She certainly wasn't complaining, but she was surprised he had devoted so much time to her already, all of it undisturbed. He hadn't once checked his communicator, wherever it was, and he didn't look concerned. "What about Rachel and Bree? Or, um . . . isn't your brother coming here too? To drop off his kids?"

"Yeah, Logan's supposed to be coming in later." He shrugged as he got comfortable, since he and Logan hadn't been getting along very well ever since the Twist had started making trips to Earthside. Now at least Liam knew a little bit about why his brother had avoided him. "I'll see him another time, I'm really not looking to go see him right this second. As for Rachel and Bree, who do you think helped me decorate the room? You're giving me way too much credit if you think I picked all this shit out myself."

Gwen smiled brighter and sunk down into the bed even more as she remained at his side. "I love them too. Not as much as I love you, but I love them too. Are you, um, going to tell people about us?" Before she had wanted to keep it low-key, but now she hoped he would want it in the open that they were together.

"I will if you're ready for me to." She made it clear before that she didn't want anything public about them at an official level, though he knew there had been all manner of rumors about the frequency with which she visited his home. "And as soon as people see you hanging out with Bree and Rachel more often, they'll start putting two and one together anyway. There's also the fact that as soon as Diego knows, his wives will know, and then everybody will know in about twenty minutes. Those women can't keep their mouths shut to save their lives."

"I'm more than ready. I just didn't know what to think or say about Logan. Or to Logan. I . . . lied to him about being with you because I didn't want him to think that I broke up your marriage, even though I had been with you. And I probably did break you up. Even if you say I didn't."

He gave her a glare for that, but tucked her in tightly against him anyway. "We can fight about that later. And Bree and Rachel will set you straight on it too, if you talk to them about it. Margo herself would tell you the same thing, though her perspective might be . . . a little different." He shook his head and sighed, then kissed her again as if to wash the taste of the conversation out of the air between them. "All I care about is that you're here and not going anywhere. We'll take care of the children, get through this war, and help humanity move on with its life. And get new pillows. For the fucking love, how do people sleep on these things? They're just . . . air."

Gwen laughed a little too loudly, but she missed his quirky sense of humor and how he could say the most random things in the middle of a serious conversation. "Oh, stop worrying about the pillows. It's not like you're going to be sleeping that long anyway."

"I mean, seriously, this is like . . . I'm going to suffocate in these fucking things." He let himself fall almost completely through one, then took it away and threw it across the room instead, preferring to sleep on his own arm. It put him in a position where his lips were close to her chest, and he had no interest in resisting the chance to lean in and kiss the side of her breast and then her lips. "I should just sleep on these instead. Much more comfortable."

She giggled again, but she knew she wouldn't be giggling if he kept that up. "Alright, fine, you can sleep on them. But you have to be nice. I saw how you treated that pillow."

"I treat you a hell of a lot better than I treat a pillow." He said with another glare, though he did move afterward so that he was laying mostly on top of her and using her chest as a pillow with his arms wrapped around her back. "Much better. I could handle waking up to this."

Gwen smiled and ran her hand through his hair as she relaxed beneath him, since there was no better feeling in the world than having Liam on top of her. She closed her eyes and took a deep breath, feeling as content as could be. At last, things were starting to feel just right.

* * * * *

Mercury wasn't thrilled to go through the Twist, let alone to go through and end up back in Logan's house. She was quiet as they walked through, and quieter still when someone gave her room assignment to Orion while she held one of the boys and he held the other. Mercury was going to keep all four children around as much as possible, and Gwen said she would assign someone specifically to help with the Bickford/Al-Jabbar children, since not only was Mercury a resident physician but also because Mercury herself was pregnant and it wasn't going nearly as well as the first time. Every time she got sick, she told herself it was normal, and it was, but that didn't mean she liked it.

When they got to her assigned room next to what would be her small clinic, she put her bag down and looked over at Orion. Orion would be going back. Back with Logan, back with Anna, and she was going to be alone. "I wish you could stay here with me."

"You and me both." Declan was asleep against his shoulder, which Orion was grateful for at least. The children were plenty of hassle while awake, and at least somewhat more manageable while unconscious. He set down the bag he'd carried right next to Mercury's, since from a first look around the room he had no idea what she would want where. Even the clinic next door was originally an entertaining space with a bar along the back. It was chosen because it already had water and a place to keep certain medications cold.

"Every week when they send supplies through, I've been told I'll be able to come through and check the perimeter with Kameron. Maybe I'll be able to talk Carl into letting me visit for a couple days here and there as things go along." No one knew exactly what to expect from the future now that the army was gathering and the rebels were starting to gain in momentum. It was a dangerous kind of world, but it was the kind Orion had trained for his entire life.

Mercury put James down in one of the cribs in her room and she sighed as she wandered back to Orion. "I hope this isn't how the rest of our lives will go. Every time things seem to go right, we get separated."

"God, I hope not." He pulled her in close. It felt like they spent every moment since her brilliant idea about the Twist saying goodbye to each other, but no amount of time would be enough. Things were too good, things were too right with the two of them together. But the mountains were no place for children, and no place to have more of them. The Estate would be safe, as much as anywhere in the world could be called such for the time being. "I know this might sound strange coming from a pilot, but I'm really looking forward to staying put someday. Preferably somewhere warm enough you can get away with wearing a little less clothing a little more often."

Mercury smiled and looked up at Orion as she shook her head. "I am incredibly pale. I would not do well sitting in the sunshine." She leaned in and kissed him anyway, even though he was still holding on to a sleeping Declan. "I don't like being here. And something just feels . . . off." She sighed as she looked around after her kiss. "Maybe it is because the last time I was here, things went terribly wrong."

"Well, the worst thing that's going to happen here is a variety of poop explosions, all of which I apologize in advance for not being around to help you handle." He kissed her to show that he really meant the apology, but sighed afterward and went to put Declan down in his own crib. "I'm done with the universe sending us off in separate directions. If the eggheads can figure out how to keep the Twist running and maybe even replicate it, though, we're never going to have to be split up again. I mean, I'll be out of a job when that happens, but I really don't mind if it means it puts me within a few steps of you and the kids at all times."

Mercury hugged him quietly after that, since she hated the idea that she had to say goodbye. Again. "I love you." She finally said before she took another deep breath to keep herself from crying. "Just promise me you won't die. I don't want to lose you."

"You're not going to lose me." He promised just as quietly, scratching her back as his fingers moved up to hold the back of her neck. "I'm pretty quick on my feet. Death is gonna have a hard time catching up with me. I'm not saying I can outrun the guy forever, but at least for the time being, I'm pretty confident about my chances."

She managed a weak smile through her tears and pressed herself as close as she could against his body. Mercury seemed nervous for a moment before she stepped back slightly and pulled something out of her pants pocket. When she opened her hand, it was their wedding rings from the first time they were married, and she looked up to meet his eyes. "I found yours when I was cleaning out our room at the house, I didn't even know you kept it with you all this time. But I'm glad you did."

He looked a little sheepish as she pulled out the rings, but he reached out to take them both to look them over again with a sigh. He had been so happy about them the first time they had acquired them, so happy to be wearing one himself, to call her his wife. "I've been looking for some time to . . . you know . . . get you away for a while, make it the right moment. I wouldn't trade the first way we got married for the world, but I felt like I needed to do something else this time around, to get that second start again. I just never found the right moment." They both knew why that was, though, since none of their family was around anymore, except for the children. "I'm glad you found them."

Mercury took hers from his hand and slid it on her finger before she took his and slid it on his. She gave him a warm kiss afterward, as if she had performed her own little ceremony all by herself. "Hopefully having this will keep you thinking of me while you're gone."

"Everything keeps me thinking of you." He said between kisses. "Most of all the sunsets remind me of you. On Eleusis and here. Only place I've seen this shade of red besides right here." He tugged at a few strands of her hair with a grin. "I don't think I've ever been stupid enough to think that having it all was going to be easy, or simple. But that doesn't keep me from wanting it. I want our life, on our terms, and whatever fight is between me and that life, that's a fight I'm gonna bust my ass to win."

"Aren't you romantic." She smiled a little brighter and held up a finger as she stepped away to the bag she'd set down. She dug through it for a moment and came back with a small item that looked like a piece of glass, but she knew he recognized it. A lot of people used them to store small clips of information in space. Mercury put the small square piece in his hand and tapped on it a few times. What came up was a short video clip of her sonogram of their girls and their little hearts beating. There wasn't much to them, but they were two distinct little people inside of her. "If you get homesick. The girls will help you." She swiped her finger and there were little clips of Leo and Lynnette too. Leo's laugh was unmistakable from the rest of the children.

He smiled at the video clips and took the data glass from her with a few taps of his own just to try it out. He wrapped it up tightly in his fingers once he'd looked through them, and pulled out his communicator to insert the glass so he could hold onto it. "Thank you. I miss them already. And you." He double checked the glass in his communicator and put it back in his pocket, glancing over at her device. "You'll, um, you'll find a few pictures on your communicator that weren't there before. I'm not much of a photographer, but I did what I could."

Mercury fished out her communicator and quickly went through the photos, since she wanted to see. "Are they naked?" She asked with a smile, though she had no idea what he would put on her communicator.

"Maybe." He said with a grin. "I admit nothing."

"You *are* trouble." Just the first one she found made her blush. "So you won't let me take pictures of you, but you'll pose without me? I let you take pictures of me."

"The only reason you didn't get to take pictures of me is because I enjoyed taking pictures of you too much. We never got to the part of you photographing me." He remembered the night in question a little too well, and he knew his communicator remembered it even more accurately. "I'll be taking more the next time I get back to you. And you can take whatever pictures of me you want."

"The next time you see me, I might have a bigger baby bump." She said with a teasing smile, since she liked knowing about his special kind of kink. Anything that made him more attracted to her was a good thing.

"That just makes it less likely that we're gonna spend much

time taking pictures." He said with a grin, kissing her one more time and then going down to one knee to kiss her bump as his hands caressed along her legs. "Be good for your mother. She's being plenty good to you."

"I doubt they will be, given their track record." Mercury mumbled with a smirk before she ran her hands along Orion's head. "I love you. I'm not going to say goodbye. I'm just not. But I am going to call you every day."

"Good. It'll give me something to look forward to." He kissed his way back up her body slowly, appreciating her for the work of art that she was. "I love you too." It sounded like goodbye, but he didn't want to say it any more than she did. "I'll see you as soon as I can get through with the next supply opening."

Mercury glanced back at the boys before she followed him to the door, and as soon as he opened it, she reached for his hand and pulled him back so she could kiss him one more time. Her kiss was hungry and desperate at the same time, since she didn't want him to go even though she knew he had to.

He kissed her against the door frame for a long time, not caring that the people in the mountains were probably waiting on him to close up the Twist for the night and move on. He needed more time with Mercury. He needed a world where he could be with Mercury without anything tearing them apart. It occurred to him that he might need a world that didn't actually exist, but he dismissed the thought quickly. If that world didn't exist, then he would help create it. It was that simple.

Mercury didn't move as they kissed for as long as they possibly could before eventually the sound of his communicator chiming reminded them that people were waiting. She broke the kiss slowly and looked up into his dark eyes before she gave him a small but reassuring smile. "Go kick some ass and come home to me." Cursing wasn't usually a part of Mercury's vocabulary, but she wanted to make him smile even though they were parting for the moment.

It had the desired effect, and he kissed her one last time for good measure before he sighed and pulled away. "I'll do that. When I do, your ass is next." He looked her up and down with a grin that was mostly forced for her benefit, then squeezed her hand as he pulled away. He looked back at the end of the hall, just to get a last look at her against the door frame, and his hand lingered on the corner as he moved around it as if he was physically restraining himself from going back to her. He had a war to fight. He needed to be elsewhere to fight it.

Mercury couldn't help the flood of tears once Orion was gone, and she stayed in her room with her sleeping babies without moving until she heard a soft knock on her door. She knew anyone and everyone probably had her room number since her makeshift clinic was next door, but it didn't mean she was emotionally prepared for a patient. Regardless, she wiped her eyes and got up to answer the door. Mercury certainly wasn't expecting to see Logan on the other side of the door, but she kept wiping at her eyes anyway. It had been a long time since she had seen him for more than a few minutes at a time, and even that was rare, since more often it was Anna who would bring the children over to swap or they would just pick up the other set of children from the care center and cut out the other parents completely. The attempt at therapy had been a bust, mostly because both of them were too busy to commit. "Logan." She said softly before she cleared her throat. "I didn't know you were here."

"I just got Leo and Lynnette settled in one of the main sleeping rooms. Leo took some time to get to sleep." He wasn't sure why he felt the need to explain that to Mercury, since they weren't her children, even if she would be caring for them for the foreseeable future. "I wanted to come see you before I head back to the mountains. It's unlikely I'll have a chance to come out here for a while." Unlike Orion, clearly Logan was already focused almost entirely on the work ahead. He'd have a lot of coordinating to do between the various sites.

"You wanted to see me?" She asked with confusion, but she invited him inside anyway, since his sons were sleeping and she figured he really meant he wanted to see them. "Or you wanted to see the boys?"

"Both." He lowered his voice dramatically once he was inside, and walked over to the boys' cribs to look down at them and smile at how peaceful they appeared. It wouldn't last, but he had long since accepted that about having children. "Do you have everything here you need for the time being?"

"I think so." Mercury nodded as she moved to stand next to Logan and look down at James, who always looked so much like Logan, especially while he slept. Mercury didn't know what Logan knew about her or her life now, if he even knew she was with Orion, but now that she had a ring on her finger, she thought she should explain herself to him. "I'm thankful you sent additional medical help for us. I'm going to need it as my pregnancy progresses."

When he nodded, it was clear that the news didn't surprise him, but he did look her over afterward anyway, making eye contact for the first time in a long time. "I've meant to say congratulations during one of our exchanges, but it never quite seemed like the right time. I'm happy for you." He gave her an attempt at a smile, though it was clearly sedated from the rest of the circumstances around them. "Is everything going alright so far? You seemed to dance through your pregnancy with these two. I hope karma isn't attempting to balance that out for you this time."

"It is not as easy this time. I'm attributing it to having girls versus boys the last time." She shrugged and leaned in a little to pull a thin blanket up over James. A silence stretched between them as they watched their sleeping twins and she finally looked up at Logan again. "I don't know what's going to happen from here. You know better than I would." As she looked up at Logan she thought about all the good things they had shared. Even the first day she met him, they worked together and he had saved her life on the shuttle without even knowing her. "I do know that I'm tired of being angry. And it's pointless at this point to hold a grudge, because if something happens, I don't want that to be the last memory I have of you. Being angry."

"I imagine there are going to be a lot of people whose last memory of me is being angry by the time all is said and done here." He kept his voice low so as not to disturb the children, and couldn't quite look over at her. "You've got more right to be angry at me than anyone."

"Other than both of us being ridiculously busy too often, our marriage was a good marriage even up until the last day." Mercury had gone through a lot of hours of therapy alone since Logan decided to go back to Anna, and training on self-defense with Orion had helped her too. "I have nothing left to be angry about, Logan. I still don't understand why you wanted to give up what we had, but you made your choice, and I hope that you and Anna are happy together." She was sincere as she looked at him, even though he wasn't really looking at her. "I depended on you to make me feel safe, and I felt lost without it. I should not have put that on you in the first place."

"I never minded." He finally looked over at her, both hands still on the rails of the crib in front of him. "And it was never because I wanted to give up what we had. I was grateful, I'm still grateful, for everything that we had together."

Mercury tried to give him a reassuring smile, but she wasn't good at being reassuring when it came to Logan. He hadn't considered what it would do to her when he left her, or if he had, it wasn't enough to keep him from hurting her. It didn't matter now, though. She reached over, touched his arm, and squeezed it once before she let go. "You said you wanted to see me. Were you just checking on our accommodations?"

"No." He admitted, looking down at her touch on his arm as if it was a foreign presence before he looked back up in her eyes. He didn't move away from her touch, and moved slightly toward her as he looked her in the eye.

"Most of the people involved in this rebellion are going into it thinking we're going to steamroll the Consortium and waltz over to Eleusis with no resistance. Neither you nor I are that stupid. A lot can and will happen, very soon, and there are no guarantees for any of us. I didn't want to go into that without seeing you again. I wanted to tell you how grateful I am to have known you. To have had the life with you that I did before things changed." He took in a slow breath, since he wanted to get through what he wanted to say, even if it wasn't easy for either of them. "I wanted to tell you that it's been a privilege to love you. In case I don't get the opportunity to tell you in days ahead."

Mercury wasn't exactly sure what to say to something like that, especially since it was unexpected. She just stared at him for a moment before she took a deep breath and stepped up closer to him to give him a hug. As angry as she had been, as hurt as she had been, there was always a part of her that loved and missed Logan. That part would probably always exist, since she had loved him so deeply. Mercury was happy with Orion and she had no doubts about him, but she was also grateful for what she had with Logan. The memories were currently tainted with her lingering negative emotions, but time would help that fade. "That's kind of you to say. You changed me for the better, Logan. I'm grateful for that too. We'll see each other again. You're too stubborn to let the Consortium kill you."

He didn't hug her back at first, but his arms eventually worked their way around her, one of his hands moving up to the base of her neck beneath her unbound hair. The sensation of holding her was so familiar and yet so foreign at the same time, it had his senses spinning. "I'll make sure they have a tough time doing it, that much I can promise."

He didn't let go of her quickly, since it was just too easy to stay there in that moment a little longer. "When I applied for the Initiative, it was because I felt like I had nothing left, and I thought I might as well throw my life in somewhere I thought it could do some good. When I chose to go, my reasons had changed, and I thought I knew why I was getting involved. When things went south on Nine, though . . . whatever else that place was, it was also where I learned the real reasons why I'm in this fight at all. You're still a big part of those reasons, Mercury. You always will be."

It wasn't easy for Mercury to feel like she was important to Logan when his actions had shown otherwise, but all she could do was hug him in silence for a little while longer. They could have had a good and happy life, even with the difficulties they had, but he chose otherwise. Now, so had she. "Thank you for wanting to fight for me. And for the boys." She eventually replied as she pulled back from the hug she had initiated. "If any of us have a future, it will be in large part because of what you sacrificed and what you have done."

"If any of us have a future, then I'll consider it all worthwhile." He took a step back after she let him go, just to put space between them again, and looked back down at the sleeping children. "Give them my love. The next time I see you or them, it will probably be on the other side of the sky." He reached into the crib to put a hand gently on the boys' backs as they slept, to say a quiet goodbye to them, then gave her a last brief look before he headed for the door.

Mercury watched the door as it closed behind Logan and she took a deep breath and sighed it out slowly as he left. She didn't cry for him, but there was definitely a hole in her heart he left behind. She didn't want him to die. She wanted her sons to have their father, and she wanted Logan to have a happy life. Mercury wanted it for all of them, even though she knew it was unlikely that even half of the people going to fight the Consortium would come back alive. Only time would tell.

26

Carl snarled at the man on the other end of the holo-call and he hoped the resolution on the device was sensitive enough to pick up the scowl on his face. "Maybe you didn't understand me the first time because your translator was trying to sugarcoat me. I don't do sugarcoats. You submit your people, every single one of your people, to the standard vetting codes and background check, or you sit back in Sumatra for a few more months while the rest of us go kick some ass. Got that? Yeah, word for word as close as you can get it. That's what the word translate fucking means, doesn't it?"

He waited for the message to be delivered and reluctantly accepted, and he glared at both the commander and the translator as they talked it over. "Pleasure talking to you as always. Get me the manifest and we'll get it in the works. We'll be opening to your location at 21:30 tonight, so you've got until about 1800 to get it done. And yes, that's my time. Your world runs on my time now. Get used to it."

He turned off the communicator and shoved it back into his pocket, then turned to head back up the slope to rejoin Orion, who was standing on the side of the road as the world of the mountains changed. Only days before, there had been people going about their lives, carrying children, enjoying the sunlight, carrying food or laundry back and forth from one house to another. Now the black and red of the rebellion were everywhere, people moving in uniform rows wearing similar uniforms as they turned houses into barracks.

Orion had some shouting of his own to do, looking down from the rise he was standing on to yell at a group of recruits coming up the road. "Hey, does this look like a fucking running trail to you? Unless you've got wheels, get off the fucking road!" He waved on the truck that paused around the corner at Orion's signal, and the vehicle moved through the sea of rebels who had parted at Orion's barking. "These people, I tell you." Orion shook his head as his friend approached. "No fucking excuses. I was raised on a space station and even I know better than to run in the middle of a road."

"I expect they're just excited and not thinking straight. At least, that's what I'm afraid of." Carl sighed as he looked up the slope at the Labyrinth, where yet another group of soldiers exited and got their first look at the valley, courtesy of Xander and Tatyana's tour guide status. He'd have to go introduce himself eventually, but he wasn't about to be official when he didn't absolutely have to be.

Instead, he looked down at Aiko, who was standing nearby tending to some of the late summer flowers that had been planted by the community years before, in honor of all those they had lost on Nine. Carl made it clear that anyone who interfered with anything explicitly marked would have hell to pay, and he was grateful that the shrine, at least, had gone undisturbed. So far.

"Did you get the message from Xander earlier about wanting both of us by the Twist later? What's that all about?" Carl was too busy sorting out the army under his command and growing by the day to be present at every induction, so the fact that he'd been requested made him a little nervous.

"I don't know." Aiko replied in a distracted tone until she turned her attention back to Carl. She was turning into a comical balloon of a person in the middle with her second pregnancy, but Carl could not convince her to go to the Bickford Estate even though they sent William with Kameron and Melissa. "He usually doesn't like to talk to me at all."

"He doesn't like to talk to anybody except Tatyana these days. He probably thinks we all think he's an asshole. The fact that he's right doesn't really excuse it." Carl checked his communicator just in case there were more messages from the various commanders, but blissfully, there was nothing for the moment.

"Whatever he wants, I'm fairly sure I'm not gonna like it." He moved a little down the slope so he could sit down, mostly so that Aiko would have an excuse to do the same right beside him and get off her feet for a little while. "I talked to him yesterday about letting us go back to our house on Eleusis." He said in Japanese. Orion was distracted with more barracks issues anyway, so it wasn't as though he was excluding his friend from the conversation. "He said he'd consider it this time, which is more than I've gotten from him in a while. Logan looked like he would overrule the guy if Xander didn't give in, so we should be able to go home pretty soon."

Aiko smiled, since she was excited to go home, especially after staying in the mountains. Home was better than being stuck in a tiny little unit in a dark labyrinth. "Are you happy about that? Or are you still going to try to convince me to go with Will?"

"I know better than to try to convince you of anything. Unless it's a new sex position. That almost always pays off. And takes very little convincing." He grinned over at her and leaned in to kiss her once. "No, I'm glad to be going home. Eleusis is . . . just a better place than here." His smile fell a little as he looked around. "Even if I will end up being remembered as the first man to wage a war on a brand new planet that doesn't deserve to see any."

"The Consortium started this. Not you. Don't you throw any guilt into this." She kissed him again. "I don't want that around our son." She teased as she held out a finger before she leaned back a little in the grass and ran her hand over her belly. "Do you think you're ever going to give me a daughter? I thought for sure I would get someone on my team this time."

He smiled over at her and shrugged. "Hey, I had the requested conference with my balls prior. That's all I can do. I'll have a talk with them again whenever you're ready for round three, but I can't make too many promises. For all I know, I might've been designed to only pop out little carbon copies of myself." It wouldn't have surprised him, after all the other revelations he'd had about his own nature since leaving the Consortium's control. "You and me might be getting peed on a lot for the foreseeable future."

Aiko sighed dramatically. "And we would have made such beautiful girls." She relaxed a little more in the grass since she didn't want to see more soldiers marching around. "I asked Logan if I could have someone else shadow me sometimes in case you need a break from having me around." She admitted softly, since she knew he would glare at her for it. "He said he doesn't trust anyone other than Orion or Anna to do it. He said he wouldn't put it past some of these men to . . . well, you know. Take advantage."

"I'm not sure I can even trust Orion around you. He's got a pretty deep-rooted thing for pregnant women." He teased her with a grin and poked her belly lightly as he looked down at her. "At least it'll only have to be until we get home. If even half the traps I left are still in place, that house is safer than anywhere else

I think I've ever been in my life."

"I will definitely feel safe there. Hiding out until the war is over." She sighed and looked around again before she turned her attention back to Carl. "What am I going to do if something happens to you?" Aiko was genuinely concerned that he was going to be killed, since he wasn't indestructible. He was still human, after all, just different than she was.

"You mean besides getting more sleep?" He said with a grin that quickly grew a little more serious. "If I die and the war turns into a losing battle, then you'll take down as many of the fuckers as you can your own way, for the sake of the boys. If I die winning the fight, then you'll be too busy helping everybody on Eleusis get their colonizing right to worry or mourn about me."

"That's not true." Aiko argued as she attempted to prop herself back up again. "You matter much more than that. Even though I wasn't supposed to fall in love with my Match, I did. I don't know what I'm going to do on Eleusis if you're dead."

He gave her a slight glare, but he reached out to take her hand anyway. "I love you enough not to want to be the end of your world if I die, Aiko. If I die, you'll live, and whatever you do, you'll make the world a better place. It's just what you do."

"You're not my *entire* world." She said defensively. "Just most of it. Look at you, you're huge. You take a lot of space." Aiko held tighter to his hand. "And what about if I die? Do you already have my replacement lined up? Is that why you're being so relaxed about this whole thing?"

"Oh yeah. Absolutely. I've got a list, in fact. Though they weren't easy to find. Beautiful Japanese women of childbearing age aren't as common as you might think." He smiled over at her and helped her sit up with a hand against her back. "Anything happens to you, I go on the warpath until somebody manages to stop me or I run out of people to kill. One or the other. Kam already knows she gets custody of William."

"I see how it is. You get to go crazy and I have to live on with the boys. This second one doesn't even have a name. Are you going to help me do that, at least?" She teased as he helped her stand up in turn, since they really did not have the time to sit around very often. "If we want something like William, we could use . . . Charles? Charlie is cute."

Carl shook his head at that suggestion once they were up. "I've spent too much time talking to Xander lately, Charles is not a name I'd like to pass on to our son." There was a story behind his eyes that he wasn't sharing, but the time they had together, he wanted to spend talking about them and focusing on them. Not on other people's problems. "If we wanted to go full revolutionary, we could have our first son named William and our second one named Wallace. That would give you a Wally. Rhymes with Charlie."

Aiko wrinkled her nose at that and shook her head. "Wallace isn't bad, but I don't like Wally." She held his hand firmly as they started back toward the labyrinth to see why Xander wanted to meet with them. "What about . . ." She sighed dramatically. "I can't think of anything."

They passed a multitude of soldiers in the hallways on their way down, some of whom stopped to actually salute him as they passed, and some of whom gave him dirty looks instead. He imagined he had probably insulted their commander in some way, and couldn't have cared less. "Thomas is another good one. I had a good friend named Thomas growing up. Not sure what actually happened to him. Thomas, Tommy?"

Aiko shook her head again. "Not a fan of that one either. What about Owen? Owen is a nice name, I guess. Or . . . we could name him Cameron after Kam."

He winced a little. "I don't know. They're both about as likely to be in trouble with me. I want to be specific when I'm yelling at people. That would blur the line a little." He sighed, since they had been going back and forth about names ever since they'd been told she was carrying another boy. "Kid's gonna be born without a name. I didn't know we were gonna make that a family tradition, but it seems to be headed that way."

Aiko pouted a little but she tried not to look too disappointed about it. "I wanted to have a name before we go back." She paused and then continued. "Just in case."

He couldn't answer that right away, since behind all the jokes they told about it, they both really were trying to prepare for anything. "Orion and I hung out with a guy named David back on Three. Parents died in some kind of trouble with the Consortium brass when he was younger. Said his name meant 'loved' or something like that. His parents gave it to him so he would know, since they weren't around very much. Seemed like a pretty good name for a kid to have."

"Hm." She said as she looked up at Carl briefly. "David isn't too bad. Do you like it?"

"Wouldn't have suggested it if I didn't." He said as they got onto the lift. A glare from Carl was enough to tell those standing by that they weren't invited into the lift, and the doors closed behind him as he pulled Aiko's back against him so he could massage her shoulders and along her spine. "William and David Tanaka. They definitely sound like transplants, that's for sure."

"They are. Well, kind of. I guess William isn't, or won't be, if we get back to Eleusis where we belong. He was born there, after all." Aiko appreciated the massage, and she leaned back into him easily. "Magical hands. I swear, you have magical hands."

"They're not magical. They were just designed this way." He went through a long period on Eleusis where he struggled with how much of who and what he was had been drawn up in some geneticist's sketchbook before it became his. But ever since, it had become something he was capable of joking about. More than anything else, he learned just how little he knew about his own capabilities.

He had been shot straight through his side just a few days before, and it was nearly healed already. He barely even felt the pain when he dug the bullet out from between his own ribs. It was sore when the adrenaline faded from his body, sure, but at the time, it had been like he was working on somebody else. He kept pushing, and finding little or no resistance to the expansion of his own physical abilities. "I need to get you back to the unit after this meeting so I can massage your feet for you again. I saw the way you were shifting back and forth earlier."

"Don't worry about my feet." Aiko closed her eyes briefly while the lift traveled. "There is enough for you to worry about without worrying about me. David and I are fine." She gave a reassuring pat to her bump. "He agrees."

"Oh, he does, does he? Funny how you're always talking about being outnumbered but I'm the one who always gets outvoted." Carl smiled as he leaned down and kissed her forehead, his hands moving over the rest of her in a warm caress. He never passed up an opportunity to touch her whenever it presented itself, even if the lift was only semi-private. "I prefer worrying about you over everything else."

Aiko turned around so she could look up at him and she smiled. "You're a softie at heart, but I won't tell anyone. You have a pretty fierce snarl when you want to." She tugged him down into another kiss and stayed that way until she heard the lift doors open behind them. "We're here already?"

He glared at the lift gate and nodded. "Looks that way. We're gonna finish this later." He promised her with a last kiss, taking her hand to head toward the heavily guarded Twist room.

Aiko wasn't exactly happy to be anywhere near the Twist or Xander, but the sooner they talked to him, the sooner she could rest. "You called, we came." Aiko said as they got closer to Xander. "What do you need?"

"You know, for a guy doing his best to save the world from itself, I get a lot of shit from people who don't need to be shoveling." Xander glared daggers at her from one of the control panels, a few others around the room on calls with various rebel locations. Clearly there was an entire operation underway about which Aiko was not informed. "You're also early. I didn't ask for you to be down here until this afternoon." He was growling as he said it, and he turned away from her dismissively to look over at one of the other techs. "Ready on mid-continental location 6.93, confirm lock."

"Are you bringing someone in?" Aiko said as she stayed behind Carl. She didn't have any problem going through the Twist, but she didn't want to be sucked back through without any preparation all over again.

"A few someones, yeah." Xander tossed back, focusing on the technicians and their work to make sure they were accurate. They had a dozen people in training to be operators, with the renewed need for local travel, but Xander didn't trust any of them completely.

"6.93 locked, targeting confirms area clear. Power levels well within margins, area surveillance mitigated. Ready for bridge lock." The attendants were clearly reading off a script, but they were learning the way Xander wanted things done, and Xander seemed to approve.

"Bridge lock approved." He didn't move away from the Twist, since the blast from its opening for an Earth-based transport wasn't anywhere near as violent as it was for a Eleusis transport, localized to the opening of the Twist itself and just the few feet surrounding it.

When it stabilized, the scene on the other side of the Twist opening was brightly lit and filled with green in shades and patterns that Aiko vaguely recognized from another life. The plants had grown and been moved slightly in the time she had been away from the greenhouse, but everything was more or less the way she'd left it.

Xander turned around to face the two of them, looking down at the watch on his wrist with an impatient sigh. "Your family's been vetted and has been approved. Your parents can stay here and help with operations. It's twenty minutes from now until our next scheduled pickup from the Ethiopian contingent. You've got that long to get them and anything they want to bring with them."

Aiko looked stunned as she stared at Xander before she grabbed Carl's hand and started moving quickly. She didn't even allow herself to register that her parents were alive as she ran. He said parents. Her other siblings too? Twenty minutes wasn't very much time, so she just scrambled. "Really?! Come on!"

Carl was right behind her, though he glared at Xander on his way through because of the theatrics. He let Aiko lead the way, since he had no idea where he was going, even though she had described her home to him before while they were on Eleusis. He was just grateful that her childhood home wasn't right in the middle of St. Louis. Their appearance in the middle of the city might have raised more than a few eyebrows. And alarms. And guns.

Aiko rushed up to her house and knocked on the door, loudly, even though she knew her father would probably answer the door armed, he always had. She backed up quickly and stood in front of Carl, since she didn't want her parents shooting a gun at some stranger that happened to be the father of her children. She waited and watched, her heart racing and the baby kicking inside of her as a result. "Twenty minutes? That's not enough time to do much of anything!"

"He's not gonna close it again behind us. He just gave us twenty minutes because he wants us to move our asses and doesn't want to be seen as nice." He wasn't in as much of a rush as Aiko was, because he was the commander of the army. It wasn't as though Xander was going to leave him in the midwest.

She'd lived in the house most of her life, and she could tell from the sounds of the floorboards creaking inside when her father got to the door. There was a pause as he looked out through the peephole, then the door was thrown open almost viciously as her father attacked her with a hug.

"Aiko!" He apparently didn't notice she was incredibly

pregnant at first, since he put her down almost as fast as he picked her up, looking down at her bump. "Oh, I'm sorry, I didn't . . . whoa, you're really far . . . who is *that?*" There were too many questions pouring out of her father all at once, and it was a very different thing for her to see from him. He had always been so calm and collected before, so controlled about everything he did. The man in front of her was haggard, stressed, jumpy, looking everywhere at once as if the pillars in front of his house would draw a weapon on him at any given moment.

Aiko hugged her father for as long as he would let her before she smiled back at Carl. She was smiling because she was with her father, but she was also smiling because she knew Carl understood her father. He was as fluent in Japanese as she was, nearly. "That's my husband. Match. Whatever. His name is Carl. We have a son, William, but he's somewhere else so he can be safe."

"You have . . ." He was still breathing heavily as he looked back and forth between her and Carl, but he glanced away furtively afterward and pulled her almost bodily back into the house. "You have to get inside. They're watching. They've been watching . . ." He even tried to manhandle Carl, though it was incredibly ineffective and Carl was coming along anyway of his own accord. "They'll be here any minute. They've probably already seen you. You have . . . You're alive! You are alive, right? I'm not . . . this isn't . . ."

"Dad." Aiko said as calmly as she could. She couldn't believe *he* was alive. They'd been rumored to be killed after the fall of Nine. "Come with us. We're going to go with the rest of the rebels, we're going to go to Eleusis. I'm alive. This is real." She moved her father's hand so he could feel the kicking baby in her belly as a reality check. "Come on, we don't have a lot of time."

He held onto her belly for a moment in wide-eyed amazement, but she could tell that reality was setting in the longer he looked down at her. "Okay." He finally agreed, nodding almost frantically. "Okay. We'll go. We'll get . . ." he shook his head and started moving back into the house. "Your brothers and sisters . . . went to live with your aunt on Prime. The Alperts asked themselves. Said they'd be going to school. Couldn't refuse. Hitomi!" He called through the house as they walked, still a little dazed but at least appearing slightly more focused. "Hitomi! Aiko is home!"

"The Alperts?" Aiko felt sick as she looked back at Carl, but she didn't want to worry her parents as she attempted to hurry them out of their house. Her mother came rushing in and then ran to her to hug her and fawn over her, even though they had no idea that she was even pregnant. "Get what you want to keep. We're going through the Twist to get back to the other rebels."

"The Twist?" Her father almost exploded at the mention of the word, but though he seemed like he was going to say something else, he stopped with his mouth open and backed off, nodding ineffectively. "I'll . . . our things. We have bags just in case . . . You . . . large . . . Carl, husband, right? Help with . . ." he was speaking in slow English, and clearly it had been a while since he had needed to do so.

"I'll help with your things. Just show me what to grab." Carl was already moving, speaking fluent Japanese as he moved through the house with her father to gather up what they deemed necessary.

Aiko rushed around the best she could, but being pregnant wasn't helping her. She was winded before she was finished helping, but she didn't stop moving until Carl had to command her to stop. Aiko waited for her parents and their things, and they were quickly out of the house. "I'm so happy you're okay." She said as they hurried out. "We'll have to do something about everyone else. The Alperts aren't to be trusted."

Her father didn't look particularly 'okay' on his way out the door, but he was hurrying as well as he could. "They said . . . for their safe . . . keeping. I don't . . . it's like you." He said as his voice broke. "Most of a year . . . we haven't heard . . . no letters. They just keep telling us they're fine, not to worry, they'll be able to call soon. But they never do. I don't know what more they want."

"We will find them." Aiko promised, since she didn't want her father to worry any more than he already did. "You'll be safer now." She held onto her father like he was going to shatter right in front of her while Carl helped her mother. "I'm going to do everything I can. I promise."

They all hurried back out of the house and into the greenhouse as it approached their limit of twenty minutes, but her father looked even more confused when Aiko headed into the greenhouse rather than the road nearby. When he saw the open doorway of the Twist, he stopped, and had to shake his head a few times to understand what was in front of him.

"This is . . . that's it? That's the . . . it's . . . where is . . ." he stopped when Hitomi came up to support him, and just nodded, squeezing his wife's hand. "Okay, I . . ." he looked around again as they all heard a car door close outside, and suddenly his eyes were clear. He stepped away from his wife to look out one of the transparent windows of the greenhouse, and ducked back in the next moment as a bullet ricocheted off the door near him. "Go! Run! They were watching!"

"I don't care, come on!" Aiko ducked herself, but she was more worried about her parents and Carl. "Just run through!"

Her father hesitated, but moved when Carl shoved him in that direction, staying behind to make sure Aiko and her parents had gotten through safely. He took his time heading through himself, and when a few Consortium guards came around the corner, he took out each one with a bullet each from the handgun he was holding. He shot through the Twist at those who came afterward, all of whom were stunned for the first moment they saw the Twist itself, giving Carl the moment he needed to gun them down.

"Anytime you're ready, Xander." He said without looking away from the opening, still firing whenever someone came around the corner. "That's half a dozen less we've gotta deal with eventually, but still, I'd rather not right now."

When the Twist finally closed, Aiko felt like she could breathe again, but when she did, she realized her arm had been grazed since it was bleeding and it started to hurt. "Ouch." She said calmly as she looked at her arm, but then she looked at her parents. "Are you two alright?"

Her father was limping, but her mother didn't appear to be hurt. He fell against one wall nearby with a few of the technicians calling for a medic. "Two shots." He groaned as he clutched at his thigh. "One lodged in my tibia, one that feels like it might've hit my femoral artery."

Aiko was down on her knees without a second thought to look at her father's leg before she was ripping at fabric to tie around his leg to stop the bleeding. "Usually I have my bag with me . . . I could sew it up, someone will be here . . ."

He groaned loudly to cut her off, and his teeth started chattering with the pain as she worked, but eventually the bleeding began to slow, and Oliver came rushing down the stairs in a hurry, throwing himself at her father as the worst obvious injury in the room. Strangely, though, her father looked relieved by the injury rather than actually angry about it. He looked around the room with something like his old curiosity in his eyes, before he settled on Aiko again. "This is real." He said, still in Japanese, but he actually broke out into a laugh as Oliver began stitching him up, hissing in pain with every one, but laughing afterward each time. "You're really alive. We're really here."

"You're really here. I'm really alive." Aiko said as she looked at her still-bleeding arm. "The rebellion is alive and nearly ready to attack. We're going to Eleusis. It is real too."

He took deep breaths to help with the pain, but each one sounded like a sigh of relief at the same time. "I knew you were alive." He closed his eyes and turned back toward his wife. "Things will be better now. We'll get them back. All of them." He turned and took a few more quick breaths to steady himself, clearly gaining in strength. "Where is your brother?"

Aiko looked back and forth between her parents and she knew she couldn't hide the pain in her expression. "They wouldn't help him." She breathed the words through the pain that sliced through her chest anew. "They could have. But they wouldn't." Aiko pulled out her communicator and pulled up a picture of Kassie and William together. "He has a daughter, though. Kasumi. She has a beautiful and fierce mother that was his Match. She did everything she could to change the Consortium's mind and they still didn't."

She could see the denial in both her parents expressions. They had been holding on to the possibility that the Consortium had been lying about Kazuo the same way they had been lying about Aiko. Hearing her confirm what they had refused to believe was true settled in on them like a weight, but it was mixed with the sight of their grandchildren. "They're beautiful children." Nobu Tanaka had always been the kind of man who dealt with what was in front of him, but he wasn't afraid to let the tears fall as he thought about Aiko's lost brother.

"We knew the risks." Aiko reminded her parents, but it didn't make the pain of losing her brother any less. She watched as her mother moved to sit as close to her father as she could while he was being fixed up. "Just another reason to take the Consortium apart. They didn't have to let him die. But they did."

Oliver had done his fair share of triage and emergency medicine, having to deal with hospice patients who often disregarded their own better sense. He stitched up Nobu's leg and removed the bullet from his shin as quickly as possible, but he knew the man would need more work than he was able or trained to do. "That'll keep you in one piece for the time being." He pulled Aiko over to where he had set up his suture kit, cleaning off her arm as he spoke. "You'll have to see Chiamaka to have her finish you off. She's the actual trauma surgeon around here. But that should hold off the bleeding for a while until she can get in and make sure there's no other damage."

Aiko watched her parents as she let Oliver work on her arm. She didn't want to look away from them, as though she thought they would be taken away in an instant. When she did look away, though, she was looking for Carl. Did he get injured? "Carl?" As she came down from the adrenaline rush, she was starting to feel queasy.

"I'm here, I'm fine." He reassured her quickly, finishing up with the last checks of his gun to make sure it was appropriately reloaded. She could see he was bleeding from a shot through his upper arm, but it wasn't impeding his movements. He looked down at the wound when she looked at it, and shook his head.

"Just a through and through. It can wait to get stitched until you're all seen to. I'm just glad we got back through." He turned to glare over at Tatyana, who was the only person in charge who was close enough for him to yell at. "You couldn't have checked on their surveillance and disabled it before we went through? I thought that was supposed to be your specialty?"

"It is. You got here early and I ran out of time to check everything perfectly." Tatyana said with a glare of her own. "I did the best I could on short notice. No one is dead."

"At least four people are dead. Just none of ours. Those are still lives that could have been avoided. As could these injuries." Carl was still glaring, but there was nothing that could be changed after the fact. "So whenever you and Xander are done trying to be cute about dealing with people's lives and want to get serious about fighting this war, let me know. Until then, I'm gonna be with my wife and her family. And you will work on finding coordinates for the rest of her siblings so we can work on that extraction. They said the Alperts are holding them on Prime."

"I'll find them." Tatyana said confidently before she nodded back to his family. "Take your wife to see Dr. Woods. She looks ill. You don't want her to lose that baby."

"No, I don't." He took Aiko's hand once he was able to get her away from her parents, and squeezed it gently. "You really should go get checked out. I'll keep an eye on your parents and make sure they find their way to our spare bedroom."

Aiko didn't want to leave her parents or Carl even for herself, so she held onto Carl's arm. "Come with me. Please. I don't want to be alone. I feel dizzy and nauseous."

He wasn't going to refuse a request like that from his wife, so he reached down and scooped her up without any other conversation. "Oliver, make sure they find our house. We'll see you back there as soon as we can." He nodded to Nobu and Hitomi on his way out of the room, still sparing some time to glare back at Tatyana as he hurried to find Barry.

Aiko felt weak and tired as Carl carried her to see Barry, and after a quick examination and some IV fluids, he determined it was stress-related, but her blood pressure was still higher than healthy. She laid there on a small bed in Barry's clinic with Carl next to her and she was still shaking a little.

The last thing she wanted was to see her parents killed right in front of her, and it nearly happened. "I'm sorry." She apologized for taking Carl away from his duties and being shaken so easily. "I . . . I wasn't prepared to see them, and then we were being shot at, and I . . . I just didn't handle it well."

"To clarify, I'm the weird one here." He was sitting on the bed beside her at her waist as if his body would form the bulk of protection for her against the rest of the world. "I'm the guy who just shot and killed at least three people, and I don't anticipate losing any sleep over it tonight. I get dibs on weird." He was running his free hand over her slowly as they waited to see if her blood pressure would normalize, but they had already talked about the fact that it might not.

David was due very soon, after all, and it was hard to even tell how soon, since days on Eleusis were longer than days on Earth and neither Carl nor Aiko had been particularly detailed in keeping track of the passage of time. They weren't even sure precisely when William's birthday had been, and had assumed based on the due date Mercury had estimated for her before they were trapped on Eleusis. "I wish I could say it was the last time you're likely to have someone shooting at you, but that's really not the business we're in."

"I know." She said softly as she reached out to touch his arm, since touching him kept her grounded. Aiko was afraid of what could happen to her and her baby, and her previous stubbornness was faltering. "What if the baby comes early? What if we're supposed to be fighting on Eleusis and I'm in labor?"

"Then we'll deal with it. The same way we dealt with it when William decided to come along while we were supposed to be gathering twilight flowers for medicine." He wasn't fazed by the possibility, since he had long since gotten accustomed to the fact that children complicated everything around them. It was hard, but he didn't expect anything in his life to be easy.

"I think babies are going to continue to be a complication for us. Apparently you can't keep your hands off of me, and I can't say no." She gave him a small, teasing smirk. "And we're really good at making babies."

"I really can't, and neither can you." He returned the grin, and leaned over her on the bed to kiss her. He knew it wouldn't do her blood pressure any favors, but he couldn't resist. "I love you. They're not complications, they're our family, and they come first. If this kid decides to join us soon, so be it. No matter when he gets here, I'm not kidding myself about how long this war is gonna take to fight. It's not gonna be over in a few days or even a few weeks. So whenever he gets here, he's welcome, and we'll take care of you both."

Aiko looked up into Carl's eyes as she reached up and placed a hand on his cheek. "How are you so confident about all of this?"

Carl smiled, and ran his hands over her scandalously before he kissed her again with every bit of his usual confidence. "My friends are fond of saying I'm too stubborn to be anything but confident. I can't say they're completely wrong about that. Most of the time when I make something work, it's because nobody told me it shouldn't be possible and I'm just persistent enough to keep trying. For this, though, I'm confident because I've had dozens of chances where the world's tried to kill me and none of them have even come close. I also know that so long as I'm alive, I'm going to be fighting the Consortium and taking care of our family. So if they can't kill me, and I know I'm not going to stop so long as I'm alive, it all comes down to what my next target is. Fuck everybody and everything that gets in my way."

"You're the best thing that has ever happened to me." She grabbed his large hand with both of hers before she kissed his knuckles lightly. "You give me confidence because you are confident. Thank you for that."

"You've got more reason to be confident than just about anybody here. You're one of the few people who actually knows what the fuck you're doing." His fingers moved over her cheek as he rested close to her, feeling the constant need to place himself between her and the world as much as physically possible. "Xander is an asshole for the way he handled it, but I'm glad we've got your parents here. Your dad seems like he's gonna need a bit of looking after, but they're in the right place to get it, at least."

"I hope so." She enjoyed his touch more than just about anything in the world, so she ran her fingers over his hand before she scooted away from the edge of the bed. "Lay here next to me. Please? I really think cuddling will bring down my blood pressure."

When Aiko asked for something, nothing else in the world existed, not the war they were fighting, not the troops waiting for orders or the operations waiting for his oversight. He moved easily up onto the narrow bed with her and laid on his side to pull her in against his chest, since he took up most of the room on the mattress.

Aiko smiled as he pulled her close and enveloped her into his side, even as pregnant as she was. "The best place in the universe is right here." She clung to Carl and closed her eyes to try and get some rest, even though she didn't think it was possible. Then again, just about anything was possible with Carl.

* * * * *

Logan walked beside Anna on the way down to the Twist with the same conflicted air between them as there had been since she had decided to stay. Neither of them had talked about it since that fight, but neither of them had budged on the subject either, even if they had continued living together and sleeping in the same bed most of the time.

Without the children there to tie them both to the house, it felt empty, but they still kept coming back to each other. "I'm not fully convinced of how moral or ethical this assignment is either." He agreed with her as they walked. "But in circumstances like these, I can't imagine it's only the Montgomeries who are going to end up believing in a moral grey area by the time all is said and done. As it is, you're one of the best marksmen we've got. Having you on this, plus Orion, means we eliminate only the people we've already reviewed and determined need to be eliminated. You're the ones least likely to miss and kill somebody else on accident." Carmina's people were likely better suited for the job, but they weren't trustworthy enough for something like this.

Anna didn't say anything at first, but she finally looked over at Logan. "You know, when I begged my dad to let me learn how to use a gun, I never thought I'd end up in a situation like this. I just wanted to be able to go hunting with everyone else." She watched him for a moment before she peeled her eyes away from him. "It was fun, going out with you and the guys. This is an entirely different ballgame."

"It's a whole different world, you're right about that." He looked over at her to agree wholeheartedly, then shook his head. "There's a lot of things I never thought either of us would be, but it seems like we keep turning into them anyway." He reached out to take her hand as they walked, even though things between them hadn't been particularly bright or good for a long while. He still *wanted* things to be good, and he had never been particularly conflicted about how he felt for Anna. There were just other things going on in his mind at the same time. "Some of those trips you went out on with me and the other guys are my favorite memories. You were always so mean about bringing down more animals than any of us could. Even if you couldn't carry them all yourself on the way back."

Anna gave him a small smile at the memory and squeezed his hand as he held onto hers. "You know me. Competitive to a fault." She held his hand even tighter and paused for a moment on their walk toward the Twist. "I'm . . . I hate to admit this, but I'm . . . really scared."

He stopped with her, glancing down the hall toward the first of the posted guards in the hallway near the all-important chamber. "Everyone is. Me included." He pulled her into a hug against the wall and sighed into her hair as he held her. "Fortunately or unfortunately for both of us, being scared isn't something that's ever stopped us before when there was something we wanted to get done. The war we're about to start is just one of those things, I think. Even if it's easily the scariest thing I've ever done in my life. Give me shitty diapers and crop yield problems any day over this."

"No joke." Anna agreed as she folded into the hug and held as tightly to Logan as he held onto her. "I know we've been having a hard time. But once this is all over, things will be good. I promise."

"It's gonna be a long time before all this is over. But I want it to be. Both over and good." He kissed the side of her neck as he held her, guilt moving through him as he could feel conflicting emotions in her as well. He had no idea what she'd been doing on days or nights when she'd been away from him, and he knew she still didn't know about the time he spent with Gwen. But in a lot of ways, he knew no matter what had been going on with her, it wouldn't have stopped him from loving her. They just needed to get past the war they were fighting so they could go back to living life on their own terms. "I love you, Anna. Always have, always will." He gave her a kiss that was tentative because it felt like they themselves had been tentative for so long. "Let's go pick a fight."

After the tentative kiss, Anna didn't feel like it was enough, so she hauled Logan back to give him the most passionate kiss she could manage. "Kiss like you mean it. Always." Her lips tingled after a kiss like that, and it made her want to kiss him again. "I love you too, Logan. Forever. Whatever it looks like."

With that kind of encouragement, he responded as her younger, teenage self had always wanted him to, lifting her fully into his embrace and spinning to put her back against the wall to kiss her. It felt like some kind of goodbye, but it was just Logan's way of saying goodbye to the relative peace under which they'd been able to live, since they would have none of it in days to come. Even after the kiss broke, he held her there for a long time with his lips against her neck to cherish the peace of the moment. It was one small breath of what he wanted out of life, one sliver of a dream he continued to feel was out of his reach. "I do mean it." He said against her skin, without letting go of her.

Anna ran her fingers through his hair as he held her in place, and he could feel her shiver a little from the way his lips felt pressed against her skin. "You're going to get me all hot and bothered if you keep that up." She teased as she held onto him. "Unfortunately, there's no time for it right now. So sad."

"Very sad." He agreed wholeheartedly, since they both needed some make-up sex in the worst way. He kissed her neck one more time to make their situation worse, then he let her slide back to the floor. "You'll just have to make it back safely after tonight's excursion."

"Talk about a hell of a motivator." Anna said with a smile and as the space between them widened just a bit. "Oh, I'll be back. Sex with you is going to be one amazing reward." She couldn't help but steal one more kiss. "Alright. No more teasing. Let's go."

The room housing the Twist had never been particularly comfortable, but it had somehow grown even more close and claustrophobic with added bodies and a number of added barriers set all around the room. There were a dozen or so commanders who had been picked out by Carl or foisted on him by Carmina, all of whom were there to supervise operations and occasionally participate.

Near the Twist itself, Xander and Tatyana occupied their accustomed place on the central control console. In front of a new barrier Anna had never seen in place before, Orion was getting comfortable in a kind of forward-tilted seat with a shelf in front of him. There were a dozen rifles laid out on the table beside him, and a second seat near him, clearly waiting for her, according to the orders she'd been given. He was going through each rifle methodically and checking them to make sure all the moving pieces moved to his satisfaction, and didn't look up as she came in.

"Good of you to join us, Ms. Prince." Xander said with his usual acidity, but he didn't double down on it when it didn't seem to have any effect on her. "Have a seat and we'll start going through today's targets."

Anna gave him a sarcastic salute before she headed to her seat, and though she looked over at Orion, he didn't even acknowledge her presence. Anna had basically given up on ever talking to Orion unless she had to, mostly because even though apparently Mercury and Logan could have some kind of polite conversation, Anna was a bug or worse to Orion. He never wanted to look at her or say anything to her, and eventually she'd stopped trying to get her friend back. It wouldn't happen. He wouldn't be a friend or even an acquaintance. Just the father of her son. Anna looked over the guns and turned her attention back to Xander, since he was going to give her instruction.

"There are two key objectives here." Xander continued, though Anna could see that Carl wasn't happy about Xander running the operation in question. Or happy about Xander running anything, really. "From the west coast, Jason is going to utilize the Consortium's own tracking system to target every current member of their Board of Directors. All nineteen of them."

He let that sink in for a moment, since they were the nineteen richest and most powerful people in the world, most of whom were famous or infamous for something, or had been at one time. "There are five of them he tells me he hasn't been able to locate, including both the Alperts. We think they might be on Eleusis right now, but we don't know for sure, only that their tracking system can't target them and hasn't had a pin on them for weeks. The rest of them we've got locations on as of this exact moment. We'll be opening the Twist to a space in the same room with each of them in turn, at which point you'll eliminate them as quickly as possible. Once they're each confirmed deceased by the Consortium's own sensors, the Twist will be closed and we'll move on to the next target site."

Xander paused, heaving a brief sigh at the hit and run tactics they had to use. "Our best estimates show that we should be able to get through every one of the targets before the Consortium realizes we're using their own program and shuts it down to lock us out, but there are no guarantees. The faster we can move, the more of this we'll be able to accomplish and the more we'll be able to get done."

"So now we're assassins." Orion said as he hefted another gun, not happy about the task, but not shrinking away from it either. "And we're a thousand percent sure that every single one of these assholes is worth killing?"

"A thousand percent? No." Tatyana replied instead of Xander. "Not even a hundred. I can give you eighty to ninety five. Most of them have families, spouses, some of them have children. However, all of them have been involved in one way or another with the Initiative, upper Consortium projects, or rebel elimination programs. Every one of them has blood on their hands in one way or another. And all of them need to be eliminated in order for us to get anywhere. Is that enough cause for you, Mr. Al-Jabbar, or would you like another assignment?"

"We all have blood on our hands, Ms. Sery." Orion spat back, but he cocked the rifle in his hand, apparently choosing that one to start with. "And my rank is Captain. Mr. Al-Jabbar is my father."

"Speaking of your father," Xander stepped in, just to keep the argument from escalating any further, "when the Consortium takes their location tracking system offline, we'll have a rare window of opportunity to retrieve some personnel from the various Stations. It's been decided that there are a few key targets for kidnapping that will have strategic value. Carmina's team will be handling these extractions. But there are also several people on the Stations who we'd all like to see returned to Earth if possible." Xander gave Orion a pointed look.

"If all goes according to plan, we have a lock on your family, Captain. They've all relocated to Station Three, including your sister-in-law and her son. We intend to keep the Consortium from holding any more hostages than absolutely preventable, and your family is included. If we can get the Consortium to shut down their tracking program, we'll be sending you and a small team to extract them."

The shock on Orion's face was mingled with gratitude at first, but rage replaced the gratitude quickly. "Two years, we've been living in these mountains, and you've given me barely more than a quick reassurance that they've all still got a pulse, now you're finally letting me bring them in? When the Twist has been working for months?"

"Timing, Captain." Xander said without any hint of apology in his voice. "You have your orders. Are you ready to proceed? Both of you?" He looked back and forth between Orion and Anna a few times, waiting in what approximated as patience, his hand hovering over the control panel.

Anna picked up her gun of choice as well, and as she was about to say she was ready, she glanced at Orion and over at Xander again. "What about the Finnegans?" She clicked off the safety on her gun. Anna and Mercury didn't have a relationship even approaching friendship and they barely tolerated each other, but Mercury was important to both Logan and Orion, and she knew the minute he heard about his family he was wondering about Mercury's too. "Do we get to bring them back as well?"

"The Finnegans are also off the grid at the moment." Xander seemed frustrated about that fact, as well as a little surprised that Anna had asked the question and not Orion. "They're on the list for extraction as well, though, as soon as we get a lock on their current position. The last we knew of them they were on a shuttle leaving Six headed for Prime after being summoned for a meeting with the Alperts. After that, they fell off tracking, but we have no reason to believe any harm has come to them."

"I'm sure you'll do your best to find them." Anna replied with a tone that meant he better do his best, or she would have something to say about it. "I'm ready." She wanted to look over at Orion, but she didn't. Anna knew he didn't want her there and would have vastly preferred Fitch or anyone else, probably, but he was stuck with her. "Whenever."

The Twist flared into life, and in front of the two of them along the inner curve of their personal shield, the image of their first few targets flashed up in holographic form. There were four of them all in one place, it appeared, two men and two women, all of them middle-aged or older, looking austere and professional in pictures that had clearly been edited to be as flattering as possible.

"If you could target the women, I would appreciate it." Orion said beside her in a low, almost-friendly voice. It was the first thing she'd heard from him in months that didn't have some kind of harshness behind it, even if he still wasn't looking directly at her. "I'll target the men first and work on taking out whatever guards are in the room with them, but I've just . . . never shot a woman before. I'd like to avoid it, if that's possible. Even if it's not possible forever."

"Sure." Anna replied like it was the easiest thing in the world, deciding who to kill, but she was trying to remove herself from it so that she didn't become consumed by guilt. It was about survival now. She had to survive, and she had to do whatever it took to make that happen. "You're the Captain. What you say goes." She replied in all seriousness, since she was willing to do whatever he asked. He was in charge and he knew better than she did.

Being a soldier had always come easily to Orion. Following orders, following discipline, working within rules, had been as natural to him as breathing. The minutes that followed, however, were easily the most difficult thing he'd ever done in his professional life.

The Twist opened into a clearly exclusive cafe somewhere on Prime, where the four Board members were sitting at dinner with drinks and beautifully-crafted food spread on plates around the table between them. People started screaming and fleeing the area as soon as the Twist stabilized, but by then, it was too late.

Orion and Anna together mowed down the wall of security personnel who sprung up from surrounding tables around their wards, and all four of the Board members dropped within seconds, two bullets to the head and heart each. The place had gone from a peaceful cafe to a bloodbath within half a minute, and the first to rise and sprint from the room had yet to even reach the doors when Orion leaned back from the window to begin reloading his rifle. "Confirm and close. Next window."

Efficiency. That was what mattered. Keep it clean. Keep it moving. Stick to the plan. Follow orders. That was the most important thing. Objective, Effort, Completion. Life was that simple. Life had to be that simple. Allowing it to be more complicated at that moment meant a greater possibility of failure. Failure was not acceptable. The world became simple, because it had to.

"Ready?" He looked over at Anna, for once looking her in the eye. She had known him as a dozen different things, and among all the rest, it wasn't the first time they had gone to work together. Whatever else had happened between them, they were still on the same side, and he still had her back, just as he knew she had his.

Anna nodded as she looked him in the eye, but there were tears falling down her cheeks from what she had done. She never thought of herself as a soldier. She was just a farm girl with exceptional aim, a farmgirl they happened to trust. The things she had killed prior to their escape from Nine were wild animals or farm animals that needed to be slaughtered. She wasn't trained in defense, and certainly not an assassin, but there she was anyway. Anna had never been in it for a war, she was in it for a future. Her body was trembling enough for him to see, but her arms and hands seemed still and sure.

"Ready." She attempted to say, even though her voice cracked when she did.

The Twist refocused itself completely apart from their own reloading and preparations, and Orion turned his attention to the next pair of faces in front of them, a man and a younger-looking woman with a harsh aspect to her that no amount of photo editing could erase. "You're doing well. I didn't see or hear any extraneous fire from you in the last window. Just keep it tight like that and you'll be fine." He encouraged her without looking over at her again.

When the window opened, they were slightly higher up in the perspective, looking down at a wide avenue somewhere beneath glass that looked up at Earth beneath the station. Their two targets were walking below, with guards shadowing them at a distance. Orion quickly adjusted his seat to angle down into the corridor below and took careful aim. The gunshot from his rifle was barely even audible, but the man in their targeting images dropped with a burst of red from the side of his skull a moment later.

Anna wasn't exactly comfortable with being praised for being a good murderer, but she did her best not to fuck anything up. She took a steady aim at the woman but the only good shot she could get at first was in the chest, and she managed to get one through the head before she had to turn her gun onto the guards that gave them return fire. God, she was going to have nightmares. Probably forever.

They returned fire at the guards as well as they could, and they were too far away with too much protection for any of the guards to get anything through. Everything was caught by their own shield wall, and the Twist eventually snapped shut, whirling back into life again immediately as it moved to the next target.

Over and over again, it spun through different faces, different places. Two of the targets were actually on Earth, out under the open sky doing business with other Earth-bound dignitaries at the time, but Orion and Anna took them down all the same, leaving the Earth dignitaries alone. Unlike some of the others, Xander took a piece of paper and threw it through the Twist at the Earth officials just before the Twist closed, but it opened again before Anna or Orion could ask any questions.

"They're starting to close it down." Jason's voice said from a nearby console, since he was working on the targeting along with them, just remotely. "Eleven down out of total nineteen, three more targets available. Two are in the same place."

Xander nodded at the hologram of his brother. "We'll hit those two and then move on to extractions."

When the Twist opened again, the last two men they were targeting were in a medical monitoring room, each hooked up to a dozen machines with masks over their faces to keep them breathing. Orion didn't fire, looking up over the shield at Xander and Tatyana. "You are shitting me, right? How are they on the Board? They're shitting into a bag and they have a tube shoved down their throats."

"Let's just pretend we're ending their misery." Anna said in a voice smaller than anyone had ever heard from her. "I don't want to think about it. I can't think about it." She squinted as she aimed her gun, even though she didn't want to.

Orion spared another moment to glare at Xander, but the faces and identities were a verified match, and he knew there had to be a reason why two people on life support were still on the single most powerful legislative board in the world. Whatever that reason was, killing them would disrupt it, which would create chaos, which was what they wanted. He took Anna's lead and put three bullets into the man directly in front of him, two in the chest and one in the head, before setting his rifle down harshly and grabbing a pair of handguns. "Confirm and close. Next window, show me my fucking family."

Anna put down her gun and was slower to grab another one, and it was clear that she was traumatized over the entire thing. She wanted to be excited for Orion on his behalf that he would get to see his family, but all that occupied her mind was one face after another that she had murdered. "At least you know they'll be safer now." She croaked as she shakily looked down at her loaded gun. There was no telling if there would be unwelcome company between them and his family. They had to be prepared.

"They're wise to us." Jason's voice was saying from the console nearby. "The Consortium is in full panic mode. Everything on every station has been locked down and they've declared a universal state of emergency. Long story short, they're shitting their pants." Jason didn't sound particularly happy about that fact, only reporting data. "Your family got stuck on two different sides of a lockdown. I'm working on overriding the door between before we send you through. Stand by."

Clearly it was easier said than done for Orion to sit still after what they had done, but he took up his guns and waited as Jason worked with the Station security to get the access he needed. "Carl?"

"Right behind you, brother." Carl said from nearby, loading up a few guns of his own as he joined Orion and Anna behind the shield wall, along with a few others. "You're lead on this one. I know Three as well as you do, but it's your kin we're after."

"I'll follow." Anna said softly, since she didn't know his station at all, but she was still able to shoot her gun. More or less. "We'll get them out."

The Twist eventually stabilized on a hallway Orion recognized, but he had severely mixed emotions when he took a running head start and leapt through the opening of the Twist into the greatly-diminished gravity of Three. The aperture opened up on a mostly-broken stairway around the corner from his old unit, and he pulled himself up through the lessened gravity with no difficulty whatsoever. Every bend and twist in the metal was as familiar to him as his own name, and he didn't mind it in the slightest.

Your parents are in your old unit. Xander's voice said into his earpiece, guiding him as he made his way up the broken stairs. *Your sisters are trapped right outside and being escorted away. Your parents have the boy inside and the guards aren't having any luck lifting their own override. Jason's working on it. Get to your sisters first, we're working on relocating the Twist somewhere it's not going to cut anyone in half.*

Anna looked back and forth between Orion and Carl but she kept up with them as quickly as she could, even though it was strange to attempt to readjust to partial gravity when she hadn't lived in space that long previously in the first place. She opened her mouth to say something, and then shut it and then opened it again. "Should we split up? Carl knows where your unit is, right? We risk your sisters' safety even more if we have to take them along with us to get your parents. This way we can minimize their exposure to danger. Especially your little nephew too."

"That makes sense." Orion said with a nod in Carl's direction. "You and the others get to my parents. They'll remember you and they won't go crazy about seeing you the way they might when they see me. Anna and I will deal with Khadi and Misha."

"Anybody or anything else we need to get while we're here?" Carl asked, both to Orion and to the ever-listening voice in all their ears.

"Yeah." Orion said as they all stopped on a landing, watching as a hallway cleared of a burst of security personnel and went silent. "If they're still alive, pick up my ferrets. I miss those little fuckers."

Carl shook his head, but he was smiling anyway. "You are certifiably insane, Captain. No wonder we're friends."

"I mean it, General. Parents and pets. I want them all alive and unharmed." A pair of security officers approached down the hall, but Orion stepped out and dropped both of them with a single bullet each before they even knew they were being attacked. He hurried down the hall in long, bounding strides made possible by the lower gravity.

Anna followed after Orion quietly as Carl went separately to get his parents and the little boy. She did her best to keep calm, though her heart was racing, especially when she had to down two more guards. "It will be nice to put faces with names." Anna finally said in a hushed tone, even though she didn't think he would care to introduce her as anyone important to him. "You told me a lot of stories about your sister."

"You'll like her. And she's gonna love you to pieces." He said with his eyes focused ahead, moving through the corridors with his gun down at his side so as not to attract any undue attention, even if they did have security personnel trying to call out their location whenever they were encountered. None of them got the chance. "Misha's a little quieter, but you'll still like her. She may speak softly, but she takes no shit from anyone. Especially not where Ahmed is concerned."

They came out onto a broad access corridor between rows of residential units, where there was general shouting from both citizens and from security personnel, everyone trying to be heard over everyone else. The chaos was tangible in the air, and as they found cover, they saw several of the Station citizens assault the security officers who were trying to hold them back from their homes and beat them senseless. The tide of chaos didn't last long before security was shooting back into the crowd and people were quieting down, but clearly nothing was getting resolved, and even the security personnel were clearly confused.

"I highly doubt they'll like me. I'm the ex." She replied in a whisper as they crouched and watched. "We need a diversion." Anna said before Orion could say something that would remind her that she was the one who had destroyed things between them. "I can go hide down that other hallway and shoot off my gun. They'll come running."

"There's two dozen of them lining this place, and yeah, they'll all come running to shoot you. Not happening." He gave her a protective glare, and started looking around the corridor as more pushing and shoving started. Things were going badly for the crowd and would only get worse the longer people went without answers.

He found what he was looking for after only a few minutes of searching, and moved closer to Anna so he could point over her shoulder while still keeping them both concealed. "There. Back corner, over by the fountain, where the bodies start thinning out. Woman in a full *hijab* next to the one with the huge gold earrings. That's Misha and Khadi." There were easily two hundred people between him and his sisters, though it didn't appear the two of them were in any immediate danger.

Anna nodded as she looked at the women for a moment in silence, but then she turned her attention slightly toward the fountain. "The fountain. What if we . . ." She was moving up and down a little so she could get a better look. "If we can shoot at the right place, we can get water going everywhere. It'll scatter the crowd. And the guards."

Orion agreed, and looked around the corridor to make sure he was looking at the right thing. It had been a while since he'd been home, but he'd spent most of his life looking at the corridors in Three, and he remembered them vividly. "Feeder pipe is running down the far wall just past the two of them. Aim high, where it hits the plastic connector, and that'll shatter the whole thing, send it everywhere. I'll hit the main back here closer to the cops." He settled in to take his aim, keeping out of sight along with Anna as well as he could.

"Three, two, one . . ." their shots rang out in unison, but the spray of water from the ducts and piping all around the area as a result was more of a distraction than the gunshots, and most people were looking up at the ceiling as if the gunshots had just been the sound of the pipes bursting. Predictable chaos erupted, along with more than a few other gunshots, but the security forces were quickly overwhelmed by the panic of the crowd as people rushed in every direction.

Anna and Orion remained ducked down in hiding until it was clear that they could get up and look like part of the crowd, and Anna got up first. She shoved her gun into her pants and looked back at Orion. "This is going to be our only chance. Just jump into the chaos and get a shower."

He hadn't seen his family in years, and he had just subjected them to even more chaos, so the look of conflict on his face was one that prevented him from moving immediately, even when it appeared safe. Eventually, though, he forced himself into motion, running through the spray of water from pipes nearby toward the spot where he'd seen his sisters last.

They moved away with the rest of the crowd, looking for a way back up to a different residential level along a set of staircases on the far side of the chamber. Orion stopped just below the huge staircases, his voice slightly louder and clearer than the rest of the screams as he yelled in Arabic. "Khadi! Misha! We need to go! Get down here, I have a way out!" There were no security officers in sight, he just hoped his sister and sister-in-law both recognized him and they still trusted him.

Misha was the first to stop even though Khadi kept pulling on her, and she looked back down the stairs and stood there frozen in shock as soon as she saw Orion. He had a small, water-soaked woman next to him, but he looked the same as the last time she had seen him. His eyes were still depthless dark, his features were the same, if not slightly hardened. Was he really alive? "Khadijah, is that . . ."

Khadi stopped as soon as her sister-in-law turned into dead weight, and she looked back. First she looked at her sister but then she looked further down and cursed in a way that was entirely inappropriate, and her parents would have scolded her if they heard. "That can't be."

"Yes, it fucking can!" Orion screamed up at them both, completely heedless of anyone else listening in on the conversation. "Now come on and move your asses! We've gotta go! Now!" His eyes pleaded with them where they stood on the stairs, but he lowered his voice the next moment. "Base crew, tell me you're making progress with that Twist site that's not gonna cut anybody in half."

"Nearly there." Tatyana answered, but that was all the answer she gave, since she didn't have a timeframe.

Khadi hurried down the stairs and dragged Misha after her even though it was clear that Misha was in shock. She found herself looking up at Orion for the first time in over two years, and she didn't know if she should cry or yell at him. She did know they were in danger if they were with him. The Consortium questioned her and their family for months after what happened on Nine. "Go where? What about mom and dad? What about Ahmed?"

"Carl is getting them out of the unit. We need to get down there and meet up with them. My people are working on an extraction point for all of us." He looked down at Khadi once she was down on the floor with him, though he didn't have to look down very far. She had grown since he'd been home last, just as he had, and she was easily even taller than Mercury, though more thinly built. "Merciful god, I missed you. There's a lot to catch up on, but right now we need to get moving. The waterworks aren't going to keep security personnel occupied for long, and pretty soon they'll figure out a way to bring tracking back online."

"I'm glad you're not dead, you big idiot." Khadi said and was scolded by Misha, but she was good at getting scolded. It didn't phase her.

"You look well." Misha said politely as they ran, always and ever so polite and soft-spoken. She had met his wife once and hoped that his redheaded match was safe.

Anna looked over at the polite sister-in-law and the tall, brash sister and she couldn't help but scratch at the back of her neck. She had Al-Jabbar tattooed on her hand and Orion's constellation on the back of her neck and she hoped no one would notice and ask questions she was sure Orion didn't want to answer. "Carl is heading to the Twist location now. We need to hurry."

They encountered chaos wherever they went, with citizens of the Station attempting to resist the security officers and the security officers attempting to instill some kind of order on an unruly population. It made enough of a mess that very few people were free to pay any kind of attention to the four of them as they ran, for which Orion was deeply grateful.

When they got to his old unit, the corridor itself had turned into a war zone, several groups of citizens armed with household implements fighting against security officers who were doing their best not to kill anybody while not being killed themselves. Carl and the others who had come along were across the corridor from where Orion's old unit had once been, and Carl was busy smashing his shoulder into someone's door. As Orion came in sight, he hit it a few times and they finally managed to cave it in, hurrying Orion's parents and nephew into the unit ahead of him as he waited for Orion and his sisters.

"Good, you found them. This one's unoccupied. Base said they were able to set up in . . ." Carl let out a roar as Orion saw a spray of blood from the man's shoulder. They both turned around immediately to open fire in the direction of a gang of security officers who identified Carl and Orion as the fugitives they were.

"Go!" Orion shouted at Anna and his sisters, physically shoving Khadi through after the other rebel soldiers.

His sisters rushed through after Ahmed was safely with them but Anna turned and started firing her gun like a madwoman. She hit one square in the forehead without even trying and then nailed a second guard in the chest three times. Anna didn't glance back to see if the Twist was even still waiting for her, she just kept shooting at guards.

Orion was left beside her once everyone else had gotten through, and he had to physically grab her by the arm to drag her into the unit, since there was no hearing anyone or anything over the chaos in the station and the gunfire everywhere. "Leave it! We're done here!"

Anna seemed to snap out of whatever trance she was in once Orion touched her and she moved with him toward the Twist. Everyone else had gone through and she and Orion were the only ones left.

Once they were through (and not without injury) Anna didn't even look up or back. Just knowing the Twist was closed and no one else made it through, Anna collapsed to her knees on the floor. She didn't even know what to feel or how to react. She felt too disconnected for emotion.

When she hit the floor, Orion was on one side of her, pulling her up to stumble away from the Twist, but a much stronger set of hands hit her from the other side to pull her the rest of the way to her feet, as Logan helped her away from the Twist opening. Behind her, Xander and Tatyana were already working to regroup the soldiers who would go on the next jump. Carl stayed behind, but dismissed Orion to take care of Anna and see to the disposition of his family. Carl hung back and barked orders to get his people into line for the next incursion, but it was all just a haze in the background.

"Are you hurt?" Logan asked beside her in a low voice.

"I don't know." Anna replied honestly, since she just felt so numb. "Is everyone okay?" She looked dazed as she looked up, but she was oddly surprised to see Logan, since she had been next to Orion. She had expected to see Orion. Maybe even hoped for it?

"I think so." Logan said quietly, looking up at her other side for confirmation.

"Carl was hit on the way into the empty unit." Orion answered, helping her stand on her own but not holding on any longer than necessary. "But you know him, he's alright. I caught a graze on my leg that's gonna mess up my uniform, but other than that, I'm fine. I don't think anybody else was hit."

Anna leaned into Logan as soon as Orion let go of her, since there was no way she could hold herself up. "I'm glad your family is safe." Anna glanced up at Orion, though she didn't look at him for long. "You have a lot of catching up to do."

"Yeah, I do." He gave his family a smile across the room, since they were currently being cleared by some of Xander's personnel so they couldn't be tracked. "Thank you." He turned back to Anna rather than going to see his family immediately. "For helping me today. And for helping retrieve them. I'm grateful."

"I've got your back." She said with what she hoped looked like a smile, but she knew she was fried. She didn't even feel like herself. The Anna she knew wasn't a murderer. Not until that day. "You, uh," Anna started to say as he turned away. "You don't have to say anything about me when you tell them about Leo." Though maybe he would, maybe he would want to tell them how terrible she was. Anna shrugged and scratched at the back of her neck again. "It's okay. Whatever you want to say."

He shook his head. "Things are complicated sometimes. Believe me, my family understands that better than most." He gave her another tentative smile, then moved away to help his family, giving out hugs all around, including one for little Ahmed, who only knew Uncle Orion from pictures.

Logan helped Anna get away from the Twist room just as it flared to life again with the next target, but he stopped in the hallway outside the room. "Alright, no more bullshit. What do you need?"

"I don't think I can walk back." She said softly before she started crying, though she held herself back from sobbing. "I can't do that again, Logan." Anna was shaking all over again, since one murder after another ran through her mind. "Defending is one thing . . . I'm not a murderer. Or I wasn't. Before."

He nodded and pulled her in close against him, rubbing her back to help her feel like she was back in control somewhere, not shooting people she'd never met. "It wasn't my favorite idea that Xander and Tatyana have ever had, but it seems to have worked. If the news reports we've gotten while you were away are any indication, in the last hour we've set all of Earth and Space on fire." He rubbed at her back again and held her with a sigh. "Not that it makes it feel any better."

"There were people already dying. On life support. And I had to kill them." She closed her eyes and let Logan hold her, she would be on the floor otherwise. "I'm not . . . what does that make me? What kind of person can do this and then go back to being a mother to innocent babies? I'm . . ."

"You and Orion were right about those two, though you didn't know it at the time. They were being kept alive because the people who held their power of attorney weren't their direct heirs, so they couldn't inherit their Board positions, but they could exercise their power on the Board so long as those two were still alive. They got fucked into a life of pain and suffering because of a technicality.

As for the rest of them, you can look over their files later. I didn't do much more than glance at the ones I didn't already know, and I wouldn't recommend losing much sleep over them, even if I know that's not going to help either." He sighed against her hair. "Orion was right. You did what we needed to do without doing any more damage than we needed to do."

Anna relaxed just a little bit as Logan gave her more information, but still she was exhausted and felt broken. "I thought it would feel justified, after what they did to us. It just felt wrong. Even if you say it wasn't." Anna was limp in his arms and she kept her eyes closed. "Can you take me home? Please?"

He nodded against her neck and picked her up easily, carrying her through the corridors to the lift heading out. He was supposed to stay and supervise several of the missions that day, but Xander and Carl had those things under control, and some things in the world were just more important.

Once she was home she stripped down and showered to feel a little bit removed from what she did. After that she hurried to get into bed. It was strange that their children weren't there, and she missed them even though she knew they were safe. When Logan showed up in their room with a glass of water, she almost cried at his thoughtfulness. "Can you stay with me? Please?"

"Yeah, of course." He put the glass on her side of the bed, then went to sit next to her once she slipped under the covers. It was only mid-afternoon, but there were some days that needed to be over as quickly as possible. "I'm not going anywhere."

Anna reached out for his arm and pulled him closer even though he was fully dressed and she was hiding underneath the sheets. "It's a good bed." She said from under the cover. "But only when you're here."

He kicked off his shoes and took off the formal shirt he wore to toss it aside, then moved over her to his side of the bed so he could lie down and hold her. "It is a pretty good bed." He kissed the side of her head as she hid from the world. He wouldn't tell her that it was going to be alright, he was just going to be there for her when it wasn't.

Anna curled into him as soon as he was on the bed with her, and she buried her face into his large chest. "I love you." She said out of nowhere, but in that moment she was even more grateful for his closeness and willingness to hold her and be with her. "I hope all of this makes a difference in the end."

"It will." He promised against her hair, his fingers smoothing it away from her face as if he could banish her troubled thoughts with the same motion. "What kind of difference, that's anybody's guess right now, but it will make a difference. I believe for the better. We'll find out soon enough. Just get some rest for now."

"Don't leave, okay?" She said sleepily as his fingers worked their gentle caress. "Please don't leave."

"I won't. I promise I won't." He pulled the covers tighter around her to keep her warm and help her feel just a little more comfortable, but he knew there was only so much he could do.

27

Information about the ongoing fight with the Consortium was everywhere as soon as it began in earnest, and there was more of it with every passing hour. The Twist allowed Xander and Tatyana and Carl to coordinate attacks everywhere in the world at once, bringing down not just the Board members that had been their initial targets, but weapons depots, transportation hubs, supply chains, and anything else they could think of to keep the Consortium off its feet.

The latest news, after an assault on Prime, was that the Consortium deployed a significant number of its fighters to Earth, where a dozen different governments decided to take advantage of the chaos and pledge their own independence from the Consortium. The soldiers were sent 'to enforce diplomatic peace agreements' between the various factions, but no one, especially there in the mountains, was buying the line.

Even so, the fact that they had inspired the countries of the world to stand up and fight meant that their strategies were working. It also meant the time had come to hit the Consortium where it would hurt the most.

"Are you up for this?" Oliver asked as they got into their gear near the Twist room. They were no longer in just jumpsuits and careful Eleusis camouflage gear. Parts of their equipment were body armor and heavy weaponry, and neither of them had any illusions about what they were about to walk into.

"Probably not." Anna said in a sedated, yet honest, tone as she finished fastening her jumpsuit and grabbing her gear. She put most of it on with ease, but she was still fumbling here and there. Clearly she wasn't built to be an assassin. "But I'm in this now. There's no farm to go back to if we can't get this done."

"That's true enough." He agreed, then spun her around so that he could help her with some of the fastenings along her back. "I'm glad we have the assignment we do, honestly. Going to any of the fights here on Earth or in Orbit seems . . . too close to home for some reason. I guess because it *is* home. Fighting on Eleusis to remove the Consortium feels more . . . justified, for some reason. I'm not sure why."

"I don't know what I feel about any of it." She stared at him for a moment before she reached out and touched his face lightly. Anna wanted to feel anything other than guilt, since staying numb was not going to help her or anyone else. "All I ever wanted was the chance to live a full life with someone that I loved. This is way beyond any of that."

He nodded against her touch, since he could certainly understand that. "The road to peace is, by definition, not peaceful. Otherwise you'd already be where you're going." He gave her a sad smile and continued working on both their gear, fastening small weapons and ammunition cartridges where they would be in easy reach. "I used to get told that exact thing quite a lot a few years ago. I've never been a particularly patient person when it comes to waiting on things in the world to improve."

"I just . . . can't shake the images." Anna let him do more for her than she really needed, but she was just out of it. She needed something to re-ground her, and she hoped Oliver could help her. Anyone, really. "Does it make me just a terrible, unforgivable person that I didn't ask questions? That I didn't try to figure out if all of those people deserved what we did to them?"

"No, it doesn't." He continued his work without asking questions. He understood the haze she was in a little too well. "It makes you a soldier. Or it means you were a soldier for that day. That hour. And that's what we need to be when we're over there. So we can work together to get this done." He straightened out a few pouches at her belt and then seemed satisfied that she was adequately equipped and got back to his own gear.

"Taking orders isn't something you're good at, and that's not a character defect on your part. Taking orders means letting some other bastard be responsible for what you're told to do. That's not something I've ever been very comfortable with myself." He had a few things to grab, but it didn't take him very long, since he was only carrying a single gun and enough ammunition for an emergency, not for an assault. "When the history of all this is written someday, your name is going to be listed with the revolutionaries, and no one will be laying flowers on the graves of the people you've killed or you may yet kill."

"I just hope, at this point, no one is laying flowers on *my* grave any time soon." She watched him as he finished getting ready, and she took a deep breath before she stepped up to him again. "I'm glad you're coming with me again. Maybe you can help me keep my head on straight." Anna chewed on her bottom lip, but clearly there was something she wanted to say to Oliver and she hadn't seen him in a couple of days. Weeks had passed since they had first been together. "There's something I want to tell you."

He got a look on his face that was almost comical whenever he was curious about something, and he gave it to her completely when she said so. "Is there? What would that be?"

Anna cleared her throat a few times and forced herself to make eye contact with him again. They were alone at the moment, but it wouldn't last long, since they would need to get moving. "I'm pregnant. And I'm pretty sure it's yours . . . I didn't ask for a paternity test or anything, but due to timing and, well, frequency . . ."

His eyebrows shot up and whether they were going to be alone for long or not, he didn't bother stopping himself from leaning in and kissing her in celebration. He laughed afterward as he held her by the waist with the bulk of their equipment and armor between them. "That's great, Anna. I mean, I know it's complicated, but it's more great than it is complicated. You're certain?"

Anna kissed him back first before saying anything, since the kiss helped her to relax a little bit. Kissing Oliver and talking to him was much easier than thinking about the task ahead of them. "About being pregnant, yeah, I'm certain. I'm pretty predictable, but other than that, I've just been cranky and horny. Similar to the last time I went through this. I, uh, I want to ask Barry to run a paternity test, but I wanted to know what you want to do first."

"Well, if we're being personal, what I want is to hear more about how being pregnant makes you horny, since that's the first I've heard of that being a symptom. Lucky you. And me." He chuckled and kissed her again, but his look was more serious afterward. "Paternity isn't going to matter to me. You matter to me. I want to see you happy, no matter what that means."

She smiled a little when she heard him laugh, and she kissed him a few more times. "You matter to me too." Anna kissed him harder and let the kiss linger for a little while. "I know what you lost, and I didn't know if you would want any part of a baby after what happened. Logan and I have had a hard time and we've been distant for a while. I don't know what is going to happen between him and me. I . . . he and I are complicated. It doesn't matter. If this is your baby, then you should be a part of its life. Especially because if you aren't, it won't be able to pick up your perfect accent."

"Yes, well, I'm glad we at least have our priorities straight for the child's development. The accent is a necessity." He laughed again and ran his hands over her, even though she couldn't really feel the touch due to the stiffness of the body armor they were encased with. "We'll figure everything out as time goes on, but right now, the only thing that would make me happier than finding this out is finding out that you'll be staying back because of it." He sounded conflicted on that point, but he didn't look away from her. "I know you fought with Logan on the same subject, I just worry about you being in harm's way, more so now that it's both of you."

"I thought about it." Anna admitted, since she didn't want to put an unborn in harm's way, but she shook her head by way of final explanation. "Aiko is going. She's getting close to popping, and she's going. I committed to this. What kind of life is this baby going to live if we can't defeat the Consortium anyway? I killed people for this cause. I need to see it through. Somehow."

"Alright. We'll take good care of you both." He promised with another kiss, then sighed as he glanced down the hall toward the Twist room. "Let's go see what kind of damage we can get up to."

Anna stole another quick kiss before she started walking with him, since she was grateful that he didn't argue with her to try and change her mind. She was in it now, and she didn't want to turn back. "Thanks. For not pushing me away or pushing to change my mind."

"Oh I know better. No way am I going to try and contradict something you've decided on. I want to live." He smiled down at her in their last moments together, then tried to appear normal as he stepped past the rows of guards and into the Twist chamber itself. No one needed any complications going into their venture, and Orion and Logan were both present in the room waiting for them.

When Anna came out of the room where she and Oliver had their moment and she saw Orion and Logan, she felt like her life was a mess all over again. She was excellent at making fucking messes, but she had a little more sympathy for Liam. It wasn't easy to love three people at once. Anna walked toward the Twist and stopped at Logan. "I'll be back as soon as I can be."

Logan still looked every bit as worried as he had since the assassinations. Not just for her, but for the entire world around them that was plunged into chaos. "It's going to be a long day. For all of us." He reached out to hold onto her by the waist, unwilling to let go of her even as the Twist began cycling up across the room. "Be smart out there. They're not going to just sit back and take this."

Anna nodded and looked up at Logan for a little while, as though she was memorizing every bit of his appearance and his features. "I'll be smart. I want to survive this thing, after all."

"Good. That makes all of us." He knew better than to think that everyone would, though. No one present had any illusions about making it through unscathed. They had already lost people in the attacks conducted, but each death only seemed to push everyone who survived deeper into their own convictions. "I love you, Anna. Go kick some ass."

"I love you too, Logan." She gave him a hug even with all her clothing and equipment, and she was hesitant to back away, but she knew she needed to. Anna walked away slowly after that and then went to stand next to Orion as they waited for the Twist to open completely. "Did you send your family to Mercury?"

He shook his head as he rechecked the last few of his weapons. "I tried, but they wouldn't go. They said if I'm going to be running missions to Eleusis, they'll stay here so they can be here when I get back. I think Misha and my parents would've listened if it was just them, but Khadi dug in and wouldn't leave."

"Sounds like someone I would get along with." Anna gave him a small smile as she looked up at him and then turned her attention back to the Twist. "They'll take care of them here. Are you ready to do this thing?"

"I don't think we have much of a choice at this point." He picked up a bag of charges waiting nearby and hefted it to his shoulder, along with Carl and several of the other officers nearby. It was a larger group than they had ever taken to Eleusis before, but they weren't worried about keeping a low profile any longer, and the more guns on hand, the better. "I just hope Wack-job Montgomery isn't waiting for us."

She glanced over her shoulder at the rest of the assault team and felt her heart wrench all over again at the sight of Cory among them. He wasn't going to be with the forward assault, but he had come to the mountains to help, and wouldn't be denied his choice. She had personally seen to it that he was assigned with Aiko to keep an eye on the Twist to guard their exit. Even that was closer to danger than she had ever wanted to see him, but stubbornness ran in their family.

"He probably is." Anna forced her eyes forward until their Twist opened up completely, and fortunately, it looked as though the area was clear. At least for the moment. "Here we go."

Every other time they went through the Twist to Eleusis it had been with cautious observation, tests in hand, and eyes open to watch for anything new they could learn about the planet. Every other time they had set a sedated pace, careful of every other step where dangers unknown could spring up to trouble them. But as soon as Carl and Carmina charged through the Twist ahead of everyone else, the ranks fell in behind them at a run, Orion and Anna right along with them.

They jogged through the Twist room and then they were jogging across Eleusis' surface, fanning out across the countryside in prearranged patterns to split up and hit the Consortium compound as hard and fast as they could before they were detected. Over two hundred fighters poured through the gate, some of them shouting back and forth to each other, making bets on the damage they could do, remembering fallen comrades, remembering stolen homes. Most ran in vengeful silence, their hands on their weapons and their eyes locked on the target ahead.

As they ran, projectiles began to fly from behind them, where the launching equipment had been dragged hastily through the Twist by another squad. The explosives were comparably small and thin against what Anna knew they could have used, but the Twist would only admit so much artillery at once. All the runners around her had a clear vision of the first bomb as it hit the Consortium compound, setting up a huge plume of fire and smoke from one of the walls closest to them. Another projectile flew, and then another, just as quickly as they could be dragged through the Twist and deployed, taking out entire sections of the barrier wall at once and sending Consortium soldiers spraying into the air.

Anna certainly wasn't prepared for bombs and that kind of warfare, but she kept going and waited for orders as they continued making their way toward the compound. She looked over at Orion and then over at Carl. They had a plan of action to split up the group to make maximum damage and impact, but she didn't know when she should break off.

Once they got closer to the Consortium wall, there were people on the defense shooting back at them, and Orion quickly moved to take cover, along with most of his squad nearby. He bent himself around the tree he was using to hide behind and began picking off people one at a time, swearing under his breath. "I was hoping we could make it at least to those rocks." He glared down the slope at the den of open stones he had hoped to use as a defense. "Anna, get up the hill to that outcropping and see what you can do with some sniper work. Oliver, Koskei, cover her."

He took a few more shots down the slope as the entire landscape was rocked by another explosion farther up the wall, and they could see Carmina's team taking full advantage of the chaos the blast caused, even if their enjoyment was relatively short-lived. "Lawrence, take your squad down the ridge and keep your focus on the Consortium's Twist. If they try to bring in reinforcements, I want them dead before they get off the ramp. The rest of you, with me." He looked over at Anna as Lawrence started to lead his team away between volleys of gunfire on every side. "We'll keep their focus on us so you can get up there. Ready?"

Anna nodded and took off when she was given the signal to do so. She ran her ass off to get up the hill as quickly as she could, but not without gunfire zipping past her at every chance. She ran zig-zag to make herself a more difficult target, but she did pause from place to place to return fire. Hell, if they were going to shoot at her, she was going to shoot back.

Koskei and Oliver did their best to add their own cover fire on the way up the ridge to her assigned station, but neither of them was an accomplished marksman. As she got in position behind a set of rocks and took aim at the Consortium compound below, she heard Koskei grunt behind her and felt him hit the ground. Oliver was there beside him in a heartbeat, pulling him behind a set of rocks near her so he could get a look at how badly the man was hurt. "Are you alright?" He yelled over the chaos at Anna, pushing away Koskei's shirt from the gunshot wound in his chest.

"My ass may have taken the brunt of it again." She said as one cheek felt like it was on fire, but she didn't care. Anna hid behind the rocks and got her gun into position without pausing even once, and she kept herself low as she returned fire. "Is he okay?"

"Well, he's not singing." Oliver said as he worked, trying to keep himself low to avoid any stray fire. The hilltop protected them fairly well, but he wasn't taking any chances. "But his heart's still beating for now, so I'll take that as a start. Koskei, can you move?" She couldn't hear or concentrate on most of the conversation that followed, but there was a good deal of grunting from Koskei and attempts at direction from Oliver as he worked to get at the bullet.

It was good news, at least, that no one seemed able to follow them up the hill, and Anna managed to keep herself low and to take out a few of the Consortium assholes. "They know my spot. We have to move again."

"He can't move." Oliver said quietly, Koskei's grunting growing weaker with every passing moment. "Where are you going to go?"

Anna looked around after she glanced at Koseki, who didn't look great. "There's a bigger ledge over there, and the rocks are thicker. It'll provide more coverage. Can you hit him with some morphine, at least? I don't want to leave him behind, but if we take him . . . we'll be just as dead."

"No." The word came from Koskei, not from Oliver. The man was shoving Oliver away as he struggled onto his side. "No morphine. Makes me itchy. Can't stand the stuff." He grunted in pain weakly one more time and pulled himself along the ground until he was wedged into the same rocks where Anna was. "Go on. I can still shoot. I'll hold here, you get to the . . . to the ledge." They all winced as another explosion hit below, but it provided a lull in the firing from the Consortium walls as everyone checked on what had happened, at least. "Go, now!"

Anna didn't hesitate after she was yelled at, and she and Oliver moved further away from the core group of fighters so that she could get to a better vantage point. She got herself into a spot that felt safest with Oliver behind her and waited for the dust to start to settle from the explosion. "I don't think anyone imagined it would be like this as soon as we walked through."

"They were ready for us." Oliver said as he looked over her shoulder. "They expected more than us, from the looks of it. God, they've got reinforcements and reserves and a whole mess of artillery they aren't even using." He pointed past her to the hazy area between two buildings where there were armored cars outfitted with launchers similar to what they brought. "They just don't even need them with a group as small as we've got, so they're not bothering. They're just picking us off a few at a time."

Anna felt angrier at that kind of information, so she aimed where the air was clearest and killed another Consortium idiot straight through the skull. "Where's everyone else? We'll have to move back toward the Twist and regroup."

"I'm checking. Keep shooting." He didn't move away from her as he brought up his communicator, but he did flinch involuntarily every time she fired. Out of the corner of her eye, she could see the terrain they mapped around the compound, and small pinpoints of light showing their own people spread out to cause mayhem. "Carmina's squad is making some progress over on the north short wall, but it doesn't look like they've got the space to do much more than they're doing. Carl and Orion's squads are taking every wave that comes up, but the Consortium's Twist is still open and people are still coming through. Right now it's just . . . it looks like a fucking meat grinder."

"Fuck." She replied after hearing that news, and she re-positioned so she could take down a few more goons. "So there's no clear path back? And no one is close enough to help us get back?"

"Everyone's pinned down." Orion's voice came over their earpieces, since he'd been listening to their conversation. "We're trying like hell to get that Twist down, but they've got some kind of shielding on it that we haven't been able to crack. Carl's on it. The Argentinians are having a fucking field day down here, you should see these guys." Even when he was in the middle of a fight, Orion was incapable of being a hundred percent serious. "There's some higher-ups who look like they're too old to be front-line fighters standing back from everything. Can you get a clear line on them? Up by the flatbeds near the glass building? One's shorter, kinda stocky, one's older and thinner?"

Anna looked around for a moment and once she saw what he was talking about, she repositioned her gun and looked through the high powered scope. "I can probably get the short one." She bit down hard on her bottom lip as she evaluated for the best shot, finally settling on a hit to the neck and then to the chest. She aimed as carefully as she could and managed to get the first shot, but her second one was off.

"Fuck. Well, he's down, but I don't know if I managed to hit anything important the second time. The first went right through his throat."

The older one started running when his companion was shot, but he ran the wrong direction, and Anna saw him take a bullet to the brain the next moment when he stopped to look around frantically. "Team effort. Thanks for the help, I didn't have a clear shot." Orion sighed in her ear as a flurry of gunshots erupted wherever he was, but he didn't sound concerned when he spoke next.

"Even if Carl gets that Twist down, we're not gonna be able to deal with this many. We need a way out of here and back to the other side so we can come back and finish what we've started later. Anybody have . . . oh no you fucking didn't." A few more gunshots went off, and she could hear Orion yelling unintelligibly in Arabic for a while.

"And stay dead!" He finally shouted. "I swear, the nerve of some people, swarming up over a flank like that. You see anybody else who looks like they might be in charge?"

"No, I don't see anyone else. They're probably all hiding in there, like fucking cowards." Anna looked back at Oliver, but he shook his head. He didn't see anyone either. "Maybe we can try to move again, get closer to you somehow? We're fucking sitting ducks up here if a group heads our way."

"Swing back and away from the walls and get as close as you can to the Twist, see if you can pick off some of the idiots giving Carl a hard time that way. I'm gonna see if I can have some fun with the toys they brought for us to play with." She heard Orion giving more orders as he turned to speak to his soldiers instead of her, and actually heard some laughter break out among those fighting with him. They were up for anything, and clearly so was he.

Anna looked at Oliver again and she sighed. "I guess we need to get closer. I don't like the idea of getting closer, but if Carl needs us . . ."

"We can manage it. Double back, stick to the trees, there's a good position near the wall. We can get there." He pointed out the spot he was talking about on the map, but shrugged afterward, since it was just a guess on his part. "There's only so much more good we can do here, and like you said, they're gonna come out here and try to sweep pretty soon. We need to go."

She gave him a nod and started moving toward the position near the wall so that they could try and help Carl. Anna didn't hear any more from Orion as they moved, but once she was nearing the wall, she decided to try and speak with Orion. "We're approaching the wall. Can I get any insight about the best place to be?"

"Carl's going to bring his team up from the coastline about a hundred meters to your left." She could finally get a visual on Orion where he stood just barely inside the wall, he and the rest of his squad hunkered down inside a pile of rubble that had been left by one of their own explosives. It was providing them good cover, but there was a lot of open ground between where she was and where he was. Ground that had a few bodies on it that belonged to the resistance, some of them moving, some of them not. "If you've got a clear shot from where you are, you should be able to pick off some of the reinforcements the next time they send a wave. There's too many of them right now, and not enough of us."

Anna's heart was thundering in her chest as they remained close to the wall and she looked over at Oliver with obvious fear in her eyes. "Something feels off. It's so quiet."

"They're pulling back." He agreed, and Orion echoed him a moment later. While Orion sounded triumphant about it, though, Oliver sounded skeptical. "But they don't look like they're doing it because they're scared." He listened to his earpiece and watched the ongoing scan of the area on his communicator a little longer, but he shook his head when nothing else emerged. "They want us to get in there farther. That's the only reason they would . . ."

"Pull back!" The order came from Carl in no uncertain terms just a moment before they saw explosions plow down the line of the outer wall. It damaged parts of the outer wall in the process, but it didn't seem as though the Consortium particularly cared about it, so long as it could do some damage to the rebels. The explosions marched down toward them almost in slow motion, but the size of the blasts and the pace at which they were coming spelled out Anna's death long before it got close to being delivered.

Anna cared less about being seen than she did about dying, so she turned around and grabbed onto Oliver and took off running. She had a better chance even in the open than she did staying near the wall, but she knew it wasn't a good chance. All she could think about as she ran was Leo and Lynnette, and how she wished she could run through a portal and straight to them. She didn't want them to be motherless, and she didn't want to die.

The cascading blast from the wall hit her like a wall of invisible bricks in the back, sending her and Oliver flying across the ground. A piece of shrapnel from the wall sailed into her and knocked the side of her head just before she hit the ground, sending her head whipping forward as she tumbled. Pieces of wall fell nearby, and the dust cloud was enough to choke the air right out of her lungs.

Beside her, she could still feel Oliver shaking from the impact, reaching out for her even though he seemed incapable of moving. There was something wrong with her entire body as she looked back through the debris, since she couldn't move. She could still feel every part of herself, most of it bruised or battered, but nothing moved when she tried to get up to run.

Figures moved all around her, some of them rebels, some of them Consortium soldiers. As the explosions from the wall destruction began to die down and the dust began to clear, she could see that from the way she'd landed, she had a near-perfect line of sight to their Twist. It was an open mouth of darkness in mid-air against the bright blue afternoon sky, but it was also a massacre. Carl and his squad appeared unaffected by the wall bombing, or if they had been, he still had plenty of fighters with him. They had taken the mouth of the Consortium's Twist itself and were shooting both into Prime and behind them at the Consortium fighters remaining in the compound.

As she watched, though, Carl ordered his people to fall back and focus their assault on the compound. They flowed down the ramp and directly into the fight, pushing the Consortium back a few dozen meters before there was a split-second explosion on the other side of the Twist. It winked out of existence in a flash of firelight, and the remaining rebels sent up a cheer.

"Everyone fall back! Fall back and regroup!" Carl was yelling over the communicator, though some kind of sand had filled up Anna's mouth and prevented her from answering. Thick debris surrounded her, but that didn't stop her from hearing Orion yell for her.

"I saw her go down!" He was in a rage at someone, pushing them to keep looking for her even though the order to withdraw had been given. "She was here! She was right here before the blast!"

Anna could feel her eyes burning with tears as Orion yelled out for her, but her whole body was useless, even though she didn't understand why. The blast had fallen around her except for the piece that had hit her head. Maybe she was paralyzed. Maybe she was dying. The shock of everything was preventing her from processing pain. It didn't matter now. They were going to leave her. She was going to die in the middle of a field on Eleusis, and she didn't miss the irony. All this time she'd been fighting to live on Eleusis only to die before she lived.

Orion was trying to watch behind him for enemy fire while he picked through the rubble around where he had been sure he had seen Anna last. Gunfire still saturated the air through the ringing in his ears, people running both toward the fight and away from it as quickly as possible. There were bodies everywhere, and through the dust and smoke he could barely tell who was theirs and who wore the uniform of the Consortium.

All units . . . Carl's voice came a little more calmly, though the sound of gunfire through his comm was close and quick, *all units, fall back to the Twist. We've done everything we can do here today, and they need us on the other side of the door.*

That kind of message was ominous enough to throw Orion's mind into even worse confusion. He could feel himself torn in four directions all at once. He wanted to follow orders, to retreat back to the mountains, but he had to find Anna. It wasn't a choice and it wasn't a want, it was a need. He *wanted* to stay and put his fist through every face wearing a Consortium-style shit-eating grin. But he needed to defend his friends, and that meant complying with orders.

Orion ignored the rest of his unit fleeing all around him and went about picking through the debris, going from one broken body to the next. She couldn't be dead. She couldn't be. The smoke would hide him for a while. He had to find her. He had to.

No one came. Why didn't anyone come? Anna tried to move again, but she couldn't. When she opened her mouth, a croak barely escaped. "Ol . . . Ol . . ."

Oliver couldn't answer, and when the smoke began to clear, she could see why. A few feet away, with an arm still reaching out for her, Oliver looked even worse than she felt. He had a long gash across his forehead and the stone that had hit him was still leaning on his skull. Past him, though, she saw Orion scanning the area, looking for her, and she saw him find her.

His eyes were only on the bloody mess of her for a split second when more gunfire rang out, and she saw him jerk to one side just out of her limited field of vision. Carl and what was left of his squad swept into her line of sight afterward, and she could see Carl bend down to scoop Orion up. No one saw her or Oliver where they were lying behind the rubble. No one stopped to pick them up, just two more corpses on the battlefield to be cleaned up later.

Anna started crying since she couldn't cry out, both for herself or Orion. Orion couldn't be dead. She didn't want to die. She didn't want to watch Orion die. Or Oliver. They were all going to die.

Orion tried to move or do anything else as Carl carried him away, but the man was too strong and too big and whatever had just hit him in the back hurt too much. He could barely breathe, but he kept on thumping at Carl's shoulder. "Anna . . . Anna . . ."

"I know, brother. I saw her go down." Carl corroborated, eyes still straight ahead as he ran. "Last I looked, we've lost a hundred and thirty three out of five hundred ninety six. We have to get out of here. We'll come back for everyone when we can."

Aiko, who had been far away from the attack but who had remained out of sight near their Twist was the voice that came over Carl's radio. "Divert! The attack on the other side . . . the Twist . . ."

Gunshots rang out on the same audio channel Aiko broadcasted through, which only had Carl running faster to cover the kilometers between them. He could see the field where the Twist had touched down from a hundred meters away, and he looked for Aiko first. She was still in her position with the launchers, but when he looked at the Twist itself, what he saw made his heart sink.

He couldn't see through the doorway of the Twist because it was blocked by a wall of half a dozen people all firing into it. The few flashes he got from the other side of the Twist were of a bloodbath, but he didn't get to see much before a familiar face turned around and actually smiled down the slope at him.

"Alright, enough fun! Shut it down!" The vaguely-French accent yelled across the distance, as half a dozen of the fighters behind Henry switched their guns out for the grenades at their belts. They were all tossed through the opening in sync, and the entire group immediately got back onto their idling truck and pulled away quickly.

A few seconds later, there was a flash of orange from the control room inside the mountains, and the doorway vanished.

Aiko stared from where she was positioned, clearly shocked that their only way back to Earth was destroyed once again. "Carl . . . you know where to go, right?" She asked over the radio, since she was talking about their home. It was the only safe place she could think of, and Orion clearly needed medical help. She had a stash of medical supplies at her side in a bag and whatever she had left behind before.

"It won't fit everyone still stuck out here." His heart seemed to slow to a crawl. All around them, the rest of the rebels were catching up in groups, a few hundred of them left in the retreat, and all of them looking to Carl. He shook his head and handed Orion off to a few other soldiers who came up to take over for him, and glanced down at himself to see why they thought he needed help. Blood flowed from his shoulder and both arms and explained their reason for concern, even if Carl honestly couldn't feel the cause of the bleeding. All he could feel were the hundreds of eyes on him waiting for direction.

"Three squads. One with the wounded and still walking, one for rear-guard and one for everybody else. Rear-guard, dismantle these launchers and the remaining artillery and get them outfitted for transport. Wounded, with me. Everybody else, we're about to head deep into the woods. Form a perimeter around the rest of us, I don't want any surprises from the flanks and I don't want anybody waking up any Behemoths on our way through. We've taken enough losses for one day. Carmina, you still breathing?"

There wasn't an answer at first, but eventually her voice crackled through. "The radio is damaged." She sounded garbled after that, but then her voice crackled through again. "Directions . . ."

Carl looked back down toward the Consortium compound, looking around at everyone around him afterward for confirmation, but everyone was shaking their heads. "Say again, Carmina, that didn't come through. What's your position?"

"East of . . ." her voice came in and out, and then one of the soldiers nearest Carl finally spoke up. "Don't tell me we're risking our lives standing out here for her and her assholes. Sir. Can't we direct her later? When we don't have people bleeding out?"

Carl rounded on the soldier with a glare, pointing at the space where the Twist had been a moment before. "You see that? You see what's *not* there anymore? We're gonna risk our lives for every single beating heart that's still willing to fight for our own on this side of the galaxy. That includes Carmina and her assholes. And for speaking up, you get to lead the team. Take a dozen able-bodied and retrieve her and whatever other stragglers you can find."

Clearly the woman was not pleased but she complied, at least. After that, everyone followed Carl's directions. What he said was law, since he was one of the few who knew how to help the rest of them survive. Orion was taken ahead of the rest, and Aiko caught up with the soldiers carrying him so she could attempt damage control.

* * * * *

Xander pushed himself up to his hands and knees in the hallway just outside the room that previously housed the Twist, coughing in the cloud of dust and debris. He was scratched in several places and he was pretty sure at least one of his ribs was broken. He could see Tatyana moving nearby, so he wasn't too worried about her, but everything else, everyone else, everything they had worked for, it was all gone.

"Can you walk?" He croaked through the dust filling up his throat. "They threw tracers before the grenades. They've got our location by now."

"Shit." Tatyana cursed but coughed up whatever was in her lungs. One of her arms was definitely broken and one of her legs had twisted the wrong way. "We need to . . . prepare to fight or evacuate."

"Evacuating isn't an option. Not anymore." He said with a furious look back at the Twist room. He felt around in his pockets for his communicator, and managed to pull it out and get it up to his ear. "Bickford, are you still there?"

"I'm still here." Logan said through the connection, though his voice sounded more deflated than anyone in the operation had ever heard. The comm line had been open during the entire attack, and even from his perch up in his office rather than right beside the open Twist, Logan heard and watched every detail of the attack as the Eleusis team's sensors reported it back. He had seen the wall erupt, he had seen where Anna was when it happened, and he hadn't heard anything from her afterward.

615

"Renata." He said quietly, singling out his secretary from the group of people scattered around the office on watch with him. "If Martineau or any of his people are still on this planet, I want them up here now, and mobilize every single person in the barracks. Establish defensive perimeters. We need everybody awake and armed in five minutes."

"Yes, Sir." Renata said just as quietly since she knew the severity of what just happened. Whoever was still alive on Eleusis was now more or less permanently stranded on the planet. Their Twist wasn't only damaged, it was destroyed. Hundreds of people on an alien planet without many tools and no place to live. At least they had Carl and Aiko. "What about your Estate? Do I notify them . . ."

"I'll make that call." He got up from his chair along with everyone else in the room, all of them heading for the surface level of the Labyrinth. "You all have your teams to oversee, get busy on it. I don't know how long it's going to take the Consortium to scramble their people and get them here, but you can bet they're not going to give us time to run. Get moving."

Everyone jumped at Logan's command except Renata who still looked over at her boss with a sympathetic look. She moved slowly to do what she was told, but only because she was hesitating on his behalf. "I'm sorry, Sir, for your loss."

That kind of sympathy reminded him of the walls that he could feel crashing in on his own understanding of reality, and he couldn't even respond to Renata at first while they walked. "A lot of people are going to lose a lot of things today." He couldn't even process what happened as he felt the spiral begin to take hold on his brain. They had known the risks, but Anna had wanted to go anyway. She shouldn't have wanted to go, she should have sat it out, especially after what happened with her sniper attack. But there was no use blaming her or anyone but the Consortium for it. But she still shouldn't have gone. And on and on it went until Logan himself was at the middle of the cyclone of blame swirling in his mind and there was no escape. "Get Martineau. Now."

Renata didn't hesitate anymore after that and rushed out of the room to do as she was asked, since she knew Logan was right. There wasn't a lot of time, a lot of people would lose people they loved or their own lives, and now was the only opportunity they would have to curb that number as much as possible. Her one hope was that the people in the Midwest were at least safe and unknown. Innocent children didn't need to pay the price.

It wasn't Martineau who responded, but one of Carmina's lower flunkies. The man still made most of the other rebels shrink away whenever they saw him, marked as he was by the tattoos around his ear, but he didn't seem to notice or mind. By the time he found Logan, he was up on the exterior of the Labyrinth, watching everyone hurry inside from their homes in the valley, but mostly watching the sky as if the pleasant summer clouds would open any moment and pour down death on them all.

"Valdez reporting for Commander Martineau." The man said brusquely, trying to remain confident in the face of everything he clearly knew had happened. "You wanted to see me, Sir?"

"Get word to your squadron. We're going to need them now." Logan commanded without even looking at the man.

"We had agreed that the squadron would be kept in reserve until we could . . ."

"Those circumstances changed the moment the Twist was destroyed and we lost the upper hand we've had for the past weeks. The two of us standing here arguing about it means they're going to be twenty seconds later getting here than they would've been if you had shut your mouth and done as you were told." Logan's voice was still quiet, but it was sharp enough to cut glass. "Move your ass and get them here."

The man clearly wasn't pleased with the order, but he nodded and gave a kind of salute Logan didn't recognize, and wasn't entirely sure he was comfortable receiving. "As you say, Sir."

Logan returned his look to the sky, waiting for any sign of anything different from any other summer day. "Did you get that, White?"

"I got it." Jason said into the communicator seed in Logan's ear. "I've got a relay channel open for him to get to them. I put them on standby as soon as the attack began. They shouldn't take more than half an hour to reach you."

"Shoulds and shouldn'ts aren't going to help anyone out here right now." He said with a repressed sigh. "What are you seeing upstairs?"

"Your location's been broadcast through too many levels of command for me to erase in one sweep. They've got the first wave in motion already, as well as some other players I don't see the purpose of yet. They've gotten wise to my access with most of their communication channels."

"How long?" Logan asked without taking his eyes off the sky.

There was a pause before Jason answered, and Logan knew the man well enough to know it wasn't because he was uncertain of the answer. "Twenty minutes for atmospheric entry. Maybe a little longer."

There was no point in arguing against timeframes, so Logan just nodded, even if Jason couldn't see him. It wasn't Jason he was really acknowledging, after all. "Patch me through to the Estate, White. They need to know what happened on Eleusis. And what's about to happen here."

Kameron was on patrol when her communicator rang with Logan's specific tone, and she immediately picked up. She wasn't one to ignore a leader, especially when she never knew what would happen from one moment to the next. It was quiet at the estate, and the peace of it had her on edge. She was not built for peace. Her life had always been busy in one way or another. "Fitch here."

"Fitch, it's Logan." He couldn't say Bickford, since she was living with his brother in his house and their voices still sounded mostly identical. "Don't have time for drawn out details. This morning's attack on Eleusis was a successful failure. The wall is down, so is their Twist. Casualties for the attack have been set at roughly twenty-one percent, including Koskei, Oliver, Anna, and Carmina. Orion was hit at the last we saw, but was being carried away from the wall when our data stream ended. The Consortium took out our Twist as well, but sent tracers through first. Jason puts their ETA here in the mountains at roughly nineteen minutes. I have everyone pulling into the Labyrinth to effect our defense and buy some time until Carmina's squadron of Ascenders can get here. Unless you have a better strategic suggestion."

Kameron was stunned, but she only let it keep her silent for ten seconds at the most. "Well, fuck." She said at first and then her mind was spinning through options. "You're right, the best option is to have everyone pull in, but remain in the upper portion of the Labyrinth so you have some chance of getting the fuck out of there. If you go any lower than five floors, you're likely to be buried alive." Kameron put her hand up to her head as she shook her head slowly.

"Goddamn. I'm going to take preventative action here, just in case our location has been compromised. Oh, also, there's an emergency exit through the Labyrinth on the opposite side of the entrance. It was mostly used as a utility shaft to haul up and to lower big machinery. I say make it a trap, lure some of the fuckers back there, let them go down past the fifth floor and then blow some shit up. Better for them to be trapped alive than you."

"I'll see that it's conveyed and have O'Hara see what she can do about dropping some of them back there. Thanks for the tip." He hadn't known about that particular aspect of the place, but he also hadn't been head of security. "Get me Mercury, please. If I can get in contact with you on the other side of this, I will."

"Sure. I'll send you to her directly." Kameron was still stunned as she patched the secure connection through with a shit-ton of password-protected codes and transferred the connection to Mercury. "Doc, it's Logan." It was the only warning she managed to give Mercury before she was off the connection and running toward getting her own security team ready for anything that might happen on their end.

"Logan?" Mercury sounded surprised, since she had no idea why Logan was contacting her and why Kameron did it so hastily. Except that something must be wrong.

"The attack today worked and failed at the same time." He said quietly, knowing that Mercury would understand the complications of a description like that. "Both Twists are down. Theirs first, then ours. Anna went down when they set off explosives to blow their own wall. Orion wasn't far away when it happened. He got hit with another one of the blasts down the line. Carl had everyone in retreat toward the Twist, but some Consortium troops circled around them and got to the opening before they did. They bombed our Twist and sent tracers through. We lost connection with Eleusis, and the Consortium is going to be here in less than twenty minutes." He felt almost grateful for the need to repeat the information, since it allowed him to wrap his head around it, in order to deal with what was in front of them.

Logan could hear her gasp and hear the breath get stuck in her chest, since she couldn't breathe at the news that Orion had been hit, but Anna too. Mercury was in her clinic, but since it was in the room next to her home, she could hear the children through the wall. All four of them. "I . . ."

What could she say? What did he want her to say? Again, she was useless to stop anything worse from happening to her world. Her life. One of her hands absently went to her stomach where her daughters were still growing. Orion's daughters. Even if he was okay, which was unlikely after what Logan described, he was injured and trapped on a planet with little medical assistance except for emergency kits. They weren't enough. If he wasn't dead yet, he was dying. Mercury was holding back tears as her shock still kept her immobile and struggling to breathe. "Then you have twenty minutes to make sure you're not going to die." She finally responded with a shaky exhalation of breath. "Because we're the only family they have left."

"There's been enough dying today. I don't intend to let any of our people do any more of it." He eventually said, his eyes still fixed on the sky as he waited for what he knew was coming. "Kiss my children for me, Mercury." It might have been a command, but she could hear the same shock and pleading in his tone as she could feel moving through her own heartstrings. "We're going to do the best we can here, I can promise you that. Even if I don't know if it will be enough."

Mercury nodded slowly, even though she realized he couldn't see her nod. "No matter what happens, your best is more than enough." She said as her voice cracked. "I'll be with the children. Contact me as soon as you can."

"I will." He promised, but didn't close the connection. "You know me, Mercury." He eventually said, blinking a few times rather than giving the sky the satisfaction of seeing his tears. "I'm never going to stop fighting."

"Thank goodness for that." She said gently as her own tears betrayed her and fell down her cheeks. How, in all the world, did she end up with Logan as the last person alive that cared about her? He was the one who had broken her heart, and now he was the only one left? How did that happen? How did Orion . . . he . . . . Mercury couldn't even think without wanting to break into sobs. "You should go. You're running out of time."

He agreed, but didn't say anything about it right away. "I'll call again soon if I can. I . . ." he stopped, pausing again with no other sound from the other end of the line. "Be safe, Mercury."

"I will do my best." She said just as softly before she let out a shuddering breath that was the only indication of her inner turmoil. "Don't die." She pleaded, even though she knew she should have just kept her mouth shut. "Please."

He considered answering, but he couldn't bring himself to give her the answer that he knew she wanted to hear, so Logan just closed the connection and put the communicator back in his pocket. He reached up to tap his earpiece to pick up on his connection with the rest of the Labyrinth personnel, and listened to the chatter over the lines for a few minutes before he took in a deep breath and got back to work. If he was ever going to see Mercury or his children again, they needed to be prepared for what was coming. "Valdez, what's your status?"

* * * * *

"Kameron." Jason's voice interrupted her in the middle of her conversation with one of her squad leaders on the other end of the Estate grounds, breathing a little faster than normal. If something had White stressed, it generally wasn't a good sign. "Sorry to interrupt, but we need to talk."

"Shitballs, don't give me a fucking heart attack when you break into the middle of important conversations, White. What the hell do you need to tell me that's more important than this?" Kameron was obviously annoyed, but she was scared too. Before, the danger only concerned her. Now she had to be worried about her wife, her daughter, and her nephew. "Make it quick."

"Two ships entering the atmosphere on a trajectory to your location." He said quickly, hoping that was concise enough for her. "Neither of them are fighter or bomber class, or personnel carriers. I'm working on obtaining the manifest for either, but they seem to be getting used to my tricks. They're both usually in service in the ferryman line between Prime and the ground, though this is the first time the Bickford Estate has had its own stop on the tour."

There was a long string of curses that escaped Kameron's mouth and she squeezed her eyes shut for a moment. "What I wouldn't give for a fucking fighter ship right now. I need some big artillery." She ran her hand over her face and then let out a sigh. "We're already moving people into what Bickford assures me are 'impenetrable bomb shelters'. He called them panic rooms or some shit like that, but there aren't a lot of them and they're not that big. A few of my guards and Ben moved to take a group toward the Prince estate because they have a shelter too." Fitch's mind was spinning all over again, since she couldn't believe this was happening. "How did they fucking find us?"

"I'm still working on that. Everything about that estate has been off the radar in every single way for months now. But I doubt they would send two heavily-staffed ships just on a hunch." Jason said with a sigh, sitting in the middle of what seemed like a thousand holograms, none of them particularly helpful as he watched the situation deteriorate on every front all at once.

"Look, that trick I said I could pull months ago? I set it in motion as soon as I knew things were fucked up in the mountains and on Eleusis. But it takes time to execute and it's not going to do shit for any vehicles not currently docked and in standby. The best I can do right now is what I've been doing for the past five minutes, screw with the GPS relays all over the planet just to divert a few of these ships. The whole world is gonna be pissed off at that system once they notice what's happening, but it should at least buy both you and Logan a little more time to prepare for what's coming at you. There's not much else I can do from here right now."

"My fucking wife and kid. It would be one thing if it was just me . . ." Kameron wasn't usually one to lose her cool, but she'd never really had anything to lose before Kass and Melissa. "I have to go. I have to find Liam."

"I'll let you know if I discover any more miracles on my end. Good luck." Jason said quickly as she cut off the communication, watching in horror as the paths of all the inbound ships began to converge from all over the globe on the mountain settlement. His processes were doing their best to break into the guidance and targeting systems of all the ships involved, but whoever the Consortium had working their defenses, they had learned a lot about his methods, and he was getting blocked at every turn.

He closed his eyes to all the data pouring into his brain at once, and turned to look back at Jessie across the room, holding Bekah in the small kitchen of their nondescript apartment near the seashore. None of the ships were headed even vaguely in their direction, which meant they were still undiscovered. For the time being. "I love you." He said to her, even as grief already began to paint itself all over his face. "I'm glad we're here. Not there."

"Me too." Jessie said softly as she held Bekah a little bit tighter. "They're our friends. Sort of. I don't want them to die, but I'm glad we aren't there." She shook her head as she kept away from his screens and any more information. She just didn't want to know.

Gwen was with Mercury and her children when Liam contacted her communicator, but she already knew what happened since Mercury came back from her clinic sobbing.

Gwen was doing her best to comfort Mercury and her children without freaking the fuck out herself, and so she tried to sound calm when she answered. "Liam? Where are you? People are losing their minds, I'm with Mercury . . ."

"I'm down here helping everybody get down into the shelters, where are you and Mercury?" He had been grabbed by the news while he was in the middle of playing with his kids, and he had rushed to get them downstairs into the cellars with their mothers without getting trampled by everybody else. A few others had managed to get everyone more or less stable for the sake of the children, but the noise behind him was a mass of screaming kids and scared adults. The bunkers had been in the process of getting prepped ever since they all arrived on the Bickford estate, but they hadn't been there nearly long enough to truly be prepared. "If you said anything, I couldn't hear you, say again? I'm on my way back up to get you, where are you?"

"I'm in Mercury's room." She said a little louder as she held onto Lynnette. "She talked to Logan, she's incredibly upset, I can't leave her."

"Alright. Get the kids together, I'm on my way." He assured her as he shoved his way through the halls. He was moving against the tide, since most people were trying to shove their way down rather than up, but he kept shoving his way through even though the bunker beneath the house was incredibly narrow near the entrance. The bunker could hold maybe a hundred people, and there were already more than six hundred staying at the house.

"Kameron!" He called above the chaos, people screaming everywhere for their children and for their friends as everyone tried to push into the chamber. "Kameron! Gwen is up there!" He didn't know if she could hear him over the chaos, but she was a great deal closer to the door than he was, and people were actually listening to her when they told her to move.

Kameron met eyes with Liam and she looked at him with sadness in her eyes as she shook her head. "We have to close it! Get back in! I'll go find her and Mercury!"

"No!" He screamed right back at her, still fighting toward the door, but there were too many people shoving their way in, and it was too late by the time he got there. Kameron had already gotten out of the room and tasked several of her people with shutting off the various layers of protection the bunker afforded. Liam had done maintenance on some of the countermeasures himself, and he knew they all worked.

As soon as he heard the first huge door crank itself into place, he slumped against a wall just to stare at it, his communicator momentarily forgotten in his hand. Even over the screaming, he could hear the locks of the door clicking into place, and the massive thud of the secondary door falling into place beyond. They were almost four hundred feet below ground, encased in solid rock in every direction, with a stairway leading up to the house that currently had hundreds of people trapped on it as they tried to get to safety. The house had never been designed to be permanently full, let alone overcrowded. There simply hadn't been space.

"Gwen?" He lifted the communicator to his ear again, hoping he could get some kind of connection up to her, that she was even still on the other end of the line. "Are you there?"

"I'm here." She said in a voice that sounded so small and distant. She'd heard everything, and it didn't take a genius to realize that she could end up dead in a matter of moments and he was locked away with Rachel and Bree without her. Gwen took a deep breath and held a little tighter to Lynnette, and she went to pick up Leo as well, since Mercury was clinging to her boys. "I guess you can't come after all, huh?"

All she could hear was him breathing heavily on the other end of the line for a while as people's screaming began to devolve into sobbing, the entire world breaking down as people began to realize that the separations might be permanent. "In the single bedroom down the hall from Mercury's clinic, the one with the Bowie knife hanging on a rack over it, that's my old room. There's a shotgun and two handguns just inside the closet. Ammunition is right above them on a shelf. I know Kam's people are gonna try to make some kind of stand, but whatever you need to do to protect yourself, grab the guns and do it. I'm gonna get out of here, and I'm gonna get back up to you."

A few tears slid down Gwen's cheeks, even though she was moving to get up with the two children she had in her arms. She held the communicator with her cheek until she could put Leo and Lynnette in a playpen so she could go get the guns. When she looked back at Mercury, she told her she would be right back, but Mercury was still crying and holding onto her twins. Gwen understood her pain, but she also understood that while Mercury had seen death as a doctor, Mercury hadn't experienced life quite as fully as most. Clearly grief caused by death was a fairly new thing for the doctor.

Gwen was trying to keep her head clear as she continued to cry and wander toward what she had been told was Liam's old room. Once she was inside, she cried a little bit harder. "I'm sorry I wanted to keep us a secret for so long. And that I stayed away from you for so many months. It was stupid. I wasted so much time, and now . . ." Now what? Was she going to die? What was the Consortium going to do? "I love you so much."

"I love you too." He said as he slumped against the wall, glaring at the door he himself had helped to maintain as a hated object between him and a piece of his family. "We're going to get through this, you hear me? We're going to . . ." he stopped talking as the lights in the shelter flickered for a moment and a few bulbs popped before the lights came back on in a slightly subdued glow. The emergency generator had kicked on. Which meant something happened upstairs. There had been no impact, no thud of something hitting the ground or of a detonation, but his communicator's line was dead and he could tell by the renewed screaming around him that he wasn't the only one.

Every light in the house went out at the same moment. Every viewscreen, every communicator, every piece of electronics in the entire home went immediately and eerily still, a moment before a sound wave smashed into the house in the wake of the electromagnetic pulse that had disabled everything. Outside the house, two ships were finally visible on their last approach, settling down in the front lawn of the house with their hulls freshly blackened by atmospheric re-entry. Kameron could see the mounted turret on the side of one of them that had been the culprit of delivering the blast that had single-handedly sent the entire house back to the stone age.

Kameron sent Melissa with Kass to find Mercury in her room next to her clinic so they would be all together, and she knew Gwen was there, hopefully with a few guns of her own by now. Kam looked around at the men around her that were her security team, since they were the husbands, mostly, of women inside the house. There were some women too, but their security wasn't enough to take on whatever would come out of two Consortium shuttles. They could handle just about anything else, she felt, but not that.

"Don't shoot." She ordered loudly, since she didn't want to

provoke a beast. "Not until I give the go-ahead. I don't want them bombing this fucking house if we can avoid it."

There was no motion or activity at all from either carrier as they set down and stabilized themselves in the front yard, but eventually, one of the hatches opened near the ground. When it did, the opening remained empty for a long time before two figures walked out. Both of them had their arms up and out to the side to show that they were unarmed, and they were both dressed nicer than any soldier would have been.

"We've been sent to talk!" The man yelled across the distance as he walked down the ramp, a beautiful redheaded woman at his side. "Please don't shoot!"

"You can talk from there!" Kameron shouted back, though she was a little taken aback by the man's accent. It reminded her . . . Mercury. His accent sounded like a heavier version of Mercury's. "Who are you?" Kam didn't lower her gun, and she kept it fixed on the man who approached, even though she told him to stay put.

"My name is Marcus Finnegan." He kept walking, though he did stop a few dozen paces away from Kameron. The engines of the crafts behind him were silent, as were the plains all around them, but he was close enough for Kameron to see just how red and thoroughly splotched both his face and his wife's were. There were tears streaming down both their faces, but Marcus was doing his best to focus. "Is our daughter safe?"

Kameron finally lowered her gun and nodded to the men around her to lower theirs as well, even though she wasn't sure this wasn't a trap. These people definitely looked like Mercury, though, especially the woman. "Mercury is inside. I assume that's who you're talking about."

The man gave a brief gasp, and nodded as he took just a few steps closer, his hands still out to the sides so that Kameron could see that they weren't there to trick anyone. "I . . ." he took a deep breath and steeled himself for what he had to say, though it seemed to bring fresh tears to his eyes. "They have two hundred soldiers on the ship behind us. Maybe another hundred on the other one. But they're only here to guard you. They sent us out here to tell you that if you offer any resistance, they'll take off again and bomb this place until there's nothing left standing. Instead, they're demanding that everyone inside surrender and agree to come quietly."

Kameron closed her eyes and growled softly. "Motherfucker." Her gaze was angry when her eyes snapped open again. "I highly doubt your daughter is going to want to see you if she knows that you came here with the fucking brute squad, Governor Finnegan. You would let them do that? Bomb a house full of children? Babies? Your own fucking grandchildren?"

"Do we look like they're giving us a fucking choice?!" He shot back just as angrily, his hands trembling as he kept them in the air. "If you've got some kind of master plan, whoever you are, some kind of secret artillery hidden away in that mansion that's capable of blasting these two out of the sky, by all means, pull the trigger and let's be done with it. I sincerely hope you do. We've been trying to help you, to get to Mercury, for months now, and we've been nothing but stalled along the way. I dunno what more we could have done from our end, but we're dragged here now, and they mean what they said. They want every man, woman, and child disarmed and packed away in those cruisers within the hour, with no resistance, or this whole place is going to get remapped as a crater."

Kameron took some solace in knowing that the people tucked safely away in the bunker wouldn't be found, so at least some people were safe. The bunker was made to be undetectable, even to the Consortium. Unfortunately, her own daughter and wife hadn't made it into the bunker.

"Fine." She threw her gun down on the ground. Kameron sure as hell wasn't going to risk her daughter's life, her wife, or anyone else just to test the Consortium. They didn't have the resources to resist anyway. All of the big artillery had been transferred to the mountains way back when the midwest had been deserted in the first place. "This isn't over, but I won't resist. For now." She paused and followed the threat up with an eerily calm tone. "I assume you want to see her. Your daughter."

Marcus nodded weakly, since he had clearly hoped they had some kind of weapon that would be effective against the carriers behind him. "Please." The word begged all by itself, even as people began coming out of the carrier behind him with guns drawn. No one fired, but they were clearly marching out to escort Kameron and the others back into the ship.

Kameron looked at the Consortium soldiers and looked back toward the house. "I'll take you to her." She said loudly so the soldiers would leave her alone. "I need to go inside and speak to the rest of the house so they know not to resist. Let's go, Governor. Maybe you can soothe her tears, since the Consortium just killed her husband."

Marcus stopped and hung his head before he followed Kameron into the house, reaching to clutch Claire's hand tightly as he did. They were well-dressed and carried themselves with the authority of their station, in spite of their present circumstances. They looked around as Kameron escorted them and some of the exterior guards began to give themselves up. Each one of them was manhandled and shoved toward the carrier ships to be restrained for prisoner transport, and there were more soldiers pouring out.

Kameron knew eventually she would be manhandled herself, but she was trying to prepare herself for it so she wouldn't fight back. She shouted out, "No resistance! Go with them!" as she walked through the house and led the way. She didn't say another word as she stopped at the door and knocked on it before she did anything else. She didn't want Gwen or Melissa to get antsy with a loaded gun. "Girls, it's me. I have some visitors with me, then we have to get moving. It was either agree to go with the Consortium or get bombed."

When there was no immediate response from inside the room, Marcus took a hesitant step forward, with a hand lingering on the door frame. "Mercury?" The room was dark inside, since all the power was out in the house, but there was some small light coming in through a window farther along that made the room seem darker and more blue than the mood of those already inside.

Mercury was huddled on her bed with her sons but through her tears, she could have sworn that she heard her father's voice. Was she hallucinating? She knew, based on her studies, that sometimes extreme grief could produce hallucinations. Mothers hallucinated holding their babies when they had lost them. "Da?" She asked tentatively, since she hadn't called him that since she was a little girl. "Is that really you?"

Marcus pushed his way into the room at her tentative voice, and the two of them rushed across the room to get to Mercury as soon as they saw her. "It's us, little one." He collapsed next to her, pulling her in against him to crush Declan between the two of them.

Mercury was stunned to see her parents, let alone be surrounded by them, but she started crying even harder as they held onto her. Her boys whimpered in fear, since they didn't know her parents and because Mercury herself was crying, but she was doing her best to hold them and reassure them.

Mercury's mother was the first to lean back out of the hug to look at the babies in Mercury's lap, though they didn't look the way she expected them to look, when she heard that she had grandchildren. Neither of them looked like the husband Mercury had left with, since they were both fair-skinned. They were adorable, however, and Claire's heart squeezed at the sight of the two little boys. "Two boys, and I didn't give your father even one. Looks like you have Finnegan boys now, Marcus. Especially that one." Claire nodded toward Declan, the obvious redhead of the two.

Marcus nodded against Mercury's hair, still holding her with one arm as he looked down at the squirming boys and tried to give them a smile to reassure them. "It's alright, lad. I promise you're a sight prettier than I am, don't be thinking this old face is the shape of things to come for ye." The boys seemed to settle the longer he and Claire stayed there with Mercury, but even if the boys were calming down, it didn't change what was happening. "We've been trying to find you for so long, lass. Ever since Nine went sideways, we've been trying to find where you and the rest ran to, but we could never . . . there's just so much that's happened."

"I know." Mercury said softly as the never-ending tears continued to stream down her face. James was always the more curious one, and so he wasn't nearly as tentative as his brother. Mercury released him so her mother could hold him while she tried to calm herself down. "I didn't know if I would ever see you again. They cut us off at the Initiative and things just got worse." Mercury ran her fingers over Declan's wild hair and she leaned down to kiss the top of his head.

"Orion . . . went to Eleusis this morning . . ." She struggled to say anything about him, since her heart was shattered. "And then Logan . . . Logan Bickford, he and I were matched . . . he was attacked too . . ." She looked up when she heard voices in the hallway, and she looked panicked. When guards appeared at the doorway, she started shaking her head. She was terrified to go back to Orbit, even though she knew it better than Earth. But she knew it would be hard to ever escape if she was in space. "We can't go back, Da. Please. We'll never leave."

"We'll think of something." He reassured her, still holding tight to her as some of the guards moved on to check the rest of the hallway but one of the guards moved inside to check the rest of Mercury's rooms for occupants. "It was either go peacefully now or they were going to bomb this place down to its foundations. The foul-mouthed captain outside decided to lay down arms, and I thank her for it."

They could already hear Kameron threatening the guards if they touched her daughter or wife in the wrong way, but clearly the guards didn't care enough to listen, since she continued to threaten them until Mercury couldn't hear her anymore.

Gwen was sitting quietly on the other side of Mercury's room with two babies in her lap, but she didn't want to interrupt the reunion. She had already put down her gun and resigned to going to Orbit, even though she'd never left Earth in her entire life. She didn't have the skills to resist, not with babies to care for. Maybe it was karma telling her she didn't deserve Liam, since she was getting ripped away before she could really have a life with him and his family. They had started to become her family, a real family for her, and now she was playing mother to two babies who may be orphans by now. She had no idea.

When the guards looked at her, Gwen stood up and hefted both babies to both of her hips. "Don't worry, I have no intention of resisting, but I'm not letting go of my children." She claimed them as her own, since she didn't want anyone getting ideas about connecting them to Anna and Logan. Gwen wasn't stupid, she knew Anna and Logan were some of the biggest names in the resistance and she didn't want anyone taking it out on their children.

"If you think we're here because we've got a thing for taking care of screaming kids, you need to get your head examined. You take care of your own bastards." The guard laughed, nodding into the room. "Get their shit together, both of you." He glared across the room at Mercury. He didn't like the fact that the Governor and his wife were permitted to come down to make their daughter feel better and ease the surrender, since they were traitors every bit as much as the rest of the idiots in the house, but he had orders not to shoot them. At least not on purpose. "You've got five minutes. Get moving."

Gwen already had bags packed for the children since she was always prepared, especially with the four children in the room.

She'd spent a lot of time with them, after all. She got up and took a bag over to Mercury before she grabbed a couple of bags for Leo and Lynnette and left her communicator in her back pocket. It was fried, but she hoped somehow she could still get pictures off of it. Someday. "Pushy, pushy." She snipped as she moved ahead of the guards. "You really should learn how to treat a lady, boys."

"Oh, we know how." The guard said as he shoved her with the butt of his rifle, forcing her to stumble a little with Leo and Lynnette in her arms along with their bags over her shoulder. "You tie her up, for starters, which is what's gonna happen to you on the way upstairs. After that, you'll find out exactly how we treat a lady." He looked back at Mercury, waiting for her to get a move on. "You too, Gorgeous. I think we'll actually 'treat' you first, now that I'm thinking about it."

Gwen glanced at Mercury and she looked back at the guard before she kept walking. She would do whatever it took to protect a friend. "You don't want her, she's from space. Your space women don't know shit about good sex. You all are way too prude up there."

"Sounds like you've met all the wrong Orbitals." Another guard said with a laugh, though he still had his gun at the ready as everybody moved through the halls. They were steadily joining other cowering women and children and men who had been trying to stay as far away from the descending ships as possible. "And now on, you better get used to speaking when spoken to. You're gonna get that mouth of yours stapled shut."

"You don't want my mouth stapled, big guy. I can do better things with it open." Gwen gave him a charming smile and kept moving, though she felt more and more dead inside with every step. She glanced back at the mansion once they were outside, and she turned away from it and kept going toward the shuttle. Gwen was never going to see Liam again, and she never even had the chance to really say goodbye.

One of the guards on the way to the ship tried to shove Mercury along the same as they were doing with the rest of the parade of victims, and Marcus stepped up to push the man back. "They're coming peacefully, you moron! Leave your hands off . . ." he didn't finish what he was saying, since something cracked across his jaw and sent him sprawling in the grass, quietly gasping to breathe after the shock of the impact.

"Dad!" Mercury cried out, since she had only just gotten her parents back, she didn't want anything to happen to them, and she held her children tighter. "Please. Don't hurt him. I'll do whatever you want, just don't hurt him."

"You'll do whatever we want whether we hurt him or not." The guard responsible jeered as Claire helped Marcus back to his feet. "Back in your restraints."

Marcus didn't say or do anything else outwardly defiant as they were herded onto the ship along with hundreds of other crying and screaming people, some of them to one ship and some to the other with no apparent rhyme or reason for the division. Rather than seats with straps for traditional take-off and landing, the inside of the carrier ship had been converted to a massive array of dozens upon dozens of cells, each of them locked with bars from the outside with padded interiors to protect people during the craft's more violent movements.

Mercury and her parents and sons were herded into one by themselves and the door was thrown shut. Gwen was thrown in with her hastily adopted children and another sobbing mother in another nearby. All over the ship, the doors were being slammed shut, setting the whole chamber ringing with the sound of hope being destroyed.

28

Logan looked up at the sky from the entry cavern above the Labyrinth, watching people scatter across the valley in front of him like ants in a flood. The orders had been given, the strategy completed. It would be a good plan right up until the moment the first shot was fired. That was how every plan for every fight in history had been. Theirs would be no different.

"White." Logan kept watch, listening to the sound of boots receding behind him. There had been some argument from those still with him in the mountains that they wouldn't be able to be of any help in the deep passages leading to safety, but Logan had accepted none of their protests. There were plans in place, but there was nothing anyone could do to help those plans. They would either work or they wouldn't. If it progressed to a ground fight, Logan knew better than to think they had a chance.

"White, this is a very bad time for you to be away from your communicator." Logan almost growled when the man didn't answer.

"Busy." White finally answered tersely. "Trying to salvage something from this . . ."

"There's not going to be any salvaging." Logan said quietly, calmly. He should have been grieving. Anna was dead. Mercury was about to be taken. His children . . . He should have been frantic, but he wasn't. Being frantic would do no one any good.

Rage. That was the only thing to feel anymore.

"I don't need you trying to save anything right now. I need something that's going to fuck with their fighters and save the lives of our people here. What do you have for me?"

Jason hesitated on the other end, and the sky remained silent above. "It's not finished yet, but I have a disruption . . ."

"Don't talk. Finish it." Logan ordered in a low voice. Rage was simple. There were enemies that needed killing. That was the end of it. It wasn't political, it wasn't social, it wasn't economic, it hardly even had anything to do with emotions. Rage was even simpler than that.

He was glad when Jason didn't answer again. It meant he was working on whatever brilliant thing he certainly had in mind.

"Xander. Ready in the valley." Logan almost whispered, his eyes never leaving the sky.

"Ready here, Bickford." Xander said reluctantly. "But all this is going to do is . . ."

"Shut up and wait for my order, Xander." Logan snapped, but still without actual anger behind the words. It went beyond that for him. "You're going to say that you've been fighting this war all your life. That you know better than I do how it's done. If that were true, we wouldn't still be fighting it. Don't leave your post and we might get through this."

Xander's silence was all the answer Logan required, and besides, he was sure the artificial man saw the same thing coming over the horizon that he did. Black dots barely visible through the clouds, coming in his direction.

The first strike confirmed everything he had come to expect from the Consortium.

Dozens of missiles came pouring out of the sky and rained down on the mountain around him, every one of them taking chunks of stone and metal with them. Pieces of the mountain were more vulnerable than others, and he saw each of the generators ripped apart in a single moment. It was a sensible priority for attack, Logan couldn't blame them. That was why he had made sure there was nothing important in those places any longer besides the targets that had made them obvious.

"First wave cleared!" Logan had to shout to be heard over the sound of falling debris, but he hoped it was still enough for him to be heard. "Arena One, fire at will!" As the fighters of the first wave of missiles passed over the valley stronghold to get visual confirmation of their damage, a wave of energy weapons let loose from the far side of the valley, buried deep within the rock to evade sensors and make targeting them difficult. Dozens of rays put up just enough resistance to fry circuits and stall every engine they touched, and Logan couldn't help but smile as the ships began to fall straight out of the sky.

"Not expecting an actual fight, were you, assholes?"

He watched the remaining fighters regroup, avoiding the energy weapons the best they could as they pulled back for a second run. Some of the fighters let off volleys at the apparent source of the weapons, but Logan wasn't worried. The perimeter defenses had been designed by somebody even more paranoid than White, and that was saying something.

"Arena Two and Three, ready on my order. Three, it's gonna be on you first, they're pulling back to the fourth quadrant . . ." he broke off, looking above him at the overhanging stone of the entrance to the Labyrinth. He grabbed the case that was enabling his communications and ran, but barely made it out onto the mountainside before it collapsed behind him.

He glanced up as he ran, somehow keeping in mind that the battle was more important than his pressing need to run away from the rockslide behind him. "Go for Arena Three!" He jumped over a rise and scrambled up a short incline to get some distance from the rockslide. Some of the falling debris caught one leg and twisted his knee and ankle wickedly, but he managed to pull free and limp to something that resembled safety.

"Stand by Two!" He panted and watched what happened, another battery of weapons drawing fire and attention from the fighters that engaged the energy weapons. It was a multi-pronged net of weaponry in which the Consortium had to get caught. If they managed to slip away and regroup, come at the Labyrinth from some other direction, they were all cooked.

"You alright, Bickford?" Xander's vaguely-English accent came through the comm unit, broken up by some of the interference caused by the energy weapon discharge nearby.

"Still breathing." Logan grunted as he tried to climb to a better vantage point. "There's a personnel carrier coming down on the west side." He groaned, spotting one that had managed to slip through the trap of the weapons assault the rest had been caught in. "You and Grey are gonna have to deal with them."

"Copy that, we see it. We're on our way." Logan could hear Xander giving orders, but he didn't listen in on them any longer. He had the bigger picture to keep an eye on.

He wrenched himself free of a tangle he'd gotten into on the rocks, but did his best to stay low so he could still see the entire theatre of the battle. He could see what the Consortium wanted to make of it, but after the retaliation his people presented, they had fallen back to rethink while their ground forces moved in.

"We're not gonna let you sweep this one under the rug, you fucking bastards." He growled as he watched the sentry ships massing miles away through the sky, each of them turning every which way as his energy weapons continued to spray fire occasionally. He needed them unstable, he needed them just a little off balance. That was always when the giant was at its most vulnerable. "You murder innocent people, you twist every word in every fucking language until it means whatever you think it should, and you excuse it with whatever scientific doubletalk will get you into your next luxury suite. You're not gonna shut us up, and you're not gonna kill what we've started here."

They couldn't hear him, but he wouldn't have cared if they could. It was the truth. They had taken everything from him the moment they convinced him to agree to join the Initiative in the first place. Whatever he could take back from them, he would take, even if it would never be enough.

"Valdez." Logan grunted through the communicator when he was confident there wasn't going to be a missile headed for his face in the near future.

"Seventeen minutes, Sir." Clearly the man didn't even need to hear the question to know what Logan wanted. "First flight only has six Ascenders coming with it. Eleven in the second flight, five minutes behind."

Logan's eyes flicked back over at the personnel carrier, touching down in a blind spot between the energy weapon ranges, and he wondered if Xander had the manpower left to deal with them. *Twenty minutes for the air support and this is going to be over in ten.*

There was nothing more he could do but wait as the Consortium's fighters moved quickly to surround the mountain, covering every approach and every side of the community Logan had tried to help build.

I refuse to believe that this is going to be the way the world works from now on. He thought as he glared at the fighters, any one of which could be carrying a missile or a bullet fated to end his life. *I refuse to believe that hope is always going to die like this, cold and cornered at the edge of the . . .*

A thought occurred to him, and his fingers scrambled in the dirt for his communicator. "White, get me an open comm to whoever's in command here."

"I do that and they'll have your position . . ."

"Just fucking do it!" Logan screamed into the communicator. He didn't have time to explain what he was going to do or why. Time was exactly what he didn't have and exactly what he was trying to get more of.

Jason groaned on the other end of the communication, but he did as he was ordered. "Turn to channel seventeen on your comm, you'll get their attention."

Logan complied just as some of the fighters opened fire on the outlying buildings of the compound, all of them thankfully abandoned. "This is Logan Bickford, commander of the forces here in this valley and presiding officer of the organization known as United Earth. I want to speak to the commander of the forces sent here to murder us all. There are some things you should know about the complex you're blowing up." There was no answer, and more fire rained down from the attacking ships, so Logan tried again. "More specifically, there's information the people in charge of you are going to be pissed you didn't stop to learn once we all get to the other side of this. It involves the Twist. Or should I say… Twists."

The line was quiet for a brief moment, but the outlying ships soon stopped firing and drew back a few hundred yards, out of range of Logan's energy weapons. A click on the comm finally answered him. "This is Colonel Tisdell. Your Twist has been destroyed, or you wouldn't be standing there trying to make a deal." The woman's voice was harsh and clipped, and Logan could almost feel her irritation.

"Yes, you destroyed the Twist we stole from Nine before we blew it up. Well done. Just like we destroyed the one Twist you had left on Prime. And the one we left behind on Nine. Way too big, would never have managed to fit it in my carry-on luggage." He didn't even crack a smile, since he was in no mood for really making jokes. What he needed was to appear calm. People only joked when they felt comfortable. Comfortable people put their enemies ill at ease wondering why they were so comfortable. "Before you carpet-bomb this entire valley, though, you should know that the copies of the Twist we've made are quite viable. Your bosses are going to want those intact. So you might want to reconsider just nuking this place and going about your day."

Silence greeted him, but no fighters moved in to further the attack. *Just wait. Every second is fewer bullets flying, fewer missiles launched. Every second is another life spared. Maybe. Maybe.*

"You have no other Twists. The process for manufacturing the materials . . ."

"Was a *bitch* and a half to figure out, believe me. But then again, we've had a year and more up here, isolated, none of the distractions of terrorizing the world you Consortium people have to put up with all the time. Not to mention some of the finest minds on the planet working on it. I'm not gonna say it was easy, but it was certainly worth it. You fistfuck this entire valley and you're gonna find yourself on the short end of a very short stick as you deliver the broken pieces of what we've accomplished to the benevolent overlords upstairs."

He shrugged, and hoped it was somehow audible over the comm. "So if I were you, first off, I'd be better looking, and second off, I'd do this operation on the ground with bullets and bayonets, just to be on the safe side." Silence answered him, but still the ships didn't move. "Of course, if you prefer *not* to be on the safe side, by all means, keep bombing us. A lot of good it'll do you when we've had the whole place more or less abandoned for days now."

He got no answer, but he wasn't really expecting one. The conversation had taken up a few minutes, and that was all he had needed. He hoped.

Down in the valley, a few people began running from one house at the far end up toward the Labyrinth entrance. O'hara was coordinating them, Logan knew, but he still clenched his knuckles in anxiety as they presented themselves as a target. Sure enough, one of the fighters took the bait and set in pursuit of the people on foot, only to place itself in the line of fire of an anti-aircraft setup in one of the buildings. One of the runners was down, but so was the ship. Logan hated himself for being grateful that the exchange had gone in their favor. As if anyone's death was ever in anyone else's favor.

The exchange repeated itself four more times before the other fighters caught on, but all that meant to Logan was that he could move his people without them being immediately targeted. It was the opposite of crying wolf. *You make sure there's a wolf on hand every single time you cry wolf, then everytime you cry it the rest of your life, guaranteed somebody's gonna be on high wolf alert.* "Xander, how's it going with our guests?"

"Ten injured, four fatalities. We've got them pinned at the ship landing now and we managed to disable the engines. They're going nowhere. You have fun with that speech?"

"Hey, I'm just trying to make sure people don't get yelled at by their bosses. Nobody likes a hostile work environment." He eyed the rest of the ships, hovering on the edges of the community with their guns pointed at everything he had known for over a year. A single bluff was keeping them at bay, and only temporarily. For all he knew, they had some method of scanning down to the lowest depths of the Labyrinth to try and call him on it and they were just waiting for that scan to complete before they dropped Hell on him again.

If that was the case, so be it. He just hoped the scan would take another three or four minutes. "You keep doing what you're doing. O'hara?"

"Second ship down by the rear entrance. Waiting for them to get comfortable now before we send through the welcome party. Tell Commander Fitch thanks the next time you talk to her, in case I don't get the chance."

"Tell her yourself after we're done mopping up the party-crashers down here. I want updates on your progress as it goes." He rubbed at his forehead, the strain of keeping constant watch on the Consortium fighters beginning to knot his brow together. "Valdez?"

"Seven minutes for the six, thirteen for the eleven." He kept his update short, but clearly still had his eye on the countdown.

Two minutes later, the Consortium opened fire.

Logan vaguely remembered rolling down the mountainside after something struck just below his location. The sound silenced the world temporarily and sent him tumbling uncontrollably over rocks and scrub grass clinging in vain to the scant dirt covering the stones. His shoulder hit a tree trunk just before a second explosion uprooted the tree and sent him flying through the branches. He remembered thinking that it was amazing he was even still alive, let alone conscious, when the rolling and tumbling finally came to a stop.

He was bleeding in a dozen places and he was sure he had broken his shoulder. It only made matters worse that he couldn't stop coughing because of all the dust. He crawled away from the tree as well as he could, though he couldn't see more than a few meters in front of his own face through the debris in the air.

Had it been seven minutes yet? Other bombs were going off all over the valley, the entire area strafed over and over again with merciless firepower as the Consortium called his bluff.

His communicator had been lost somewhere in the explosions, and Logan couldn't bring himself to even look around for it. He didn't even want to check in with Xander and O'hara to get their damage report. He knew what they would say. Instead, he focused on getting himself out into clear air so he could see what was happening.

When he finally did, he came out on a fallen slide of stone that had previously been the side of the mountain. He pulled his way through the dislodged gravel and barely managed to get a decent look at the sky when it exploded in a thousand colors.

The Ascender squadron.

Logan couldn't see well enough to appreciate the magnificent exchange of death in the sky over him. He didn't know enough about aerial combat to understand what was happening even in the places he could see. All he could do was cheer every time a fighter came down that he didn't believe was theirs. Even when one came careening toward the mountainside not fifty meters away from him, he didn't stop his celebrations. He laid on his back and attempted to push himself along the ground to get out from under all the dust, all the fallen branches . . .

He heard the explosion of the fighter as it hit the mountainside behind him, saw the debris flying through the air, mingled with everything else. He flipped onto his stomach as he tried to crawl, saw pieces of the fighter blown in every direction from the blast. He saw one piece come directly up in front of him, felt it darken the sky directly above him as it fell . . .

Everything went dark as the screaming pain drowned out every other sensation.

* * * * *

"Logan." A voice was calling to him. He didn't know whose voice it was. All he knew was that it wasn't anyone whose voice he would have done anything to hear again. It made answering seem not worth the effort. Answering was so hard. Why was answering so hard?

"Yeah." He finally managed to grunt, though he still didn't think answering was a good idea. Where was he? Who was talking to him? Couldn't he just rest?

"Good, you're not dead." Xander. Why was Xander talking to him? Couldn't the man see he was sleeping? "It's been over an hour since the attack. Took us a while to find you up here. We need to move."

"Move?" He asked dumbly, hating himself for the ineffectiveness of his response.

"Yes, move. I'm pretty sure the Consortium didn't enjoy getting spanked, so if they have the chance for payback, you know they're gonna take it."

Logan managed to open his eyes, but the world looked almost exactly the same as it had when he had last closed them. He closed them again immediately, hoping it would change when he opened them again.

That hope turned out to be ill-placed. He looked out at a valley on fire, with crashed fighters and Ascenders everywhere, people roaming the valley looking for survivors among the dead. "The Ascenders weren't enough." He eventually said, since the numbers they faced had been so much more than the firepower on their side.

"Jason sent out a call to some we thought we might be able to rely on as friends. Turned out it worked. The Ascenders kept everybody busy for a little while, but when the Colombians showed up, things started getting really interesting. The Argentinians too." Xander gestured up at the sky, where Logan could see some large transport vessels he'd never laid eyes on in his life. "It's still your fault that anybody here survived that at all. You kept them busy just long enough for us to get by. You should feel good about that."

Dozens of ships hovered in the air above the mountain community, of all sizes and uses, all volunteered for their cause. Logan had his eye on one particularly large transport, which he knew they would need to get everyone remaining in the valley out of there.

Logan closed his eyes again and shook his head. "They're dead." He didn't need to explain what he meant, least of all to Xander. "There's nothing to feel good about." He put his arms behind his back and pushed to get up, but nothing happened. Confused, he tried again, and still nothing happened. "I . . . what . . ."

"You shouldn't try, you might wrench something." Xander said in the quietest voice Logan had ever heard from the man. "We need to get you into a scanner, but from the way we found you . . ."

Logan winced at the memory, since he knew exactly what happened, he just hadn't been willing to admit it. "I'm sure there's others that need a scanner worse than I do. So long as I'm not going to bleed to death, just get me into a chair and get me a report on the survivors once you have it."

Xander paused, but he looked away to wave forward a gurney that was standing by with a pair of soldiers to carry it. They made short work of getting Logan on it, though he winced and grunted the entire time.

Once he was up in the air and being carried by the attendants, Xander stood with him and looked down into his eyes with a reassuring hand on Logan's forearm. "This rebellion is alive right now because of you. Don't think anybody's gonna forget that. Including the Consortium. They haven't had their ass kicked like this in centuries."

"Right." Logan agreed, looking up at the sky from his stretcher. "This is what alive feels like."

* * * * *

Aiko fixed Orion up as well as she could manage before she gave him an Eleusis-made medication that would help with the pain enough to allow him to be coherent without being drunk.

When Orion started to wake up, Aiko was working on stitching someone else up, but she turned her attention to the cot where his legs were hanging off because they didn't have anything long enough. Not yet, anyway. "Take it easy, big guy. You got nailed with some shrapnel pretty bad, but you're lucky, it didn't hit anything vital."

He groaned as he leaned back on the cot, both because it was so uncomfortable and because his back felt like it had been put through a cheese grater. "Lucky." He repeated with his eyes screwed shut, sighing as he tried to listen for anything else going on around him. He had no idea where he was, but if Aiko was sitting there stitching someone up, then they were fine, at least for the time being. "Not sure that word really applies to any of us right now."

"Well, we're not dead. So that's something, I guess." Aiko said gently as she finished up with her stitching, put a bandage over it, and sent the man on his way. She poured some tea for Orion before she went over to him. "The medication I gave you should help with the pain, but this tea will help too. I did what I could, but I'm not a doctor. Just . . . the closest thing to it out here."

He took the tea with something he hoped came across as gratitude. "How many of us are left?" He asked over the steam, sipping at it slowly and hoping it was more helpful than it tasted. "The last casualty count I saw before the wall started to come down on my face was ninety-six."

"The last that Carl told me was a hundred and twenty." She said gently as she looked him over to check on his wounds. "You've been out for about a day and a half. The Consortium sent out forces for the rest of us, but they don't know this forest like we do. The rest of us are scattered in places Carl scouted out, but we're all still close together. A whole team of Consortium idiots got eaten by a Behemoth, so that was a cause for celebration a few hours ago."

She shrugged and sighed as she looked up into his eyes. "Carl took a team back to where Anna was last seen when he felt it was safe. There were no bodies. The Consortium picked up all of the bodies."

Orion's eyes were still closed as he sipped at the tea, but there was no look of surprise on his face. It was the way the Consortium operated. "How very hygienic of them. Wouldn't want to leave the corpses around to infect the not-quite dead." He sipped a little more and winced as he tried to move his shoulder a little. "Do we have an estimate on how many personnel the Consortium has left in their compound? Or have they already re-established their Twist and started importing the whole fucking army?"

"It seems like they're in a panic, since they've been buzzing around their compound, and a shuttle left the compound early this morning. I'm assuming they would not have sent someone off in a shuttle if their Twist was working." Aiko shrugged again. "Carl is pretty certain their Twist is going to be down for a while. He said it took a lot of damage." Aiko moved to take a seat and she leaned back to ease the pain in her back brought on by being far too baby-heavy in the front. It was a miracle that nearly-dying hadn't put her in labor. Apparently her son thought it was much safer to stay put. "We're trying to re-establish communications with Xander and Logan, but it's been iffy at best. We don't even know if there's anyone there to hear us."

"I remembered somebody screaming about tracers before I passed out." The news didn't alter his mindset, though, since Mercury was safe in the midwest. Even if the mountains had been wiped out, she should have been safe. "How soon are we going to get mobilized to finish the job we came here for? Has Carl given orders on that yet? We can't stay scattered forever to just let them pick us off."

"We are trying to make sure we take care of the wounded the best we can before we do anything else." Aiko sighed as she looked at Orion. "We don't have the people to take on the Consortium, Orion. We're stuck here. This is about survival now, not war."

"They have the luxury of not thinking that way." He said without looking at her, though he did finally open his eyes, staring malevolently down into the tea as if he could see the bleeding corpses of the people who killed Anna. "For them, it's still going to be about war. And our extermination. The only way we survive is if we destroy them first. Those are the terms the way they've set them."

"How? How can we possibly survive except to outsmart them out here? Their compound is their playground. Out here, they are incapable of doing much of anything. Rushing headlong into a fight we can't win isn't going to bring Anna back from the dead."

"Maybe not, but I'll sleep a whole lot easier." He downed the last of the tea, which was even more bitter than the first few sips, eliciting a grimace from him. "And there's no guarantee that she's dead. When I saw her, her eyes were open. I didn't see her long enough to know if that's because they were stuck that way or because she was looking for someone."

"If they picked her up, she's dead or as good as." Aiko said as gently as she could. "She's a known face in the resistance. She's been a known face since even before she joined the Initiative."

"And you've never been privy to a Consortium military briefing." He said with a snap in his voice that had nothing playful to it, even if his anger wasn't really directed at Aiko. "They don't just kill the people who bother them. They destroy them. If she was alive when they took her, she's alive now. And she'll be that way long enough for us to get in there and find her."

Aiko held up her hand to indicate she didn't want to argue with him. "You'll have to convince Carl if you want to attempt to break into the compound. I don't think he will be easy to convince, though." Almost as if he overheard her talking about him, Carl came into the small home he had built for himself and Aiko, but he had a crackling communicator in his hand. They could hear Tatyana asking if anyone could hear her.

"We're here." Carl said without explanation, hoping that something, anything, was getting through to the other side of the galaxy. "How are you getting this through?"

"Sending voice data to the other side of the universe uses some of the same technology as the targeting scanners for the Twist." Jason's voice interjected, clearly on the same line with Tatyana, "But it's a great deal less complicated to send audio data than to open magic doors. I've had this set up for a while now, but it's easier if the Twist itself isn't blown up. What's your status?"

Carl sighed, since he despised Jason as a coward, among other things, but he had to be grateful for the man's genius. "A hundred twenty four confirmed dead, ninety-seven during the attack, the rest in the day and a half since. Another thirty-seven not yet confirmed dead, currently missing. Six . . . absconded." He said even more reluctantly. "One squad ran off into the forest when they were supposed to be on patrol. Their signals have been heading south and it's not worth the manpower to send people after them just to force them back to fight. We'll deal with them on the other side of this if Eleusis doesn't do it for us. Four hundred and sixty-three remaining in the forests south of the compound. At least two hundred of those wounded, but the majority able to fight one way or another. What about you in the mountains?"

"We lost about a third." Tatyana said in a strained voice, but she knew death was inevitable, even if she had hoped the numbers wouldn't be as high. "We managed to blow up most of the Consortium vehicles and send the survivors running. It was hell, but at least some of us are still alive. We're mobilizing the remaining weaponry and going to the Midwest." She paused before she continued, since she knew Carl would not take the news well. His son had been in the Midwest. "The Consortium found them. Satellite images show that the house was cleared of all inhabitants. The reports we've been able to steal since . . . have not been promising about the well-being of those who were there."

Aiko felt like the breath was sucked out of her chest, and she started to shake as she thought about Will. Her sweet baby boy. He couldn't . . . he couldn't be dead. The Consortium wouldn't kill babies, would they? Harmless little babies? She thought about her brother and how the Consortium hadn't cared about him. Why would they care about a bunch of unknown children?

"They found . . ." Carl was clearly on the verge of an explosion, but shouting would only wake and attract the wildlife to their relatively-secure home. "How the fuck did they *find* them? You all said there were no eyes on the Bickford place! Where did they take my son?"

"The shuttles went up to Prime. But the count . . . the reported count of prisoners was far less than the number of people that were sent out to the Estate." Tatyana sounded defeated, since clearly she thought that a solid majority of innocents were dead. "The Finnegans were reported to be onboard, as was Mercury. They were transferred to the psychiatric unit. The charts Jason found said they were being evaluated for 'unusual and violent behaviors'. That's all we could really find."

"So they left the prisoners they took alive?" Orion asked from the cot where he sat, even though he hadn't been invited into the conversation. "Why would they do that?" She was still alive for now, but if she was in the custody of the Consortium and pregnant with his children, one of the things the Consortium had been keen to prevent, he had no doubts she would lose that status very quickly.

"For now, I suppose. There was a medical request for a large supply of lethal injections. The prescription was sent by Dr. Maria Kaplan." She knew Orion would remember the name and know it wasn't good news. "We are trying to find a way to get off-planet and get to Prime, but all travel is being heavily monitored and no doubt Prime has tripled their security . . ."

"When she says travel is being heavily monitored," Jason broke in with obvious annoyance, "she's doing her damnedest not to give Logan or me any credit for what happened in the fight, since her boyfriend was fucking useless. The only 'transportation' still going to space is the kind that's owned by the nations of Earth. The Consortium's own fleet is either compromised or at the bottom of the Pacific, for the most part."

That lightened Carl's mood, but only by a hair. "You pulled it off, then." Carl shook his head. "Congratu-fucking-lations. We'll make sure you get a medal and a cookie in the aftermath. What about getting the Twist back up and running?"

"Ours is in a hundred melted pieces." Tatyana shook her head as her voice crackled in and out. "It cannot be repaired. The only known remaining Twist that might be useful is on Prime."

"So it wasn't completely destroyed in the attack." Carl wanted to be a little disappointed about that, but given the circumstances, he wasn't. At least not entirely. "Well, we did our best. It should at least take them a while to repair it."

"They're currently in the process of harvesting as much of the active ingredient from it as they can." Jason's voice cut in again. "I won't bore you with the details, but the Consortium spent most of the fortunes of the entire board gathering the resources just to make the three they did and they've never been able to synthesize more. At least not that I've found with a hell of a lot of digging. Their best option right now is to reclaim what they can from the damage and hope it's enough."

"And you're sure they're doing that?" Orion had to hold onto the one possible chance any of them had of getting back to Earth. The irony of needing that particular destination so desperately was not lost on him.

"It's what I would do if I was them, therefore it's the smartest thing they could be doing right now. They're working on it. But like you said, we've got a window of non-transport until they manage to pull it off."

"But it also means you are stuck and we cannot send you more supplies. We also cannot get to Prime. So we all will have to do what we can with what we have." Tatyana added.

"We're supplied here." Carl said confidently. "Aiko and I spent most of yesterday morning briefing some of the soldiers on how to find food and how to hunt some of the tastier game. The Behemoths alone are capable of feeding most of us comfortably on a protein and mineral-rich diet. We've already downed three, so dinner tonight is steak all around. Until the Consortium starts making moves against us, we'll manage."

"Or until we make our move against them." Orion turned it around on his friend with a meaningful look that Carl only sighed to answer.

"We'll be fine. But every single satellite is gonna be looking for you assholes out there." Carl said with no little concern in his voice. "I know you're good, White, but you can't hide everybody forever."

"We'll play that dance until we're able to get a strategy together that works. Meeting up with whoever's left in the midwest is the first step." Jason seemed more resigned than excited, but then again, he was half a continent away from danger. "Most of our point in contacting you was to reassure that as far as we know, no harm has come to any of your family members. We're sending a full file of known information along with this transmission, it should link to everyone's feed once you give the go-ahead to send it out."

"Fantastic." Carl didn't sound very excited about it, but it wasn't really very exciting news.

"Good luck to you." Tatyana said as nicely as she could, which meant not rudely. "We will try to contact you again when we can."

"Good luck to you too." He had never been particularly fond of Tatyana either, especially since he had initially been the one to investigate her as a traitor to the Consortium and a downright bitch. Neither opinion had changed, he just no longer had a problem with the first part. "I'll send the list of casualties from our side as well, make sure you can inform . . . whoever's left to inform."

Carl closed his eyes at the bleakness of their situation. Months, years, of careful planning, of positioning, of gathering resources, building an armory, an army, a strategy, all destroyed in a day. The Consortium had taken nearly as big a hit, true, from the way Jason described it, but still, it was diminishing, on both sides. "I'll keep updates in a log on my device and keep it charged. This sun works just as well for that as ours. Any time you can patch in to retrieve an update, I'll make sure something is waiting for you. Right now we're going to make sure we've got what we need here, keep an eye on them, and do our best not to get killed until we can fully regroup. I'll keep you posted."

As the communicator went dead, Aiko just stared at it in Carl's hand before she got up and went and threw up just outside her home. Thinking about Will being dead made her insides churn and her brain turned to mush. William was supposed to be safe. Not dead. Not . . . not dead.

Carl didn't leave the house to go after her, but he did take a moment to hang his head and lean against a wall nearby before he activated his communicator again. "Get me Carmina, Wilkes, and Grier. I don't care where they are. I want them here in an hour." He cut off the impromptu call and put his communicator back in his pocket to give himself time to process the news. "I'm glad you're awake." He said eventually to Orion as he put together another cup of tea for Aiko whenever she came back inside. "I hate looking for new commanders."

"I'm going back for her." Orion said without skirting around the subject. He didn't look away or flinch when Carl looked back at him disapprovingly. "Once I get my bearings here and we get a good look at who's left in that compound, I'm gonna take anyone dumb enough to follow me and go back in to get her. Even if I have to defy my CO to do it."

"We can fight about what we're doing and what we're not doing later. I'm not gonna have it right now. Not today and not tomorrow. The day after that, we'll revisit it." Carl understood his friend's grief, but he wasn't going to allow for any kind of division in the ranks. Not when the ranks weren't that big to begin with. "Today and tomorrow, if she's dead, she's still dead, and if she's alive, they'll be sitting around figuring out what to do with her the same way we're going to be sitting around trying to figure out how to get to her. And everybody else they might have who we think is a corpse right now. We need to be solid before we move, otherwise we get more fucked by the minute."

* * * * *

In the few days that passed after the Consortium took most everyone from the Bickford estate, the lingering hundred or so remained in the bunker even though Liam had opened it up hours after the Consortium had gone. They were all in a sort of daze that was fueled by survivor's guilt and grief, since families had been already torn apart by war, now further torn apart by the Consortium. Bree and Rachel felt the loss just as much as anyone else, over Gwen, but also over Margo. Chrissy was safe in their care, but Margo and her new husband had been taken. While they might have been mad at Margo, they certainly didn't wish her dead.

Bree made a small dinner for the group of them with the rations they had, and when she set it down in front of Liam, she sat in his lap afterward. His mind had been occupied the entire time Gwen was gone, and she knew he was frustrated by how limited he was in doing anything to get her back. "Logan will be here soon, right? He will have a plan. They took Mercury and his children. He'll have a plan."

Liam didn't seem comforted at all by that possibility. "My brother might be a good leader and apparently some kind of tactical genius, but that doesn't mean whatever plan he's gonna have is gonna be a good one. Or good enough." He stared down at the food in front of him, leaning on the table with one elbow and his other arm around Bree's waist. "Plus, he's gonna want to rescue his kids, sure, but they just killed Anna. There's no way Logan's going to be thinking straight."

"Are any of us thinking straight?" Bree asked as she looked back at Liam and then over at Rachel and sighed. "How are we supposed to get up there to rescue Gwen? What if they send her off as a slave somewhere or something?" Bree clearly knew very little about what kind of life people lived in Orbit, but she didn't care to know. Their lives were separate from her own. Until now.

"The way every news outlet in the world is telling it, the Consortium's entire fleet just about dropped out of the sky. Logan controls the largest fleet in the world right now, aside from what a few countries down here on the ground might be able to put together. But that doesn't mean we're gonna be able to do shit once we actually get to Prime."

Liam didn't know anything about life in orbit, but he'd seen enough by way of documentaries and other television shows that were set on Prime to know what the place was like. It was bigger than any city on Earth, and more densely populated than most countries. Finding anyone in that place would require a lot of work, even more so people the Consortium was keeping as prisoners. "But the station is gonna have its own kind of defenses, so it doesn't matter that we've got the ships. I'm not going anywhere just so I can get blasted out of the sky before I get there. That doesn't do anybody any good."

Rachel, who usually kept quiet, finally spoke up. "It feels like we failed her." She said softly as she looked over at the babies who were oblivious to the dire situation, thankfully. "We're supposed to protect each other, and they took her anyway."

"We're not going to fail anybody." Liam's denial was gentler than anything else he'd said that day, but he did look over at Rachel past Bree. "They put Logan and all the rest of them in the Initiative through all manner of behavioral experiments, fucked with their meds, their chemistry, do you think this is just the next phase of that? I expected them to come down here and just bomb us straight back a few centuries. Them taking people doesn't make any damn sense. It's not like anybody fighting for this is gonna back off because they have hostages."

"They would not have pushed so hard for people to make babies if they didn't want the babies." Rachel replied with a sigh, since it seemed like once the Consortium had collected all of the people in the house, they didn't sweep further. They didn't even bother the Prince farm, where a few people had fled to safety with Ben and his family. "So yes, I do think this is the next phase of that."

Bree looked deeply disturbed and she shook her head. "That's so fucked up. What kind of psychopaths do they breed up there?"

Rachel shook her head again. "It's just someone's good intentions centuries ago gone completely wrong now. The whole point of Eleusis was to re-establish the human race, which to some people meant making a *better* human race." Rachel kept up with news and current events as much as she could, especially because she had once been pursued to join the Initiative for her intelligence and quick, tactical mind, but she hadn't had any interest in it. "I'm sure the Initiative didn't go away, it just went into hiding due to the reputation it acquired after the fall of Nine. So who knows what will happen now."

"Whatever they want with those kids, they're gonna get kicked in the teeth for it." Liam half-growled from the table, his fingers drumming anxiously, since he needed to be doing something. Anything. "Without the Twist and with most of their fleet grounded, pretty soon the Consortium is gonna start feeling the pinch when it comes to resources. They recycle and produce as much as they can up there, I know, but they're gonna have to start leaning on Earth shipments and start commandeering shit from different countries just to get what their stations need. I'll have to figure out a way to be in the right place when that happens and get to Prime that way. Maybe all of us can, all of us under Logan who are left. Then once we've got enough people there by those means, we can make a move." It was just a thought, and he had no idea how any part of the plan would work, but he had to have something to hold onto.

"So when Logan comes, you're going to go with him? Go up into orbit?" Bree asked as she turned toward Liam more on his lap. She didn't seem surprised, but she was more interested in confirming what was going on in his head.

He didn't look happy about it, but she and Rachel could both tell what the answer was just from the look in his stormy grey eyes. "I can't stay down here and run while they're up there at the mercy of somebody that wants nothing good for them. It's just not in me." He looked like he wanted to apologize for that, for the fact that he would be leaving, but he couldn't bring himself to do it.

Bree leaned in and kissed him warmly before she pressed her forehead to his. "She's one of us. Or she should be, but you still have her ring." She chastised before she kissed him again. "You better save my ass if I get taken by aliens. I would not be happy. So you need to save her too."

"If we start throwing aliens into this mess, we are all fucked. And not in the way I like." He kissed her back, but he was clearly still distracted, and would be until things were back to the way they ought to be. He looked down at his pocket as it began vibrating beneath Bree, and moved her slightly to get his communicator, even if he didn't want to remove her from his lap entirely. When he saw that it was Xander, he immediately became nervous, since he didn't need any more bad news. "Who's dead this time?"

"Nobody else yet, more's the pity." Xander answered, more grumpy than usual ever since the fight and his own failed part in it. "Just wanted to notify you that we're five minutes out. Didn't want you or anybody else in the house thinking you were being invaded again. It's the good guys this time."

"You sure that's what we are?" He mouthed the message to Rachel and Bree, so that they could start notifying people and forestall a renewed panic. "Seems to me I'm just a guy who wants the rest of his family back."

"Yeah, that makes two of us, Bickford Junior." Xander didn't go on to explain that comment, and groaned into the phone. "Anyway, get your people together. We've got the equipment now and it's best we all stay together."

As soon as the convoy showed up and it was confirmed it was 'the good guys', Larissa was one of the first to run out, since she wanted to see Logan. They were fortunate enough to not have lost him, at least. She was young enough to run while still quite pregnant, though it was still a bit comical to watch.

The convoy was impressive to look at, even if everyone insisted that it wasn't enough to make for an offensive against the Consortium directly. Dozens of ships moved through the air to land all around the expansive Estate, some of them larger transports, some of them small one- or two-man fighters. There was an entire swarm of what looked like hundreds of tiny person-sized pods that moved like a flock of birds behind the rest of the fleet, but there didn't seem to be any actual people inside them.

As soon as they landed on the ground, they all opened

themselves up to expose solar charging panels, as did most of the other ships on the ground once they had landed. The ones that landed closest to the mansion were transport ships, though of a very different class than the ones that had arrived to steal away the rest of their families.

When the loading hatch of one of the ships opened and people began coming out, there was initially no sign of Logan. Eventually, when most of the traffic had cleared, a wheelchair rolled up to the top of the ramp and began its cautious descent. It rolled smoothly onto the ground, Logan's strong arms pushing it along by way of the wheels so he could cross the distance between the ship and his childhood home. The shirt he wore was still ripped to hell, and Larissa could see hasty bandages across one of his shoulders and peeking out from beneath his shirt, wrapped around his ribs. Otherwise, there was no sign of damage to his legs, but there was no sign of movement from them either.

Larissa didn't slow anyway, since she didn't care what state her brother was in as long as he was alive. She met him as quickly as she could, which left her short of breath. "Logan." She breathed as she remained at his side. "I'm so glad you're alive. Even if you're not okay." Larissa looked him over and hoped that he would be, since she knew he wanted to keep fighting.

He pulled his sister down into a hug, which was difficult for both of them in their present conditions, but he still held onto her tightly. "Same to you, sis." He kissed her cheek and held onto her for just a little longer before he resumed pushing himself toward the house, a little more slowly so he could roll beside her. "Cory is okay." He knew it was abrupt, but he knew she would want to know up front. "Or he was, the last we heard."

Logan could see she relaxed a little bit when she heard that Cory was alright, but she was trying not to worry about Cory. There was nothing she could do about the fact that Cory was gone and there was no way to get him back without the Twist. She had resigned to waiting and hoping, as long as she knew Cory was still alive. "Thank you for letting me know. I . . . did my best not to assume the worst when we heard about Anna."

"Good. Assuming the worst is my job." He knew his own home well enough to know which portions of it were amenable to the newly-handicapped and which were not, so he steered toward the side of the main entrance, grunting at even the small bumps of the entry doorway, but saying nothing about it. "Did they damage the house at all, or just ransack it for the occupants?"

"Some doors and windows, but not very many." Larissa followed alongside her brother and sometimes behind him. She wanted to ask about his injuries, but she also knew Logan would tell her if he wanted her to know. "They just took everyone in the house and left. They didn't look for anyone else, didn't try to break into the bunker. We don't know if they didn't find it or didn't care. Ben said he saw the shuttles leave, no one bothered the Prince farm or any other. When we came up from the bunker, it was like everyone just took their bags and left, except for the few broken doors and windows. We heard shouting the entire time, and lots of crying."

"They were probably here after certain people. Once they had them, and as many hostages as they could ever want, they must have decided nothing else was worth the effort." Logan couldn't say he blamed them. They had taken so many people that almost everyone still involved with the rebellion had lost someone, either killed on Eleusis or taken as prisoners to Prime. "I'm getting awfully tired of saying goodbye to this place." They weren't sure what their plan was now, but currently they didn't know if it would be safe to remain at the estate.

He couldn't be much help to anyone in his present condition, so he just stayed in the grand entry hall and watched people come and go with their belongings and whatever they could take from the house that seemed like it might be useful. No one smiled, and no one had a reason to.

"Eventually we'll come back. We're Bickfords." Larissa reached over and touched her brother's good shoulder tentatively. "Are you going to tell me what happened to you or are you going to just keep it to yourself?" Apparently she couldn't keep herself from asking after all.

He shook his head, not in a refusal to answer the question, but just because he wasn't entirely sure himself. "It's war. A lot worse has happened to a lot of people already." He looked down at himself and glanced at his shoulder, moving his arm tentatively with a wince just because he could. "The field medics aren't sure what's going on with me yet. They've got worse cases they're tending to back on the ship. It's not like we've got full medical scanners available on fighter ships."

"Sierra might have a portable one, it wouldn't be as good as a full-body scanner, but it might be something. You should have her look at it before we go." When he started to shake his head, she glared at him. "You're not going to be any good to anyone if you don't get fixed up. Also, what, are you never going to have sex again either?"

"You think my sex life is really first on my list of priorities right now?" He hadn't gotten angry at his sister very many times in his life, and he had been away from her for most of the past two years. He knew he was a far cry from the older brother she had once known. He glared up at her for the comment and went back to watching people hurry in every direction in front of them. "We're gonna have a long flight ahead of us once we leave here. Sierra can scan me then, but I'm pretty sure I know what she's going to find."

"People may be calling you the President of Earth, but you don't know what's best all of the time, Logan." Larissa was one of the few people that didn't back down from her brother when she felt like she was right. She was usually quiet, but she was stubborn too. "I don't know a fraction of what happened to you while you were gone, and I don't need to. But a little humility and self-preservation wouldn't hurt you."

"I'm not the president of anything." He knew what was circulating and what Jason encouraged after the attack on the mountains, but that didn't mean he needed to encourage it himself. Just because he was the first person in three hundred years to win any kind of military victory against the Consortium didn't mean he was anyone to look up to. "You should go get your things, sis. I made sure to reserve a cabin on my command ship right next to mine. It should be big enough for you and for Liam's family."

"You *are* the President." Larissa pressed as she looked at her brother a little bit longer and shook her head. "But if you want to do any more good, stop being so stupid about it." She turned and walked away, since clearly he didn't want to talk or listen. So much for being excited to see him when she wondered if he wished he had died anyway.

He didn't try to stop her as she left, and just sat in the corner of the grand entryway to watch people for a long while without really seeing anyone. His communicator beeped a few times in the pocket of the wheelchair, but he ignored it, even though he knew he probably shouldn't.

He had fought like hell for two years to try and either get to a new world or save the one he had, first for Anna, then for Mercury, then for both of them. Now neither of them was ever likely to see it in peace. Hundreds of other stories had already ended the same way, fighting for something the Consortium didn't believe in. Millions had died in the centuries since the Crisis because of some kind of accident he knew was somehow linked to the Consortium in the first place. No amount of pain or suffering would satisfy them. No sacrifice was too great for them to demand of the human race in the name of their deluded vision of progress.

And people thought he was morose on account of being confined to a wheelchair for an unknowable amount of time. It was almost comical, if there were still any part of him that knew how to laugh.

He didn't know what else to do but fight. It was the only thing he had done the entire time he was with Anna or Mercury, and it was the only thing that made any sense to him anymore. It was the only thing he could do to honor either of them, even if it was also the thing that had taken him away from them both.

He wheeled himself back out the door, since he didn't need to see the rest of the house. It was one of his only opportunities to see the place utilized and really alive, but it no longer seemed to matter as much to him as it once had. No quantity of life within it would matter to him if the right lives weren't part of the mass.

He took his communicator out of the pocket of the chair and set an earbud in place before he reconnected one of his missed attempts. "What is it, Tatyana?"

"You asked to be notified if we obtained any more information about Mercury." Tatyana was there with the rest of them, but she rarely went outside if she could be busy doing something else. "She's being confined with her parents, but all of the prisoners are being held in a separate wing of Prime. Previously unoccupied, but now slated for only the prisoners' confinement. Her last vital scan showed that she's alright, though incredibly distressed. But she's alive. None of the children have been actually named, only given code names. It's hard to tell who they would belong to."

"Eventually they'll get around to doing genetic sequencing on all of them. Bounce that against Mercury's own records if we've still got them anywhere and identify them that way. I guarantee the records *she* kept had names. We need to be able to get a status on people's children to reassure everyone that we've still at least got eyes on the situation." He wheeled himself up the ramp of the ship with no difficulty, but the interior was actually more difficult to navigate than the outside world had been, narrow and efficient as the spaces tended to be. "And there's still been no response from the Consortium about the attack? Even after Jason's broadcast of the attack footage?"

"They've been running cut footage and images. Calling the entire transportation shutdown an act of terror." Tatyana sighed and then she continued. "They've been publishing reports about how the Crisis Virus alters mental stability and capability. 'Any contact with Earthlings who have joined Orbit within the last three years is heavily discouraged. Even the smallest traces of CV could alter your mental health.'" Tatyana repeated in a mocking tone, since clearly she knew what the Consortium was doing. "They're basically telling people that we've gone crazy down here on Earth and we want to blow them all out of the sky. Every station has sent representatives to Prime to take a vote today, but everything says that they're going to declare war against Earth before the end of the day."

"Good." Logan said without reservation, even if he knew Tatyana might not agree with his assessment of that particular vote. "That should make it a whole lot easier for most of the supposedly United Nations to get their head out of their ass and realize exactly what the Consortium's endgame is here. I thought it would take more than just a single defeat for the Alperts to become quite so stupid."

"They can't openly retaliate without proving there is reason to do so. By providing that to every Orbital they've got, they can then start retaliating without recourse. To them it seems like a genius move, I'm sure. I'll let you know when I've heard about the official vote."

"Do that. And keep sending the invitations I asked Xander to send earlier to the heads of state. I know he blew me off when I told him to start sending them. You're smart enough not to do the same." He felt strange giving that kind of order, huddled in the corner of a transport freighter as he was, dirty and injured, possibly handicapped, with his last shower more than three days in the past. But he still wanted those communications sent.

"They'll get sent. We'll discuss next steps shortly."

Logan didn't bother saying goodbye as he closed the

connection, tucking the communicator back into its pocket on his wheelchair. Out there somewhere in the world was the means to victory against the Consortium. Out there somewhere was a strategy, a set of allies, a weapon, a tool, something, that would allow him to continue fighting. He just didn't know where. But he'd be damned before he stopped looking for it.

* * * * *

Mercury felt strange being back in Orbit. This time there was no Orion. There was no Logan. No Anna, even. Mercury sat on the edge of her pristine bed in her grey uniform with her hair braided just so. Everything felt so familiar, and yet so… wrong at the same time. All of the prisoners were together, more or less. Everyone had their own sleeping unit, but it was just a bed and a single chair with a small desk, two cribs for her sons. They weren't allowed to sleep in a crib together, since they weren't supposed to become dependent on the other. Mercury thought back to years before when she would have agreed with the command, but now Mercury felt it was inhuman after the trauma. Distant and cold.

There was a training room for their daily exercise. There was a cafeteria for their meals. A recreational room for socialization and for communal childcare. Everything was standardized. They were all seen by the best doctors Prime provided. It felt like a previous life. It felt like a cage. It *was* a cage. She knew the difference now.

Mercury heard a knock on her door and she looked over at the boys, but they were still napping. They still had another hour before they would be forced to wake up, so Mercury got up from her bed and walked quietly over to the door. She wasn't surprised to see her father on the other side. Only a few people talked to her anymore, since most of them blamed Mercury for being the beacon she didn't know she was. She had no idea that the Consortium was hunting her specifically.

"Hello, Da." She said softly as she stepped out of her room and closed the door quietly behind her so her boys could sleep in peace.

"Hey, Mer." She couldn't miss the look of guilt on his face that had never gone away since the first moment she'd seen them. "Have you slept?"

"Not much. Or well." She admitted as she glanced back at her closed door. "I'm afraid someone will come and take them. Or I keep seeing Orion die, even though I didn't see anything in the first place."

"So far as I know, they haven't been able to restore the connection over the Twist. So we don't know anything about how things went on Eleusis." He had been trying, all day long, to establish some kind of meaningful communication with any of his old contacts, but it was slow going at best. "If he was still in the mountains, though, chances are he's still alive. The defeat out there was a lot worse than any Consortium outlets are letting on."

Mercury nodded slowly and looked down at the floor instead of at her father. She found it hard to talk about much of anything without getting extremely emotional. "You should not push for too much information. I don't want the Consortium to do something to you to punish you for it." When she looked up again, it was hard for him to decipher the emotion in her eyes. Mercury used to be so easy to read, but not anymore. "They came to Earth for me, didn't they? Everyone is accusing me, but I want to know the truth."

He had once been so confident, so certain about everything he did at all times, but when he shook his head, he didn't look completely certain at all. "No, it wasn't just for you, but you were one of the main reasons, yes. They wanted you, and as many of the children of the Initiative as they could round up."

"They want my children?" Mercury instinctively took a step back toward the door and her other hand went to her stomach. She couldn't do anything to protect herself or her children, but she wanted to. She wanted to keep them safe. "Because they're different? Like me?"

He shook his head, but the look in his eyes confirmed almost everything she'd ever considered about herself. "Like you, yes, I'm sure they are, but no one . . . no one is ever going to be exactly like you, Mercury. Not unless they cloned you precisely, and even then," he shook his head again. "They want to know about your children. They want to know what they're capable of."

"What does that even mean, no one is going to be like me? I started to do some research, but it was so limited in the mountains. I couldn't get much. What . . . what am I? Why am I this way? You told me that you and mother had struggles conceiving, but I didn't know that you went to someone to alter my genetics."

"We didn't go to someone to alter your genetics." He said in the political tone she had always taken for granted from him as a child, but she had learned to read straight through it after hearing it so much from Logan while he was conducting business. "Your mother and I weren't able to get pregnant on our own, even after years of marriage. We already knew we would be trying in-vitro methods next, after everything else had failed. The number of times your mother miscarried . . ." there was nothing political or hedged about the pain in his eyes at that particular memory. "The Eleusis Initiative had just been formed, under the deepest terms of secrecy. I was involved because I was already on the executive board of Station Six."

By the sigh that followed, that had been the easy part of the story to tell. "Another project had been started a few years earlier, to which I was privy only because your aunt Deirdre was involved. It's never been publicized, but the name by which it's been known ever since is Project Clay." He looked increasingly uncomfortable as he talked about it, but he went on anyway. "The board had been reconstituted and the Muriels had gone into a coma, so their votes were taken up by their executors . . . it doesn't matter. The point is, the landscape shifted. The Alperts took control of the Board and greenlit . . . a dozen projects that had been tossed out for decades. Clay was one of them. It dealt with human genetics, exploring the limits of what's possible in genetic manipulation."

Genetic manipulation. In humans. Why would her father ever think that it was . . . morally . . . okay to participate in something like that? As a doctor she would never . . . would she? Would she participate in human trials, if it meant she thought she was going to do something good? Mercury's conflicting emotions showed in her eyes, but she remained silent until she felt as though she could speak again. "So what am I, then? A project?" She tried not to sound hurt at the fact that, yet again, she was some kind of experiment, but apparently it was her whole life's purpose in the first place.

"No, of course you're not a project." Her father stepped up closer to her, but it had been over two years since they had really seen each other, and clearly a great multitude of things had changed in the intervening time. "You're my daughter, and I love you." He knew that wasn't sufficient explanation, since it never had been with Mercury, so he continued, within arm's reach but not actually touching her.

"Clay inherited some massive storehouse of data from another unauthorized study that was conducted almost a century ago, so they started with that and worked from there. They . . . designed . . . twenty-four codes, twelve male, twelve female. Their plan was to place them immediately into the foster care system and follow them over the course of their lives to monitor their development and place them in situations where they could be tested. Your aunt Deirdre was involved from the beginning, and she knew your mother and I were having trouble conceiving on our own."

What followed was clearly the most difficult admission of all, since he hesitated longest before actually saying it. "In each of the created codes, they realized that outward appearance didn't really matter all that much or make much of a difference with the way the rest of the code was expected to work. You'll understand that better than I ever will, I'm sure. So the plan was to alter the twenty-four codes to make them as diverse in appearance as possible, to remove suspicion, apparently something they said they learned from the previous project a century ago. Your aunt Deirdre interfered, using some of my genetics and your mother's to alter one of the female codes. When you were placed in the system, I used my captain status to pre-empt the adoption process. You've been with us since the day you were born."

Mercury certainly didn't know what to think about that, since she didn't even know what it made her. She wasn't . . . her mother hadn't given birth to her? If she was only partially genetically attached to her parents, who else was biologically a part of her? "So I assume you had to take part in some kind of agreement to keep me." All of her life she had been monitored, and she hadn't even once wondered why. It was just her life. It was a part of everyone's life, though she didn't realize hers had a different purpose. "What was the agreement? What were they hoping to find?" She crossed her arms, since she didn't know if she was more angry or hurt, but the secret-keeping definitely felt more painful than anything. "You knew I was studying genetics along with my CV research. You didn't ever tell me the truth."

Guilt was a new emotion for her to see on her father's face, and it made him look weaker than she had ever seen him. "I wasn't supposed to know anything about Clay. I didn't have clearance. When we adopted you, it was just like any other adoption from the central network. When they found out that we knew, that we had been involved at all . . ." he shook his head again. "The ones running Clay were trying to do their best. They had good intentions, even if that doesn't matter. You weren't the only one who was placed with a family against the wishes of the project's oversight. The administration saw that kind of tampering and placement as a betrayal of the integrity of the experiment. Your aunt Deirdre and everyone else involved disappeared. I've never been able to find out what happened to them."

He clearly missed his sister, and felt guilty about her loss even though he had been permitted to keep Mercury. "When the overseers on the Board figured out that I knew more than I should, they decided to hold it over me. If I ever told you, they would kill all three of us. Every time they needed to force my cooperation on something, every time they wanted me to change policy aboard Six, the same song and dance. Every time you made a decision that took you closer to genetics and CV research, I can't even tell you the kind of scrutiny each of those received. But every time, they came back knowing you had made those choices for yourself."

Every time Mercury wanted to speak there were ten more questions in her head, but she knew interrogating her father wouldn't do much about what had already been done. "I'm getting very tired of adjusting my understanding of my life only to find out what I believed to be true, isn't. Again and again." Mercury sighed and lowered her arms, since she was already too exhausted to hold onto anger for very long.

"Orion has . . . had a friend . . ." She replied hesitantly, since it hurt to mention Orion. Especially in the past tense. "That I researched briefly, because his wife was one of my patients. After seeing his medical history and genetic code and doing a comparison to my own, I can only assume he was also a part of this . . . project. Orion described him as nearly indestructible, and his medical record proved it. Except he had to take medication to survive. I've never had to take any medication other than a temporary pain-control regimen. When he came back from Eleusis, he seemed healthier than ever."

Mercury paused to glance back at her unit where she still didn't hear anything from her boys, but she was considering them carefully. Logan wasn't genetically altered as far as she knew from his explanation of his life, most people of Earth didn't care to include the government in their lives that way. Mercury blinked a few times before she put a hand back on her stomach. Orion, however, had been altered. He told her as much. What would their daughters become, as a mix between the two of them? They'd been Matched, but now she wondered if someone had their fingers in that as well. The Matching program was an excellent way for the government to do whatever 'experiments' they wanted without ever owning up to it. "They're making a very specific kind of human, it looks like." Mercury finally replied as she looked back at her father. "The perfect fighters. The perfect doctors. Made and controlled by the Consortium. I'm just a prototype, I'm sure. Incubating what they really want."

"What they want doesn't matter." Her father defended, with more rebellious fire in his eyes than she'd ever seen in them before. He had never been particularly friendly with the rest of the captains under the Consortium, but he had still always played their games and done their work. "You're not an experiment, or a machine, or a set of damned code. You're who you choose to be. Just like the rest of us."

Mercury shook her head and held out a hand. "Look around, Father. We're all an experiment now." She looked cold and distant as she took another step back so she was standing against the door to her unit. "No one is going to get us out of here. No one even knows we're here."

"If they don't yet, they will soon. I can promise you that." He didn't move any closer, since she didn't want him nearby and he couldn't blame her. "The Board met a few hours ago and formally voted to declare war on Earth. They wouldn't do that unless they knew there was still someone left to fight. Means your rebellion isn't as finished as they wanted us to think it was on the flight up here. Someone knows you're here. They'll come for you."

"Us." Her expression softened as she looked at her father again. "I'm not leaving you and mother behind if someone does find us here." Mercury looked at her father again and decided to step away from the door and into a hug with him, even though she was still hurt and angry. "I'm glad you both are alright. You're my parents, and I love you."

He put his arms around her tightly, as if she was ten years old again and he could make everything better in the world by saying it was. "I'm so proud of you, Mercury. You've done what you knew was right every step of the way. You've got more courage than I ever did."

"You raised me to do the right thing and to be strong. I don't know if I always do, but I have tried my best." She agreed with that part at least, and hugged him for a little bit longer before she pulled away. Mercury tried not to show her vulnerability, but she knew she did more often than she should. "Will you stay in the room with me? I have a hard time sleeping if I'm alone, it will feel safer if you're there. There is still an hour left before the boys have to wake up from their nap."

"Of course, Mer." He went in with her quietly, and looked in on both the boys before he went to take the one seat in the room by the desk so she could lie down and get some sleep. Even as isolated and restrictive as the cell seemed, Marcus sat in the chair as if it was his own personal office back on Six, but it was completely out of habit. A long life being in charge of most of his world had left him without any other option than to appear in control, even if he wasn't.

Mercury went to the bed, laid back, and stared up at the ceiling for a moment before she closed her eyes. She wanted to cry. She felt like she always wanted to cry, but she was trying to be strong. It was so hard, especially now that she knew how closely the Consortium was watching her. She had her boys to think about, if nothing else. Mercury had no idea if someone would ever get her out, but she would keep a little hope. Maybe they *would* get rescued. All she could do until then was play the game the best that she could.

EPILOGUE

When Anna opened her eyes, she thought she would either be looking in the faces of her dead relatives or she would be in a fuck-ton of pain. She was met with neither. Anna turned her head slowly side to side to test if she would find any pain or resistance, but she was on a hospital bed, surrounded by curtains.

When she sat up slowly, a soft beeping started, and Anna could see she was hooked up to a few monitors that were watching her heart rate, her oxygen, along with other things that she wasn't quite sure about. Anna was amazed when she looked down at herself, dressed in grey, but no longer injured. She remembered being injured. Paralyzed, even, though she hadn't been sure at the time. The only sign of potential injury was that one of her hands was partially wrapped, though her fingers were free from the wrapping, so she didn't really try to move it more than she had to.

Where the hell was she? How was she . . . okay? Better than okay? Was she in some kind of fucked-up dream? Limbo? Oh god, she was in limbo, wasn't she? Both God and the devil didn't know what to do with her.

Before her thoughts carried her down that particular rabbit hole, a computerized voice spoke above her.

Patient Anna Prince. Please remain calm, you are in recovery room one. A physician will be with you momentarily. Please feel free to review your information. A holographic image showed up in front of her, showing her a somewhat-detailed report of what she had gone through, and Anna's head started to spin.

Apparently she had somehow recovered from multiple internal bleeds, broken and fractured bones, as well as a partially severed spine. And, above all of that, she was *still* eight weeks pregnant. How did her baby survive all of that? How did *she* survive all of that? Where was Oliver? Where was anyone else?

"Hello?" She finally spoke up, and found her voice was hoarse from disuse. "Is anyone else in here, or is it just me and the computer?"

There are presently fourteen patients in this recovery ward. No other patients are currently conscious. A physician has been alerted of your consciousness, and will be with you momentarily. The computer voice replied, assuming that she was still speaking to it since there was no one else awake or present in the room.

A moment after that answer, Anna could hear a door slide open somewhere off to her right, and she heard soft footsteps along the tile floor heading toward her. The man who opened her curtain did so gently, giving her an expression that wasn't quite a smile, but was filled with professional courtesy. He was a small man with the kind of face that made him look too young for the doctor's coat around his shoulders, but he looked fairly comfortable in it nonetheless. He carried a tablet in the crook of one arm, on which he had been alerted of her consciousness.

"Good afternoon. I'm Dr. Kunal Sidana. You're awake somewhat ahead of our expectations. That's a good sign." He gave her another almost-smile and a once-over, then tapped a few times on his tablet. "Please remain on the bed for the time being and rest against the pillows. Have you reviewed your historical information?"

"Yeah, I looked it over." Anna said as she did as the doctor asked and rested back against the pillows. "Kinda sounds like I should be dead. I'm not, though, right? Where am I?" She looked up at the ceiling again, but it was just white everywhere. "I don't think this looks like heaven, since no one I know is here. And there's a pretty convincing argument I would certainly deserve to get stuck in limbo."

"I admit, I'm not very familiar with that particular religious paradigm. I was raised Hindu. The paths of morality don't always jive with more Western ideas of heaven or the other alternatives." He gave her the same non-smile again as he worked on his tablet, then seemed to complete what was on the tablet for the time being, since he held it against his side to look at her directly.

"Your injuries were quite extensive, but taken individually, there was nothing that couldn't be overcome. You have been unconscious for just over two weeks while your injuries were processed and addressed." He paused for a while and looked back at her as she waited for an answer to her question, then went on without any indication of feeling apologetic or remorseful about what he reported. "Some of your questions will be answered.

Others will not. It is my advice that you become accustomed to a lack of information in this regard. But I can tell you that you are not, in fact, in limbo."

"Wait, what? Huh? You can't tell me where I am?" Anna went from feeling like somehow she had been saved miraculously to feeling very wrong in a matter of seconds. Why would a doctor say something like that to her? Anna sat up a little bit straighter but decided not to push it too much with the doctor. "Alright. Can you tell me if my baby is okay?"

"Yes, I can." He actually seemed pleased, for some reason, that she asked a permitted question, and he gestured to the monitor beside her bed where she had read about her own history a few minutes before. "Your baby is developing according to expectations for its gestational stage. During your numerous surgeries, the blood supply to your reproductive system was placed on a bypass in order to minimize stress to the fetus and maintain resources for your own body's healing process. When stress hormones in your blood began to return to normal levels, the blood supply was restored. Genetic testing revealed no anomalies that you have any reason to be concerned with at the present time. Would you like to know the gender of the child?"

"I, um . . ." Anna shifted uncomfortably since she was starting to really question everything around her. "Sure. What's the gender?"

"It's a girl." He pronounced with slightly more of a smile than before, as if his face remembered what a legitimate smile felt like after a long period of absence from the expression. "In terms of appearance, it seems she'll favor you quite strongly, judging by the percentage of genetic similarity, but of course these things do tend to shift and change as a child grows."

Anna smiled a little bit as well, though she still couldn't shake the feeling that trouble was looming just overhead. Even with the news of a baby girl, the world just didn't feel right. A hospital like this would have to be Consortium-run, right? So was she back in space? How did that happen? "I don't suppose you have any way to determine paternity, do you?"

The man raised a curious eyebrow, then gave a slight shrug. "If you provide us with a list of potential fathers, we would have the ability to screen the child's code against any potential matches to determine likelihood, yes. So long as the father's code is also in our files."

She knew they would have Logan's information on file, but she didn't know about Oliver. Was Oliver even alive? "There's only two potential fathers. One is Logan Bickford. If this is a Consortium hospital, I know you have his code on file."

"I believe we do. I'll verify and let you know. The other?" The man's conversation wasn't much better than the computer, and appeared to be just about as pre-programmed, every response careful and concise, even though it wasn't clipped. It wasn't as though he didn't care about her or about being there, he was just tightly restrained in what he said and didn't say.

"Oliver Masterson. He was with me . . . I don't know where he is now, but I don't suppose you're allowed to tell me that either?" Anna questioned carefully, though she was really trying not to freak out or be pushy. It was harder than she thought it would be.

"I . . ." he shook his head, after appearing to make an effort to tell her, but apparently not choosing to do so. Or was he unable to do so? "We have Nurse Masterson's code on record as well. Are they the only two possible candidates?"

"Yes. They are the only two." She was a little frustrated that it looked like he was going to tell her about Oliver, but then he just didn't. What was the deal with this guy? They must have Oliver too, somewhere, if they had his information. "How long until I can know?"

"That's not for me to say." He said without hesitation, looking her over one more time. "Are you reasonably assured of your present well-being?"

"Am I reasonably assured? I'm fucking skeptical as hell, but you seem infuriatingly short on information. So take that however you like." She sat up again, even though he told her to lay back. When she sat up, she remembered the wrapping on her hand. "Oh, hey, what the hell happened to my hand? I didn't read anything about it in the report."

"The report details all procedures that were involved in healing you from your injuries sustained during the assault. Any procedures conducted afterward are not listed in the report." He said by way of explanation, even though it felt like he was having to circumvent some kind of rule to tell her even that much. "I'll inform our Chief Medical Officer of your status. Please remain in the bed. We'll be back when it's convenient."

Procedures after? Anna looked down at her hand, but she

decided against unwrapping it. If it was infected or something, she wasn't about to make it worse. Anna closed her eyes and tried to sleep, but she couldn't. She was getting more and more anxious until finally she heard a door open. Maybe it would be someone with more answers. She needed answers. More than that, she needed a way out of wherever she was.

The first person she saw was Kunal again, carrying the same tablet as before, but the next person she saw walking after him was one of the last people she ever wanted to see again, walking beside one of the last people she ever expected to see alive.

Maria and Stephen Kaplan both looked every bit as antiseptically perfect as they had the first time she'd met them on the first day of the Initiative, but the look in their eyes was no longer fake politeness or guarded malevolence. If anything, the look in their eyes was utterly apathetic and almost bored.

Rather than any kind of introduction or reunion, though, it was Kunal who spoke, reading from the tablet in his hands as if he hadn't just been there talking with Anna a few minutes before.

"Test subject Echo-23 emerged from the induced comatose state at 14:26 this afternoon. Subject is female, native to the Midwest district, currently pregnant at 8 weeks of gestation. The fetus is female, with no observed abnormalities. Subject is 1.73 meters in height, weighing 66 kilos. Subject reports that she feels reasonably assured of her physical well-being as of 14:39. Subject's implant was successful in saline administrations prior to subject regaining consciousness, and subject has been marked with identification in accordance with project protocols."

Kunal finished his report and took half a step back away from the foot of the bed, looking over at Maria rather than at Anna, as if she had ceased to exist the moment his boss stepped into the room.

"What. The. Fuck." Anna replied as she actually physically attempted to get away from the Kaplans, but there was nowhere to go. "This is not real. You two . . . *you* . . ." Anna said pointedly at Stephen, since he was not supposed to be breathing her air. "You're supposed to be dead!"

Maria stepped up as though Anna wasn't beginning to escalate, and she took a tool resembling a gun and grabbed Anna's arm. She injected a solution quickly before Anna could even react. "We'll start with a mild sedative, since you're new at this."

When Anna started to calm against her will, Maria looked back at the other doctor as she slowly unwrapped Anna's hand and Anna could see what was wrong with it. There was no injury or deformation, just a black-ink tattoo with her identification number along her palm.

E-23.

"We'll begin trial number one with test subject Echo-23." When Maria looked back at Anna's sedated gaze, she just smiled. "Welcome, Echo-23. I appreciate your sacrifice."

The story concludes in

The New World

ABOUT THE AUTHOR

D. Brumbley is a husband/wife duo from Kansas City who spend most of their time in each other's heads. In suburbia the duo lives in a simple house with a dog and two feisty kiddos. One half of the duo loves football, baseball, libraries, and romance. The other half of the duo likes D&D, Fantasy novels, Marvel Comics, and cheesecake. A country girl and an east coast boy met online, became best friends, fell in love, and somewhere along the way decided that telling stories together would be fun.

Best. Decision. Ever.